The Cosmos in Her Hand

A Novel

Jennifer Cyphers

Table of Contents

Kali, Ju, and Olivia

Kali and Lev's Lunch Date

Lev and Kali

Experimental Passport Pilot Needed

Kali and Lev Travel Together

Lev, Marina, and Arjun

Lev Returns

Lev, Kali and the Ginger Wine Crime

Days that Don't End

Kali and Tracy

Kali and the Cannonballs

Lev and the Team at John's Camp

Kali, James, and Dave

Kali in the Crow's Nest

James and Bolin

Kali in the Crow's Nest

After the Battle

The End of the Cannibals

Night Shift

Lucifer Wins

After the Boozy Bonfire Celebration

Lev Tells Kali the Plan

Lev and the Intel Team Say Goodbye

Lev and the Intel Team Arrive in the Kingdom

Lev in the Kingdom

Lev Meets Bas

Maren in the Kingdom

Olivia in the Kingdom

Back at Ivy- 8:30am ET

Kali Goes to the Lab- 9:15am

After the Meeting- 11am

Lev and Bas in the Cages- 7pm

Lev and Kali- 8pm

Kali's Not Like Everybody Else- 5:15am

Kali, Bas, Rollo, and Pele

Kali and Lev

Lev

Traffic was light and he was making good time despite already being late. Her plane had arrived on time, but the property manager had not. He had given her a heads up about the possibility of him not getting to the airport in time to pick her up yesterday after the AC had gone out at the new rental. It was only the end of May, but already the warm temperatures and humidity had required some occasional use of the AC to keep their new upstairs apartment cool. They had rented the apartment a month before finals week, and she had spent almost two weeks with her parents in Connecticut after graduation before flying down to Northern Virginia to be with him in their new place. Both of them newly graduated with hard-earned degrees. She had earned her Bachelor's degree and was going to start on her Master's in education this fall. He had completed his degree and planned to take at least a year off before looking into what was next, academically speaking. He had options and some time to consider them while he worked with Dave and his team at the lab.

New adventures, a new city, new jobs, a new apartment, and a fair amount of school loans, but hey, they had a plan to tackle that part. For instance, the apartment was not nearly as upscale as they would have preferred, but the rent was better than they had hoped for when they'd estimated their cost-of-living expenses. Plus, they each managed to get hired at their new jobs prior to graduating. Everything was on track and expectations were being met. He was feeling really lucky in life. Especially when it came to Yuna.

He had been to the airport a few times in the past when flying back and forth for job interviews and then when they had spent a weekend apartment hunting during their final spring break. He knew the exit was just a few miles ahead and prepared to make his way across the highway. Before Siri could tell him to get into the right lane, he flicked on his blinker and looked into the rear-view mirror and then over his right shoulder to see if it was safe to start getting over from the left lane. This was a really good time to head over to the airport, he thought to himself. Very little traffic right now. He made his way to the lane second from the left, and looked into the rear-view mirror again before looking to the right. He got over again. Siri decided it was time to let him know that his exit was coming up and that he should get into the right lane. Way ahead of you Siri, he thought.

He was excited to see Yuna after not having seen her since the day after their graduations. His parents had flown in from the west coast two days before graduation to spend some time with them and to help them pack boxes for their move to Washington D.C. Yuna's parents had driven in from Greenwich the day before the graduation ceremonies and they'd all had a great time catching up over a celebratory restaurant meal and drinks. Hoshi and Minato Mori were very wealthy and enjoyed lavishing their only daughter and their future in-laws with generous meals in great venues.

Yuna was an only daughter, and he was an only son. All four of their parents were committed to being life-long friends through their relationships with their only, and beloved, children. In fact, every winter break since he and Yuna had begun dating during their freshman year at college, her parents had flown with Yuna to the west coast to spend the holidays with him and his parents. That first visit had been casual with the Mori's spending a good portion of their time exploring sites in San Diego and Los Angeles, but both sets of parents hit it off and it just became a yearly thing for them to gather on the west coast during the winter and then at the Mori's place on the east coast for a week in the summer. At this point, their parents were friends with or without Yuna and himself.

He was thinking about his mother now and how she'd asked him if he and Yuna planned to get engaged during the week prior to graduation while the two families were briefly together. Even though he and Yuna wanted to make their intention to marry official with an announcement and a ring, they had decided to wait until the winter holidays and their yearly winter family get-together at his parent's house in San Diego. For him, there was a moment of disappointment when he realized that all of their college friends would not be around to celebrate their engagement news once they left Massachusetts. But Yuna, with her usual candor, looked him straight in the eyes and explained to him that all of their friends would be celebrating their own graduations with their families. It would be selfish of the two of them to demand some of their friends' joy at their own personal academic accomplishments and congratulations for their entirely expected engagement. So, ok. She wasn't wrong. She also wasn't wrong when she followed up by adding, "They better all come to our fucking wedding, though!" He smiled thinking about it now. She definitely had a way about her that he appreciated. Yuna. All straight talk.

Siri was telling him that his exit was half a mile ahead just as he read a highway sign he was passing informing him of the same information. His excitement at being reunited with Yuna after two weeks of separation started to grow even stronger. Her plane had landed on time at 11:30am. It was now nearly 1:30pm. She had texted him when the plane landed that, of course the plane was on time when he was going to be late, and added a rolling eyes emoji. She followed up with a reminder that she was content to wait and would be sparing no expense on fast food options until he arrived. He hadn't had lunch yet as he had been dealing with the AC guy and had then bolted to the airport as soon as the problem had been fixed. He was hungry. He was definitely going to need some food for the ride back to their apartment. They might hit the beginnings of rush hour traffic on the way home. Their home. Had a nice ring to it. He smiled at the thought.

He put his blinker on earlier than was necessary as he approached the exit to the airport. He considered his early action a courtesy to the drivers around him and not a result of a mixture of hunger and excitement that had dictated his decision. He wasn't speeding, but he suddenly found himself approaching the car in front of him at an alarming pace. It was as if the driver in front of him had taken their foot off the gas pedal and the vehicle was losing momentum rapidly. No brake lights? he thought. "*Fuck!*" he whispered out loud as he stepped hard on his brakes to avoid a collision. He watched as the car in front of him suddenly careened sharply to the left and into another car that was also suddenly slowing down. It was horrifying and he felt like he was in a nightmare as many of the vehicles around him and in front of him started slowing down and taking dramatic turns out of their lanes. He tried desperately to see an opening where he could pull over to the right of the roadway and onto the shoulder.

Some cars were still accelerating at a normal speed as he had been just before he began to slow down for the exit. They crashed violently into the cars that had slowed down and entered their lanes. Everything happened so fast. As he tried to navigate his own car to a safe space on the right side of the highway, he watched as cars crashed into one another all around him. If he hadn't switched lanes early, if he'd waited until Siri had told him to start getting over for his exit, he might have been trapped in one of the left lanes and not able to drive off the road onto the shoulder area as he was attempting to do now. He found an opening as the cars behind him slowed dramatically or swerved out of the right lane altogether. He kept driving off the shoulder of the road and headed closer towards a fenced-in field set back away from the highway which was surrounded by wooden fencing. Grazing cows were contained inside the fenced field. He steered his car straight towards the wooden fencing trying to get as far away from the highway as possible.

Worse than what he could see happening around him on the highway was the noise made by all of the metal colliding and rubber tires squealing as conscientious drivers braked as hard as they could to avoid collisions. He swore again as he panicked and abruptly turned his wheel to the left to avoid crashing into the wooden fence surrounding the pasture. He had been driving faster than he realized when he drove off of the highway towards the safety of the field. He found himself parked alongside the fenced pasture with his car now pointing towards the airport exit. The cows appeared oblivious to what was happening on the road alongside their enclosure.

Behind him, cars that continued accelerating, crashed into the cars that had been in front of him before he'd driven onto the shoulder. It didn't make sense to him. He had stopped and avoided a collision. How were cars that had been behind him still accelerating and driving into other cars?

He put his car in park and turned to look to his left at the scene unfolding on the highway. His heart was pounding as he realized the oversized pickup truck that had been behind him was now in the backseat of the car that had been in front of him just a minute earlier. That could have been him. He could see cars in front of him that had also driven off the road and towards the pasture. Some seemed to be piloted intentionally by drivers intent on getting out of the way of the pile-up, while other cars appeared to be drifting haphazardly off the highway. It didn't make any sense to him.

His hands were shaking as he gripped the steering wheel and stared wide-eyed to the right of him at the cows, still unperturbed and lazily grazing in the pasture. With his car in park, he turned off the engine and grabbed his keys out of the ignition. He grabbed his phone from the change holder in the center console and went to open his door to get out on the driver side when he noticed a small white car drifting slowly off of the highway towards him. It was then pushed slowly by another car into his driver side door. His body lurched gently to the right when the small white car drove into his driver side door. He felt stunned more by the events of the past few minutes than stunned by the impact of the white car against his own. Eyes still wide, he looked to his left into the windshield of the white car as it continued to gently push against the side of his car. He was just feet away from the driver of the white car and could see her body slumped forward, suspended by her seatbelt.

He scrambled across to the passenger side of his car and fumbled with the door lock before opening the door and getting out to run away on shaking legs before anyone else drove into his car. As he was running, he turned and looked in back of him to see if any cars were heading towards him. Outside of his car, the noise of the crashing cars up and down the highway was deafening. The sounds were all around him. What he saw paralyzed him with disbelief. It wasn't just the southbound side of the highway that was experiencing a massive pileup. He could see semis on the northbound side of the highway crashing into cars. Some were going full speed and crashing violently into drifting vehicles. Others were simply careening about the highway, as if the drivers had fallen asleep. A semi jackknifed and the sound made him shudder as he watched in wide-eyed horror. Cars from the northbound lanes were driving into cars in the southbound lanes by driving right through the median.

He was taking it all in as he stood there in the grass. A few other people were exiting their cars as he had. Some were screaming, adding to the noise of the car crashes that were still happening, but there was something else. Something louder. The air felt like it was pulsating around him and he felt weak as he turned to his left and looked up at the sky. It was a plane. A plane was coming down right onto the field where he stood. Its approach was rapid. Despite the fact that his senses were already overwhelmed, it took only a split second for him to absorb what was about to happen. His hair stood up on end and the air felt electrified but it may have been adrenaline and fear causing the sensations he felt now.

He ran and leapt over the wooden fencing and into the enclosure of the grazing cows and sprinted with all his might towards a distant, tall line of trees marking the start of a small forested area beyond the cow enclosure. Adrenaline propelled him towards the tall trees with speed he never imagined himself capable of reaching. The plane approached with a deafening roaring sound and he yelled out as he threw himself to the ground in a desperate attempt to avoid the imminent crash. The plane was just yards above him as it passed over his prone body pressed into the grass of the pasture. When the plane smashed into the ground immediately beyond the exit he had intended to take to the airport, the ground he was pressed against vibrated from the impact, shaking his body. The air exploded with the energy of the impact and it seemed like a singular event until, lying there, he realized he could hear the screaming of more planes as they made free-falling descents to the ground. All around him, coming into the airport just a few miles from the pasture where he was pressed into the grass, he could feel more impacts shake his body as the earth beneath him absorbed the force of additional crashing planes.

He could make out explosions coming from the direction of the airport and a horrifying thought occurred to him. Yuna was waiting for him at the airport. He had to get there immediately to find her. He could hear explosions coming from the direction of the airport, and the thought of her running for cover as he had, terrified him. What if she were injured? He felt for his phone in the grass around him as he remained lying prone on the ground. Trembling all over, he finally got up on all fours and desperately searched with his eyes and hands for his phone in the unmanaged grass of the field. A few feet from him, he found it where it had landed when he had thrown himself to the ground. His hands were shaking as he tried to call Yuna's cell phone.

People were entering the pasture as he had in an effort to avoid being hit by the ongoing car crashes on the roadway. A woman was running towards him carrying a small child with another slightly older looking child running behind her. He looked back down at his phone which was letting him know that it was calling Yuna's phone, but she wasn't answering. The woman was near him now and yelling at him to help her, but he could only stare at her from the ground where he was sitting, perched on his knees gripping his cell phone. His legs were too weak to trust. He just wanted to hear Yuna's voice and to tell her he was on his way. He'd run the rest of the way to the airport, but he was going to get there. He looked back down at his phone as the woman continued to try to find a person in the field who would help her. He texted Yuna's number and asked, 'Are you Ok OMW.' He hit send and tried to call her phone a second time. When there was no answer, he left a message saying, "It's Lev. I'm ok. I'm at the airport exit. Text me or tell me where to find you. I'm going to be on foot. I'll get there soon. Let me know where you are."

The crowd of people in the field was small given the number of disabled vehicles which were strewn across both sides of the highway. The sound of crashing vehicles had subsided but was suddenly replaced by explosions as some cars had caught fire. Smoke began to billow from the highway and mingled with the rising smoke from the fallen airplane just beyond the exit overpass. Behind him, more smoke was rising from the direction of the airport. The sound of explosions as cars caught fire surrounded him as if every single road beyond his field of vision had also experienced a massive pileup. Where were the sounds of sirens letting them know that help was on the way?

The woman with the two children was talking to a man who was crying and unable to make eye contact with her. Lev watched as she put the small child she had been carrying down onto the grass and turned to the young girl on her right. As she bent down to speak to the crying girl, the smaller child darted towards him. The child's eyes were open wide and fear and confusion were painted all over his face. He ran with his mouth open as if he were screaming, but he didn't make a sound. It was a little boy, and he was running right at Lev. With the terrified child heading towards him, he found the strength to get up off the ground and onto his trembling legs and attempted to speak to the child, saying, "It's ok, guy. Let's get you back to your mom, ok?" But the little boy ran past him and headed towards the tree line across the wide pasture. Lev found his voice and shouted towards the woman who was still speaking to the little girl.

"Hey!" he shouted to her, "Your son is headed towards the trees!"

"He's not my son!" she shouted back with a tone that sounded as angry as it was fearful. "I found him crying in a car. His parents are dead," she said, turning away from him to console the little girl.

He stared at her in confusion. "Well, we can't let him get lost in the woods!" he shouted back at her.

"I have to take care of my daughter," she screamed at him with fury rising in her voice. Lev looked back at the small boy who was struggling to run as fast as he could through the field, away from the carnage.

The young boy was running towards the trees. He was small. Only about three years old. Lev started towards the child, realizing he was the only one who was going to prevent the kid from leaving the pasture. It was still a good distance across the pasture to the trees for such a small child, so he tried to compose himself as he began to jog towards him. When two other adults from among the survivors in the pasture jogged up to him and offered to help him catch the young boy, Lev slowed his pace to a fast walk and told them he had to get to the airport, but he'd help get the kid if one of them could take over after that. They agreed, but the woman looked at him with glassy eyes and suddenly told him and the older man that both of her children were dead in her car on the highway. She explained in a monotone that their car had not crashed, but that they were both dead.

Lev stared down at her as they walked quickly. There was nothing to say. The older man responded, "We'll get this kid and you look after him until help arrives, ok?" The woman nodded in agreement even if she was in shock. They started running towards the small boy again who had increased his distance from them.

Running quickly now, Lev kept pace with the older man who appeared to be quite athletic and fit. There were a lot of current and former military members living in D.C. and the surrounding areas, so Lev calculated that it was likely the older man was in the military or had been previously. Maybe a police officer. In alignment with Lev's thoughts, the older man shouted to the running child, telling him to stop, but his voice was deep and loud like an angry drill sergeant and the child made his first sound by screaming loudly and picking up his pace as he ran towards the trees ahead of him.

"There's a fence around this entire pasture," the older man said, looking at him as they picked up their pace and closed in on the boy. He looked towards the trees where the older man was pointing and saw the wooden fencing, but also noticed something else, something dark, woven through the wooden fencing.

"Hey," Lev said, looking to his right at the side of the face of the older man running along with him. "Hey, I think there's barbed wire in that section of fence."

"Fuck. Run faster!" the older man growled, keeping his eyes firmly on the child ahead of them. But they were outpaced by the increasingly terrified child who had already created distance between them earlier.

It was clear now, though, that the back end of the pasture was protected by the addition of barbed wire. The two men ran as if they were being chased and not actually the chasers in the situation. They were both trying to catch up to the boy before he reached the fence wrapped in sharp barbed wire which was meant to deter predators from entering the pasture. But it was too late. The boy desperately scrambled into the space between the first and the second rail of the wooden fence not understanding the danger imposed by the barbed wire. The two men ran towards him watching in horror as the child flailed in a desperate attempt to get free of the razor sharp barbs piercing his body.

"Oh, fuck, fuck, fuck!" the older man yelled with increasing volume with each 'fuck' he uttered.

A sickened, "Oh my God," escaped Lev as they quickly approached the screaming child and saw the extent of his injuries.

Deep new wounds continued to form as the young boy struggled to get free and barbed wire could be seen tearing at his clothes and shredding his small arms, face, stomach, legs. The older man was using a much kinder voice now as the child screamed in agony at the wounds that continued to be inflicted on his small body. His neck ripped open as one section of barbed wire scraped over the top of his small head and wound its way around his tiny neck.

The older man was encouraging the boy to hold still and let them get him out of the fence. Lev was flustered as he tried to find a limb he could free as the child flailed about making the situation so much worse. Both Lev and the older man had the skin on their arms torn at by the barbed wire as they worked together to free the young boy.

The wound in the child's neck was bleeding but it was the wound across his left eye that made Lev gag. His eye was essentially cut in half, and his lid was ripped off. Lev and the older man worked together lifting the tangled wire around the child's head and body until he was free and Lev took his small, heaving body which was wracked with quiet sobs, a few paces away to the grass where he laid him on the ground. The woman who had agreed to care for the child was nearby, and Lev could see by her expression that it was too much for her to bear. She was repeating the word 'no' and covered her mouth before turning to vomit. When she was done, she didn't say a word to Lev or to the older man. She just turned around and ran in the direction of the highway and left the two men with the severely injured child.

Lev was overwhelmed and realized he didn't have any skills to help the child. Basic life support training from his time spent as a junior lifeguard a decade earlier was useless to him. He only knew enough to begin to look for places where he could apply pressure to some of the more serious wounds on the child's body. There was a frightening amount of blood coming from tears in the boy's neck, but Lev struggled to stem the flow applying pressure where he believed it would be helpful to do so. The boy had a glazed look in his one good eye and he was whimpering and gasping for air between quiet sobs. His skin was shredded and he was bleeding from multiple areas of his small body, not just his neck. Lev noticed the flesh on his small arms was severely torn with alarming amounts of blood flowing into the grass beneath his body.

The older man was standing over Lev and the boy when he suddenly crouched down across from Lev alongside the boy. He put his large hands on the child's head, and Lev imagined he wanted to get a better look at the enormous wounds across his small neck. In an instant, the older man turned the boy's head violently to the right and Lev heard the sickening sound of the child's neck snap. The whimpering stopped. There were no more gasping breaths. His uninjured eye was still open with a look of wide-eyed terror, but he was silent. He was dead.

Both men were still crouched over the boy's lifeless body when, horrified and confused, Lev shouted at the older man, "What did you do?" And answering his own question, "You killed him!"

The older man was staring down at the face of the dead child as Lev shouted at him. Slowly, he turned his face up towards Lev's and, sighing deeply, responded, "This kid was already dead. Do you hear sirens? I don't. He'd have laid here and suffered until he died. You know that. That would have been worse. Look at the cars over there!" he said as he waved his left arm towards the highway. "There's at least one plane down right over there on the other side of that exit ramp. I heard a whole bunch more go down even if I didn't see them. I know you did, too. No one was coming to save this kid." He stared into Lev's eyes and Lev could see the despair all over his face.

"Yeah…. Yeah," Lev said with a tone of defeat while still looking at the face of the older man. But he couldn't stop himself from suddenly crying even as he realized the older man was right.

"Listen," the older man said to him, "Whatever this is," he gestured around the pasture towards the highway and then up to the sky, "is bad. This kid isn't the only one that's going to die in front of you today. You come across someone this fucked up, you don't let them suffer. You fucking do the right thing and end the torture for them. If you can help, then help. But neither of us was going to help this kid. We tried. Ok? We tried."

At that, the older man suddenly stood up and started walking back towards the highway leaving Lev still kneeling alongside the dead child, wiping away his tears with his own blood and the blood of the dead child on his hands and mixing with them. He reached into his pocket and pulled out his phone. Still no response from Yuna. He wiped his eyes again no longer crying now, stood up, walked a few paces away from the lifeless body of the boy, and involuntarily dry heaved a few times before standing back up. His stomach was empty. There was nothing to throw up.

Standing there, dazed by the assault on his senses, Lev looked towards the highway and at the people standing around in the pasture. Survivors had moved into the pasture as cars were catching on fire and the threat of explosions loomed. Some of the living were still trying to drag lifeless bodies from vehicles. When he had headed out for the airport, the sun had been shining and the day had been warm and humid. Now, the sky was darkened by the numerous car fires and plane crashes. He looked up and down the highway and saw billowing black smoke clouds dotting the horizon in both directions. The air tasted of burning fuel and other things he did not want to contemplate. He was walking now, heading towards the airport exit at the far end of the stretch of pasture. The cows showed no interest in any of the people in their expansive enclosure and did not seem bothered by the constant sound of explosions near and far.

Lev took out his phone again to see if Yuna had sent him a message. She had not. He brought up her name and tried calling her again, but his phone told him there was no service. He felt his stomach drop as he realized she had not gotten back to him and, with no service, finding her at the airport would be difficult, at best.

He began jogging across the pasture believing that getting to the airport as quickly as possible would be his best chance at finding her. The older man was right when he said he didn't hear any sirens from rescue services. The sound of crashing vehicles and crashing airplanes was over, but the sounds of people crying and pleading for help along with intermittent explosions filled his ears now.

His legs were weak after the adrenaline rush he'd experienced, but his feet continued to pound the soft grass of the pasture beneath him as he ran haltingly towards the airport exit. The compassionate part of his being slowed his momentum when he heard cries for help from people inside and outside the highway wreckage, but the words of the older man propelled him forward towards the airport exit. It was more than likely that he could not help these people. He wasn't trained in medical care. He didn't want to know what their injuries were. He didn't want to be confronted with a choice to help a person or to end their suffering. He had to keep going towards the airport to find Yuna.

As he neared the far end of the pasture, he scanned the wooden fencing to make certain there was no barbed wire at this end. There wasn't. He put his right foot on the middle beam of the fence and hoisted himself out of the enclosure and continued sprinting up the gentle incline of the airport exit. Cars had driven off the road and crashed beneath the exit ramp, fires were burning, and smoke filled his lungs and burned his eyes as he made his way up the ramp. He was increasingly fearful of the vehicles that were already on fire, afraid they'd explode like bombs while he was running past them. The fear increased his determination to get away from the wreckage all around him if possible, and he continued to sprint at a pace that caused his lungs to burn as he took in deep breaths of the smoke-filled air.

At the top of the exit ramp, he looked left and the sight caused him to stumble as his legs weakened at the sight before him. He suddenly stopped running and came to a dead stop unable to look away from the scene. The plane that had crashed just beyond the exit had created a deep crater where it had landed. Exit ramps on the other side had been impacted and Lev had a difficult time comprehending the level of destruction before him. With extreme effort, he tore his gaze away from the carnage and forced himself to keep moving ahead so that he could get to the airport and find Yuna. He wondered how long he could keep going on foot and started to consider the actual distance to the airport. At least three more miles. Maybe five. He wasn't out of shape. In fact, he was in great shape. An avid athlete, actually. It was the shock, the adrenaline, the filthy smoke-filled air making it difficult to breath and burning his eyes. It was all of that, but mostly the shock.

While the exit had not been densely littered with wrecked cars and injured people, he discovered that weaving on foot through a mass of tangled vehicles at the traffic light at the top of the exit was a dangerous, smoldering obstacle course. The airport exit was a particularly busy exit with several exits converging at the top of the small hill.

Leading to the airport, the road sloped gently downward towards a usually bustling area with many businesses lining the main drag on both sides of the triple lanes. Fast food restaurants, gas stations, car dealerships, grocery stores, all vying for recognition from airport travelers. As he continued to run in the direction of the airport, he heard cries of help from dazed people, some bloodied, some holding dead loved ones, some who were insisting he come help assist another. He kept running.

He could also hear cries for help coming from inside cars. Children in car seats crying, the sound of a dog barking from inside another car. The amount of people outside of the burning, mangled vehicles seemed small. Why were so many dead inside their cars, he wondered. The thought persisted. It grew and he wondered to himself what killed the woman who drove her small white car into his car back at the pasture? He had to find Yuna before he could help anyone else. He wanted to help, but he had to find her before he could stop and help another person.

His lungs were burning from the smoke, and the heat and humidity were suddenly even more noticeable to him. The air he was breathing in was dense and not providing him with the oxygen his physical efforts demanded. He slowed down as he tried to find a space to get past vehicles which had all crashed together in one massive pileup under an intersection. The traffic lights were still working, but no passage was possible by way of a car. He heard the cries of a woman coming from one of the cars in the pileup, looked in the direction of the calls for help, but quickly looked away and headed towards the right of the intersection looking for a path around the tangle of automobiles. His heart pounded in his chest and he ducked for cover as one of the cars across to the left side of the intersection exploded. The force of the explosion shocked him and he felt the power of it in his trembling body. As he regained his composure, he looked in the direction of the explosion and realized a combination of his wanting to avoid the crying woman trapped in a car and his thirst had saved him from heading left around the intersection. He had seen the fast food restaurant on the right side of the road beyond the intersection and made the decision to see if he could catch his breath there and get something to drink. The woman wasn't screaming anymore. He'd have been killed by the explosion if he'd chosen to help her. That realization mattered to him as he made sense of the fact that he had just avoided being killed and, as a result, was able to continue his mission to find Yuna at the airport.

Shaking off the ugly fortune of having avoided being alongside the car that had just turned into a bomb, he ran the rest of the way down the street towards the familiar fast food restaurant. He consciously made the decision not to look for water at the gas station next to the restaurant because he saw smoke coming from a car that had been pushed off of the road and into the gas station parking lot. The driver of that car appeared dead. Not from an impact, but just slumped over dead.

Lev was barely jogging past the gas station when he told a small group of bloodied people standing in the parking lot that the nearby car was smoking and could cause the gas station pumps to explode. They all stood motionless, mute, watching him warn them, but none made an effort to distance themselves from the smoking car. He told himself the effort he had made was enough. He had to get to Yuna. He waved his right hand in the air as he passed them and shook his head no as he muttered, "Fuck it." Even when he tried to help, it was no use.

Lev and Aisha

The parking lot and sidewalk surrounding the fast food restaurant was moderately filled with cars and bodies lying about on the asphalt and cement. Some bodies could be seen slumped over in still running cars, some bodies were strewn lifeless at the outside eating area, and some were crumpled on the ground near and within the entrance he was approaching. Again, he thought, Why are they dead?

Cars were wrapped along the drive thru and more than one had impacted another. The door to the restaurant was propped open against a large man lying on the ground with his drink spilled out in front of him. His face was flat against the sidewalk, his torso was outside, but his legs were sprawled out in back of him still within the restaurant. Lev pulled the door all the way open and side stepped his way around the dead man in order to enter. He could see two people alive at a table in the corner of the restaurant, but the dead far outweighed the living . Bodies were strewn about tables and the floor. Many appeared to have died while eating. Just died while eating their burgers and fries. The two living souls in the corner were talking when Lev walked in and they stopped to look up at him.

"You know what's going on out there?" the guy asked him.

Lev looked over at him. He wasn't asking for actual help. He looked about Lev's age, probably mid 20s. The woman he was with was a lot older. Her hair was white, and she looked at Lev, hopeful that he could tell them what was going on.

"No," he said. "It's everywhere, though. I just came off the highway heading to the airport. Everything is fucked up. Planes went down, too. Just…. everything…." he trailed off. Talking seemed so unusual all of a sudden. Why words? He wondered to himself. Why bother? His mind continued to question. He had no answers.

He looked down at the floor trying to avoid bodies as he made his way to the counter. Was he going to order a drink, he wondered to himself. He shook his head no to shake off the useless thoughts that wanted him to return to normal. No, he thought again and walked to the end of the counter where he entered the service area and quickly went to grab a pre-made sandwich which he noticed resting under the heat lamps. He also noticed the cups for drinks which customers were handed in order to fill their own orders from the self-serve fountains. He felt a sense of relief that he'd be able to clear his mouth of the taste of fuel and the feel of the debris from the burning particulate in the air which was coating the inside of his mouth.

The smells of burgers and fries ignited the hunger he had felt earlier despite the events of the last 20 minutes. He grabbed a burger wrapped in familiar purple paper identifying it as his usual order and looked down at the cup dispenser grabbing for the largest cup available. He saw his hand take hold of a cup and didn't recognize the hand as his own. It was filthy with blood and dirt and numerous slashes. His legs were spread wide open as he straddled the dead body of a petite food service worker sprawled lifeless on the blue tile floor.

As he shifted his weight and turned to go fill his drink cup at the self-service station, he saw movement at the opposite end of the counter out of the corner of his left eye. He turned his head to get a better look and noticed a wide-eyed employee perched on her knees over the body of a large man. She was holding the man's hand in hers. An act of comfort for the dying man, Lev determined. The man's uniform indicated he was a manager, while her uniform indicated she was a server. The large man labored to breathe, and the skin on his face appeared to be a disturbing shade of blue ash. His labored breathing held Lev's attention for a moment, but the way in which the young woman kneeled beside the man caught in his mind and forced him to recall himself kneeling above the body of the young boy as he laid dying from the wounds caused by the barbed wire.

He looked at the young woman. She wasn't crying, but she was staring at him with wide eyes and a look of concern etched in her forehead. Even crouched down on the floor, Lev could tell she was tall.

"No one's coming to help you. He's probably having a heart attack. I think that's what it is. He's going to die," Lev said to her without emotion.

She looked down at her coworker who continued to breathe laboriously, and looked back at Lev. "You alright?" she asked him with a hint of concern for his well-being that he had not been able to muster for her coworker or even her.

"Yeah. I need to get a drink. I'm trying to get to the airport on foot. How far is it from here?" he asked absently as he walked towards the drink machines in the customer seating area while stepping over dead bodies. He pushed his cup under the pink lemonade faucet and watched as the pink liquid began to fill his empty cup. Normal. Not normal. You can't have both at the same time, he thought. It's one or the other. The young man and the older woman who were sitting at the table in the corner were still there. Lev looked over across the room at them, but his attention was quickly grabbed by the flames of the car in the gas station parking lot.

"*Hey*!" he shouted at the pair. "Get away from the window! There's a fire at the gas station!" The young man turned his head to look out the large wall of windows overlooking the gas station in order to see what Lev was telling them. "*Run*!" Lev shouted at them. His cup of lemonade was overflowing onto his fingers and, without caring, he dropped it and ran back to the front counter and went around it to the young woman who was now standing over her coworker with a frightened look in her eyes at the sound of Lev shouting and running towards her. The words of the older man in the pasture were loud in his mind. He would save a person if he could. She could be saved. This would not stop him from getting to Yuna.

The young woman looked frightened and confused and demanded of him, "What's going on?!" But Lev didn't respond except to grab her hand and run with her to the back of the kitchen area as quickly as possible. She didn't make him drag her, she kept pace with him despite not knowing why they were running. The explosion of the gas pumps came in an instant and the force ripped through the restaurant. The sound of breaking glass as the wall of windows was shattered made both of them scream in terror and drop to the ground just as they flung themselves into the employee break room. Still on the floor, Lev scrambled to turn around and managed to kick the employee break room door closed as a second explosion followed the first one. Before Lev or the young woman could speak, a third explosion, which shook the interior walls of the restaurant went off.

The lights in the break room had gone out as soon as the first explosion ripped through the restaurant. There were no windows in this corporate designed place of employee relaxation. Four cement walls and a windowless door sheltered them from the force of the explosions next door at the gas station. Probably the only good use of a room like the one they found themselves in.

Lev and the woman huddled together in the dark under the one small break room table. She wasn't crying, but she was holding onto his arm as if he could offer her some sort of protection. He couldn't. They waited a few minutes in silence in the dark, anticipating another explosion, but when none occurred, she said to him, "We need to get the hell out of here before we can't."

Lev nodded in agreement, but said nothing. He felt completely out of words. She couldn't see him nod in agreement in the darkened room, so she crawled out from under the table while telling him to come with her using her most authoritative voice. As she fumbled in the dark, and finally reached the handle of the break room door, she heard Lev behind her coming out from under the table.

Opening the break room door and stepping into the kitchen area, the smoky air quickly filled both of their lungs. The air was so thick that Lev noticed he could feel it on his tongue, and when he bit down with a grimace, he realized he could bite the air between his teeth.

"We can't breathe this," the young woman said to him. She didn't turn to look at his face when she said it, just turned back towards the breakroom where she grabbed two clean dish towels from a shelf and emerged from the darkened doorway and handed him one saying, "Try to tie this around your head. Keep this air out of you."

Lev struggled to comply. She still had words, and they were good and useful words. She looked at him as he failed to tie the dish towel around his face. She couldn't do it either. They realized that the dish towels were too short to tie effectively around the width of their heads. Turning towards a row of industrial sized sinks near them, she reached above to a metal shelf with a clear plastic tray and pulled out a couple of rubber bands.

"Use a rubber band. Like this." She proceeded to turn around and demonstrate how he could gather the ends of the dish towel and secure it to his head. He did as he was instructed. As she watched him secure the dish towel around his mouth and nose as a makeshift face mask, she realized that despite his appearance, he might not be dangerous after all.

"Are you injured, sir?" she asked him, pointing to the still bleeding injuries his hands and arms had acquired trying to free the young boy from the barbed wire. "You have blood all over you. Your face, too," she said with more concern than curiosity and waving her hand about the various areas he was presumably covered in blood.

"It's not all my blood. We were trying to help a little kid. He didn't make it," Lev said in a tone devoid of any emotions.

"Ok. I get it," she said to him more kindly now that she was beginning to trust he might be a decent guy.

"My name's Aisha," she said as she adjusted the dish towel around her mouth and nose.

"Lev," he responded as he fumbled with the dish towel still trying to secure it well enough to keep it above his nose without it sliding down.

"It doesn't have to be perfect," Aisha said to him. "Just get it so that you won't suffocate from all the particulates in the air. Leave your nose out if you have to and breathe through your mouth. You can find something better later." Lev nodded in agreement but managed to properly secure the dish towel so it covered his nose as well. He might have to adjust it more later so it wouldn't fall off when he began running again. For now, it was fine.

Aisha rubbed her eyes. "Jesus, it's burning my eyes, too," she said. Lev silently agreed. His eyes were also burning and they had been for a while. Aisha grabbed his right hand and led him towards the front of the restaurant. He allowed himself to be led by her. Did she want to check on the manager? he wondered.

As they left the kitchen, he noticed Aisha look to her left at her manager. He was no longer struggling to breathe. His chest did not move. She quickly turned around and faced Lev. With the dish towel covering everything except her eyes, he found it difficult to guess what she was thinking. He thought she was going to say something to him about her deceased manager, but instead, she said a forceful, "Move," and dropped his hand only to gently push him aside so that she could grab two large sized cups from the cup dispenser.

"Here, go get us some drinks. Whatever's working. If the machine is damaged, the iced tea dispenser will probably still work." She stepped over her petite coworker and grabbed two large paper bags. "Go get the drinks," she said to him. "I'll get some food." He stared at the back of her head and realized he didn't have a plan, so he might as well do what she commanded him to do since her plan included him finally getting some food and a drink. She shook open the first paper bag and reached for several of the burgers which were still perched under what was recently a working heat lamp. He turned around and walked towards the drink dispenser trying not to look left over at where the young man and the older woman had been seated. He didn't want to know if they were dead, alive, or suffering. He just did not want to know anything anymore about other people and what they were going through. He needed to get the drinks and take the bag of food Aisha was making for him and get to the airport to find Yuna.

Aisha was right, the dispensers were damaged and not working, but the iced tea container was a separate, manual machine that was shoved against the right side of the drink dispenser. This placement had kept it protected from the multiple blasts from the gas station.

As he filled the first cup, Aisha yelled to him to hurry up in case there was another explosion. She also asked him if he thought cash would be needed. He blinked hard at that question and turned his head to look over at her in wonder.

"You're really thinking this through, aren't you?" he responded.

"I'm taking cash," she muttered affirmatively as he watched her open the cash registers with the manager's key. "You never know. Credit cards won't be working. Don't let me go to jail for this," she said as she looked up at him and half laughed.

As she continued to open cash registers and remove cash, Lev finished filling up the second cup and turned to join her. He heard a sickening groan from the floor near the destroyed window overlooking the gas station. He closed his eyes and steeled himself for what he would see if he dared to look towards the sound of human suffering. He slowly turned his head to the right and saw the charred body of the young man who had been sitting by the window minutes earlier.

Lev turned his head away and coughed hard enough to suppress the feeling of needing to gag. He turned his gaze back towards Aisha who was still busy adding food to the two bags she was filling for each of them. He watched as she put a handful of cash and coins in each bag. Time slowed. He looked back at the charred body of the young man who was visibly trying to reach out a hand to him from across the room.

"Help me," he whispered.

Lev walked over to the counter where Aisha was standing on the other side. He stood there as if he were a customer on a regular day. He put both of the drinks down on the counter in front of her and held her gaze in silence as the dish towels they were wearing as face masks obscured all other facial features.

"What?" she asked him. He said nothing. "What's wrong?" she asked with greater insistence this time. Still looking at her eyes, he slowly pointed to the dying young man on the floor. "We can't help him," she said quietly, shaking her head no firmly and taking a step backwards. She was clearly upset at the sight of the injured young man.

Lev looked away from her and slowly began walking over to where the grievously injured young man was laying on the debris strewn floor. His burns were severe. His clothes had been burned away in many areas and there was a shimmer to parts of his open burn wounds. Lev realized it was glass from the window embedded into his body. He removed the dish towel from his face by lifting it over the top of his head and placed it gently over what was left of the young man's mutilated face. Gently, but firmly, he placed one hand on each side of the young man's head and then, quickly, he twisted his head until he heard the same snap he had heard earlier when the older man had ended the suffering of the young boy.

"Oh, shit," he heard Aisha whisper from behind the counter. "Oh, shit, Lev. You ok? It had to be done. I couldn't have done it though. I couldn't even kill my manager when he was laying there dying, and I hated that motherfucker...." her voice trailed off.

Lev got up and walked back to the counter and said, "I need a new dish towel."

"Yeah, you do!" Aisha said with reverent enthusiasm.

He walked around the counter and back to the darkened break room and grabbed a new dish towel and a new rubber band from the clear plastic box and secured it around both his mouth and nose like a pro as he walked, stepping over the bodies of the kitchen staff and then back to Aisha. She was sipping her iced tea under the dish towel covering her face and reached over to grab his cup from the counter and handed it to him.

"Here. You need this," she said. "You need this with some fucking vodka in it, but this is all we serve here. Fucking G-rated establishment."

He took the cup from her, and slid the cup up under the dish towel, and drank half of the contents before stopping to catch a breath. This is what he had come in here for in the first place.

She handed him his paper bag full of food, cash, and change.

"Here. There's enough food for your airport friend, too," she said. Lev took the bag from her and asked her how far away the airport was from where they were. "Less than five miles, but..." she shook her head, looking outside the broken windows of the restaurant, "...how are you going to get quickly past all those cars? You hear that? That's another one exploding. Well, something's exploding. You're going to need to hustle past whatever you see smoking." She looked at him and sighed and shook her head. Lev could tell she was contemplating something, so he waited for her to finish.

"Listen," she finally said, "you saved my life. I didn't know the gas station was going to go up like that. I might have walked over to that guy and tried to talk to him if you hadn't shown up. Follow me," she said and walked away from him back towards the kitchen area and into the break room.

Lev stood in the doorway of the darkened room and watched her open a locker. She pulled out keys and walked over to him.

"These are the keys to my moped. It's parked out back, so maybe it didn't get damaged in the explosion. Let's go check it out. If it's usable, take it to the airport to find your friend. It's skinny enough to fit between that shit traffic mess out there and it has a full tank of gas. I only have one helmet, though," she ended.

Lev had been looking at the keys she'd placed in his hands while she spoke, but when she was finished, he looked at her eyes, and said, "Ok. Thanks. You've been really helpful."

"Yeah," she said with a surprisingly upbeat tone, "That's what you get for saving my life. Me being helpful and shit." She playfully tapped his upper arm and told him to follow her out to her moped. Along the way, she asked him if he had ever ridden one before or if he needed a quick lesson. Growing up in southern California, Lev and his friends had done plenty of dirt bike riding in the desert, so he said so and assured her he was skilled on two wheels.

Aisha opened the back door of the restaurant which led to a large dumpster protected by three cinder block walls. Her yellow moped was parked inconspicuously to the left of the dumpster along one side of the cement wall.

"My manager lets me park here because my last one got hit by some drunk guy when I was working nights over spring break," she explained to Lev.

"Spring break?" Lev asked politely, realizing that despite her impressive resilience and ability to think critically during all this, she might only be a high school student. With the dish towel still on her face, he'd already forgotten what she looked like, but he remembered he thought she looked young. "Are you a student?" he continued.

"Yeah, just finished my first year of grad school and was looking forward to quitting this shit job and doing my internship, but I guess that's not going to happen," she remarked matter-of-factly. She was older than she looked, then.

Not needing to fake his curiosity, Lev asked, "What are you in grad school for?" He put the paper bag full of food into the small storage compartment she had opened for him. He actually was mildly curious, but more surprised at how she kept managing to hold conversations despite the events they were both living through.

"Physical therapy, and I had secured a paid internship for the summer with my mentor who owns a practice in the city. I mean, given the state of things, I would think an internship this summer would have me learning a lot of skills working with whoever the hell survives this little apocalypse, but maybe Bob is dead, too. Who the hell knows?"

The first hint of defeat entered her voice, and Lev felt responsible. "Well, no wonder you said you couldn't kill your manager. You're training to help people heal," he said, hoping to reignite her attitude. He didn't want to take her moped and leave her feeling defeated.

The moped looked new and Lev hopped on and started it up.

"Hold on," she said and darted into the back door of the restaurant. She emerged quickly with a pink helmet and handed it to him. "No one's gonna save you if you get into an accident on this thing, you know?" she laughed. He heard an appreciation for dark humor in her voice and realized she was coping the best way she knew how.

"Hey, I'll try to return it to the same spot when I get back. I'll leave the keys under the back wheel of the dumpster," he told her.

"Or," she said seriously, "you and your friend can bring it back to my house. See that intersection up ahead?" she asked him pointing in the direction of the airport, "If you take Walnut Avenue south at that intersection, and turn right onto

Forrest Road, my house is the obnoxious yellow two story house at the end of Sunnyvale Lane. My mother thought it would be funny to paint our house yellow because of the street name. It's not hard to remember. Walnut south, right onto Forrest, and then remember it's a yellow house at the end of Sunnyvale. I mean, I don't know if you can get yourself and your friend back to wherever you're from if this is what the highway looks like," she finished. Lev was shaking his head yes as she spoke.

"Yeah. You know what? Yeah. I'm going to take you up on that. I'm not even going to lie and say I have a better plan. I don't have any plan except to find my girlfriend," he said to her.

"Oh, goddamn. I hope she's ok. I'd offer to come help you look, but three people on my bike won't work and anyway, my mom's at home because she had knee surgery two days ago, so she's laid up and I want to get back to make sure she's ok."

"Do you want to drive with me to your house and drop you off there first?" Lev asked her suddenly concerned that he was not being at all considerate of her needs while looking out for his own.

"No. It's not far at all, and I need to walk off this stress. I have my dish towel to protect my lungs, got some food for me and my mom, and walking will help me chill out before I get home. I don't want to be freaking out because my mom sure will be! One of us has to be calm!" She laughed at the thought of the dynamic between herself and her mother and Lev realized he was really fortunate to have found this person during this crisis.

"Ok," he said looking at her, "I'll find my girlfriend, and we'll make our way back to your place. I appreciate the help you've given me. I really do. We just moved here two weeks ago. I'm not even sure how we'd find our apartment without Siri."

"Definitely. I'll expect to see you later," she said and stood there as he made his way out of the parking lot and towards the airport.

The Airport

He was glad he helped Aisha. Helping her had helped him to have a better way of getting to the airport to find Yuna. There was no clear path down the main road, and he found himself weaving the moped from the shoulder of the road, back into open spaces in driving lanes, and he even entered a large parking lot of a shopping center which provided him the most clear space to move forward. He noted people walking towards their own destinations, groups of people standing about talking, and disaster heroes who were still trying to save others. He noted the complete lack of emergency services attending to any of the infinite number of crises and considered what 'survival of the fittest' meant in a situation like this. Is it the most physically fit who survives something like this? Or is it the most emotionally resilient? The ones with the hardest hearts and a strong sense of self survival? Aisha was emotionally resilient in a crisis, he thought. But did she have a strong sense of survival? She'd given him her means of transportation. That wasn't too smart if you really thought about it. He also thought of the small boy torn apart by the barbed wire and his own reaction in that situation from start to finish. A small terrified child running towards him during an unfolding tragedy, giving chase to rescue the child, and just the absolute horror of how it ended. Was that a good use of his physical, mental, and emotional strengths? Probably not. He needed to make better choices for himself and not worry so much about others for a while. It was an uncomfortable thought. He considered himself a nice guy.

He stopped the moped at the base of a small overpass which appeared completely blocked by tangled vehicles. The largest, a moving truck, was flipped on its side with smaller cars beneath it, and it was blocking all of the lanes. Access to the shoulder was completely blocked by several cars including one which was smoking. After carefully scanning for a passable space, he began to back up the moped and headed towards the left side of the overpass. The lanes going in the other direction were not completely blocked, but to get over to the other side, he'd either have to turn around and drive a bit further down until the center lane guard rail ended, or he could hoist the moped over the guardrail right here and keep moving forward on the opposite side of the roadway.

He decided to hoist the moped over the guardrail. He was a big man standing six feet four inches tall. He wasn't an athlete of a specific sport, but he was an avid outdoorsman and had worked out faithfully since his youth. In middle and high school, his peers and physical education teachers all assumed he would join a sport and be a star athlete for the school, but he lacked a competitive edge that would have propelled him to do so. He wasn't a team oriented sportsman. He liked to play tennis, but he didn't like to keep score. His parent's signed him up for sailing lessons, but as talented a sailor as he was, he never accepted opportunities to participate in races. He was raised in California, so he surfed. He golfed with his father because it was fun to spend time with him, and his father understood that it wasn't a competition for him. As he got older, he initiated pick-up games with friends because he really did like playing baseball, basketball, soccer, etc. He just wanted to avoid the aggressiveness of competition. He enjoyed running in the early morning before school, skiing in the winter, and his parents converted the third bedroom of their house into a workout room with all the equipment one could want in a home gym.

Lifting the moped over the silvery grey guardrail he thought of his first date with Yuna. She had expected him to keep score when they went to play mini golf, but he told her he didn't want to keep score. She had responded enthusiastically, "Oh, good! I thought you took me here just to show me how great you are at it and beat me. I would definitely lose. I've never even played before. Not keeping score is so much better. Now I can relax!" She had laughed and shrugged at that and he thought she was the most adorable human he had ever interacted with. He recalled a first date he had gone on with another woman he had met before meeting Yuna. A really nice woman named Melissa he had met in an Intro to Something class he couldn't recall. They had gone bowling and she had lost. She was seriously pissed off about losing. Going out for pizza afterwards, she pouted and kept complaining about having lost despite him assuring her it didn't matter and insisting it was just a game. What a miserable date that was. But Yuna got it. Got him. "That was so fun!" she had declared after her first game of scoreless mini golf. It had been fun. They missed shots, they laughed and encouraged one another. They got holes in one, they cheered for each other.

With the moped on the opposite side of the road now, he stepped over the guardrail and opened the storage compartment to get a burger or whatever he could from the bag Aisha had packed. He was really hungry. He grabbed a burger wrapped in purple paper and ripped the paper off tossing it to the street at his feet. He lifted off the pink helmet and put it on the seat of the moped. He ate the burger by going under the dish towel. He ate it in less than a minute. He ate so fast that it hurt swallowing and he wished he had a drink to wash it down with. He reached back into the bag and grabbed a mystery sandwich wrapped in blue paper. Tossing aside the paper, he noted that this one was a chicken sandwich and not a burger. There was lettuce and tomato on this one. It was easier to swallow than the burger. He'd spent about a minute on his meal. He needed to get going.

His eyes burned. He wiped his greasy, bloody hands on his shirt and then wiped his eyes. The wounds on his hands caused by the barbed wire stung. He suddenly noticed that the cars around him contained dead bodies, but he noticed with surprise that this fact didn't horrify him or make him sick despite just having eaten. He looked around him. A man was walking towards him with a noticeable limp. Lev nodded to the man who was staring intently at him and said, "Hey." The man raised a hand in a feeble attempt to acknowledge Lev, but dropped his hand quickly and kept walking towards him. Lev let out a sigh, he did not want to make any more friends today. He wanted to keep moving. Eating had been necessary. This impending social interaction, not so much. The man was getting thirty seconds of his time, and no more. He had a pathway to the airport for now, and he wanted to get going. He could feel the food in his stomach begin to turn to fuel. He wanted to keep going.

"Man, I'm heading out. I can't help you," Lev shouted absently at the man as he continued his approach, limping through the wreckage of cars. Lev picked up the pink helmet off the seat of the moped and put it back on then closed the storage compartment to secure the rest of the food.

As he threw his right leg over the seat of the bike, the man spoke up in a voice that reeked of desperation asking Lev, "Hey, my leg is messed up really bad. Can you take me to a hospital?" Lev felt a sense of incredulity rise up in him as he processed the man's request. Quickly, the incredulity faded to a mixture of anger and disgust.

"No, man, I cannot take you to a hospital. Look around you. Jesus Christ," he said with rising contempt for the man. The man stopped his approach and stared at Lev as if he had just broken some indestructible human contract which demanded you help a fellow human in need when asked, and perhaps, Lev had done just that. But he didn't care. This man had nothing he needed or wanted which would help him find Yuna. This man was intent on taking from him. Taking his time, his focus, his energy. He couldn't allow that to happen. He turned the key in the ignition and drove off through the spaces provided by this side of the roadway. He shook his head at the thought of the desperate man. Not my problem, he told himself. That's how you survive.

Riding through the traffic on the streets leading away from the airport provided Lev with more clear routes for him to navigate the moped and he felt he was suddenly making good time. He had to back up once when a path that seemed clear was suddenly discovered to contain three cars with growing plumes of smoke coming from them. He also noticed a small fire visible under the backside of the smoking car closest to him. He didn't want to risk riding past the smoldering vehicles and have them become a problem for him. He backed up quickly until he could sufficiently turn the moped around and made his way to the grassy median which, unlike the overpass earlier, did not contain a guardrail.

People were mostly congregating in the grass along the median, so he had been trying to avoid the area concerned they'd want him to stop and help them or see if he had any information they could use. He purposely drove the moped at an aggressive pace as much as he could in order to convey to survivors that he wasn't going to stop to help or chat. Some raised their hands to get his attention, but the helmet helped him to pretend he hadn't seen their non-verbal requests for assistance.

Still, survivors were few and many of the cars contained dead bodies not killed by impacts of cars against cars, but, instead, by whatever it was. Was it a chemical attack? Had they been attacked by a terrorist group? He was closing in on the airport now. The smoke rising from the direction of the airport gave him a sick feeling deep in his stomach, and multiple areas across the skyline with more billowing black smoke reminded him of the sound of the multiple airplane crashes earlier. His eyes burned sharply from the smoke and pollutants but his lungs were doing better with the help of the dishtowel Aisha had instructed him to wear.

He continued across the grassy median to the right side of the roadway and slowly made his way to the congested entrance of the airport parking lot. The cars entering the airport were tangled in a disastrous and impenetrable mess of metal. At least, impenetrable with the moped. The vehicles were turned every which way, some were billowing black smoke, and a few had already gone up in flames earlier by the look of it. Lev surveyed the scene looking for a reasonable way to get into the airport parking lot. Beyond the parking lot was the actual airport facility, and he could see where parts of some of the buildings had been destroyed by at least two downed planes. His heart raced as he tried to recall the layout of the airport and which area Yuna would likely have been in while waiting for him to come get her this afternoon. The food courts for her airline would have been further to the left, he sighed in relief. She wouldn't have bothered to walk much further than her arrival gate. There were plenty of food choices in that area.

He quickly rode the moped back towards the cell phone parking lot down the street. The cell phone parking lot was encircled by a low cement wall with tall metal bars at the front entrance. He leaned the moped against the cement wall where pleasant looking shrubbery had been planted to make the lot look more inviting. The lot was large, and he was not parked directly near the entrance. He scanned the location of where he was leaving the moped slightly concealed by shrubbery and put the keys in his pocket. He tucked the pink helmet under the bushiest part of the shrubs and realized he didn't care if it was gone when he got back. He didn't care if the moped was gone. He just wanted to find Yuna. They could walk to Aisha's Yellow house and he'd buy her a new moped to replace this one if it came to it. He scanned the remaining tangled pathway towards the airport. He snorted a small, disgusted laugh and wondered if anything would be easy today.

He started back towards the road scanning for a passable entrance along the exit leading into the airport. There were no people around him now. Any survivors had walked away already. He realized he could climb over several of the cars to the left of the mess. He'd be dangerously close to at least one large pickup truck that had black smoke coming from its engine. What if it went up in flames as he scrambled over and around it? He kept looking for a better way to navigate into the airport. He heard a child crying from inside one of the cars and closed his eyes as he tried to suppress his concern and empathy for the helpless kid. He couldn't rescue a child and carry it with him over smoking cars, across the entire airport parking lot and into a semi-destroyed airport facility while looking for his girlfriend. He thought of the older man in the cow pasture telling him to help when he could and end the suffering of those who were too far gone to save and he decided that the child would still be in the car when he came back with Yuna. He would rescue the child then. Yuna would help. A dark thought crossed his mind. What if the car goes up and the child is killed in an explosion? Or worse. What if the child is burned to death as a slow moving fire overtakes the car he or she is in? He shook off the thoughts as quickly as they flowed into his mind. Survivors are not the fittest, he told himself. Survivors are the most strategic, the most determined to survive. He had to prioritize himself and his ability to find Yuna. The crying child was not his responsibility right now. It felt cold hearted, but he didn't bother to linger on the thought.

He scanned the scene again looking for the safest way through the cars. Nothing looked good or easy. He accepted that he would have to climb over vehicles quickly and take his chances getting through to the area up ahead. He realized this was the first action he was taking that truly was a risk by choice. He could have made it this close to the airport only to be killed by some bullshit like a car going off like a bomb as he scrambled across the hood of it. He climbed on top of the car in front of him, looked around, and confirmed his only option was to sprint across the majority of cars and trucks. The route that made the most sense included running across the top of a minivan which happened to be smashed into the rear of one of the cars that was billowing more and more smoke from its engine. He took a deep breath and jumped over from the hood of the car he was on and into the back of a blue, short bed pickup truck in front of him.

The dead didn't complain about him using their vehicles as his obstacle course. He climbed on top of the pickup truck and slid down its hood where he then sprinted forward across the back of one small sedan and then to the right onto the hood of another small sedan. The front of this sedan was crumpled into the SUV in front of it, so he dropped into a space along the passenger door where he was able to stand on the ground and squeeze between the SUV and the cement wall to the right. As he passed by the passenger side of the SUV, he came face-to-face with a dead woman whose face was pressed against the glass window. The airbag had deployed and her glasses were crooked and pressed against the window but held in place by her nose.

He stared for a second. His face was blank as he looked at her. He turned his attention to the front of the SUV which was too bent to climb up and over but he saw a space under the car in front where he could possibly crawl underneath and get ahead by one car length. He dropped to the ground and looked under the car in front of the SUV but realized the plan would not work. He couldn't see how he'd get clear of the car from beneath it given his size.

He looked behind himself at the cement wall that served as a protective guide to traffic heading into the airport parking lot and considered how it could be useful. He leaned against the cement wall and placed his feet on the passenger door of the SUV. He looked at the dead woman's face again before using his feet against the car, his hands against the cement wall, and the force of his back against the wall to move sideways in a forward direction. The space between the wall and the car in front of the SUV narrowed and he used his feet and hands to maneuver himself higher until he could pull and push himself onto the roof of that car. He was sweating as he found his balance and stood on top of the car. He looked across and saw more than one way forward which was a relief. He quickly darted across the remaining stretch of vehicles and ended by jumping off the hood of a car which had crashed into a ticket distribution machine. The arm of the machine was lifted high into the air above a small car with two dead in the front seat. The way forward was less impacted and he started running towards the entrance to the airline Yuna's flight had arrived on earlier in the day. Someone called out to him to turn back shouting at him, "Everyone's dead!" but he kept running. Not everyone's dead, he thought to himself. I'm not dead. Lots of people aren't dead. I'm not dead. Aisha's not dead. Yuna's not dead.

Yuna's airline occupied the space furthest away from the entrance to the airport. Entering the building wasn't an option as so much of the first sections of the sprawling building appeared to have been damaged by several downed airplanes as well as airplanes that had simply meandered into the structure rather than taxiing down the runway to depart. The air here was thicker with smoke, and it was painful to breathe even with his makeshift mask.

Jogging forward along the pedestrian sidewalk alongside the exterior of the airport, gave him a new perspective as to how many people had not survived whatever it was that had happened. On the roadways, and when passing by commercial outlet stores, the dead were contained inside vehicles or within stores for the most part. Here at the airport, the dead littered the sidewalk areas where convenient baggage check-in kiosks were available for every airline. He noted that people standing in line, entire families with their luggage, children in strollers, elderly in wheelchairs, all of them just dropped where they were standing or sitting in line and died. His mind struggled to make sense of the number of dead. Bullets didn't kill them. What he'd witnessed earlier on the highway when it all started was nearly five miles from the airport. How was a chemical or biological weapon possibly responsible for this number of deaths across such a vast distance?

It made no sense. What killed these people? Why was he alive? What was different about the others who also survived and were milling about dazed? He swallowed hard, blinking harder. His eyes were tearing as if the thoughts he was trying to make sense of were making him cry, but in reality, it was the smoke filled air that was making them burn and tearing up was their best defense against the particulates circulating in the smoke.

He was out of breath, in part because the air was so polluted so close to the burning structure of the airport, but also because of the never-ending fear. Adrenaline and fear were impacting his ability to maintain the high level of physical activity needed to keep running towards Yuna's airport terminal. He stopped near a kiosk where a dead man and woman lay haphazardly, one in front of the kiosk, the other in back of it. They were valets for airport parking. Their customers were also lying dead in front of the kiosk where they had been standing in line waiting for their turn to hand their keys over to one of them.

Lev was panting in the hot polluted air with one hand on the service counter of the bright red and white kiosk. It occurred to him that the employees manning the kiosk might have water under the back of the counter, so he stood up straighter and walked around to the back of the counter to search, hopeful for a brief moment. On a hot day like this, even if their shift had begun in the cooler hours of the morning, they would have likely prepared for the heat and humidity to come by bringing along some water or some other beverages to get them through the day. Under the kiosk, Lev saw a medium-sized red cooler with the airport's logo on it. He had to move the dead customer service worker's legs by pulling her towards him a couple of feet, but was able to grab the handle of the cooler afterwards and bring it to the side of the kiosk. Opening the white lid, he let out a deeply grateful sigh. A small layer of ice on the bottom was keeping no less than six bottles of water cold. There were also a couple of energy drinks which Lev would not normally choose over water, but he grabbed an orange colored one and twisted the top off and drank the contents until finished. He grabbed the bottle filled with a red energy drink and put it on top of the counter of the kiosk. He grabbed a bottle of water and opened it and drank half of it before putting it down on the counter alongside the bottle of red energy drink, then he grabbed all the rest of the waters. With all of them on the counter of the kiosk, he walked over to the line of dead valet customers and scanned about them for a tote bag he could use to carry the drinks. Yuna would be thirsty, too. He grabbed a tote bag off of a dead woman surrounded by three dead teenagers. He dumped the contents of the tote bag onto the sidewalk to make room for the drinks, but noticed the contents included a bag of trail mix that he decided he wanted to keep. Packing the cold drinks into the tote bag, he shoved the trail mix on top and slung the bag over his shoulder before grabbing the half-finished water from the counter and finishing it. He threw the empty bottle to the sidewalk. He kept heading towards the far end of the airport towards Yuna's arrival terminal.

The inside of the building was far less smoke-filled than the outdoors at this point, so he found an entrance way that was propped open by a dead body and entered the dark interior. The dead were strewn about, and he scanned the scene. This was close to Yuna's arrival area. He called out her name and was startled by the gruff sound of his own voice. He considered that the smoke must be impacting his vocal cords. He grabbed a water bottle from the tote, unscrewed the plastic cap, and took some sips to clear his voice. He coughed a few times and tried again. Loudly, he called to Yuna. He listened to the silence intently. No one responded. He remained inside the front section of the airport, but did not venture deeper inside. He wanted to keep an eye on any people outside the facility who might be Yuna. He wanted her to be able to hear him calling to her if she was outside. He continued traveling towards Yuna's terminal by walking alongside the glass wall that contained the entranceways and walked outside to call for her at each of the numerous doors which led outside. He kept yelling out her name and waiting for a response. Waiting. Walking. Inside. Outside. Calling out to her again. No one responded to him. He walked over to an open door leading outside and shouted her name three times. He waited in between each call of her name. Was she waiting for him inside? The air quality was much better inside. He went back inside the terminal.

There were no living that he had encountered at this end of the airport. He stood still and looked around. All of the power appeared to have gone out and much was dark inside despite the time of day. The air outside was dark, the sun obscured by smoke, so the inside of the airport had a dark and gloomy look accentuated by the numerous dead collapsed all over the floor. He stood still and tried to listen for any signs of the living before calling out Yuna's name again. He waited and thought he heard something. He listened intently. He called out Yuna's name and stood wide-eyed desperately trying to hear if another person would respond. He heard what sounded like crying coming from behind him and turned around calling out Yuna's name again. He walked briskly back to where he had just come from and listened intently for the sound of another person. He heard faint crying coming from the women's restroom and dropped the tote outside the bathroom entrance and ran quickly into the serpentine, doorless entrance to the restrooms. It was completely dark inside the windowless space, and he fished out his cell phone to use the flashlight feature. He used the flashlight to scan the room and called out to Yuna.

"Mommy," a child cried, and Lev let the disappointment wash over him as he realized what he had heard was the cries of a child calling for its mother. He stood there with his cell phone flashlight steady on a line of female bodies collapsed along the row of sinks in the dark. He looked at each one trying to see if any were his Yuna. None were. He sighed a mixture of relief and bitterness and moved the flashlight towards the far end of the restroom where a stall door larger than the others was located. The door contained a plaque that indicated it contained a baby changing station. Lev pushed on the door and confirmed it was locked from inside.

"Kid, can you open the door?" he asked the sniffling child locked behind the closed door. "Kid, the door is locked. Can you unlock the door? he asked again, trying to sound comforting.

"Mommy," the child said again.

"Can you reach the door lock and unlock it so that we can find your mommy?" Lev asked the child.

"Mommy is here," the child responded.

Lev shined the flashlight on the floor to see how much space there was for a grown man to climb under it and unlock it himself. "Ok, kid. My name is Lev. What's yours?" he asked as he got down on his knees to crawl under the door of the bathroom stall.

"Prisha," the child whimpered quietly.

"Prisha, I'm going to crawl under the door and then I'll unlock it so that we can get out of here. Are you ready? I have a flashlight. Do you see the light on the floor? That's my flashlight. I'm going to crawl in now."

He grunted as he made himself small enough to fit under the open space at the bottom of the stall door. The light from his flashlight bounced all around the walls, ceiling, and floor of the bathroom stall and even caught the wide-eyed face of the frightened little girl who was strapped into an umbrella stroller. Lev felt sick at the realization of how many small children were in similar situations right now. Better off dead, he thought to himself. He felt parts of his body, his hands and arms, push against something soft on the floor and realized it was the body of Prisha's mother. He imagined she had taken her toddler into the bathroom and died as all the others had. Prisha had not. The thought of all the helpless children left living while their parents dropped dead in their tracks sickened him again. He felt a wave of empathy wash over him. Where was that empathy when he heard the crying child locked in a car, he wondered. He was at the airport now. It was easier to stop and help a child now that he was where he needed to be in order to find Yuna. He would give this child to some other survivor and keep looking for Yuna.

He stood up and used his flashlight to survey what had happened in the bathroom stall. Prisha was strapped into her stroller facing away from the toilet. Her mother was collapsed alongside the toilet. She had positioned Prisha facing away from herself as she'd used the bathroom, so Prisha might have avoided seeing much before the electricity had gone out while she'd been locked in the stall with her dead mother. He shined his flashlight towards his face so that the little girl could see him. He removed the dish towel from around his head and made an effort to smile a friendly smile hoping it would help her be less fearful. He tucked the dish towel into his back pocket.

"Hey, Prisha. I'm Lev. You ready to get out of here?" Lev asked the little girl kindly.

"Mommy is sick," Prisha whimpered between soft cries.

"I know. I know," Lev responded soothingly. "We can't stay here, so I'm going to open the door and we're going to go outside and see who we can find to help us," he added. He unlocked the door, but thought of all the dead women laying on the floor beyond and hesitated.

"I'm going to turn off my flashlight for a minute and carry you and your stroller out of here, ok?" he said to the little girl.

"Ok," she responded.

Lev thought she sounded resigned to whatever plans he had for her, so he turned off his flashlight, stuffed it into his back pocket with his mask, and unlocked the stall door. He opened the door wide and bent down to lift the stroller containing Prisha so that he could walk both straight out of the bathroom. She must have weighed the equivalent of a butterfly because Lev noted how incredibly light and easy the lift was given how exhausted he was beginning to feel from both the physical exertion of the day and the emotional exertion he was going through every time he had to stop to interact with another still-living soul. He quickly walked through the bathroom towards the small light at the entrance to the exit of the serpentine doorway of the restroom.

Once out of the restroom, the minimal light shining in from the glass wall of windows leading outside felt like a relief. The dark bathroom had unnerved Lev as he considered nightfall would arrive in a few hours and who the hell knew what would happen then. The world was in a state of chaos. Still no sound of rescue services in the distance. An airport destroyed. Small children dying trapped in cars, in bathroom stalls. He put Prisha and her stroller down on the ground and felt in his back pocket for the dish towel. He'd leave it off for now.

"Prisha, I'm going to have to call out to my friend to try and find her, so if I'm yelling loudly, it's because I want her to hear me. Do you understand? I'm going to be loud. My friend's name is Yuna. I'm going to keep calling for her and then I'll wait to see if she hears me. If you hear anyone calling to us, you tell me, ok? You listen, too. Yeah?" Lev asked the frightened child.

"Ok," Prisha said meekly.

"Are you thirsty or hungry?" he asked her, remembering the tote bag he'd left by the bathroom entrance.

"Yes. I want my snacks," Prisha said absently.

"I have both! I left my water and snacks near the bathroom. Hold on," he told her. He jogged the few feet over to his tote bag, grabbed it and held it up and smiled warmly at the child as he jogged back to her. Her expression was still blank, but she was making eye contact and not afraid of him at all. He knelt beside her stroller and pulled out a water bottle and removed the cap. He poured a little onto the floor in back of the stroller because it was so full that it had spilled slightly when he removed the cap.

"Here you go. Can you handle the bottle without spilling it?" he asked her.

"Yes. I'm a big girl," she responded with confidence in her ability.

Lev watched as she did a pretty good job of drinking from the bottle and then sighed at him loudly to indicate she had really needed the water.

"Alright then!" He smiled at her. He dropped the cap to the bottle on the floor and pulled out the bag of trail mix. "Dude, you have any allergies?" he asked her seriously.

She shrugged and sipped from the water bottle.

"Can you eat peanut butter and jelly sandwiches?" he asked her with a look of concern to convey to her that he was serious.

"I like peanut butter and apple slices," she said to him.

"Ok, well those are good, but I don't have any of those for you. What I have is trail mix. There are peanuts, raisins, chocolate candies, and other stuff in here," he said as he shook the bag at her.

"I don't like raisins."

"That's fine. Just throw them on the floor when you get one from the bag!" Lev said with humor. Prisha liked that and kicked her feet happily in her stroller. Lev opened the bag of trail mix and placed it in her lap. She handed him the water bottle, and he told her to ask for it if she needed more water.

Lev headed back on his way towards Yuna's terminal pushing Prisha in the stroller. She tossed raisins to the floor and offered him brightly colored chocolate candies in an effort to share the best part of the trail mix. Lev accepted her gifts and the two of them moved forward with no other communication while he shouted Yuna's name into the silence of the airport. They hadn't walked far when Lev heard a female voice respond to his calls.

Outside a woman yelled back to him. "Hey! Hey, outside. Where are you?" Clearly, the voice did not belong to Yuna, but he had Prisha, and he knew he had to find someone to take her so that he could continue searching for Yuna on his own. He scanned for an open door and saw one ajar with multiple bodies on the floor keeping the doors open. He bent down to Prisha and told her to hang on and that he was going to make her fly out the doors. He lifted up her stroller and carried her over the bodies in the doorway, kicking the doors open wide enough to fit the two of them through to the outside.

Once outside, he yelled for the woman to find them. She emerged from behind a cement pillar that probably served a functional structural purpose to the building as well as an architecturally aesthetic purpose. The woman was dressed in comfortable travel clothes and looked in her mid-thirties. She was small, just a little over five feet tall, and lean like a fitness instructor. Her blonde hair was swept up in a tight pony tail and she had no makeup on. She looked terrified, but relieved at the same time to see Lev and Prisha. It could have been that Lev's size and appearance frightened her at first, but the little girl eating trail mix in the stroller before him lessened her fear as she assumed he was a good guy. She could not have known that Lev had left many people to die today, including children.

"Hᵢ!" she exclaimed with excitement looking at both Lev and Prisha directly. "I'm Liza. Do you know what's going on?" she asked Lev.

Lev shook his no head and blinked hard at the question. "No. No idea," he said to her. "I'm looking for my girlfriend. She came in on a flight earlier today. I just found this little beauty in the women's restroom. This is Prisha."

"Hi," Prisha said cheerfully to Liza and tossed a raisin to the ground in search of more colorful chocolates.

"Prisha does not like raisins." Lev half laughed at Liza.

Liza seemed confused and Lev decided to take advantage of her confusion by taking control of the conversation. He didn't even know he had it in him to be so manipulative, but there it was. A sense of survival rose up in him and dominated his decision making in his own best interests. Not in the best interests of this woman Liza. Not in the best interests of Prisha. No. His own best interests because his best interests were aligned with Yuna's best interests. And Yuna's best interests were aligned with her parent's best interests. And every decision he would make would also be in the best interest of his own parents. He was overwhelmed by the power of the self-interest that suddenly dictated his decision making.

"I'm going to leave Prisha with you now. I'm not good with kids. I don't have any. Don't want any. Here's a bag of water bottles for you two. I'm taking the sports drink, though. And actually, I'm going to take one water bottle. You can have the rest. The kid has trail mix. I have to go now." Lev dropped the tote bag next to the stroller and turned to walk away. It took Liza a minute to absorb what was happening but, when she did, she shouted to him something about his not being allowed to leave a child with her because…. it wasn't fair. Lev heard her and scoffed at the idea of fairness in this situation. Yuna's terminal was the next one. He came all this way to find Yuna. Not finding her, now that would be unfair. Fuck everyone else and their fucking problems. He didn't turn around to respond to Liza. He kept walking towards the doors up ahead ignoring Prisha as she called his name.

When he and Yuna had traveled through this airport previously, they had gone to the vegan restaurant at the far end of this entrance. She had declared that particular vegan airport restaurant superior to well-known vegan hot spots in his hometown of San Diego. She would have gone there for lunch, he thought. He kept walking. He could hear Prisha calling loudly to him now, and it hurt him deep inside for some reason. It was a pain he didn't expect. He'd known the kid for about 10 minutes. It fucking hurt him when she desperately screamed his name that last time before he pulled the door open and ran inside of the terminal to find Yuna at the vegan restaurant. He was going to find her. She would be there. He sprinted over bodies and luggage to the darkened front of the Vegan Experience restaurant and squinted hard looking in booths and on the floor for Yuna. This was end game stuff he didn't want to acknowledge. This is where she needed to be. Dead or alive. He coughed hard to clear his lungs and call her name. He stopped walking, leaned forward, put his hands on his bent legs, closed his eyes and breathed in deeply through his nose and exhaled long and slow through his mouth trying to clear his anxiety and the feeling that he wanted to be sick.

He had wanted to find her before he got here to her terminal. There was nowhere else to search after this. He had hoped to find her walking along the sidewalk outside. He had hoped to find her in the previous two terminals that were not filled with smoke. He had hoped she would be in the women's restrooms. He had shouted her name inside loudly hoping she'd hear him and come running up to him, so happy to be reunited despite the odds. He stood near the hostess desk of the restaurant and scanned the darkened room and tables for signs of Yuna. A lot of bodies were slumped on top of tables, but many were also on the floor. The hostess was crumpled behind her pillar of a desk, and Lev stepped over her arm in order to enter the dining area.

He left no stone unturned. He methodically went to each table throughout the restaurant and made certain every female body was not his Yuna. He went into the women's bathrooms and checked by using his cell phone flashlight that each deceased female was not Yuna. He went back into the dining area and double checked every dead body to confirm none were Yuna. He called her name loudly over and over. She was not in the restaurant. He walked back past the dead hostess and left the area to stand outside of it and survey other options Yuna might have taken. She knew he liked the cookie shop three stores down, so he walked over there to see if she had stopped in to buy him some cookies. She wasn't there. He started to panic. How could he leave the airport unless he had checked every single body to make sure it was or was not Yuna?

The impossibility of his situation started to wash over him. He could have passed by her at the first terminal. Why hadn't he been calling her name the minute he hit the exit? Because, he told himself, those areas were destroyed and on fire. Maybe she had been walking nearby with the intention of getting to their apartment? Maybe she had been walking outside the airport while he had been in the women's restroom getting Prisha out of the locked stall. Maybe Yuna was walking past the yellow moped right now as he looked for her in the cookie shop. He didn't fucking know. How the fuck could he know? Did anybody ever really consider the immense value of a goddamned cell phone until they couldn't contact their loved one in an emergency? No. He hadn't. He took it for granted that he'd always have access to people he cared about through technology.

He stood there with frustration and desperation rising inside him and replaced those feelings with rage and screamed into the darkened airport terminal with both fists clenched tightly by his sides. He was an idiot. How could he find her? Should he go back to their apartment? How would she even get back there? It was 22 miles of mangled highway between here and the apartment. He barely made it through the wreckage from the fast food restaurant with Aisha's helpful moped. He needed to know if Yuna was dead or if she was looking for him.

Could he spray paint a big message for her against the airport walls? That was movieland bullshit. Where was a can of spray paint when you really needed one? Not here. Not in the last terminal of a fucking collapsing, smoldering airport.

The realization of the hopelessness of his situation washed over him in waves. He felt like he was drowning in a thick sea of filthy water determined to smother him and kill all of his hope. This was it. He'd walked past dying people, desperate people, children trapped in cars, and calls made specifically to him for help in order to get to the last terminal of a destroyed airport where he had hoped to find his girlfriend alive despite 9 out of 10 people being dead in an instant. But his girlfriend would be alive. Oh, yeah. And waiting for him in their favorite vegan restaurant. Because he was so special and so was she. Reality. Reality check. Check mate.

He stood there and waited for some sign that he should leave, go back to the moped, find Aisha's house. He felt paralyzed. He waited and felt numb, but didn't feel compelled by any outside force to leave the spot he was standing in. He realized he would have to decide to move. Decide to leave the airport. Decide to go to Aisha's house. Yuna didn't know Aisha. Yuna would have no idea where he was. There was no spray paint and there would be no romantic discovery of how he had tried to find her and all she had to do was follow his spray painted messages to their hero's romantic reunification. No. He had to decide to leave the airport and leave any hope, no matter how small, of finding Yuna. He had to abandon Yuna. That was the choice he was going to have to make. Stay here in a smoldering airport filled with dead bodies, or leave the airport. He had to give up trying to find Yuna and go find Aisha's house.

After standing in the same spot for some time, he finally decided to walk back outside. His movements felt robotic, and his joints were stiff in their reluctance to obey his decision to leave the terminal. His mind tried to reason with his body by assuring himself that he was just going to step outside to clear his mind and consider his options. But his body knew his mind was lying. He was going outside so that he could begin to depart the airport. There was no hope inside this terminal. Yuna could have survived. But where would she have gone? To the apartment 20 plus miles away? He was struggling to contemplate the nearly five miles he was going to have to travel to get to Aisha's house. Vehicles were still exploding in the background of every minute. The air was completely polluted by smoke and dangerous particulates from the downed aircraft and whatever else was going up in flames. Still no rescue sirens in the distance. The sun would eventually set, and there appeared to be no power in the airport. What about the rest of the area? His phone was still without service. His battery was at 52%. That was his flashlight for the dark hours.

Once outside, he turned to his left to look for Liza and Prisha. They were gone. Liza had done the right thing, he told himself. She took Prisha with her and would look after her. The main exit to the airport was nearby to the right of him. The direction of the entrance he had come in through was obscured by billowing clouds of black smoke as the airport and planes continued to burn. He started to walk towards the ticket booths set up along the exit area.

Cars were jammed in a mangled mess here as they were at the entrance to the airport, but not as tightly as at the entrance. He didn't need to carefully survey the exits in order to see clear pathways out of the airport parking lot. He walked slowly towards the exits carrying his two bottles of drinks in one hand. With his free hand, he wiped his burning eyes which had only experienced relief as he had cried silently as he made the decision to leave the airport and leave behind any hope of finding Yuna. He said nothing, but the screaming inside his head was deafening. He felt weak and plodded forward with almost no energy and imagined reaching the airport exits constituted an insurmountable feat. His lungs burned, but he didn't care enough to get the dish towel from his back pocket. He walked through the smoke filled air not caring.

He walked around vehicles and the ticket booths set up to take fees for day parking. He did not see any living souls and wondered which direction Liza and Prisha had headed. Did Liza take Prisha back inside the terminal to continue to look for her own family? It wasn't his concern. Liza seemed like a normal enough person. Prisha would be better off with her than with him. If he had found Yuna, it wouldn't have been an issue. She was excellent with children. She had earned her degree in elementary education and had been hired as a second grade teacher at an elementary school near their apartment. She was supposed to start this fall. She was so excited. She was going to earn her graduate degree in special education because she loved working with kids with special needs. She spent time during the summer months working at a day camp for special needs children in Connecticut.

When he had discovered Prisha, he thought to himself that Yuna would be able to make her feel better once he found her. Yuna would be distracted by caring for Prisha while he figured out how to get to Aisha's house. He wondered if he was actually a good person as he realized he had considered Prisha a tool for potentially distracting and comforting Yuna. Maybe Yuna would have asked him what the hell he was thinking by bringing a kid into the situation and expecting her to suddenly become a mother figure to an orphaned toddler. Yeah. Yuna might have gone down that path. No sense romanticizing the sensibility of a direct and practical woman like Yuna. She might have offered him a verbal beat down to rival any physical altercation he could imagine with a man his same size. At what point had he turned this effort to find Yuna into some stupid fantasy where he saved the day by saving his woman? This ending? The one where he leaves the airport without the woman he loves, having let countless people die rather than even attempting to save them…. This was always the eventual ending to today. He wasn't a hero.

He kept walking towards the roadway ahead where airport traffic merged with traffic traveling east on the road he had ridden in on. Explosions suddenly sounded behind him and the force of them brought him immediately and violently to his hands and knees on the street. The bottles he had been carrying rolled away from him on the ground. The exit ramp he was on shook with the force of the explosions and his ears rang and a pain in his head appeared suddenly. On his hands and knees, he turned himself slowly around to look at the airport buildings and watched as a second massive explosion ripped through the lengthy interconnected buildings. His mouth hung open and the bottles he'd been carrying rolled further away from him as he crouched there in the street looking in horror at the sight of the airport collapsing as supporting structures gave way.

The black smoke was mingling with dirty brown dust clouds produced by the crumbling cement and Lev realized the clouds of pollutants would reach him quickly, compromising his lungs. He scrambled to his feet and reached down to grab one of his drink bottles. He ran with renewed vigor as fast as he could, but he could feel the energy of the explosions catching up with him as he ran. Cars were crashed all along the merge lanes, and he tugged on door handles to find one that would open for him. The third vehicle, an SUV with hazard lights blinking, had a slightly open driver-side door with no driver taking up space. Lev quickly jumped into the driver seat, slammed the door closed, and looked at the dead male body leaning forward onto the dashboard in the passenger seat. He reached down and unbuckled the seatbelt of the passenger and pushed the lifeless body back against the leather bucket seat. Reaching across the dead man, Lev pushed the unlock button and wrenched the passenger side door open. Despite being a grown man, the passenger was a smaller person and Lev simply outweighed him while also being considerably larger. He shoved the dead man out of the passenger seat and onto the ground below. Then he climbed into the passenger seat on his hands and knees and reached over and grabbed the door to slam it shut against the incoming smoke, soot, and chemicals that were heading his way in the ominous cloud caused by the latest explosion. If Liza had taken Prisha inside the building, they were certainly dead now. By that same logic, if Yuna had been alive waiting for him inside, she was also certainly dead now. How could he ever know for sure? He wouldn't. And he would never make peace with that reality.

Sitting in the car, he realized it was still running. The driver had left his or her dead family member sitting in the car and had left it running with the AC still going. He shook his head as he accepted that the driver had done what they thought would be best for his or her dead passenger. He looked into the rear view mirror hoping to get a glimpse of the toxic cloud that was hurtling towards him when he saw something that crushed what was left of his spirit. There were two small toddlers buckled into car seats in the back seat. Whoever had been the driver of this SUV, had left their front seat passenger, a man, and two small children in the AC of the still-running car. Did the person go to find help? Lev felt the grief of the person who had left these people behind. He believed it was probably a wife, a mother who had survived and looked at her dead family and ran to get help, leaving the car running with the AC on so that they would be comfortable on this warm day.

He heard a noise and looked around him. Smoke enveloped the SUV, and a day which was already frighteningly dark, turned to night as the black cloud from the airport surrounded the vehicle. The noise grew, and Lev wondered if a smoke cloud could create a noise like the one he was hearing all around him. It took a few more seconds of trying to understand where the noise was coming from before Lev realized the noise was coming from himself. It was the sound of utter despair, rage, and fear. It came from deep inside him and was coming up and out of him in a slow building scream. He gripped the steering wheel as the emotions came flooding out of his body, unstoppable and untamed. He sounded inhuman. He sounded like a dying animal. His eyes were wide with fear as he realized he was powerless to stop this flood of emotion from emanating from his own body. He had lost control when he lost all hope, and he knew that seeing those two lifeless bodies strapped in their car seats behind him had been the last thing he was capable of processing.

During the time it took for the debris cloud to pass over the SUV he was in, Lev submitted to the demands grief created. He wailed without a hint of self-consciousness and without restraint. He gave in to the various horrors of the day and cried openly for the young boy in the pasture, the young man at the fast food restaurant, and all of the others he hadn't stopped to help. He cried bitterly for himself and Yuna combined and had no idea how to make anything better or how to find her. When he finally became conscious of himself again, he wiped his face only to realize he was covered in tears, snot and drool. He felt barely human in this deep level of grief. He wiped away all that he had expressed onto the front of his shirt and didn't care in the least if, by doing so, he was also wiping the blood of numerous others onto his body. His shirt certainly contained the blood of several others he had encountered this long day. Eventually, he sat without expression, not making a sound in the driver's seat of the SUV, a parental figure to two dead children strapped into car seats inches behind him.

The air was slowly clearing. The clock on the dashboard said it was 4:34 pm. The last time he had looked, it had been around 1:30 pm. All this had happened in such a short amount of time. How was that possible? It felt as if time had slowed down and he'd lived multiple lifetimes in the past three hours. He felt older. He felt he had personally lost so much in only three hours. Aisha. It was summertime. The air was clearing and the sun would be out for a few more hours even if darkened by smoke. He was only about five miles from Aisha's yellow house. He had to get there before nightfall. This side of the roadway was more clear than the other side as evidenced by his efforts to travel west to the airport.

He looked around the inside of the SUV for anything useful to help him get to Aisha's house. He took his cellphone from his pocket and plugged it into the car charger. Reluctantly, he looked back at the dead toddlers and saw a baby bag on the floor beneath the seat of the toddler in back of the front seat passenger.
He twisted his body and got up and reached down for the baby bag and pulled it up to the front seat with him. Upon opening it, he discovered nothing he could imagine would be useful. Maybe he simply lacked imagination. He didn't know for sure. He thought of his parents in California. He couldn't save Yuna and she was realistically less than a mile away from him. He loved her. He would die for her. He would let other people die for her. He had most likely let other people die for her today. But he couldn't save her. He knew this because he hadn't saved her. Where was she? His parents were 3000 miles away from him. He had no power. He felt ashamed and the sense of powerlessness enraged him to the point of frightening him, so he made an effort to ignore the feeling. He could deal with that later. Maybe. Maybe not. How do you deal with all of that, he asked himself.

Mentally, he made a plan he could accomplish before nightfall. He would get himself to Aisha's house. He tried to come up with a second part to his plan, but nothing made sense other than to get to Aisha's house. Maybe once he was there, he could come up with part two to his plan. He pulled his homemade face mask from his back pocket and secured it around his head. He opened the car door and headed east in the foul air towards the intersection Aisha had pointed out to him. The intersection before the fast food restaurant. Aisha wasn't getting her moped back tonight.

Aisha and Bob

Aisha watched Lev pull out of the parking lot on her bright yellow moped. He was a large man, too large for her moped. The pink helmet on his head made her think of statement jewelry. The thought made her chuckle to herself. For sure, he looked like a man on a mission during an apocalypse. She was a realistic woman. She didn't expect to see him again. She had to get home to her mother. One thing she hadn't shared with Lev was her concern for the well-being of her mother. She loved her mother. Her mother was her everything. Fuck kids who disrespected their mothers. Moms were the best. At least her mother was.

She walked back inside the dilapidated fast food restaurant, clearly her former place of employment given the state of it, and headed towards the women's restrooms. She had to pee. Walking over the bodies of her co-workers, she felt nothing. The job had been necessary these past three years as she had completed her bachelor's degree and then the first year of her graduate degree. Her manager was a goddamned idiot. An abusive cog in the machine of a bullshit corporation. He probably wouldn't ever admit he was a racist, but he lowkey was. He never realized she wasn't a desperate black woman working in fast food. He never seemed to understand she had goals she was working towards. He treated her like her life depended on this job. He spoke to her about her 'career' in fast food, ignoring what he knew about her academic goals. Instead, he talked to her about her potential as management due to her intelligence that only he could perceive.

He always seemed surprised at how bright she was. His meaty hand on her shoulder whenever he walked by her. Gross.

She walked past his lifeless body behind the cash registers and exhaled a sound of disgust at his form. Her coworkers all had aspirations for themselves which he was incapable of respecting because he had no respect for any of them. Heading towards the restrooms, she wondered if an asshole of a human being was capable of realizing they were an asshole of a human being. She stopped walking as she rounded the corner of the dining hall. The wall leading to the women's restrooms was gone. Destroyed in the explosion from the gas station. She looked to the left and saw the men's bathroom door intact. Hopeful, she entered and stepped over two male bodies in order to enter a stall and relieve herself.

She exited the men's restroom and made her way to the front counter. Grabbing her bag of food and money, she turned to exit through the front doors, but realized the gas station explosion had made the area impassable. She headed back through the kitchen and out the back doors where she had seen Lev off minutes earlier.

The air was thick with smoke. She had been camping many times with her mother and the air did not smell like a campfire. The smoke was toxic, burning fuel, burning materials no lungs should breathe in if they wanted to remain healthy. She kept the dish towel tightly against her face, secured by the rubber band, and walked towards the intersection leading towards her home. Two days earlier, her mom had had surgery on her knee for a recent problem that had developed. She was recovering with her daughter who was a graduate student in physical therapy attending to her needs. Aisha loved being able to take care of her mother during her time of recovery.

44

Her mom had worked at the airport for 15 years as a ticket agent. You would have thought her wrists would have given out after decades of hauling luggage onto scales and onto the conveyor belts, but no. Her mother's right knee had been the weakest link. It was a surprise. Thankfully, the airport union members had excellent health insurance and Rhonda had her knee issue addressed promptly. Surgery had been deemed a success, and she was to rest at home and begin therapy quickly. Aisha considered how fortunate she was that her mother had a health situation that related to her studies. If she had been diagnosed with breast cancer, or even high blood pressure, she would have been at a loss. But a situation that required physical therapy? Wow. Now that was some good luck.

When she had turned 14 years old, their neighbors Bob and Lisa had asked Aisha if she wanted to babysit their boys from time-to-time. She had enthusiastically agreed seeing as they were neighbors and her own mother would be available if a problem were to come up. She thought the world of Bob and Lisa. Lisa had been her sixth grade English teacher and Bob was a physical therapist at the nearby children's hospital. Their youngest son was born with a moderate form of cerebral palsy and Aisha found herself drawn to the magic of helping to heal bodies with physical therapy due to the time she spent with the family. Over the years, Bob had encouraged Aisha's interest in physical therapy and let her spend hours at his practice as a high school intern. When she showed an interest in occupational therapy, Bob arranged for her to spend a summer month working with a colleague of his who specialized in OT just to see if that was truly where her interest lied. She came back to physical therapy. OT was fascinating, but PT was where her passions found their home.

Working towards her bachelor's degree, Bob had encouraged her to explore other interests but leave her degree choice open to a graduate degree in physical therapy in case she decided that was her ultimate career path. It was. She spent every summer interning for Bob at his practice and learned from the ground up. She worked with the administrative staff and learned about insurance and customer service. She worked with a variety of patients and interacted with children with Down syndrome and high school athletes who had sustained injuries. She worked with middle aged women whose bodies had declined due to injuries and even pregnancy, and middle aged men who experienced physical breakdowns due to sedentary corporate lifestyles or whatever else got to them as they aged. The variety of issues fascinated her.

Bob's enthusiasm for the recovery of the human body was contagious. Movement. Diet. Inner joy. It was the inner joy that threw Aisha. Recently, Bob was big into eastern medicine including acupuncture and mediation for total health. He knew exactly what a human body needed to do to heal, but he insisted the mind was connected to the ultimate healing. Aisha considered his enthusiasm for eastern medicine, holistic healing practices, massage, acupuncture, meditation, and more. She respected him and listened to him as he preached a whole mind/body approach to physical healing. Lisa did not. Lisa voiced increasing disdain for Bob's evolving approach to physical therapy.

Sometimes, Aisha felt trapped between the two conversations she found herself involved in with Bob and Lisa. Their youngest son had made impressive improvements over the years given his original prognosis regarding his cerebral palsy. Even though it was deemed moderate, he still had significant limitations. Eventually, he reached the pinnacle of his improvements and Bob was delighted in every way, but Lisa continued to lament their child's disabilities. He required the use of a wheelchair. For Lisa, this signified a failure on the part of Bob to completely heal their child. For Bob, Lisa's reaction signified an unrealistic expectation of how their youngest son would thrive in the life he had before him.

Between the two of them, resentment grew and festered. Only a few months earlier in the spring, Lisa filed for divorce from Bob and he moved from the house across the street from Aisha to an apartment near his practice in D.C.. Aisha was now considered an essential part of Bob and Lisa's family as one of the only people they trusted to care for their youngest son. His disabilities required a certain knowledge about how to care for and assist him in discreet activities such as toileting. Aisha had been involved with the care of this child for so long that, even as he entered his teen years, he accepted her assistance as a matter of fact, not as an embarrassment.

As devastated as Aisha was that Bob and Lisa were divorcing, she tried to believe that they were doing their best to continue to provide for their children in a way that honored their family. Aisha's mother counselled her to remain neutral in the situation. "Don't choose a side. Both are hurt," her mother cautioned her. "What they say about each other will be unflattering, but neither is spouting gospel." That was really good advice, and Aisha took it to heart over the ensuing months. Bob said little about Lisa and the kids, but Lisa just would not stop bad-mouthing Bob. It was difficult to listen to her mentor be described as a bad parent who was reluctant to do all that he could to heal his youngest child, and Aisha wondered if Lisa was suffering from some other emotional or health related issue as she continued to bad mouth Bob. Bob said very little. He affirmed his love for Lisa and his three children. He kept Aisha on as an active intern and his practice thrived due to his increasing availability once Lisa made a successful and unkind effort to reduce his time with their kids.

The past month had been the most difficult for Aisha. She made an effort to remain neutral, but Lisa had begun to hint that if Aisha took a summer internship with Bob, she would be, in effect, aligning herself with the opposition. Aisha balked at the threat that she had to choose a side, and told Lisa that the internships Bob offered her were essential to her graduate studies and career goals in physical therapy. She appealed to Lisa to consider her years of care for their youngest son as a sign that all she wanted was to be an excellent physical therapist capable of caring for those who needed assistance. Lisa relented and acknowledged that the internships provided by Bob were probably valuable to Aisha's career goals. But the confrontation had set Aisha on edge. She no longer trusted Lisa and didn't have the confidence to confide in Bob. She had completed her first year of graduate studies and was in the home stretch. She wanted to work at Bob's PT practice this summer, possibly throughout the school year, and graduate next spring. She did not need this fucking drama.

She walked outside to the parking lot from the back door of the fast food restaurant with her bag of cold food and cash. She had done the walk many times before. It wasn't a problem. The cars in the roadways weren't an issue. She knew what yards she could walk through to make her way to her mother's bright yellow house. She just wanted to get home and make sure her mom was ok and had everything she needed. She had filled her mother's prescriptions the day she came home from the operation, so she knew she had at least two weeks' worth of medications on hand in the event that pharmacies could not fill prescriptions due to whatever was going on. Two weeks should be enough time for authorities to figure out what had happened and get the world back on track she thought optimistically, even while surveying the carnage outside. This thing where bodies were lying all about was unsettling to Aisha. Not orderly. She preferred order. None of this made any sense. Bob was very analytical. She would call him to ask him what he thought was going on, but her cell phone was not picking up any signals. She walked briskly towards the intersection ahead so that she could get home to her mother. She did not even consider her moped or Lev's integrity in returning it to her. She didn't care about those types of things. She had done right by him and the rest was his business.

The side roads were not nearly as impacted as the main roadways. These were residential streets. Aisha and her mom lived at the end of a cul-de-sac of a residential street with no outlets from any other nearby streets. You had to want to enter their neighborhood with a predetermined destination in mind because no street in their development, except this one, had an outlet to a main roadway. Aisha and her mother were one of two black families living in what was essentially a private development. It wasn't designed that way, but in the end, by not creating any exits, the neighborhood was able to maintain an exclusive and private feel.

Fifteen years earlier, Aisha's mom found herself newly widowed from Aisha's father and $54,000 richer thanks to a settlement from the insurance company of the drunk driver who had killed him. It wasn't a fair settlement at all, but Aisha's mom had just been hired at the airport which was a union job and offered a fair wage. She didn't want to continue to fight for more money. She wanted to move on, start her new job, get Aisha into a new home and a new school. Heal. Aisha was only 9 years old, and her mother decided the low cost of a small house near the airport and an elementary school was a good investment. She was right. The airport offered many stable jobs for middle class people. The nearby public school did as well. With a decent down payment for a small house located at the end of a cul-de-sac, basically the last house in the development, Aisha's mom had secured for herself and her daughter a respectable lifestyle complete with a brand new public elementary school which fed into a highly rated public high school. Aisha wasn't ignorant to the fact that her widowed mother had beaten the odds stacked against a black woman. She marveled at her mother's resilience and resolved to rise even higher in an effort to make her proud of her only child. It was the two of them together always. Not against the world. They weren't in a constant battle against society at large. But they worked together for the best interests of one another. Aisha always worked. She babysat, she worked fast food, she earned good grades and was offered a very small scholarship to the nearby state college. Her mother worked at the airport and enjoyed union benefits. She worked holidays and overtime. She worked only five miles from Aisha when, as a little girl, she had to put herself to bed at night and make breakfast for herself before school. They knew they were each doing the best they could for one another. She considered her mother to be her best friend.

The yellow house loomed up ahead of Aisha. The walk had been largely uneventful even as the air reminded her of the surrounding destruction. When the event had happened, school was still in session, people were still at work. Appointments were being kept. Many people in her neighborhood were not home until school got out or the work day ended. So, Aisha's walk home was through a small neighborhood where many people had not yet returned home. She had not seen anyone after leaving the main road that led to the airport. She wondered if her mother was sleeping due to having taken her pain meds, or if she was awake and knew what was going on outside her house.

As she passed by Bob and Lisa's house, she wondered how she would be able to find out if they were all ok. She wanted to be able to call and check in on them and wondered if land lines would have continued to work during apocalyptic events. She walked up the steps of the porch and placed the paper bag full of food down on the small table between two rocking chairs and went to grab her house keys from her purse. She closed her eyes and swore softly as she realized she had left her purse in her locker at the restaurant. "Oh, my fucking god," she muttered completely pissed off at herself. She turned the door handle and discovered it was locked. Well, it should be locked, because she locked it this morning when she left for work. She rang the doorbell and felt badly about having her mother have to get up and use the walker to come let her absent minded ass inside. She rang the doorbell again and muttered aloud quietly, "Sorry mom."

She stood there waiting and rang the doorbell a third time before walking over to the front windows, peering inside to see if she could spy her mother making a slow approach to the door. The interior of the house was dark because the power was out and the sky was darkened by the smoke which filled the air. She pressed her face against the glass window and tried to see better. The house was a medium sized two story with two bedrooms upstairs and one small bedroom downstairs. Her mother would normally be in the master bedroom upstairs, but due to the surgery, she was spending her time recovering downstairs in the spare bedroom.

Aisha couldn't see her mother approaching the front door, so she decided to try the sliding doors out back. She circled around the left side of the house where the gated fence was perpetually broken and would allow her access to the backyard. After jiggling the broken handle several times, she was able to open the gate and jogged around to their wooden deck and up the stairs. She was hopeful when she grabbed the handle of the sliding door. It was also locked. She shook her head in frustration. The window of the lower level bedroom was too high for Aisha to see into and possibly tap hard on and wake her mother, but she remembered the side door to the garage was sometimes left unlocked by, well, herself because she was a little forgetful about that particular door.

She walked back the way she had come around and twisted the door handle. It was locked. She rolled her eyes thinking that her mother had probably locked it because she sure had not. She stood there with her hands on her hips and wondered what she should do. The world was a mess. Power was out. Her mother was on pain medications and sound asleep in bed. She couldn't find a way inside her home. She sighed and lifted her foot up off the pebble walkway that her mother had chosen rather than less expensive cement and kicked the door as hard as she could saying, "Really sorry about this mom!"

Aisha learned that kicking in a locked door was a lot easier to do in movies than in real life. She lifted up her foot and kicked as hard as she could multiple times before feeling the door start to give way. "You are kidding me with this right now," she muttered to the Universe.

"Come on!" she shouted as she kicked the loosening door as with all her might. Almost. One more kick would do it. She was unreasonably tired and attributed it to the stress of the day. She gave the door another hard kick and it bounced open, relieving her of the thought of having to muster the strength to do it again. She walked inside their single car garage and around her mother's car parked inside. She closed her eyes and sighed loudly as it occurred to her the door from inside the kitchen leading to the garage was most likely locked as well. She walked up the two cement steps leading to the door, and turned the handle. Yep. Locked. She stood there for a minute with her eyes closed and tried to clear her mind and figure out how she would kick open this door which was perched atop two cement stairs and opened towards her and not away from her as the outside door did. She was not going to be able to kick this door inward. Maybe she could find a tool in the garage to pry open the door, she thought. She would need more light to search for an appropriate tool for the job. She walked around her mother's car to the automatic garage door and pressed the interior button to raise it up and give her more light. She pushed the button several times before remembering that the power was out and lifting the garage door was going to be on her. As she slowly lifted the garage door up, she wiped sweat off of her forehead and unclipped the dish towel that was around her face. It had been loosened during her ninja moves to knock open the side door. She secured the dish towel again quickly because the air really was foul with smoke and debris. Three houses down on the other side of the street, she saw a person walking towards the back of Bob and Lisa's house. There were no cars parked in the driveway or out front just as there hadn't been when she had walked into the cul-de-sac earlier.

She didn't think she could get into a physical fight with a burglar and win, but she felt a protective sense of urgency come over her that demanded she at least try to see who it was snooping around the house of her adopted extended family. She walked out of her garage leaving the garage door open and went back up onto her front porch which was slightly concealed from view from the street due to the evergreen shrubs planted along the front of the railing. She waited to see if the person would re-emerge from the back of the house where she could get a better look at him. Maybe it was a neighbor she knew who could help her break into her own house. Maybe it was a murderous stranger who was taking advantage of the lack of emergency services during this apocalypse party.

She waited and watched scanning both sides of Bob and Lisa's house looking for the person to walk back out front. Instead, the front door suddenly opened and Aisha realized it was Bob. He was standing in the open doorway, looking up and down the cul-de-sac. He retreated back inside and closed the door. Aisha was thrilled. Bob would help her get inside her house. Why had he gone around back and not in through the front door to begin with, she wondered. She ran off her porch and kept running straight to Bob and Lisa's front door. She removed the dish towel from around her head and shoved it into the waistline of her work pants. She rang the bell repeatedly until Bob opened the door. She was beaming, so happy to see a familiar face. A face that made her feel safe. A face that would say yes to her when she asked him to help her get inside her own home. But his expression was dark. He looked stern in a way she had never seen in all the years she had known him.

"Aisha," he said flatly. "Thank god you're alright. How's your mom?" he asked her still wearing the dark expression the entire time he spoke to her.

"I'm so happy to see you!" she said flustered now by his behavior and tone. "I'm locked out of my house. My mom is sleeping and isn't answering the door. I kicked in the garage door on the side of the house, but I can't get in because the kitchen door is also locked. I need you to help me. What are you doing here? I was watching you because I saw you go around the house, but I thought you were a stranger breaking in." She looked at him waiting for a response and watched as his expression softened before he responded.

"Lisa changed the locks, so my key to the front door doesn't work. I have a key to the back door and hoped that she hadn't changed that yet. I got lucky, I guess. Thanks for looking out for the house. Let's get you inside yours and check on your mom," he said kindly. He stepped outside and pulled the front door of his former house closed behind him. Aisha was full of questions, finally having a person she trusted to talk to after all that had been going on.

"How did you get here? Where's your car?" she asked him.

"Lisa had asked me to pick up Brendan from school at 1:45 today because he had an orthodontist appointment and she couldn't get a sub for the second half of the day. I got there a little early and was parked out front when she texted me that she had gotten a sub and was already on her way to the orthodontist with him. I think she was screwing with me, but when I called her and Brendan answered, I said to tell mom I'll pick up your brothers and hang out with them until they finished up at the orthodontist. You know? I was trying to not get into an argument and call her out for playing games with my time. But she got on the phone and said she had decided to take all three boys out of school since it was the end of the day and they were going to go shopping afterwards. Can you believe that? When did she become such a bitch? I mean, I think it's the craziness of the day making me lose it like this. I'm sorry. I apologize for speaking to you like this. I don't know where they are. I'm losing my mind. I don't mean to vent at you like this...." he trailed off as his dark thoughts took over.

"It's ok. Today has been insane. You must be so worried. I only got here about 15 minutes ago, and her car wasn't here," Aisha said to him, trying to use a soothing tone. She was worried about them, as well. Lisa was a pain in the ass recently, but she loved Lisa and the kids.

"What does shopping mean? How do I narrow that down? Food, clothes, what?" Bob asked absently as they walked up to Aisha's front porch. "I was at the school when everything happened. She takes them to the orthodontist over on Mitchum. I went there on foot. I can't even tell you how awful it was. I looked in the parking lot for her car. It wasn't there. I've been looking for her car in piles of wreckage from the school, to the orthodontist's office, to here. I haven't seen her car anywhere." Bob stopped talking and grabbed the handle to the front door of Aisha's house to confirm it was locked.

"I'm going to kick it in if that's ok with you," he said to Aisha, looking at her for permission.

"Yeah, do whatever it takes," she told him in earnest.

With one kick, Bob broke down the front door to her mother's house, and Aisha cringed at the sound of the frame breaking apart. She went to enter the darkened house, but Bob suddenly put his right arm out in front of her and stopped her from entering.

"What?" Aisha asked him.

"Honey, there are a lot of dead people out here. A lot. They were alive, and then they just died for no reason. You understand what I'm saying?" he asked her, looking at her intently with that unfamiliar dark look taking over his face again.

"No. My mom is just sleeping because she's taking pain medication because of her knee surgery. She's sleeping." Aisha insisted. Bob's arm was still blocking her from entering her own house and he made no effort to lower it.

"Which room is she in?" he asked with authority, staring at her face.

Aisha felt small and suddenly very afraid. "The downstairs bedroom. It's to the left of the dining room. Down that hallway." Aisha pointed inside the house towards the back where a dining room table could be seen from the light entering in through the sliding glass doors.

"I'm going to go check on Rhonda first. Then I'll come back to let you know if she's ok? Aisha, are you hearing me?" He hadn't broken eye contact with her since he'd kicked open the door, and Aisha felt herself giving over her authority in this situation to a man she had known most of her life and trusted completely. Neither had broken their gaze upon the other, but she couldn't find words to speak at the thought of what he was suggesting. She nodded in the affirmative, a small quick succession of nods to indicate they would do this his way. He lowered his arm a bit but pointed to the rocking chairs next to them on the front patio.

"Go sit, and wait for me. I'll be right back."

She turned silently and walked the few steps to the pair of black rocking chairs and sat down slowly. Her body felt like it was full of cement, and her limbs felt impossibly heavy. A feeling of dread crawled around her skin, and she shuddered. Bob was still looking at her until she had settled onto the chair.

"I'll be right back," he said and turned and entered her house.

Inside, Bob walked quickly towards the room where Rhonda should be asleep. He liked Rhonda. She was a class act in so many ways. A hard worker, raised a fantastic daughter by herself, a great neighbor, and funny as hell. She had a wicked sense of humor enhanced by her exploits working in customer service at the airport. Her stories could bring the house down at a dinner party. He desperately did not want her to be dead. He did not want to have to tell Aisha that her mother did not survive whatever was going on today.

The door to the spare room was ajar and he called, "Rhonda, it's Bob. I'm here with Aisha. We want to check on you and make sure you're alright." He waited. No response. He tried again, louder this time and gently began to push the door to the bedroom all the way open. "Rhonda, it's Bob. I'm here with Aisha." As the door to the room opened, Bob could smell the death in the room. "Oh, no…." His voice trailed off as the smell hit him first and then the sight of Rhonda sitting up in her bed with one leg resting atop two pillows. The book she had been reading was in her lap, but her hands were not holding it up. She was slumped backwards and to one side with her mouth hanging open. He walked into the room and took her wrist to check for a pulse just to be able to tell Aisha he had done so. No pulse. He turned and opened both windows of the small room to clear the smell because he knew Aisha would want to come in and confirm for herself that her mother was indeed deceased. He had to go tell Aisha now.

Aisha watched as Bob walked out the front door and back onto the porch. They stared at each other for a few seconds, and Bob closed his eyes and slowly dipped his head towards the ground before lifting his face back up to deliver the news of her mother directly.

"Sweetie, your mom is not alive," he said, trying to avoid the word 'dead.' Aisha sat perfectly still in the rocking chair and continued to stare at him.

"Your mom passed away. Do you want me to walk you in so you can see for yourself? Or would you like me to wait outside? I'm here for you, ok?" He walked closer to where she was sitting and stood just off to her right side. He was looking at her and offered her his hand to help her make the walk into her home to confirm her mother's passing. Rather than taking his hand, she turned her head away from him and continued to sit motionless in the rocking chair. He gave her time to process what was happening and didn't rush her to respond.

After a few minutes, she turned her face up towards his as he stood above her. "I'll go in by myself," she said and stood up slowly.

She didn't doubt Bob. If Bob said her mother had died, she was dead. She felt numb, but she wasn't in denial. She started walking towards the front door and turned to Bob and said flatly, "At least she won't be mad at us for kicking in two of her doors today."

Bob pursed his lips together in a small tight smile and nodded in agreement adding, "Yeah, can you imagine her telling everyone how we kicked in two of her doors while she was recovering from surgery?"

Aisha added, "And every time she told the story, she'd stare at each of us, too."

"None of that weak, side-eye bullshit, either. Your mother was all about the direct stare. Yeah, it would be a long time until we heard the last of that." Bob agreed.

Aisha sighed, closed her eyes for a second, and gave Bob a small smile before heading inside by herself. Bob breathed in deeply and exhaled hard. He turned around to locate a rocking chair and sat down on the one vacated by Aisha a minute earlier. He leaned forward and put his head in his hands and then rubbed his hands through his hair. He shook his head absently. He was terrified at the thought of Lisa and his sons being alive and trapped out there in the mess of it all. He stared at the house he and Lisa had shared and hoped they would come walking up the cul-de-sac and be reunited. He was not a romantic man, he had seen too much human suffering working in his field, so he quietly prepared himself for what was the likely outcome of the day. One or more of his family members might be dead. All of them might be dead. Whatever this was, it crept into closed homes and killed healthy people. It took down airplanes. It killed indiscriminately and instantly. And it let others live. What was it about Aisha, a 24 year old black woman and him, a 44 year old white man that protected the both of them against whatever killed all the others? Her mother was dead. She clearly didn't have the same protection, and they were related and both female.

He was so confused. A biological weapon made sense, but not when trying to figure out how some people survived and others did not. It got to people flying airplanes as well as people on the ground. How did that make sense? He waited in the silence for Aisha to reemerge from her house so that they could decide together what they would do next. Aisha was family. He wasn't going to leave her to deal with what was happening by herself. They would stick together.

Aisha walked out of her house and nodded to Bob. She had been crying but had composed herself before coming outside. She swallowed hard and pointed to the paper bag on the table between the two rocking chairs. Walking to sit on the other side of the table in the other rocking chair, she told Bob, "That's a bag of food from the restaurant. I grabbed what was there before heading home." She sat down and looked out across the front porch through the evergreens to their neighbors' homes. She turned and opened the paper bag and pulled out a burger, unwrapped it, and began to eat.

Bob looked into the bag and went to pull out a sandwich but paused and asked her about the money that was also in the bag.

"Oh, yeah. I thought maybe the ATMs wouldn't be working and credit cards would be useless, so I grabbed all the cash from the cash registers in case I needed it. Don't worry," she said, turning to him, waving her half eaten burger in the air in front of her. "Everyone is dead there. The gas station next door blew the hell up and nearly took the whole place down. *Oh*!" she added with renewed enthusiasm. "I forgot. There was this guy who showed up. He was heading to the airport to find his girlfriend who had flown in earlier." Bob watched her telling him about the earlier part of her day and was amazed at how resilient she was. She continued, speaking with enthusiasm. "He saved my life. For real. He noticed the gas station was about to blow up and grabbed me and ran with me back to the break room seconds before the first explosion. There were three huge explosions, one after the other. Took down the entire side of the building. Killed a couple of survivors who were inside with us, too. Well, actually, Lev, that was the guy's name, Lev actually killed the guy who survived the explosion because he wasn't going to make it. His injuries were *not* survivable. So, Lev walked over and snapped his neck and killed him. It was really awful, but it was necessary." She stopped talking and took another bit of her cold burger.

Bob said, "I'm glad you made it, and I'm glad this guy Lev was there to help you. Sounds like he had to put that other man out of his pain. I don't know if I could have done it, though."

"Me, either," she agreed. "I told him I couldn't have killed the guy even though it was the right thing to do. I gave him my moped so he could get to the airport and find his girlfriend. I told him they could come back here tonight."

"Ok, so what does he look like so I don't immediately assume a dangerous stranger has come to our quiet cul-de-sac?" Bob asked her.

Aisha considered what Lev looked like for a minute and described him to Bob. "He's really tall. Easily over six feet tall. He's built like he works out a lot, and he's got short black hair, thick eyebrows, and really, really intense eyes when he's looking at you. They're brown, and maybe on a good day, his eyes look friendly. But today, not so much. A little scary, actually. No facial hair. When I saw him outside the restaurant heading in, I ducked behind the counter and grabbed Ray's hand because I was kind of afraid of him just by the way he looked. I'm not good with guessing other people's heritage, but he looks like he's Indian, or got that in him. His skin has some color. Anyway, it turned out that he's a nice guy. Just having a shitty day like the rest of us, I suppose. Probably upped the intensity of his natural appearance." She finished her burger and reached back into the bag for another. "I'm so hungry," she muttered absently as she tossed the second wrapper onto the porch floor.

"Me, too," Bob said as he reached for another sandwich. He'd eat whatever he grabbed. "So, we're looking out for this Lev guy and his girlfriend coming in on your moped, then. I'm going to be honest here. I don't think this guy is going to find his girlfriend alive at the airport."

"Me, either," said Aisha. "But, I could tell he had to try. He was that way. He had to go and see for himself."

Bolin and Ryan

It had been about a week since the extinction event had occurred. That's what survivors were calling it, anyway. Truthfully, he didn't know what had happened that day, but extinction event did capture the totality of the destruction of life and civilization all around the streets. The government wasn't calling it an extinction event, and the news wasn't calling it that, either. They weren't calling it anything because they had no way of communicating with everyone who had survived. No one really knew who in the government had survived even after a week to figure some shit out. Was the President alive? What was going on in other countries? The survivors just walked around the burning landscape with bandanas tied around their faces and desperation in their eyes. Some people had crazy in their eyes, though. Bolin was wary of each kind of person. The desperate tended to be either needy or greedy. They'd either beg you to help them get what they needed or they'd try to overpower you to get what they wanted from you. He wanted nothing to do with those types.

Where were the people who wanted to work together and cooperate towards some kind of meaningful progress? He wasn't thinking about rebuilding from the ashes at this point. Hell, the ashes were still accumulating because, apparently, the world was entirely flammable in an apocalypse. Something the end-of-the-world movies never contemplated. Would have been a lot more comfortable if the event had happened during the winter, he thought. Fires would have kept the living warm during a cold winter. Surviving in a burning hellscape apocalypse during a humid heatwave in June in Philadelphia was not ideal. Walking down the sidewalks, stepping over the festering dead, remaining alert in an effort not to trip like he had two days ago when he broke his fall by landing on top of the remains of a putrefying dead woman, Bolin contemplated his need to get out of the city and head to either the coast or the mountains. He remained undecided at this point. He would most likely be walking in either case.

Transportation was a luxury of the old world. This was the new world. Water and good shoes were the tools that would serve him best now. Would he head east to the coast, or west towards the mountains? Where was the catalyst for this important decision, he wondered? Usually, his important life decisions were made once he encountered a clear reason for making the decision. He was not the type of man to answer the call of random impulses, so he remained in this rotting, burning city, a stranger in a dying land, waiting for knowledge that would inform his next move.

He had come to Philadelphia to meet up with a couple of navy friends who had retired three years ago and settled in the city. He, himself, had been over in D.C. attending an event for Memorial Day, and they had invited him to come stay at their home and do the whole barbeque and beer thing with them. He had been driving a rental to their restored brick townhome in the city when it happened. Suddenly, traffic all around him either stopped completely or careened in every which way. A guy on a motorcycle drove directly into the passenger side of the car he was driving and he had watched as the body landed on the hood of his engine and slid to the center. Just like that, too. The guy was dead before he landed on the hood. Bolin hadn't even seen the guy coming. Must have been cruising through the intersection to the right of him and come up over the sidewalk to have hit him the way he had. He kept thinking about it. He had been two cars deep at a traffic light and in the right lane, so much of what he witnessed occurred in front of him and from the left and right of his lane. Cars in back of him were hit and pushed into the back of his small rental, but he was never in any real danger of being severely impacted. The car in front of him, though, and the other first cars at the traffic light, they had cars from across the intersection career straight into them. They buffered the impact felt by Bolin.

He was seven years in the navy now after completing his bachelor's degree in civil engineering at college. He had spent his youth trying to convince his parents he had no interest in pursuing medicine or academics as they had. He rationalized the need for world order brought about by a well-educated American military which could support the goals of civilian citizens and even their own medical and academic careers. He had eventually gained their reluctant acceptance of his goals for himself apart from their own goals for him. They were the quintessential tiger parents. First generation Chinese American, extremely successful in their fields due to hard work and self-sacrifice, and they had waited a long time to finally commit to having a child in order to give their only child all of the best opportunities they could possibly provide. He was fluent in three languages and proficient on multiple musical instruments. He did not enjoy summer vacations at the end of a school year as his classmates did. He attended a prestigious and private NYC school. He attended rigorous academic classes year round in programs thoroughly researched by his parents and deemed essential to his intellectual development.

He was fortunate to have his grandmother provide the role of nanny until he entered high school. She had passed away suddenly during his freshman year in high school when he was 14 years old. Her sudden loss shook him deep inside and, if asked, he would admit that her death was the catalyst for his breaking away from the expectations of his parents. But he wasn't asked, and he didn't like the thought that his parents would essentially blame his beloved Zumu for his choices if they knew how he truly felt. His grandmother had been a constant in his life. She took him to his numerous extracurricular activities and helped him master Mandarin as the two of them were only allowed by his parents to communicate in the language in order to build his skills. As a result of his parents' dedication to his excellence, he was a man of many skills and only a few close friends. They denied some truths about their only child, but Zumu had instilled in him respect for personal character. He relied on that as opposed to an easy charm. There was nothing wrong with candor.

For all that he could do as a result of endless training, he had limited confidence in his own social skills and struggled to form deep friendships. He wanted to share his knowledge and skills with others, but he could not develop the ease needed to facilitate dialogue with people he met in social settings. He had not lived a life full of opportunities to practice those essential interpersonal communication skills. Perhaps he was also naturally inclined to be a little reserved, or shy, even. When with others, he came across as quiet or, as someone in a group project had once put it, 'unapproachable and judgmental.'
But he was not those things. Inside he felt a deep desire to connect with others, to learn about their interests, and to share his own interests. He wasn't looking to boast, he wanted to connect. But academics had taught him to argue and prove himself, and the navy had taught him discipline. His parents had taught him to focus with pathological myopathy or risk disappointing them. His grandmother had taught him to be patient. He was patient. His grandmother would be proud of his ability to be patient.

On the other hand, he was losing patience with being a bachelor because he was getting tired of forcing himself to engage in the meaningless conversations one must subject themselves to in order to meet someone for casual sex. Sure he was socially awkward, but he was by no means celibate. He found that sex, as intimate as it had the potential to be, as intimate as he longed for it to be, did not actually require a deep level of communication with a casual partner, and he did not have any moral hang-ups about hookups that limited those interactions even though he was becoming bored by them. It helped that he was a good looking man with a well-exercised build. He was the same height as his father at five feet nine inches. He was a nice guy even if a bit quiet and awkward. He could easily attract a partner for one night.

After the incident at the intersection, he found he had to climb into the back seat of the rental car in order to get out through the passenger side backseat door. He had scanned the chaos of the scene trying to make sense of how the pile up had occurred, but noticing drivers were dead in their vehicles confused him. They had not all died on impact. There were too few survivors emerging from cars, from local businesses, and pedestrians were lying about the sidewalks dead. People in crosswalks were on the ground dead. And if the visuals were not enough to secure his utter confusion at what was going on before his eyes, there was the sound of screaming in the sky above him which dragged his gaze mercilessly upward where he witnessed the first of several airliners nosedive out of the blue sky and aim deliberately for the ground below. He grabbed the top of his head with both hands and shouted in horror, eyes wide at the crash of the first plane and began to look for a safe place to run for shelter as he spied a second plane making its descent into oblivion.

Bolin had chosen to seek shelter inside a combination bar and restaurant that had a large open outdoor dining area on the sidewalk. The entire front wall of the place was open, and the entry to the interior was dictated by metal railing which encased the outdoor dining area. His rental car was visible to him as he entered the darkened space, and he jumped and ducked at the sound of another explosion. He turned around to look outside. This one was not the sound of a crashing plane, but of a vehicle possibly. Maybe something else he was not considering. He turned his attention to the interior of the bar and realized the air was still and silent inside. There was only one person alive, other than himself, inside the room as far as he could see. He had to walk carefully over bodies strewn about the floor to get to the bartender who was still alive behind the counter.

"Holy shit, man! What the fuck is going on out there?" the young bartender asked him with eyes opened wide.

"No idea," Bolin replied. "It happened all at once. Cars slamming into one another in the intersection. I thought maybe the traffic lights had caused it, but…." Bolin turned his head to the right and to the open air patio leading to the sidewalk with what looked like a hundred people dead where they sat or stood. He waved his right hand in the direction of the dead and turned his attention back to the bartender shaking his head vigorously asking, "See? Not a situation caused by a broken traffic light."

The bartender nodded his head in agreement. "I think I'm the only one alive in here," he whispered to Bolin. "You want a drink, man?" he asked with wide eyes and a shrug that conveyed helplessness in an impossible situation.

"Yes. Please," Bolin responded.

The bartender looked relieved, and a sense of comprehensible purpose invigorated him momentarily. "Yeah, I'm having one or more with you. What do you want? Name it," said the bartender.

"Shots. Anything you feel like pouring. I just want it to hit my system quickly," Bolin said as he turned away from the bartender and stared at the dead inside and outside. He turned back to the bartender and the row of dead bodies lining the counter of the bar. Some of the dead were sprawled face first on the bar counter, while others had fallen off their bar stools and were in a haphazard arrangement of half on their stools, or in another dead person's lap, and a woman had one of her legs caught under the counter so that she was hanging upside down with her head on the floor. Bolin pulled a slender man from his death perch on the barstool in front of the bartender and dragged him to rest on top of another dead body a few feet away. He stepped up onto the bar stool inspecting it for anything revolting before taking a seat. Meanwhile, the bartender poured them shots from a bottle of golden brown liquid that Bolin couldn't bother to name. He poured a total of four shots, and they each downed one quickly.

"My names Ryan," said the bartender after downing the first shot.

"Bolin," Bolin responded.

He grabbed for the second shot as did the bartender named Ryan. They both tossed them back and placed their glasses on the bar at the same time. Ryan filled all four shot glasses again.

"Oh, I'm going to see how hard these hit me before I have any more," Bolin said with a knowing tone. "I don't know what I have to be prepared for next."

Ryan did not share Bolin's concerns for what could possibly happen to them next and refilled all four shot glasses drinking his third immediately.

"Did you call 911? I don't hear any sirens," Bolin asked, looking at Ryan.

"I tried as soon as I saw what was happening, but the line went dead mid ring. I think the plane crashes probably took precedence over car accidents. But then there's all these dead people. I don't understand. Do you think it's like, I don't know, chemical warfare or biological warfare?" he asked Bolin.

"Well, then why are we alive?" he asked Ryan.

"Yeah, true. I feel fine other than, I don't know, shocked."

They both looked outside when they heard a woman call to them from outside on the sidewalk. She was hysterical and difficult to understand, but when Bolin motioned to her and called for her to come inside, she quickly took off towards the intersection not bothering to continue her interaction with the two men.

"So, we're not the only two people who survived this." Ryan half laughed.

Bolin suddenly stood up and patted his back pocket looking for his cell phone. "I must have left my phone in the car," he said to Ryan. "I'll be right back."

He made his way over the bodies on the floor and outside to where the sun was still shining as if life on planet earth had not just come to an abrupt stand-still.

The rental car was totaled, but access through the back passenger door wasn't a problem for him. He reached in and grabbed his cell phone which was still in the cup holder between the two front seats. As he made his way back out of the car the way he had come in, he jumped at the sound of a vehicle exploding about a block ahead of him through the intersection. He banged the back of his head on the door frame and muttered, "Jesus fucking Christ!" His parents would not have approved of such coarse language. They didn't approve of much about him anyway, so he really didn't care. In fact, he realized he had not considered their safety in this situation until he swore and considered they would be disappointed in him for coarse language. So the benefit of swearing turned out to be that it made him remember to consider their well-being during what appeared to be a crisis. Well, he hoped they were both ok. Not for his own sake, but for their own sakes. If they were still alive, it meant they could possibly apologize for disowning him when he rejected their script for his life and let them know he'd be making his own decisions. Decisions such as leveraging his degree in civil engineering to join the navy and the Civil Engineering Corps. According to his parents, he had wasted all of their efforts. So disappointing. Alright. He hoped they were still alive and could recognize his value outside of the failed expectations they claimed he represented. Maybe, one day, they could have an actual relationship with him and finally embrace him for who he was.

Phone in hand, he had tried to call 911, but there was no service. He turned to walk back into the bar and talk with Ryan about what was going on for a bit longer. He knew he couldn't make sense of anything he was seeing on his own, but the walk back into the darkened bar provided him with a broader view of the city streets than he had taken in a few minutes earlier. "Holy shit," he involuntarily muttered to no one but himself as he took in the complete carnage on the streets. It looked to him that all streets, as far as he could see, were at a standstill. Smoke was rapidly filling the air and darkening the skies. He could see small flickers of red and orange flames through smoke coming up from cars. He could make out some people walking around on the corner about two blocks from where he stood. He walked briskly back into the bar where Ryan stood downing another shot.

"I'll take my third now," Bolin said, realizing Ryan would have to re-pour it for him.

"Here ya go, man!" said Ryan with renewed enthusiasm for the bartending life.

Bolin downed the shot and told Ryan what he had seen outside. That there were more survivors even if most people appeared to be dead, and that the threat of cars going off like bombs was real.

"Yeah, well the fire in the kitchen might be a problem soon, too," said Ryan, pointing towards the back of the room. Bolin looked in the direction Ryan was referring to and saw smoke just beginning to fill in the air surrounding the western themed swinging doors that were the entrance to the kitchen.

"We should get out of here before the place goes up," Bolin said to Ryan with growing concern for an impending fire.

"Yeah, I guess so. But first, I'm going to grab some of the good stuff here for the road," Ryan said resolutely.

"Which way to the bathrooms?" asked Bolin.

Ryan pointed towards the back of the restaurant again and added, "Left side. Hallway in back of the stage," to enhance the directions he offered.

Walking towards the bathrooms, Bolin considered how serious the kitchen fire was going to be a few minutes from now. He half ran and hopped over bodies and entered the darkened hallway that led to the bathrooms. He turned the handle of the first door on the left and had to pull out his cell phone to use the flashlight in order to see inside the darkened room. The room was not a bathroom, but looked like a storage room for the equipment of the house musicians. He saw a couple of large amps, and his flashlight picked up some extra bar stools, and an assortment of peddles. As he turned to exit the room and go find the bathroom, his flashlight caught the soft orange glow of an acoustic guitar behind one of the spare bar stools. He walked inside and reached over the stool to grab hold of the guitar. He scanned quickly around some shelves above the guitar and saw one packet of strings. He grabbed those and put them in his back pocket.

Walking out of the room, he held up the guitar towards Ryan and shouted, "Hey! Is this yours?"

Ryan looked up and shook his head no, adding, "No, man. It's yours now!"

Bolin leaned the guitar against the wall and pushed open the next door on the left. With his flashlight, he confirmed he was in the men's restroom. He navigated around the deceased.

When he got back to the bar, Ryan was on the customer side of the bar counter holding a plate with a burger and fries that had formerly belonged to a customer. He was eating the burger without any hint of remorse.

"I missed my lunch break earlier because we were really busy," he said to Bolin as a way of an explanation.

Bolin didn't care. He was hungry too, but he could wait. It suddenly occurred to him that his friends might be alive and waiting for him. He told Ryan he was heading to the home of friends when everything had gone down and asked if he wanted to go with him to see if they were ok.

Ryan declined and tipped his head in the direction of the kitchen saying, "Nah, I gotta go check on my girlfriend. We broke up last weekend, but I gotta go see if she's ok. We need to get out of here before some shit blows up in that kitchen. You hear all those cars going up outside? Crazy."

Bolin agreed and said, "Yes, ok. Well if you can't find anyone else you know alive and want to meet back up with me, I'm heading over to 1641 Independence. All these buildings and townhomes are connected, though. That kitchen fire makes me think once one goes up, they're all going to go up like flaming dominos."

Ryan looked annoyed and said, "Shit. My ex lives in a townhome over on Regents. I need to get over there. I'll be at 729 Regents and then my parent's house at 2187 Lexington."

Bolin was using his phone to make a note of the addresses Ryan was giving him. The military had taught him to always respect a potential resource in a war zone. "1641 Independence," he repeated to Ryan.

"I know where that is," Ryan responded, looking at him chewing the last bite of burger. "That's a rich neighborhood. I'll try to find you if that's how this plays out, man." He dropped the plate onto the table absently, not caring if it hit one of the dead. He wiped his hands on his apron and removed it and tossed it to the floor. "You want to take a bottle to go with you to your friend's house?" he asked Bolin with a friendly smile.

"Yes. Whether they're alive or dead, I think I'm going to need another drink before the day is through," Bolin said to him, not returning the smile. He was serious. He didn't drink much at all as he tended to be called upon by others to see them home safely, but those three shots had done a lot to warm him and calm the stress he felt building inside. He wasn't responsible for anyone but himself right now.

"Here. New bottle of the whisky we just had," said Ryan enthusiastically.

Bolin took the bottle from him and thanked him before exiting the restaurant.

Bolin and James

About a week had passed since Bolin had seen Ryan. Maybe five days. Time was hard to keep track of now. At the townhome of his friends, Bolin had discovered both of them dead inside their kitchen. It looked as if they had been busy preparing for the barbeque with him. Tameen had her long black and grey hair held back with red ribbons that were visible to Bolin as she laid flat on her back on the kitchen floor. She was laying under the contents of a salad she had been carrying. He imagined she had prepared the salad and was going to put it in the refrigerator where it would wait until she deemed it time to serve. Her eyes were closed in death, but Alex's eyes were open. Bolin leaned down and closed them for him while continuing to imagine their last living moments. He considered the broken glass and spilled drink on the floor near Alex. There was a lemon wedge still within the broken remnants of glass. A pitcher of iced tea was atop the kitchen island. It looked to Bolin as if Alex had just filled a glass of iced tea for himself and would have been asking Tameen what he could do to help her get ready for his impending arrival. That's what husbands do. They stand around and ask their wives what they can do to be useful before guests arrive.

Tameen and Alex were in their early 50s and had met while both were members of the navy more than twenty years earlier. They had gotten married a few weeks after meeting when both were stationed at the naval base in San Diego. They were the best example of a loving relationship Bolin had seen in his own life. His parents didn't really care for one another. They were more focused on the objective elements of life rather than the subjective elements. Their practicality dictated all decision making including unions between people.

Tameen and Alex were the opposite even as dedicated members of the navy and having to spend quite a bit of time apart from one another over the years. They each possessed a passionate awareness of their individual spirits as well as the other's spirit. When Bolin had met Alex during a deployment to Afghanistan, Alex took an immediate liking to him. It surprised Bolin to be accepted so quickly and without any fumbling and awkward effort on his own part. He was used to being grudgingly accepted and occasionally included in social events, but Alex had taken an immediate shine to him despite his presupposition that Alex would not be interested in striking up a friendship. On the contrary, Alex insisted that when they returned to the States, Bolin would have to meet his wife Tameen.

So, with little effort made by himself, he found himself friends with two of the nicest people he had ever met. He was a young navy officer at the time, and valued Alex's friendship, but also his approval. By approval, he did not mean approval for small incidental actions and minor personality quirks, but approval for himself as the person he was. It came at a time when his parents had resoundingly rejected him and his decision to join the navy with the goal of putting his civil engineering degree to use in the Civil Engineering Corps division of the United States Navy. Alex already had a decade in as a member of the CEC and filled a much needed role as an enthusiastic and supportive mentor for Bolin.

Seeing his two friends, really his only friends, lying there dead on their kitchen floor suddenly hit Bolin hard and he found himself leaning against their refrigerator with one hand against his mouth trying hard not to cry. He stepped away from the refrigerator suddenly and straightened his posture, angrily wiping away tears that had not yet fallen. He looked around the kitchen and turned to open the refrigerator door. He saw a covered ceramic baking dish and took it out and walked over to the counter carefully avoiding Alex and his spilled iced tea. He removed the tinfoil from the baking dish and looked at the marinating meats ready to be grilled. He looked towards the back of the kitchen through the paneled glass french doors and headed outside to the gas grill which was visible from inside the kitchen. He cooked the food Tameen had prepared for them, he ate, he drank iced tea with shots of whiskey, and when the sun set and the townhouse became dark, he went outside and played his newly acquired guitar beside the gas flames of the barbeque.

The air quality was bothering his eyes and throat, so he went inside to find some cloth he could use as a face mask. He returned to the outdoor patio wearing a bandana he found in a bedroom drawer. He sat outside and played guitar but didn't sing beneath the bandana despite being able to carry a tune. The music he played on the guitar was punctuated by explosions which he imagined to be cars, homes, businesses and whatever else he didn't bother to imagine. He supposed all of these old brick townhomes would eventually be burned to the ground because in the hours that had passed, he had not heard even one emergency siren.

Eventually, he fell asleep outside on the new patio furniture his friends had purchased for their forever home. The air was bad, his eyes were watering to clear themselves of the soot, but he didn't want to be inside the townhome if a fire broke out.

He had looked for Ryan at the two addresses he had for him the next morning. He had not found him. This morning was now approximately a week since the day it had all come to an end. There were not a lot of survivors. The dead far outweighed the living. By a lot. Dead bodies were still visible locked in cars that had not burned. Roads were not cleared in the slightest. The electricity remained out. The air quality had been, at times, horrendous. It was easy enough to find food and drink if you had some training in resourcefulness. He had that training. He'd been to war zones. One of the most surprising things to Bolin was the amount of material that burned. Once one object, be it a house, a store, a car, whatever, began to burn, with no one to put out the flames, the surrounding materials burned. It kept up like that for two long days before a change in the weather brought a deluge of rain that continued for three days straight. Many of the fires were extinguished, or at least tamed, at that point. The rain also provided some relief from the poor air quality.

Much was still burning, but with so much potential fuel being wet now, the fires were not spreading as easily as they had before. The pollutants were pushed into the ground from their lofty heights in the air and Bolin was able to walk around this afternoon without a mask breathing freely while searching for something to eat before the sun went down. He was unfamiliar with the city of Philadelphia, so he found himself wandering the streets looking for essentials he would need before he departed. Maps were not easy to come by in the time of Siri and ubiquitous technology. He had a map of the city itself from a tourist shop that he'd found before it burned to the ground. Healthy fresh food was not easy to come by in a burning city. He had taken some fruit from Tameen and Alex's house before leaving to find Ryan, but a continuous supply of fresh produce was hard to come by.

A lot of what he had with him now came from the house of his friends. They had excellent gear. He had taken one of their hiking backpacks and filled it with items he believed would be of value to himself once he departed the city. He had the backpack and the guitar on his back now as he walked down the street. He had chosen a hard case for the guitar at a large music shop down by the water the day after leaving the townhome. The music shop was nestled between two tourist shops which had not burned yet. He took his time in the music shop to gather guitar strings, a tuner, and other things which would fit inside the compartments of the new case. He had taken two guns from the house of his friends along with bullets and a knife. He figured finding more guns in an American city would be easy enough, but he wanted to be armed as he left their townhome. He did not know what to expect on this new day. He grabbed their first aid kit, a flashlight, batteries, and a can opener.

He continued to consider what he would need to collect now in order to survive outside the city. He wanted to leave. He still deliberated between the coast to the east and the mountains to the west. He wished he was more familiar with the landscape of Pennsylvania, but he simply wasn't. Up ahead he saw a street he hadn't been down yet. The streets were blocked by vehicles that still contained the dead, but the living were also milling about down at the far end. Maybe someone had some news. It was after noon, but still early, maybe around 3pm. He had time to look around the city some more before it began to get dark. It wasn't that it was dangerous on the streets at night now, but it helped him sleep better if he secured a place to sleep that wouldn't burn in the night. In general, the living were still shocked and trying to make connections, and not behaving in dangerous ways. There was still time for them to become dangerous. Hopelessness would eventually set in and survival, anger, despair, and ruthlessness would follow. In any case, he found that no one he had met had any information even nearly a week after everything went to hell. A lot of people had ideas. Really stupid ideas, but no one had any real information. The real zombie apocalypse was the living staggering around the dead. He walked up the street and saw that the people gathered together were waiting outside a restaurant at the end of the street. Prior to the apocalypse, the place must have been popular because it was quite large from the looks of it on the outside, and as he rounded the corner past the people standing on the sidewalk, he saw the establishment continued on into a large outdoor dining area complete with some large pieces of modern art statues placed throughout. Two entrances meant it had been a popular establishment.

He walked back around the corner and asked a man who looked at least 20 years older than him what was going on.
"Oh, the owner's nephew survived, and he's been giving out meals every evening to anyone who shows up. Said they had a delivery the afternoon the shit hit the fan and they had been the first stop on the delivery route. He told me that when everyone dropped dead, he ran all the fresh food from the truck into their freezers to keep it from going to shit, and now he's making meals until the food runs out."
"That's really nice of him," Bolin said, surprised at the gesture. "How long has it been since, you know...? I feel like it's been a week, but I'm losing track of time," he asked the man.
"Me, too," said the man. "It's five days, though. Not a full week yet. Feels like a fucking eternity. I only know how long it's been because I had two weeks' worth of medication left for my dog, and I'm getting nervous about running out. I've gone to a bunch of brick-and-mortar places in the city looking for her medication, but I always ordered it online. I can't find it here in the city."
The man looked at Bolin. His eyes held genuine concern for the situation regarding his ailing dog, and Bolin felt uncomfortable in the silent request for

sympathy. He felt sympathy, but he struggled to find the right words.

"I really hope you can find what your dog needs," he told the man. "Does this kid just open the doors eventually and let everyone in? What happens next?" Bolin asked, changing the subject from the man's dog to a potential meal.

"Yeah, around this time each day, he comes out and, he's super friendly, not from around here, he starts waving his arms and telling us to come in and line up at the bar. He dishes out the food and we all eat until the food runs out. No leftovers because he can't save anything with the power out. He told the group of us last night he has maybe three days' worth of food left but after that, he's worried about it being fresh, so he's going to quit then."

"Am I allowed to be here? Or is it only for people he knows?" Bolin asked the man.

"Yeah! You're allowed to be here and get some food. I'm telling you, the kid is really nice. This restaurant has been around for something like 40 years now. It's a family thing. The kid is the owner's nephew. He's come around for a few summers now to work for his uncle during the summers. He's from Ireland, hence the name of the place." The man pointed at the words above the front of the restaurant and waved his arm trying to show Bolin. "Monaghan's Pub and Kitchen. A great place before the end of the world and a great place, at least for a while, after the end of the world," the man summed up.

The crowd grew by two more and Bolin counted a total of 14 people standing about waiting for the owner's surviving nephew to open the door and let them inside.

"He cooks for everyone and doesn't ask for anything?" Bolin asked.

"There's nothing we can do. Can't wash the dishes, the water's out. We throw our dirty dishes in the dumpster behind The Grotto restaurant down the street to try and keep the rats from overrunning this place."

"Makes sense," said Bolin.

The two men stood silently for a few minutes before a woman approached the man and said, "Hey, Mike. How's the search for Honey's medicine going?"

"Ah, not good," he said dejectedly.

The woman looked at Mike with sympathy in her eyes. "Sorry to hear that. I hope James opens up soon. I'm looking forward to pretending to be a normal person and sit down, eat, shoot the breeze, get a little buzzed…. Seriously takes the edge off after staring at dead bodies all day."

"Same," said Mike. "Hey, Imani, this guy is new here. What's your name, man?"

"Bolin," said Bolin.

"Bolin, I'm Mike and this here is my new best friend, Imani. Best thing that happened out of this apocalypse is I got to meet this wonderful lady."

Bolin nodded towards Imani and told them it was nice to meet them both.

She asked him if he was from the city and he told her how he had been in the city to meet up with some friends, so he had spent the past five days wandering around trying to get his bearings before figuring out where he should go next. He mentioned that after the torrential rainfall of the previous days, finding a physical map to help him navigate was the main issue hampering his desire to leave the city. Imani clapped her hands together enthusiastically and told the men she would be right back with a map for him.

"I live a block away. I'll go get it for you. I'm staying right here in the city and don't need it. If James lets you in before I get back, save me a seat by you, Mike," she said.

"You got it!" he assured her as she darted quickly down the sidewalk towards her home.

Bolin thought Mike might have someone to help him get over the loss of Honey when the time came.

"James is the kid," Mike said unnecessarily. He motioned towards Bolin's back and asked, "You play guitar?"

"Yes," Bolin replied.

"Maybe you want to entertain the crowd after dinner?" Mike asked hopefully.

Bolin laughed at that and said, "Truthfully, I will sing for my supper tonight if that's what it takes to be invited in."

"Everyone's invited. You'll see," Mike said confidently.

Their conversation ended as the door to the restaurant slowly opened outwards towards the small gathering of hungry survivors. A very tall and lanky red-haired man with pale skin, a face full of freckles, and bright blue eyes was looking straight at his dinner guests as he smiled broadly and pushed open the door. He used his foot to prop it open by lowering the door stop. "Dia Dhuit, friends! Come along inside!" he said loudly to them as he ushered them inside. He had stepped back inside the doorway and was partially obscured from the view of those still outside as Bolin approached the entrance.

"Ah, a new face tonight!" he said as Bolin began to pass through the doorway. He quickly reached out for Bolin's right hand while gently applying a friendly slap to his right shoulder with his left hand. "Name's James. And what should I call you?" he asked with sincere interest in learning Bolin's name which had the negative effect of immediately engaging Bolin's anxiety.

"Oh, yes. Hello. My name is Bolin. I hope it's ok if I join you all tonight. I was passing by earlier. I was told it would be ok?"

He regretted his best effort to communicate confidently almost immediately, but James' expression continued to convey his sincere interest in what Bolin was struggling to say, and he responded, "Well you heard right, Bolin! I'm so glad you decided to join us. If you go line up behind that fellow named Mike over there, I'll be coming around in a minute to serve everyone. Go on!" he finished with a beaming smile that might have been just a tad infectious because Bolin began to feel a little lighter inside and genuinely welcomed to the gathering of hungry survivors.

This was a really good environment to be in tonight, Bolin thought to himself. He did like the idea of a night of comradery offered by this little group of survivors. Especially James. He was gregarious in every communicable way, engaging guests with his voice, his mannerisms, and his confident social interactions. He had a youthful face, but he offered the confidence of a much older man who had some life experience and expected to find a way to navigate the current situation with at least some measure of success. Although Bolin had doubts about what the future held for everyone, he decided he would happily take in some positive energy at least for the duration of one meal. As he lined up to be served, he continued to listen to James enthusiastically and warmly welcome dinner guests behind him.

With everyone who had been on the sidewalk now inside, James left the door open to encourage stragglers, or the curious, to enter and walked briskly across the room and behind the bar. The bar counter was lined with an eclectic mix of serving bowls and pots and Bolin recalled Mike telling him that, without running water, dishes could not be cleaned for a second use. James clapped his hands together once for no one but himself, and pulled over a stack of clean plates to serve each person waiting in line. The restaurant was quite large, so they must have a decent supply of plates, if not pots, still available with the post-apocalyptic nightly crowd sizes of 14 or so guests.

An attractive young woman was behind the bar with James standing to his left. She was taking drink orders and handing them out as people had their plates filled with food by James. They had bottled water and cans of drinks as well as the contents that remained behind the bar. Bolin approached the bar behind Mike and James raised his red eyebrows high at him while fanning his long arms across the top of the prepared food.

"What'll ya have, Bolin?" he asked him with a smile. "The freezers have given us one last night of meat. Unless you're a vegan, I highly recommend you go for one of these stakes tonight as there won't be any left tomorrow." He pointed to the salad and potatoes and said, "The fruit and veg will last a few more days, but, sadly, these are the last days of their high quality. Starting to decline, I'm afraid. Oh, and this is the lovely Maria who will be taking your drink order. Maria, this is a new guest by the name of Bolin." Maria waved and smiled at Bolin as she handed Mike a full glass of whatever he had requested. "She has a heavy drink-pouring hand by order of the proprietor, so you might want to take a bottle of water along with whatever she makes ya," James said, winking at Bolin.

"This all looks great. I was just thinking how much I miss fresh vegetables today," said Bolin surveying the spread of food laid out along the bar. He looked up at James' smiling face and felt the infectiousness of his friendliness once again. He tried to shake off his social anxiety wanting to enjoy the people who he was fortunate to be around this night. "Yes, so steak sounds great. I'll have that, and I'll have whatever else you're offering."

"You sure?" James asked him. "Because I've got broccoli over here and I know some people are just adamantly opposed to this very fine vegetable. They say horrible things about it which I definitely do not agree with!"

Bolin let out a small laugh and felt a growing ease at communicating with him. "Well, I don't know who these broccoli haters are, but I guess it just means more for us because I like it, too."

"Double ration for you then, sir!" James said while placing an extra spoonful of broccoli on Bolin's plate. "Second serves are self-serves here, so if you want more after this, come on up and don't be shy about it, ok?" James added that last part minus some of the theatrical enthusiasm he had been displaying up to that point opting to speak to Bolin in a quieter tone making sure Bolin understood he was welcome to help himself.

"Thank you," Bolin said and turned his attention to Maria who was waiting to fill his drink request.

"Water, please," Bolin said to her.

"And a shot of my favorite Irish whisky for the newcomer," James said to Maria with a nod to Bolin.

"Yes, ok. A shot of Irish whisky along with that water," Bolin agreed, smiling. Maria filled a shot glass with whisky and nestled it among the broccoli on Bolin's plate then handed him a water bottle.

Walking back towards the tables, he saw Imani enter the restaurant carrying a large road map. It looked like the kind gas stations used to sell decades earlier before technology rendered them obsolete. Bolin had his hands full as he made his way towards the table where Mike was already digging into his plate of food. He placed his food and drinks on the table next to Mike. Mike raised his free hand and waved to Imani and she walked over and placed the large road map book in the middle of the table for Bolin. Bolin noticed it was a comprehensive road map for the entire United States.

"Took me a minute to find. It wasn't where I thought it would be. Oh, steak tonight, huh? Oh, I'm so into that right now. I'll be right back," she said, walking away from them towards the bar.

"Thanks for this!" Bolin said to her as she departed. He removed the backpack and the guitar from his shoulders and placed them on the empty table next to theirs. As he took his seat, he noticed James engaging Imani, his last full-serve customer.

Bolin was starving. He really wanted the vegetables. Oh, yeah, and the steak, but the vegetables were, to him, the best part. So hard to come by in a food desert like a city. Maybe he should head towards the mountains where he would possibly be able to farm. The coast might not be the best place to figure out how to grow vegetables. He never had a taste for fish or the other seafood dishes his grandmother was so fond of making for him as a child. He just loved her more than he disliked what she prepared for him. The fact that he had eaten plenty of seafood prepared by her was no indication of his appreciation for them as a food source. He might have found the reason why he should choose one destination over the other. No taste for seafood.

Imani came back with a plate heavy with food and did a little dance of joy as she placed it on the table.

"Oh, this looks good! How does he do all this without power?" she asked them.

"There's a brick grill in the kitchen from the old days," Mike said with authority. "Place was built more than a hundred years ago. They always kept the brick fireplace. I worked here for one summer when I was a kid. It used coals and wood. I'm sure it's how he's cooking. I haven't asked. I'm just glad he is."

Bolin noticed Maria making her way over to a table to his left with her own plate of food and drinks. She had a bottle of vodka tucked under her arm and the man she was about to sit next to relieved her of the bottle with an enthusiastic, "Hell, yeah! Thanks, James!" She sat down next to the man laughing and Bolin turned to his right at the sound of his name being spoken on his other side.

"Bolin, Mike, Imani! Room at the table for one more?" James asked them. The three of them encouraged him to take a seat, but Bolin noticed James had waited to be encouraged to join them rather than pulling out the available chair presupposing it would be alright with them. As James sat down, he noticed the large road map in the center of the table and asked them about it.

"Are you three planning on heading out of the city?" he asked with interest.

"Bolin is," Imani replied. She nodded her head towards Bolin to let him explain himself. James was clearly hungry after cooking for what must have been hours and then serving everyone else. He was eating food from his overflowing plate quickly while waiting for Bolin to speak.

"I had come to visit friends in the city when everything went to hell. I found my friends. They're dead like most are. I'm currently stationed at Camp Pendleton over in southern California, so I'm too far from home to get back anytime soon. I've been looking for a map because I'm not familiar with the area, and I don't know the best routes out of the city or even where to go honestly."

"Kind of like me!" James beamed after swallowing a mouthful of steak and washing it down with a sip of water. "How do I get back to Ireland?! This is my third summer here, but I really don't know my way around outside of the city. I know the city pretty well, though. What are the options you're considering?" he asked Bolin.

"All I had in mind was the coast or the mountains. I know, really vague. I was waiting for a sign to help me decide and then I was served a plate full of vegetables and I think I have just decided I'm going west or someplace where I can farm."

"You've done some farming then, yeah?" asked James, impressed with the thought.

"Actually, no. None at all. I grew up in New York City, and we didn't even have a houseplant I could practice my plant care skills on. I sprouted a bean once for a science class though." He laughed at his own joke and expected to be the only one, but James laughed out loud with him and said something about if the spark exists it can persist with a little care and encouragement.

"Maybe touch base with me here before heading off on a farming adventure. I've got two days' worth of food left here and I have no reason to stay after that. I've also got a bit of knowledge about agriculture rolling about in this head," he said, pointing his fork at his head.

"You do some farming back in Ireland then, James?" asked Imani before Bolin had a chance to inquire.

"Oh, yeah. Grew up on a working farm just north of Dublin with sheep, goats, horses, chickens, the whole lot. In my third year at University earning my agricultural degree with an emphasis on sustainable and organic farming."

The other three looked at him, surprised and impressed with the new information he had shared about himself, but it was Bolin who spoke first and said, "So you're a farmer then, and not a chef? Because I thought for certain you were a chef and a master of the culinary arts."

"Oh, yeah. I'm a farmer first, but I do love to cook! Whole family are farmers for generations back. My father's a farmer and so on. Mum was raised on a farm and my brothers, sisters, and I were raised to follow. I grew up on family land. Respectable 35 hectares. I don't know what that translates to in your American measurements," he finished.

"That's about 86 and a half acres," said Bolin with authority.

"Good with maths, are ya?" James laughed while taking a sip of whisky.

"Yes, my degree is in civil engineering and I've been with the navy's Civil Engineering Corps for seven years. I do well even without a calculator," he laughed.

"Well, well, well," said Mike cheerfully. "Aren't you two just full of surprises? Here I thought, you know, first impressions and all," he pointed at Bolin, "I thought you were probably a tech wizard from silicon valley because, New York? You don't even have an accent! How is that possible? And then this kid! I seriously thought you were still a kid. You're tall, but you look like a teenager, James! Not more than 19. I saw you drinking whisky and thought maybe the drinking age is lower in Ireland and you know, apocalypse rules apply these days anyway."

Imani shook her head in agreement. "Mike and I did not consult one another about any of this, but I thought the same things," she laughed.

James was clearly enjoying the conversation and got up from the table laughing assuring the three of them he was of legal age to consume alcohol internationally. "Make your best guesses while I go fetch us a bottle to share!" he said amiably and headed back to the bar.

When he returned he remained standing and pointed to Mike and asked,

"How old am I?"

"21," said Mike, slapping the table.

"Eh, wrong! Your reward is a full glass of the best Irish whisky my uncle keeps." James filled Mike's glass to the very rim and pointed at Imani.

"Your turn, Imani," he said to her. "It's impossible to tell because you have a youthful spirit that's going to influence any guess I make, but I'm going to say 26 because working on a farm and earning a degree at the same time probably takes a little extra time," she laughed.

"Oh, so sorry Imani! You are also incorrect, but here is a full glass of the best Irish whisky you will ever have in this lifetime or any other!" He also filled her cup to the rim while she laughed and declared that she wasn't going to be able to get home tonight without assistance, and Bolin saw Mike nod reassuringly at her.

James turned to Bolin and looked firmly at him with a glint in his eyes, "Bolin, my new friend, how old am I? And don't worry. As you can see, there are no losers here. We all win. In fact, I'm going to win right now and pour myself a drink while you decide on a number."

As James topped off his glass with the Irish whisky, Bolin said, "Being good with math doesn't make me a good guesser, but I'm going to say 23 and a half to split the difference between Mike's guess and Imani's guess."

James lifted the bottle of whisky high above his head and let out a whoop of excitement. "Bolin! Almost to the day. You're too modest! You are in fact good with maths and an excellent guesser, sir! Let's fill up your glass shall we?"

They were all laughing when James sat down and raised his glass and proposed a toast, "An Irish prayer for my new friends" he said. They all raised their glasses to meet his in the middle of the table and he recited from memory, "May God give you, for every storm, a rainbow. For every tear, a smile. For every care, a promise. And a blessing in each trial. For every problem life sends, a faithful friend to share, for every sigh, a sweet song, and an answer for each prayer!" They clinked their full glasses together and all voiced their approval at the sentiments James had so eloquently recalled in his choice of a toast.

Placing his glass on the table, James turned to Bolin and asked, "That guitar. You play? Or were you planning on picking up a new hobby now that none of us have real jobs anymore?"

"Oh, yes, I play. I found it in a bar the first day."

"Would you be willing to play something for us while we finish our food and drinks?" James asked him without actually sounding like he was pressuring him.

Bolin's parents had made him take years of piano and violin, but the guitar was his secret passion. Away from them at college, he had bought himself an acoustic guitar first, then an electric. He hadn't found the end of his musical talents. He found playing music a true joy that resonated deeply inside of him. That wasn't something his parents put in him through hours of mandatory practice. He was born with the passion for music. When playing the guitar, he did not suffer from the same anxiety he felt when trying to interact socially. The music flowed through him like some separate and vital energy only dependent upon his willingness to let it access the use of his body. He was never self-conscious when he played. If he had a natural state of being, it would be playing. Even piano and violin, which his parents had succeeded in making so unenjoyable by their demands when he was young, became instruments he could appreciate once he was free from their judgement. Without his parents around, he had learned to enjoy music from those sources as well.

He looked at James and got up from the table saying, "Yes. I would like to play. Does anyone have a request?" He unlocked the guitar case and pulled it out. A tuner was clipped near the top and he removed it. "It's already tuned," he said absently.

"Play something you love," said James.

"Yeah, don't let us choose," said Mike.

Bolin noticed that the other dinner guests were beginning to realize that he was about to play. He suddenly felt so normal and at ease knowing he was going to get to play to a small audience.

"Don't be nervous," said Imani enthusiastically. "We haven't heard music in a week. We'll enjoy anything you decide to play." Others agreed with her and added their encouragement.

"This is a song I wrote before joining the navy," he said. It was meant to capture my feelings about making a life altering decision with little real understanding about the consequences. Everything worked out in the end, and I made the right choice for myself. I kind of feel like I'm on the precipice of another decision just like that one. Trying to make a decision about where to go next." He pulled the guitar strap over his head and immediately started playing his song. It began slowly and he made the decision not to sing the lyrics he had written nearly a decade earlier, but to simply let the music do the talking for him. In his mind, he felt that each of the people sharing a meal together on this day were making a personal decision and they could, themselves, supply their own words.

The music Bolin played gradually built in intensity and his musical talent was revealed as true artistry to his small audience. Had his eyes not been closed, he would have noticed several listeners had been moved to tears because of the feelings being addressed through his music which resonated with the survivors gathered in the restaurant. In his own mind, and with his own ears, he could hear the complexity of a hard to make decision unravel and become clear. This followed with music meant to convey settling on a decision and the realization that no path is ever entirely known to the traveler. You simply have to keep moving forward in this life and have hope. The music ended with what Bolin interpreted as peace in the final decision and any potential outcomes. He opened his eyes as the final note hung in the air, and noticed his audience all staring intently at him. He suddenly felt awkward and said quietly, "Well, that was the end."

Someone started clapping, and others joined in. Mike, Imani, and James who were closest to him motioned for him to come sit back down with them while James added, "That was absolutely fucking brilliant, Bolin. Sincerely beautiful. Like you felt it in your soul and so did everyone else."

"Thank you. Playing is about the only time I feel right. Pre apocalypse and post apocalypse, actually." He laughed a little laugh and picked up his still full glass of whisky and took a sip.

"Does the song have lyrics?" asked Imani.

"Yes. I chose to leave them out because I figure we are all on the verge of making important decisions for ourselves. Maybe listeners can come up with their own lyrics to match their unique situations," he finished.

James blinked hard and turned to face him. "You're an enigma, Bolin," he said. Then, looking away from him, he took a big sip of his whisky before asking Mike and Imani if they had any hidden musical talents. Neither claimed to and the conversation turned to future plans for individuals at the table once James ran out of food to serve and the early evening dinners came to an end.

Mike noted Bolin's concern for access to food and water offering that end of the world movies never bothered to explain how fires would consume so many resources. He explained that he and Honey were currently living in an abandoned boat over at the marina because their townhome had burned to the ground just before the rains hit. Imani remarked that her apartment building had been spared for now, but that some of the surrounding buildings had been destroyed by fires already. She told how the first couple of days she had hesitated to believe she would need to break into the homes of others to gather supplies, but by the second day of rain, with bodies still laying in the streets, she decided no one was coming to help and began to break into stores and homes that were not destroyed in order to find nonperishables. Today, she had found the heat and humidity combined with the recent rains made entering closed homes nearly unbearable due to the stench of the decomposing bodies inside. Outside on the streets, the smells were increasingly overwhelming, but the bandana she kept in her back pocket helped when she found herself walking through particularly dense areas of decomposing bodies. She said how lucky they were to be having meals with James, and thanked him with a sincerity that warmed the mood at the table further.

From there, the hours passed in an easy-going exchange between exhausted, scared people who were thankful for the opportunity to socialize in a familiar way. Good food, good drinks, good people. Bolin was encouraged to provide more background music for the group if he was so willing, and a teenage girl named Katie, who was a regular member of the nightly dinners, shyly offered to go to her home and bring back her flute to join in. They all encouraged her enthusiastically, particularly Bolin, and were rewarded by her skillful accompaniment to Bolin's acoustic guitar. They discovered she was the daughter of two accomplished Philadelphia Orchestra members who had died the first day and that she had been staying in the hall since day one. A woman named Jayden, whose family had also died, asked if she could stay with Katie explaining she had been spending her nights in the hammocks down at the harbor. Mike listened to Katie and Jayden and told them there were plenty of boats available down at the harbor along with a growing friendly and supportive community that looked after one another. He added that one benefit was the cool nights on the water after long hot days. He turned to Imani and told her she was welcome to come back with him tonight and check out the available boats and joked that they could be neighbors. Bolin thought Mike was making a clever move on Imani and watched as she knowingly accepted his offer of an after-dinner real estate tour.

Prior to the apocalypse, Mike had been a widowed public utilities worker five years out from retirement. Imani had been a real estate agent for 30 years and was widowed only eight months earlier when her husband had passed due to a cancer she declined to specify to the group. "Cancer is cancer and I won't name it and give it a fancy title," she said, waving her hand at their request for specifics. They respected her opinion and the conversation moved on to other topics.

As the summer sun began to set outside after a long day of sunshine and the light within the restaurant began to fade, Maria stood up and let everyone know that it was time to begin cleaning up and head out until tomorrow. She let their guests know that there was still plenty of food which would eventually go to waste if more people did not show up tomorrow and the following day. She encouraged everyone to bring a new friend to the next meal. "Same time tomorrow everyone. Around 3pm. You know where the sun should be by now. But really, bring someone. James and I are going to have to use up a good amount of what's left for the next two days."

People began to get up and take their dirty dishes with them intending to bring them to the dumpster behind the Grotto as a way of assisting James and Maria with the clean-up process. Not wanting the evening to end, they milled about saying goodbye to each other and thanking James and Maria for the food and company at the end of the day. Bolin headed over to James to offer to help clean up, but Maria got to him first and said, "James, the wine. Don't forget the wine. You left eight cases in back."

"Oh, right!" he said, clapping his hands together with enthusiasm. "Hey, before you leave," he said loudly to the group, "I have loads of a very fine red wine here for those interested in having a nightcap later at your own place! Take some glasses if you need them, too! Or drink it straight from the bottle, eh? Same effect. Getting wasted, right!? That's the goal now, admit it! Go ahead and place your dirty dishes over there. We'll take care of those tonight. You should leave here with arms full of wine instead!" He walked to the kitchen and re-emerged with two cases stacked one on top of the other. "Here ya go! More in the back. Take two bottles if ya want. Three even. I've got at least 48 bottles and there's what? 17 of us? I don't like red wine. Someone else can have mine," he said cheerily. "It's all going to go to waste if this place catches fire before we can enjoy it."

As James placed the first two cases of wine on the bar, Bolin approached and said he'd go get the other cases for him so James could hand them out. James seemed delighted at the offer and remained to open the two cases he had brought out. He passed out the wine bottles while offering friendly wishes of goodnights to his guests. Maria asked if anyone needed food to take back with them, and handed Mike a bowl with food for Honey which she said James had already made for him to take back to his ailing elder dog. "I hope your little Honey is feeling better, Mike," she said to him as he thanked her and James. James nodded silently at Mike's gratitude. He and Imani headed out with a single case of red wine that Mike was carrying while Imani carried Honey's dinner, and James turned to Bolin who was placing two more cases of wine on the bar saying, "Someone's getting lucky tonight, ya think?" He winked at Bolin who turned as Imani yelled back to Bolin that it had been nice meeting him and they'd better see him the following evening. Bolin turned back to respond to James, but he was already engaged in a conversation with Jayden who asked if there were any non-alcoholic options for her and Katie to take with them. "Well, I'm sure we can find you two ladies what you need," he said,
continuing to empty the two additional cases of wine bottles onto the bar counter which Bolin had brought out.

"Maria, my love, can you look over there for some non-alcoholic drinks for Miss Katie and Jayden, please?"

"Can I have their bottles of wine," asked a man who looked barely out of his teens.

"There are some other survivors near where I've been staying. I haven't met them yet, but I'll bring them some wine tonight and suggest they come here with me tomorrow," he added.

"How about four bottles for ease of carrying?" asked James without hesitating to question the kid's story.

"Yeah. Four is fine," said the likely teenager.

"Ah, what am I thinking?! Here, just take this case. Even easier to carry!" said James sliding an unopened case of six wine bottles forward. He turned to Bolin. "If we run out of red before you head out, I'll let ya grab anything else here that you want instead. Whatever you like."

"Sure, ok. I'll go get the other cases," Bolin responded, not worried about whether or not he was going to be walking out of the restaurant with red wine. He was planning to take his still half-full glass of whisky with him, so he felt like he had plenty to get through the night, anyway.

Bolin brought the last two cases of wine to the bar and James turned to thank him saying, "Mighty helpful of you, Bolin." Bolin had wanted to offer to stay behind and help clean up the place earlier, but he was anxious that his offer would be unwanted. He was enjoying the easy acceptance of a group of strangers and did not want to put anyone off. He wanted to return to the group for a meal the next evening. He wanted to be welcomed. Still, he decided to take the chance and possibly get to spend more time socializing before the night ended.

"I wanted to offer to stick around and help clean up since, well, it was very nice of you and Maria to go through all the work of preparing everything. Whatever needs doing. Tell me what it is and it will get done," he added hoping his offer to help out would be accepted.

James turned to him and smiled broadly saying, "You know what? I'm going to take you up on that offer. Send Maria home early and let her take the night off, hey?"

"Yes. That's great. Tell me what needs to be done. I'm all yours."

James listened and continued to smile at him. "Sounds good to me." Turning towards Maria, he said, "Maria, Bolin has agreed to close up with me tonight. Why don't you head home and let us finish up?"

"Hell, yeah! Thanks, Bolin! Nice to meet you tonight. You coming back tomorrow?" she asked him.

"Yes. I plan to," he said to her.

"Great! See you then. James, I'm taking this," she grabbed a full bottle of scotch from the back wall of the bar, "....and this!" she said, grabbing a half full bottle of Grand Marnier.

James shook his head sadly and said, "Disgusting. I don't even know ya!"

"More of that Irish Whisky for you," she said smiling as she headed out the back through the kitchen.

Bolin was the type of person who thrived in the military. He liked knowing what needed to be done, and he could be counted on to accomplish any task set before him. Cleaning up after a small dinner party was not going to be the type of task that challenged him, but it felt good to take orders from James and know he was helping out. As a navy officer, he had thrived in all aspects of his assigned duties. So, clearing the dirty dishes and walking them down the street to another restaurant's dumpster where James hoped to que rats and avoid their encroachment upon his own restaurant, made him feel useful.

They had finished cleaning up and were now sitting together at the bar finishing their glasses of whiskey surrounded by the small light afforded them by the four oil candles James had lit earlier. James was showing genuine interest in the work Bolin had done for the navy in the Civil Engineering Corps. "So, construction projects, infrastructure and infrastructure repairs, and even natural resources management? That touches upon areas of my own interests," he clarified with Bolin after Bolin had described to him some of the work he had carried out in the Middle East and various areas around the world.

"Yes. I've even built greenhouses of all sorts, pit types like the walipini, underground, and lean-tos. I've tried to be helpful when interacting with people in places the navy sent me. Finding resources to build a greenhouse that suited the area, spending an afternoon helping dig wells to water crops, even parabolic solar cookers to help with food preparation and water pasteurization... I probably need to find some seeds and a book about how to grow things. I've never actually grown a plant. Greenhouses I build for myself might remain empty," Bolin laughed, adding, "I don't feel any better prepared for what's going on now having had military training. I can't say I'm bringing my military experience into any of my reactions to this so far. Most of that stuff I mentioned, I did on my own time. I want to get out of this city. A dense city like this is never a good place to ride out bad weather or food and water shortages. There's plenty of land just west of here. North, too. Fertile land and rain are really great resource advantages America has over other places. Thankfully, I was here in Philadelphia when this happened. Otherwise, I'd be in southern California, and there's not a lot of rain out there. There is a lot of desert which I wouldn't have any idea how to farm. I mean, I don't know how to farm the land anyway, but I know you need rain and fertile soil. I feel like I have a lot of good options today. Imani's map will help."

James sat and listened quietly as Bolin spoke and contemplated all that he was telling him. "Well, it looks like a war zone in need of a civil engineer out there already," he said with raised eyebrows. "Your next deployment will probably be to an American city."

Bolin shook his head and said, "What's going on outside is going to require a functioning government. I'm becoming increasingly concerned that what we see here on the streets of Philadelphia is actually everywhere. If other cities had fared better, why haven't they sent us help? I can't imagine what New York City is like right now."

James nodded, "That's right. You said you're from New York. Do you need to get back there to family?" he asked with concern.

"No. My family consisted of my parents and my grandmother. My grandmother passed away years ago. My parents and I are not close. We haven't spoken in years. Not since I joined the navy seven years ago."

"Wow. I mean, sincerely, Bolin. That's tough. I'm really close to my family and I'm devastated thinking about what's potentially happened to them. There's no way I'm getting back to Ireland any time soon the way things are now." James sighed deeply at the thought of not being able to get back to his family. He continued, "The thought of them being alive and worrying about me is also a heavy burden. You must have all the same deep emotions even if for completely different reasons."

Bolin was listening to the words James was speaking and noticed the heavy heart with which he expressed his feelings of helplessness in the situation he found himself in. He didn't want to be at a loss for words as he had been when Mike had told him about his sick dog, and said, "That's a tough reality for you James. I'm sorry it's not easier. A big family that cares about each other is a gift. If they were walking distance, I'd walk with you and help you get back. You know, an adventure. I'm always up for one. For instance, if they were in Alaska. Alaska's walkable from here. But, even after years in the navy, I don't know how to sail. Certainly not all the way to Ireland. We really don't all learn how to actually sail in the navy." Bolin shook his head and offered a small shrug.

James laughed at that and tapped his own heart with his right hand and looked at Bolin. "Well it means a lot to me that you'd wear out your walking shoes to get me to Alaska! And we share an inability to sail. I wouldn't even pilot an inner tube in a kiddie pool. Truly. Do you have anyone special you need to get back to in San Diego?" he suddenly asked him.

"No. No one," Bolin said, shaking his head. "But speaking of someone special, I guess I should head out and let you get back to Maria."

"Maria?" James asked, looking puzzled.

"Yes," Bolin said. "You and Maria. You're a couple, right? Maybe just a summer in Philly couple or an apocalypse couple, but a couple."

James was looking at Bolin with a growing smile and eyebrows that couldn't find the ceiling. Finally, laughing, leaning forward, and slapping his leg lightly, he stood up straight and tall from his chair accentuating his full height and said decisively, "Maria and I are not a couple. She and the fella she was seated next to at dinner are a couple and have been for years. They both survived whatever this is together which I'm inclined to believe is going to turn out to be a rare event." James was still smiling, but not looking directly at Bolin as Bolin followed James' lead and also stood up. It was probably time for him to leave anyway, he thought.

James looked back at Bolin with a more serious expression and added, "I had someone back home. We'd been together for four years, but we broke up shortly before I came here this summer. Told me someone better came along. Someone who enjoyed the city life and who didn't want to live on a farm for the rest of their life. I love the farming life, have I mentioned?" He paused and looked reflective for a moment. "No," he shook his head, still looking at Bolin. "No. You know what Bolin, maybe my intention has been lost in translation due to the differences in the languages we're speaking. Maybe that's it. You know? I've been flirting with you in Irish all night and I just realized it might not be translating to American. I can be less subtle, though." He walked up close to Bolin and tipped his face down to look at him. "I'm interested in men. Specifically, you. How about yourself? Are you interested in men? Me, perhaps?" James pointed to himself smiling while he said this.

Bolin was looking up at James who had decreased the space between them to just a couple of inches. He took a small step forward and closed the space between himself and James and pressed his body against the taller man. He slowly wrapped one hand around the side and lower back of James and felt both of James' hands being placed gently on his shoulders and then moving slowly down his back. It felt good to be touched. As they continued their embrace, James leaned down and kissed Bolin's mouth slowly and softly. They continued kissing each other slowly while exploring each other's bodies with their hands in the silence of the empty restaurant with just the light from the oil candles illuminating the large space.

James broke their kiss, but not their embrace and asked Bolin, "Ok? Is my flirting effectively transcending our language barrier now? Or should I stick with being as direct as possible to avoid future misunderstandings?"

Bolin laughed slightly looking up at James and said, "Your flirting is great. It's probably my fault. Being direct is appreciated and might continue to help me keep up with your intentions. I'm going to have to go back over everything you said to me tonight to pick up where you were trying to get my attention because I honestly thought you were with Maria. I mean, I considered that you're an attractive man, but I didn't consider you were interested."

James leaned forward slightly and said, "I'm very interested," before continuing to kiss Bolin with a noticeable increase in intensity. "I want you tonight if you want me, too," he told Bolin between kisses that became harder and more insistent.

"Yes. I want you," Bolin said as they kept kissing. He pulled away slightly and looked at James asking him, "Where are we doing this? I don't have a place. Where are you staying?" He was stroking James' chest with one hand and placed his other hand on James' arm.

"Upstairs is an apartment where I'm staying." James spoke quietly to Bolin while still kissing the side of face and neck.

"I'll follow you," said Bolin with eyes closed as James ran his hands down his back and over his ass squeezing gently with both hands. James slowly broke their embrace and grabbed a half empty bottle of whisky from the counter along with one of the oil candles.

"This way," he said, leading Bolin out of the soft light of the bar towards the kitchen.

The stairway to the upstairs apartment was dark but easy to navigate with the light from the oil candle. At the top of the stairs, James opened a door that led to a massive open space with walls of tall windows that let in some light from the night sky. The vast room contained only a few interior walls dividing some spaces. Bolin recognized the windows from the outside view of the building. An entire loft, not just a small apartment.

"My uncle and his wife lived up here for a few years before buying proper residential properties," he said to Bolin in a voice that suggested he didn't want to talk about anything unrelated to the sexual activity they were both pursuing.

"I'm very interested, but tell me about it later," Bolin said while turning towards James and stroking his arm.

"Yea, right." James smiled. "Bed's over here," he said, pointing across the space of the loft to one of the few areas that contained three walls for at least a little privacy. James led the way and Bolin followed him watching how he moved and thinking how close he had come to missing out on this opportunity. Other than really liking the idea of having sex with just about anyone tonight, he was surprised at how much he liked James as a person. He had written him off as unavailable early in the evening. He did hook ups. In general, he didn't expect to truly enjoy the company of the people he hooked up with, but he always enjoyed sex. What was going on with James felt different. It felt exciting. He enjoyed James' company. He seemed like a really good person. Inside the bedroom that only had three walls, Bolin noticed that the bed was made. Not made well, but still tidy and effectively made. James placed the oil candle on a tall dresser and took off his shirt as he walked to the other side of the large bed and lit a candle on the nightstand with a lighter that had been nearby. Bolin was undressing on the other side of the bed as James walked back around to him and touched his arm as he leaned in to kiss him.

"It'll get really dark in here fast and I want to be able to see you. Is that ok? Or no candles?" he asked Bolin as he walked over with the lighter to light a second candle on the nightstand closest to Bolin.

He waited for Bolin to respond and lit the second candle as Bolin said, "Yes. Light is good. Are you concerned at all about fires?" he suddenly asked James.

He could see James smiling at him in the flickering light as dropped the lighter noisily on the night table and approached him saying, "No, not really. But there's a fire escape behind those curtains," he said, pointing across the bedroom to the exterior wall. "That's the exit if there's a fire or you want nothing more to do with me after we're finished."

Bolin closed his eyes, shook his head and laughed at the comment asking, "What?" and James quickly added, "Oh, but you're gonna want a lot more to do with me after tonight, Bol." He leaned down and kissed Bolin while also gently leaning his shirtless chest against Bolin's.

Bolin sighed. "I want to feel your entire body against mine," he told James as he moved away from him and finished undressing. James did the same and the two men laid down on the bed together and kissed and touched and explored each other's bodies becoming less patient for what they each wanted as the time passed and their sexual desires increased. The lights from the candles flickered on their skin illuminating areas where each man desired to be touched by the other. The shadows cast by their bodies as they wrapped themselves up in each other played against the walls of the bedroom. For Bolin, there was nothing else going on in the world that night that could tear his attention away from James' touch on his body as James went down on him, and nothing that could stop him from pleasuring James in return.

Afterwards, as the two men were lying in each other's arms, Bolin turned his face towards James' and quietly asked him, "Were you going to let me leave after dinner?"

"No." James laughed. "I had a plan that involved running after you if you walked out the front door. I was keeping my eye on you in case it became necessary."

Bolin laughed at the thought of James running after him.

"I'm serious. I'd rather be rejected than miss an opportunity," James said emphatically.

They both laughed, and Bolin offered to go get his guitar while James poured them each some more whiskey. They sat on the couch together for several hours talking, and Bolin played his guitar softly in the background of their various conversations. James hummed some Irish folk songs he liked, and Bolin tried to capture the sounds with his guitar. "We'll look for a music store and see if there's any sheet music for traditional Irish folk songs that survived the fires," Bolin told him.

"I think you did wonderfully just off of my clumsy, drunken humming, Bol," James said encouragingly while kissing him for his efforts. Eventually, they went back to the bedroom and drifted off to sleep together in each other's arms.

Rollo and Mick

Mick was shaking which terrified Rollo. His older brother was braver than he was, and if he was shaking in fear, then he knew this was the end.

"You listen to me. We didn't come this far to have you blow it just to pretend you can save me now," Mick said to him with a tremble in his voice. "Go, before you're locked out. Put the extra tech back in the safe and get back to Pop's house before they come looking for you."

Rollo was taller than his older brother by a lot, but he never felt taller than the man. He looked up to him in everything. Looking at him now, he was terrified it would be the last time he would see his brother alive. Worse, he was afraid if he did see his brother alive again, it would be at an imprisonment ceremony.

"You're almost finished. We can go together. Come with me and …"

Mick turned towards his younger brother with fury and grabbed both of his arms unkindly, shaking him as hard as he could. "Get the fuck out of here now! You're going to ruin everything and get both of us captured!" He suddenly pulled Rollo towards him in a tight hug and said, "If we see each other again, if you get yourself killed in front of me, I'll Rewind you and kill you a second time. I love you. Go!" He shoved Rollo away from him and turned back towards the computer he had been working on leaving Rollo to stare at his back.

"I love you, too, Micky," he said loud enough for his brother to hear as he turned away and walked towards the door of the small room.

As he reached for the handle, he saw it twist downward and watched in horror as the door jolted open in front of him. "Vespry's over here!" shouted the man in the doorway looking back over his shoulder into the hallway at his search team. "Got a second Vespry making this a family affair," he shouted to his team in the hallway while staring at Rollo. "Someone inform Bas we have both Vesprys in custody." The man in the doorway shoved Rollo forward towards his brother who was still standing with his back to the door typing into the computer in front of him.

Mick turned suddenly and growled at Rollo viciously, his face contorted with

82

rage. "You fucking piece of shit, Rollo! You turned in mom and pop, too, didn't you!?" He suddenly reached around him to the computer and grabbed it pulling it with all his might from off the desk and threw it at Rollo's head hitting him and leaving him stunned and staggering. Lunging at Rollo, he managed to punch him in the face hard knocking him to the ground before jumping on top of him to continue to rain down fierce blows on his younger brother's face and ribs. Rollo felt at least one rib break after his brother's first blow had broken his nose. "You killed mom and pop and now you turned me in you fucking piece of shit! Fuck you! I'll kill you!" Mick screamed in a rage as he pummeled Rollo without mercy.

The man in the doorway was trying to drag Mick off of Rollo as others entered the room and surveyed the scene. For his efforts, Mick struck his elbow backwards and caught the man straight in the face breaking a second nose in about as many seconds. He turned and suddenly grabbed the man's gun as several other soldiers entered the room. Mick shot the man in the chest three times as he staggered backwards holding his bleeding, broken nose. Lying on the ground dazed and beaten with blood pouring down his face and a desperate ache in his ribs, Rollo watched as his older brother killed the first man and turned to shoot and kill the others as they entered the room. "No! Not gonna kill you bastards. What's the point?" he said laughing bitterly. "This bullet's for my squealing pig of a little brother." His eyes showed madness, as he reached up and wiped his nose with his left hand and aimed the stolen gun at Rollo with his right hand. He suddenly lurched backwards as a hail of bullets pierced his body as the other soldiers opened fire on him. Rollo watched his brother stumble backwards, losing his footing and then falling in slow motion to the ground, still alive, but mortally wounded. Rollo struggled to get up off the floor with the pain from what might be more than one broken rib and managed to get himself into an upright seated position on the floor. He stared at his brother's dying face. "Fuck you, Mick!" he shouted at him. "You fucking high and mighty piece of shit. You wouldn't know the winning side if it bit you in the ass."

"Move," a soldier growled at another. "Where's a Rewind? Bas, over here. Fuck. Marshall's dead. Out of time. The older Vespry killed him. Tried to kill his brother, too. Called his brother a traitor before beating the fucking hell out of him."

"Is Mick alive?" Bas asked as he entered the room and surveyed the three men on the floor.

"Yeah, he's alive," said the soldier.

Bas walked over to Mick and looked at him with disgust. Shaking his head he asked, "So it was you. How could you? You were going to be a King. I was going to give you a goddamned kingdom. Why? Fuck you. I don't care. You're not dying today. Give me a Rewind immediately!" Bas shouted furiously at his soldiers standing behind him. "I want him in a time cell for fucking ever!" he said as he turned towards the men standing in the doorway. "Where's a fucking Rewind?!" he screamed at his soldiers through his rage with eyes bulging.

"You'll never get to me in time," Mick said with a tone of disgust through a mouthful of blood. He suddenly pointed the gun he was still holding in his hand to his head and looked at Rollo. "Pop would hate you for siding with this prick," he said to his little brother and shot himself in the head. Rollo stared coldly at his brother's lifeless body and suddenly spit a mouthful of blood over at it. He looked up at Bas and snorted a bitter laugh. "15, 14, 13, 12... Where the fuck is the Rewind? I'll take that kingdom since you got no one to give it to now," he said with another bitter snort.

Bas looked down at the younger Vespry. He had never given the younger brother of his right-hand man much of a chance. Mick had always seemed indifferent about the value of his younger brother to the overall mission. He had told Bas that bringing family into this wasn't always about how valuable to the mission they could be, but that, for practical purposes, every society needed janitors, landscapers, cooks, someone to wash the dishes, etc. The brother wasn't too bright as far as Bas could tell, but Mick thought he could still serve a purpose other than in research or in a governmental capacity. It would also make his parents happy, and both of them had value. It occurred to Bas that perhaps Mick had been keeping his role in the opposition from everyone, including his own brother. He reached down and offered Rollo a hand up. Rollo grabbed the hand of the Almighty Bas firmly and accepted the agony of getting himself upright knowing that a hand offered by the Mad King himself was a positive sign he might actually survive the day and avoid endless torture.

"Oh, he fucking broke my ribs. Jesus that hurts," he said out loud to no one in particular but needing all witnesses to hear. He stood up in front of Bas holding his ribs with his twisted nose bleeding profusely down over his mouth and chin. He wiped it roughly with the bottom of his shirt trying to convey righteous anger as Bas continued to stare at him blankly.

"You in on this with your brother?" he asked him pointedly.

"Nah. I got suspicious the past couple of days after my pop was caught stealing that tech. I asked Mick what he knew, but he acted like he was surprised. Said his loyalty was not an issue. The way he looked at me though…. When he said it, I didn't believe him."

"Why are you here now?" Bas asked icily.

"I followed him last night when he left the house really late. I saw him talking to that woman Lacy. The guard from the Cells. This morning, I followed him here. I wanted proof before I turned him in. I caught him. Your guys couldn't catch him. I did," he said proudly with a quick sneering glance towards the soldiers standing nearby.

Bas stared at Rollo without saying a word to acknowledge anything he had just told him. Rollo stared back and didn't flinch. He suddenly shook his head in annoyance adding, "Look, man I don't know what Mick was up to, but this felt like some bullshit worth reporting given what my pop just did."

Bas continued to stare at him in silence. "What was Lacy up to?" he asked Rollo without emotion.

Rollo knew exactly what Lacy had been up to. He hadn't spied on his brother having a secret meeting with Lacy. He had met up with Lacy himself as part of his own plan. He, himself, had given Lacy the stolen tech his pop had tried to bring to their tech person before getting caught. She had to get it to their tech now that pop was dead. They needed working tech for their team. As he answered Bas's question, he hoped that Lacy had already delivered the tech and was back. If she got caught, she would have to be a sacrifice, just as Mick was a sacrifice. She knew the dangers and accepted them.

"I saw Mick hand her something in a box. They talked for a few seconds, not even minutes, and she walked off and he headed back to the house. So, I ran back around and got inside before he saw me. I have no idea what was in the box. I know they're friends. I thought it could be nothing. That's why I followed him here this morning. I was suspicious, but I didn't have any proof. I think the shit with my pop has me fucked up. Like I don't even know anyone the way I thought I did."

Bas watched him intently as he spoke. When he stopped talking, Bas turned to the soldier nearest him and told him to go get Lacy and bring her to the Cells so she could be interrogated about the meeting with Mick the night before. "Don't tell her why she's being brought in. Just bring her in," he told the soldier. Looking at Rollo he said, "I don't trust you. How about we toss you into a time cell for a week and see if that changes your story?" He stared at Rollo coldly.

Rollo knew there really was no mercy in Bas. He was a complete psychopath who got off on hurting others, but he could be manipulated. His brother had figured him out and had worked him into complacency allowing for them to try and subvert Bas's plans. Rollo sighed deeply and rolled his eyes dramatically while blinking. He tipped his head a little to the left and then put it straight up again and looked at Bas.

"Fuck. Fine. What's a week, like four seconds? So I'll be tortured for a week and come back with my nose still bloody and wet and with broken ribs?" He stared at Bas for a second as if bored by the thought before shrugging and taking a step forward saying, "Alright. Let's get this over with then."

Bas let Rollo walk past him to the nearest soldier standing in the doorway. Rollo looked down at the soldier who was shorter than he was, a man he knew to be named Sheng, and muttered to him, "Well, c'mon, Sheng. Let's get this over with. Take me to a time cell." Sheng looked across to Bas for permission to take Rollo, but Bas silently shook his head no. Sheng looked back at Rollo and said nothing. Rollo turned around to look back at Bas and manufactured his best look of confusion to really sell the act he was putting on. "My King, do I go now?" he asked Bas.

Bas ignored him and looked at Sheng saying, "Take him to the hospital to have these injuries treated and tell them he's to remain there. They are not to release him until I give the order. I want five inspectors to meet me at the Vespry house immediately to search for evidence that Rollo is not as innocent as he claims to be. Which team members were supposed to have Rewinds?" he asked Sheng. "Marshall and Kasper," Sheng said, knowing what would happen next.

"Marshall's dead. Kasper's not even worth service work now. Torture," Bas said. Kasper was standing towards the back of the hallway and groaned before fainting.

"How long?" asked Sheng.

"Until I forgive him for costing me the pleasure of dealing with Mick," he snarled. He walked past Rollo and said nothing else as he headed down the hallway.

Sheng looked at Rollo and said, "God help you if you're lying. You're gonna wish you had died rather than what he'll do to you."

Rollo scoffed at Sheng and said, "You see me not worrying, Sheng? That's because I'm not a bitch traitor like my pop and my brother. Get me to the hospital already."

Sheng turned and walked past other soldiers who were deciding who would carry Kasper off for eternal torture. "Get the bodies," he told one of them.

Rollo walked behind Sheng. His confidence in not being caught was due to the fact that his brother was not the architect of the plan, he was. His brother and his father had been working for him. He knew his brother wanted him to do what was necessary to win. He had managed to be killed which was an enormous relief. Rollo walked behind Sheng suppressing every emotion he felt in the current moment. His brother was dead. He consoled himself with that thought. It was better than him being alive. Another thought crept in now. Why had the soldiers been looking for Mick? Did he make a mistake? Did Mick make a mistake? Did he have a traitor in the opposition? It wasn't Lacy. Not a chance. Lacy would go to the cells for the cause and not turn any of them in. Especially if Bas bragged to her that Mick was already dead. They had nothing to lose, and she knew that. Eventually, he'd find a way to get her out. He had to hope she was strong enough to survive in there mentally until he could free her. Death would be easier, but her fate was already sealed. He couldn't kill her to save her now. She was going to be sent to torture today.

Lev, Aisha, and Bob

Lev didn't bother to go back to the cell lot and retrieve Aisha's moped or the food and money she had packed for him. The explosion that collapsed the airport facility had filled the air with a thick layer of soot that was not clearing from the hot humid air. Instead, it was mingling with all of the smoke from the numerous other fires burning on the roadways and in buildings. The road leading out of the airport converged with another and Lev considered the effort to get across the tangled roadways to the moped through the toxic air a task he wasn't up to after everything he had just failed at accomplishing.

Walking towards Aisha's house in a daze, emotionally spent, feeling like giving up, he moved forward bloodied, covered in his own and others' filth, surrounded by even filthier air. For a while he didn't bother to put the dish towel back around his face, not caring to make the effort. But breathing became difficult as his lungs protested against the thick air. He decided to make the effort to put the dish towel back across his mouth. Coughing was annoying. It felt like his body was trying to save him when all he wanted to do was die. He walked dangerously close to cars which appeared to him to be capable of going up in flames. He didn't care. He walked past all manner of living beings trapped in cars, appealing for him to help. He didn't care. He was numb to everything, even his own grief. He had a plan. He was going to walk to Aisha's yellow house. That was all he could focus on now.

People did not approach him as they had earlier when he was trying to make his way to the airport. Back when he believed he could find Yuna like some mythical super hero. No. Now people noticed him and then hesitated and reconsidered asking him for help. He knew why, too. It disgusted him. Before, he looked like he could help. Now he looked like he needed help. They were all just opportunists earlier. Not one of the people he passed by as he walked to Aisha's house offered to help him. Not one asked if he was ok. That's how it is, he thought to himself. Just a bunch of fucking takers. And he had felt shame earlier when he didn't stop to help people. But the truth was, no one was helping him. Take care of yourself first. That was his new approach to surviving. He wasn't going to feel guilty about it either.

The traffic intersection before the restaurant where he'd met Aisha earlier loomed ahead of him in the distance. The long June day meant the sun was still out somewhere behind the smoke filled air, so despite the hours having passed since the world had stopped making sense, it was still light enough outside to see. He came to the intersection and turned right making his way into the community of homes. These streets were largely devoid of cars and he walked down the streets rather than on the sidewalks. "Walnuts grow in the Forrest of Sunnyvale," he said aloud, utilizing the mnemonic he had created for himself when Aisha had given him directions to her house. He turned onto Forrest and saw it was a dead-end street with several cul-de-sacs branching off of it. Sunnyvale was the last street up ahead. He held no thoughts in his head but to get to the yellow house at the end of Sunnyvale.

Aisha had told Bob she needed to stay at her own home overnight in order to wait for Lev and his girlfriend. Bob had shaken his head and tried to insist she couldn't do that with her mother inside. He let her know that Lev was probably not going to show up and he certainly wasn't likely to return with the person he had gone to find. He waved his hand towards the direction of the airport when they both heard the rumblings of what could only have been a massive explosion coming from the facility. He had touched her arm gently to get her attention while he told her the explosion likely destroyed the airport. He tried to reason with her to no avail. She was adamant that she would wait for Lev outside on her front porch until the next day. Lev had saved her life. Bob argued that she had also saved his life by giving over the keys to her moped, packing him food, and making sure he had a helmet.

"Jesus, Aisha. You've done enough. You need sleep tonight. Come across the street and sleep in Lisa's room. I'll sleep on the couch."

"No. He might not even come here, but I told him he could, and I told him I'd be here, so I want to follow through. You have to be able to count on a few people in a situation like this. He said they just moved here. He doesn't know anyone else. I want to stay here in case he shows up," she told him.

Bob shook his head telling her, "Ok. Then I'm staying here with you. You don't know this guy. He's probably alright, but no way am I going across the street and leaving you here alone overnight."

He looked at her and she could tell he wanted to say something important. "What is it?" she asked him. "Just say it."

"Your mom. What do you want to do about your mom?" he asked her quietly, as if by saying the words softly, they would be less painful. Aisha had lived a good life with her mother. She had grown up happy, having her needs met. She was also exposed to details of her mother's life. The life of a black woman in America. A widow. A single mother. A life of overcoming tragedy, embracing pragmatism, laughing at challenges, believing in the power to overcome. Her mother wasn't religious in any sense. She didn't even say 'God bless you' when Aisha sneezed because, as she told Aisha once when she asked why her mother never said God bless you after a sneeze, 'God doesn't exist. I don't say anything after you cough, do I? No.' When Aisha had protested and said it's polite to say God bless you after a sneeze and lots of people say it, her mother responded, 'That's their indoctrination. This is yours. Count on yourself. Not some made up God.'

Aisha looked at Bob. Her mother wasn't sentimental about things just because someone else told her it was the polite way to be. Her mother was dead. Her mother, if she were standing here beside her right now, would tell her to do what needed to be done and nothing more. No theatrics. Theatrics didn't solve problems. No endless weeping. She had watched her mother endure the grief caused by her husband's death. No useless weeping. Do what needs to be done. 'Get up or be dragged,' as she liked to say to Aisha. Aisha looked at Bob.

"We need to wrap her body in the bedsheets and take her outside." She turned and headed into the house and Bob only hesitated for a second before following behind her to help do what needed to be done.

Inside Rhonda's temporary bedroom, Aisha and Bob lifted the edges of the bed sheets to cover her body. Bob went to the foot of the bed and Aisha went to the headboard and together they lifted Rhonda's lifeless body wrapped in sheets off the bed and walked it out of the bedroom, down the hallway, and into the dining room.

"Let's put her down for a minute so I can open the door," Bob said, indicating he wanted to open the sliding doors leading to the backyard deck. Aisha gently placed the top portion of her mother's lifeless body onto the dining room floor, and

Bob went around the dining room table to unlock and open the sliding glass doors. They walked Rhonda outside to the wooden deck and Aisha indicated she wanted to place her mother's body on the lounge chair on the left.

"That's her favorite place to read when it's nice outside," she told Bob with authority. None of this quiet talk bullshit. Whispering wasn't necessary around the dead, she thought to herself.

With Rhonda carefully placed on her favorite lounge chair, Bob turned to Aisha and put his arm around her shoulder. "You ok?" he asked her kindly.

"No," she said matter-of-factly staring at her mother's body wrapped in her favorite purple colored sheets. She loved color. The more the better. Aisha's bed sheets were white. Did she prefer white sheets just because her mother preferred colored sheets? She didn't know. She turned her head away from Bob and looked over their backyard. The daylilies her mother had planted years ago were blooming along the border to the deck, and Aisha walked away from Bob's hand and down the wooden steps of the deck to them. She picked them all. Why not? They all belonged to her mother. She had loved them each and every year. Coaxed them to bloom to bring her joy. With her hands full of the daylilies, Aisha walked back up the steps of the deck and walked past Bob to place all of the blooming flowers on her mother's wrapped body. "There you go, mom. All for you," she said to her mother. She walked back towards Bob and he wrapped both of his arms around her in a big hug and pulled her close to him. He didn't feel the need to say anything, but kissed the top of her head as she pressed against him for the hug she so desperately needed at that moment.

After a minute, he released his grip on her and said, "Let's go wait for this guy and his girlfriend out front." Aisha wiped her eyes and they walked back through the quiet house to the front porch together.

"Are we going to sleep out here, then?" asked Bob.

"I'm hoping he shows up before it comes to that," Aisha said with a small laugh.

Lev could see the canary yellow house at the end of the cul-de-sac now. He didn't stop walking towards it. He hadn't stopped his forward momentum since he had left the SUV with the dead babies in the back seat. He had one goal and that was to reach the yellow house on Sunnyvale. His steps were purposeful, but his ability to think was limited to the goal of reaching the yellow house. He looked like a man on a mission, walking with purpose, strides that looked full of intent. But his mind was not connected to his body any longer. He didn't have a plan once he arrived at the yellow house. Maybe Aisha wouldn't be there. Didn't matter. He only knew he was going to the yellow house. Didn't matter why. He would stop walking once he got to the yellow house. He was close.

Aisha and Bob were sitting on the rocking chairs outside on the front porch of her mother's yellow house discussing how they could find Lisa and the boys. Bob was trying to think of places he should look for his wife and children once the sun rose in the morning. Aisha said she would go with him or branch off to other locations to cover more ground. Whatever Bob needed. Suddenly, Bob stood up and looked intently down the street to the entrance of the cul-de-sac. "Hey. Is that your guy?" he asked Aisha.

Aisha stood up and squinted through the dimming daylight to the entrance of their cul-de-sac and pursed her lips tightly as she considered the figure striding purposefully towards them. "Yeah, you know what? That's him. That's definitely him." She looked at Bob and went down to the driveway with him following behind her. She kept looking towards the man approaching them trying to assess the situation.

"He's alone," she said as she turned her head to Bob. She looked concerned. Bob understood immediately.

"He'll be devastated after trying to find her," he said to Aisha, adding, "He might even be injured. You heard that explosion coming from the airport. That was really bad."

"Do you have first aid equipment at your house?" she asked Bob while still looking intently at the figure rapidly approaching them.

"Yeah. We'll see what he needs first," Bob said, also watching the man approach. He was a broad shouldered, tall man like Aisha had said. No wonder she had been frightened of him immediately following everything in the world coming to a violent stop.

"Shit. Here goes," Aisha said to Bob while looking at Lev.

"Lev!" Aisha said as she walked up to him. Lev looked down at Aisha's face completely ignoring Bob. "Hey. You made it back. That's good. What do you need?" she asked him as his eyes stared down at her. The rest of his face was concealed by the dish towel she'd sent him off with for protection from the smoke filled air.

"She's probably dead," he said without emotion looking at Aisha.

"I'm so sorry. I know you did everything you could. You need to come sit down. Ok? This is my friend Bob. He's a good guy. We'll help you."

Lev looked at Bob, noticing him for the first time.

"Hey," Bob said to him with a small nod.

"The air is better here if you want to take off the mask," Aisha told him.

"Should I take it off?" he asked her.

"Yes," she responded, looking at Bob with concern.

"I think he's in shock," he said to her quietly, but not caring if Lev heard him. "Lev, my name's Bob. I think you're in shock. I want you to come with us and sit down where we can help you. Ok?"

"Ok," Lev said, looking at Bob. He didn't feel Bob's and Aisha's hands on his arms as they led him up the walkway to Aisha's house and to the front porch, but he felt relief as he got closer and closer to the bright, canary yellow home knowing this was where he needed to be in order for the day to finally come to an end.

90

Aisha and Bob walked Lev into her living room and directed him to sit on the couch in the darkened room.

Bob told Aisha, "I'll go grab him some clean clothes from Luke's house. They're both about the same size," and then left Aisha to try and talk to the large, traumatized man.

"Hey, Lev. You're really kind of a fucking mess. I think the water is still working. Let's find out because you seriously need a shower and some clean clothes. You're covered in blood, and I honestly don't know what else. Bob's getting you some clean clothes." Lev looked at her with a blank expression and said nothing. "Come on, man. Work with me!" she said as she tugged on his arm to bring him up off of the couch. He slowly got up and let himself be led up the darkening stairway to the shower upstairs. She told him to turn on the water and she'd grab him some clean towels from the hallway closet. Aisha heard Bob enter the house and called downstairs to him letting him know they were upstairs. She looked at him with wide eyes as he got to the top of the stairs and pointed towards the bathroom and shook her head silently. The door was open, so Bob walked into the doorway and looked at Lev who was standing in the bathroom motionless with the water running in the shower.

"Hey, here's some clean clothes for you. Take a shower. You'll feel better after you get cleaned up," he told Lev. Lev turned and looked at him and asked him to leave. Bob walked into the hallway and Lev didn't bother to close the door as he undressed and got into the shower.

"I have a few candles and flashlights around here somewhere. Do you have any?" Aisha asked Bob.

"Yeah. Lisa's big into candles," he said. "I'll be right back." He went downstairs and headed over to his former house to retrieve what he could find.

Aisha leaned on the wall of the hallway and slowly slid down to the floor where she sat in her own, less severe, version of shock. In times like these, she rationalized, it was important to prioritize the needs of every individual if survival was the goal. Right now, Lev was clearly the weakest link in their three-person chain. Who knew what he had seen on his way to and from the airport. Who knew what he had seen relating to his girlfriend. Who knew what he was just naturally capable of processing. Sure, she'd lost her mother today, but her mother had made sure she was a strong and independent woman, capable of confronting any variety of hardships and riding them through rough waters to the shoreline where she could be safe again. I love you mom, she thought. I'm gonna help Lev, and someday, maybe he'll help me. Right now, I'm strong. I've got this. She sat on the floor of the hallway and didn't shed a tear.

She started to get up off of the floor when she heard Bob coming back up the stairs. "Lots of candles, and several flashlights, too. I left them all downstairs. How is he?" he asked Aisha.

"I don't even know," she said. "He's in the water as far as I can tell. He's completely out of it mentally. I don't know if he's planning to come out anytime soon. I kind of picture him just standing there."

"Ok," Bob said, realizing he should take charge of getting Lev moving. Bob entered the bathroom and said loudly, "Hey, Lev. Save the rest of us some water. You got towels and clean clothes here on the counter." He waited for a second to give Lev a chance to respond. Lev remained silent, but he shut the water off which Bob took as a positive sign.

He exited the bathroom and looked at Aisha and quietly whispered, "I heal bodies not minds. I thought I knew the mind-body shit, but I don't." He offered a small grimace with wide eyes while shaking his head.

Aisha touched Bob's arm lightly and said quietly, "I want to help him."

Bob nodded in agreement.

Aisha called out to Lev, "Lev, Bob and I are going downstairs. Come join us when you're dressed."

They went downstairs together and sat next to one another on the larger of the two living room sofas.

"He's completely fucked up," Aisha said to Bob.

"So am I. How are you?" Bob asked as he put an arm around her and pulled her close to him.

"I'm doing ok. Better than him, for sure."

"I need to find my kids tomorrow," he said to her.

"I know. I'll do whatever you need me to do. I want to find them, too," she said as she leaned into his side.

"I want to look for the minivan. I... I'm realistic about this. I'm not stupid. I saw a lot today when I was looking for them. I saw... I know. I...." He sighed and inhaled deeply before speaking again. "I... I believe my boys are dead." Aisha wrapped her arm around Bob tightly and said nothing while he tried to find the words to speak. "I saw the dead. Is it wrong? I don't want Bryan to be trapped in his seat, alive, surrounded by his dead brothers and his dead mother." He gasped and grabbed his mouth as he said the last words. "I don't want him to be alive overnight like that, strapped into his seat, surrounded by dead bodies. That would be worse than him dying." He started to cry quietly and Aisha held him tighter with her arm around his stomach.

"We'll make a plan and we'll find them tomorrow," she said as she hugged him tightly.

"There's nothing we can do tonight," Bob said. He continued to cry quietly as he thought of his boys and their mother out overnight in the destruction. They would look tomorrow. The lights were all out, the roads and buildings were burning, the air was filled with smoke. They couldn't look for Lisa and the boys until the morning. Maybe Lev would be able to help. If not, he could stay and rest a bit longer. Bob understood where Lev was at right now. It was a place he dared not to go as he contemplated the fate of his wife and his three boys.

Lev stood in the shower and tried to remember what he was supposed to do next. Get dressed. He touched the wall of the shower and ran his hand down the sleek surface of the shower wall. He took his hand and ran it down his hairy, wet chest. The wall felt smoother. He ran his hand down the shower wall again. His head lowered and he felt an emotion overcome him in the absence of any feeling at all. Rage. Was it rage? Indifference. Was indifference an emotion? He was confused by his feelings. Aisha was here. She was a decent person. She would help him. Bob said he would help. Who was Bob? Bob just showed up at the yellow house. He stepped out of the shower and looked at the clothes Bob had left for him. He hadn't given Bob anything and Bob had helped him already. He considered that Bob might be a decent person. He would always protect Aisha. They came from nothing and helped each other without concern for personal costs. He wasn't sure about Bob yet. What did Bob want? He got dressed in the darkening bathroom. Killing Bob to save himself or Aisha was an option.

Lev walked out of the bathroom and called for Aisha. Aisha got up from the couch, leaving Bob, and stood at the bottom of the staircase looking towards Lev.

"About time you were done in there," she said with a friendly tone. He looked at her emotionlessly. "Lev, you're so fucked up right now, and I have no idea how to help you. Did you find your girlfriend?" she asked him as he headed down the staircase towards her.

"No." Lev answered.

"Do you want to talk? I'm not a psychologist. I don't know what you need, but we can talk. Bob's really good with trauma like this. I don't even think he knew he was until today. He's my physical therapy mentor I told you about back at the restaurant. He's gonna stay with us tonight. My mom…. My mom died today. He helped me. Come downstairs and be with us. His kids and his wife are all… he can't find them. You hear me, Lev? Bob's got three kids and a wife he can't find. We're all fucked up. Ok? We understand." She looked at Lev, her eyes pleading with him to believe she understood his loss. He looked down at his bare feet and then back up at her again.

"Ok. I think I'm feeling a little better now. I just don't want to talk about what happened at the airport," he told her.

"Yeah, that's fine with us. We can talk about something else. I know Bob wants to try and find his family tomorrow. Maybe we can come up with a plan before we get some sleep."

Lev looked at her but didn't tell her what he thought about a plan that involved trying to find the people you love in this new world. He honestly didn't think he could be a part of that effort twice in a row. He'd had enough false hope in one day to last a lifetime.

Bolin and James

It was the final night James would be preparing meals for guests. He and Bolin had spent the previous two nights together in the loft and Bolin had made himself entirely available to the meal prep that was important to James. Right now, James was going through the remaining fresh foods from the restaurant, inspecting each item for overall quality. He was throwing out a good deal of what he had hoped to be able to use, but he didn't seem worried. The power had been out for a week, and the frozen foods were all defrosted and no longer safe to eat. James wanted the final meal for his guests to be the best it could be. He had laid in Bolin's arms with his head against his chest the previous morning explaining to Bolin, "The final meal may be the last meal a person might enjoy for a while. Maybe it would be the last time a person experienced a large friendly gathering. It should be as nice as possible." Bolin understood. James' passions were sincere. He recognized food, drink, and good company as important to James' efforts to help others during this time of crisis. What was important to James, was important to him, as well. That was a fact now. James wasn't worried while he disposed of the restaurant's foods that were no longer usable because Bolin had already seen to it that James would have fresh food to work with while preparing the final meal.

Bolin had been learning about what was important to James since they had met two evenings ago at the first meal he had attended. When James had woken up the morning after their first night together, he had quietly told Bolin to go ahead and sleep in. "I'm gonna go decide what needs to be cooked tonight," he said as he gently kissed the back of Bolin's neck and shoulder several times while slowly running his hand down his side. Then he got quickly out of the bed and disappeared before the sunrise.

Bolin had not been able to fall back to sleep, so he eventually got up and made his way back down the darkened stairway to the kitchen below the loft. He saw oil candles lit throughout the kitchen and that James had been busy bringing clean dishes and pots out from large shelving units and had left them on a long counter in the kitchen for use later. Bolin scanned the rest of the kitchen looking for James from the bottom of the stairwell for a moment before he noticed him as he walked into a large food pantry, holding a candle, where he began to gather industrial sized cans from shelves. Bolin headed over to him.

"Let me help you with that," he said, reaching for the cans James was holding.

"Oh, grateful for the extra arms," James said, handing over what he was holding to Bolin. "I'll just grab a few more, but go ahead and place those atop the shorter counter in the kitchen."

"Will Maria be here to help you cook later?" asked Bolin as he walked the cans to the counter.

"No, she usually shows up an hour before I open and starts drinking with Greg, though," he laughed. "I mean, continues drinking. You notice she was completely hammered last night?"

Bolin shook his head no.

"Yeah, got a bit of a problem, those two," he said with a laugh and a nod. "Her mother worked for my uncle for decades before she passed a couple of years ago. He kept Maria on here despite her drinking problem. Every time he wanted to fire her for stealing money or alcohol, my auntie would stop him. Told him every family has a problem child." James laughed.

"Oh, are you related to her?"

"In the adoptive sense. You know, friends can become family, too. Maria's like a cousin. A very problematic cousin with serious addiction issues. I don't think alcohol is her only vice, eh? Ok, actually, I know for a fact that alcohol isn't her only issue. Family, right? What can you do except accept 'em?" James nodded with a shrug and a smile.

Bolin listened to James and said, "I don't want to stay in Philadelphia. When I leave, do you want to come with me? Maria and Greg can come, too. Family is important."

James looked shocked and his smile disappeared as he stared at Bolin for a second trying to process what he'd just said to him. "Yeah, I wanna go with ya," he said as he walked closer to Bolin and put his arms on top of his shoulders.

Bolin wrapped his arms around James' waist and nodded. "Yes. That's good. We can decide where we'd like to go by looking at the map later. You want Maria and Greg to come with us, right?"

"I really do, and I appreciate you saying you'd share that burden, because they would be a burden, but, in all honesty, I don't believe either of them will want to leave the city. Neither of them is well. They've had access to a lot more alcohol and prescription drugs this week than ever before. I think they're enjoying themselves here," he said in a serious tone.

Bolin considered what James was telling him. "I have to ask, do you want to stay here in the city with them? I'll stay here if you do." Bolin offered sincerely.

James smiled. "No. Not at all. I'm simply explaining their reality. My reality is a much different thing. I prefer barns to high-rises, dirt roads to freeways, and pastures to parking lots. I'm ready to leave," he said assuredly.

Bolin was watching James speak and smiled as he realized they wanted similar things. He told James, "These are things I prefer, as well. Please let me know if you need to stay in the city longer in order to be available to Maria and Greg. I'll wait for you to be ready to leave."

James nodded and kissed him saying, "I'm going to invite them to come with us, but I expect they'll decline the invitation. I'll tell them where we've decided to go once we know what our plan is, but I don't expect to ever see either of them again. They're good people, I'm not speaking ill of them, but I might be understating their addictions," he said somberly.

"I understand. What can I help you with today?"

James kept his arms around Bolin and nodded thoughtfully. "I have a plan for tonight and all the ingredients are here. I'm distracted by what I want to serve tomorrow night. I'm going to need some ingredients."

"Well, tell me what you need. I'll start looking today," Bolin had told him.

With the help of Mike, Bolin mapped out several nearby urban farm share sites around the city as well as a couple of urban city farming sites he could search for potential produce James might be able to serve to his guests. Mike asked Bolin to keep his eye out for any pet stores that hadn't been burned to the ground and asked him to look for Honey's medication if he had an opportunity. "I will," Bolin told him.

Bolin set off on a mission to find James fresh produce and anything else that he might like. At the first farm site, he realized that the rains had pushed much of the pollutants that had been in the air into the soil and around the growing produce. He wasn't sure the food was safe to eat. It didn't look safe to eat. Much of it was coated in a black, greasy film. He focused on finding sheltered vegetables inside greenhouses, but the small farm co-ops in the city he checked out didn't have greenhouses with growing vegetables inside now that it was June. He consulted the map Imani had given him and noticed a large farm located about 15 miles outside of the city and walked around the city until he found a scooter rental shop and a scooter with enough gas for the trip. He left immediately and headed out to the farm weaving in and out of the tangled mess on the city streets. When possible, he avoided riding over dead bodies, otherwise, he accepted the fact that getting out of the city required a reluctant acceptance of the reality. There were far more dead bodies on the sidewalks and in the streets than there were vehicles. Some things could not be avoided.

A great deal of the distance to the farm was along roads that were fairly unencumbered by either vehicles or dead bodies. The ride took less than an hour, and Bolin arrived to see that the effort had been worthwhile. James would be pleased with what he would be able to bring back to him. In fact, he was going to ask James to ride back out to the farm with him. It was stunning and it had not burned to the ground. From the greenhouses, Bolin gathered an eclectic assortment of fruits and vegetables in order to show James the variety available. He also gathered all of the seed packets the farm had on display for purchase. This was a working farm without a farmer. Perhaps James would be interested in moving here. He'd still be close to Maria and Greg and be able to check in with them from time to time.

Bolin noticed the grazing farm animals and went to check on them. Their water containers were full from the three days of rain, but Bolin worried about the quality of the water they were forced to drink. He located their feed inside several different barns and used a wheelbarrow to fill various empty feed containers, ensuring all the animals he could see were fed. In the chickencoop, he gathered eggs in a large basket and figured some would break during the trip back to the city, but some would survive the bumpy ride. He tossed food to the chickens and hoped he had done enough to sustain the animals until James could check on them. He really didn't know what he was doing. He only knew that food and water were essential to all living creatures.

He returned to the restaurant about six hours after having departed, and James stood up straighter from his work of preparing food in the kitchen to look at him as he walked in carrying all that he had managed to ride back with on the scooter.

"Hello. I found eggs," he said, smiling but in an exhausted tone.

James continued to stare at him but suddenly started laughing. "Bol, did you ride all the way out to that farm on Flourtown Road?!" he asked in amazement.

"Yes. You know it, then?"

James dropped what he was doing and walked over to Bolin to relieve him of some of the many bags he was carrying as well as the basket of eggs. "Yeah, I know of it. I've been once, three years ago. I remember it was a great farm, but I don't take days off when I come here to work for my uncle. I work every day to earn money so I don't have to work while I'm at Uni. Let's get you something to drink, eh? Have a seat. You look sunburned." James laughed while getting him a bottle of water.

Bolin nodded his appreciation for the water James handed him and said, "I imagine I did get sunburned."

"Oh, look what you brought back!" James exclaimed as he brought out the various produce items from the bags Bolin had filled.

"I only took what had been sheltered from the rain. The local produce in the city looked unhealthy from what the rain dragged down out of the sky."

"Oh, smart." James nodded in agreement. "Look at all these seeds, too." James looked at Bolin, trying to convey his appreciation. "This is amazing, Bol. You really went above and beyond. I can do so much with what you brought back. Thank you. The eggs are fantastic. Ah, you look exhausted. Was the trip difficult?" he asked, concerned.

"Not really. I had to feed all the animals, though," he said as he finished his water.

James stared at Bolin and shook his head suddenly. "Alright. Seriously. I'm asking you this. Will you marry me?"

"Yes. Seriously," said Bolin, nodding his head and walking up to James saying, "Come here. Let's seal our marriage with a kiss."

"Right now?" asked James, smiling happily while wrapping his arms around Bolin's dirty, sweaty, sunburned body.

"Yes."

"Alright," he said as he leaned down to kiss Bolin. "So, we're husbands now?" James asked, beaming.

"Yes. We are," Bolin said, smiling back up at his husband.

Rollo

In the hospital, Rollo relaxed on the bed provided by his benevolent King, that crazy, evil fucker. He thought of his pop, his mom, and his older brother. His heart broke, shattered into a million pieces over and over again. When he felt better, he allowed his heart to break again, and again, and again. He screamed internally while thanking his nurse for her gentle attendance to his broken nose and his broken ribs. He had three broken ribs to be exact.

Mick had beaten the living fucking hell out of him, even broke his left eye socket as he should have done, and had given him a concussion when he launched the computer at his head. No mercy. You can't fake rage. Dig deep. Find what infuriates you. Use that. Convince your audience. Every member of his family was dead except for one. That was good. Better to be dead. Lacy was probably being put in a time cell now for refusing to talk. He would try to rescue her if that was the case. He would rescue her, though. Mick had cared for her. She was family forever. He would have to bring her back even if only to kill her.

His family and Lacy would tell him there was no fault, but it felt like their deaths and Lacy's impending imprisonment were on him. He had been the first in the family to speak up.

"Hey, I think this is fucked up. Anyone else having second thoughts?" he had asked his family.

His pop had stared at him for several beats before agreeing. Mick was a momma's boy and needed their mom on board before he would agree. It didn't matter if he believed Rollo was right. Mick looked at their mother and waited for her answer. They all looked at Tonya, waiting to see how she felt about the suggestion by Rollo that they reconsider their loyalty to Bas.

Tonya, shook her head, and Rollo felt a sickness form in the pit of his stomach while he waited for her to speak. "He's insane. We're all in danger either way. Let's go down fighting. Maybe we can save some people even if we can't defeat him," she had said in a hushed tone. Hearing his mother, Mick was completely onboard with trying to stop their self-appointed King, his best friend.

Tonya had grabbed Rollo's arm tightly when he had suggested they go against Bas. When she finally let go, she whispered to all of them, huddled with their heads together, "He has to be stopped." But it was Rollo who initiated their involvement in the revolt. No one would ever suspect the meek and lanky younger teenage brother of the exalted Mick Vespry, himself, the best friend of the most insane on high ruler of planet earth, to be the one to initiate and organize a revolt. Not even his own family members were aware he'd been secretly leading an opposition for more than a year. Only Lacy and Soren had known how deep into the fight Rollo actually was. But then Soren had been put into a torture cell by Bas.

He was glad to finally feel it was safe enough to ask his family to join him. He had doubted them. Their commitment to Bas was long-standing, but things had finally started to change. Mick saw things he wasn't comfortable with. Lacy was in Mick's life now. His parents were questioning Bas's intentions in hushed tones around the breakfast table. Rollo had hoped they would be ready to come around. He was relieved they were. He could forgive them all now.

Rollo laid in the hospital bed and contemplated what Bas could possibly find at their family home. Nothing. Lacy hid the tech already. Hopefully, she had hidden it for the later part of the plan. The advantage of a family led revolt was that they could all gather without arousing suspicion, and they all spoke a familiar language. They didn't need to record shit or write anything down. They could communicate with nods and benign looks to one another. Rollo had spoken to Lacy about being a stooge if necessary. She had dug her nails into his arm drawing blood and told him she didn't want to live in a world ruled by Bas. He'd imprisoned her husband, Soren, a year earlier, and she had waited for an opportunity to exact revenge since then. Falling for Mick had been unexpected, but it was a sincere relationship. Rollo imagined her commitment to rage and revenge after learning her second partner had been killed. Bas couldn't comprehend the eternal nature of an adversary fueled by loss. Rollo knew to respect the power of loss. Even before he had felt it by losing his parents and his brother. Bas might not lose the war. Hell, maybe Bas would win. Rollo knew Bas was powerful. But Bas would suffer. He would be made to fight for what he was taking. Rollo would make him fight for what he wanted. He wouldn't just hand it over to him. Lacy wouldn't stay down no matter what he did to her. Two partners lost. No God could help Bas if Lacy was free. If Bas had any sense at all, he'd kill Lacy immediately. Torturing her wasn't worth the risk of keeping her alive. That was the best Rollo could hope for Lacy right now.

He was woken in the night as a person was brought into the bed next to his. Behind the curtain, he could hear the scuffle between the hospital staff and the patient. Someone suggested they strap the patient to the bed, which they immediately did, but another voice suggested a second shot of sedatives. The ensuing scuffle made Rollo laugh involuntarily and grab his side as the pain from his broken ribs wracked his body. He muttered a long and quiet "Fuuuuuck," as he gripped his sides and winced at the pain. The people behind the curtain paid him no mind.

"Get her off of me!" Someone screamed loudly, and Rollo breathed deeply to suppress his laughter.

"Bitch bit me!" A woman cried out.

"Get out of here! You're useless," someone with authority said in anger.

The patient wasn't a wallflower. She screamed obscenities and made threats she couldn't possibly keep. Rollo laid in his bed holding tightly to his sides to minimize the pain he felt in his broken ribs. He listened as the hospital staff was clearly overcome by the passions of their newest patient.

A voice, female and stern, sounded suddenly. "Bas wants her taken to his residence. A staff of five is expected to accompany her. Tend to her injuries there, not here. Whatever you have going on now, offer to drop it and accompany her to his residence. If your patients die without you, so be it. Go," the voice said.

"Can we pump this bitch up with more sedatives?" someone asked.

"Yes, but Bas wants her, so don't hurt her. Only he can," said the authoritative voice. Rollo wasn't laughing anymore. He laid in his bed and listened as the hospital staff prepared a second sedative for her. She was lucid. "Who are you people?" "Don't touch me!" "I'll kill you when I get a chance!" and his favorite, "I won't forget your face!" That was a really good threat, he thought. It would stick with a subordinate. He had no idea who she was, but she was electric, alive, aware. All aspects that would make a time cell more painful, but also characteristics of a fighter. He needed fighters. He'd lost his mother, his father, and his brother. He probably lost Lacy, as well. He might have a traitor in his organization, or maybe he simply made a mistake along the way. He wanted to know who this patient was. She was exactly what he needed.

He listened as the hospital staff wheeled her down the hallway and she shouted at them, "I'm not afraid of you!" Oh, but you will be, Rollo thought to himself. Oh, you will be. He wondered how he could learn the name of the fearless woman being dragged off to Bas's residence. This was intel he never dreamed of possessing. Bas might have a weak link.

Lacy and Soren

When she met her future husband, she had been serving ice cream samples to obnoxious tourists who demanded samples of all of the flavors offered by their ice cream shop. Patiently, she handed out small unrecyclable plastic spoons, one after another to the group as they tasted samples such as 'peanut butter fountain' and 'strawberry mango.' Really? She wondered, you need to remind yourself what fucking peanut butter tastes like?

The man not connected with the group waited patiently for his turn at the counter. "Hi sir, can I interest you in a sample of one of our flavors?' she asked him politely, but with a hint of irritation he could definitely detect.

"No, I know I want a chocolate cone. Thank you," he said to her politely.

She stared at him waiting for the inevitable additional requests, but they did not follow.

"Ok, So just a chocolate cone?" she asked him, daring to hope this customer would be that easy.

"Yes. I like chocolate," he said to her with a friendly smile.

She laughed and shook her head while scooping chocolate ice cream for his cone. "Sprinkles or anything else?" she asked him before handing him his cone.

"No. It's perfect the way it is," he said to her.

She looked at him for a beat before handing him his uncomplicated ice cream cone. "Here you go sir. Thank you. Pay at the register. That way," she pointed towards her coworker Chima, who was in charge of the financial transactions.

"Want to go out tonight after work?" he suddenly asked her, throwing her off her script.

"What? Wait. What?" She laughed and looked down, embarrassed. The customers behind him would be waiting for their orders to be taken.

"What time do you get off?" he asked her without embarrassment.

"4:30."

"I'll meet you out front at 4:30. Tell me if you want to go out," he said as he moved towards the cash registers.

She blushed and shook her head as the next person in her never-ending line asked to taste the sample of the pink ice cream next to the white stuff with colored bits in it.

At 4:40 she walked out front of the ice cream shop tired and feeling like she smelled of ice cream and cones. She was irritated. She didn't want to meet some guy or go on a date. She wanted to go home and shower and eat a fucking salad. Cucumbers, radishes, carrots. Ice cream was nauseating after nearly a full summer of dishing it out to selfish customers who were willing to dramatically overpay for a tiny cup of frozen dairy product. Embarrassing. He was waiting outside near a bike rack outside the ice cream shop. He smiled at her as she approached him.

"No," she said, putting up a hand. "I'm tired and I smell like ice cream. I don't want to do anything that involves impressing a man I don't know."

He laughed at her and said, "Yeah, so you want to maybe go change and meet me at the first bench over by the dog park? We can watch people throw Frisbees for their dogs."

She stopped and looked at him long enough for him to finally speak.

"I'm Soren. I don't know your name yet." He looked at her and waited.

"Lacy," she said mildly. "I'll go home and change and decide if I want to meet you at the dog park. What's your number? I'll text you. I'm really tired. Honestly, I can't imagine walking back down here..."

He recited his phone number and watched her type it into her phone. "Try it first to make sure you got it," he said to her. She did and his phone rang.

"Nice. Now you have my number. Maybe I wasn't going to text you," she said aloud, annoyed at herself.

"Don't worry. I won't bother you. Call me if you want to meet up. I can come get you if you're tired," he said.

She walked away and considered how she was absolutely as rude as she could possibly be and he was still interested. It made her laugh. She'd forgotten his name already. Did she give him hers? She couldn't remember. It had been a long day.

She showered and changed her clothes before having a salad for dinner. Her curly red hair dried without assistance, and she looked at her freckled face in the mirror and thought, well, of course he was attracted to me. I'm cute, even if I'm rude. She didn't own makeup or have the patience to apply makeup even if she could have afforded some. Even though she couldn't remember the details he had shared with her, such as his name, she considered that he was attractive. He looked about her age, had blonde hair, and his clothes hung on his lean frame. He definitely didn't go out for ice cream frequently. She liked his attitude. It accommodated hers.

A little after 7pm, she pulled out her phone and texted the number he had given her. She wrote, "I forgot your name. I'm Lacy. I can meet up tonight for a little while. Where? Dog park?" and hit send.

Immediately her phone let her know she had a text. "Name's Soren. First bench at the dog park. Saving you a seat."

"Be there in 15," she texted back. She looked down at her phone and laughed. She was probably going to be murdered by the Ice Cream Killer tonight. She didn't care. She was only 21 years old and her life was already bullshit. She grabbed her mace and walked out the door of the apartment she shared with too many people.

Lacy met Soren on a bench overlooking the dog park at the beach. He smiled at her as she approached the bench, but she held up her hand and said, "I feel bad about this because I'm really tired and not into it at all."

"That's ok," he said kindly.

"Ok. Well, let's get ourselves introduced and if we like what we find out, maybe have a proper date later when I'm not so tired?"

"Sounds good," he said, smiling at her.

They liked each other after their talk on the bench at the dog park and found their conversation went on for hours. They spent most of the time laughing at people, society, and cultural expectations foisted upon the latest generation. Soren walked her home like a proper gentleman even if she secretly believed his impeccable manners were designed to discover her residence. She figured if he was a stalker, she'd move. She'd moved a couple of times in the past three years. She carried her life in a backpack. No problem. If he was a stalker, she'd just move again.

But he wasn't a stalker. He was kind of amazing. She hated to think of him as something other than just another guy who was into her temporarily, but after the first time they slept together at her place, she couldn't help but notice the shift in his commitment to her. She tried to lessen his responsibility by telling him she'd been on her own for a long time and was happy with her latest group rental, but he suggested to her that maybe just one roommate would be better. It threw her. Threw her mind into a confusion she wasn't prepared for, wasn't prepared to contemplate.

"You need to slow down," she told him reflexively.

"You need to know when you've met a partner worth considering," he said thoughtfully. They had a stare-off after that. Different from a standoff, but possibly more intense. She broke it by saying, "Stop. Stop," and shaking her head.

"You should come live with me," he said suddenly.

"I don't even know where you live."

"It's different."

"Like a group thing?" she asked him.

"No. I'll whisper it to you and you think about it, ok?" he said to her very quietly. It was confusing, but when he leaned over and started to tell her where he lived, she felt her body get ridged and pulled away from him.

"So, you're crazy, right?" she asked him with complete sincerity.

"No. And I can show you without you having to be committed, but you'll have to swear to keep it secret after I show you... or your life will be in danger. Do you want to see?"

"Why would you even offer?" she asked him seriously.

"Because I want to be with you, and soon, I won't be able to leave," he said.

They stood facing each other in complete silence for a long time. Minutes easily passed. Soren didn't move or ask her to respond. She stared at him. More time passed.

"Ok. Fine. Yeah. I get that. You might be crazy, but maybe I am, too. Show me," she said. He rolled up his sleeve and told her to touch his arm. They looked at each other as he touched the screen on what looked like a wrist watch. He pressed his forehead against hers and grabbed her firmly around her waist. She felt fear for the first time as he gripped her shoulder and told her not to worry.

Lacy and Mick

"What was Soren up to?" Mick demanded harshly of Lacy. She was scheduled to enter a time cell if his interrogation didn't go well.

"Fuck you, supreme sidekick!" Lacy snarled at him.

Mick closed the distance between them and looked at her kneeling before him and knew that the witnesses would want theater they could talk about to others who weren't present. He lifted his foot, but instead of kicking her forcefully, he used his foot to shove her backwards and onto the ground. He lunged menacingly forward and straddled her, bringing his face close enough to hers to ensure his audience wouldn't be able to hear everything he said to her.

"Help me help you," he whispered. "Bitch, did you know what your husband was up to?" he shouted for the interrogation audience. She laid on the ground silent and motionless for a few seconds and Mick felt the opportunity to save her slip away.

Suddenly, she shouted loud enough for the witnesses to hear, "Soren loved our King! He never said anything against him. If you say he was a traitor, I believe he was framed! He always told me to honor Bas. He was devoted to him!"

Mick knew this was a lie. Soren worked for Rollo, worked for Rollo even before he, himself did. Soren was an original member of the opposition. He looked at Lacy beneath his body, pressed against the floor. Her husband had been sent to the cells and would likely end up tortured forever. Dead would have been better. He had to sell it or Lacy would end up receiving the same punishment. He grabbed Lacy by the hair and wrenched her head towards him.

"You telling me you had no idea your own husband was a traitor?" He demanded of her.

She gasped at the pain and shouted defiantly, "My husband wasn't a traitor. He served our King. He would never turn on him. He threatened to kill me if I ever questioned my service to our King and the mission. My husband was framed."

Mick bent forward and pulled Lacy's head to him by her hair. "Fight harder," he whispered to her. "Your traitor husband was found with tech meant for survivors of the first wave. Caught with the tech!" he yelled for the witnesses.

"I'm a fucking food server. I serve meals to residents. Kill me. I know nothing including who will cover my next shift. Fuck you all. I serve our King. Maybe my husband used me. I don't fucking know what's going on. I came here willingly. I was serving ice cream to tourists before this. Let me fucking go, you asshole. I'm not my husband!" she shouted under Mick's body weight.

Mick lifted himself off the ground and off of her body. He flicked a hand at a soldier to his right and said to him, "One year in a time cell. Break her." He reached down and grabbed for Lacy's arm pulling her violently up from the ground. "Talk the entire time you're in there. It will help keep you sane," he whispered to her.

"Sir, a year is a long time for the spouse of a traitor. I want to run this sentence by Bas. Three months is the usual sentence."

"Fuck you, Rufaro. Fuck you questioning me. I don't believe she's innocent. She knew what her husband was up to. Break the bitch. Find out if others are in on it." He glared at the lower ranked soldier. One thing he knew for sure was that Bas liked to overrule his decisions. By sentencing Lacy to a year in a time cell, he was sure Bas would intervene in a grand gesture of showing mercy. He would use his benevolence to remind citizens that if they turned in a family member for being a traitor, he would show them mercy. If Mick had sentenced her to less time, Bas would have let her rot.

Mick already knew she was a traitor. She worked for Rollo. Soren had been one of Rollo's most loyal team members in the opposition, but he had tried to keep his wife out of danger by not telling her what was going on. Lacy was just frustratingly clever. She could read people easily. She wanted to fight against Bas, too. He had been told after the fact that Rollo had only reluctantly accepted her into the fold because she had insisted on working for the opposition once she learned what her husband had been up to. Their mother had scolded Rollo for not letting a woman take an important role in the rebellion early on once she herself had joined them and discovered how long Rollo had waited to allow Lacy to join. She reminded him that women were quite capable of espionage. The truth was, Rollo had waited patiently on the sideline for permission to use Lacy. He knew her value. He had waited on Soren. Rollo was a chess master. He could see years into the future, but Mick was beginning to think Rollo had help with that skill.

Lev, Aisha, and Bob

Aisha slept on the couch and Bob slept on the love seat. She was a little taller than Bob. Lev, as tall as he was, slept on the living room floor between Bob and Aisha. Earlier, Lev had been sitting on the floor with his back against the larger couch where Aisha was sitting. He wasn't adding much to the conversation about how to search for Bob's family. He'd told them how he had only moved to the state two weeks ago and was unfamiliar with the area. They decided searching together would be the safest way to approach looking for Lisa and the kids since there would be no way to communicate with one another if they separated. After the plan was decided, Aisha got down on the floor and sat next to Lev. She wrapped an arm around his shoulder and asked him what she could do to help, but he didn't have an answer for her.

"I'm so stupid," he said to her suddenly. She felt a wave of compassion for him wash over her as she contemplated the hopelessness of his situation.

"You're not stupid. You thought you could save the person you love. I couldn't save my mother today, and tomorrow, we're probably going to help Bob realize he can't save his wife or any of his three sons. Then Bob will go temporarily insane just like you are now."

She made the comment with sincerity and Bob, who was lying down on the loveseat listening to her, didn't take offense. Instead, he spoke up quietly and offered, "Hey, we have to try. Lev had to try, and I have to try. We're all alive, so we're going to have a future. We have to be able to say we tried to save the people we love, right?" he asked them.

"Yeah. We have to try. Right, Lev?" she asked him encouragingly. She saw him nod his head slightly in the affirmative and said, "Lev agrees, Bob."

"Tomorrow we turn this town upside down looking for my family," Bob said with determination. He watched as Aisha continued to encourage Lev to pull it together. Her strength in the face of the loss of her mother amazed him. He watched her get up from the floor and take her place on the larger sofa and settle in for the night. Maybe, he thought, this was all a terrible dream. Maybe Lisa and his boys were alive. Maybe Rhonda was asleep in her spare room recovering from knee surgery. Maybe Lev didn't exist. He drifted off to sleep trying hard to think of nothing so that he wouldn't end up having nightmares.

Bolin and James

Bolin helped James prepare the final meal for his guests. This meal, the final meal, included all of the food they could find to serve to the people James had come to know over the course of the week. James was grateful for the eggs and produce Bolin had brought back to him after his ride out to the farm. Bolin wasn't an expressive man, but he recognized and valued emotions in others. James was clearly overwhelmed by the thought of leaving the city and not feeding the people he had come to know even if he had only provided meals to them over the course of a week. He would miss Mike, Imani, Carl, Maria, Katie, Jayden, Louis, and more. He would miss all of them. He cared about their well-being.

"My mum, she grew up poor. There was a hard decade for farms when she was younger," he told Bolin. "She taught me that feeding people was a kindness. People don't need expensive gifts. They need a good meal and friendship. I took that from my Mum." He explained.

Bolin thought about the coldness of his own mother and the warmth of his grandmother. He wasn't the type of person to dismiss what was important to others. Sometimes, he genuinely disagreed, but in this instance, he agreed with James. James wanted to have a nice final meal with the survivors who had come to count on nightly meals at his uncle's restaurant. People whose company he genuinely enjoyed. Food was important to James. He considered his own limitations when it came to social interactions. James liked to feed people. He brought seemingly disparate people together and enabled them to discover their human connections. Mike and Imani were a good example of this. So were he and James. They prepared the meal together as husbands now, and Bolin talked to James about the farm where he'd gotten the eggs.

"You can carry on with what's important to you, but do it 15 miles from here at the farm. Come back to the city, check on Maria and Greg, invite people to dinners at the farm."

James stepped closer to Bolin and leaned over to kiss him as he sliced onions.

"I like that plan, love," he told Bolin.

Bolin nodded. If you cared about a person, you supported their ability to engage their passions. James had a passion. It was farming, food, and feeding people. In that order. He intended to support his husband's passions.

17 Years Later

The sharp knock on his door woke him up from a dream-filled sleep. It took him a moment to shake off the images and remember where he was. Raiders. Last night had been a nightmare. People died. James. He was still fully dressed and wearing his boots when he put his legs on the floor and walked to his door to see who was knocking, to see what they needed him for now. He was still in a daze from waking up in the middle of a dream. He realized quickly how much of his body hurt from fighting overnight. The muscles in his arms ached as he used one to open the door and lifted the other to rest a hand on the wall for support. At least he'd made it out alive. They took losses last night. Rare for them. They were usually over prepared for these types of attacks on their community. Raiders were usually small groups of rag-tag survivors who were not truly prepared to take on their well-armed and trained fighters. He was the Head of Security for the community, and as such, demanded vigilance against attacks. No mercy in combat. No sympathy for raiders who survived. He had no patience for weakness, or insubordination in members of his security teams, or his security team leaders. Weakness and insubordination lead to deaths of others and even of yourself. If you displayed either characteristic, you would be taken out rather than cause the death of another through your failure to perform.

"Lev, you requested a wake-up at sunrise. Do you need more time?" the man asked him with efficiency. It was Vivek standing before him now. Maren's husband. He had seen her go down in the inner yard last night. Bolin must have sent Vivek to see if he'd be ready to gather second shift to relieve first.

"Yeah, tell Bolin we'll be on time to relieve his shift. How's it out there this morning? How's Maren?" he asked Vivek. He hoped for good news. Maren had skills other than fighting. She was an expert IT addition to the Research Team's IT duo. She managed to keep their systems up and running when others couldn't. He didn't want to lose her. In fact, if she had survived last night, he was going to insist she be declared essential and removed from her security team. Others could fight in her place. Others could not replace her IT skills. Two years ago, she had two apprentices assigned to her at his request and was training them between working with Ivy's two IT guys and working on a security team. She kept busy and was definitely essential. She'd have to go to the towers with the others during future battles. He would be adamant about the proposal to remove her from security at their next team meeting. She could fight from the towers. He didn't care. But no more ground combat.

Vivek looked at Lev with appreciation for the inquiry into his wife's condition and said, "Medical says she's got a concussion and lost two teeth, but she's going to be fine. I think the guy who hit her thought he'd killed her, so he kept going after she was on the ground."

"Good to hear," Lev said, honestly relieved. "Let Bol know I'll be out in 15 minutes to give them a break."

"Will do," said Vivek, already jogging down the hallway to the exit.

He closed his door and observed the condition of his bedsheets. Covered in mud.

Lev walked into the small bathroom that was part of his adequately sized dorm. He turned on the water in the small sink and looked in the dirty mirror at his reflection. He was covered in crusted mud and his skin and long black hair looked greasy. There was blood mixed in with the mud for sure. His beard was getting too long and he could see bits of mud and grasses in it. He bent over the small sink and cupped his hands to gather the cool water to run it briskly over his face and through his filthy facial hair. He pulled his fingers through it in various areas and rinsed his hands of the dirt into the running water.

The night before, he had found himself face down in the wet mud of the long dirt roadway leading up to the facility after a brutal fight with a guy as big as himself. He always made a point of finding the biggest adversaries in a fight because he knew the unfair advantage size leant to the process of intimidation in battle. He'd seen a large guy heading towards Maren and ran with his axe through the fray to stop him before he had a chance to take her down. He hit the man with deadly precision. With his axe lodged in the back of the large man's neck, he was then hit from behind himself and slipped in the wet mud of the road and landed face first, his hands failing to break his fall. Laying there, he turned in time to see Maren stab a smaller man before being struck hard along the side of her head by a stick wielded by a raider. He watched her go down to the ground and felt instantly it would be an unacceptable loss to lose her. The raider who had assaulted her looked at her barely moving body lying on the ground and kicked her hard once in the head before taking off to fight others. That must have been when she lost two teeth, he thought. At least she'd survived.

Lev thought about what had happened next as he tried to work out some of the mud from his long hair. The man who had taken Lev to the muddy ground slipped and ended up alongside him. Lev wasted no time or effort and reached around to the man's head and managed to grip his hair. He used the man's hair and body weight as leverage and pulled himself onto the man's chest while he was lying there confused for a split second as a result of his own fall. Lev beat the man's face with his own muddy hands until he was certain the man was either dead or too injured to move again that night. He hauled himself off of the man's limp body and pulled his axe out of the larger, dead man's neck and ran towards his team to help kill more raiders.

Raiding was such bullshit. Pathetic losers who wanted to take from others who had worked hard to get something functional going. Raiders went from one working camp or town to another and destroyed the efforts of more organized groups sometimes just for a fucking meal. In the end, they ruined possibilities and set back efforts to recreate a functioning society. Frontal lobotomy morons with no ability to think more creatively than to overpower and take for immediate self-gratification. Lev and his community had plans. Long standing plans. They were working towards something better. They made personal sacrifices in an effort to reach their goals. He had no problem killing raiders. Hell, he had no problem killing. If there was a God, even it would have stopped keeping track of how many people Lev had killed over the past 17 years.

Lev stared at his face in the dirty mirror. He recognized the man in the mirror. He looked mean, cruel, even. His eyes were still a dark shade of brown. Nothing illuminated his dark features and his even darker nature. He didn't bother to dry off his face or hair as he turned to take a piss. He walked past his muddy bed and out of his room and headed towards the ground level barracks of his team. He steeled himself for the fury he would need to suppress if any team member whined about not being rested enough to head back out this morning. Lev was the Head of Security, but he was also a commander of a Security Team. Of the four facility commanders, Lev was the scariest by far. Everyone had heard the whispers about Security Team members who had disappeared over the six years since Lev had arrived and taken command of Team 4. Did he take out team members who he had no faith in? Probably. That was the accepted sentiment of the entire command structure of the facility. Was the place better protected from outsiders since Lev had arrived six years ago? Definitely. That was also the accepted sentiment of the entire command structure of the facility. He headed downstairs to his team.

Lev had earned a reputation years before coming to the Ivy facility six years ago. He was the leader of another community that had been established on the campus of the University of Virginia in Charlottesville back in the early days of the extinction event. The campus had been largely empty when the extinction event occurred because graduation events had already occurred and the school was mostly closed. Summer classes had not yet begun. He named his community Campus, and he ran it with a ruthlessness that succeeded in weeding out the physically weak as well as the emotionally weak. He had no sympathy for those who lacked resilience. He hadn't survived just to wipe the asses of weaker survivors.

In the early days of Campus, survivors would approach looking for shelter, community, an opportunity to be a part of something again, something that resembled society. That was not what Lev's community offered. As time wore on, word got out to uninitiated travelers that if you poked a sleeping tiger, you had better have something to offer. Something was going on in that community led by Lev, but what, was not known. Over the years, Campus gained a reputation as a place you should travel around, give a wide berth to, avoid altogether unless you had something valuable to offer. You would be expected to explain your specific skill set and defend your ability to contribute to his community. He didn't like to have his time wasted by sniveling, hungry, tired, cold, useless survivors. He didn't care about your problems. He wasn't a vessel for mercy. He was a vessel for rage.

He had set up Campus about a year after the extinction event, and he had immediately learned about the small group of survivors over at Ivy. During his first months at Campus, he had sent his people to see what the small group of survivors were up to over there buried in the woods as they were. They claimed they were a small group of, at most, 15 survivors. They appeared to pose no threat to Lev's community. They claimed most of them had been tourists to the Foundation when the extinction event occurred. Eventually, new people arrived at their facility and they developed a small trade agreement between them as their farming abilities flourished. Both communities benefited from their relationship with the other. It wasn't until years later that Lev learned what was actually going on at Ivy. Both communities had their secrets, but Lev took it personally. So much wasted time. The deception was unforgivable in many ways. It burned him to his core. Some people he forgave. Some people he did not.

Lev opened the door to the barracks of Security Team 4 and noticed with some pride that most of his team looked up and ready to relieve Bolin's team. "Nice," he said to them darkly but approvingly from the doorway. "Wait by the gate for me while I get an update from Bolin. Maren's going to be ok. Williams, you're in charge." He turned and walked away from the doorway leaving the door wide open and heard as his team scuffled about getting ready while Williams shouted loudly about them having one minute to be ready to head out to the gate.

Lev turned the corner and ran as fast as he could over to medical on the other side of the large facility. He wanted a personally procured update before heading out to the field. He needed to know. There were some things, some people he cared about. Those were the only people who reminded him that he was human. For them, he could make room for things like vague emotions and patience. But only for those very few in his small inner circle.

It was early in the morning. The sun was just high enough to share its light on the landscape. Lev walked out of the facility through the gate where his team was already waiting. He walked past them and nodded to Williams. "Give me a minute," he said curtly as he walked by him. He stopped and stood still on the calm grounds that had been a battlefield the night before and scanned the field for Bolin. He saw him carrying the legs of a dead raider in the distance. Bolin would be a fucking disaster this morning, and Lev steeled himself for their interaction. After the battle the night before, he had at most three hours of sleep before this morning's shift. He was fucking tired and pissed off. But Bolin had been awake longer and had less sleep at this point. Then there was what had happened to James. Bolin was also going to be an emotional wreck. Lev wanted to get him off the field and back inside for some rest as quickly as possible. He didn't need to be out here.

Lev walked with determination towards Bolin and shouted his name as he approached. Bolin turned at the sound of Lev's voice and dropped the legs of the dead man. He turned to his left and shouted to a subordinate to take over for him and walked quickly over to Lev.

"I've been to see James. He's ok," he said flatly. He knew his friend and knew that it was sometimes best to speak to him in a monotone using as few syllables as possible. Crucial if you wanted to penetrate his way of processing information. Especially if he was already upset as he was right now.

"Is he conscious?" asked Bolin sternly.

Lev knew Bolin would want details, so he came prepared to offer them. He had left his team in their barracks and had run to medical telling the attendant, "I need info on James now, before I relieve Bolin." Confronted by the unexpected presence of Lev in the hospital ward, and hearing Bolin's name thrown in, the attendant called loudly to their facility doctor and she came running at the sound of urgency in her attendant's voice. She wasn't intimidated by Lev or Bolin. She had been with Lev for the past 15 years and knew how to work with him. When he had come to this community, she had come along from Campus at his request. She gave him the information he needed quickly and he left immediately without so much as a pleasantry passed between the two of them.

"Yeah. Doc says he has at least two broken ribs. At least two. And a concussion. And, this is the worst part, his nose was broken. He'll never be as handsome as he was before." Lev looked at Bolin to assess his level of humor and found it lacking immediately. "Ok, seriously, he's going to be fine, and he'll be ruggedly handsome with the new nose, but his arm is broken, too. Did you know about his arm?" he asked Bolin.

"No. I didn't," said Bolin.

"It's been set. A clean break, thankfully. You know they can't handle much more than a clean break. Fucking Christ. Thankfully, it was a clean break. That raider that attacked James, Eymen took him out. Killed the son of a bitch. James is ok. You ok?" he asked his friend, concerned for his emotional state. James shouldn't have been involved in the fight. He was a fighter and quite strong, but he was an essential member of their community. Rules said he had to go to the tower.

Lev looked at Bolin and tried to gauge his level of emotional fitness and said to him firmly, using his Head of Security authority, "Your shift's over. Take your crew and head in for rest. My team will finish this up. Give me some quick details first and then go see James. He's probably still sleeping, but it will make you feel better."

Bolin was listening and breathed deeply as he was agreeing with Lev. He turned his head to survey the remaining carnage from the battle the night before and hesitated suddenly while looking out towards the northern edge of the compound.

"What's that?" he asked Lev suddenly with concern in his voice.

"Where?" Lev asked him, looking in the general direction being pointed at by his trusted friend.

"There. Down by the main road headed this way. Off the dirt road and in the grass," Bolin said, pointing to a small speck in the distance.

Lev squinted and looked intently in the direction where Bolin believed he had seen something worth questioning. He made out the shape of a small figure working its way towards the compound.

"Can't be a raider," said Lev. "Can't be this late. Some traveler with piss-poor timing," he added.

But Bolin was looking to make someone living pay for the damage done to

James. He lifted his gun and said, "No one's innocent these days. You coming?"

"Yeah, I got you," Lev said, adding, "Williams is in charge of my team right now. Who should he get an update from while we check this out?"

Bolin turned to his left and shouted to his second in command, a woman named Anna.

"Anna!"

She came running towards them, gun ready, and a look of determination on her face. "What's up, Bolin?" she asked her team leader.

"Lev and I are going to find out who this dipshit is walking up to our front doors," he said, using his chin to indicate where in the field they were headed. "Williams is in charge of Lev's team till we get back. Tell him what needs to be done and let both field teams know what Lev and I are investigating. Be ready for a signal if it turns out to be something other than a traveler."

"Got it." She ran towards Williams and the rest of Lev's team waiting by the gate to deliver the first part of the message. Bolin knew Anna would inform the rest of her own team about what was going on and both teams would be ready in the event the approaching stranger was initiating a new fight.

"Bol, I think this is simply a traveler.

"Yes. I know," said Bolin as he continued with a strident and angry pace towards the person approaching their facility.

Lev kept pace with Bolin's pace and continued, "We lost some people last night. Let's check if this one has any decent skills before we commence with the killing, eh?" he asked, still trying to diffuse the bad temper of his friend. "Could be a doctor. Maybe a dentist. God knows we need a dentist. Maren could use a dentist," he added, continuing his efforts. It looked to Lev like Bolin was having none of it. He was mentally locked in to his rage.

"We need a barber. You look like shit," Bolin said to him.

Lev felt a small sense of relief creep in at the casual insult offered by Bolin and snorted a mild, "Fuck you, man," at him as they continued walking towards the stranger.

In any case, both men were ready to make a split second decision the other would never question. If someone needed killing, neither would hesitate.

The Traveler

She had been walking for days towards her destination. She didn't know how many days. She had lost track of time which her friends had warned her was likely. Her best guess was that she had been walking for six days, maybe seven, or maybe five. She walked slowly, enjoying being outside. It was still very early in the morning. The sun was just beginning to rise. It was supposed to take her five days to find the scientists.

While walking this morning, she thought of the events of the previous day. She had stopped walking early in the morning when the rain had begun. The rain had been a welcome relief as she had been able to take off all of her dirty clothes and stand naked outside in the downpour getting herself clean. She let the rain wash away the days of accumulated dirt, the sweat, and the smell of fear from the adrenaline that coursed through her body. It had come down hard all day, finally stopping just as the sun began to set. She had water now because she had wisely set out some containers to gather the fresh rainwater. Thunder and lightning had lit up the sky for a while, and the electricity in the air made her feel liberated as she stood outside and watched the streaks of lightning light up the sky. Then the world got quiet again, and she was left to explore the small apartment behind the gas station before going to sleep for the night.

She had already decided to stay in the little apartment behind the dilapidated gas station for the night in anticipation of the rain. A man and a woman had lived there as evidenced by the clothes that hung in the closet and which were folded neatly into some drawers. She was still naked from showering in the pouring rain when she entered the apartment. She walked into the bathroom and took a folded towel from a small stack she found in a cabinet. She dried her body and hair and tossed the towel over the top of the bathroom door before walking into the bedroom to look for clean clothes to wear. She saw several candles on a night table next to the bed and opened the drawer looking for matches or a lighter. Would a lighter even work after 17 years, she wondered. She hoped they had matches. She rummaged through the drawer and found two lighters and a matchbook with three matches left in it and placed them next to the assembled candles. She would try and light them when it got darker.

A purple silky looking box she had moved aside in her search for matches caught her attention and she took it from the drawer and opened it. Inside was a purple silky drawstring pouch which she withdrew. She opened it and smiled at the sight of the purple vibrator. She opened the battery compartment and removed the useless, ancient batteries, tossing them onto the floor. It would do its job even without vibrating.

The bed looked unmade and she didn't want to dirty her skin after having just cleaned off in the rain, so she stripped the top layer of blankets and sheets off and tossed all but one of the pillows onto the floor. She reclined backwards onto the bed and used her fingers to stimulate herself. Her breathing slowed down as she relaxed and slid her fingers inside her vagina to see how wet she was. She reached inside herself and reached up towards the interior of her clitoris rubbing gently against the familiar landscape. She felt her excitement increase and removed her fingers and began rubbing the vibrator slowly against the outside of her vagina and clit. She tried inserting the vibrator and met little resistance and breathed in deeper as she pushed it in as far as she could. She slid it back and forth inside of her with her hand for a while enjoying the sensations which increased her desire to orgasm.

Eventually, she reached for the pillow she'd left on the bed and placed it firmly between her upper legs squeezing tightly against the vibrator and rolled herself over on top of the pillow moving rhythmically against it on the bed. She began to breathe more quickly and moaned out loud as she moved faster pushing her clitoris against the vibrator using the pressure from the bed and the pillow to rub her as well. The vibrator pushed against her from inside and she moaned loudly and repeatedly as her impending orgasm built up in intensity. She moved her hips faster pushing harder against the bed. When she came her eyes were shut as she moaned obscenities mixed with words of approval. As her orgasm weakened, she slowly stopped moving and laid on her stomach on top of the pillow with the vibrator still deep inside her as she felt the aftershocks on the floor of her vagina. She laid there for a minute letting the release of sexual energy relax her entire body. Slowly, she turned over and slid the vibrator out of her and put it on the night table. She was keeping that, she thought to herself, as she sighed deeply and laid there for a while with her eyes closed.

Getting up, she grabbed the vibrator from the night table and walked outside to one of the bowls she had left out earlier to gather water. She picked up the bowl and walked it over to the small car parked near the building and used the water to rinse the vibrator. She poured the remaining water out and walked to another bowl. She grabbed that one and took it inside to clean herself off with one of the towels from the stack.

After she was clean and dry again, she found dark blue denim jeans with multiple rips throughout the leg areas and was happy when they fit her well. She could have done without the once trendy rips in the legs, but still, it was nice to wear jeans again. She found a drawer full of black t-shirts and chose one to wear while stuffing two more into her backpack. The bras left behind by the former occupant of the apartment were too small for her, though. That was disappointing. She had rinsed her only bra out in the downpouring rain and it was now hanging inside the apartment over an open window as she looked through the rest of the contents of the abandoned apartment. She hoped her bra would be dry by the morning. The apartment was getting dark and it was difficult to see. Neither of the lighters were working, but the first match did and she lit the three candles on the night table. The light they offered was enough for her to continue looking through the contents of the room.

She looked around for more jeans in the closet and stuffed another clean pair into her backpack without trying them on. These ones were not ripped to shreds. Too bad she didn't find them first, but she wasn't changing now. She put on two pairs of socks because her feet hurt from the blisters she'd acquired during the days and hours of walking. Plus, the elastic in the socks was wrecked by the effects of time, and she needed to layer them on her feet to keep them up in her shoes. She found a hairbrush and a toothbrush in the bathroom. She brushed her hair and teeth and packed both brushes in the side pocket of her backpack along with the purple vibrator in its silky purple drawstring pouch inside its purple silky box. She had been without food for at least a couple of days, but she had plenty of water now. She didn't know how long it had been since she had eaten, but she knew staying hydrated was more important than eating. Neither the apartment nor the gas station had any food that looked edible after 17 years.

She went to sleep on top of the comfortable bed. The sheets she had removed earlier were still piled on the floor and the air was warm enough that there was no need for a blanket. She slept in her newly acquired dry clothes minus her bra. She kept her shoes on her feet just in case she had to run, and she kept the flowers she had picked from a field the day before on the night table alongside the bed. She had them in a water bottle with just enough water at the bottom to keep them satisfied. She had opened all of the doors and windows of the small apartment to make herself feel safer. It helped. She was tired. Falling asleep wasn't difficult.

That was the night before. She had woken up before the sunrise this morning and put on her still-damp bra before heading out. Maybe she would reach her destination today, she thought hopefully. Walking in the dark before the sunrise was easier because the air was cool and invigorating. Her feet hurt, but she wasn't hungry anymore. She drank the water she had collected during the heavy rains the day before and carried the plastic water bottle with flowers in her left hand. The flowers still looked healthy which made her happy.

As the sun began to rise, it revealed a cloudless blue sky after the day of heavy rain. She had been walking for a while in the cool predawn air, following the road she knew she was supposed to be on when she suddenly noticed a large clearing coming into view now that she had finally walked over the aging bridge she had expected to find at the end of her journey. As she left the bridge behind her, she saw three windmills and the large main facility with several smaller structures up ahead. The entire compound was much larger than she had anticipated. She saw several enclosures with spots inside that must be grazing animals, and several large farmed areas. The grounds were not encircled by any formidable perimeter. It did not look like a castle with a moat or a wall. It looked more inviting than that, but there were several towers which she assumed must be lookouts.

Trees and forested areas had clearly been reduced over the years. This was more than she had been told to expect. She had to leave the cracked pavement of the main roadway and take the dirt road leading into the compound. Once on the dirt road, she quickly decided the rains the day before had made it too soft and muddy to walk along and stepped to the right of the mud and puddles and onto the firmer soil held together by the tall grass alongside the dirt road. There were scattered trees dotting the landscape far out from the compound where she was walking now, and she wondered if anyone would notice her approach. She could see people milling about the area and wondered what they were doing since it didn't look like they were working a farmed area.

She felt excitement at completing this part of her task. This was definitely the place her friends had told her about. The windmills gave it away, but it looked larger and more organized than she had expected. Hopefully, she would find the people she was supposed to meet. Afterall, a lot of time had passed. People might be dead by now. The sun continued to rise and brighten the blue color of the clear sky. She shifted her backpack and tipped her head back to finish the water in her bottle. She dropped the empty water bottle on the ground and continued to hold the water bottle with her flowers in her left hand. She stared intently at the little dots of people ahead of her in the distance.

It suddenly appeared to her that two of the dots were approaching her. She kept walking, wanting to be certain before waving a friendly hello. She had gotten a good night of rest in the apartment behind the gas station, so she had a lot of energy with which to greet these people she had been walking for days to find.

Lev, Bolin, and The Traveler

"Kill first, ask questions later doesn't work," Lev said to Bolin as they continued forward towards the stranger.

"Yes," Bolin responded curtly.

"Put your gun down. I got this. Don't kill people we might need. You know I'll kill him if he's useless," Lev said to him. They walked together, closing the gap between the stranger and themselves. Bolin did not lower his gun as Lev had told him to do. Lev shook his head a bit and pursed his lips. Very few people could get away with disobeying Lev.

The stranger suddenly waved an arm high above their head and Lev could see more clearly that the stranger was a woman with shoulder length, unruly masses of wavy blonde hair. She was quite thin and hardly looked like a threat. He could see she was holding something in her left hand, but couldn't quite make it out as it blended in with the tall grasses she was wading through as she approached them. He decided it wasn't a gun that she was carrying.

They were within 40 feet of her when Lev registered a look of happiness emanating from her face, and noticed the water bottle containing cosmos in her left hand by her side. She was striding with a spring in her step towards them as Bolin suddenly stopped walking and raised his gun shouting, "Drop your weapon! Get on the ground! Now!"

Lev almost never hesitated, but he did for a second as he tried to reconcile the forceful, angry demands being made by Bolin with the non-threatening approach of the smiling woman carrying flowers and no visible weapon. Did he not see the same thing he was seeing, Lev wondered to himself.

"I said get on the ground!" Bolin yelled at her.

Lev had stopped his approach as had the woman. He watched as the woman's friendly smile lingered and slowly took on a look of amusement while staring intently at Bolin. She even laughed slightly and shook her head as she smiled and asked him, "What?"

She looked at the angry man. She wasn't going to get on the ground. The ground was wet and muddy, and she was fairly clean. Her clothes were clean. "Yeah, hey. Not going to get on the ground. It's wet," she said to Bolin still wearing a friendly smile. She pointed to the ground. "It's wet," she said again for emphasis.

Both of her hands were down by her sides now. One empty and one holding the bottle with flowers. She was slender and maybe five and a half feet tall or a little more. Her hair looked surprisingly clean for a traveler and was hanging around her shoulders in full, wavy blonde mounds framing her face. She looked neat, but still unkempt, as if she'd been standing in the wind.

Lev kept his eyes on her while saying to Bolin, "I think she's a traveler. I don't see a weapon."

Bolin was still feeling defensive from the events of a few hours earlier and didn't listen to Lev or the woman. He knew from personal experience that travelers could be assholes, too. "I said get on the fucking ground and drop what you're holding or I'm going to blow your fucking head off!" he shouted at her. Lev didn't doubt the threat and looked at the woman expecting her to comply.

She looked at Bolin with eyebrows raising higher and lost her smile as she tipped her head to one side and said slowly and thoughtfully, "Well, if you're going to threaten to kill someone, you should make sure they're afraid of dying first. Otherwise, what's the point? I mean, really, what's the point?" She shrugged as she asked him the question twice adding, "I'm not dropping my flowers. They're cosmos and cosmos are my favorite. So, yeah. Not dropping them. Not getting on this muddy ground, either."

She continued to stare at Bolin, not acknowledging Lev at all until Bolin started advancing on her with his gun raised, still demanding she get on the ground. That was the moment Lev noticed her head turn ever so slightly in his direction. She blinked hard and slow at him, asking as she sighed loudly, "Is he always this intense?" Her full smile returned as she looked directly at Lev, completely unconcerned about Bolin advancing on her with every intention of roughing her up if not outright killing her.

Lev took two large steps forward and walked in front of Bolin's line of fire as he advanced towards the woman with his gun pointed at her, ready to shoot.

"Hey, she's unarmed. She's fine. It's fine," he said to him.

"Get on the ground!" Bolin yelled at her a third time menacingly as he shifted his position around Lev.

"No," she said mildly, shaking her head and shrugging again.

"Jesus, stand down. I've got this," Lev whispered to Bolin. He didn't wait for Bolin to respond, beginning now to feel like he was trapped between two children who were fighting and realizing neither was about to give up their position. He turned to the woman and looked at her asking, "What do you want? What are you doing here? You part of the problem we had here last night?"

She looked at him as he spoke to her, choosing to ignore the shorter man who continued to seethe and point his weapon at her. This man was much taller and larger all around than the one with the gun pointed at her, but she had the feeling he could kill her more quickly even without a gun. The shorter man was furious, shaking with his rage. His hair was cropped close to his skull, and his facial hair was cropped closely to his face. He was sporting a lot of grays throughout his once black hair. The taller man had shoulder length black hair that fell in soft greasy curls around his face. He had a full and unmanaged beard that looked like it extended up to his full unmanaged eyebrows. His eyes were dark brown and might have been friendly enough were they not framed by the deeply arched eyebrows which made him appear perpetually enraged. His hands, one of which was holding his partner back now as he had slowly crept forward, were enormous but fit the scale of the rest of his body. Still, she wasn't afraid of either of the men. Not the one who could kill her with his gun and not the one who could kill her with his bare hands... or maybe a deadly glare. The thought made her smile faintly to which Bolin responded with immediate aggression.

"You think I'm fucking joking? Were these your friends that came in here and attacked us last night? You think you're going to walk up here and play games with me?"

"I just got here," she said, turning her attention away from Lev and towards the animated angry man. "I come in peace," she said, and Lev couldn't tell if she was taunting Bolin on purpose for her own amusement or if she meant to be friendly.

Lev took his hand off of Bolin's shoulder in an effort to signal that the trio had established some parameters. Namely, Bolin wouldn't shoot the woman, the woman wasn't part of the raider's group from last night, and Lev was going to take over trying to figure out what she wanted. To further his intention, he took another step ahead of Bolin trying to move, once again, in front of his line of fire.

"You weren't with the raiders?" he asked her flatly.

"No," she said, smiling at him.

"We got hit pretty hard last night. Now you just show up here. Not like we get a lot of visitors. If they were your friends, they're all dead now," he said, staring blankly at her while searching her face for a reaction.

"Yeah, so no. I don't know the people who attacked your people. I'm by myself. I did notice..." she said, turning around and pointing at a tree off in the distance, "there's a dead guy over there by that tree. Kinda lying next to it. Definitely looked dead to me, but maybe he was faking. I didn't check." She looked back at Lev. "Maybe one of yours? Maybe one of theirs. Not anything to do with me either way," she said, looking directly at him with an inscrutable expression of her own. Just the faintest smile seemed to linger on her face no matter what was being said.

"Why is she here?" asked Bolin, resigned to his demoted status as second interrogator.

"You looking for supplies or what?" Lev asked her.

She looked around Lev's side as she noticed Bolin signaling to some crew members to approach. Lev noticed her eyes looking at Bolin, and he turned slightly to look over at him as he signaled the team members he was ushering towards them. He looked back down at her. It occurred to him that she was fairly petite for someone with such a fearless attitude.

"What do you want?" he asked more firmly, hoping to hold her attention and finally get a useful response from her.

"I'm here to speak to some scientists. Do you have any scientists here?" she asked casually while looking up at Lev's face and directly into his eyes.

He looked down at her and exhaled loudly before choosing his words. He knew Bolin would also be listening to what was said next. "Whether we do or do not have scientists here at this facility doesn't change the fact that you're not getting any closer unless you tell me exactly what you're doing here."

"Well, I'm here to talk to some scientists and you and the extra angry guy here don't look like scientists to me. So, I will wait until I can talk to some scientists. If you have any around," she said with an intentionally antagonizing tone.

Lev almost laughed. Almost. Instead he said, "Give me a clue. Farming, water treatment, electricity, what? Something I can work with," he said to her, realizing he'd have to work with her because threatening her was not likely to motivate her at all given how she'd already responded to them.

"I'm supposed to talk to scientists not soldiers," she said with no room for negotiation.

She looked at Bolin who had his body mostly turned towards the approaching team members but his face was now firmly set on the conversation between Lev and herself. His mouth was hanging slightly open as he looked from her face to Lev's back. She looked back up at Lev and he felt he was unwillingly conscripted into her standoff.

"What resource do you need information about from scientists in the event we have some here? I'd have to give them a reason to speak with you," Lev told her.

She turned to look up at his face and whispered, "This should be confidential. Ok?" she asked him.

He nodded a quick flick of his head in the affirmative.

"I need to talk to them about time and space travel ...stuff," she said quietly while waving her right hand through the air. She spoke to him as if whispering a secret to a trusted friend. Even though she said the words quietly, Bolin, who had been listening intently, heard her and immediately raised a clenched left fist in the air while turning back to his approaching team members. As quickly as she had said the words, Lev had also turned around and raised his own fist to stop the approach of the team members. They stopped and Lev shouted loudly, "Go back! We've got it!" to them.

Bolin walked up alongside Lev now and looked at her. "You think you have something we need?" he asked her, conveying his doubt.

"Oh, definitely. Yes. But I can't talk to you about this anymore because I'm only supposed to talk to the scientists. Kill me if you feel you must. I'm not saying anything else about it." She was looking at Bolin when she said this, but turned her head to look back up at Lev now. "Have you got scientists, then?" she asked him hopefully.

He looked away from her and over at Bolin standing along his right side. "We bring her in and put her in a room. Talk to her. Have the teams clean this shit outside."

"Yes," Bolin agreed.

"Hey guys? What room? I'm happy to wait out here for the scientists to come to me. I don't want to go to a room," she said pensively and Lev took note of a hiccup in her fearlessness.

"It'll be a nice room," Bolin said to her snidely.

"No thanks. I'll stay out here," she said, turning to walk towards the tree where she said she'd seen a dead body. "I'll hang out with the dead guy!" she called back to them as she walked away, waving her right hand in the air.

Lev felt his patience start to wane and rolled his eyes and muttered a barely audible, "What the fuck?" as he took several large strides across the grass and caught up to her as she walked heading towards the tree.

She felt him alongside her but continued ahead saying, "I don't want to go to a jail cell. I don't want to be a prisoner. I'll wait outside."

"I'm not going to put you in a cell. It's a room. It's gonna have a guard, probably two, but it won't be a jail cell."

She stopped walking but didn't turn to look at him. "You're bigger than me, so I know you can make me go into a jail cell, but I won't talk to your scientists if you put me in a jail cell." She made this statement while staring at the landscape before her.

Lev listened and heard her reveal a weakness. She might have been a prisoner in the past. She definitely did not want to be jailed. Over the 17 years he had survived the apocalypse, he had become a master of exploiting weaknesses in others. He decided to try and build trust with her about his intention for her and the difference between a room versus a jail cell.

"I can't walk you into our building after a night when we were attacked and lost good people and just let you roam around the place. I won't put you in a cell, but, you understand, you need to go to a room and have guards. That makes sense, right?" he asked her while staring down at the top of her head. He noticed how blonde her hair was while waiting for her to contemplate her limited options. She was right, he and Bolin could force her into a jail cell, but he honestly wasn't suggesting that. "It's a room. It's going to have guards. I'm going to insist you stay in the room."

"Can I leave the door open?" she suddenly asked him, turning to look up at him.

Her expression was serious and Lev made a quick decision aimed at getting her to comply. "Yeah. The door can remain open. But don't leave the room. Deal?"

"Deal," she said.

Lev noticed she had successfully controlled a good deal of her current situation despite not having the advantage. She wasn't going to be allowed to wait outside in the field while their teams cleared bodies and burned them. But, she was going to wait inside in a room, not a jail cell, with guards watching her, in order to be allowed to speak with their scientists. She was going to be allowed to keep the door to her room open. She had negotiating skills. She might have been nervous, but she certainly didn't panic. She kept her wits about her. She turned around quickly and deliberately to head towards the facility with Lev and Bolin and said nothing as the three of them began walking through the swaying grasses in the light of the early morning.

As they walked Bolin told her, "I can't believe you were willing to get shot over some flowers."

"They're cosmos," she said lightly as if that made all the difference.

Lev kept his mouth shut while he listened and walked slightly ahead of them towards the gate. His brooding expression was darker than ever as they approached the entrance to the facility.

His and Bolin's teams were scattered about the compound working hard to make repairs and clean up the bodies. The burn pit would be going most of the day. Leading Bolin and the woman, Lev shouted to Williams and waved him over.

"There's a body by the tree down there," he said, pointing. "We missing anybody?"

"Everyone's accounted for as far as I know. I'll send two over to bring it back and double check it's not one of ours."

Lev pointed to the woman as Williams was looking with curiosity at her standing behind him next to Bolin. "Bolin and I are taking her in for ..." he rolled his eyes, sighed and suddenly waved a hand in the air..."a talk, I suppose. Isn't that right?" he asked her, looking down at her to confirm his intention for her.

"Yeah. To a room, not a jail cell," she said, confirming their verbal agreement with confidence.

Lev turned back to face Williams and said quietly, "We don't believe she's a threat, and she wasn't part of the raiders group last night. She might have some other information. Bolin's team is relieved for now. Take our team and carry on where they're leaving off. I'll be out in a bit. I'm not sure how long this will take."

Williams confirmed his understanding of the expectations Lev had for him and the team and walked away to find Anna and relay the information.

Lev turned to Bolin and the woman and asked Bolin, "I'm thinking second floor, Aisha's old room. Yes? No?"

"I'm thinking the basement," Bolin said seriously. But Lev looked over at him across the top of the woman's head and shook his head no silently.

"Aisha's old room will be fine," Bolin muttered with a shrug as Lev pulled open the door to the facility and entered ahead of both of them. The door wasn't usually guarded, but after last night, Team 3 had been put on interior facility duty. It was easier than any other assignment being that it was out of the sun and the humidity. No bodies to clear. They gave Team 3 interior facility duties for the morning because their team had lost three people in the fight overnight. It gave the surviving team members something to do other than feel like shit about their losses. They were a battered and demoralized team right now. Lev looked at the woman from Team 3 and told her he needed her to arrange to have two guards posted to Dorm 17 asap.

"I should probably have three guards," the woman said to Lev, while craning her neck to look down the hallways.

He watched her looking down the hallways and said, "I think two will be enough." She said nothing in response. "Send two guards to Dorm 17," he repeated to the member of Team 3 who then dared to sigh loudly. "Don't," Lev snarled at her.

She suddenly stood up straight and offered an apologetic, "Yes. Sorry sir. I'll get the guards right now." She departed her post quickly, terrified at having Lev angry with her.

Interrogating the Traveler

Lev led them down several hallways and up two short flights of stairs to the second floor. They walked down several more hallways and took stairs that went up and then some that went down again as they navigated towards Dorm 17. The final hallway was short with only two doors, one on each side. It didn't make sense and she asked, "Did the builders forget to finish this hallway?" The layout was perplexing, but Bolin looked at her and shrugged silently by way of an explanation which meant she wasn't going to receive a satisfactory explanation, probably because they didn't have an answer.

Lev used a key he fished out from the depths of his pocket to unlock the door and pushed the door open and walked in first. She noticed a large window above a twin bed and some useful furnishings such as a night table, a small dining table with four chairs around it and a loveseat against the wall alongside the open door that led to the hallway. There were two doors inside the room other than the door that led to the hallway. One was open a bit and she could make out that it was a bathroom. The other door was closed and she wondered if it was a closet or if it led to an adjacent room. The bed had no sheets and there were no small useful items to be seen anywhere in the room. No lamp, no books, nothing except a bed, a night table, a kitchen table, four chairs, and a small loveseat. The walls were bare. There was no carpeting. There were no bars on the window. She noticed a light switch near the door they had entered through and looked up to see a single light in the ceiling.

She decided it was not a jail cell, but she was concerned that the abbreviated hallway left her with little options for escape if the need arose. She had the window and one length of hallway to navigate. That was it. Unless the second door led to a second room with other options. She didn't know yet. She would need to find out. She walked over to the nightstand and placed her plastic bottle with the cosmos on the nightstand and removed her backpack and placed it on the floor next to the bed. She turned and looked at Lev.

"Sit down," Bolin told her gruffly as he closed the door to the room.

She turned her gaze towards Bolin but didn't make a move towards the table. Instead, with an uncompromising tone, she said, "I'd like that door to remain open."

Bolin was already pulling out a chair for himself, so Lev stepped back to the door and opened it all the way, an action which caused Bolin to raise both hands and shake his head with a confused look on his face.

"We discussed leaving the door to the room open before she agreed to come inside," he explained to Bolin as he pulled out a chair for himself.

"Oh, now I'm not confused anymore," Bolin responded sarcastically.

Lev looked at her still standing alongside the bed across the room from the table where they were waiting for her and decided to try a new tactic. "Would you please join us?" Lev asked her while pointing to the two remaining available chairs. Bolin scoffed loudly again and Lev turned to look at him and said patiently, "I can handle this if you want to go down and take care of some business." He actually wanted Bolin present when he spoke to the woman because Bolin had a way of getting to the heart of a matter when he wasn't an emotional mess like he was right now, but he also wanted Bolin to know he would understand if he wanted to go to medical and check on James.

"I'm sticking around for now," he said, looking at Lev.

Lev looked at her still standing by the night table and added, "You can stand if you prefer."

She walked purposefully over to the table and pulled out a chair and sat down across from the two men who wanted information from her. Well, she thought, this will teach them to deal with disappointment. She smiled at the thought.

Lev saw her suddenly smile and hoped Bolin wasn't going to react negatively to her unpredictable social behaviors the entire time.

"What's your name?" Bolin asked her, hoping for an easy start to their conversation.

She tipped her head to the right and looked at him with raised eyebrows and said, "Let's start with something easier, huh?"

"What the hell's easier than 'What's your name?' Unless you have amnesia?" he asked, instantly annoyed at her. He turned to Lev. "Your turn," he huffed, leaning back into his chair aggressively while folding his arms against his chest.

She didn't care. She turned to Lev looking as bright-eyed as she did in the field when Bolin had threatened to kill her if she didn't drop her flowers and get onto the wet ground.

"Do you know the names of any of the scientists you want to speak with?" he asked her, unafraid to jump into the more pointed questions.

"No," she said.

"Why do you want to speak with them?" asked Bolin.

"I have information and tools they can use," she said to him promptly.

"Where are these tools? In your backpack?" asked Bolin.

"It's tech. I hid it," she said to him. "

Are you a scientist?" Lev asked her.

"Oh my god, no!" she said, laughing and tossing her head forward. "Oh, yeah. No. I'm not a scientist."

"Do you specialize in math?" Lev asked her.

"No. Not even a little," she said, still laughing.

"I want to look through your backpack," Bolin suddenly said. "May I?"

"Sure, go ahead. There's nothing in it except some clothes and other things you don't need."

Lev noticed that Bolin had waited for permission from her to search her things before he got up from the table and grabbed her backpack. Maybe Bolin was figuring out how to work with her.

Lev asked her, "Where is your group based? Where did you walk here from?"

"I came from "New Zealand," she said, putting New Zealand in quotes with her fingers.

He was confused. She was confusing. Was she crazy? Just flat out crazy after 17 years living through an apocalypse? Was that it? He preferred to put crazy out of its misery rather than let it wander about. Crazy caused unnecessary problems for others. Had she heard about their scientists? Had rumors escaped their facility? Was she a spy? Did she have information they needed, or was she on a fishing expedition? She was inexplicable on so many levels that his head was spinning as he tried to come up with more questions for her that she wouldn't easily deflect.

"Where did you hide the tech you say you brought with you?" he asked her.

"Not in her backpack," Bolin chimed in as he headed towards the table with her backpack in his hand.

Bolin brought her backpack to the table minus the clothes he had removed and left on the bed. "What's this?" he asked, holding up a small bottle of hotel shampoo and another bottle of hotel conditioner.

"Shampoo and conditioner," she said, looking at him as if he should know what they were.

"They expired at least 15 years ago, you know? Everything has an expiration date. This is garbage," he told her with authority.

"No, it's not," she said with confidence. "Anyway, what do you care?" She looked up at his thinning hair and smiled at him. She saw him scowl at her reference to his impending baldness and felt herself warming to him.

"You don't even have a weapon here," Bolin said with surprise and a bit of disappointment in her lack of consideration for self-protection.

"Well, maybe I'm a weapon," she offered.

"Is confusion your weapon?" Bolin asked her suddenly slightly amused by her relentlessly confounding approach to conversation. He unzipped the side pocket of her backpack and pulled out the hairbrush and toothbrush and put them on the table. Then he pulled out the purple silky box and held it up shaking it, asking, "What's in here?"

"A vibrator," she said with a small laugh that displayed no embarrassment for herself or for either of them.

"Oh, really?" he asked in disbelief, raising his eyebrows while pulling off the lid.

"Uh, Bolin," Lev said, putting a hand up while still staring at her, "I think it's gonna be a vibrator." He couldn't help smiling as Bolin dropped the box onto the table and pulled open the drawstrings on the purple pouch.

"Ok," he said, nodding his head rapidly. "Yes. It's a vibrator." He quickly pulled the drawstrings tight again and put the pouch back into the purple box and then into the center compartment of her backpack. He left all the other items displayed on the table and her spare clothes remained on the bed. He sat down in his chair and shook his head lightly hoping Lev would continue the conversation.

Lev looked at the woman across the table from him who had managed to elicit a small moment of humor from Bolin and suddenly wondered if she was, indeed, the weapon. Maybe manipulation was her weapon. Had she been manipulating them this entire time? She was inside their facility a few hours after a serious attack. She was in a room and not a cell. The door was open as she wanted.

"Ok, ok. Hold on. We're here to find out what you want from us," he said to her firmly. "Bolin, you sure there are no weapons?"

"Yes. She's got some hotel items here. They're from some Australian hotel chain. Hey, I stayed here once on a deployment," he said suddenly, turning to her.

"How'd you get soap from this hotel?" his face was screwed up in perplexity as he looked over at her and waited for an answer.

"Maybe I found them when I walked here," she said without commitment to the likelihood. "When can I speak to your scientists?" she asked them.

Lev couldn't decide if he'd had enough or if he was entertained for the first time after 17 years of living through the dark ages of humanity. "They're not at the facility today. We expect them back later tonight or sometime tomorrow. The rains held them up. There are several here now, but the higher ranking ones are gone until whenever they return today or tomorrow. You'll need to stay here until then." He looked at her sternly and hoped he could end the games she was playing with them. It was beginning to feel like games. He was beginning to feel like the mouse to her cat and he preferred it the other way around.

Bolin was experiencing the opposite effect from her levity and asked, "Are you hungry? Have you eaten?"

Lev noticed her expression turned to unabashed appreciation for the question and watched as her shoulders dropped as she said, "I haven't eaten in days. I don't know how long. I can't keep track of time here. I'm so hungry. I'm so very hungry."

Bolin looked genuinely interested in her declaration of hunger. He turned to Lev and said, "I'm going to check on some things downstairs and then I'll come back and bring some food. Did you want something, too?" he asked him.

Lev was actually hungry because he hadn't eaten yet and shook his head yes adding, "Anything is fine." Bolin left them with the less erotic contents of her backpack still displayed on the table before them.

"What's your name?" Lev asked her pointedly.

She looked at him quietly and squinted at him. "I don't think you understand time and space travel. I get it. You're the muscles and not the brains of this operation."

He scoffed and smiled at her description of him but kept eye contact with her.

"I don't want to give you my name. Some day this will be the past. What if it comes up in the future? What if I tell you my name, and in the future present, or the other one, they realize it was me? You know, they won't kill us for being a part of this. They'll capture us." She looked at him with raised eyebrows to convey how serious a problem that would be for both of them.

"Well, what can we call you then? Make up a name," he said to her, leaning back in his chair. "My name's Lev. What do I call you?" He watched as she looked around the room for inspiration.

"I don't know," she said as her gaze drifted across the bare walls of Aisha's old room.

She stared at her cosmos and Lev felt like he was losing her to her thoughts.

126

He asked her, "What name do you like?"

"My own, but I can't use it," she said.

"Then what state were you born in? We can call you by your state name."

She pondered that suggestion for a moment and asked, "Well what if I was born in New Hampshire?"

"Were you born in New Hampshire?" he asked her.

"No."

"Then don't worry about it," he said.

"What if I was born in Georgia? That would be easy. Or Virginia? Or North Carolina?" she said with enthusiasm. Some of those would be easy. "But what if I was born in Florida?" she asked, looking directly at him with a gotcha expression on her face.

"We'd call you Flo," he said.

She smiled. "Ok, that's true. That was easy. What about Washington State?" she asked, looking back at him.

"How about Mary for George Washington's wife?"

"Ok," she nodded her head in agreement. "Oregon?"

"That.... I don't know. I don't know what we could do with Oregon," he admitted. "Were you born in Oregon?"

"No," she said.

"Then let's not try to figure it out," he told her.

"Well, what if I was born in Texas?" she asked him suddenly.

"Are you just trying to come up with states that don't translate easily into names for you?" he asked her.

"No. Maybe. But I can't think of a good name for myself if I had been born in Texas. Maryland would be easy. So would Delaware."

"Delaware?" asked Lev.

"Yes. Della or Delta. Those are both good names I could enjoy," she said.

"What state were you born in?" he asked her, smiling slightly and shaking his head, giving in to the game she was enjoying.

She looked at him and got very quiet. She had a pensive expression on her face, but he knew she was about to tell him. Maybe she felt it was giving up a piece of her privacy to do so.

"I don't want anyone else to know my name is made up," she said to him with a serious tone in her voice.

"Sure. Ok. What state?" he asked her.

But she remained silent and looked at him with that pensive expression, obviously concerned about the fact that she was about to share actual information with him. Finally, she said to him, "You know, I do realize you don't believe me and you probably think I'm crazy. But imagine that I'm telling you the truth. What if I reveal information about me to you and doing so leads to me being discovered in the future? That could also lead to today being discovered when this becomes their past? Then you're involved. Imagine that could happen even if you don't believe that's what's going on." She looked at him but he said nothing. "That's not how it works today, but he's always working on how to change it," she said almost to herself. She looked like she had more to say, and he waited for her to finish her thoughts. "I'm from California."

He slapped his leg and sat up, leaning forward on the table. "How about Cali? We can say your name is Cali."

She looked at him and her face conveyed a lack of security in her own safety at having revealed to him where she had been born. She was right, he did think she was probably crazy, but she was also entertaining him in ways that people who were terrified of him never would. She clearly had not gotten the memo that he was dangerous to her well-being. She spoke to him in such a way that she also demanded he respect her. Plus, he'd been having the same conversations about survival for nearly two decades and she was suddenly here with an abundance of unpredictability and weird sentences that he had to stop and consider how to respond to. She was interesting. Maybe even a little fun if not frustrating. She was difficult to be angry with when she maintained that benign expression and never once looked fearful of him personally. She wasn't afraid of him or Bolin, actually. And she said she was from California. Maybe she was lying. He didn't know. He suddenly looked at her and was reminded of his hometown. How did she wind up in Virginia? He actually wanted to know.

"Ok," she said. "Cali, but I want it to be spelled with a K. K A L I," she said, spelling it out. "Not with a C, because if it's spelled with a C, it might remind people of California. They might find me if they find it written down like that. So, if you spell it, spell it with a K. Actually, don't ever write it down. Don't keep records. Do you people keep records?" She looked at him, demanding he agree to the terms she was presenting.

"Kali with a K. Like the goddess?" he asked, amused.

"What goddess?" she asked.

He laughed and waved his hand. "Never mind."

"Don't write it down," she demanded.

"It's a post-apocalyptic world. We write very little down these days," he said, laughing at her with a genuine sense of humor at the conversation they were having. He ran his hands through his long greasy hair and shook his head.

He got up from the table and pointed towards the bathroom saying, "You have a private bathroom here, and when your guards arrive, I'll tell them to go get you some sheets for the bed."

"I need three guards," she said, looking at him with an expression of concern.

"Why? Tell me why you would possibly need three guards on the second floor of a compound that's on edge from an attack the night before?" he asked in exasperation.

She looked at him and asked, "How do I get out of this room? How do I get back outside?"

He stood up even straighter, displaying his full height at the question, and scoffed. "Why?" he demanded.

"So I can run if they find me," she said seriously. "The hallway ends. What the hell is that about? That leaves me only one way out unless I go through this window which, thanks for the second floor accommodations, but I'm not liking my chances. At least if you'd put me on the third floor, I might be able to count on dying if I jumped."

He was flustered. What the hell did that even mean? She could come on strong when she wanted to. He kept thinking he understood her communication style and then, bam, she turned. They had been getting along and now it was unraveling because she needed the floor plans of the building for an escape from people who were possibly hunting for her.

"Who's looking for you? No one's getting up here. No one has before. Not in nearly two decades. You're safe up here," he said with confidence.

She looked at him and rolled her eyes. "You have no idea. You said you wouldn't put me in a jail cell, but it turns out you've put me in a big comfy jail cell." She sat before him posturing defiantly with her head tilted to one side, defying him to question her conclusions.

A woman appeared in the doorway and excused herself for interrupting their silent standoff. "Excuse me, Lev. I'm here for guard duty," she said, looking from him to Kali.

"You know what?" he said tersely to the guard who looked perplexed. "You wait at the bottom of the stairway. Wait over there until the second guard arrives. Stay there until I get you. I'm *talking* with the... guest... and we need privacy." He turned his attention back to Kali as the guard walked out of view from the open door and headed to where Lev wanted her to be.

He looked at Kali with more than a little irritation and demanded, "Tell me about the people who you say are after you. We need to protect this facility in the event that people are actually after you as you suggest." He thought he was being reasonable, but when she sat there silently looking at him, he closed his eyes for a brief second and said in a calmer tone, "It would help if I understood your concerns about the people you say are looking for you. I need to know what your concerns are in order to properly protect my community and protect you while you're a guest here. Ok? Can you help me out?" he asked, throwing his large arms out in front of him in exasperation.

She considered his appeal and finally said, "Just don't tell anyone why I'm here. Don't tell the guards. I'll talk to your scientists and they can figure out the best way to deal with me being here. Do you think Bolin is telling anyone why I'm here?" she asked him with genuine concern.

"No. Bolin is not going to mention to anyone why you claim to be here. Until I know more, two guards are enough for you while you're here. And based on your persistence, I'm going to tell the guards not to tell you how to get out of here, so don't bother asking them. They won't tell you."

Lev saw a little darkness cross her face but not despair. If anything, determination settled into her expression and she turned her body in her chair and pointed to the extra door in the room asking, "What does that door lead to?"

"A small closet. It's empty," he said as he walked over and opened the door to show her the empty space. "See? Empty," he said to her again. He watched her expression as she crossed off the door and its possible contents as a potential useful resource. He walked back to the table and sat down looking at her face. Again, her expression was at best benign, and at the very least blank. She suddenly smiled at him and said nothing.

"Where did you come from?" he asked her mildly, hoping to retain a more gentle mood.

"I arrived in a place and walked from there," she said to him without conflict.

"Well, that's really fucking vague. Who told you to come to our facility and speak to our scientists?" he asked her with the same tone, hoping for actual progress.

"My two friends," she offered quickly.

"Are they scientists, too?" he asked her.

"No. They're both....traitors," she whispered, and then looked up at his face and nodded her head adding quietly, "Don't even tell Bolin that last one. Don't tell anyone."

"How do they know about Ivy? Have either of them been here before?" he asked her suddenly feeling like he was getting somewhere with her.

She looked at him. "I think that would be information for the scientists."

"You said you brought proof and you hid it. What kind of proof?" he asked her, trying not to lose momentum.

"I brought tech that will help your scientists," she said, smiling at him brightly. "They're really going to like it, too." She let out a small laugh at that.

"Where's the tech hidden?" he asked with a tone he struggled to keep calm and friendly.

"After I talk with your scientists, I'll know how they want me to go about getting it and bringing it back here."

"Why didn't you just bring it to begin with?" he asked her, trying not to sound accusatory.

"Because it's been 17 years for you guys and I wasn't sure who was alive and who I might run into on the walk here, and if, you know, they'd find me. If I had the tech on me... That would be really bad," she said and opened her eyes really wide.

He watched her. There was simply no evidence to support her overall claim, but there was a possibility that she had heard rumors about what was going on in their facility. Maybe she believed what she was saying. She had to believe it in order to walk up here and start talking about time and space. She had to believe what she was saying to antagonize him and Bolin the way she had been doing. But here she was. No evidence. No names. No hard knowledge. No science background. No math skills according to her own assessment of her abilities. In the past, he'd have killed her already. He forgot why he hadn't. He looked at her and the contents of her backpack still on the table. He looked over at the bed where Bolin said he had put her clothes. He saw the cosmos in the water bottle on the side table. Oh, yeah. It was the cosmos. That's why he hadn't killed her. He looked back at her.

"Where'd you get the cosmos?" he asked her.

"Not yesterday, but the day before, I was walking down the road to get here and there was a huge field of cosmos swaying in the breeze. I haven't seen cosmos in nearly forever, at least it seems. They're my favorite flower. They looked so beautiful. I didn't expect them. I took a few and kept walking," she said, looking directly at him as she spoke. She kept doing that to him. It wasn't so much that she was looking at him and discovering him, but more that she was looking at him as herself being an open book and challenging him to see her. For all she was hiding, she kept looking at him insisting she see something in her. Was it her intentions? Was she trying to reveal her intentions by looking directly at him, directly at Bolin?

"What are your intentions coming to us?"

"To give you what you need!" she said excitedly, looking at him and smiling.

Bolin walked in carrying a bowl of food and walked over and set it down on the table in a space not covered by the contents of her emptied backpack. He was clearly proud of the food he'd brought to them. James' influence had seeped into him over the years and become a part of his own identity. Food was caring. Food was love. Planting it, nurturing it so it grew and thrived. Harvesting it. Cooking it. Serving it. An entire cycle of caring wrapped up into a single meal. James was recuperating in a hospital bed, but Bolin was determined to honor his husband by feeding the stranger they had decided to bring into their facility. James would have it no other way if he hadn't been injured. In his absence, Bolin would see to it that the stranger was fed. Personal feelings aside, this weird bitch was going to have a great breakfast, he thought.

"The kitchen was serving this for breakfast this morning," he said as he lowered the large metal bowl with five hard boiled eggs, several small red potatoes, and numerous vegetables onto the table.

She breathed in deeply, overwhelmed at the array of food being placed before her after not having eaten in days. "I'm so hungry. Thank you so much, Bolin," she said as she sat up straight in her chair. There was no silverware, so she grabbed an egg which had already been peeled.

Lev watched and felt the complete break in their conversation was at hand for the moment. She was focused on eating. Would it be worth it to remind her of the conversation they were just having. Maybe he could pick up where they left off. Lev considered how this could be problematic. He was organized, methodical even.

He had focus and he retained it. Frequently for years. Kali was living in the moment. She bounced from one subject to the next. One emotion to the other in an instant. She seemed reckless, like a child unaware of danger, but all too aware at the same time. Was she here to speak to their scientists about time and space travel, or was she just here to be a momentary storm? After 30 minutes alone in a room with her, he had no clear answers, and it left him feeling completely confused about how to manage her going forward. Was she actually managing him? Maybe she wasn't flighty and disorganized. She claimed to have walked to Ivy over the course of days. She claimed she was following a plan. She was making his head spin. He couldn't figure her out and predict her next move.

"Bolin, this is Kali," he told him.

"Why was that so hard when I asked?" he asked her.

She had a mouth full of food and shrugged.

Bolin excused himself, satisfied that he had supplied both Lev and the newly introduced Kali with a more than adequate meal. He still hadn't been down to see James and let Lev know that was where he was headed as he left.

"Is the second guard downstairs?" Lev asked him, following him into the abbreviated hallway.

"Yes. You have Moore and Lemming on guard duty."

"No. Not Lemming. He won't do at all. He'll fight with her right away. I need a diplomat for her. Someone who won't fall into the arguments she's provoking."

"I'll tell him to take a hike as I leave. Tell him to go get … Who do you want? You know her best by now."

"Tell him to get my guy, Bautista. I trust him not to be easily manipulated by her."

"Ok. So, Kali. You think she's for real? Time and space information for the team?"

"The more time I spend talking to her, the less I know. She might be for real, or she might be batshit crazy. She's all over the place and… She's evasive as hell one minute and offering information the next. This woman, she'd take on you while you were locked and loaded. I'll check in on her after my team passes to third." He stopped and considered what else he wanted to run by Bolin. "I didn't like how she asked for three guards. I don't want an 'I told you so' opportunity to arise. She's convinced the people after her are a threat to whatever precautions I've offered her," he concluded. Bolin looked at Lev but didn't speak yet. He had known Lev for nearly a decade now and he'd known of his reputation for longer than that. Lev was, by far, the scariest human he had encountered after the demise of civilization. It seemed to him that Lev was working out his concerns. If Lev was concerned, so was he. Lev began again, "She's worried about people who she says are after her which could be problematic for the entire compound."

"You left Williams in charge, right?" Bolin asked Lev.

"Yeah."

"I'll go tell him our guest has concerns about a search party looking for her."

"Ok. I'm going to try to find out something useful until we're finished eating. Thanks for the meal, man. She's giving me an uneasy feeling. She knows I can overpower her, she said as much out in the field, but at the same time, she seems willing to physically fight. Like, sure you can fuck me up, but I'll fuck you up, too, in the process." He laughed mildly at the thought and looked at Bolin.

"I got that too when she didn't flinch when I threatened to shoot her," Bolin said, raising his eyebrows.

"She didn't fucking care at all," Lev laughed.

Bolin went to walk away but turned around and added, "I smelled that shampoo. It smelled fresh. That was weird." He shook his head and walked away from Lev yelling, "I'll have your guy Bautista sent up."

Lev walked back inside Dorm 17 and looked over at Kali still eating from the bowl of food Bolin had brought them.

"I saved you some. A lot some, don't worry. I was so hungry. This is so good. I thought maybe Bolin poisoned it because he's wanted to kill me a couple of times since meeting me, but I don't even care. It's really good," she said, smiling. "Whatever poison Bolin seasoned this with is delicious!"

He couldn't stop a small laugh from escaping when she said that last bit, and he walked over to the table assuring her that Bolin would never poison the food or drink of another.

"Bolin knows someone who considers it a divine mission to feed humanity," he said to her as he grabbed a hard-boiled egg and bit it in half. After eating quietly for a few minutes, he said, "Listen, I know you don't want to tell me anything because I'm not a scientist, but can you tell me more? What do you have that a scientist could possibly want?" he asked her.

"I told you already, I have words and I have tech. I hid it. The tech. I didn't want to have it on me in case I met, you know, shitty people along the road. I ended up about five days out from your compound. I think it took longer because of the rain, and I admit I was walking slowly enjoying myself a bit, but I hid it. I figured I would find the scientists and then I would walk back and get it." She looked at Lev for his understanding and found the doubt in his eyes hardened as he absorbed what she was saying.

"So, you want me to believe you have tech that... What? Proves time and space travel are possible, but you hid it days away from here? God damn, lady. You're asking a lot," he said, laughing as he bit into another egg.

She laughed too, and said, "Yep. That's about what I'm asking!"

"I don't even know how I'm going to promote you to my people. You're not giving me much," he said to her with a serious look on his face.
"Well, I can meet the scientists today or tomorrow and then I'll go get the tech and bring it back here once I know for sure that I've found the right people. I know the route now. You can give me a knife," she said breezily as she scanned the

food bowl considering what she wanted next.

He looked at her. She was probably completely insane, but so was the idea of time travel until it was a reality. He thought of Yuna and their parents. He thought of all the dead. He thought of Aisha and her mother, and Bob and his family. He looked at this person they'd decided together to name Kali, which amused him even if she didn't get it, and considered his options. "You have tech that can help our scientists?" he asked her, grabbing for a potato.

"Yes. This is Ivy, right?" she asked him.

"Yeah. It was known as Ivy Creek Foundation before the event."

"Then this is where I'm supposed to find the scientists," she said confidently and pushed the remaining food towards him. She was full and said so.

"You need to be patient while guarding this woman," Lev said to the guard named Moore. "Her name is Kali. I sent Lemming away because I don't need an antagonist on duty with her. She's antagonizing enough all by herself. Bolin's sending up Bautista. She may have enemies who are after her, and she may be important to Heather. I'm not saying she does or that she will be, I'm saying she might to both. You understand?" he asked the woman from Team 3.

"Yes, sir."

Lev looked at her unsure of what additional information might actually be of help to the guards. He added, "She's not to leave. She's persistent. She talks in circles. You understand?"

"Yes, I understand."

Lev stood silently for a minute contemplating what tricks Kali might pull with the guards after he left. "She needs to stay in this room. I'll be back later. Do not let her out, but don't treat her like a prisoner. Be ... Jesus.... Just be nice to her and assure her that I'll be back after my shift." He noticed the confused look on the guard's face. "Listen to me. She's manipulative. But she's not the enemy. She doesn't trust us, and I don't trust her. I'm giving this small, unarmed woman two guards not because she can physically overpower you with your gun, but because she could manipulate the shit out of you if you were left on your own. You understand?"

"Yes."

"She's smart. But she's scared, too. That makes her clever."

"Understood, sir."

"Tell me the minute Bautista arrives."

Lev walked back into Dorm 17 and looked at Kali who was sitting on the unmade bed. "Take it easy on my guards, ok?" he asked her. She looked at him without responding or conceding and Lev felt compelled to appeal to her better nature if she had one. "Hey, I have to clean up from the bullshit of last night. I'm going to get you an audience with our scientists. Ok? Yeah, we have scientists here and they might be interested in what you want to tell them. Ok? So, all I'm asking is that you take it easy on the two guards I'm putting outside your door. Can we at least agree that I'm trying?" He looked at her and raised his usually menacing eyebrows to new heights and smiled at her.

She laughed lightly at his effort to be agreeable. "Ok. Ok. But can I have directions out of here?" she asked him seriously.

"You throw both of your guards at anyone who makes their way up here and you run back down the hallway I walked you through. Ok?"

"I can sacrifice my guards?" she asked him in a decidedly serious tone.

It concerned him the way she said it, but he responded, "Yeah. Throw them at anyone who comes for you."

"Ok, then," she said looking at him minus the smile that had previously shown up so easily. "Some people have to die for the cause."

"I have to do my shift and then I'll be back to check on you. Sleep. Eat. Shower. Don't mess with my guards but feel free to sacrifice them to any assailants that make their way up here. Agreed?" he asked her.

"Agreed," she responded.

Bautista tapped on the doorframe at that moment and Lev introduced him to Kali quickly before walking out and leaving her to her thoughts.

She watched him go and felt invigorated by the human interactions after days alone. Lev seemed reasonable enough given the situation. He was obviously trying. He seemed like a man who had survived for a long time in a terrible situation. The world ending. Loss. Fear. Despair. She knew those feelings. She sat on the edge of the unmade bed and looked over at the empty bowl of food Bolin had brought to them. Bolin was ok. He had brought her really good food when she was hungry. People thought of food as sustenance, and it was, but it was hope, too. Once fed, you had hope because your strength returned and you could think more clearly. She had hope after the meal Bolin had provided her. Why would you feed someone you planned to kill? That would be a waste of food. She knew the scientists were here. When Bolin had fed her, he had confirmed them. Lev was trickier. He was a This-for-That kind of guy. Everything was an exchange for him. She didn't feel compelled to give him anything but the smallest amount of information to keep him interested. But he made her laugh. She laughed at him, though, not with him. She wondered how he managed his relationships. Completely transactional or did he reserve the transactions for survival. She had noticed how the guard inside the building feared for her life when she hesitated to comply with Lev's order. Was he without mercy? Or was he trying to survive? Her friends had told her to reserve judgement, to contemplate the individual situations she would encounter. Good people killed others, too. She knew that. She, herself, was a good person. They told her to kill anyone who stood in her way or who threatened the mission. She could kill Lev, and she could kill Bolin. She wasn't planning to. She wondered if they held any value to the mission. She needed to get to the scientists. They would be imperfect, too. She would try not to judge them or kill them. They were different.

Lev walked back outside and scanned the field for his team members. His mind was overwhelmed by interactions he had had with Kali. He shook his head and tried to shake off his conversation with her. She was probably crazy. Plain and simple. Crazy. She brought nothing physical to demonstrate her claims. She admitted she wasn't a scientist and said she didn't know math that could assist. He stopped and wondered, but who was she? He had only found out who she wasn't. Who was she? He asked himself. He suddenly felt uneasy. This apocalypse Kali told him who she was not, but she hadn't told him who she was. He considered this fact. Who was she? A woman from California? He shook his head. We're all somebody from somewhere. He had to deal with the needs of his team before trying to deal with her. He'd go back to her room after his shift. He'd be tired, but he'd have more time and demand answers from her.

She got up off the bed and walked into the bathroom and ran the water in the sink. They had hot water. She looked at the shower. She was thirsty after eating the meal. She didn't have a cup. She walked out to her female guard and asked for a cup to drink from. The guard looked at her considering all the admonishments Lev had levied upon them and said, "I'm not to be distracted by you and your demands." She laughed at that response and walked back into the room and grabbed the bowl Bolin had brought to the room earlier. It was empty now, but had some debris from the food it had contained earlier. She rinsed it in the bathroom sink and added water to it and drank. She added more water to the bowl and walked out of the bathroom and placed it on the night table next to her cosmos.

She dragged the mattress to the doorway and laid it down on the floor in the open doorway. The male guard watched her with a quizzical expression and questioned her intentions, but she waved him off. "I'm still in the room, so what are you worried about?" she asked him defiantly. When the female guard questioned whether they should allow the mattress in the open doorway. The male guard said, "Lev said she's not a prisoner, right?" and shrugged it off. Kali laid on the mattress in the doorway and fell asleep after having had the full meal brought to her by Bolin. The two guards watched over her as she slept in the doorway for several hours.

Lev suddenly appeared at the end of the short hallway and went up the stairs two at a time. He stopped and looked at the two guards and pointed down at Kali who was still asleep.

"What the fuck is this?" he asked them quietly.

"She said you told her she could keep the door open. Then she dragged the mattress over here and fell asleep on it," said Bautista.

Lev thought for a minute. He was tired. "I did tell her she could keep the door open." He considered the situation. "I also told her I'd be back to talk with her tonight. Let your relief know she's waiting to talk to me, and I'll be back later."

"She also argued until she fell asleep about having directions out of here," said Bautista. "She kept asking for explicit directions out of here. Every turn. She said if she didn't have the directions, she would have to sacrifice us."

Lev couldn't suppress a small laugh at that information. "I'm taking command of third and their shift this afternoon because Candace is still recovering in medical. The security meeting will have new information you two are going to want to make sure you get from various team leaders when you're finished guarding sleeping beauty. It'll be late before I'm finished and get back here. Whoever relieves you, give them a heads up about her," he told them. He walked away from the sleeping Kali and told the guards as he departed, "When she wakes up, tell her we'll talk tonight."

He said that and left, not realizing how Kali might act upon the meaning of his words.

Kali Does Things Her Way

It was later in the evening before Lev was finally able to pass along security responsibilities to another security team. He went to his room and stripped naked first then stripped the muddy bed sheets off of his bed. He stood naked in his doorway and tossed his bedsheets and clothes outside his door. He'd take them to laundry tomorrow. He'd worked two shifts in a row on top of everything else. At least 12 hours, possibly 14. It was getting late. He was exhausted. He walked back into his room and to his shower where he spent a lot of time rinsing the dirt off of his body. James had been making castile soaps for years and Lev had his most recent concoctions. He rubbed the thyme scented castile soap through his hair and along his body. The soap smelled good. James was very talented at a lot of things and his soaps made everyone feel more civilized. Lev used a torn cloth to move the homemade soap along his body and thoroughly washed away the accumulated dirt of too many days. His hair and body felt clean as he felt the warm water start to wane. The day had been long and hot, the work hard on his tired body. He stood under the running water as it became cooler and enjoyed the feel of the cool against his sunburned skin, sore muscles, and darkening bruises.

He turned off the water and dried off with a small towel hanging on his bathroom door. Walking naked into his studio-sized dorm room, he opened the closet door and pulled out clean sheets to remake his bed. Did he make sure Kali had sheets, he wondered? No. He might have forgotten. He'd go check after he was dressed and went over to talk with her some more. Maybe he should have someone bring her dinner. The 'scientists' weren't back from Campus by now, so he suspected they would be back tomorrow. Traveling at night was a bad idea.

He was putting a clean sheet on his bed when he heard the knock on his door. He stood tall and turned towards his closed door.

"What?" he asked sternly.

"Sir, it's Gorman. Kali is adamant that she speak to you."

Lev looked confused as he shook out a clean bedsheet. "Now? I'll be there in ten minutes. Tell her I'm on my way."

"Sir, she's here with me in the hallway. I could not stop her without forcefully restraining her and you asked us not to treat her like a prisoner," Gorman said with a tone of evident exasperation.

"I also asked for her to be kept in her room," he muttered aloud for only himself to hear. Lev considered his options, and killing Gorman for not being able to control Kali wasn't a reasonable option considering what he had himself experienced earlier.

"Bring her back to her room. I'll be there soon," he said absently.

"I'll wait here," he heard Kali say through his closed door with assumed authority over her choices, and effectively dismissing Gorman. "Lev, I'm going to wait here," she said to him through the door a little louder after not getting an immediate response from him.

Lev hadn't paid attention to his nudity until then. Suddenly aware of his lack of clothing, he stopped making his bed and walked over to his closet and pulled out some clothes and put them on. When he opened his door, ready to be furious with Gorman, he was confronted by a smiling Kali with Gorman standing decidedly in the distance.

"Hi," she said with a friendly smile. She motioned with her hand and body to enter his room. She was holding the bottle with the cosmos and gently pushed past him on his left side and entered his room without an invitation when he didn't step aside for her.

Lev watched Gorman's eyebrows raise as he shook his head to indicate that he, too, had struggled to control Kali just as Lev was struggling now. Lev glared at him from his doorway and said, "Get your partner and both of you stay out here until she leaves."

"Yes, sir," he said attempting to convey a tone of commiseration.

"Gorman, I'm leaving this door open. If you and your second aren't here in three minutes, I'll have you caged for a week. And Gorman, two guards is two guards at all times. I can't believe you walked her down here without your second. Both of you, double farm for a week."

Caging was a serious threat. No one with power made that threat unless they meant it. Gorman ran to Kali's room to get his second. They would have to make it back to Lev's doorway in under three minutes.

"So, you have a nice room," Kali said to Lev as she walked around the space surveying his accommodations. He noticed she had placed the cosmos on one of his tables. He'd been in the same room during the six years he'd been at Ivy. He didn't collect much, but the items he had around his room were useful. There was no art on his walls, but he had hung dark sheets over his windows to black out his room on mornings when he could sleep in or on days when he could catch a nap. He had books, so he had wooden shelving that he had built over the years as his book collection grew. His book shelves were full. He had a table with two chairs and a large couch that a man of his size would be able to stretch out on and read a book when he had the time for such luxuries.

Kali sat down on his couch and looked up at him. "You said you'd come back. Did you forget?" she asked him.

He considered her as he had earlier. She was exasperating, but what she did, that he appreciated, was disrupt the flow of the monotony of living through 17 years of the apocalypse. Even raiders weren't enough to break up the flow of daily life. They had a tornado come close to wiping them out about three years ago. Most people at the facility thought that was a terrible experience, but Lev kind of wished it had gone right through the compound and given them something to focus on other than the usual. Kali, she was a bit like a tornado. And now she was seated comfortably on his couch in his room, and he had no idea what she was going to do or say next. He found himself, a demonstrably dangerous man, explaining himself to a waif of a woman who was sitting comfortably on his couch, completely relaxed, as if she owned it.

"I didn't forget. I took a shower and was going to go over soon," he said to her.

He watched her looking at him as he explained himself to her. This wasn't how it was done. He was used to demanding explanations.

"You know, I don't think the guards you have guarding me are going to be enough. I just don't have the same faith in them that you do. It was fine during the day when everyone was awake and, you know, if something were to happen, like if my people came after me, it would be the daytime and maybe it wouldn't end badly. Actually, it would. It would end badly for a lot of you. But maybe I could have escaped. Thrown my guards at people coming for me. Found my way out. Being the daytime, I would have had better odds. Now, it's dark and I still don't know my way around this place." She looked at Lev intently.

"Are you going to ask me for three guards again?" he asked her, slightly amused and honestly considering relenting to the request.

"No. Now I feel differently about, you know, everything. I've had some time to think about it and the truth is, only you and Bolin know why I'm here. So, even if you doubt me and maybe think I'm crazy, I can't help believing that if you were suddenly confronted by people coming after me, you'd realize I was right. You'd respond to the actual situation. The guards, they wouldn't know what to do. I don't trust them. They can't protect me." She wasn't smiling anymore as looked at him.

"You don't want three guards, then?" He clarified.

"No. I want to stay here in your room with you. And, yeah, have guards outside."

He looked at her and laughed a big hearty laugh. "Yeah, so that's going to be a no from me. You cannot stay here in my room tonight. The two guards will be enough. I know these people. Two guards outside your door are enough."

He turned to finish making his bed and waited for her to protest. He was using a flat sheet to cover his mattress, so he shook out the clean sheet and let the air help him lay it across his bed. He heard Gorman and his second arrive outside his open door. He decided they had made it back in under three minutes. He was reminded that she didn't have sheets for her own bed and said, "We can chat here for a bit and I'll have one of your guards go get you some bed sheets to bring back with you." She was silent behind him, so he finished making his bed by tossing the extra sheet he'd be using as a blanket onto his bed. He turned to look at her and was met by a determined and unyielding expression on her face. Was there boredom mixed in with the rest, he wondered?

"Look. We just don't work that way here. I don't work that way. Ok? You're going to be fine staying in the room you have. You noticed when you walked over to my room, you're basically on the same floor as I am, right?" He waited for her to acknowledge this fact, but she continued to stare at him. Since she wasn't arguing, he continued. "It's a few turns down long hallways, but you and I, we're on the same floor. You'll be fine overnight and I'll come get you tomorrow as soon as our scientists are ready to meet with you. I'm thinking mid-afternoon. So, sleep tonight, hang out in your room tomorrow. Someone will bring you food."

He looked at her to confirm this was how things were going to proceed. Again, she sat there on his couch, looking at him with a determined expression, the smile long gone now. "Kali, be reasonable," he said quietly. "Look, I have a lot of books here. Take a few with you. Take ten. Keep busy and take a break from whatever you're worrying about. If anyone shows up here looking for you, it's like you said. This place is a maze. They're not going to get in, but if they did, you're basically a needle in this haystack." He walked over to his wall of books and pulled one down. "Here's a good one. It's about rabbits," he said, looking over at her.

"I've read that one," she said flatly.

"It's good enough to read twice," he said as he offered it to her. She stood up, and he thought she was going to come take the book he was offering her. Instead, she walked over to his bathroom and went inside and closed the door.

He waited for a minute before putting the book back on the bookshelf and walked over to the bathroom door. He knocked and asked, "You alright in there?"

"Why wouldn't I be?" she asked him from behind the door.

"Because the light switch is out here, so I'm assuming you're in the dark in there."

"Why the hell is the light switch out there and not in here?" she asked him through the closed door.

"I don't know," he said, flicking the light switch into the on position.

"Thank you. Where's the door lock?" she asked him next.

"There is no door lock. Why would the door need a door lock in this small room?" he asked her.

"Well, just so you know, I'm going to stay in your bathroom tonight."

He closed his eyes and rested his head on his bathroom door. He had fought for hours against raiders the night before and had almost no sleep. It had been an exhausting day cleaning up from the fight. He'd worked two shifts. Every part of his body hurt. When he had taken a shower earlier, he noticed the bruises covering his body. He wanted to go to sleep. Now he had a likely unstable woman in his bathroom who was probably going to fight to remain in there. He knew how to fight post-apocalyptic raiders, not people who suggested they might be time travelers and demanded to sleep in his bathroom.

"Listen, you cannot stay in my bathroom tonight. Go back to your room. Take some books. I'll come by after I wake up just to check that all's good. I'll come by early."

"No. I'm staying here tonight. I feel safer around someone who knows what's going on."

I don't know what's going on, he thought to himself.

"Also, I'm leaning against the door so don't kick it in or something like that because I'll get injured."

"I won't kick in the door because I like having a bathroom door and they're not easily replaced post hardware stores," he said to her.

"Ok good. And also, I am not able to stay in this bathroom with the door closed, so I'm just going to open it a bit and then that's how it will be," she said with a tone of authority. "Again, I'm right here, so don't go kicking in the door."

"I'm not going to, but you cannot stay in there overnight. What if I have to use the bathroom?" he asked her.

"If you have to use the bathroom, I'll leave and wait on your couch. Then I'll go back in. I'm fine sleeping on the floor."

"Not gonna happen, Kali," he said, feeling fatigue set in. He wasn't even mad. He was just tired.

"I'm opening the door just a bit because I can't be in here with the door closed like this," she said.

He removed his forehead from the bathroom door and stood up straight as she slowly opened the door a few inches.

"I need it open more," she said, and opened it halfway. "That's good." She looked up at him and slowly got down onto the floor in front of his shower stall.

The bathroom was small. Her body took up the floor space in the doorway. She sat with her back against the exterior tile wall of his doorless shower.

He looked down at her and said, "I'm serious. You cannot stay in my bathroom overnight."

"If it's because you have a girlfriend or a boyfriend, or whatever, just introduce us and explain that I'll only be here for one night."

"It's not about another person. You have a room. You can't stay in my fucking bathroom," he said, closing his eyes and rubbing his face with his hands hoping she would see reason.

When he opened his eyes he looked at her sitting against his shower stall and remembered the warning that a cornered animal is the most dangerous animal. She looked like a cornered animal, not so much afraid, just determined to survive. He suddenly considered the amount of fight she would put up if he... If he what? If he grabbed her and dragged her out? If he had her guards drag her out and down the hallway to her room. Would she scream the entire time? If he wasn't so tired, he could think better and maybe find a solution that didn't involve her sleeping in his bathroom. If she hadn't said she'd come to their facility to talk to scientists about time and space travel, he wouldn't care if she was dragged off and put into a cage in the basement. If she wasn't moderately entertaining, he'd drag her out himself and lock her in her room for annoying him. He was more tired than annoyed, if he was being honest.

"It's fine. I'm fine here," she said to him from the floor where she was sitting.

He looked down at her and turned around and walked over to the still open door of his room. Both of her guards were outside in the hallway.

"You listening to what's going on in here?" he asked them.

Gorman spoke first saying, "I heard her say she wants to stay here tonight and not go back to her room."

"Same," said the second guard.

"Do each of you know who's assigned to relieve you overnight?" he asked them. Neither knew who their replacement was going to be, so he told Gorman to go to each of their teams and let them know that guard duty would be by his door when they sent replacements. The door would remain open. Nothing untoward was going to happen. She would either be on his couch or on his bathroom floor, depending on her preference.

As he was about to send Gorman to inform their commands and future guards of the new assignment, Bolin came down the hallway heading towards his own room.

"Hold up," Lev told Gorman. "You coming from seeing James?" he asked Bolin.

"Yes. He's doing well. Sleeping now. How's our guest?" he asked him, looking curiously at the two guards flanking Lev's doorway.

"Funny you should ask. She's in my bathroom insisting she sleep there overnight rather than in her own room."

Bolin let out a big laugh and said, "No fucking way! You're kidding. Let me see." He walked around Lev and into his room and looked over at the bathroom door and saw Kali sitting on the floor. She smiled and waved at him. He waved back at her. He walked back into the hallway with wide eyes and whispered to Lev, "Holy shit. Are you going to drag her out and put her in a cage now, or what?" he asked him half seriously.

Lev shook his head and closed his eyes and said, "If I wasn't so tired right now, if I didn't want to know what the hell she had to offer at the meeting tomorrow, I'd drag her down the hallway myself. I just... I don't know. It seems like one night. Man, I need sleep."

He looked at an amused Bolin who said, "Ha! You're going to let her sleep in your bathroom!? Seriously?"

"Well, I'm thinking I'll tell her she can sleep on my couch. I'll keep two guards here and keep the door open. I swear, if I get wind of anyone talking shit about this situation, I'll commit a public murder." He said that last part looking from one guard to the other. Both guards muttered their absolute understanding of the situation. The door would remain open. She'd be on Lev's couch. Bolin was informed and that gave Lev his second for additional approval of an unusual situation.

"Come on. This is kind of funny. You should have let me kill her out on the field today," Bolin said to him, smiling.

Lev raised his eyebrows and nodded his head in agreement saying, "Ok, so in the interest of putting last night's fight, our ensuing losses, this bullshit of a full day of cleaning, repairing, and burning the dead, coupled with a nearly complete lack of sleep to an end, Kali will stay in my room tonight and tonight only. We'll avoid dragging her down the hallways to her room and dealing with whatever she would have thrown at us. This decision is being made in the interest of getting sleep tonight and finding out what she has to offer the RT tomorrow." He looked at Bolin and the two guards.

Bolin spoke. "Yes. I agree with the decision when you put it that way. I would not want to be a part of dragging her back to her room. I had trouble dealing with her when she was in a good mood. I wouldn't want to know what she's like when she's in a bad mood. So, yes. She stays with you. Hell, if she wants, she can stay with me. Do you want to ask her? I'm fine with that. I don't care. I sent Meabh to stay with Aisha earlier this afternoon."

"I think she's made it clear she wants to sleep here, but thanks for the offer. I'll let you know if I need to take you up on that."

They all agreed, and Gorman went off to tell their commands to send replacements every six hours to Lev's room.

Lev walked back into his room and began to close his door when he remembered he was leaving it open for the night. Kali watched him as he approached her where she sat on his bathroom floor. She wasn't afraid of him. He even looked nicer now that he'd had a shower and was clean. She'd heard them talking but couldn't make out what they were saying. She'd heard Bolin's voice. She'd seen him when he entered Lev's room and looked at her on the bathroom floor. She didn't care. She wasn't embarrassed. She felt this was the safest place to be overnight. She intended to stay here and would fight to remain exactly in this spot.

Lev stood in the doorway now and looked down at her. He looked exhausted.

"Hey, you can stay here tonight, but I would like it if you'd stay on the couch instead of the bathroom floor. Can we agree to that arrangement?" he asked her, sounding more tired than defeated.

"Sure. That sounds good to me. But are you going to suddenly drag me out of here and put me in my room or a jail cell? Because I'll just fight and fight and fight. I will. I won't be able to stop myself," she said to him as both a fact and a warning.

"Yeah, no. We had a talk out there, the guards, Bolin, and myself, and we decided you could stay in my room on the couch, or in the bathroom if you really want to do that, with my door open and two guards on all night. Ok? And just so you know, the light from the door shines directly on my bed, so I'm not thrilled about making that sacrifice for you." He smiled even though he meant it, and she slowly stood up and thanked him for the sacrifice and offered him a smile of her own.

He didn't have extra sheets, so he offered her the sheet he had planned to use as a blanket. She laid it down on top of his couch and sat on top of it looking at him.

He said to her, "I need sleep. If you're not tired, maybe read a book. There's enough light coming in from the hallway. Or, if you're hungry, I can send one of them for food." He waved his hand towards his open door indicating he would send a guard to get her something to eat.

She considered the options he'd presented her and said, "I'll go to sleep now, too." She pushed his small coffee table further away from the couch with both of her feet and laid down on her side facing him.

He noticed she had put her feet up on the couch while still wearing her shoes. "You can take off your shoes," he said to her, motioning towards her feet.

"I always sleep with my shoes on. You know, in case I wake up and have to start fighting or running. You should sleep with your shoes on, too."

"I only do that when I'm too tired to take them off." He shook his head and turned towards his bed. "If I were wearing shoes now, they'd stay on because I'd be too tired to take them off." He sat down on the edge of his bed and looked at her across the small room. She was watching him and he suddenly felt self-conscious for the first time in a very long time. He laid down on his back and closed his eyes against the light from the hallway coming into his room through the open door. The light crossed the room and landed directly on his face and he thought about turning over and sleeping facing the wall. He opened his eyes and looked over at Kali. She was still staring at him. She looked concerned about something.

"What is it?" he asked her adding, "I thought you said you'd feel safe spending the night here with me."

"I do feel safer here in your room. I know you'll fight them if they show up, and I believe you'd even be able to take some of them out. That will give me time to escape."

Lev stared across the darkened room at her. Her face was a little obscured by the dim light on that side of the room, but his face was completely illuminated by the light from the hallway.

"So, do I run to the left or to the right when you're fighting?" she asked him.

He remained quiet for a few seconds before responding. "Head left all the way until the end of the hallway. Then go right all the way down that hallway, going up and down the random stairs. After the green door on the right, that's Bolin's room by the way. Actually, knock on Bolin's door and send him over to help me fight the assholes you're running from." He let out a small, amused laugh at the thought.

"After the green door?" she prodded him.

"It's the end of the hallway. There are two doors. One is a locked storage room, the other is the back stairwell. Go down the stairs until you see another green door. There are other doors, but ignore all of them. Just find the green door. That one leads outside and opens to the gardens on the far side of the building. Run to the woods. I'll look for you there after I take out your boogeymen."

"Ok. Goodnight," she said and closed her eyes.

He watched her for a few minutes not certain she would remain quiet or if she'd suddenly want more information. He had told her the way to get out of the building and wondered if he should have. In any case, he continued to be amused by her willingness to sacrifice him for her own escape. He looked over at her, eyes closed, shoes on, no blanket. If she was playing them, she wasn't sparing any details. If she was crazy, she was in deep. If she was neither of those.... He sighed. He sat up slowly and quietly on the edge of his bed and reached around to the foot of his bed and grabbed his boots. He quietly put them on over his bare feet and laced them up. Kali didn't move. She appeared to be asleep already. For his part, he slept on his back with the light from the doorway on his face. He didn't want to turn away from his door and lose seconds getting up if it came to that. It took him a long time to fall asleep and he knew it wasn't the light on his face that kept him awake. It was the thoughts. Kali had his mind spinning.

Plausibility and Confusion for Breakfast

She woke up and looked over at Lev who was still sleeping. She saw that he was wearing his boots and was glad. It meant he listened to her. The cosmos she had placed on his table still looked nice enough and made her smile. She went to the bookshelves and took down the book he had offered her the night before. She leaned back into his large sofa and started to read with the book quite close to her face in the dimly lit room.

After a few hours of reading, she got up quietly and went to the doorway to speak with the guards on duty. They were new people she had not met earlier.

"Can I have food and something to drink?" she whispered to them.

The hallway was not as quiet as it had been overnight. People were entering and leaving their rooms. Most tried not to make eye contact with her as they passed by. She tried to be friendly and smiled at those who she caught looking at her. The female guard snapped, "Keep walking," to a man who slowed down as he walked by. Kali watched as he picked up his pace and didn't look back.

Lev woke up to the sound of Kali talking to the guards and sat up and tried to rub the sleep away from his face.

"Ugh. What's going on?" he asked, standing up ready for anything.

"I asked for some food," Kali offered innocently.

"What time is it?" he asked the guards while turning to lift his curtain and look out his window. He shoved one side of the makeshift curtain aside to look at the sky. By the position of the sun, he guessed he had slept in considerably. He looked at where Kali had spent the night on the couch and saw the book he had offered her the night before. It looked like she had read quite a bit while he slept.

Looking back at her he asked, "You've been up awhile? You're hungry?"

"Yeah. I didn't want to wake you. It's been a few hours."

Lev walked to the doorway and looked down both sides of the hallway ignoring the new guards. "Hey, Chase! Come here a minute."

"Sir?"

"You on your way to breakfast?" he asked him.

"Yes."

"Well, do your thing, but when you're down there ask Marco to have someone bring me two breakfasts."

"Ok, will do."

"Hey, order the breakfasts before getting your own."

"Got it," Chase said and left quickly.

Lev looked over at Kali and said, "I need to make plans for the day, but I can't think just yet." He walked into his bathroom and closed the door and she heard the water come on.

Kali walked over to Lev's bookshelves and looked at what he had collected over the years. She looked at the doorway and couldn't see the two guards she knew were right outside the door. She walked over to the small dining table and pulled out a chair and sat in front of her cosmos. They were actually beginning to look a little tired.

Lev emerged from his bathroom looking wet. His shoulder length hair dripped water onto his shoulders and when he turned around to turn off his bathroom light, she could see the water running from his hair down the back of his shirt. He walked over to the table and pulled out the other chair and sat down. He placed both of his elbows on the table, crossed his arms, and leaned forward on them while looking at her. "So, we'll have some breakfast and talk about what's likely going to happen today when you meet our scientists. Ok? And then I have to take you back to your room. Do not, for fuck's sake, do not ask to stay here in my room," he said with a weary smile that intentionally conveyed humor.

"No, I won't." She laughed back at him. "I was thinking that my friends said I should try to identify a person who I could trust and I think maybe it could be you," she said.

He liked the sound of that but he also didn't want to sound too eager and scare her off. Instead he offered, "I don't know. I mean, I think I'm a pretty trustworthy guy, but I'll also kill you if I have to. I'm kind of committed to the whole killing-to-survive thing. It's the apocalypse vibe. It permeates the air. I've definitely embraced it over the years," he said in a friendly tone.

"Oh, that's ok. I understand that completely. I'd kill you in a second, too, and I didn't even live through the apocalypse," she said enthusiastically.

He closed his eyes briefly, shook his head, and laughed a small laugh while saying, "Ok..."

"So anyway, let me know if you want that responsibility."

"I thought you were only going to speak to scientists," he said warily, getting up to grab some socks from a pile of clothes near his closet.

"Well, yesterday, after I woke up from my mattress nap on the floor, I was thinking about how my friends told me to find people or a person I could trust, and I realized I need to find someone I trust who has some muscles. Some fighting skills. And you know, scientists aren't always known for their murdering skills."

"True," he said, sitting back down in the chair across from her and removing his boots from his bare feet. He continued in a reflective tone. "None of our scientists are part of the brute squad."

"I told you I hid the tech I brought. In my mind, I was thinking I'd take a scientist with me to retrieve it. Or maybe go alone and bring it back once I was sure the people I needed to bring the tech to were here. Now, I'm thinking maybe you or Bolin could go with me to get it and bring it back here." She was looking at him with that inscrutable stare again as she told him things that made his own mind spin.

"You said you hid the tech days from here," he reminded her. "You think Bolin or I can just leave and walk for days to retrieve something you claim exists, but may not because, if I'm being honest, I haven't decided if you're straight up crazy as hell or if you're for real. And then we'd have to walk back. So, be gone from here for what? Eight days?" He looked at her and tipped his head saying, "That's a lot to expect." His socks were on now and he was putting his boots back on and lacing them up.

"Eight days, maybe 10. I don't really know how long it would take to get there and back," she offered, not helping to make her case.

"We could take horses," Lev said, pondering the possible ways to make this happen. Find out if she actually had tech that would help them.

"I'm not going to ride a horse. I don't ride horses. Ever," she said firmly.

He looked at her in disbelief. How could a person spend 17 years after the apocalypse and not ride a horse? "Well, we can't be gone that long, so a horse or two would shorten the trip considerably."

"Then I'll go with Bolin. Can he be gone long enough for walking and not riding fucking horses?" she asked calmly.

"Man, you really don't like horses, do you?" he asked, laughing.

"No. I'm not riding a horse," she said firmly, not laughing along with him.

"You could tell me where you hid the tech and I'll ride and go get it then," he offered, not wanting to lose her good will. The food he had asked to be delivered had arrived and one of the guards interrupted them with the news. "Thanks," Lev said, getting up from the table to take the bowl and the carafe from the guard. Kali moved her cosmos closer to her, and he placed the bowl and the carafe down on the table between them and sat back down.

"Is this coffee?" Kali asked him.

He realized he might lose the flow of their conversation. He wanted to redirect her back to the discussion about retrieving the tech she claimed to have hidden. "Uh, no. This is chicory. No caffeine, but it's a nice substitute. Makes the post apocalypse lifestyle just that much more bearable. So, how about you tell me where you hid the tech, and I'll ride and retrieve it. Then you don't have to ride a horse or walk all the way there and back." Lev poured the hot chicory into the two mugs that had been resting on top of the food in the bowl.

She took the mug he offered her and sipped it with a suspicious expression.

"Mmmm. This is good," she said, taking another sip.

"We could spare a scientist for that length of time. You could go with one of them," he offered, hoping she'd bite back at the offer he expected her to reject. She did.

"Don't be stupid," she said in good humor with a quick shake of her head. "I just told you I want you for your muscles and deadly abilities. I'm not taking off on a potentially dangerous journey with an intellectual." She sipped her fake coffee and reached for a handful of blueberries while smiling at him.

"Hey, now," Lev said with a laugh, "I'm starting to take offense. I'm a pretty decent combination of muscles and smarts."

She laughed with him and waved a hand towards his bookshelves. "I did notice you have an impressive collection of reading material." She added, "You might be well-rounded with some hidden talents I'm not tuned into yet."

"Might be," he agreed. "So, no way around it, someone or some people are going to need to go and retrieve the tech you say you hid. This tech will be of value to our scientists and it relates to time and space travel?"

"Mm-hmm," she said as she chewed her food.

"And yesterday, you mentioned information, as well. Where's that information? Hidden with the tech?" he asked her.

"Yes, and no. There's a book hidden with the tech. Then there's the information that's in my head." She reached for what looked like a piece of meat and held it up to Lev asking, "What's this?"

"Probably deer," he said, grabbing a piece for himself.

"I've never had deer meat," she said and took a bite.

He looked at her and scoffed.

"Doesn't taste like chicken," she said after considering it and kept eating.

"The information in your head, are you going to share it this afternoon when I bring you to meet the scientists?"

"Mostly, no. I'll wait until they have the tech. Things will make more sense that way."

"I'm struggling to figure out how we go about retracing your steps and finding this tech and then bringing it back here. It's a long time for any team member to be gone. My job, I can't just leave for that long unless I have a replacement. Bolin's not going to go with you, but I'll let him know you were willing to travel with him. He'll be touched that you trust him that way." Lev laughed a little and continued. "Bolin's partner was injured the other night in that fight. Hence the overt aggression in your direction when you arrived in our field. He wouldn't want to travel now. I wouldn't ask him to."

Kali sipped her chicory. "I guess that leaves just me as the best option," she said.

"Or just me on a horse." Lev countered.

She shook her head no while surveying which food item to take next from what remained.

"Why not?" asked Lev.

She looked up at him with wide eyes and raised eyebrows and an expression of incredulity. "Because the tech I brought with me is fucking dangerous, man!" she said. She shook her head and looked past him and then back at him again. "Plus, you wouldn't even be able to get it. You have no idea. Fuck it. I'll go alone. I know the way here now." She sat back in her chair with a small piece of a sweet potato and said, "Yeah, I'll leave tomorrow morning and go get the stuff myself. I'll be back in like, I don't know, depending on the weather…. Anywhere from eight to 10 days. Give me a gun or some kind of weapon."

"Ok, ok. No, to the you going alone plan and definitely no to me giving you a weapon. What the hell? Come on, now!" He was amused as he leaned back in his chair, wiped his hands on his pants, and grabbed his cup of chicory.

"I got here by myself. I can go get what I brought and make my way back. I didn't even see any other people on the way here. I thought I'd be in more danger than I was."

"I could send you with like four of my people. Strong people. People I trust," he offered.

"What? And then all those people would know about what I brought and what's going on? That's… That's the worst idea so far. I'd rather go alone. Worse, I'd rather go with a scientist. I reject that idea in its entirety. Clearly you haven't accepted what's going on yet." She looked at him across the table. "That's the problem. You don't believe me yet," she said.

"I'm trying to. If I'm being honest, I want to believe you. But no. I feel like this is going to be a fool's errand and I don't like being made a fool of," he said to her with a hint of resignation in his voice. "Everyone should be back by this afternoon. I'll let them know what's going on, what you're saying, and what you're offering. I'll send for you, and your guards will bring you down to the meeting. You'll get the floor, say your piece, and we'll make a decision about how to proceed. Sound good?" he asked her, sounding hopeful that she would approve.

"Yeah. That all sounds good. Just no horses. And I'm fine going alone. Oh, and I'm not telling anyone how to retrieve it on their own because they can't anyway. We can negotiate my need for a weapon before I head out," she said, looking at him with a playful smirk.

"Not gonna happen," he said, smiling back. "You done eating?" he asked her without trying to sound like he was rushing her.

"Yeah."

"Grab some books if you want to, and your guards will take you back over to your room. Don't forget your cosmos," he said, pointing to them. She picked up her bottle of cosmos and walked over to his couch and picked up the book she was reading and they walked out of his room.

"Take her back to her room. Door stays open, she stays in the room. Kali…" he said, turning to look down at her, "I would appreciate it if you would stay in your room." He nodded his head at her looking for confirmation that this request would not be a problem for her before he returned to get her for the meeting.

"Yeah, yeah. Ok. What if they get back too late to have a meeting?" she asked him suddenly.

"I really think they'll be back today. Most likely before the sun sets. I'll send someone to let you know when they get back if I can't do it myself. It'll be a few hours after they return that I'll send for you. You can put your feet up and read until then. There's nothing to do until they get back." He was using a calm and reassuring voice in anticipation of counterarguments she might present. He felt their dialogue over breakfast had been productive and wanted to send her off to her room trusting him enough to wait for what might be quite a few hours.

"Let's go," one of the new guards said roughly to her while taking her arm equally roughly. Kali tossed her arm away from his grasp and immediately raised her other arm to strike the guard, dropping the book she had been holding in the process. Lev reacted swiftly and grabbed her fighting arm in midair stopping her from striking the guard. These two new guards had not been on duty with her before this morning.

"Hey!" Lev snapped at him. "She's not a prisoner. She's a guest. Treat her like a guest, except for the part where she needs to stay in her room. Door stays open. Got it?"

"Yes. Sorry, Lev." The guard could barely make eye contact with Lev as he realized his mistake.

"She tells me you treated her like a prisoner, you're gonna be sorry," he said sharply, and Kali watched as his face contorted into a menacing glare. His eyes could be so benign and even convey a bit of humor, but they could also show he was a threat waiting for an opportunity. He lowered her fighting arm and looked at her, his eyes losing some, but not all, of their rage. "If any of my guards fuck with you, let me know," he said to her.

"I will."

He picked the book up off of the floor and handed it to her. He watched them walk off down the hallway to the right and he figured she was calculating this second exit strategy after his directions for escape last night. He was right.

Passing the Hours

Kali didn't hold a grudge against the guard who grabbed her, but was fairly certain Lev would. The guard looked agitated and let his partner take a primary position in their walk to her room. Kali calculated the steps from Lev's room to hers and took note of as many details as possible along the way. From the outside, the main building appeared quite large, but she didn't understand its shape. Having had an opportunity to peer through several windows, she still didn't understand the layout of the interior of the building. Why did her hallway end abruptly? It didn't make sense to her. The stairwells were not all located in predictable areas. The building was a bit of a maze. Lev said they were both on the second floor, but there were half staircases between his room and hers. It would have helped if her friends had provided her with the layout of this enormous building.

The door to her room was still open and the mattress was still in the doorway on the floor. She picked it up by one end and dragged it over to the metal bedframe and laid it on top again. Her clothes were on the table with her backpack and its contents still displayed on the table. She walked to the door and told her guards she wanted to take a shower. The one who had grabbed her arm asked if she needed soap or a towel. He was clearly trying to make up with her and treat her like a guest. "Yes, I'll need a towel, but I have my own soap," she said to him. He told the other guard he'd be right back and headed out of view.

She grabbed her small bottle of hotel shampoo from the table and walked into the bathroom and removed her bra from under the black t-shirt she had been wearing since the night she'd spent at the apartment in back of the gas station. She hand washed her bra under the running water using her shampoo sparingly. She emerged from the bathroom and looked at the large window above the twin bed. She wanted to hang the wet bra in the sunny window and let the sun and warm air dry it, but she couldn't see how she would hang it from the cement walls. Lev's window had a curtain or a sheet hanging from it somehow, but the window was framed by cement cinder blocks of which the entire building appeared to be constructed.

She called to the remaining guard and asked, "Hey, can you come in here for a minute? I need some help."

The guard appeared in her doorway immediately and asked, "What do you need?" She looked at Kali standing on the mattress holding a dripping wet bra in one hand with her other hand steadying herself by leaning on the wall.

"I washed my bra, and I want to hang it here in front of this open window to dry, but I can't find a way to hang it," she said to the guard. "What's your name?" she asked suddenly, interrupting the guard just as she was about to speak.

"My name's Ju. I hang mine like this," she said as she walked over to the bed and climbed up alongside Kali. "Use the corner of the open window and wrap the strap tightly over the edge here…. And make sure it's jammed in there good because no screens means if it falls, it either lands in the room, or on the ground outside. The breeze will help dry it, but it will also loosen it and might make it fall." She paused to consider what she had said and added, "Unless you have a rooftop under this window?" Ju peered outside the open window and saw the top of one of the first floor roofs. "Ok, so if this falls, we'll have to go downstairs and climb out the window of the room below yours to get it off the other rooftop." She looked at Kali.

"This building is shaped weirdly, isn't it?" Kali asked her.

"Oh, it's like an Escher drawing!" Ju exclaimed in enthusiastic agreement. "Took me months to figure it out. I don't know who the architect was, but he or she was a little crazy bringing this into reality." Ju was smiling while talking to Kali and focused on jamming Kali's bra strap tightly into the sliding space at the top of the window. "I think it's secure, but if you look over and it's gone, don't worry. We can get it back."

Kali liked Ju. She raised a hand for a high five and Ju obliged.

"What did you use to wash it? It smells really good," Ju asked her.

"Some shampoo I have," Kali said.

"Wow. Most everything expired years ago. You got lucky. James makes really good castile soaps, but the smell of yours reminds me of twenty years ago."

"Who's James?"

"Oh, never mind. I know we're supposed to treat you like a guest, but naming names probably isn't something I should be doing."

"Ok," said Kali, curious, but not offended by Ju's reluctance to reveal more about the post apocalypse soap maker.

As they went to get off the bed, they noticed the first guard standing in the doorway with a towel for Kali.

"Here's your towel," he said but remained standing in the doorway with his arm outstretched waiting for Kali or Ju to come take it from him. They got off the bed and Kali walked over and took the towel from his outstretched arm. She thanked him but she didn't ask him his name. Kali decided he was really out of place as a guard. He didn't have the requisite social skills to be a successful guard. She would know. She had had plenty of guards over many years. He was harmless, but he wasn't guard material. She walked into the bathroom leaving the door wide open and turned on the water. She was undressing when she heard Ju tell her partner to stand on the other side of the door to give Kali privacy. Kali hoped she wouldn't have to kill Ju at some point. She really liked her friendly personality.

She washed her hair and body properly, not as she had done outside in the rain a few days earlier. She didn't use a lot of her hotel shampoo and conditioner, but was happy to learn some guy named James was able to make soap for the people who lived here. The shower ended as the warm water began to run cold. She exited the shower and dried off. She hung the damp towel over the top of the open bathroom door and walked through the room to the table and picked up the jeans that had no tears in them, one of the black shirts, a pair of black socks, and the hairbrush and toothbrush. She walked over to the bed and dropped the handful of clean clothes and the brushes on top of the mattress and got dressed with her back to the door. She couldn't see her guards, but she didn't care if either of them saw her body. She was used to having no privacy. She didn't say anything to her guards and they didn't say anything to her. She went back into the bathroom and brushed her hair and teeth. She gathered her dirty clothes off of the floor and washed them in the small bathroom sink one at a time using a small amount of her shampoo. She hung them on the shower head and the knobs in the shower stall not caring how long they took to dry. She'd like her bra to dry in time for the meeting though. She had gotten plenty of sleep the day before during her hours long nap and then when she slept in Lev's room last night, too. She wasn't tired. She sat at the table and read from the book she'd brought with her from Lev's room.

She had been reading for a while when Ju tapped on the door frame to get her attention. Kali looked up from her book and Ju said, "Hey, we're taking off. Thing One and Thing Two are going to take over from us. It's after lunch time. I'm headed down to eat. Can I bring you up something when I'm done?" she asked her.

Kali had been deep into the story she'd been reading and felt like she was waking to a new world while Ju was speaking to her. "Sure. I'd like anything you want to bring me," she said, smiling.

"Ok, I'll see you in a bit. Oh, I see you haven't lost your bra." She smiled and pointed to the open window.

Kali turned around to confirm the continued presence of her bra and said, "Good. I didn't want to go on a rooftop rescue mission for it anyway."

Ju left and Kali stood up and stretched. She walked over to meet her new guards. She recognized one from yesterday. "Bautista?" she asked him.

"Yep, that's me. How you doing this morning?" he asked her.

"Fine. Been reading. I might start getting bored, though."

"Nah, you'll probably stay entertained and happy until my shift is over," he said, laughing at her.

She laughed, too. She didn't want to ask him if their scientists had returned. She didn't want to engage anyone other than Lev or Bolin in her quest for information. She had noticed when Bolin had stopped his people from approaching them out in the field the day before. When she had mentioned time and space travel, he'd held up his fist and stopped their approach. So had Lev. It made her think she shouldn't say anything. Neither man had told her not to say anything, but she had made it clear to them that she didn't want them to talk about why she was here except with their scientists. She wasn't certain where their secrets and hers collided, if at all.

"Have you seen Lev or Bolin today?" she asked him.

"No, I was out in the field earlier and came back, ate, and headed up here after another guy was pulled. I heard Lev didn't want him on duty with you. I was requested. You might be a little bit of trouble, hey?" he asked her, chuckling in a friendly way.

"Well, I mean, not on purpose. And even if a little on purpose, it's likely I'm just having fun. I'm still learning your customs. I haven't caused any problems today," she said, laughing.

"Yet," Bautista laughed. "There's still time!" he added as Kali nodded in agreement.

The other guard remained silent and didn't try to join in their discussion.

"Well, I'm just going to keep reading for now," she said, turning to walk back to the table and her book.

"Whatcha reading?" Bautista asked her.

"The book about the rabbits," she said as she picked it up and showed him the front cover.

"Oh, yeah? I heard about that one. Never read it. It must be good. I feel like I'm the only person who hasn't read it yet. Can I borrow it when you're finished?" he asked her.

"It's Lev's book. I'm borrowing it from him. I'll ask him if I can pass it along to you when I'm finished." She heard the second, nameless guard scoff and mutter a quiet, "Jesus."

Kali couldn't see her where she was standing outside the door against the hallway wall, but she definitely heard her. She stopped smiling and tipped her head and looked at Bautista who was standing in the doorway as he shook his head in frustration at the guard Kali couldn't see.

He snapped at her. "Jesus what, Tracy?" He turned back to Kali. "Ignore her. You know what? Enjoy the book, but don't bother Lev with lending it to me. I'll make it an adventure and try to find another copy on my own. Just don't mention to him that I want to borrow his things. It doesn't work that way here. Ok? You catch my drift? Learning our customs?" he asked, laughing knowingly.

Kali understood. There was a hierarchy and Lev was at the top and Bautista was somewhere beneath Lev. "No, I won't mention it to him. I get it. I'll keep an eye out for a copy for you, too. In fact, I'll bet I can find you a copy before you can find yourself one."

"Yeah, ok," Bautista said and waved her off in a friendly manner as he departed the doorway heading towards the opposite side of the wall along the hallway.

"No, I'm serious," Kali said with a voice that pulled him back into her line of sight. "I'm going to look for a copy of this book for you. You have to look, too.

Whoever finds a copy for you first wins."

He filled in the open door frame with his large body and pointed out the obvious with a mild laugh. "Sounds like I'll win either way because I'll end up with a book."

"Sure, you can think of it that way, but I'm going to find a copy of the book for you before you do. I'm gonna win," she laughed and added, "I'm laughing, but I'm serious."

"What do you win if you find a copy of the book for me before I do?" he asked, smiling.

"Satisfaction."

"Are you going to be pissed off if I find a copy first?" he asked her, feeling just a little worried.

"No! I'll be amazed though. I'm really good at finding stuff."

"I guess I really can't lose, so it's a bet," he said with a smile and a shrug.

"You won't lose, but I'm going to win," she said confidently, and opened the book and started reading again.

Lev left his room after Kali had departed with her guards and did his mandatory time on the farm as everyone who wanted to eat was expected to do. He spent an extra hour working in the garden and then cleaning animal enclosures before writing the letter K by his name indicating her meals, as well as his, were paid for on this day through his manual labor. He made two additional water trips just to be sure no one would question the meals she was receiving. There were plenty of community members in the field today earning their meals after yesterday when so much time and energy had been spent cleaning up from the fight and sleeping off injuries. They all saw him earning Kali's meals.

Generally speaking, a guest could stay without contributing for three days. This was day two for her. Prisoners got one small meal at the end of a day if there were leftovers. Prisoners could go days without eating. They got water, though. He knew Bolin was going to have to add James' shift to his own on the fifth day of his recovery. Sick and injured community members had five days to recover before someone had to take over their essential labor. You didn't have to work the farm every day of the week, but a minimum of three times a week for an hour each time was required. Any more time than that, you were likely an assigned farmer working for James. Keeping a farm this large running smoothly required all hands involved. Ivy had never gone hungry under Lev's system. Before Lev had arrived, they had had a couple of rough seasons. There were a lot of problems at Ivy before Lev arrived, but Lev's Campus community was well run. Lev didn't allow chaos. He ran a tight ship. The world was chaotic enough.

Bolin Meets Lev

James and Bolin had found Ivy four years after the extinction event. Bolin described the way the place was run at that time as success by pure luck, failure by ineptitude. He and James had spent seven years at Ivy before Lev moved in and became a permanent resident, but they knew each other well before Lev moved in. There were a lot of adults and even more small children at Ivy back then, but it wasn't a family atmosphere. James and Bolin were on their way out, ready to leave Ivy due to the lack of cooperation from the community to work the fields and participate in producing better outcomes. Bolin said it hadn't begun that way.

When they'd arrived, the community was small with no more than 30 people. It was being led by a group of self-identified environmentalists who claimed they were looking for possible natural causes for the death of so many during the extinction event. They were welcomed into the small community, and James was quickly put in charge of all of the farming responsibilities and found he had some good people to work with. Bolin was put in charge of security and infrastructure and met Lev as a result of his role. They worked out some friendly trade agreements between the two communities right away as Bolin decided Campus was an undeniably valuable resource to Ivy. His former military training informed his decision to seek out a friendly relationship with Ivy's more powerful neighbor. That was also how James finally got his bees.

Bolin and Lev built their relationship around their shared disdain for disorder. Each man considered the other dependable. Lev understood Bolin wanted stability for himself and James. Bolin understood Lev wanted a thriving community with no bullshit. Lev also wanted the neighboring community of Ivy to be free of bullshit that might impact Campus. He had largely ignored Ivy and their very small community until Bolin had moved in. Ivy's community numbers were slowly increasing and, to Lev, Bolin appeared interested in establishing a better dialogue between the two communities.

Bolin didn't see a reason not to inform Lev about the environmentalists who had started the Ivy community. He told Lev they believed something in nature had caused the extinction event. Lev didn't have a problem entertaining Bolin's enthusiasm for the conclusion the environmentalists were seeking, but he shrugged and said he believed it was something else.

Their relationship was initially transactional, but Lev enjoyed doing business with Bolin, as well as enjoyed their conversations, and grew to respect him. Bolin found Lev to be committed to a thriving type of survival rather than just being a psychotic killing machine like the rumors and body count over the years suggested. It was a fine line, but Bolin appreciated the distinction. He had been to war zones while in the military. Bolin also appreciated the protection Lev's Campus community provided Ivy. Roughly five miles separated the two communities. They could go months between communicating with one another, but they could also make contact whenever either needed something from the other.

James' farming methods improved crop yields and everything at Ivy was running smoothly for a couple of years. Their community numbers increased to 42 which paled in comparison to Lev's community which contained more than 200 members. But then a moderately sized band of 17 travelers arrived around their fourth year at Ivy. Bolin understood they were only passing through and needed a place to rest on their way north. He accommodated their request as he usually did for travelers who sought a night or two of food and rest on the way through to other locations. Travelers were not entirely uncommon but a group this size was unusual. They only usually entertained travelers in numbers of one or two. Bolin described them as a traveling community, not just travelers. In any case, the occasion provided James with an opportunity to cook for a large, hungry crowd of guests.

The leader of the travelers was a religious woman named Moira who was on an intense campaign to promote her idea of rebuilding society by devotion to God and supplying the earth with as many babies as possible. 'Be fruitful and multiply,' was her favorite sermon theme. On their first night at Ivy, she rose to speak at the dinner James had prepared for them and for the rest of the Ivy community, and she didn't stop speaking for an hour. The display was uncomfortable for many Ivy community members, but Bolin noticed a few approach Moira after dinner. He wondered if Ivy would lose a few people to Moira when she and her group left the next day. If only that had been the case.

Over the course of the next few days, Moira found reasons for why her group could not depart Ivy just yet. Instead, Moira appealed to many within the Ivy community to allow her group to stay and become a part of Ivy. She quickly won over a few members at Ivy for whom her brand of zeal appealed, and a meeting between Bolin and the environmentalists led to a decision to give Moira and her group time to assimilate. Bolin didn't like the 'wait and see' approach, believing that he'd seen enough, but a case was made for growing their community and allowing different voices to be heard by some of the others in the meeting, so he relented.

According to James' interpretation of events, things had been going really well at Ivy since he and Bolin had come along. The farm was producing more than enough to sustain them and to trade with Lev's community, the animals they'd collected were healthy. They had bees, thanks to Lev, and a reliable irrigation system thanks to Bolin which saw them through the hot days of summer. Bolin's skills as a civil engineer had been put to good use throughout the compound. They had built their first greenhouse into the side of an embankment they'd dug and had plans for a second one. They had two root cellars and James was fermenting wine. Bolin would whisper that James was fermenting everything during that time, and James would laugh and own it.

But James also blamed their successes in providing for the community members at Ivy for the growing complacency that began to take hold in the residents of the well-run, well-fed community. According to James, the lack of daily challenges and the lack of a constant threat of death after their first few harrowing years as survivors, increased the susceptibility of some people to the charismatic Moira and her brand of supernatural divine assistance in their quest for survival.

Bolin had a slightly different take on events. Bolin described what followed as a full-on takeover by a cult with a deranged religious leader who started to feed on the fears and hopes of people tired of living through a post-apocalyptic society. Moira continued to preach to her followers that if they wanted to have blessed lives, they would need to bring new life into the dying world. Every good harvest was taken as a sign from God that they were righteous in their quest to repopulate the earth because more food meant they could feed their growing population.

But it didn't actually work that way. More babies were born and more mouths needed feeding while less workers were available to feed the increasing population. Childbirth might be a natural process of the female body, but it also takes a toll on one, too, and no one at Ivy had medical training. Women and children died in surprising numbers, but Moira convinced her followers that they had to have faith and produce more offspring. People needed to be available to care for the babies and small children that threatened to outnumber the adults. Some parents found it all too much trying to survive while caring for their children and simply left in the middle of the night leaving their babies and toddlers behind.

Nearly three years after Moira's arrival, the community had an uncomfortable amount of parentless small children and babies and an emboldened, or possibly desperate, group of men who were organizing to find more women to care for their children and continue to repopulate God's creation. One evening, Bolin stood out of sight at a meeting being held by Moira and listened as the fervor for a need to bring in new female members escalated. They talked about kidnapping women and girls on a mission planned for the following week. They would avoid Lev's community and described Campus as a Hell they would one day overtake with their own numbers. He heard Moira as she claimed God approved of their plans. He quietly walked away from where he had been secretly listening in to the meeting. He needed to consult with James before making a final decision about how to proceed. James told Bolin he'd had enough after hearing about the details of the meeting Bolin had listened in on that evening. In addition he, himself, had experienced too many unrealistic demands to produce crops for the entire community which community members weren't, themselves, willing to help cultivate throughout the unusually dry summer season. Not even their irrigation system built by Bolin could help overcome the lack of people willing to participate in maintaining the gardens. James assured Bolin that Ivy would barely have enough food in their root cellars to last through the winter even before adding kidnapped women and girls to the community. He explained to Bolin that fall crops were not even being prepared as they already should have been if they expected to have an adequate fall harvest. He told Bolin that he believed a lot of people were going to starve this winter at Ivy and that it would be safer for them if they left sooner rather than later even though Ivy had once held so much promise for them to live a good, stable life together. Bolin had heard all he needed to hear.

Lev had been working with Bolin for years when Bolin approached him the following morning and asked if he and James could join Campus. Lev was surprised to see Bolin at that early hour at his door, but not surprised when Bolin skipped past all customary pleasantries and simply requested his small family be permitted to join Campus. At this point, he and James had taken in an abandoned baby girl they'd named Meabh after James' mother. Meabh's own mother had died in childbirth and no men claimed to be her father, although it was well known who her father actually was. Lev asked Bolin to elaborate on the reasons he and James wanted to leave Ivy and Bolin explained to Lev that he and James felt the environment at Ivy had irretrievably deteriorated beyond what was acceptable to either. He told Lev about the men in the community suddenly discussing plans to abduct females for procreation, assuring Lev that they intended to avoid Campus in their upcoming quest for women. He spared no details and told Lev how Moira had described Campus as a Hell on earth which they planned to one day address. In any case, it was certainly no place to raise their daughter.

Lev wasn't opposed to the idea of Bolin and his family moving over to Campus. He already knew he liked Bolin and James, and he knew both would bring valuable skills, but he questioned Bolin asking him, "Who the fuck is in charge at Ivy?" He'd thought it was Bolin, but Bolin surprised him by describing Ivy as being run by the elusive environmentalists who barely associated with the community. "I'm in charge until an important or difficult decision has to be made. They agree to a meeting at my request, listen to me present the issue, then overrule what I believe will be the best solution. They might even fight for weeks between themselves fighting to be the one whose solution is implemented. It was fine while the issues were small. I could work around their dysfunction. But Moira's a big problem. The environmentalists can't or won't deal with her. I can't do it on my own."

Bolin also explained to Lev that once the community numbers had grown, the environmentalists didn't help farm or produce food. They believed the work they were doing was more important than tending to crops or infrastructure maintenance. They expected community members to do the labor. They didn't care about Moira and her expanding cult that was now plotting ways to bring in women any way they could.

What he described made Lev laugh at him and slap him on the back. "Man, I thought you were in charge!"

"I am as much as they allow me to be." Bolin explained he was more into building up the infrastructure of the larger facility. The repairs to the windmills, the construction of greenhouses, and irrigation systems. Lev respected that. But Lev was more interested in the anti-social, work-averse environmentalists that Bolin had told him about. "What are they up to?" Lev wanted to know. Bolin wasn't entirely certain.

Lev offered, "How about I help you get rid of your cult and you show me where your environmentalists are holed up?"

Bolin knew that by aligning with Lev, he was taking a chance that Ivy would be up for grabs. He made no attempt to hide what he was thinking. A man like Lev would either respect you for your candor and work with you, or show you respect you for your candor by killing you quickly. He decided he was willing to take a chance with Lev and told him, "I don't want to run Ivy. I just want the cult members out. If I had my way, James and I would stay at Ivy with Meabh. We would be happy to move to Campus, and I appreciate you saying we'd be allowed to, but we would prefer to stay at Ivy where we've both put in a lot of effort to make it a good place to live. There are a few good people there that feel the same way, and the environmentalists are negligent in running the place, but they seem to know a lot about the facility and seem committed to whatever it is they spend so much time working on. I think they're just… really smart people with no discernable people skills."

"Well, let's go rid you of your cult first and then go have a word with your environmentalists second," Lev had said to him. "Decide where you want to live after we do that, huh?" Lev asked him.

"Yes," Bolin agreed.

For better or for worse, their deal was struck. Bolin never denied he knew what the outcome would be by striking the deal with Lev. He'd discussed his concerns with James and had gotten his approval before speaking with him. It wasn't so much that Bolin had made a deal with the devil as it was that a deal had been made between two devils- Bolin and Lev. James had told him, "When the world's on fire, it's the devils who survive." He wasn't wrong.

The Scientists

Lev finished his and Kali's farm work and went back to his room to clean up. The sheet Kali had slept on was still on his couch, and he decided to leave it there for now. He washed away the dirt and sweat from his body under a quick shower and changed into clean clothes. He tossed his dirty clothes into the hallway on top of his muddy sheets from the day before. He'd get to his laundry later. His team had duty for the next six hour shift, but he needed to speak with Bolin before that began. Finding Bolin wasn't usually difficult. He was either wherever James was, on the field somewhere, in his room at the compound, or at the small house he'd built for himself, James, and Meabh.

The five room house sat to the far left of the grazing fields and provided space for James and Bolin to be parents to Meabh. There were two tire swings hanging from a tree near their house and, of course, Bolin had built his daughter an elaborate tree house in that same tree which Lev called Meabh's Mansion. Meabh was the only child living at Ivy, but she had frequent visits from her friends at Campus. Campus had a few children, most of whom were children who had been spared when Lev and Bolin drove out Moira and her cult. Meabh was also considered family by Aisha, Bob, and their son Otis who was a year older than Meabh.

The route between Campus and Ivy was well worn now with the two communities basically operating as one giant organism at this point. Everyone knew Lev was still the leader of Campus, but he chose to live at Ivy and be their Head of Security. Aisha was his second at Campus and in charge of daily activities at Campus.

Generally, Bolin worked steady six hour evening shifts with his security team and kept a fairly consistent family life routine with James who worked mornings and afternoons overseeing the entire food cycle for the community. But sometimes, events occurred which disrupted schedules. Events such as their compound being attacked. Then Bolin's shifts would become round-the-clock temporarily. Having a room at the main facility made it easier for him to sleep when he could and not disrupt James and Meabh. In general, James and Bolin shared parenting duties equally, but with James injured and Bolin having his schedule made unpredictable for a couple of days, Bolin had sent Meabh over to Campus to stay with Aisha and Bob. Lev went down to medical to see if Bolin was with James before looking for him elsewhere. Even if he wasn't there, James might know where to find him.

James was standing in medical talking to Santi, or Doc, as only Lev ever referred to her. "Lev, it's about time you visited me," James said, pretending to be insulted.

"I was here before Bolin was, but you were sleeping." Lev informed him proudly.

James laughed and instantly winced from the pain laughing caused his broken ribs.

"Ugh! That's painful. You looking for Bolin? Because he left about thirty minutes ago for the farm," James said to him.

"Yeah, I am. I was just out there. Must have passed each other. Hey, Doc. How's the patient?" he asked Santi.

Santi looked at James with a confident expression and spoke to Lev while still looking at James saying, "Sending him back to his place to finish recuperating right now, but he's being an asshole about orders to rest and not returning to the gardens, or tending to his animals, and you know, the kitchen, and... all the rest." She turned to look at Lev and her expression was an appeal to his authority.

Lev looked away from Santi and over at James saying, "Man, you listen to Doc and go home and fucking rest until she tells you you're cleared. I catch you anywhere you're not supposed to be, I'm sending you to Aisha's to let her mother you until you're better. Yeah?"

"Fine. Fine!" James said, throwing his one good arm up in the air, exasperated at being ganged up on by the two of them. The movement caused him to wince again and he said defiantly, "I'll go and fucking rest and die of fucking boredom."

"You need the rest!" Santi scolded him. "You need time to heal. You're going to prolong the healing process if you do too much too soon. In a week, you're going to be significantly better if you take it easy for now. Probably need two weeks before I'd suggest bringing Meabh back, though. Get those ribs settled, give your nose time to lose some of that swelling. Your arm's going to take a couple of months. Just do what I say, especially when it comes to your arm or you're going to have serious regrets," she scolded him angrily.

"Ok, I'll do what you say! Now, come here and give me a careful hug. You're mad at me, and I can't have that. We need to make up," he said, leaning in to get a hug from Santi.

Santi's shoulders relaxed and she obliged James with a hug. The two of them came from completely different backgrounds and practiced different professions, but they had formed a sibling bond underscored by genuine concern for one another.

Lev asked James if he needed help walking back to his house, and he said 'no' at the same time Santi said 'yes,' so Lev left with James and walked him across the expansive grounds and gardens over to his front door.

Lev had hoped to meet Bolin along the way, but he was nowhere to be found. Lev and James chatted during the walk and Lev reminded James to 'stay in the goddamned tower with Meabh' the next time the facility was attacked. James defended himself by explaining he was already on the field talking to Eymen when they were ambushed.

"I can fight, you know?" James said, slightly annoyed that his injuries suggested otherwise.

"I know you can. Just, you're important in other ways, and then there's Meabh. Bolin's already security. Both of her parents can't be on the field at once. For now, at least until she's older. You know, just head to your tower. Or maybe you can run her there and join future fights. I don't know. Talk it over with Bolin. I'm not opposed to you being on the field as soon as you're healed. We can always use more fighters on the field. Actually, I'm staying out of this. You and Bolin talk it over. I'm certainly not ordering you onto a security detail, though."

James seemed to appreciate Lev's suggestion and patted him on the arm, assuring him he planned to talk over his role in defending Ivy from raiders with Bolin.

They arrived at his house and James said, "Ah, thanks, Lev. That was more difficult than I thought it would be. Ribs, eh? Jesus, broken ribs hurt. We need Bolin to lay some smooth sidewalks throughout this place."

"Yeah, I'll leave it to you to tell him he needs to pave the grounds." Lev laughed as he waved and headed back out to find Bolin. "Tell him I'm looking for him if he shows up!" Lev said as he departed.

Bolin was talking to the recovering Maren in the cafeteria when Lev finally spotted him. He ended his conversation with Maren as soon as he saw Lev approaching him, recognizing the look on his face as one that implied there might be a problem.

"Outside?" Bolin asked him, wanting to suggest a private space to hear what Lev had to tell him.

"Yeah," Lev said, and the two men walked quickly out of the nearest doors and headed into the back fields.

"What is it?" Bolin asked him pensively. He steeled himself for whatever Lev was about to tell him. Lev launched right into the conversation after having been thinking about it since his conversation with Kali earlier in the morning.

"She's getting to me, man. I don't know if it's because I want to believe her, or if she's telling me things I honestly believe are plausible."

Bolin looked like he was about to say something, but Lev held up his hand to stop him.

"No, I gotta say all this or I'm gonna forget a detail. She says the tech that she brought is hidden about five days from here. But I don't trust she knows how far away she hid it. You know, assuming she actually had tech and actually hid it. Anyway, the number of days she said she walked fluctuates by a day or two. I've decided to call it five days to split the difference. She said she wants to go back by herself and get the tech and bring it back to Ivy now that she knows we have the scientists she says she was sent to find. Or, she wants one of us to go with her to retrieve the tech. Me or you. She said she'd go with either of us. She says she's decided to trust me and you, no one else. How about that, huh? She trusts you. And she refused to go on horseback. I'm telling you now to save you the effort later. She won't be convinced to take a horse. She refused to take a team. She refused to go with a science nerd. She says the tech is dangerous. She wants a weapon for the trek if she goes alone. Did you notice the scars on her arms yesterday?" he asked Bolin suddenly.

"Yes," Bolin said with a look of concern.

"Those are bite marks, aren't they?" Lev asked him.

"That's what they looked like to me," Bolin agreed, sighing.

Lev continued, "That's fucked up, right? So, I see that, and I'm not about to ask any questions, but I have to wonder if she's just out of her fucking mind from some other shit she's been through."

"Definitely could be," agreed Bolin.

Lev looked around the field as both men stood without saying anything. He was clearly agitated and Bolin gave him time to say what was on his mind.

"Did I ever tell you my mother was a hairdresser?"

"No. I didn't know that," Bolin said to him.

"Out in the field yesterday, I noticed something about her hair. It was when she decided she was going to go wait under the tree where she'd seen the dead raider. I was standing next to her, trying to negotiate with her to get her to come inside, and I'm taller than her, so I could see the top of her head. I could see how blonde her hair is compared to the roots coming in. I spent a lot of time in a salon after school, you know, doing my homework while my mother worked. I know a surprising amount about goddamned hair that I shouldn't know. I know what her hair looked like to me. It looked like she had her hair bleached about five fucking weeks ago, man. How?" He stopped talking and looked at Bolin demanding an answer to his question.

"I don't know anything about hair. Asians, you know? We generally don't color our hair. But could it be lightened from the sun? Being outdoors?" he asked Lev.

"No. No fucking way. Her hair was "processed,"" he said, putting the word 'processed' in air quotes. "That's a fucking salon term I'm dragging out from my childhood memories now because I know what I saw. How does she have bleached hair? I saw the fucking roots."

"You want to go with her to look for the tech she claims exists based on the roots of her hair. That's what I'm hearing from you right now. That's five days there and five days back. You might get to where she claims she's hidden this tech and discover there's no tech and she's absolutely fucking crazy. She might hand you some silverware and say, 'Hey, here's the tech I told you about.'"

"Yeah, I know! I know! But tell me this. What has the RT been working on all these years? Why do we keep it a secret? Why go through this in our own little bubble and when Kali shows up, dismiss her?" Lev asked him.

"Maybe because she's come across as a little fucking nuts so far. Is she a scientist?" Bolin asked him.

"You heard her. She said she's not," Lev said, looking at him.

"And she's not a mathematician," Bolin said to him.

"No, but she's calculating all the fucking time," Lev said, raising his eyebrow and scoffing.

"What was she before the extinction event?"

"I don't know," Lev admitted.

"And yet, you believe there's a possibility she might be telling the truth? Enough of a possibility that you want one of us to walk, not ride horses, for five days from here, possibly find technology she brought from the future, and then walk, not ride horses, five days back here?" Bolin asked him.

"Yeah."

"Ok, I'll go with her if you want me to. Just say so. Are you asking me to go with her? I'm really uncomfortable with her being armed for this, though." He put his hands on his hips and laughed while shaking his head.

Lev shook his head and laughed, too. "No. I'm not asking you to go with her. I'm thinking I should go with her. She's fucking difficult even when she's being agreeable. But I'd need you to take over as Head of Security while I'm gone. And I'm thinking Williams can take over my team while I'm gone. You know I've been training him to run a fifth team anyway. This would let me know his strengths and weaknesses before I actually hand him a team. Also...." Lev sighed with annoyance before continuing. "Where the hell are Heather and the others?"

"Oh, I saw them arrive before I hit the cafeteria. They're back. They had a shitload of tech being dragged by their horses and were also all wearing heavy looking packs on their own backs. I told Heather we have a guest and that you needed to have a meeting with the team. She asked for more details, but I said I was leaving those to you."

"Ok. That's good. Jesus, they were gone a long time. Was it a full three weeks? I lost track. When their rider got here yesterday and said they were resting at Campus overnight, I was a little concerned because Kali isn't the most patient person I've ever dealt with. I had hoped they would get back by noon, but looks like the meeting with Kali will be around sunset. I'd actually better stop by her room and let her know. I think staying in more frequent contact with her makes her less unpredictable."

"Yes. Heather mentioned that Aisha told them to stay with her until this afternoon to give us time to get Ivy straightened out. I kind of appreciated that. Who needs Heather and her crew walking around pretending they almost died in the attack despite being safe in the tower?" Bolin laughed sarcastically.

"I hope the trip they went on to find tech and hardware was worth it," Lev said.

"I wonder if they made it all the way to William and Mary," Bolin said as the two men began walking back to the main building.

"I was told the goal was Norfolk to look for anything useful that might still be laying around on the navy bases," Lev said.

"I thought they were going to the college campuses around Richmond and if they didn't find anything useful, they'd head down to William and Mary in Williamsburg. I mean, I never expected Heather to be that ambitious. That's a hell of a trip even with horses. It's good your people at Campus went along with them."

"My team picked Richmond apart years ago, so I kind of think they would have had to go down to at least Williamsburg, but I'm hoping they went as far as Norfolk. I was in Norfolk sometime during the second year, but I wouldn't have known all to collect back then."

"Would you now?" laughed Bolin.

"Well, Heather is the boss and says she knows what she needs, so I guess it had to be her." Lev agreed. "I hope she had fun." He added coldly.

As they approached the building Lev said, "I'm gonna go tell Kali they're here. Then I'm going to find out when Heather and the team will be ready for the security debrief. I'll tell them about the raiders and Kali, and once the debrief is over, I'll send for you and Kali. You'll need to put someone from your team in charge in case you don't make it back in time for duty. Same for me. I need to find Williams, actually. I'm supposed to be out there, maybe now, I'm not even sure to be honest. I don't know what time it is anymore. Williams is about to get used until he drops. Any questions?" Lev asked him.

"Yes. I want to be clear. You think the meeting with Kali will go on so long that it will cut into my shift?" Bolin asked.

"Yeah, it could. I have no fucking idea. You're covering for Candace today, right?" Bolin nodded. "You should be there for the entire meeting with Kali, though. I'm not about to predict how that will go. I don't know if she'll continue to be evasive, making getting information from her take longer than it should, or what. Maybe she'll refuse to talk. Also, I want you there because I want to make a plan to go get her potential tech. If we all agree I'm going to do this, I want to leave tomorrow morning, so you need to be there to agree to that and take over as Head of Security while I'm gone."

"Ok, yes. That makes sense. That could take a while. You think it's necessary to leave tomorrow?" Bolin asked him as they walked through the cafeteria.

"Yeah. I'm positive if I don't go with Kali immediately, she'll climb out a window when we're all sleeping and go by herself," he said with a laugh.

Bolin looked at Lev without envy for his situation. "Why don't I go tell your team you're in a meeting and Williams is in charge? You go deal with Kali before she detonates. Yes?" Bolin asked him.

"That would be great, man," Lev said and started jogging towards Kali's room on the second floor.

Lev walked up to Kali's room and motioned silently to her guards asking if everything was alright. One nodded and said Kali was still reading quietly. The other guard, who he recognized as Bautista, shook his head no and motioned to Lev that he wanted to discuss what was concerning him at the bottom of the stairs out of Kali's hearing.

Lev walked with Bautista to the bottom of the stairs and said, "What? Just tell me." His tone was less impatient as it was resigned to deal with whatever problems had built up in the time he had left her waiting.

"She's not reading. She's had the book open to the same page for hours. She's sitting there... Like a ticking time bomb is all I can think," he said, trying to convince Lev he should be concerned.

Lev didn't need convincing. "Ok. I needed to know that," he said.

He took a deep breath and stood quietly for a minute before turning and heading back up to Kali's room. Bautista followed him. Lev reached his hand in to tap on her open door, but she had heard him arrive and was already sitting at the table with the book on the table, looking up at him from where she was sitting.

"Hi. Are they back?" she asked him.

Lev turned to the guards and told them to go wait at the bottom of the stairs. He didn't want them listening to his conversation with Kali. He walked into the room and pulled out the chair he had been sitting in the day before.

"Yeah, they got back a little while ago. I'm going to see about having a meeting with them now. I need to talk with them first. I don't know how long that will take. After I have a meeting with them first, I'm going to send someone to have your guards bring you down to meet with them. I want you to know that I've spoken with Bolin about the various ways in which you could go get that tech you say you've hidden to bring it back here, and he and I agreed that I'll go with you to get it. No horses. We'll walk. You'll be unarmed. Does that sound good to you?" he asked her.

"When would we leave?" she asked him.

"Tomorrow morning. If that works for you." He'd added the 'if that works for you' part as an afterthought because he believed he'd picked up on her disdain for being told what to do yesterday during her interactions with Bolin. If he'd said to her, *'You will go with me tomorrow morning,'* he imagined she'd have said, *'Fuck you! The hell I will!'* even if she really wanted to go at exactly that time. Anyway, it was a tactic he was experimenting with when it came to interacting with her. He felt he was having some success with it.

"Yeah. Let's do this," she said with no real enthusiasm.

He considered that tomorrow morning was a long way away for her to contemplate and that she wanted to go to the meeting with the scientists.

"We'll have this meeting soon. Ok?" he said to her. "To be clear, I'm going to have a meeting with them first. I don't know how long it will take, but I'm definitely going to send for you eventually. It'll happen today. If you feel like you're waiting a long time, don't start getting antsy and trick your guards into taking you to my room or to find the meeting. Your guards might not even know where the meeting is being held. Whoever I send to go get you for your meeting, won't be able to find you and it will take longer to get you there. Understand?" he asked her in an effort to preempt any problems she might create.

"Yeah," she said flatly.

"You're making this really easy, and it's making me nervous. Is there anything I need to know?" he asked in a serious tone.

"I'm very anxious to have this meeting, and I feel like it's taken all day for you to get here and tell me they're back." She closed her eyes and shook her head as she sighed loudly.

She was clearly frustrated, but Lev was more concerned about the anxiety underlying her frustration. "Well, I appreciate your honesty. And so you know, I didn't see them when they returned, so my timing is basically off by an hour."

"Being in here is really difficult for me. All this waiting," she said to him, sounding agitated beyond what was reasonable.

He sat there looking at her for a few seconds before saying patiently, "This is a process. I'm getting you to a meeting soon. How can I reassure you that I'm making this meeting happen today?"

"I really need to get out of here. I feel like I'm in a jail cell here in this room, and I don't want to be here anymore. Can I go wait outside?" she asked hopefully while staring at him.

Lev knew that wasn't an option. He looked away from her gaze and said, "We're going to leave tomorrow morning."

"Yeah, but you don't really believe me. Why would you go if you don't believe me? Maybe you'll change your mind before tomorrow morning," she said, looking at him intently.

"That's a possibility." He agreed. "But consider this, you can see me right here, right now making it happen just in case you're not totally batshit crazy and just looking for an excuse to go get some replacement cosmos," he said, smiling at her.

She smiled at his attempt at humor and looked up at his face and rolled her eyes and shook her head. She looked at him again and sighed and said seriously, "I'd appreciate a different room after the meeting. Or I can sleep outside. I hate being in here. I want to get out of here."

"Yeah. Yeah. Ok, we'll find you a different room. Maybe another hour until I send for you. You going to be ok for another hour?" he asked her thoughtfully.

"I don't know," she said, and he knew she was being honest.

He couldn't believe he was saying it, but he asked her, "Do you want to wait in my room until I send for you?" He swore at himself for doing it, but he saw her shoulders relax and her demeanor change instantly, so he let himself off the hook and listened to her accept his offer.

She tipped her head back and then looked at him and said in a relieved tone, "Yeah. I'll sit on the couch and read books. I won't touch anything except books. I won't snoop. I'll just sit there. It doesn't feel like a prison in there, and I think I know at least three ways to escape from your room." She mentioned the potential escape routes in earnest and didn't appear to consider how he'd react to her comment.

In his mind all he could hear was a long drawn out version of the word 'fuck' as she added the part about potential escape routes, but he tried to control his reaction and said, "Ok. I'll walk you down with your guards. Let's go." He stood up from his chair at the table. "You want to put on your bra and grab your flowers and the book?" he asked her pointing over to the open window where her bra was still hanging.

"Yeah, ok. It's probably dry now."

"I'll tell your guards what we're doing and meet you in the hallway when you're done. I hope I can trust you alone in my room," he said with a nervous laugh as he went to inform her guards of the new plan.

She stood up and said, "Lev, I promise you can trust me in your room."

He watched as she then turned to climb up on the bed and get her bra from the open window. He watched her for a second then turned to leave. "Looks like you got a shower," he said, pointing to her clean hair.

"Yeah, I really didn't expect hot, running water when I got here."

"Ivy has water and electricity thanks mostly to Bolin," Lev said from the doorway where he waved to her guards.

"No, I meant here in the post-apocalyptic world," she said and walked into the bathroom to put her bra on.

Lev hoped she didn't see him hesitate as she said that. It was those little things she said that were working on his inability to discount her the way Bolin thought he should. He walked out of the room as she began to change with the bathroom door open and thought to himself, plus, I can see her goddamned roots even better now that her hair is clean. Was Bolin right not to think her roots were a big deal? He told her guards they were going to head down to his room. He sent Bautista, who had informed him of Kali's state of mind, to inform his command and the second guard's command where to send their replacements.

Lev considered Kali's craziness might be a virus he'd caught. How could he leave her alone in his room?

Kali watched Lev leave his room. She had promised him she wouldn't snoop around in his belongings. The sheet she had slept on the night before was still laid out across his couch. She walked over to his bookshelves and tried to figure out if he had arranged them in a system. It appeared to her that he had used a theme for their arrangement on the shelves. He had books on philosophy, history, science, math, art, fiction books, biographies, and more. He really had quite a large collection. She had been so anxious all day stuck in that small room with no reasonable escape routes. She felt her anxiety melting away as she stood in Lev's room and looked around at the items he surrounded himself with. She had told him she wouldn't snoop through his belongings, but she felt she was keeping her word if she merely looked at everything that was visible. That wasn't snooping. Even though she hadn't done much during the day, and she had barely moved a muscle for hours, she felt tired enough to consider taking a nap. She walked over to the couch and laid down on top of the sheet and closed her eyes. She fell asleep before Bautista returned and remained asleep after new guards relieved Bautista and Tracy.

Lev knocked on Heather's door and waited for her to open it. He knew she was inside because some of the other 'scientists', as Kali called them, told him she was sulking in her room. Lev and everyone else at Ivy just called them the Research Team or the RT. He was going to tell Kali to refer to them as that. He corrected himself: He was going to suggest to Kali she refer to them as that. He knocked harder on Heather's door a second time and called her name loudly through the closed door. This time she opened her door quickly.

"Lev. Sorry, I didn't realize it was you."

"So you make other people wait? What if it was someone I'd sent down to get you?" he asked her without waiting for an answer. "We need to have a meeting with the entire RT immediately. Meet in the conference room. Bring your sheet there to cover the board," he said, pointing to her bedsheet.

"Listen. I'm exhausted. We're all exhausted. Can we do this tomorrow?" she asked him.

"You're not exhausted. You just had at least a day off over at Campus. Don't tell me Aisha made you work for your meals. And everyone here has moved on from the attack. I just spoke to Margie and Sathindar. They're both ready to go. We can't all be waiting on the boss to debrief about the results of a three week expedition for useful tech, an attack on the community, lives lost, and a traveler who showed up asking to speak with our scientists about time travel. Time and space travel to be exact." He watched as her face lost its nonverbal plea for sympathy and turned to one of hopeful surprise. "Yeah," he said to her, nodding his head. "Get down to the conference room immediately. I'm shutting the door and moving ahead without you if you're not there in five minutes."

He turned and walked out of her room and heard her yell, "Wait up, Lev!"

"Grab the sheet!" he yelled to her without turning around to wait for her.

Rollo and the Research Team

The eleven original environmentalists at Ivy were actually members of the scientific Research Team that were now meeting together at Lev's request. They had never been a group of environmentalists. That was just how they'd presented themselves to anyone who entered Ivy. Each member of the RT represented a specialized branch of mathematics or some niche field of science. They had found themselves together at Ivy 17 years ago as members of a scientific panel assembled by an anonymous benefactor who had awarded each a sizable research grant at their various universities or corporations. Each grant stipulated that the person named as the recipient must attend the panel at Ivy in order to use the grant money they had already received. Some had flown in from various institutions from around the world, while others had flown in from various universities and research laboratories throughout the United States. None knew the names of the others until arriving at the Education Center at Ivy. As they arrived, they discovered some had known of one or the other in the group through professional endeavors and some were friendly across their academic disciplines. During the early days of the extinction event, none could point to a specific defining relationship between the individual group members other than that they were each considered highly skilled in their areas of expertise.

They had been instructed to meet for a private audience with their benefactor at the Education Center at Ivy and that was what they did on that hot, humid day at the end of May. After they had all arrived, they socialized with one another outside the locked building using the time they waited as an opportunity to get to know the others who had been so generously gifted with research funds for their different fields of research.

Eventually, the doors to the Education Center were unlocked and a tall, young looking black man stood before them smiling nervously. He was dressed in a red t-shirt and blue jeans with black sneakers. He waited until all eyes were on him before speaking to those he had assembled.

"I suppose you are all wondering what you are doing here," he said loudly with a voice that lacked confidence but was striving to take on a bold tone. "My name is Rollo Vespry. I'm so sorry to inform you that it is likely that everyone you know is already dead."

Members of the group before him suddenly started to ask him questions, but he held up a hand to quiet them and when they didn't cease their overlapping conversations and questions, he finally shouted loudly over them, "I don't have long! I also don't have a lot of answers for you. I'm not a scientist. I barely passed high school algebra, ok? It's going to take me a long fucking time to figure out what the hell I can do to help you, but in the meantime, you have to figure out how to help all of us. It turns out the one thing I'm good at is being a spy and a traitor to an evil fucking villain. Too many movies and too many video games, right?" He laughed nervously to his audience which was now paying attention to him.

"Hey, kid," one of the women from the group called out to him while stepping forward. "Listen, the grant money. It was deposited, so I know that part is real." She turned to the others in the group. "Did your grant money deposit?" she asked them. Everyone agreed their money was received. She turned back to look at the young man and asked, "What's the rest of this about?"

He looked agitated and said, "I've got no time for this. I'm gonna be yanked. Everyone's dead. It's got to do with Time. You have to figure out the formulas to help Time, and travel, and unlock spaces. Others can already do it, and it's not good, man. It's really bad. Don't tell anyone what you're doing. If they find out, it's going to be easy to deal with you. Keep this shit a secret. Don't ever say my name to anyone outside of this group. I told you my real name. I'm working over here to help, but it's probably going to take a long time for you, but it's going to take so much fucking longer on my end. There are so many more years there. I had a place built for you. It's mostly done, anyway. It's a huge building north of here closer to the reservoir. Go check it out. I didn't know what you'd need. I just put as much shit as I could in there to get you started. There are books and computers and all sorts of science and math shit. I didn't know what half of it was. I'm gonna try to get you some tech. Stay away from everyone and like, all distractions. Figure it out. Keep this shit secret or they'll find you."

"Are you crazy?" a man in the group asked loudly.

"Yeah, I'm fucking crazy. I work for a crazy motherfucker who just killed most of the people on the planet. So, yeah, I'm fucking crazy. I'm fucking 25, asshole. How the fuck old are you? 50? Go back to town and check it out if you don't believe me. Everyone's dead. Go check out the new pad I had built for you, keep your mouths shut, and figure this shit out. Figure out the formulas for Time. Don't get caught. If they find you, you'll get to meet the most crazy son of a bitch in the fucking Universe. Trust me. I'm the good kind of crazy. You want to deal with me!"

"Ok, Rollo? Is it Rollo?" the first woman asked him.

"Yeah, it's Rollo. Rollo Vespry. Don't you people listen? I hope you nerds are list..."

In that moment, he disappeared before their eyes.

A woman named Heather walked up the steps of the education center and turned to face them. "I want everyone to use their cell phones to write down everything The Benefactor just told us. Swear words, and all. Every word right now to the best of your recollection. But," she admonished them, "do not write his name. Just use 'The Benefactor' in place of his name. No one said a word, but they all pulled out their cell phones and began entering what they remembered hearing. Some people sat down in the grass, others joined Heather on the steps, while others went to their rented cars and sat in the air conditioning.

When it appeared that everyone had done their best to record the words of The Benefactor, Heather walked inside the education center and searched for something to write on and something to write with. She emerged and sat down on the top step of the building. Together, they all reconstructed the words of The Benefactor to the best of their ability. Heather stood on the top step and read aloud the final version of the assembled speech he had given them and made sure the entire team agreed those were the words and instructions he had given them. It was the only information they had to go on as to what he needed from their research team. Not one member of the research team ventured into town that day to prove The Benefactor wrong. They knew they would find the dead if they did. None of their cell phones had service. None were tempted to discover if their loved ones were ok. Every member of the research team agreed to never say his name out loud, not even to another member of the research team. He was simply referred to as 'The Benefactor' from that day forward. They had all seen him disappear. They walked in silence as a group, heading north to find the building he told them he'd had built for them.

The Research Team Meets

Lev entered the conference room to see Margie, Sathindar, and most of the other members of the RT already seated at the conference table. He scanned the room quickly to assess who was still missing. He noticed Charles seated at the table already, which was a pleasant surprise. He was usually the last person to arrive. Next to him were Kendrick and the always punctual, Jim. Other members were standing in the room talking to one another, but started to break up their conversations and head towards their seats once Lev entered the room.

The original RT consisted of 11 members assembled by The Benefactor, but Campus had contributed nine more team members after Lev and Bolin rid Ivy of Moira and her followers. During the 17 years that had passed, two of the original 11 RT members had died. One had committed suicide at the end of her first year at Ivy, the other slowly became ill over time and eventually passed away in his sleep. No one really knew what his diagnosis was. It had happened recently. His death was a loss to the team. He had contributed a lot.

"Kath, Where's Peter?" Lev asked a woman seated at the far end of the table.

"He was working in the coops when I found him. I told him to run. He understood. He'll be here in a minute."

Lev looked over at another empty chair and asked, "Olle, where's your wife?"

"She was in the shower after farm this afternoon when I told her we had to get down here. She'll be here quickly," he said, assuring Lev. Before Lev could respond, Olle looked past him and said, "Araceli! See? There she is." Lev turned and looked at the tall Spanish woman with closely cropped wet brown hair and big eyes looking from her husband and back to Lev.

"Hey, Lev. I hurried. What's up?" she asked as she took an empty seat next to her husband.

"I'm waiting until we have everyone in the room. There's a lot to discuss, but I need to get to it all quickly. We have a guest we have to meet with afterwards," he said to the entire room. "We're missing Niels, Jessica, Peter, Genji, Andrew, and Angelo. Anyone else?" he asked the present team members.

"Heather?" Margie offered sheepishly.

"No. I'm here," Heather said loudly from the hallway as she entered the room carrying the sheet Lev had asked her to bring. "I saw Cara from the kitchen on my way over and asked her to bring us some food and water in case this goes as long as I suspect it will. I want everyone alert."

"Good thinking." Lev acknowledged.

Peter walked in saying, "Sorry it took me so long. I was covered in chicken shit and feathers after cleaning out the coops." He pulled out his usual seat next to Kath and threw his arm around her shoulders. "Sounds like we're going to have some fun today," he offered enthusiastically, looking at Heather.

Lev was getting aggravated and it showed in his darkening demeanor. He glared at the assembled team and said, "Five people are holding us up." He fumed from his seat, looking at no one in particular.

Sathindar tried to appeal to Lev's waning patience by saying, "All of them have been informed and are on their way. No doubt, they'll be here momentarily, Lev."

Lev looked at him and sighed loudly. "Hang the red flag on the door," he told him.

Sathindar rose from the table and picked up the red flag that hung from a string and walked to the conference room door to hang it on the nail that had been there for nearly two decades.

"How will Cara know she can knock?" asked Shirong.

"She'll leave whatever she brings us on the floor. We'll check for it after we cover some ground," Heather said to him.

While she spoke, Niels, Angelo, and Genji arrived together and quickly took their seats at the table.

"Who's still missing?" Heather asked Lev.

"Jessica and Andrew," he said gruffly.

"No, no! I'm here," said Jessica from behind him, floating by him quickly as she made her way towards her seat.

"We're waiting on Andrew, then," said Lev. "Who informed Andrew to get down here?" he asked the team members.

"I was supposed to," said Margie. "He was down at laundry. It was too far to go to and still inform the others I had to find, so I sent his neighbor, Leigh-Anne, to get him. She understood he was to be informed immediately and get here asap. I watched her run to go get him."

"So, you didn't see him?" Lev asked, annoyed.

"No. I had to find four others. Laundry is too far. I believe I made the right choice, but I also believe he'll need some time to get back here."

"Ok, ok," Lev calculated the distance between their laundry facility and the meeting room and admitted defeat. It was a haul. He paced out of the room and into the hallway looking both ways and walked back into the conference room. Waiting for Andrew was going to be difficult, but they couldn't start without him. The minutes passed by and everyone sat around the table talking quietly amongst themselves except for Lev and Heather. They tossed the sheet she had brought with her over the top of the board to cover some of their most valuable work.

"You think the guest would understand this?" she asked him incredulously.

"I think it's a precaution worth taking. Not likely she would, but the team has put a lot of work into this. Let's just cover what's been accomplished. Let's figure this woman out before we let her see what's been going on here," he said.

Cara appeared in the doorway with two members of the kitchen crew behind her. Between the three of them, they were carrying enough food and drink to feed the entire team and then some. Members of the team hopped up from their seats to take the items from Cara and the men. Cara and the rest of the residents of Ivy knew never to enter the RTs conference room. Just never enter it. That was a rule.

The food and drinks were laid out across the length of the table and team members were pouring themselves water into the ceramic mugs brought by the kitchen team. The mugs and plates had been piled into a plastic bin and each team member had grabbed a set, placing Andrew's set in front of his empty chair. Food was being passed around and loaded onto empty plates. The person seated next to Andrew's empty chair placed some meat and vegetables on his plate for him. They were just about all seated again when Andrew came striding quickly into the room looking red-faced with sweat pouring down his face and large wet sweat stains growing under his armpits.

He walked up his chair and pulled it out saying, "Thank you for waiting for me. I got here as quickly as I could."

"Have some water," Lev said to him, indicating to the rest of the RT that he wasn't going to continue to be angry at being made to wait.

Lev sat down in a chair at the head of the large conference table to the left of Heather. She asked if everyone was ready to begin. They were all more than ready to hear what Heather and Lev had to say.

Heather raised her hand to begin and turned to Lev, asking if he felt security information should begin the discussion as it was likely the least complicated information they would cover. Lev nodded in agreement.

"Two nights ago, the compound was attacked by a sizable group of raiders. We counted 23 of their dead and burned the bodies. We don't know how many escaped. We had four of our own dead when all was said and done. This was the biggest loss Ivy has suffered in years. The group of raiders that attacked was large enough that there's concern about how neither Ivy or Campus knew about them prior to the attack. Crow's Nest One spotted them coming in from the south road, so there's a question about whether or not they even knew we were here, or if they were just a raging band of assholes who came up on Ivy and decided to wage war without first contemplating some kind of civilized diplomacy.

"One alerted the other Crows as soon as they spotted them, and Team 3 was on shift on the ground and was notified immediately. Candace's team took three losses almost immediately after she approached the raiders. She was also injured but is back in her room, out of medical, and resting now. It had rained hard most of the day. The team had a quick consult before walking up to who they believed to be travelers. They had decided to approach the strangers as possible travelers looking for shelter overnight because of the conditions outside. They approached the strangers with the intent of turning them around to shelter in the barn. Before they even had a chance to offer accommodations, someone in the raiders let out a yell and they attacked.

"It was a fucking melee after that. Total hand-to-hand combat. They didn't have guns. They were armed with bats, axes, shovels, knives. We had the advantage due to the guns and numbers on the field. Crows lit up the night and rang the alarms. Everyone came out. It was a fucking bloodbath. Essential were injured. James is going to be out for a few more days before Doc will let him back to work just to oversee his crew. He won't be able to do more than that, though. He won't be able to do more than oversee his crew for a long fucking time while he heals. That brings me to my first request.

"I want to remove Maren from the security teams. I know she's a badass on the field, and it's going to piss her off, but she's gotta be deemed essential. She's too valuable to our maintenance of IT to be on the front lines of an attack. I watched her go down on the field. I thought she was dead. If we lost her, we'd feel her loss on the RT. She's a reliable team member on her security team, but she's a more valuable asset with tech. She needs to train more community members in her skillset, too." He looked around the room. "Any questions or concerns about my request to deem Maren essential?" he asked the research team who all remained silent, and then turned to look at Heather.

"Confirm or deny Lev's request now," Heather said without emotion.

They went around the table and waited as each team member responded to Lev's request to deem Maren essential. All were in favor.

Heather nodded. "She's going to be angry, but we brought back a lot of tech today. She'll be really busy with that and her two new team members."

"I'll inform her tonight," said Lev. "One other thing, making her essential, I want her to have clearance along with the other two techs."

Heather turned to him. "You think it's wise to bring in someone else? The more people who know, the more exposure we risk," she said.

"You said it yourself, you just brought in a bunch more tech. We've had the other two techs since I brought them in six years ago. They've solved more problems than they've ever caused. Have they caused any problems? We need to have a skilled IT crew with clearance. We lose one of our current two, then we're down to one IT crew member who knows what's going on. I want her to have clearance," he said, looking at her.

"I understand. Ok, I agree. We brought back a lot and I would like skilled team members who are informed through clearance to go through what we have."

She was nodding her head in approval as Lev turned to the team and asked, "Any questions or concerns about my request to grant Maren clearance?"

Jim's arms were resting on the table and he lifted one hand from his elbow. "She's married to, or, with Vivek, right?"

"Yeah," said Lev.

"Well, it's not easy to keep secrets from a spouse. Bringing her in, do we accept that Vivek will then know? We've all worked so hard to maintain absolute secrecy regarding our work, to protect the identity of The Benefactor, to protect ourselves. I'm uneasy about adding a new member to the RT. That's my piece. I have to say it, man," he concluded, looking around the table.

"Anyone second Jim's concerns?" asked Heather. Angelo and Charles raised their hands, but all others stayed quiet. "Same concerns? Or do you have additional concerns you'd like to express?" asked Heather. Charles and Angelo said they shared Jim's concerns regarding Maren keeping the work conducted by the research team a secret from her spouse.

Lev sat back angrily in his chair.

They needed complete agreement in order for any request to pass. He leaned forward on his elbows and was about to speak when Heather touched his arm gently and asked, "May I have an opportunity to address the concerns of these three men before you do?"

"Go for it," he said, letting his annoyance have free reign of his voice.

"Honestly, if Lev hadn't suggested giving Maren clearance, I would have eventually. How can we have an IT crew member who doesn't know all that we are doing here? Why we are doing it? The nature of our relationships within the team. Without clearance, she will be denied access to meetings such as this. I know Wong and Carter aren't here right now, but they're sorting the tech we brought in today. They'll get debriefed later. They're very busy. So we have Wong and Carter who have been working with Maren for three years now, but they won't be able to tell her what she's working on with them when she sees all of the new technology? They have to dance around conversations with her, as it is. It would benefit the work all three of them do if they could communicate honestly with her. Sometimes, they have to exclude her when they would prefer to work with her.

"Margie, Sathindar and I just brought in two carts filled with new tech to add to what we have. We spent three weeks out there gathering new tech to assist with our work. Like the majority of you here, I haven't left Ivy since we arrived 17 years ago. All of Lev's people have seen it first-hand. I finally saw what it looks like. Anyone who hasn't, should. Maren has. She's been out there. Lev brought in nine new team members when he got here. Both of our current techs are from Campus. All three of you know Maren," she said looking at the faces of Angelo, Charles, and Jim.

"Is this some sexism? Do you want to deny us a third tech because you think a woman won't be able to keep our secrets from her husband? She needs to have clearance. We need a third tech. We lost Christo to whatever cancer he had only four months ago. We're getting older. We need to consider that. The facility was raided two nights ago and we lost four community members. James was on the field when they were attacked and he was brutally beaten. He's essential. Even essential community members can die. But James, he has an entire farming army! He's got all of us involved in food production and animal care. God forbid he had died two nights ago, but he's prepared us to continue on without him. What do we do? We are not being smart for such an illustrious group of academics.

"I know we need consensus to give Maren clearance, but I want everyone to know, I back Lev's request to give it to her. We need to have a separate meeting soon and deal with some harsh realities about who to bring on to the team so that we have replacements who are informed and ready to carry on our work."

She stopped talking for a second before starting again. "I am still pissed off because I believe it's because she's a woman that you three suggest she won't keep our research work separate from her relationship with her husband."

Charles began to protest against Heather's accusation, but she cut him off saying, "Oh, please, Charles! None of you implied Maren would tell community members! You implied she'd tell her husband. It's bullshit." Charles looked away from Heather and shook his head while looking at his plate full of food before him.

Heather was still hostile when she asked Lev to continue.

"Any questions or concerns about my request to grant Maren clearance?" he asked.

Everyone remained silent but a few stole looks at Charles, Jim, and Angelo. They had had far more contentious votes in the past, and everyone knew they could defend their concerns and not face backlash from the team or when they were out in the community. They had to have consensus according to their protocols. Concerns must be addressed. If Jim or any other member of the team wanted to deny Maren clearance, they would be tasked with demonstrating the threat Maren posed with facts not just baseless fears. If Jim had said to the team that Maren was a known liar and represented a threat, that would have been a valid reason to investigate. But implying that she might divulge their secrets to her spouse when others in the room were currently married to community members who did not have clearance was not enough. Maren was already a valued member of the tech team, now she would be an informed RT member with clearance.

When no one voiced an objection the second time, Heather spoke up. "Confirm or deny Lev's request now," she said. They went around the room and all confirmed Maren's clearance.

Lev was satisfied. If she broke the rules of her security clearance, he'd kill her and everyone she'd spoken to himself. He'd do it right out by the gate in the middle of the day in front of Vivek and anyone else. He wouldn't ask permission from the team. He'd just do it. Heather knew that, too. They all did, and it pissed him off to waste time on nonsense.

Heather looked over at Lev. "Any other issues security needs to address?" she asked him.

"Yeah, lives lost. We lost three team members from team 3 and one community farm member. The three from security have to be replaced immediately. I want to compare Campus to Ivy. Campus security teams currently have 25 members on each team. They have 10 teams. Their teams are divided into two divisions with five teams in each division. Division One has seniority and works three days a week. Division Two's five teams work four days a week. They basically work just under five hour shifts each day their division is on duty. This makes their security detail less tired and more alert. Our security consists of four teams of 20 working six hour shifts seven days a week. You all know I'm adding a fifth team to bring the hours down to under five a day per team. We don't have the numbers to add a 20 person security team, so Aisha is already sending us 20 people from Campus.

"I need to request four more people from Campus to replace the three security team members we lost the other night from team 3, and a replacement for Maren. We're underprepared for a multitude of security needs. We took out 23 raiders the other night. Our security detail that night was 20 members. Everyone except essentials had to come outside and fight to save the compound that night. I don't know how large their traveling fucking army was, but it was big. It's fucking amazing we only lost four people. We just had better weapons. If we had been equally matched with weapons, I don't even want to think about it."

"You want to request four additional people move here from Campus and add to our security forces," Heather stated succinctly in order to move the voting process forward.

"Yes. And I don't know who Aisha would send. They might have partners. They might not. I don't want to put restrictions on partners for security personnel. No kids, though. Any questions or concerns regarding my request for an additional four people, with the potential for partners, to move here from Campus?" Lev asked.

No one spoke.

"Confirm or deny Lev's request now," Heather said.

The vote was unanimous and Lev could bring in four additional people from Campus, who may or may not have partners, to work security detail for team three and replace Maren.

Heather looked back at Lev. "Any additional security issues you would like to inform us about?" she asked him.

"Yes. But it's a complicated situation that I would like to reserve for the end of the meeting. I would like to turn the meeting over to you, Margie, and Sathindar so that the team can hear about the mission to retrieve potentially useful tech."

Heather held out her hand towards Margie and Sathindar offering them an opportunity to speak before she, herself, did.

Margie looked at Sathindar and asked, "May I?"

Lev groaned internally at the niceties he was forced to endure during these research team meetings. He shifted in his seat noisily and stood up suddenly. "Listen, I'm trying to be patient, but I have to inform you all of something that's got me distracted right now." The room was completely silent as he stood there looking at them. It was likely none of them even took a breath while he scanned the room looking at their faces in an effort to assess their attention level.

Once he was sure they were all paying complete attention to what he was about to say, he said, "We had a traveler the morning after the raider attack. She's in a room waiting for an audience with the team as we play nice in here going over all our problems, using established protocols to confirm or deny requests and all this bullshit. How about next time I want to bring on an essential team member and grant her clearance, I just fucking tell you that's what we're going to do? Huh? How about that, Jim?" he said, looking at Jim. Jim blinked and looked away from Lev's glare and Lev continued. "Margie. "May I?"" he said, adding air quotes. "I don't have all fucking day. Tell us the fucking highlights. Sathindar, don't repeat anything Margie says. Heather, you tell us what's actually important. What we need to know. I don't want to hear about apocalyptic landscapes, ok, Margie? Save it for your friends. I don't want to hear the tourist version of the three weeks you hiked through Hell, Sathindar."

He turned and looked down at Heather. "We need to move this along because our guest is a little out there, if I'm being honest, and I need to prepare you all to meet her." He sat back down and leaned forward on his elbows looking more agitated than any team member had seen him in a long time.

Heather held up her hand to Margie who wasn't going to continue to speak anyway after being scolded by Lev. "Let me do the talking you two. Just confirm or deny if I have the information correct and if you feel I left out an *essential* bit of information, please inform us before we finish. Ok?" she asked them.

Both Margie and Sathindar nodded their agreement, saying nothing.

"Give me some water," Lev said gruffly to Dara who was seated to his left. She picked up one of the pitchers of water Cara had brought up and passed it to Lev who drank straight from the pitcher rather than pouring water into his mug.

Heather began quickly. "We found a few potentially useful items around Roanoke. We didn't just visit the universities, we also went into some businesses and residences that looked like they might have items of value inside. We didn't find anything particularly extraordinary in Roanoke, so we moved on to Williamsburg after only a day. Williamsburg institutions had a bit more hardware our tech team might be able to work with. We decided to bring back anything and everything we found that might be of value because, not wanting to belabor the apocalyptic hellscape discussion, none of us wanted to ever go back to look through the rubble again. It's my opinion that we picked Roanoke and Williamsburg clean. Do you two agree?" she asked Margie and Sathindar. They nodded their agreement and Heather continued.

"We went down to Norfolk last. This is where our plan to avoid ever having to travel that far again might have fallen apart. Honestly, there was a lot of tech down there. So much. Clearly, much had been picked over throughout the years. We weren't the first on the scene. But, some of the old buildings were completely intact, hadn't been burned, windows intact, no weather damage inside. It was exciting to see tech preserved as it was left 17 years ago. I think it would be useful for the three of us to consult with the new three-person tech team and discuss some of what we were unable to bring back. We all agreed that we will need to go back down there to retrieve some of what we decided to leave behind.

"Sathindar drew pictures of some of what we left behind, wrote down information to help the tech team identify the tech if possible. Anything we thought might be valuable and worth going back down for, we secured if we could, or moved it to a better location for future retrieval. Sathindar made detailed maps indicating where the various items were located throughout the area. Honestly, We brought back all that we could, but I would suggest having a meeting with the tech team, including Maren, immediately. We should arrange to go back down there sooner rather than later.

"We loaded up in Norfolk and headed back to Williamsburg and Roanoke where we picked up the items we had identified earlier for retrieval. That's it really. It's my belief that the mission is only half finished. We need to complete part two of the mission by traveling back down to Norfolk with a member of our newly expanded tech team and two carts once again. We would be able to fill both carts a second time. That's how much potentially useful tech we found down there," she concluded.

"Are there any questions or concerns regarding my description of the mission to retrieve tech?" she asked the team.

Genji lifted her hand and indicated she wanted to speak. "When would you want to head back down there?" she asked.

"I would be willing to travel back down again with an expanded escort as soon as next week, but let's see what Lev has going on with this visitor. The tech is secure. If we need to delay a second mission, we can do that. Any other questions or concerns?"

"When will we be able to access the new tech?" Araceli asked her.

"I think we should bring Maren onboard, get her acquainted with the tech we have, the new tech, and bring her up to speed with her new team before we bother with accessing the new tech ourselves. Some might need repairs, some might be too damaged to salvage. Any number of things. Let's let them have access to the items first."

"Any other questions or concerns?" Heather asked the team. No one responded. "I would like to ask you all to confirm or deny my suggestion that we allow Maren to become acquainted with our existing tech and our new tech before we all begin to explore what we have brought back from the mission." She went around the table and all confirmed they would wait until the new tech team was fully informed before granting them access to the new tech. Discussions about a second mission were deferred until after the tech team had been given Sathindar's drawings and a complete run down of the items by Margie, Sathindar, and Heather. It was agreed they could have that meeting between the six of them and not call the entire research team in for that.

Lev said nothing the entire time. He was interested in the tech they'd found down in Norfolk, but he didn't feel any of his inquiries would change the outcomes. He agreed with the decisions being made. He was hopeful. New tech would be great for the team.

Heather turned to Lev. "We have a guest. Please inform the team about the woman who showed up here yesterday," she said to him.

Lev didn't want to belabor any points about Kali to the team. She was what she was. She wasn't going to work well with this group of protocol based lifeforms he was sitting amongst, that was for sure. "Her name is Kali. She walked up here yesterday morning after the fight with the raiders, and Bolin and I met her on the field as she approached the facility. She asked if there were any scientists here. That part caught our attention. I asked her to elaborate as to why she was interested in potential scientists in our community, and she said she had been instructed to only speak with the scientists. When pressed, because I pressed her, she offered that she was sent to speak with the scientists about time and space travel."

The research team suddenly erupted in gasps and small excited chatter amongst themselves. He felt Heather sit up straighter next to him and saw her lean forward onto the table out of the corner of his eye.

"Lev, go on." She prodded with a tone of excitement in her voice.

"Ok, you all seem really into this information so far, but here's the part that's going to put a damper on things." The entire team became silent and he looked at their wide-eyed faces staring at him from across the table. "She's fucking difficult at best, and maybe legitimately crazy. Talking with her is an exercise in saint-like patience, but for some reason, I'm doing alright working with her." Olle snorted a quick laugh and Heather hushed him instantly. "I'm actually going to agree with Olle. I don't get it either. She wants to meet with the team. She says she was told to talk to the scientists and give them tech and information that will help them. She really won't offer much up to me, and I am hoping she gives you more definitive information. I just don't know.

"When I tried to get her to give me the tech she said she brought, she said she hid the tech five or so days from here where she was dropped off. Ok? You hearing this? She wants to go back and get the tech she hid now that she knows the scientists are here. She's got a lot of fucking conditions though. No horses, no scientists, no one she doesn't trust. Apparently, she trusts me and Bolin. Bolin and I discussed this already today. We've agreed that I'll go with her. She won't tell me where the tech is hidden. She expects me to just go on this walk with her. No information other than a conflicting number of day's walk from here." He stopped talking and said, "I'm going to let that sink in for a minute. Five days, maybe, to a location to retrieve tech that may or may not exist and then five days back." He looked around the table and over at Heather. "Heather, you have any questions so far?" he asked.

"No. Keep going," she said to him.

Lev saw Katherine raise her hand and shook his head no at her saying, "I'm only taking questions from Heather right now. A very serious point I need to make is this: She does not communicate in a normal give and take. She can be argumentative...for fun. You can lose her attention even if you do everything you can think of to keep her on track.

"She's covered in bite marks. Old scars. Don't stare at them. Neither Bolin nor I are convinced she's, you know, from the same time as The Benefactor, but neither of us is convinced she isn't, either. She's consistent in her personal representation so far. She's terrified, but not of us. No. I don't scare her. I think she goes out of her way to antagonize me. Bolin with his gun aimed at her head didn't make her flinch. She thought it was funny." He looked around at the team members whose faces were now looking alarmed and a little less excited than a few minutes earlier.

"She slept on my couch last night because she refused to return to her room. I couldn't deal with her. I agreed to let her stay. That's how determined she can be. She says people are after her, but can't explain how being on the second floor in a room with two guards isn't safe enough. She slept in my room because she said I'd fight her attackers and that would give her time to run away." He laughed. "Some of it's been kind of funny, actually," he said, shaking his head dismissively.

A serious look suddenly crossed his face. "She won't do well in here with all of you and your communication rules. Or, she'll be fine, but she'll make your heads explode. One or the other. Throw some questions at me now before I send for her. Let me try to tackle some of what you want to know. Let's be quick. One thing's for sure, the longer she's waiting upstairs to meet with you, the more agitated she's getting." He turned to look at Heather. "You first. Any questions?" he asked her.

Heather nodded. "What are some reasons why you find her story plausible?" she asked him.

"I really wouldn't call what she's presented so far a 'story.' Her information is not linear, and it's incomplete. I'm hoping she can deliver a more intelligible description of what's going on when she speaks with the team. She says she was instructed to speak with the scientists, not soldiers. As far as reasons, talking with her, she interjects offhand statements really casually. Statements like, 'I can't keep track of time here', and 'I didn't expect hot water in the apocalypse', and 'I've never had deer meat', and 'you haven't accepted what's going on yet'. She also won't reveal the names of her two friends who she says sent her here."

He decided to leave out the part about her roots growing in darker than the rest of her hair and the fact that she had told him she couldn't use her real name. That actually sounded a lot like The Benefactor now that he considered it. Still, he had agreed to keep that information to himself.

He scoffed loudly and said, "Listen, I'm not saying she's like The Benefactor. You all watched him disappear. You didn't have an opportunity to doubt him. She's different. She walked up here. She walked up here acting really fucking weird. She asked for all of you. Does that make her like him? Maybe. Maybe not. Maybe someone broke the code of silence and this fucking nut heard about us and is manifesting what we're doing here as her alternate reality. Could be. But she showed up. The Benefactor said it would take, and I quote from the holy fucking scripture, "It's going to take me a long fucking time to figure out what the hell I can do to help you." Right? He sounds like the kind of guy that would send this kind of woman to help. But it could all be bullshit, too. I don't know.

"I think we need to find out. I'm going with her to see about this tech she says she brought us. I'm not asking permission. I'm going. It's decided. Bolin's gonna take over as Head of Security while I'm gone. Williams is taking over my team. Any questions? If not, I can send for her and you can meet her and you can see what I mean first hand."

The entire team remained silent and he could see some of them looking to Heather for her decision.

"Yes, send for her. Let's see if she can pull it together to tell us something useful. I want to add this… The Benefactor, he was…. He was stressed out, too. He was a kid. He did all this for us. You don't always know what kind of package help will arrive in. Did we think The Benefactor would send us an entire second team to enlighten us? I just think we need to give this woman a chance." She laughed and looked over at Niels. "Niels do you remember you asked The Benefactor if he was crazy? Oh, that was a moment."

The mood at the table lightened up instantly, and Niels sat up straight and imitated the benefactor. "Yeah, I'm fucking crazy. I'm fucking 25, asshole. How the fuck old are you? 50?" I hope when I meet God, that's how he talks to me. No bullshit!" Niels and the rest continued to laugh.

Lev spoke up. "This is good. This is about what you're going to encounter with Kali. Maybe a little less lucid than The Benefactor," he said. He got up and walked to the door to get someone to find Bolin and someone to bring Kali down. He heard Heather say, "Lev will go with Kali on a journey to see if she brought us tech or to discover if she's insane. Confirm or deny, and I expect you all to confirm this," she said. Lev didn't wait for the results. He was going either way, so he didn't need to hear the verdict.

Lev walked down the hallway and took the usual route to the cafeteria. He scanned the vast room for a familiar face he could trust. Bautista must have been relieved of guard duty because Lev saw him sitting at a table eating a meal with Ju. He called out to him and waved him over as he looked up.

"What's up, Lev?" he asked as he ran up to him.

"First of all, thanks again for letting me know Kali was a basket case earlier," he said with sincerity. "You're good with her. That's why I requested you earlier."

"Yeah, I feel like I get her. Ju does, too. She was just telling me that, actually. And I have to tell you, I don't think Tracy should be put back on guard duty with her. She made things uncomfortable. And if that's not enough of a reason, I don't think Kali liked her. I think it added to her tension," he said pointedly.

"Good to know. Listen, I need someone to inform her guards that she needs to be walked down to a meeting with the RT in MR1. I'm listening to you, and I want you to accompany her guards for the walk. I don't even know who's got her now. But if she likes you, it would help if you were there. If you can't do it, you got duty or something, how about Ju? You said Kali and Ju hit it off?" he asked him.

"I'd do it, but I have duty in a bit. Ju is off. Can I call her over?" he asked Lev. Lev nodded. "Hey, Ju!" he shouted over to her, waving his hand to call her over. Ju got up from the table and ran up to them.

"What's up?" she asked him eagerly.

"I need someone Kali is getting along with to go to my room and walk with her and her guards to a meeting in MR1 with the RT. She's really agitated after a long day in her room. Did Bautista tell you I moved her to my room?" he asked her.

Ju's eyes widened and she said, "Yeah, he mentioned it, and yeah, sure. I got this. Kali's cool. We got along earlier."

Lev nodded but said, "I'm not exaggerating when I tell you she's really close to freaking out after waiting around all day for this meeting. I don't know who's on guard duty with her right now, but I want to send someone who can get her from point A to point B without her running off. You know she's twice as jumpy in closed spaces?"

"Yeah, door open and all that. Some PTSD. Got it."

"You sure you feel comfortable escorting her down to the meeting in the windowless basement with locked doors?" he asked her with a small laugh. "Tell me no if you can't do it," he added in a more serious tone.

"I can do it," she said confidently.

"Ok," he said, turning to Bautista. "I need someone to find Bolin. He's supposed to be at the meeting, too. Just let him know we're waiting on him. I don't know where the fuck he is right now, but he's waiting for a call down. Pick someone from a table here and send them to tell Bolin. It's an ASAP order." Bautista agreed and Lev said, "Thanks," then quickly turned and walked away heading back to the RT in MR1.

Lev walked in to MR1 and closed the door behind him. He walked to a closet door in the back of the room. He opened it and went in and pulled out two folding chairs and walked towards the large conference room table. "Dara, give up your seat," he said with authority. "I need to have Kali seated next to me."

Dara got up and took the folding chair from Lev and walked it to the back end of the conference table saying, "You got it, Lev."

Niels was seated next to her and passed her plate and cup down the table to the others who kept them going until they reached her new position at the table.

"You know what, Niels? You go, too. Take this chair. Let Bolin sit in a chair next to her."

"Wait," said Heather looking up at him from where she was seated. "Let's be clear about what Bolin knows before they get here."

"Bolin knows what he's always known. He doesn't have clearance, but this conversation isn't likely to go beyond what he can know. It's the usual. No surprises." Lev assured her.

"Okay, everyone?" Heather asked the team. When the team wasn't loud enough in their understanding, Heather asked them a second time to indicate they understood and everyone loudly voiced their understanding.

"Anyone confused about what Bolin has access to?" Lev asked them roughly. Everyone spoke louder the third time assuring Lev and Heather that they were all aware of clearance protocols.

"What's the community lie for my trip with Kali?" he suddenly asked Heather.

"Oh, um, how about she came from up north and had medical supplies with her that became too burdensome to carry after three people in her group were attacked and killed by wild boars. The supplies are in a strip mall about a week away. She says they're worth retrieving, so you went to get them with her? We can have Santi confirm the imaginary medical supplies were valuable to Ivy whether or not you and Kali actually come back with the tech we all hope she says exists. Maybe bring an empty duffle bag for the trip and pack it with leaves and sticks before you return to make it look like medical supplies."

"Sounds good," Lev said. "You all hear that one?" he asked the team. "Heather, make sure you tell Maren the community lie tomorrow. I'll tell her you're going to cover it in her clearance."

"Yes, got it," Heather said.

Everyone agreed and Lev walked over to the conference room door telling Andrew to place a cup and a plate before the seats designated for Kali and Bolin. "Pour them some water and throw some food on their plates, too," he said as he opened the conference room door. Neither had arrived yet, so he walked out into the hallway. He was actually nervous about how Kali would behave for the research team. "Fucking hell," he muttered under his breath while running a hand through his hair.

Kali and the Research Team

When Kali woke up, she saw Ju standing in the doorway saying her name.

"Hey, Lev sent me to bring you down to a meeting with the Research Team. You need a minute?" she asked her with a friendly tone.

Kali sighed and rubbed her face before sitting up. "Yeah. Just a minute," she said.

She got up and walked into Lev's bathroom and put water on her face and drank some from her cupped hands before using the toilet. She left the bathroom door open while she did these things, but Ju was already used to Kali doing that and had engaged the two men standing outside Lev's room in a diversionary conversation until Kali emerged in back of them in the doorway of the room.

"I'm ready," she said to Ju, ignoring the two new guards.

The two guards led the way with Ju and Kali following behind. They made their way downstairs and Kali asked Ju if they were now below the ground level.

"Yeah, there are four sections that are basically the basements of this place. None are connected to the others. Like I said earlier, this place was created by an architect who must have been a fan of Escher."

"Well, how can a person get out of here if they need to?" Kali asked her.

Ju knew the guards escorting Kali could hear their conversation as they walked them to the meeting, so she looked at Kali and pointed at them while making a face to indicate she couldn't answer that question. Instead she said, "I'm sure you'll be safe in the meeting. Lev will be there. He knows all the exits." Then held up her hands to Kali to let her know that was all she could say. Kali understood even if she didn't like it. She didn't blame Ju for not helping to ease her mind. The meeting didn't make her nervous, but being in the basement rooms increased her anxiety again. She decided she would have to talk to Lev about this before the meeting.

They came to a stop before a door which was larger than the others in the building. One of the guards entered a code and Kali heard an interior lock shift. The guard pulled the door open and his partner entered the hallway while he continued to hold open the door waiting for Ju and Kali to enter.

"Ju, are you supposed to walk Kali all the way to the meeting?" the guard asked her.

"Yeah. Lev specifically asked me to bring her."

He walked into the well-lit hallway and pulled the heavy door closed and Kali heard the door locks re-engage.

The guard turned to Kali and said, "We're going to the room halfway down this hallway. See the door with the red flag? That's the meeting room."

Kali saw the door and wondered if Lev would still be nice to her with all of the scientists around. He was Head of Security. She was a difficult guest. She imagined his job was to protect the scientists. All she wanted to do right now was talk to him about how she didn't want to be in their windowless basement.

She held her head up and sighed loudly and Ju said, "Don't be nervous. They're all really nice." Kali didn't respond.

When they were standing in front of the door, one guard asked the other if they should knock because the red flag was a clear sign not to knock. Ju sighed and walked around them and knocked loudly on the door despite the red flag, and the two men stepped away from the door to let her take the blame. Kali walked up beside Ju, and they turned to look at each other and smiled making fun of the two guards.

Lev opened the door immediately and looked from Ju to Kali.

"Thanks, Ju. I need all three of you to wait on the other side of the security door. I'll get you when Kali needs to go back to her room."

He turned to speak to Kali next. "Hey, you ready?"

"No. Can I talk to you first?" she asked him.

Lev stepped into the hallway and closed the meeting room door behind him while watching Ju and the guards go through the security doors. He looked at her and raised his eyebrows while sighing and asking her, "What? What is it?"

"I... this place. This is a basement. Where's the exit?" she asked him.

Lev closed his eyes and nodded. Opening his eyes and looking at her he said, "There are exits. I just trusted you to stay in my room by yourself. Can you trust me that I'll get you out of here if the people you're running from show up here in our secure basement?

She looked at him but didn't respond.

"We're going to be traveling together for days. You gotta trust me at least a little. Why would you go with me to get your tech if you couldn't?" he asked her.

She looked unhappy, but said, "I want to sit next to you."

"Yeah. Ok. Already planned it that way. Come on in," he said, opening the door and leading her inside.

Bolin was already seated in the chair formerly occupied by Niels. He lifted his hand and offered Kali a friendly wave and a small smile. She smiled at him more broadly and waved with enthusiasm that matched her smile. Lev led her to the empty seat next to his and sat down quickly in his own seat hoping that by doing so, she would also take a seat.

188

"Hi," she said looking at all of the faces of the people staring at her as she slowly took her seat at the table.

"Let's get started," Lev said. "Everyone, this is Kali. Kali this is the Research Team, or the scientists, as you call them. So you know, I've already given the team a heads-up about the information you shared with me when you arrived. Feel free to add additional information that you wanted them to know."

She was looking at him and smiled as he finished speaking. "I was only supposed to speak with the scientists. Are you and Bolin also scientists?" she asked him, still smiling at him. Her eyes were sparkling with merriment as she looked at him.

He wondered if she was serious or teasing him on purpose. He returned her smile with a small one of his own and said, "Well, we're informed about all situations regarding the work of the Research Team. They know you say you brought them tech to help with their work, and they know I'm going to leave with you tomorrow to go retrieve that tech. We keep the work being done by the Research Team to ourselves. The majority of the community members at Ivy do not know what's discussed down here, and they don't know about the work that's being done by the team. You can feel free to discuss anything you were sent to discuss with the Research Team with Bolin and myself present. We work together."

She laughed a little as he finished and turned to look at all the faces of the people around the table more closely. "There's more of you than I expected. I know my Friend hoped for that," she said as she craned her body forward to see the faces at the far left end of the table. She noticed the sheet covering the large board and said nothing.

Turning to Lev she said, "I brought five unique pieces of tech that represent some of the capabilities of…" she seemed to get stuck on the words she wanted to use and breathed in and sighed loudly before starting again. "I don't know if I should use names." She didn't take her eyes off of Lev as she hesitated to speak and he nodded his head to her to encourage her to finish. "That represent the capabilities of… our enemy, your enemy, and his fucking army. I could only bring tech that was small enough to hide in my backpack because sometimes, it wasn't hidden until I could get to it later. I might not be home, you know? I didn't want that psychopath who controls everything to find it where I was hiding it in his garage. But small doesn't mean not powerful, and each piece will provide you with new information about how time and space work and how it can be navigated. Space is weird. It includes locked places.

"Getting in and out requires a lock code. It took a long time to collect the tech and not get caught. Well, sometimes people got caught." She raised her eyebrows, rolled her eyes, and scoffed seemingly knowingly after saying that. Looking back at Lev, she continued. "My Friend included a book with the various formulas. We call them recipes. It's all above my head with physics, math, and quantum this and that, and information that will be entirely new to you, too, because it didn't originate here.

"Maybe you figured some of it out on your own. I don't know. It's possible, especially if you've been working at it all these years. Can you even move non-living stuff, yet? That would be a really good start. My Friend has included a book of hand-written instructions for creating the physical tech with things you can find here. Like a cell phone and things like that. Recipes for creating the physical tech as well as for developing working formulas to power the tech.

"Like me, my Friend doesn't have a math or science background, but my Friend knows how to get shit done by getting people to work together for the cause. We want you to be creative. Maybe you can be creative and create new stuff those assholes haven't figured out how to make yet. You know? You understand? We don't have an actual lab. Ivy is supposed to be our lab as well as your lab. You might have to create and manufacture here for them as well as for yourselves. But you'll have to figure out how to get inside in order to be helpful. Without a lab, our people can't experiment and build new weapons or technology to subvert theirs.

"Also, I've been trained how to use the tech I brought even though I've haven't actually used some of it before. I can still show you everything you need to know about how to use it. Don't worry. I know what I'm doing," she said confidently and her shoulders dropped downward as she nodded her head firmly and looked at Lev.

Bolin leaned forward and caught Lev's eyes and raised his eyebrows and mouthed "Wow," slowly.

Heather was seated beside Lev and had been listening intently and caught Bolin's nonverbal message to Lev and decided to speak up.

"Kali? Hi. My name's Heather. What is the name of your friend who gave you the tech to bring to us?" she asked her.

Kali looked at Heather as if she just noticed her sitting there. "I'm not going to say," she said succinctly and continued to stare at her.

"Lev told us that you mentioned having two friends who assisted you in coming here to us. Can you tell us the name of either of your friends?" she asked her.

"No," Kali said.

"Can you explain to us what each piece of tech you brought us does?"

"One will send you straight to Hell," Kali said in a serious tone staring at Heather, and Lev noticed Kali seemed to drift in her thoughts about what she was implying.

"Kali?" he said and tapped her forearm to get her attention.

She turned to him with the preoccupied expression still on her face but he watched her smile suddenly return as she looked at him.

"Hey, what do you mean one of the pieces of tech can send you to Hell?"

Kali sighed and let her eyes wander around the room for a second. "There's one piece of tech that I didn't want to bring, but my Friend said the formulas are all deactivated, so it won't do what it's designed to do until you input the formulas again. That's when it becomes dangerous and can send you to Hell. Even experienced people have accidently sent themselves to Hell using them. They're sharp, you know? My Friend said if you figure out how to work with that particular tech, use your own formulas that you learn by looking at existing formulas, you can use the tech to your advantage in battle and other places. You can even save other traitors. You're all traitors to him, too. He won't kill you. He'll torture you."

"Are we going to be in a battle?" Heather asked her.

Kali turned to look at Heather again and furrowed her brow sternly saying, "You have been for 17 years. You need to arm yourselves with technology and fight back now. You don't seem anywhere near ready. I'm concerned. I'm concerned for myself just being here. This room sucks. How do you get out of here? You should all leave here. Worst room ever. You're trapped."

The Research Team was quiet as Lev asked Kali, "Anything else you want to tell us today?"

"No. I think it's best to get the tech first and then I can explain more and then you'll have the recipe book, too."

"Does the team have any questions for Kali?" Lev asked, looking around the table at the team. "Go ahead," Lev said, pointing to a member of the Research Team.

"What's your academic background if not science or math?"

Lev noticed Kali instantly looked bored and annoyed, but not in the least bit embarrassed as she answered, "I have a PhD in Torture. You?"

"Your question's been answered. Who's next?" Lev asked, sounding surprised by Kali's response and irritated at the person who'd asked the question.

"You. Go."

"How can you show us how to use this tech you claim you brought us if you don't understand how any of it works?"

"Are you a fucking electrician?"

"Are you really asking me that?"

"Yeah, I am."

"I don't understand the question."

"Ok, then I'm gonna assume you're not an electrician. But I'll also assume you can show me where the fucking light switch is and how to flip it to turn on the lights. I'll also bet that--"

"Kali--" Lev interrupted.

"--prior to the apocalypse you could successfully change a fucking lightbulb. You know? Without being an--"

"Kali, he gets it," Lev said.

"Without being a fucking electrician. I understand how the tech I brought you works without being a scientist just as well as you understand how flicking on a light switch brightens the goddamned room without being an electrician," she finished.

"Jesus, I hate to ask, but does anyone else have a question?" Lev asked, looking across the faces of the Research Team warily. "Go," Lev said, pointing at a person with a raised hand.

"Kali, I'm not trying to be argumentative. I just want to understand what role you expect to play here with us."

Lev immediately closed his eyes and shook his head as the question was asked.

"You're all smart, I get it. You know a lot of math and science shit that I don't know. But you clearly don't know your enemy. I do. If this is you preparing for battle, I'm here to tell you, you are *not* ready. You're gonna lose."

"So your role is....?"

Lev watched as Kali leaned forward and pointed her finger vigorously at the Research Team member who asked the question. "Man, I'm your wake-up call!" she said loudly in a tone that conveyed her disdain for the question as well as the Research Team.

"Alright! We're done here. Kali, thank you for the information. Let's get you back to your room."

Kali stood up while taking a handful of berries off of the plate that had been before her and followed Lev who opened the door and walked out of the room first before walking in back of her to close the conference room door.

"Hey, you did really well in there. That was good information before things got a little testy at the end. Still holding back quite a bit on the good stuff in my opinion. But we'll get that tech and see what's next. I don't know how they're going to take the war talk, but I kind of think they needed to hear that."

She looked away from him and shook her head as he finished speaking.

"What? Are you gonna stay pissed off?" he asked, watching as she put a few berries in her mouth.

She chewed the berries and swallowed them, then spoke defiantly saying, "I don't want to go back to that room. I already told you that. Can I stay with you again?"

Lev nodded and offered a shrug while holding up his empty palms in front of him that registered his acquiescence even before he spoke. "Yeah. Yeah, sure. I'll finish up here and be up in a bit. I'll bring dinner. Sound good?" he asked her.

"Sounds good," she said, surprised at his offer.

He walked quickly down the hallway to the locked door and punched in the numbers to lift the security locks. He went through the door before she did and told the guards to walk her and Ju back to his room and then left quickly without speaking to her. She watched as he walked through the security doors and headed back to the meeting.

Lev walked in and sat down at the table.

"Well?" he asked.

Angelo spoke first. "I see what you mean about her communication skills. She seems to be speaking through trauma induced fantasy. Her scars are horrible.

Distracting even," he said, and Lev interrupted him.

"Ok, Ang. She's got fucked up communication skills and she's covered in scars. The trauma is evident. Probably more PTSD than all of us combined. But what did you think about what she did manage to say?"

Angelo sat silently for a minute and said, "I am a scientist. I need proof of the things I believe in. I need to see this tech she claims to have brought for us. I hear her words. I think to myself, maybe this woman heard about our research into time and space travel. Heather asked her the name of her friends. If she had uttered the name of The Benefactor, I'd believe her without hesitation. That would be proof to me. But she wouldn't name her friends who gave her this tech she claims exists. We won't say his name either, so I understand it could be that it is him. It's like you said earlier today. She gives you enough to make you at least want to believe what she's saying, but absent any proof, you are left uncertain about the claims she's making. I think you're doing the right thing by going with her tomorrow to see if the tech exists. I completely agree she presents a plausible narrative that requires we at least investigate the veracity of her claims." He looked at Lev and raised both of his hands indicating that was all he had to offer.

Several people at the table offered their agreement with Angelo's assessment of the situation and Kali.

Heather spoke up and asked, "Do any of you feel that this is a complete waste of time and not worth Lev's effort to discover if Kali has actually come to us with the intention of bringing us tech and information?" Everyone remained silent while looking around the room at each other.

Bolin raised his hand and Lev pointed at him. "Bolin?" he asked.

Bolin suddenly stood up and looked sternly at the faces around the conference table.

"We need to address the elephant in the room. It's great that we all agree Kali's story is plausible and Lev should go investigate her claims of hidden tech. My main concern is different. Whether Kali is crazy or on the level, either way, it doesn't matter. What she said about us being at war for the last 17 years... That shit is true whether or not Kali turns out to be some mentally ill traveler OCDing on a fantasy life to help her cope with this after civilization bullshit. The Benefactor told you as much.

"Sometimes I think this group forgets what Kali reminded us of tonight. We've been at war for 17 years against a man who killed seven billion people and, if Kali's on the level, apparently leads an army. We're focused on fighting raiders. We need to consider getting our own army together and being ready to fight whoever this guy is who motivated a 25 year old to travel through time and build us this place. We need to be more militarized. Ready to fight. Even if Kali didn't bring us tech. We need to ramp up our own efforts."

He turned to Lev. "Lev remembers it's a war. He's remained ready to fight all these years even before he heard of The Benefactor and the mission. Some of you would probably still question his tactics, but we all know Moira and her cult would have eaten you alive and they were nothing compared to our real enemy. You wouldn't even be here if Lev hadn't come in and done what you couldn't. She and her followers would have taken you out. You can be protected, you can be essential and go to a safe place during a raider battle, but you need to know how to fight for times that may be coming when you have no choice but to fight. Kali reminded me that we're in a war and we need to be soldiers first."

He looked at the members of the Research Team. "Every one of you should know how to fight hand-to-hand and with any weapon you can get ahold of. Being essential doesn't mean you're members of a privileged class. You can still die in a battle with this guy The Benefactor warned us about. I have a math degree. I'm an engineer. I know as much as some of you in this room. But I also know how to fight. I didn't learn how to fight and maintain the skill just to protect your secured essential asses. If you find yourself on the field in a surprise assault, you need to be able to fight."

Bolin glared at the people around the table.

"What about James? He's essential. He gets to hide out when there's a fight," Charles said.

Bolin didn't have a chance to respond before Dara spoke up saying, "Are you kidding? Have you gone hunting with James? Do you even know how the meat you eat is prepared? James can shoot, use a knife, strangle things with his bare hands, use a bow and arrow, all of that. He fucking chops wood year round to cook the meals we all eat. Do you? Or do you just assume James has a gas powered stove he and his staff use to prepare food for us? I've chopped wood. Never seen you out there." She scoffed with disgust as she finished speaking.

"I'm just saying, some people cannot fight and risk dying in raider fights if they have knowledge that can't be found in another person."

Heather responded next saying, "This is what I said at our first meeting today. We need to train our replacements. I agree with Bolin. We all need to have fighting skills. We're not kings and queens here. We tried to isolate and work and figure out what we could all these years. We've made amazing progress, but we need to participate in our survival in other ways. I think one of those ways is becoming soldiers, as Bolin says. We don't have to hide in the towers when raiders come through. We can go to the roof tops and shoot assailants. Why do we continue to hide? It's wrong. And Charles. Seriously. You need to get out and see what the world looks like, what was done to the world. I'm going to insist you accompany me to Norfolk. It's not done us any good to stay behind these walls all these years."

Lev was surprised Bolin had taken the insult Charles had directed at James so well. But Bolin had been staring at Charles since he had opened his mouth against James. "Charles. Do you remember the night we took Ivy back from Moira? I do."

Charles looked away from Bolin and said nothing.

Bolin continued. "Yes. Are you starting to remember? James heard you screaming for help as that guy Richie beat the shit out of you in the first floor north corridor. James got to you before I did because he's a fast fucking runner. He dragged

Richie off of you and beat Richie to death with his fists. Then he told me he was going to run with you to the tower to make sure you were safe. He practically had to carry you because you were nearly unconscious. You slowed him down. He could have died trying to save your ass. I'm just wondering why you, of all the people in this room, would decide to go after my husband when you know he saved your fucking life."

Bolin stared at him coldly and Charles looked up at him and said, "I'm sorry. I'm really sorry I said anything."

Bolin sat back down. Lev looked up at everyone and asked, "We all ready to move on now? I am. I agree with Bolin. Heather already said she does, as well. We'll discuss more military training for our community members and this team in particular after I return from the tech adventure I'm going on tomorrow morning with Kali. Expect me to be gone for approximately ten days. Bolin is Head of Security while I'm away. Williams is taking over my command until I return.

"I will send you, Dave, over to Campus tomorrow. Let Aisha know what's going on, and ask her to be here eight days from tomorrow so that she can be here whenever I return with Kali. We might have tech. We might not. Aisha stays informed as always. Tell her everything we've discussed here."

"Should she bring an entourage?" Dave asked while smiling at Lev.

Lev considered it for a minute and said, "Yeah, you know what? Tell her to bring her posse and leave Bob in charge at Campus. I'm not sure how long this walk with Kali is actually going to take. I told you she said it would take five days one way, and then said six. She talked about rain. I think it's best if Aisha is comfortable and plans to be here for a bit. She hasn't had a break in a couple of years. Running Campus is 24/7 work. You know what to say." He looked at Dave and nodded his head looking to confirm understanding and agreement.

"Yep. Bring some friends. Have some of James' home brews and wait for Lev."

"Exactly that." Lev agreed with a nod. He turned to Heather. "Is this meeting almost over?" he asked her.

"Any questions?" she asked the team.

When no one responded she said, "Good. I think we have to put a lot on hold until Lev returns. We have Maren joining tech. Bolin did you know we're moving Maren to IT and she's been deemed essential?" Heather asked him.

"No, but that's a good addition to the team. She can fight," he said, obviously still focused on getting the research team to embrace the expectation that they would be tomorrow's soldiers.

"Lev, don't forget to go inform Maren tonight," Heather said to him.

"Yeah, I remember. But I need someone else to notify her command. I'm going to be running around getting ready for tomorrow."

"I'll do it after I leave here," Bolin said.

Lev nodded. "And, an update. Last night, Kali slept in my room. In the hallway just now, she asked if she could again tonight. I said yes. I'm not about to stay up all night fighting this out with her only for both of us to lose sleep and have to get up early tomorrow and start walking for the next ten days. So, that's what's going on. I don't know what time we're leaving tomorrow. I'm just going to let her decide. If she's up at 3am and wants to leave, I'm not going to argue with her, I'll just head out. I've got to get going and get two backpacks ready for us and get some guns. Bolin, can you send some weapons to my room?" he asked looking at him.

"You want me to send weapons to your room with Kali there?" he asked surprised.

"Yeah. There's gonna be guards on my door all night, so no worries. I'll check out what you send me and decide if I need more or less and have what I'm bringing sent to the front gate where I'll pick them up before leaving. Anything I'm not going to bring will be sent back with a guard. I'm not fucking crazy." He laughed.

"Jesus. I was about to say…" Bolin said, looking relieved.

"I have a lot to do before I can get some sleep. Is there anything else?" he asked the team.

"No, you go on," Heather said to him.

He got up quickly out of his chair and left the room headed for the cafeteria again.

In the cafeteria, he spoke to the manager on duty and asked for two dinners to be sent to his room in 30 minutes and traveling supplies for 10 days for two people to be sent to his room within an hour. He knew it was a big request and was appreciative when the manager didn't reveal any concern over the immediacy of the need. As Lev left the cafeteria, he could hear the kitchen staff suddenly start moving about talking louder and he knew they were taking care of his request. He hoped they wouldn't bother James, but he also figured Bolin would have already let James know the request was going to be made earlier today after they had spoken.

After leaving the cafeteria, he headed over to Maren and Vivek's room which was also on the first floor. He knocked loudly on their door hoping Vivek would be on duty. Maren answered and looked surprised to see him.

"I need to talk with you privately. Is Vivek inside?" he said to her curtly.

"No, he's in a nest until later. Do you need him here, too?"

"No," he said entering her room and closing the door behind him. "This is fifty percent public knowledge and fifty percent top secret. You ready?"

She laughed and he saw where she was now missing two teeth. "Yeah, just say it," she said.

"You're off security detail starting immediately. Not another duty. You're going to be a full-time member of the RT's Tech Team. As of this afternoon, you were deemed essential. When there's danger, you go to the tower you'll be assigned. Finally, you've been granted clearance. You understand what that means?" he asked her.

"Tell me," she said to him, no longer smiling.

"You will keep secrets from Vivek. That's the most important thing you need to understand. You will keep secrets from the community. You may only share information about the RT with members on the RT who have your clearance. Here's a surprise- Bolin does not have *full* clearance. Your clearance has already been granted and approved by the team. You cannot go back now. You cannot reject the approval. If you do, you will be killed. If you speak to Vivek about anything you learn while a member of the RT, you will be killed, and so will he. If you mistakenly speak to someone like Bolin, who you might assume has clearance, you will be killed." Lev didn't add that Bolin would be killed. He wouldn't say that. He continued. "You don't have a choice in this. If you'd rather die than accept the offer of clearance, I can accommodate you right here, right now. It's not a problem. Any questions?" he asked her.

She looked at him for a few seconds and said, "First of all, I'm in. You don't need to kill me. I've been working with Wong and Carter for like three years and never said this to anyone, not even Vivek, so don't go killing him, but I felt like they've been holding back information from me. I definitely want on this team. What's this work I'll be doing?"

"It's going to blow your fucking mind," he said, smiling at her and nodding his head.

She smiled and let out a little whoop. Lev told her Bolin was going to notify her command tonight and warned her again to consider how intertwined Bolin was with the team while not having clearance.

"Yeah, I get it. Bolin doesn't have clearance. I feel like there's something you're not telling me, though."

"There is. Heather will inform you tomorrow. I'm leaving for a few days starting tomorrow. Your clearance will provide you with access to the details of my trip. Heather will tell you the community lie you'll promote. Don't fuck up, Maren. I don't want to have to kill you. It's hard at first, but it gets easier."

Lev nodded his head at her as he left and jogged upstairs to a supply closet on the third floor. Using his keys, he opened a room they used for storage and turned on the light. He grabbed two backpacks and put a first aid kit, a tarp, a blanket for Kali, because he didn't mind sleeping outside without one, and matches. He grabbed a large duffle bag as Heather had suggested. He decided not to pack much, thinking that if Kali made it here with only a change of clothes, they would be fine. When she had arrived, she'd been hungry. He figured food, water, and weapons would be the three main items they needed to bring. He wanted to get back to his room and make sure he and Kali were on track for a good night's sleep. He needed rest tonight. He was mentally tired. He wouldn't be able to deal with her without rest. She was always thinking. He needed to be thinking straight, too.

Lev walked quickly back up to his room and looked at the two guards on duty. "Hey," he said to them as he approached. "I'm expecting some dinners, some traveling supplies, and some weapons all really soon."

He walked into his room and saw Kali sitting on the sheet on his couch looking bored. "I brought each of us a backpack for the walk. Here's yours. It's bigger than the one you walked up here with. Maybe put your clothes and stuff in here."

"I washed my clothes and hung them in the other bathroom," she said to him.

He walked into the hallway and said to the guards outside his door, "One of you go to Dorm 17 and get the clothes hanging in the bathroom. Bring them here. Actually, there's a backpack in the room and stuff on the table. Put it all in the backpack and bring it all down here. If the clothes are still wet, carry them separately." He walked back in and looked at Kali and smiled. "Anything else?"

She smiled and shook her head no.

"What time do you want to leave tomorrow?" he asked her.

"I like to get an early start because it's not as hot then."

"Sounds good to me. Dinner's being delivered and food for the trip will be sent up shortly. We'll pack our backpacks and be ready to leave early. I need to arrange a wake up. What time exactly?"

"How about 4am?"

He squinted a little mouthing 'ouch' silently. "Ok, ok. 4am it is."

He walked to his door and told the remaining guard, "We need a 4am wake up. Inform new shifts."

Kali heard the guard agree as Lev turned back towards her. "Do you want me to send to medical for a sleeping aid?" he asked her.

"Oh, no. I don't take anything like that unless forced to. I can't wake up and fight or run if I'm drugged." She looked at him suddenly concerned. "You wouldn't give me a sedative without telling me would you? I don't like it when that happens," she said to him sounding angry.

He was taken aback and raised his eyebrows and asked, "What?! No, no I wouldn't do that. That's why I asked you if you wanted something to help you sleep tonight. No. I wouldn't do that. That's really uncool to do to somebody. Sorry to hear you say it's been done to you. Really."

He nodded his head at her and walked over and sat next to her on the couch. "Hey, we're going to be traveling together for days, right? I think it would help if you decided to trust me that I'm going to get you there and back without being a shitty human being. I'm going to have to sleep at night out there alone with you and trust you're not going to take off and steal my guns, hit me in the head with a rock, and shit like that, so I think we're both taking some chances here. I mean, if you think about it, and I have, you could have friends out there ready to take out Ivy's Head of Security three days into our walk. I don't know you any more than you know me. Right? So I'm deciding to just go with this and trust that you're taking me to some tech the team needs. You're gonna have to trust I'm safe...enough. Safe enough to get you there and back."

"What if I show you the tech and then you kill me?" she asked him with a smile on her face, suggesting she wasn't actually concerned.

"Well, then I'm back to being a shitty human being which I'm going to try really hard not to be," he said with a laugh.

"So no drugging or killing each other, then?" she asked him, smiling.
He agreed. "Definitely not. Neither of those."

Their meal was brought to them quickly and included two plastic bins filled with food supplies for their trip. Kali marveled at the various types of jerky and assortment of dried fruits that had been brought to them. Lev explained that their man running the farm came into the apocalypse with already honed skills. They also had a bag of quinoa, six small potatoes, two cucumbers, two zucchinis, several carrots, two onions, a clove of garlic, a bundle of firm leaves that Lev couldn't identify, a bag of dried black beans, a large bag of shelled peanuts, a bag of dried bread that lev said was their version of hardtack, a jar of berry preserves which Lev assumed was to make the hardtack edible, and finally a jar of preserved tomatoes.

"Can you cook?" he asked her in a serious tone as he pulled out a medium sized pot and dug around to find the lid.

"Oh, well, I haven't in years, or ever, but I guess I could try. I don't want to ruin the food, but it looks mostly like salad to me," she said to him with a shrug.

He laughed. "I'm only kidding. Don't worry, I can cook. Where's the water?" he asked getting up and walking out of his room to the guards. He returned a moment later and told her, "They left two gallons of water outside the door."

She looked up at him and rolled her eyes and shook her head. "I arrived with nothing except five pieces of tech and a half a sandwich and managed just fine. I might need to pour out half of my gallon of water to be able to carry my share," she said, sighing.

"I'll carry your water. And remember, we're going there and back, so twice as far, and you arrived pretty damn hungry the other morning."

"That's true. The food will be nice to have. I can't believe how much jerky they gave us," she said opening her eyes wide.

They decided Kali would carry most of the food and her clothes. Lev took half of the jerky and dried fruit from her so that he wouldn't have to ask her for any while they walked. He put some of what he took for himself into a side pocket of his backpack for easy access. Lev would carry the water, the supplies he'd taken from the storage closet, his own supplies, the cookware, the jar of tomatoes, the bag of quinoa, and the weapons. He stuffed the duffle bag into his pack and made it fit. Kali tried on her pack and Lev was impressed when she didn't ask him to lighten her load by assuming responsibility for anything else in her backpack. He didn't bother to feel the weight he'd be carrying. He'd traveled further carrying more and he knew he'd be fine. Horses would have been ideal, because they could have brought more supplies with them, but they were assuming the role of horses for this trip and Kali was basically a miniature pony to his Clydesdale.

Departure

Kali was asleep on his couch. The light from the hallway was shining on his face, but that wasn't what was keeping him awake. The thought of The Benefactor actually making contact with the RT through Kali kept his brain spinning and defying sleep no matter how badly he wanted and needed the rest. He tried to quiet the enthusiasm in his mind about having tech and formulas that would help them make more progress by rationalizing the probability as low. Looking over at her lying there asleep, it seemed so unlikely that this was the person who was chosen to deliver technology designed to save the Universe from an "evil fucking villain" as The Benefactor had described the man who had murdered nearly seven billion people in a single moment. How many others had not died instantly. Those were the ones who haunted Lev's nightmares. Even after all this time. Those the villain hadn't killed instantly, he tortured by default. Prisha's face and her voice calling out to him suddenly filled his head. It had been at least a decade since he'd thought of her. He grabbed his face with both hands and rubbed hard.

Random, disjointed thoughts were keeping him awake the more tired he became. He had decided to sleep with his boots on rather than have Kali suggest he wear them. She had refused his offer of better footwear saying that the sneakers she was wearing had already been broken in and her feet hurt enough already without having to contend with a new pair of boots.

He had decided to take two knives and two guns with extra bullets. Bolin had sent him enough for a team of six, but he wanted to travel light and figured the walk wouldn't be too bad through the area heading north. A lot of that roadway was nothing but green pastures for miles. Kali had just done it and encountered no other people or problems. There were fewer and fewer people around it seemed.

That was the last thought he had before being woken by the guards knocking on his open door at 4am.

"Ok. I'm up," he told the guard.

"Kali," the guard whispered.

"I've got her," Lev said not wanting him to startle her. She was, after all, always claiming to need to be ready to run or fight.

Lev turned on the ceiling light hoping Kali would wake up fully aware of where she was and who he was. He stood back from the couch as he called out her name and watched as her eyes opened suddenly. She remained motionless with only her eyes moving around the room to orient herself. She settled on Lev's face and looked at him blankly before saying, "I'm awake." He hadn't seen her wake up before and was glad she could orient herself so quickly. He had been worried.

"You want to go use the bathroom before we head out?" he asked her. She got up quickly and walked into his bathroom without turning on the light. He realized she wasn't going to close the door and busied himself moving their backpacks out into the hallway. There was a bag of food on the floor and one of the guards told him that the kitchen staff had sent it over a few minutes before 4am. It was breakfast. Lev stopped to consider how thorough the kitchen staff was and wanted to remember to thank James and his staff for considering all the details which would make this mission easier. Feeding them as they left was above and beyond. He hadn't ordered them to do that. Sometimes, maybe he underestimated the commitment of the community to the well-being of all members. Anyone who had already heard the community lie, which would have begun being spread last night, believed that he and Kali were going to retrieve essential medicines for the community, but even that didn't mean people needed to wake up before him and Kali to prepare a breakfast for their journey. He looked over at the bag of food and noticed two canteens beside the bag. He picked one up and unscrewed the top. Hot chicory. "Fucking awesome," he muttered aloud while looking at the two guards. "Tell them I appreciated their efforts," he said as he walked back into his room.

Kali was still in the bathroom so he pulled the sheets off his bed and grabbed the sheet from his couch and tossed them into his growing pile in the hallway. He looked at the guards and said, "One of you, volunteer to do my laundry. I offer nothing in return." Both instantly agreed to provide Lev with the service. "Ok, I offer my appreciation," he said as he waved at them and walked back into his room hoping Kali was ready. Kali was leaving the bathroom and told him she was ready to go. He asked her to give him a minute and walked into his bathroom, flicking on the exterior light switch as he entered, and closed the door. Kali went over to the doorway and tried to talk to the guards, but they seemed hesitant to speak with her, so she leaned on the doorframe and waited quietly for Lev.

Outside the front gate, Lev took the weapons he had had sent down the previous evening with the security team on duty. Someone had included a belt to secure at least one gun and one knife. Again he thought about how thorough community members were being in sending him off with Kali. Was it just for the imaginary medical supplies that they made the effort? Lev struggled with this same internal conversation even after nearly two decades. He made an effort to thank the security team members who offered him the belt making carrying the weapons easier. He hadn't been thinking earlier when he planned to carry a gun in his waistband anyway. He wasn't perfect. He knew that. He had assembled lots of evidence over the years that told him he was an imperfect asshole. But he'd rather be an imperfect asshole with a proper belt for carrying his gun and his knife. He meant it when he thanked the security team for their help.

He walked away from Ivy with Kali by his side, keeping pace.

Day 1

Kali kept pace with Lev for about 15 minutes before pointing out that his legs were much longer than hers.

"Jesus, slow down Lev. You're like a foot taller than me!" she said in exasperation. He slowed down and offered her a canteen with hot chicory. "Ooh, apocalypse coffee. This stuff is good," she said, taking her canteen from him. "That was nice of them to give us breakfast," she added as she unscrewed the top and took a sip.

Lev considered her acknowledgement of the kitchen staff. Appreciation seemed to come easily to her. He was suspicious of people when they offered him something. He was hateful when they offered him nothing. Sometimes he felt confused when the rage and appreciation swirled inside him all at once. Kali seemed unbothered. He didn't know. She was an enigma. Maybe she would beat him to death with a rock tonight in his sleep. Maybe he was tired of living this life and he wanted her to. Why was he even here walking with this lunatic? He kept forgetting. Then he'd remind himself that an entire team of academics agreed she might … might have been sent by The Benefactor. And she might… might have technology that could assist them in understanding how the "evil fucking villain" had murdered nearly seven billion people in an instant.

So, here he was. Kali telling him to slow down. Not unlike the man who had wiped out most of human life on earth, he too, had killed enough people in his own life to be deemed a mass murderer. But Kali told him to slow down, and he did.

He looked over at her. "Is this a better pace for you?" he asked her.

"Yeah," she said, smiling slightly.

He laughed internally.

They weren't making the kind of time that Lev had hoped to make, but Kali seemed able to maintain the pace they had going now. It was still dark outside, but the northern roads leading out of Ivy were clear for several miles. The sun would be up before they began to travel on roads less familiar to Lev.

The sunrise brought a warmth to the air that warned of a hot and humid day to come. She looked at him while they walked. Mostly she looked at his back as he continued to maintain a pace that didn't match her own. She was about to renegotiate their pace a second time when he spoke.

"Are you really from California?" he asked her suddenly, still marching ahead of her.

"Yeah."

"So am I."

"What part?" she asked him, sincerely curious.

"Coronado. Over the bridge from San Diego."

"Oh, I grew up in San Diego. The city. Our condo was on Ash Street downtown."

Lev stopped walking and stood silently for a minute.

She walked up to him and asked, "What? Do you see something?" She scanned ahead of them to see if she could identify anything interesting.

He looked down at her squinting and shook his head in confusion. "You're not really from San Diego, right? The whole California thing was made up."

She looked up at him and said, "No. I told you I'm from California. I grew up in San Diego."

She seemed sincere, but he wanted to test her. "Where was the best place to get a California burrito in San Diego?"

"Is this a test?" she asked, smiling and rolling her eyes. "I'm not going to fail any of your San Diego tests," she warned him while walking ahead of him now.

He waited for her, expecting her to stop and turn around, but she didn't. He conceded the battle and jogged up to her asking, "Well?"

"I was going to say Baja Burritos down in Chula Vista. Did you know that place?" she asked him.

"Oh, hell yeah, I remember them! My friends and I used to drive there going a hundred miles an hour during open lunch at school. We'd call ahead and eat on the drive back. Totally trashed my friend's car all of us eating burritos and whatever in there every day. Rolled up to school every morning smelling like a taco truck. He drove like a crazy fucker, too, as if we were involved in a high speed chase. He'd drive with one hand while eating his burrito with the other, changing lanes without signaling. Can't believe we never crashed," he said, laughing out loud at the memories. "So," he asked her, "are you saying Baja Burritos was the best place for California burritos? Because I was going to say Juan's in Pacific Beach, but now I'm going to say Baja Burritos because of the memories as well as their burritos."

"I was going to say Baja Burritos, but when you spoke about memories, I remembered the little Mexican food stand as you entered I.B. and, same reason as you chose Baja, I'm choosing that stand in I.B. because my father would take me there Saturday afternoons after we'd go surfing. Even if we went up to Sunset Cliffs to surf, or someplace even further north, we'd still drive all the way down to I.B. for lunch at that dusty little stand. Their California burritos were packed. Could eat one for lunch, dinner later, and breakfast the next morning. Plus, like I said, the memories. I miss my dad."

Lev shook his head and said, "Fuck, Kali. You're really from home?" He was smiling, but Kali saw the sadness behind the smile matched her own.

"Yeah, I'm from there, and Juan's in P.B. sucked. Fuck their guacamole. And fuck their parking lot."

They both broke into laughter at the memories, and Lev felt a little less homesick for the first time in nearly two decades while reminiscing with her.

"Was your mom around, or was it just you and your dad?" he asked her.

"My mom died in a car accident when I was seven. My dad died three days after my high school graduation. Committed suicide," she said.

"Jesus. Let's talk about something else, huh?" he said, looking over at her as she walked beside him.

He had slowed his pace after their California burrito competition which they mutually decided they had both won. Kali said neither could win against the good memories of the other. Lev agreed. They talked about surfing because Lev wondered if maybe they had crossed paths on the beaches being as he was also an avid surfer back then.

"You have a very distinct look, so, I think I would remember you if I had seen you," she said, looking him up and down.

"I was pretty clean cut when I was younger. Not nearly as hairy," he said with a laugh.

"I'm very basic, so I don't expect you would have noticed me," she said as a matter of fact.

He scoffed. "You're not basic."

Still, they concluded they couldn't recall one another from any of the beaches young southern California surfers frequented.

"How old are you? Maybe we were off by a couple of years."

"Here, I guess I'm 43," she said.

"We're both 43 then," he said while thinking about what she had said. *'Here she's 43?'* Either she never stopped playing the part, or he was walking beside a time traveling, maybe 43 year old from home. Thinking about it occupied his thoughts for a while.

They were approaching the gas station where she had spent her last night before arriving at Ivy. She pointed it out to him and said, "There's an apartment in the back of that gas station. I stayed there the night before I got to Ivy. I want to go grab some more clothes from there on our way back. The dead lady was my size."

Lev nodded and said, "Ok."

They walked in silence for a little longer until Lev said, "Talking about home brings back a lot I usually don't bother to think about. For you, too, I guess. You ok?"

"I'm ok," she said, grabbing a hold of one of his belt loops with her index finger in an effort to keep pace with him. He felt her attachment to his belt loop and kept walking without saying anything, but he slowed down a little more. They continued to walk in silence with Kali attached by a single finger to his belt loop.

They had a late lunch under a shady tree, and Lev talked about walking until sunset before calling it a day. Kali had a mouthful of hardtack and berry preserves in her mouth when he said that and quickly held up her hand shaking her head and reached for her canteen and the last of her apocalypse coffee, as she kept calling it.

"Mm-mm. No. No way am I walking until dark. I'm ready to quit now. I'm tired. I need a nap. No!" she said sternly, shaking her head.

"The sun won't set until around 7:30. We can get in a lot more wa--"

"I'm not doing that! We left at 4:30 in the fucking morning!" she interrupted him, still shaking her head in defiance of his suggestion.

"We can get in a lot more walking and get back to Ivy quicker if we just power through the daylight hours," he said quickly, hoping not to be interrupted again.

He watched as she began counting on her fingers adding up the hours they would walk if they continued to walk until sunset.

"I'm not walking for 15 hours, Lev. In fact, I quit right now. Lunch was great. I'm full. I'm going to take a nap now," she said as she laid her head on her backpack.

"Come on. You're kidding, right?"

"Do I look like I'm kidding or do I look like I'm taking a nap?" she asked him with her eyes closed.

"Ok, ok. Listen, there aren't any places I can see ahead to stop for the night. Can we agree to walk until we find a place we can set up for the night?" he asked her.

She sat up and looked off into the distance of the direction they were heading.

"Well?"

"I'm trying to remember this area. How far away a house or a store that isn't burned to the ground is from here," she said, scowling at him.

"Is it the backpack? You want me to carry your backpack?" he asked, trying to be helpful.

"No. It's me. It's my feet. It's my brain. It's my will to keep on going in this humid heat storm. I'm done, man. Done for today. I mean, if you want me to walk tomorrow, I need a fucking break today. I'm not one of your soldiers. I'm a different kind of soldier. I've been a housebound hostage for years. I didn't have an opportunity to physically train for this before coming here. I was too busy trying to remember useful things like how to find you fucking people!" She looked at him and he could see she was truly annoyed with him for the first time since she'd walked up to Ivy. "My feet hurt!" she said again angrily for emphasis while he was thinking.

He didn't want to fight with her so soon on their walk, and he realized she had made good points he hadn't considered. Was she a housebound hostage for years? That he didn't know. But looking at her, he did know she wasn't hard like the people he lived with. One look at her hands told him she wasn't farming or chopping wood to survive. The scars on her arms only indicated that she'd been abused. "Alright. We'll rest here a bit longer and then we'll walk but only to find a place to stop for the night. Deal?" he asked, trying to appease her.

"Yeah, deal," she said as she closed her eyes and fell asleep as he watched her.

He went behind a tree to relieve himself and walked back to sit near Kali while she slept. He'd let her sleep for 30 minutes. The fact that they had grown up within a couple of miles of one another boggled his mind. They had gone to all the same beaches and surfed. Probably had seen one another even if neither could recall a particular time. They ate at the same restaurants. They drove on the same streets. Shopped in the same malls. Maybe they went to the same concerts. What kind of music did she listen to? How did he and Kali both end up 3000 miles from home, only to find each other in a field at Ivy when he couldn't find Yuna all those years ago when she must have been so close by? He never spoke about it with Aisha back then or ever. He kept it all to himself, but he manifested his bitter disappointment and rage in everything he did after the explosion at the airport.

He laid down on his back and looked up at the blue sky. He missed California. He missed who he had been. He looked over at Kali. Jesus, this was not how he imagined his life would turn out.

He got up and knelt by Kali, touching her lightly on the shoulder. "Hey. Wake up," he said, expecting it to take her a minute to be roused after the short nap.

Instead, she opened her eyes quickly and looked around before sitting up. "Damn. Already?" she asked him.

"Yeah, let's find a place for the night," he said.

They got back onto the old cracked roadway and continued on, walking around the occasional car or truck. There weren't many. The traffic on this road had been light back in the day. Before they had stopped for lunch, they had walked through miles of roadway with very little other than sweeping green vistas. This part of Virginia had pockets of small towns with miles of green between them. For a car traveling at the speed limit, the distances weren't a big consideration. For Lev and his weary walking companion, it was another story.

He began to understand why she had said the walk had taken her so long. Why she was confused about how many days she had walked. She liked to stop and take breaks. He wondered if she had a touch of narcolepsy the way she could just lay down and take a nap. She made it clear that she would not be walking if it rained. It tended to rain a lot this time of year. He wanted to push her to keep moving, but he wasn't certain if they were five days from their destination or three. Maybe they were six days away. She wouldn't tell him where she had hidden the tech, insisting that if they were captured, it would be better for him if he didn't know. Trusting her went against every rational thought in his mind, but he and the team had decided it was an opportunity they must take if she had, indeed, been sent by The Benefactor.

It wasn't long before they saw a structure through the trees across the highway which appeared to be intact. As they approached the one story white house, Kali mentioned that there were no cars in the driveway which she hoped meant there would be no bodies inside they would have to step over. There were no other houses around the white house. It was sitting there all by itself out in the tall grasses along the old highway. The home was locked, and all of the windows were shut. Lev kicked in the door which gave way easily to his strength. He walked inside ahead of Kali and went through the rooms quickly for a once over with her following him.

"You're right. Nobody was here when it happened. Got the place to ourselves." He smiled, while dropping his backpack and supplies on the dining room table. He scanned the space thinking, so what if they hadn't walked nearly enough the first day? He was glad to have a decent place to sleep rather than sleeping outside or in some place with the dead lying about. Also, Kali wasn't the only one who was tired. He had gotten very little sleep the night before. He felt his body relax at the thought of getting some sleep.

Kali was going through the rooms and came back with several candles and a pack of matches. She wasn't half bad at this, he thought. She disappeared into other rooms as he looked around for things Ivy might need. Tech always wanted metals, so he went into the bedrooms and looked for jewelry.

Kali noticed and asked, "Oh, is that for tech stuff?"

He looked up at her surprised that she would know that and said, "Yeah. Good guess or do you have a hidden skill with technology? I mean, you're not a scientist, your math skills must suck because I saw you doing finger math earlier, and yet, you claim you were sent to deliver tech. So are you an IT hotshot?" he asked, hoping the answer would be yes.

"No. And IT people know math. I just know random shit like that. Keeps people guessing what my value might be," she said and rolled her eyes at him.

He laughed and said, "You're entertaining. That's your value. My life's been more exciting since you arrived," he said while he walked into the next room.

Kali claimed what looked like a spare bedroom with a twin bed and told Lev he could take the master bedroom with the bigger bed. She walked through the house opening all of the windows and walked outside to survey the property. When she came back inside, he asked her if they had to keep all of the windows open and she told him they had to because they provided quick escape routes in case the people she was afraid of came for her. He let it go. It was warm outside anyway. If it had been the winter, he might have objected. Might have, because at this point, he had acquiesced to so many of her quirky demands that he wasn't entirely certain he wouldn't have just found some extra blankets and dealt with the cold.

She came out of the kitchen and asked, "Will old coffee kill us?" while holding an unopened jar of freeze dried coffee.

"Actually, no and that might still be ok. Want to save that for the morning or have some now?" he asked her.

"I'll wait until tomorrow. Do you want some tonight?"

"No, I'm actually into this idea of getting some sleep tonight. I'm going to make us some food. Where'd you put your backpack?" he asked her. She pointed to it on the floor and he picked it up and put it in the kitchen before going outside to make a fire in a large metal pot he found under a kitchen cabinet.

Kali continued to look through the house and found a bunch of books, but not the one about the rabbits. She pulled the blanket off of the bed she was going to sleep on and removed the pillow cases from the pillows and put on clean ones she had found in a linen closet. Lev came back inside and cut up some vegetables and walked back outside with them and some salt he took from the kitchen, adding them to the quinoa. When he brought the food inside, he grabbed two bowls from the kitchen cabinets and she watched him empty the contents of the pot into their bowls. She walked into the kitchen with a glass of water she had poured for herself and grabbed two spoons and dropped one in each bowl and he said, "Look what I found," holding up a bottle of scotch. "Yeah?" he asked her.

She held up her hand and laughed while declining, telling him he didn't have to share. "What? You don't like scotch? This is the good stuff."

She responded, "Alcohol messes with my ability to have an orgasm."

He laughed and said, "Oh! See, I thought you were going to say alcohol messed with your ability to fight and run."

He was getting a glass for the scotch as he said that and she shrugged saying, "Well, you know, priorities, Lev."

He let out a big laugh and said, "Cheers, to that!" and they clinked their glasses before he took a shot of the scotch.

The dinner he made them was good and she told him so while he took her bowl from her to finish what she could not. He didn't get drunk, but he enjoyed himself having no less than two large glasses of the scotch he had found. He might have been into his third glass when he asked her where she went to high school.

"La Jolla. My father was a high school physics teacher there," she said and before he could respond added, "I wasn't thinking. I shouldn't have told you that. I don't want you to be able to identify me. Really. That makes me nervous."

"Hey, hey. Don't worry. I'm keeping your secrets. If you tell me it's a secret, I'll keep it to myself," he said to her, but he was also really surprised to learn that her father had taught physics. He suddenly said, "You mentioned blisters on your feet. How bad are they? I brought a first aid kit and letting them air out overnight will help them heal."

"I have to sleep with my shoes on," she said, sounding unwilling to compromise.

"That's right. I forgot. Ok, come on. Feet on the coffee table. Let me see so I know how hard I can push you tomorrow when we start walking." He was using his hands to motion for her to put her feet on the coffee table and she thought he looked and acted funny as the alcohol loosened him up. She imagined he was probably a fun guy at one point in his life. His stories of being a teenager in California suggested he had been.

He got up and took the first aid kit out of his backpack and sat down as she removed her shoes and two pairs of socks from each foot.

"You better not have a foot fetish that I'm unwittingly participating in, Lev," she said, laughing at him as he motioned for her to hurry up with the removal of her footwear.

He winced as she placed her feet out on the coffee table before them.

"Oh jeez. If I did have a foot fetish, it'd be over now!" he said as he looked at her feet. "You need to let your feet get some air tonight. Come on. They're going to get worse if you don't make a little effort with them."

He got up and told her he'd be right back. He went and grabbed a towel from the linen closet and laid it on the coffee table, motioning to her to put her feet on top of it.

"You ready?" he asked as he held the bottle of scotch over her feet.

"Really? Is that necessary?" she asked as he poured the alcohol on her multiple broken blisters.

He sat back on the couch and sipped his glass of scotch and looked at her. "Yeah. That was necessary. And a sinful waste of good booze all at the same time. Let them air dry. You need to sleep with your feet uncovered."

She went to argue with him, but he held up his hand and said, "Kali, you *have* to. I'm not telling you you have to... Your feet are telling you you have to. We have a lot of walking to do."

"Fine," she said quietly.

"Yeah? Ok. That was easy. What's the catch? Because with you, I'm learning that if it's easy, there's a catch."

Kali rolled her eyes and waved her hand at him. "Can I put my mattress in your room and sleep on the floor?"

"Yep. Let's do that. That's an easy fix, and I am thrilled to assist," he said, finishing his drink.

"Can I have a gun?" she asked him.

"What? No. I'm not going to sleep if you have a gun. Are you testing to see how drunk I am?" he said with a laugh. "I'm not drunk. Look at me. I'm huge. Takes more than what I've had to make a dent in me. You're gonna be fine. I'll move your mattress now. You should stay there and let your feet dry."

He got up and went to the room she had chosen and quickly dragged the mattress to the master bedroom and came back saying, "You're all set. I'll kill anyone who shows up. Let's get some sleep."

She went to put her feet on the floor and he stopped her saying, "Wait. We just killed all the germs on your feet and this floor hasn't been cleaned in 17 years." Without warning, he scooped her up from her chair and carried her down the hallway into the bedroom and placed her standing up on the mattress he'd dragged in moments earlier.

"There," he said, satisfied with his efforts.

She started laughing and said, "I have to pee."

"What?!" he asked, laughing with her. "Fucking hell," he laughed. "Hold on. Let me find some clean socks in this place." He went to the dresser in the bedroom and opened drawers to find clean socks for her to wear so she could go relieve herself. He tossed two pairs at her, giving her an extra pair in case she woke up in the night and needed to pee again. They were still laughing as she left the bedroom.

When she returned, she pulled her mattress closer to the open window, and he watched to make sure she removed the socks. He turned away as she reached under her shirt to remove her bra, saying goodnight to her.

"Goodnight, Lev," she said.

See? She thought to herself, he was probably a funny guy at one point. Too bad about the apocalypse.

Day 2

It was still dark in the house when Kali woke up. The air in the room was cool and felt good. She could hear Lev breathing deeply in his sleep. She was lying on her back and ran her hand down over her breast. She sighed and turned over onto her side. She wished she had been able to sleep alone in the other room. She had brought along the vibrator for a reason. She wiggled her toes and stretched her feet to see if they had gotten any better overnight. They still hurt. It would be overly optimistic to expect otherwise, really. She grabbed the second pair of socks Lev had given her and put them on. She removed the knife she had placed under her pillow when she had returned from the bathroom the night before and stood up noiselessly and looked over at Lev. He was shirtless, sleeping on his stomach. At Ivy he slept on his back fully clothed. Maybe this was how he slept when he'd been drinking, she thought with amusement.

She put the knife back in the kitchen drawer and walked around the house looking for shoes in the closets of the other two bedrooms and the hallway closet. The woman who had lived in the house clearly did not have an office job. The first pair of shoes Kali tried felt just a little too big for her feet. Maybe a half size too big. Better than being a half size too small, she thought to herself. All of the shoes in the former homeowner's closets were practical. There were shoes for doing yard work on the large property, shoes for walking, and shoes for hiking in the woods. None of the shoes Kali found had heels. She brought all that she found into the living room and tried them on finding the best ones for her bruised and battered feet. She realized she'd be wearing two pairs of socks and whatever she chose would fit even better then. She didn't want to wake Lev by rummaging around for more socks, but she separated out the best shoes for the walk and decided to wear one pair and pack a second. She put on some overly large rain boots while she prepared to leave the house.

She poured some of their water into the kettle on the stove and took it outside with a book of matches. The black had faded from the sky and was a shade of gray that provided enough light to see now. She was going to search around for some sticks to burn, but went back inside and grabbed two books that looked boring and lit them on fire instead. She placed the kettle on the oven grate over the kitchen-pot barbeque Lev had set up in the driveway when he had prepared their dinner. When the water began to steam, she took the kettle back inside, walking away from the flames that were already dying down to nothing. She opened the jar of freeze dried instant coffee and made herself a cup. It had an aftertaste that she could have done without, but she recognized it as coffee and was happy with the results. She looked around the kitchen and found some sugar and added that to her coffee. It was much better now. She grabbed a wooden chair from the dining room table and walked outside with it and her coffee. She sat next to the smoldering books drinking her sweetened black coffee while looking out at the lush summer greenery all around the house. It must have been paradise living out here. It seemed so peaceful to her.

Lev woke up and saw that Kali was gone and instantly panicked. He jumped up out of the bed and went to run out of the room when he saw the back of her as she made her way through the front door carrying a wooden chair from the dining room. He leaned forward and exhaled as his heart beat hard in his chest. He stood up straight and tried to catch his breath. Was that a panic attack? He wondered. Jesus Christ. Adrenaline coursed through his body and his skin prickled from it. What the hell was she wearing on her feet?

He composed himself and walked over to the front door which remained open. He watched her set the chair down and sit down with her back towards him and the house. She was holding a cup and he realized he could smell coffee along with burning paper. He looked back outside at her and saw there was smoke coming from the barbeque he had constructed last night. He walked into the kitchen and surveyed the scene, made himself a cup of coffee, grabbed a chair, and walked out to join her.

"Hey," he said as he approached her, hoping not to startle her.

"Hi," she said turning towards him. She noticed he was still shirtless and realized she hadn't put her bra back on yet. "Isn't it pretty out here?" she asked, pointing towards the landscape.

He sat down and looked at the view. "Yeah. It is. Must have been nice to wake up to this every day," he said.

"I was just thinking that, too."

He looked down at her footwear. "Nice boots. How are the feet this morning?"

"Not gonna lie. They still hurt, but I found some shoes that fit and I think that will help."

"Not those boots, right?" He laughed but then said seriously, "No, really. Not those boots."

She smiled at him over her coffee and said, "No. Proper walking shoes. The boots were just for getting around without ruining your attempts at podiatry last night. Thank you, by the way. I'm sure you were right and I needed to sleep without my shoes on. My feet are probably better even if I don't realize it yet."

"Podiatry is just one of the talents I developed in the aftermath of the apocalypse," he said with a small laugh.

They finished their coffees as the sky turned from grey to a soft shade of blue. There were no clouds in the sky and they would likely be walking in some high temperatures throughout the day. The road they needed to travel on offered little shade. The two sided highway was separated by a wide grassy median and trees on either side of the highway were set back from the road far enough that their shade didn't reach people who were walking along the paved path.

Kali brought Lev out back to show him an old hand water pump near some dilapidated raised garden beds. "I tried it yesterday and water came out," she said to him.

"Why didn't you tell me about it then?" he asked her incredulously.

"I forgot after I came back in and found the coffee," she said, shrugging. "Is it safe to wash off in? I don't know how this stuff works," she said, looking at him for an answer.

"I wouldn't drink it, but I'd definitely shower in it. Maybe wear the boots and keep the water off of your feet just to be safe," he suggested.

"Do you want to go first?" she asked him, turning to head inside.

"No. You found it. You go first and I'll have another cup of coffee and some food. You want me to heat up enough water for you, too?"

"No. I'm good," she said, heading around the house with him to the front door.

Inside, she rummaged through the drawers and closets of the late homeowners hoping to find something to wear rather than using up the clothes she had brought. Walking in the heat and humidity left her feeling sticky and greasy all at the same time. She appreciated that Ivy had running water. By looking through the clothes in the closets, she found that the practical shoe wearing, garden tending, tidy woman who had lived in the home had been taller than her, but lean like herself. Kali tried on one of the woman's bras and was extremely happy when it fit. She found five bras and decided to pack them all now rather than risk not coming back to this house on the way back to Ivy. When she couldn't find scissors anywhere in the house, she went to the kitchen and dug around in a kitchen drawer while Lev made his second cup of coffee.

She pulled out a knife and walked up alongside him. "Hey, can you cut this much off?" she asked, holding up the pants to him along with the knife. He looked down at what she was offering him and took both items and made quick work of removing at least five inches of denim from the bottom of each pant leg. "Thanks" she said and asked, "Can I get the soap you packed from your backpack?" He nodded and went out front where he sat in his dining room chair near the homemade barbeque in the driveway and she headed through the house to the back and exited a door that led from a second living room to a very light grey, crumbling wooden deck out back.

The water was cool and refreshing. She took her time and cleaned her body and hair thoroughly. It felt good to get yesterday's salty sweat off of her skin and the grease off of the rest of her body and out of her hair. She walked up onto the old wooden deck off the back door and dressed in the clothes she had placed there. She cuffed the pant legs and rolled them part of the way up her shins. The jeans were a dark blue and contrasted nicely with the white t-shirt she had found. She had two pairs of socks on now and slid her feet into the newly discovered shoes she planned to walk in. They felt better on her feet than the shoes she had walked to Ivy wearing. She brought her old clothes inside and laid them over the back of a chair hoping they would return here on the way back and she could retrieve them. She brushed her hair and then brushed her teeth using baking soda she found in the kitchen.

Lev sat outside and ate some hardtack plain while drinking his second cup of coffee. He had gone to ask Kali if she remembered he'd packed soap when he saw her standing in the back room shirtless. He didn't watch. He turned around immediately. He considered himself a gentleman. A gentleman murderer, but life after the collapse of civilization was complicated. He had closed his eyes and stepped back into the dining room hoping she hadn't seen him accidentally see her. It had only been for a second. He didn't want things to get weird. Why didn't she close doors, anyway? The bathroom door in his room? She left it open. Was she just absent minded? Well, yeah. She was that.

When she came into the kitchen and rummaged through the drawers, he wondered if he should say something, but decided not to as she suddenly handed him the knife and the pants. If she had seen him see her, she didn't care. He didn't want to make a big deal out of it. It wasn't a big deal, he told himself, shrugging. But he had let her grab the soap from his backpack which contained his loaded spare gun, extra bullets, and knife. He sat there and ate the hardtack minus the preserves which he had forgotten when making a hasty exit from the kitchen.

She had a handful of dried fruit and a piece of jerky when she sat down on the chair next to him. "There's baking soda on the counter to brush your teeth. Let's bring it with us in case we don't find more. I'm afraid of dark ages dentistry."

He laughed and said, "It's even worse than you know. We've never had a dentist in either community." Then he told her about Campus a few short miles from Ivy.

"Oh my God. We shouldn't even eat this dried fruit if that's the case," she said as she put another piece in her mouth and chewed it.

"I told Bolin not to kill you when we saw you walking up to Ivy. I told him you might be a dentist."

She laughed at that and looked at him in amusement. Her hair was wet and she looked nice. Lev turned away from her.

"Ok, my turn to clean up," he said, rising from his chair and heading inside to grab some clean clothes.

"I left the soap on the deck for you," she called back to him.

Before they left the white house, Lev came out to the living room with a box of bandages and a jar of petroleum jelly.

"This stuff doesn't expire. Put a bit on each of your broken blisters and then cover each one," he said as he handed them to her.

She rolled her eyes and threw her head back sighing loudly like an annoyed teenager before aggressively unlacing her shoes to remove them. "I'm not doing this because you told me to. I'm doing it because my feet want me to!" she said defiantly.

When she was finished, Lev had both of their backpacks ready to go.

"Did you pack the soap?" she asked him.

"Yeah, got that," he said as he slung his backpack over his shoulders. "Let's go. We're getting a late start," he added as he held up her backpack so that she could weave her arms through the straps.

Lev closed the door as they left. He had also closed all the windows. It was a nice house.

They walked for a couple of hours talking about various topics. When they discussed vacations they had taken when they were younger, they discovered they had each visited many of the same California landmarks including Death Valley, Yosemite, Joshua Tree, Sequoia National Park, and more. Both had also enjoyed family vacations to places in Arizona and New Mexico and agreed Arizona offered the backdrop to many good memories with their parents.

Talking helped to pass the time and influenced a slow and leisurely pace to the walk. Lev's mind wasn't filled with one objective that he felt compelled to plow towards regardless of the reality around him. He knew why they were walking, but he wasn't myopically focused on the end goal as he had been yesterday.

Kali had felt alone with her memories for so long that talking about shared experiences with him reminded her of details she had long forgotten. When he described the claustrophobic ascent up to the top of the Watchtower at the Grand Canyon, she remembered climbing up with her father and told him it made her happy to remember that day. As a teacher, her father had a lot of days off during the year to take his only child around on adventures. They had done a lot together.

Lev told her he had not thought about many of these memories in nearly two decades. There were no bad memories, but they each acknowledged there was a sadness associated with them now because the people they had shared the adventures with were all long gone.

"I'll remember you as part of that history now," she told Lev.

He nodded and offered a quiet, "Yeah."

They walked in silence for some time when Lev said, "Hey. I think I see your field of cosmos."

"Oh, there they are!" she said happily. "I told you it was a big field of them.

They look so pretty with the blue sky above and the green fields all around."

In his mind, Lev agreed. It was a sight to behold. The various colors of the swaying cosmos across the field lit up the landscape. When they reached the field of cosmos, Kali picked a pink one from the edge and placed it through her hair over her ear.

"Only one?" he asked her.

"Yeah. We have a long way to go. I'll get a handful on the way back," she said, smiling up at him with the flower in her hair.

Lev noticed Kali had not complained once yet during their walk. He asked her if she wanted to stop to eat and she agreed. They found a wooden bench set outside a tractor supply store and Lev went inside and brought out a large folding umbrella and placed it in the center hole of the table giving them much needed shade from the sun.

"Definitely need another shower after today. Find us another house with a working hand water pump, Lev," she said jokingly.

He laughed and said, "That was really lucky. We might not get to bathe again until we hit that place on our return trip. We'll show up at Ivy fresh and clean like we're returning from a vacation," he added.

"But we'll have tech," she said, raising her eyebrows at him and nodding.

"Will we?" He sounded doubtful, but not annoyed.

"Oh, I forgot you still aren't sure I'm not taking you on a hapless adventure. That's ok. You'll see in a few days. Then you'll know." She smiled at him.

"Well, I don't doubt you believe it. Do you want to tell me the names of your friends?" he asked, hoping to hear the true name of The Benefactor and give him the proof he so desperately wanted in order to prove she wasn't making it all up.

"Ok. But don't tell anyone else before I do, ok? I'll need to explain the relationship," she said, looking at him minus her usual smile.

"Yeah, yeah. You got it." He felt himself suddenly hold his breath involuntarily. He stared at her, unable to blink. If he'd tried to swallow he felt for sure he'd start choking.

He watched as she looked at him and said, "Time. One of my friends is named Time. And Time doesn't like pronouns, so you have to refer to Time as Time all the time. So, if you wanted to say, 'Time is concerned that he/she/they/it can't access her/his/their/its ability to regulate space around some areas,' you would say, 'Time is concerned that Time can't access Time's ability to regulate space around some areas.' You see? It gets weird, but Time prefers it that way and who are we to argue with Time's pronoun preferences? No pronouns. Just Time's proper name. I think it's because Time isn't human. Time doesn't relate to pronouns."

Lev stared at her and felt himself breath, and blink, and swallow. She was crazy. She was absolutely crazy. They should turn around right now and head back to Ivy. They could sleep in the nice white house and even get cleaned up at the hand water pump before bed tonight. Hell, he'd even grab her some cosmos right from the roots from that field on the way back and have them planted around Ivy so she could walk around them being insane but happy. He would visit her outside in her cosmos gardens and they could talk about San Diego and all that good stuff. He might even take her over to Virginia Beach every summer and they could go surfing. Mostly, she could just wander around Ivy in her cosmos gardens being a happy, harmless lunatic. She could sleep outside under the tree. He'd tell everyone to leave her alone. He could do that.

He suddenly felt depressed. He liked her, but she was bat-fucking-shit crazy.

As if reading his mind, she said, "Lev. Listen. I know how it sounds. I do. But I'm telling you the truth."

"What's your other friend's name?" he asked her quietly.

"I can't tell you that. We need to get the tech. Then you'll believe me. I'm actually probably never going to reveal my other friend's name to any of you. If you knew my Friend's name, once you realized what they were capable of doing to your body and your mind, you might break and reveal the name to them. If no one learns my other Friend's name, that Friend would remain safe. The work might still continue no matter what happens to any of us. That's the sacrifice we're all potentially making. They won't kill Time. Time is safe." She was looking at him and closed her eyes and shook her head. "I made it worse by telling you Time's name."

"Kali, can you just tell me something that makes me think you might not be crazy rather than confirming that you probably are crazy?"

"It's all so abstract, Lev. It's not easy to figure out what you need."

"Your other friend's name. That might help."

"I can't give you that," she said curtly. She got up from the table and put her backpack on and smiled brightly at him. "Let's go get the tech I brought the Research Team so you can believe me."

He looked at her with the pink cosmos behind her ear and got up and grabbed his backpack and they headed back out to the main road to continue walking.

Like Kali the day before, Lev was tired of walking and wanted to quit early. He was decidedly overcome with regret at having asked her to reveal the names of her friends. He should have continued on for the next few days reminiscing about California, remaining in ignorance rather than confirming she was insane this early in the walk.

When they had reached the road, Kali turned to him and said, "You look really upset. The only thing we can do is get to where I hid the tech. That's what will help."

Lev thought of Bolin suggesting she would hand him silverware and tell him that was the tech she had brought them.

A couple of hours passed with them walking mostly in silence. Kali's feet were doing ok in the new shoes with the bandages, so when Lev suggested they stop and investigate four houses scattered ahead in the distance, she told him there was a larger community a few more miles ahead that would offer more options. They walked for a few minutes after Kali had made the suggestion when she suddenly stopped and turned to him.

"If you want to turn back and go back to Ivy then go!" she said firmly.

"Come on, Kali. I can't deal with this right now," he said still looking down the length of road ahead of them.

"Then don't deal with it. Go back to Ivy and I'll be back in a week or whatever. I'm not walking next to a zombie for the next few days. This is bullshit. I told you the truth. It's just hard to believe. That doesn't mean it's not the truth. I'm not a flat earther telling you we're walking to the edge of the earth. The tech is hidden like, I don't know, two days from here. You'll have proof in two days. Maybe three. It's fine if you think I'm crazy but you need to decouple that from you thinking I'm a liar. I'm not a liar. I told you the truth all day today. I told you one extra thing and you're like, 'Oh, Kali's a liar.'"

"I don't think you're a liar. I didn't say I think you're a liar," he said seriously.

"You say you think I'm crazy, but what you're doing now is calling me a liar. I'm telling you the truth," she said firmly, scowling at him.

He had seen that scowl on her face when she snapped at Heather about being at war for 17 years and Ivy still being unprepared. Again, that feeling of plausibility crept up inside of him. He thought of how the entire Research Team believed she was compelling enough to warrant his mission to find the tech she claimed she had brought for them.

He looked at her and said, "You're right. I got overwhelmed by one thing you said out of a lot of other things you've told me that are not crazy, and not lies. I'm focused on one thing. I'm not saying I believe you're taking me to actual tech you brought from the future, but I don't think you're a liar. We were both comfortable with me thinking you're crazy, right?" he asked her, smiling a little.

"Yeah, I don't care if you think I'm crazy," she shrugged.

"Ok. I can do that. I think you're a little crazy, but I don't think you're a liar. I apologize for putting that out there between us. I can understand why it would piss you off. I'm not pissed off at you, by the way."

"I know. You're just completely ready to fucking quit because you think I'm a liar."

"I thought you might be more crazy than I thought you were earlier today. That's not exactly the same as thinking you're a liar, but I get what you're saying. I'm gonna stop acting like a zombie and we'll get this done in the next couple of days or so without me being such a bitch. Ok?" he asked her.

"Yeah, ok," she said, offering him a smile back.

"I do lie sometimes, though," she said as they started walking again.

"Oh?" he asked, smiling and raising his eyebrows at her. "Gonna explain that?"

"I lie to survive all the time. I lie to my captors. I haven't lied to you yet even if I haven't told you everything. It's not even like those so-called lies of omission either. I'm trying to make it so I can tell you more." She looked up at him. "I'm trying to survive, Lev. And I'm still not lying to you."

He looked at her and looked away. "I get it. I'm not lying to you either, but I'm also not telling you everything."

"Yeah, like what's behind that white sheet in your meeting room," she said inquisitively, hoping for an answer.

"Yeah, like that. I can't tell you about that," he said with a small laugh.

"So we're even," she said.

They had walked a lot more than the previous day and chose a house from among a few in a small enclave of homes in an anemic development off the main road. None of the homes had fire damage, but four revealed a tornado had come through some time back. The house they chose was a large two story home that had no deceased inside. A dead dog was in a child's bedroom on the floor near the bed, and Lev closed the door so they wouldn't have to look at the scene.

"That's depressing," he said, making a face at Kali.

"Yeah," she agreed.

Kali found candles and then went to look through books in the home hoping to find the one about rabbits for Bautista. Well, actually, she was hoping to find it so that she could win the bet she had made with him. She didn't find the book she was looking for.

Lev was using an actual charcoal barbeque he had found in a neighboring garage. He wheeled it over to the driveway of the house they were staying in for the night. He was boiling beans and quinoa in their pot while chopping some vegetables, telling her that they were going to use the still unidentified leaves as wraps and have post-apocalyptic veggie burritos. She couldn't wait. She was really hungry after walking for so long.

He told her to wear the flip flops he had found in the neighbor's garage because she needed to get her feet out of her shoes so they could heal more and she said, "Ok, dad!" but she did what he asked her to do.

She lit all of the candles she'd found and placed them on the large, formal dining room table. She took the dying cosmos from her hair and placed it next to one of the lit candles. He placed a plate with two large leafy burritos in front of her and a plate with three large leafy burritos in front of his chair. "Wow, this is a lot of food" she said to him as he returned with a large bottle of vodka.

She shook her head and laughed saying, "Wow, that's a lot of vodka!"

He swirled the bottle around and laughed maniacally while pouring himself some. "You gonna join me tonight?" he asked her happily.

"Do I have to sleep barefoot again tonight, Dr. Podiatry?" she asked him.

"Yeah. So, we'll move a mattress into where ever and I'll sleep on the floor tonight. Why? What does that have to do with you having a drink with me?"

"Because if I'm not going to masturbate, I'll drink with you. Since we're sharing a room, I'll drink with you. Last night was bullshit. I could have had many drinks. Instead I just laid there frustrated on the floor," she said, smiling.

He closed his eyes and threw his head back laughing. "No, no. Please, feel free to do whatever you want. I'll just pretend I don't hear a thing." He held the bottle of vodka up and shrugged saying, "You can decline."

"Too late. Decision's been made. We're sharing a room," she said. "I'm not getting off tonight. Pour me some."

He reached over and filled her glass while they both laughed. "I'm going to make a toast," he said, raising his glass to hers. "Here's to a mostly enjoyable walk with my new friend from home. I really enjoyed talking with you today. Thank you for the hours where I was reminded about simpler, and better times. Here's to the hours I spent today reminded of the people I continue to love even as I miss them after all these years."

They clinked their glasses and each took a sip of their vodkas.

"That was really nice, Lev," she said, smiling at him.

"Well, I meant it," he said, smiling back.

The burritos Lev had made for them turned out really well. Kali only managed to eat one before declaring she was full. Lev said her uneaten burrito would stay fresh overnight and she could eat it in the morning for breakfast, but as they sat there drinking more vodka and telling random stories from their childhoods, he suddenly asked if she would mind if he ate it. She happily slid her plate over to him and watched as he finished it in just a few bites. He offered to refill her drink again, but she declined, reminding him that she might have to fight or run if anyone showed up overnight looking for her.

Lev was a big man, and though he had been drinking, he was still not legitimately drunk. "Listen, There's nothing out here in these parts of Virginia. Small towns, not a lot of resources. No reliable bodies of water nearby. People just don't stick around these parts. I think you're safe here tonight. I'll sleep with my shoes on. You don't need to worry so much out here. Probably more likely to get attacked at Ivy because people understand we have valuable resources they want."

She considered what he was saying and said, "I'm not trying to be argumentative, but you don't understand how they move. I can handle a tiny bit more, so go ahead and give me maybe a shot's worth. But you need to agree to sleep on the bed and not on the floor. It's easier to get up and fight from the bed than scramble to get up off the floor."

He poured more vodka into her glass and nodded his head, agreeing to let her sleep on the floor again.

She raised her glass to him and drank the vodka quickly. She put her empty glass down and said, "You know, I might help you fight. I'm not sure, yet."

He looked at her for a couple of seconds considering what she was saying and looked at the bite marks on her arms. He nodded his head and drank his own shot. "Want another?" he asked her.

"No. I've had enough."

"I'm having more," he said as he poured more into his glass.

Kali refused to sleep on the second floor where the bedrooms were located, so Lev dragged a twin mattress downstairs to the living room while she quickly went into the kitchen and got a knife and hid it near where she planned to tell him to put her mattress. She tossed a clean sheet on the couch for him. All of the doors and windows were open and her mattress was only a few feet from where he would be sleeping. Lev kept his shoes on and Kali kept hers off.

She was lying on her bed looking at him in the dark when he said, "If anyone comes for you, I want you to run."

"I might. I don't know," she said.

He knew better than to argue with her, so he let her have the last word for now.

Day 3

She woke up when it was still dark outside. She listened to Lev breathing for a little while and decided to get up and heat water for the instant coffee they had taken from the house they had stayed at the night before. She got up quietly, slipped on the flip flops he had found for her, and lit a couple of the candles in the kitchen so that she could see. She grabbed some old cereal in cardboard boxes from the pantry and brought them outside to the barbeque where she got the fire going. She added water to a teapot from the kitchen and brought it outside to heat the water. She found the sugar. She felt like she had a system now.

With her coffee made, she dragged a dining room chair out to the barbeque in the driveway but this time, she continued to add flammable boxed food products to the flames to keep it going. The boxed pastas crackled loudly. It was darker this morning than the previous morning. Maybe she had woken up earlier. She looked up and realized she couldn't see any stars in the night sky. Must be clouds. Maybe it would rain today. She wasn't going to agree to walk in the rain. She walked back into the house for more flammable products to burn and came back with a wooden cutting board from the kitchen. That fed the flames for a while. She sipped her hot, sweetened coffee outside in the cool morning air and decided she would wake Lev sooner today so that they could get a head start on the incoming rain. She wanted to get him to the tech she had hidden so that he would believe her.

He woke up when he smelled the fire burning. He was a little disoriented and maybe still a little inebriated from the previous night's vodka party, but he rubbed his face and looked over to see if Kali was on her bed. She wasn't. Yesterday, he had had a panic attack when he woke up and she was gone, but today he was wiser. She must be burning household items in the driveway, he said to himself. Jesus. Getting up was harder today than yesterday. He walked into the kitchen and lifted the teapot from the counter. She had heated enough water for him. He made his coffee and grabbed a chair from the dining room table and headed out towards her. She had a decent flame going in the barbeque.

"Hey, I'm coming up behind you," he said, still sounding like he was half asleep and definitely hung over.

"The breeze is blowing this way, so sit on this side of me," she said helpfully, pointing out the preferred location for his chair.

He put his chair down where she had told him to and thanked her for leaving him some hot water.

"We need to leave earlier today. It looks like it's going to rain."

"Oh, is that why it's so dark?" he asked, looking up at the sky. "Yeah. Ok. Let's do this part where we wake up. We can pack quickly and eat on the road. No baths. I looked for a hand pump yesterday. No luck."

"Ok, but we have to brush our teeth before leaving. I'm kind of freaked out that you don't have any dentists."

He agreed to brush his teeth before heading out, agreeing with her that it was concerning that no one in Campus or Ivy had been to a dentist in at least 17 years.

She didn't make him ask her to properly address her feet before putting her shoes back on. She noticed him smugly notice her applying the petroleum jelly and bandages and rolled her eyes at him. "Yeah, yeah. You were right," she said as she finished up.

They walked down the road and ate jerky, dried fruit, and hardtack. Lev dipped his hardtack straight into the jar of preserves, refusing to eat it plain a second time. He had made himself a second cup of coffee in a covered travel mug he found in a kitchen cabinet before leaving, and when he needed to dip his hardtack into the preserves, Kali held his coffee so he could use two hands. During one switch-off, he motioned quickly for his coffee because the hardtack was so dry that he couldn't swallow it. She handed him his coffee while laughing at him. When he recovered, he coughed and said, "I think you just saved my life. The Heimlich wasn't going to dislodge that."

They walked for as many hours as they could without taking any breaks before the rain started to fall. Kali's feet were not giving her any real problems anymore, but she didn't want her shoes to be ruined by the rain. Neither knew how long they had walked because the sun wasn't out to give Lev a clue as to the time of day, but he said he felt they had walked for at least six hours, and maybe more. They had kept up a good pace, too, as indicated by the road signs. According to the last sign they passed, they had covered around 20 miles.

The rain was beginning to fall very lightly and Lev suggested they shelter overnight in a church on the other side of the street up ahead of them. Kali wanted to sleep in a real bed not in a church pew, so they walked for another mile as the rain continued to fall lightly. Lev was worried they'd find themselves in a downpour and have to wait under some trees or in an old car. He hated the old cars. They tended to have bodies in them. To their left, there was an enormous, sprawling old farm with no sign of a barn or house near it. Lev thought there should have been at least a farm stand or something along it, but it just stretched ahead. As they passed by a grove of tall trees on their right, a small farm house appeared set far back on property across the street from the old farm land. "There's the fucking house," Lev said to Kali, feeling relief.

It looked intact from the road, but the dirt driveway leading up to it was long, so they had to walk up closer to the home in order to make sure it was habitable. They entered the driveway passing by three wide, beige boulders that were about a foot and a half high each. They had once protected a mailbox from being knocked down by passing vehicles, but time and the elements had rotted the wooden post that had once held the red metal mailbox aloft. The rusted red mailbox and it's rotted post were lying in front of the circle of three boulders. Walking up towards the house, Kali said, "I think it looks ok. If it's not, we can head back to the church."

They walked up onto the covered front porch and Lev kicked in the locked front door. The rain was coming down a little harder now and they discussed their critically low water supply as they entered the house. Lev took his usual dead body tour and came back to tell Kali there were remains of a dead cat in one of the smaller bedrooms, but nothing else. Kali was searching through the kitchen cabinets for bowls and pots to place outside to gather rainwater. They were both thirsty now, but they had finished their water earlier.

Lev went out to search for containers in the detached garage and the large barn out back. He made several trips carrying various empty containers and placed them on the back patio. Some of the containers were not necessarily clean, but any water collected in those could be used to wash up in the morning. Kali found a lot of clean bowls and pots and put them out hoping they would collect enough water to fill their empty water containers.

The rain began to come down particularly hard and Kali told Lev she wanted the soap so that she could wash off now before taking a nap. He dug it out of his backpack, handed it to her, and sat on the couch exhausted and wet considering his own need for a shower. If the rain didn't let up, he would get the soap from her and take one himself when she was finished. He closed his eyes and fell asleep on the couch without meaning to.

When Lev woke up, he had no idea how long he had been asleep. It was a dark day due to the clouds and rains, and keeping track of time on days like this was difficult. He saw their bar of soap on the coffee table in front of him and picked it up sleepily. He got up and looked around for Kali. She had mentioned wanting to take a nap after showering in the rain, so he didn't call out her name, opting to look in the bedrooms. He found her in the master bedroom just off the front living room sleeping in the center of the large bed curled up on her side. The windows were open despite the wind and rain coming into the room, and she had tossed all of the bed linens onto the floor except the fitted sheet. He had noticed she always did that. She was wearing different jeans and a clean shirt both of which he assumed she had found in the house. She was wearing different shoes than the ones she had been walking in all day.

He went to go find himself a clean towel so that he could head outside to shower quickly before the rains let up. In a linen closet outside the bathroom, he found clean folded towels and washcloths, grabbed one of each, and headed out the back door onto the patio. Concerned that Kali would wake up and look outside for him, he decided to shower along the side of the detached garage rather than risk their mutual embarrassment if she noticed him showering through a window or whatever. Actually, he imagined Kali wouldn't flinch. She'd just start chatting with him and probably not even notice. Or she would notice. He couldn't tell what she considered private. It was better if he showered quickly in an area that minimized the likelihood that she would walk up on him.

The rain was coming down particularly hard as he opened a side door of the garage and stepped inside where he put the now damp clean towel on a folded ladder rung and removed his damp jeans and hung them by a belt loop onto a nail he saw in the wall. He threw his wet t-shirt on the floor of the garage and walked back outside into the downpour. He showered quickly and well enough, as he had planned to do, but the rain was still coming down hard, so he gave his hair and beard a more thorough wash a second time and then stood there with his eyes closed and face up in the rain letting his body relax. He realized he was taking too long to finish and reluctantly went back into the garage and toweled off and wrapped the damp towel around his waist. He grabbed the soap and his damp jeans and headed back inside shirtless, hoping he could find a dry pair of clean pants rather than continue to wear the ones he had been wearing.

He went to the master bedroom where Kali was napping and found her awake, lying on her back awake staring at the ceiling.

"Hey. I need dry pants," he said to her, walking in and heading towards the closet.

"I saw man clothes in the other closet," she said, pointing across the room. He turned and headed to the closet she was directing him towards, and she said, "I hope we get some lightning with this storm."

He was rummaging through the closet and said, "Yeah a storm would be nice. Maybe cool off the weather tomorrow." He had some jeans and a t-shirt, both on hangers, in his hands as he turned around and asked her, "Did you look for candles, yet?"

"No." She was still lying on her back with her arms folded in back of her head looking at him. "I'll look now." She got up slowly off of the bed as he left the room to go put on the dry clothes.

After changing, he hung his damp jeans and the towel over the shower rod in the bathroom and went to see if they had collected enough water yet to have some to drink. He brought a pot inside and poured them each a full glass of water before putting the pot back outside. The rain was letting up and the sky was beginning to clear, but he could see more dark clouds in the distance. Maybe it was a large storm system that would come and go all night long. He really hoped it wouldn't be more than a rain event. He realized he should check the house for a basement just in case a tornado popped up.

"Did you notice if this house has a basement?" he asked her as he entered the kitchen and saw her sipping from one of the glasses of water he had poured.

"That door," she said, pointing to a door across the kitchen.

He opened it and asked her, "Candles?"

She pointed to the dining room table without saying anything, and he went and got one, lighting it from a box of wooden matches she had placed near them. He went down into the basement and looked around to get a feel for it in the event they woke up in the night to the sound of a tornado approaching. He'd been through it before. This little wooden house wouldn't stand a chance, but they would now that he knew they could hide in the basement. It was tidy but it was a completely unfinished space. He found the stairs leading up to the exit outside and pushed open the old metal doors to make sure they would have an alternate exit. Everything seemed acceptable. He blew out the candle at the bottom of the stairs and left it there just in case. He went upstairs to his backpack and took out his book of matches and walked back down to the basement and left the matches next to the candle.

"What are you doing?" Kali asked him, intrigued by all the passes he had made through the kitchen while she sipped her water.

"If the storm gets bad, we can head down to the basement," he said, grabbing his glass of water and finishing it quickly.

"Why bother? Wouldn't you rather get caught up in it and end up in Oz? Get the hell out of here?" she asked him, smiling.

"Hell yeah, I'd like a pet flying monkey," he said, nodding his head in approval while she smiled amusedly at him.

The rain had stopped and there were larger breaks in the clouds that revealed the sun would be setting soon. Kali set candles around the living room and the bedroom and lit them in advance of the dark.

224

"Peanuts for dinner tonight?" he asked her as she exited the bedroom carrying the flip flops he had gotten for her the night before.

"Sure," she said as she headed towards him where he was sitting on the couch. She nodded her head and shrugged with indifference for their dinner plans.

She placed the flip flops on the floor and sat down near him on the couch then removed her shoes and socks and placed them near her flip flops. She put her feet on the coffee table and inspected their progress.

"My feet are so much better," she said, looking at him.

He looked over at her feet and agreed with her, thanking her for keeping the flip flops and for letting her feet get some air. "Barefoot tonight and same sleeping arrangements, right?" he asked her.

She smiled at him. "Yeah, it's best. You were right. You won that one."

He smiled back but suddenly turned his attention to the room saying, "Wow, it's getting really dark all of a sudden. Good thing you already lit the candles. I'll go drag one of those smaller mattresses into the master where you took a nap earlier," he told her while slapping his leg before getting up to do it.

"Did you hear that? Was that lightning?" she asked him as he walked across the living room and headed to one of the smaller rooms to get her a mattress.

"I think that was me slapping my leg."

As he made his way down the hallway, he heard her say, "I think there's going to be a lightning storm."

He pulled the sheets off of the twin bed and tossed them onto the floor of the small room because he knew she would be removing the sheets anyway. He was dragging the mattress down the hallway and towards the master bedroom off where they had been sitting in the living room when he turned to look for her on the couch to ask her where she wanted him to place the mattress on the bedroom floor. He looked at the couch where he had left her sitting a few minutes earlier and saw the flip flops and her walking shoes on the floor, but she was gone. "Kali?" He called. "Kali, where'd you go?" He waited. He leaned the mattress against the hallway wall and looked in the master bedroom expecting her to be standing there waiting to tell him where to put the twin mattress. She wasn't there. He went into the kitchen, beginning to worry now. Why did she leave without putting on the flip flops? They had just been discussing them and her feet.

He was confused as he continued to search for her in the house while calling her name louder each time. Were the people who she claimed were after her real? Did they actually show up? She wouldn't have gone outside, he thought. The thunder was starting to rumble now. A storm was clearly on its way to them. His heartbeat was increasing and he was deciding whether he would be furious with her or relieved when he found her. He walked out onto the covered patio and looked at all of the dishes she had set out in the yard to collect water. He called her name loudly and scanned the yard. He called her name loudly again and held his breath as he looked down the long driveway and saw a flash of lightning in the distance. More rain would be arriving shortly. Movement on the ground caught his eye and he suddenly realized

Kali was running down the driveway heading towards the road they had walked in on. A streak of lightning lit up the distant sky again and the delayed sound of thunder slowly rumbled through the air. He ran off of the porch and ran as fast as he could to catch up with her. Was she being chased? He didn't see anybody else. He had no idea what was going on with her.

Thunder and Lightning

She was standing on top of one of the boulders that had been used to protect the once-erect mailbox at the end of the long dirt driveway. He ran barefoot across the yard and down the driveway calling her name and wincing at the sound of cracks of lightning and rumbling thunder which he could hear approaching them off in the distance as the sky continued to darken quickly. He watched as she stood tall on one of the boulders facing the derelict farm field which faced the property, trying to understand what she was doing. Her back was turned to him, and she gave no indication that she could hear him calling to her as he got closer. He watched as she removed her shirt and threw it to the ground on her right side and held up both of her arms high above her head, tilting her face towards the sky. Every crack of distant lightning and deep, low grumble of thunder that rolled towards them told him the storm was a big one and was headed towards them rapidly.

He called her name loudly and sternly as he came up on her with her back towards him and her arms reaching out as if she intended to embrace the incoming storm.

"Kali! What the fucking hell!? Come on! We have to get inside before the storm gets here!" he said, panting in exasperation mixed with confusion and fear.

She turned around to face him quickly, and her expression revealed a complete disconnect from his own feelings which had his face contorted with concern and frustration.

"Lev!" she shouted at him happily as if they hadn't seen each other in ages. "It's a lightning storm!" Her face was beaming with excitement and he found himself momentarily speechless as he resorted to nodding his head once quickly to indicate that, yeah, there was a storm approaching.

She didn't wait for him to continue speaking and said, "The electricity! Do you feel it in the air? You know, it's the only time we're free. They can't travel where there's an electrical storm. This is the safest place to be! Right here! Right now!" She turned again to face the sky above the field across the street, and he stared up at her back for a moment and registered countless scars across her skin. Scars upon scars. These weren't bite marks like the scars on her arms. There appeared to be a large word branded into the skin of her upper right shoulder and he thought it said MINE in all capital letters, but she turned around quickly again and suddenly placed both of her hands on his chest.

226

Standing on the boulder, she was slightly taller than him, and he stood motionless looking up at her, confused and unsure what to say to her. The rain hadn't started to fall again yet, but a breeze was rolling in and whipped her messy hair around her face as she looked down at him. She leaned in closer to him with excitement in her eyes and a smile on her face and said, "This is the safest place to be. In the middle of a lightning storm. We're free right now. They can't shadow us or show up. Do you feel the electricity in the air? That means we're safe."

He was at a complete loss as to how he could respond to her as he saw a streak of lightning flash across the sky off in the distance behind her. A loud crack quickly followed and warned him the storm was getting closer and would be on top of them soon. He opened his mouth to tell her that they had to run back to the house and grabbed both of her wrists as she continued to rest both of her palms flat on his chest, but her face instantly became serious and she said, "I'm so attracted to you. Are you attracted to me?" She was looking directly into his eyes as she asked him and appeared to be waiting for an answer.

The question threw him for a second and he said, "Listen. We have to go back inside right now. The storm is going to be on top of us any minute. We need to run. Ok? Let's go. Now."

She shook her head. "No, I want to stay out here. It's the only time I'm free. It's the only time you're free, too, even if you don't know it." She tipped her head to one side and smiled. "You didn't answer my question. Are you attracted to me?"

He realized he was still holding onto both of her wrists as he felt her try to move her hands up to his shoulders. He weakened his grip on her wrists and let his hands fall down by his sides. He tried to shake off the flustered feelings that were building in him as he looked at her face and felt her hands working their way over the top of his shoulders. He tried to maintain a serious tone and said, "We can talk about that inside. Ok? Let's get back to the house and talk about that inside."

Lightning caught his eye to the right and he realized at least two storm cells were approaching the property. He heard the crack and winced, but a small, somewhat disappointed smile suddenly appeared on Kali's face and she said quietly, almost in a whisper, "That's fine. You don't have to be attracted to me." She wrapped her arms around his neck and looked down at him. "I thought you were, and I thought we could have really great sex out here in the storm." She closed her eyes briefly and then opened them to look at him again. "Do you want to consider that?" she asked him as she closed the space between them and he felt her body press lightly against his own.

He stood there with his arms at his sides and looked up into her face and shook his head no. "Kali, I... You know, yeah. You're attractive. Yeah. I'm attracted to you. But listen. I'm not... I think it's best we not, you know, because I'm concerned that, well, frankly... I think you're probably crazy. It's not right. You know? I can't. It wouldn't be right," he said half annoyed with himself for having so much difficulty saying what had to be said, but also relieved he had managed to say it.

She smiled as he finished talking and he felt her fingers play with the hair on the back of his neck as her arms entwined more securely around his neck. "So, you think I'm hot, but like a hot mess?" she laughed gently at him.

"Yeah. Yeah, I do," he managed to say, offering a small smile of his own. "Listen. I get it. Thunder and lightning... You're not concerned. But I am. I want us to get inside. Now. We can talk inside. Yeah?" he asked her.

"No. I'm staying out here."

She suddenly removed her arms from around his neck and turned around quickly to look up at the darkening sky. He was left staring at her back again and, in those seconds before regaining his composure, the breeze moved her hair away from her shoulder and confirmed the word branded into her skin was MINE. It made him feel sick, and he wanted to try and offer a better explanation to her as to why they had to run back inside right now, but she spoke first.

With her back still to him she asked him, "So what if I'm crazy? Aren't you crazy, too? Or did you survive all these years after the apocalypse and stay sane? Sane is boring, you know?" She laughed slightly and turned to face him again saying, "Yeah, I'm crazy, but I'm a good kind of crazy. I know what I want. I'm not confused. I want you. I want you now in this storm so we can both just be crazy together."

She was looking at him as he remembered the words of The Benefactor. He had said he was crazy when Niels had asked him if he was crazy that day. Maybe Kali was right. Maybe they were all crazy. Lev reached out and, despite the loud sounds of lightening cracking and thunder rumbling angrily in the air around them, he gently took her left hand in his right hand and said patiently, "If anything happens to you out here in this storm, if it starts to rain again and you slip on that rock and crack your head open, if you get struck by fucking lightening, if the storm is actually a fucking tornado, because I don't fucking know what it's going to end up being... Do I look like a goddamn weatherman? If something fucking happens, I'm walking back to Ivy tomorrow with nothing. No tech. No you. And an embarrassing story about how I couldn't get you inside during a fucking lightning storm. That's a bad look, you know? Yeah, I'm attracted to you, but I'm concerned about taking advantage of you," he said seriously while also noticing the scars covering the skin on the front of her body as well.

"Oh, I don't think that's even possible since I actually know more than you do," she said, raising her eyebrows and nodding her head.

She moved closer to him and he looked down towards his left and took her other hand in his. Now holding both of her hands, he looked back over at her face and said, "Please. Let's run back to the house together. Are you still free and safe if you're in a house during a lightning storm?" he asked her.

She considered the question and looked past him at the ground. He could tell she had a preference for remaining outside, but she admitted, "Yeah, I mean, yeah. It's all the same. I just really like being out in the middle of it and feeling the electricity in the air. But, yeah. They can't shadow us or show up in the house either." She pulled her right hand out of his hand and looked up waving it towards the sky.

228

"This is the safest place to be when he's in charge. And he's in charge even if you don't realize it," she said adamantly.

"It's also really possible that we'll get struck by lightning and fucking die. Then we won't get the tech you say you brought us," Lev said kindly, trying to appeal to her sense of survival and duty at the same time.

She looked at him with a look of genuine disappointment and took the first step off of the rock she'd been standing on. He continued to hold onto her left hand as she took the second step down.

"I'll hold your hand, and we'll run as fast as we can," he said to her.

She nodded her consent, and they took off towards the house just as the first large raindrops started falling on them.

By the time they reached the porch steps she was laughing, but he felt her resistance as he ascended the stairs. He looked back and watched as she looked at the bottom step and then looked up at him. "I'd rather die free than live locked up forever," she said, and he felt the weight of her sincerity in the statement she made even if he didn't understand what she was afraid of. She wasn't afraid to be struck by lightning. She wasn't afraid of slipping off of a large wet rock and breaking her head open and dying alone lying in the mud.

He stepped down two of the porch steps and lessened the tension between their arms and pulled her hand to his mouth and kissed it. "Thank you for understanding that I was concerned we would both die out there in this lightning storm. Thank you for agreeing to come inside with me," he said with a faint smile. She smiled lightly at him and walked the rest of the way up the stairs and onto the porch.

They stood on the porch still holding hands and Lev walked toward the front door and gently pulled her to follow him inside. He felt her resistance again and looked at her with their two arms outstretched between them.

"Come on. Let's go inside," he said quietly as the rain started to come down harder and lightning lit up the sky.

"Can we stay out here on the covered porch?" she asked him, sounding hopeful.

He walked right up to her and dropped her hand and wrapped both of his arms around the top of her bare shoulders. Looking down at her he asked, "Are you crazy?"

"Yes," she said, smiling. "Are you?" she asked him, while pushing her body against his and wrapping her arms around his waist.

"Yeah," he said with a small nod and a shrug. He leaned down and kissed her softly on the mouth. He had one hand on the back of her neck and ran the other down her bare back gliding his fingers over her scarred skin and bra strap while they kissed.

When they separated slightly she said, "Alright, I'll go inside."

He kept one arm around her shoulder as they walked towards the door, and he opened it allowing her to enter before he did. She noticed that he allowed her to enter a room first which was not typical of him and wondered if it was due in part to a fear of her turning to run back out into the storm. She was about to ask him that and turned to him, but he reached down around her waist with both arms and lifted her straight up and hugged her body against his body telling her in a throaty voice she hadn't heard from him before, "I want you. Can we do that now?"

As she wrapped her arms around the top of his shoulders and her legs around his waist, he leaned his face towards hers and she just barely had time to agree when he kissed her much harder than he had outside a minute earlier.

"Yeah. Yeah, Lev. I want you, too," she said to him between kisses that he was eagerly seeking.

He walked the two of them into the bedroom where she had taken a nap earlier in the day and walked across the room to the bottom of the bed. He lifted a knee and climbed on top of the bed and moved forward on his knees still holding her and kissing her until they were in the center of the mattress. When he started to let go of her, she loosened her grip on him and slowly slid down onto the bed. The candles she had lit earlier flickered their soft light throughout the room. He was on his knees looking down at her as she reclined before him on the bed. In the soft candlelight, he could see that her body was covered in scars, but he could also see her, the unpredictable and entertaining woman who reminded him of home.

He removed his shirt quickly, throwing it aside, and she sat up and reached around and unhooked her bra strap, removed her bra, and tossed it to the floor along with his shirt. He leaned forward putting both of his hands on the bed and pressed her back down onto the bed as he kissed her mouth hard, his tongue seeking hers. Using his right hand, he gently separated her legs as he slowly lowered himself between them and felt her lightly wrap both of her legs around his hips. He felt her arms wrap around his back and she placed her warm hands on his skin. Her breasts were pressed against his bare chest and he lifted himself up slightly to one side to put a hand on one and massaged it gently while they kissed. He ran that same hand down her side feeling the waistband of her jeans. He was excited and tried to control how forceful he was being with her when she broke away from their kissing and said quietly, "Make me cum, Lev. I want you inside me fucking me. Make me cum before I have to make myself cum."

He groaned an inquisitive, "Oh, yeah?" as he sat up on his knees between her open legs. His voice was deep and he was smiling slyly when he tipped his head down looking at her and said, "Someday I wanna watch you do that, but not tonight."

She was still lying back on the bed and smiled back at him while gliding her left hand over her left breast.

He moved quickly to get off the bed so he could fully undress and get back to her.

She sat up, and he watched her as she got off of the bed and stood in front of him removing her pants as he removed his. When she was standing naked in front of him, he stepped up to her and wrapped his arms around her, running his hands slowly down her naked body while leaning in to kiss her.

As they kissed, he felt one of her hands wrap around his lower back as she placed the other over his chest and slowly ran her hand down from his nipple, over his stomach, and down over his groin to the inside of his thigh. Her hand was warm and her touch made him tingle and his erection grew harder. He felt as she cupped his testicles gently and then released them before stroking the seam in front of them with the backs of her fingers making him groan and sigh a whispered, "Oh, fuck, Kali." He kissed her neck and caressed her body as she slowly moved her hand slowly back up over his groin and around to his ass and he wanted her back on the bed.

Kali stepped slightly back from him with her arms still around him and looked up asking, "I wanna give you head. Are you into that?"

Lev closed his eyes for a split second and nodded quickly, saying, "Yeah, I'm into that."

"You want to sit or stand? Lay down on the bed, maybe?" she asked him, as she looked up at him smiling and ran both of her hands up his chest.

Lev held both of her arms at her elbows and said, "How about I sit on the edge of the bed?"

Kali nodded and stepped aside to let him sit down. She got down onto her knees in front of him as he spread his legs apart for her to get closer. He watched her, and the anticipation of being inside her mouth made him mutter a quiet, "Fuck, yeah."

"Tell me what feels good," she said, looking up at him with a nod.

"Yeah. I will," he said and moaned as she began to suck his cock slowly before he had finished answering her. "Ok, that feels really fucking good," he said quietly as he watched her go up and down on him slowly. He ran both of his hands over her scarred shoulders, and watched her body as she moved her head up and down between his legs. She was holding his cock steady at the base while she sucked him and he could feel her fingers massage him as she ran her tongue up to his tip. She ran her other hand slowly over the top of his thigh and then around his lower back where her warm hand caressed the area just above his ass as she buried herself between his legs. He moaned as he watched her and felt her body pressed against his. He heard her moan and felt the vibration on his cock and breathed out a quiet, "Ok." He watched her as she slowly stopped and looked up at him and asked, "Do you like to have your tip played with? Like this..." and then put the tip of his penis back in her mouth and ran her tongue over the sensitive areas. "Yeah, I fucking do," he moaned adamantly, putting his head back with his eyes closed now.

"Kali, I can't keep doing this. Get on the bed. I mean, let's get on the bed," he said to her. "I want you on your back. Oh, Jesus. Ok. I mean, I want you under me? Is that ok?" he asked as he continued to rub her shoulders. She was sliding him deeper into her mouth as he tried to talk to her and she worked her way back up to his tip and said with a patient smile, "Hey. I know you're trying not to tell me what to do, but you can tell me what you want while we're fucking without worrying so much."

He groaned and asked gruffly, "Yeah? Come up here then," and motioned for her to stand up. She stood up and he quickly got up and moved the two of them back onto the bed, guiding her beneath him while she smiled at him and held onto his shoulders. "I wanna be on top of you and I wanna fuck you right fucking now," he said as he climbed on top of her and kissed her stomach and made his way up to her breasts where he stopped to slowly kiss and suck on each one before moving up to her neck.

He could feel some of her many scars under his lips, and he reminded himself to pay attention to any signs that she wasn't comfortable with him. He buried his hairy face into her neck and heard her moan as he pressed his lips against her neck and up under her ear before moving towards her mouth. He hadn't entered her yet, but he was between her legs rubbing his erection against her clitoris rhythmically when she told him between kisses, "You can come inside me, Lev. I can't get pregnant."

"I really want you right now. Can I be inside you now?" he whispered to her urgently as he kissed her neck and ran his hand down between her legs.

"Yeah, I'm ready for you," she said back to him as he slid two fingers inside her.

"Yeah you fucking are," he said and groaned quietly into her neck as he felt how wet she was. He lifted his two fingers that were inside of her and gently caressed with a 'come here' motion asking her quietly, "Is this the spot, Kali?" while kissing her mouth softly.

She was breathing heavily as he rubbed her inside with his fingers and she sighed a breathless, "Yeah, that's the spot," while lifting her hips towards him.

They continued to kiss each other as he rubbed her interior clit and he whispered, "I want to taste you, yeah?"

"Yeah," she said softly, encouraging him. He moved his face down between her legs and pressed his mouth against her with his fingers still inside of her. He felt her place her hands on shoulders and then move them up through the hair on his head as she moaned approvingly while he went down on her. He heard her breathing increase and she moaned, "Oh, yeah, Lev. Yeah, that feels so good."

He didn't want to stop, and he used his tongue on her clit and pulled on it gently by sucking on it softly, listening to her respond to his touch.

She breathed more rapidly and moaned her approval, encouraging him as he massaged her inside and out with his mouth and fingers and he looked up at her and asked her, "Are you close?" while he kept his fingers inside of her and continued to rub her.

She opened her eyes and looked down at him and said breathlessly, "I am. I'm so close."

He decided he wanted his cock inside her when she came. "I've gotta be inside you now. I want you to come on my cock," he said as he removed his fingers from her and started making his way back up over her body, kissing along the way as he made his way up to her face.

"I want you so bad. Make me cum, Lev," she said breathlessly into his wet mouth as his lips gently touched her lips through his beard.

He pressed his hips down on hers and kissed her forcefully feeling her tongue searching for his. She could taste herself in his mouth and said lazily, "Mmmm, I taste good," while stroking his bearded cheek with one hand and his upper back with her other.

He groaned and positioned himself on top of her and pushed himself deep inside her and they both began breathing harder as he moved himself in and out of her pushing deeply with each forward thrust.

Afterwards, laying on top of her with his face resting on the pillow next to her right ear, he shifted himself off of her and over to the right side of her body. Her left leg had been resting lightly atop his right leg and he felt it slowly slide away from him as he rolled his body off of hers. He reached his long arm down to her hip and slid his hand down her scarred leg and slowly pulled it back towards him to lay it over his side. His eyes were closed as he whispered in her ear, "I like this leg."

He felt her turn more towards him while positioning her leg securely across his right side with his hand still holding onto it. She pushed her left arm under his right arm and draped it across his back where she gently stroked his skin as she moved in closer to him and kissed his mouth. "Then this leg will remain here," she said reassuringly.

He let go of her leg and ran his hand up the middle of her back from her ass, over her scars, and pulled her closer returning her kisses with his own. She liked the feel of his beard against her face as she pressed against his lips buried deep in the center of it. His breath was nice and his mouth tasted good. His voice was soothing and she felt relaxed lying there wrapped up together with him. She could not recall a time in her life when she had been alone with a man who she wanted to be with, but the thought didn't upset her. Instead, she felt a kind of peace settle inside her as he continued to stroke her back and press his lips softly against hers, offering soft kisses. It helped that the storm outside continued to rage over the house. Lightning cracked in the sky illuminating the room, and thunder roared loudly in the background of the moment. It gave her a sense of peace and freedom while she enjoyed their time together.

Overnight

She heard the last of the thunder rumbling in the distance as she listened to Lev's breathing. He was fast asleep on her right side lying on his stomach with his head near hers. His right arm was draped across her upper chest and his hand was resting above her head on the pillow she was using. The rain continued to come down hard and she was glad they had found a lot of containers to put outside to collect water. They could stop back here on their way back to Ivy in a few days.

With the storm moving past them now, she wanted to get dressed and get her shoes on just in case she needed to fight because she wasn't going to run and leave him. She nudged Lev to wake him and tell him he needed to get dressed, but he was in a deep sleep and resisted waking up. Moving his arm off of her didn't wake him either, and she had to laugh a little at how out of it he was.

She left him in the bed and walked into the kitchen and grabbed the hand towel that had been hanging on the refrigerator door for 17 years. She went outside and poured a little water from one of the bowls onto it and wiped down her body before cleaning her private parts. She liked the smell of Lev on her skin, but she felt better after having cleaned up a bit. She always did. The need to get dressed and get her shoes back on forced her decision to move from the porch and back inside. The night air was cool and standing out on the porch in the rain held a lot of appeal, but she needed to get dressed first.

She turned to head inside just as Lev walked up to the open door and asked, "What's up? Is there a problem?" He was looking past her for a threat and she had no doubt he would attack, even completely naked as he was, if there was a person or animal that needed killing out in the yard.

"No problem. I was a little sweaty and came out to clean up and cool off. The storm is gone. The lightning is gone. Just rain now. I have to get dressed. I need to be able to fight if they show up."

She was moving towards him, headed inside, but he stopped her by wrapping his arms around her and pulling her to him. "Hey, we're ok here tonight. We can relax," he said, kissing her forehead.

"You need to get dressed, too," she told him and kissed just below his shoulder before pushing away from him and heading inside. He sighed quietly and stood in the doorway looking over the yard before returning to the bedroom where she was getting dressed. She had thrown her shirt onto the ground outside earlier, so she unzipped her backpack and took out a shirt and pulled it over her head. She got dressed quickly, and Lev watched as she put on her shoes and tied them before getting back into bed next to him.

He was still naked and laying on his side waiting for her when she laid down and rested on her side placing her face near his. "You should get dressed," she said quietly, while stroking his upper arm.

"No," he said, leaning in to kiss her. They continued to kiss for a few minutes until he moved away from her saying, "I'm not worried."

"I know," she said sadly, looking at him. "It's going to suck when you are."
"Why?"

"Because then you'll know what I'm afraid of." She moved in closer to him, putting her arm around his side, and he wrapped his arm snuggly around her as she nuzzled herself against his naked body.

He knew that, eventually, he was going to kill whoever had put the scars on her body and the fear in her mind.

Day 4

Lev woke up before Kali for a change. Probably, he noted, because he hadn't been drinking the night before. He looked at her lying next to him sleeping. It was dark outside but he could still see her clearly enough as his face was just a few inches from hers. Her mouth was open a little bit, and her hair was a disheveled mess all around her face. Her breathing was deep and slow. She was sound asleep, lying there fully dressed beside him. He smiled in the dark. Was this contentedness? He wanted to reach out and touch her, smooth her hair away from her face, and kiss her, but he also didn't want to wake her.

He got up quietly from the bed and walked into the kitchen to get some water. He filled a glass and grabbed a pillow off of the couch and walked outside onto the front porch where he tossed the pillow onto one of the old rocking chairs and sat barefoot and naked, staring down the long dirt driveway while drinking his water. He sat for a while, consumed with the memories of having sex with Kali a few hours earlier. He wanted her again and hoped it wasn't a one-off for her. It was hard to tell with her, but he wanted it to continue. He wanted them to continue.

He suddenly sat up as he noticed movement along the road way down at the beginning of the driveway. The sun wasn't fully up yet, and the air was wet with a light mist, but he could see two figures heading towards the house from the road. He jumped up and went inside to grab his gun and went back and sat in the rocking chair waiting for them to get closer to him. He hoped it was the people who Kali said were after her. He wanted to kill them and be able to sleep naked all night long with her tonight. None of this shoes on all night bullshit. He wanted her to stop being so afraid. Hell, even if she thought last night was a mistake and wanted nothing to do with him ever again, he wanted her to have peace. He sat there glaring at the two people approaching the house ready to find out if they were responsible for what had been done to her.

They were looking at each other, talking as they approached the front porch, so they didn't see Lev sitting off to the left of the front side on the porch until he stood up from the rocking chair with his gun aimed at them. Their faces turned toward him, and they seemed to realize they couldn't run past him up the stairs into the house and they couldn't run back towards the driveway. They were too close to him for running away to do any good, so they stood frozen, staring at the large naked man growling at them to stop.

Lev watched as the smaller person, a woman, stepped in back of the man who was using his arm to usher her in back of him.

"Who the fuck are you?" Lev demanded, while keeping his gun aimed at the man.

"No one. We're no one. We'll leave," he said as he went to turn around.

"The fuck you will. Don't fucking move, asshole. And you," he said to the woman, "stop hiding. Get where I can see you or I'll put one bullet right through your skinny boyfriend and kill you, too."

"She's afraid," said the man.

"Yeah, aren't we all. I'm not telling you again. Get where I can see you or this ends with you both dead."

The woman was coming around the left side of the man when Kali walked out of the house holding Lev's pants and his other gun.

"Good morning!" she said brightly, waving his second gun in the air as she walked over to him smiling. "Here," she said, putting his pants on the rocking chair behind him.

"These the people who've been after you?" he asked her, not taking his eyes off of them.

She wrapped one arm around his naked hips and leaned forward looking towards them to the left of where she and Lev were standing on the porch. "No. That's not them," she said, shaking her head. She slowly dragged her hand across his lower back and leaned over and kissed his upper left arm while walking away from him.

"Oh, hey now. I'm working here," he said, smiling in surprise as her hand took a long time to depart his lower back.

She was still smiling as she walked to the center of the porch and headed down the stairs to the strangers.

"I haven't cleared them of weapons yet," Lev said with alarm in his voice. He watched as Kali kept walking closer to them despite what he had told her.

She stopped in front of them and asked the man, "You got any weapons?" while waving the gun casually in her right hand.

"Yeah, I have a knife."

"Ok, so you're gonna want to place that, not drop it, place it down on the ground between us or you're gonna get shot. Probably killed. Not the worst thing to happen to a person, but it's gonna suck for your girlfriend," she said to him.

Lev was holding his breath waiting for the man to make one wrong move. "Hey, you won't have time to finish any move you make, so don't try anything."

The man looked over at Lev, but said nothing.

"Did you hear him?" Kali asked the man.

"Yes."

"Tell him not me," she said, raising her eyebrows at him and smiling.

"I understand, sir," the man said in a louder voice directed to Lev. The man slowly removed a knife from his pant leg and gently placed it on the ground between himself and Kali.

She used her foot to swipe it behind her and asked, "What's your name?" as he slowly stood back up.

"Trent."

"What's your name?" she asked, turning to the woman standing alongside Trent.

"Olivia," the woman responded.

Lev interrupted them and said loudly, "Trent, Olivia, I'm gonna get dressed now, so don't look."

Kali smiled at that and then continued her interrogation. "You got any weapons, Olivia?"

"Yes."

"What do you have?" Kali asked her.

"A gun," she said.

"Well, you're gonna need to place that on the ground between us extra slowly then," Kali said in a tone Lev had never heard her use before. You didn't need to know Kali to know that she had just implied a serious threat to Olivia through the tone she used when telling her to place her gun on the ground between them extra slowly.

Lev hurried to put on his pants and cursed himself for not sleeping in his clothes as Kali had suggested. With his pants on now, he picked up his gun and aimed it at Olivia. "Slowly, Olivia. I have you locked in," he said menacingly.

Lev walked up behind Kali on the top of the porch steps and watched as Olivia removed her gun and slowly placed it between herself and Kali.
Kali asked him, "You got them? I'm going to remove their weapons."

"Yeah, I got them both," he assured her while looking at Olivia and Trent.

Kali bent down and picked up the knife and the gun and walked up the steps with them placing them on the porch near the front door. She walked back over to Lev and stood by his side still holding his other gun loosely as he asked them, "What are you doing here?"

"We were looking for a place to spend the day. We started walking, just like, thirty minutes ago when the rain let up, but then we decided to skip a day of walking and take a break. We've been walking for weeks," Trent said.

"Where you headed?" Kali asked Olivia.

Trent went to respond, but Kali tipped her head at him and said, "Trent, I asked Olivia the question. Can you speak for yourself, Olivia? Are you Trent's hostage?"

When Kali asked Oliva that question, Lev took note of the serious tone she used. He stood still while waiting for Olivia to reveal if she was Trent's hostage. He wouldn't even kill Trent. He'd let Kali do it, because he was certain she'd be furious if he did it himself.

"No, we're friends. Yeah, I can speak for myself. We're headed to Virginia Beach."

"You two have any skills? Or are you just both lucky to have survived this long?" Lev asked them. He was thinking about Bolin and his suggestion of the development of a more militarized team at Ivy for the war Kali had reminded them they were in. "We come from a community that's run really well, but you can't just get in. We like you to have a useful skill to offer."

Trent looked at Lev and said, "I don't think I have any skills. I can farm and that kind of thing to survive. We grew up in New Hampshire. It's too cold for too long. Seems like more people died recently. There was only a few of us left, so me and Olivia decided to get to where it's warmer and set up for the winter."

"I don't have any skills either. I'm almost 17, so I can learn skills if your community can teach me," Olivia said to Lev.

"I'm 18, but I want to learn some skills, too. The most we ever had was 30 people in our group and all our skills were just to prepare for the winter and survive it. We were down to nine people including us when we left," Trent said to Lev.

Lev thought for a moment and asked, "Do you want to join my, our community?" he asked them, correcting himself to include Kali.

Kali noticed Lev make the correction and thought it was nice.

Trent turned to Olivia and asked her what she wanted to do.

"I think we'd be better off with others. We should try it," she said to him.

Lev interrupted them saying, "Hey, uh-uh. The idea of trying it out, that's a no. It's kind of like the Hotel California. You know?"

"What's that?" Trent asked him.

"Oh come on, man!" Lev said to him. He turned to Kali. "Kids today have no music history. It ruins so many conversations."

"It's tragic," said Kali who frowned, pretending to be serious.

"No, I know this one!" Olivia said proudly. "You can check out any time you like, but you can never leave. Right?" She turned to Trent and smacked his arm lightly, encouraging him to remember by saying, "Mike used to sing that when we were younger. Welcome to the Hotel California. Remember?"

"Oh, yeah! Such a lovely place," Trent said, nodding his head.

"Yeah, ok you two. So, no one walks up to this place and gets to try it out. You commit or you're killed. It's a lot to ask, but it keeps the riff-raff out," Lev said.

"Riff-raff?" asked Olivia.

"Useless assholes who take but don't contribute," Lev said bluntly.

They looked unsure about committing to the offer, but Trent asked Lev, "How many people are in your community?"

"There are two communities. One has just under 200 people, the other has nearly 500."

"I want to go!" Olivia said instantly. "I want to live with people!" She turned to Trent. "If you don't want to go, then don't. I'll go by myself." She turned to Lev and said, "I want to go. I'll be useful. I'll learn a skill."

Lev smiled and nodded. He liked her enthusiasm. "Ok, Olivia, you're in. Trent? What are you going to do?" he asked, turning to Trent who looked shocked.

"You have 700 people?" Trent asked in disbelief.

"Yeah. You in or out?" Lev asked him a second time, running out of patience now.

"In. I'm definitely in. I'll do whatever duties I'm assigned. I'll learn whatever skill is needed. I'll clean stables for the rest of my life. I didn't even know that many people were still alive on the whole planet. I'm shocked!" he said, shaking his head.

Olivia spoke up saying, "We've only seen 41 people since we left our home even after walking through big cities. Most of the people have been really desperate. You two seem like you're strong compared to others we've met."

"I'm gonna give you instructions. If you fail to follow the instructions, you risk being killed. It's basically a test to see if you have listening skills. Listening is an important skill. You ready?" he asked them. They both nodded their heads at Lev. "When you arrive at the community, walk up separated from one another by two feet. Your hands must be up in the air from the minute you can see the buildings. Walk slowly up to the buildings until guards approach you and tell you to stop. You will be asked questions. Answer them. When they ask you what you're doing there you tell them exactly this: "We need to speak with Bolin. Lev sent us." Wait for Bolin. Tell Bolin you met Lev, and he said to put you in the cages until he returns. Tell Bolin Lev said he thinks you can be useful to the community. These are the steps: Separate, hands up, Bolin, Lev, cages, useful." He told them to repeat the steps and they did. "Bolin only wants facts from strangers who enter the community. If you bore him with details, he'll shoot you for wasting his time. Any questions?"

"I'm still excited to go, but the cages sound scary," Olivia said nervously.

"We don't let people show up and give them the run of the place. Everyone starts out there."

He turned to Kali and said, "Except you."

They asked if they could have their weapons back, but Lev told them no. He also warned them against walking up to the community with any weapons on themselves. He warned them not to invite anyone else to join them, saying that when he returned in a few days, if they had broken the rules he'd given them, they'd be killed for disobeying orders.

"Are we already members of your community then?" asked Olivia.

"Exactly. You are. I'm your commanding officer. If you had rejected the offer I made to you a few minutes ago, I'd have killed you."

Trent looked at Lev and said, "Thank you, sir. I'll make sure we get there safely and don't screw up."

Lev squinted at Trent and said, "I don't know how they ran things in New Hampshire, but in your new community, women don't rely on men to protect them and keep them from screwing up. I'm sure Olivia can handle herself. Kind of like this woman standing next to me walked right up to you two and disarmed you. Kind of like this woman checked that you weren't holding Olivia hostage. Kind of like this woman came out dressed and brought me clothes so I could assist her," he added, laughing.

Olivia's face was beaming as Lev equated her value to Kali's. He walked them to the end of the driveway while telling them the directions to Ivy. He told them not to stay in the white house and described it to them.

Lev watched Trent and Oliva depart and ran back up the driveway to the house. Kali already had the teapot on the firepit in the backyard. She was burning furniture that she had broken against the side of the cinderblock firepit. She looked up at him and smiled as he approached her and he felt relieved that she was happy to see him. He had been a dumbass for refusing to sleep with clothes on and then finding himself in a naked standoff with two teenagers who were clearly not the threat he had initially imagined them to be.

"First of all," he said as he neared her, "thank you for bringing me pants."

She was very amused by the entire situation he had found himself in and walked up and gave him a big hug, rubbing his back as he hugged her against his bare chest telling her she shouldn't approach armed strangers in the future.

"Whatever. I've decided I'm going to stay and fight with you when there are problems," she muttered blithely at him.

He really liked the feel of her against him, and he still worried if she would continue to let him hug her, or kiss her, or have sex with her. He knew she wanted him during the night, but was it a one-time thing? He was lost in his thoughts when she looked up at him and said, "If I were taller, I'd give you a kiss, but I'm done growing, so you're going to have to learn how to read my mind."

He bent down and kissed her.

He went inside and brought out the coffee, sugar, mugs, and a spoon and made their coffees. She brought out two dining room chairs and Lev moved them close enough together so that they were touching. When they sat down, he scooped her legs up over his and kept one arm across her upper thighs. She ran her left hand across his upper shoulders and then ran her fingers along his neck and through his long hair at the nape of his neck. His body tingled under her touch. They sat next to the firepit as the flames used to heat their water died down.

They sipped their coffees and Lev told her how much he had enjoyed being with her during the night. He asked if they could continue on that way, or if she was ambivalent about the prospect of continuing to share a bed and sharing their bodies with one another.

Kali listened to him speak and watched how his insecurities were displayed by his mannerisms. He looked away from her briefly when he was worried about her possible answers, but for the most part, he made an effort to look at her while he asked her for answers he couldn't control. If she didn't want him again, that would be what he had to accept. He didn't want things to be awkward for the rest of the time they traveled together. He wanted to understand what she wanted.

It was all so new to Kali. She looked at the large, strong man so many were afraid of, and she knew he could take what he wanted from her, but he never presented himself to her that way. Even the first day they met at Ivy. She had told him in the field that she knew he was strong enough to make her go into a jail cell, but he had compromised with her and said he wouldn't do that.

She put her coffee cup on the ground and leaned over to him as he explained to her that he would follow her lead on how things would proceed from last night and she slid her right leg over the top of his lap straddling him in his chair. He wrapped both of his arms around her waist as she wrapped her arms around his shoulders and neck and they kissed each other softly.

"Let's make every day like last night. Ok? I want that. Is that what you want, too?" she asked him as they sat there wrapped up together in his lap, kissing each other slowly.

"Yeah, that's exactly what I want," he said, squeezing his arms around her waist tighter and pulling her against his growing erection.

She smiled at him saying, "Mmm. Then that's how it'll be."

They continued to kiss each other softly and he began to pull her against himself harder, growing more excited as she moved her hips against him.

"Can we go inside now?" he asked her.

"We can do it here or inside," she whispered to him as she kissed his neck.

"Here. Let's do it here," he said rubbing his hands roughly up and down her back and pulling her hips forward, rubbing his erection against her.

She stood up and kicked off her shoes before pushing her pants down and off her legs.

He stood up and quickly undid his pants and dropped them to his ankles and sat back down on the chair with his legs slightly apart and reached for her.

Kali spread her legs and sat straddling his lap a slight distance from his erection and watched his eyes watch her hand as she ran her hand down from her breast and down between her open legs. She closed her eyes as she ran her fingers along the outside of her vagina and over her clit. He put his hands on her bare hips as he watched her slide her fingers inside of herself and tell him, "Mmmm, I think I'm ready for you," as she played with herself on his lap.

He kept telling her he wanted her while resisting the urge to pull her forward and onto himself. "I want you so fucking bad," he said as he watched her fingers.

She ran her wet fingers across her lips and he groaned loudly leaning forward and pulled her face towards him to kiss her mouth so he could taste her for the second time.

With her legs open wide, she moved forward up against him and slid her wet exterior up and down his erection without sliding him inside of her.

He wanted to be inside her so badly that he pressed his face against hers and groaned, "Kali, let me in. Let me inside you."

She whispered, "Ok," into his ear and lifted herself up slightly and reached between their bodies and guided his erection inside her slowly. He wrapped his arms around her waist and moved his hands up under the back of her shirt to feel her skin as she moved up and down on his cock looking at him and telling him breathlessly, "Your cock feels so good inside my pussy."

At first they kissed with their eyes closed as she rode him at a moderate pace, but as they both became more excited, Kali moved faster, and Lev used his large hands on her hips and ass to pull her down harder onto himself while she leaned into him. They eventually stopped kissing as they both began to breathe harder in their excitement. Her eyes were closed now but he opened his and watched her riding him which turned him on even more. Their rhythm was fast and hard and Kali was moaning loudly and calling out his name as she began to orgasm. He encouraged her by saying, "Come on baby. Cum on my cock."

As she was finishing, he pulled her down harder several times holding her there as he came inside of her. He groaned and his voice was husky in her ear while he encouraged his own orgasm by swearing repeatedly and calling her name into her neck as he came.

After they were both finished, she slowly rose off of his lap from the straddle position and sat back down on his lap sideways with her arms around his neck and her head resting against his. Lev was naked, but Kali was still wearing her shirt. His right arm was wrapped around her lower back while his left hand stroked her upper leg. He could see the scars on her legs in the morning sunlight for the first time having only felt them in the dark the night before. He said nothing about them. They sat there for a few minutes together while she leaned her head close to his and he turned and kissed her cheek softly and told her how nice it had been to be with her again. She ran her right hand down his bare chest and back up over his left shoulder telling him she liked being with him, too.

They decided to wash off using of the some of the water that had accumulated in bowls during the heavy downpours overnight. Lev went inside and came back with their soap and some towels for them. The air was already getting warm and the water in the bowls was cool and smelled like fresh rain. They were both clean, and Kali decided to look inside for clothes that might fit her. The woman who had lived in the house was a bit larger than Kali, but she found black leggings and a safety pin which she used to tighten the waistband. She used the last clean black t-shirt she had brought from the apartment behind the gas station and one of the bras she had found in the white house.

To Kali, it looked like Lev kept wearing the same pants every day, but she realized it was difficult for him to find pants that fit his frame. He finally had clean pants again as the man who had once lived in the farm house had been tall, as well. He always changed his shirts. He would toss his dirty shirts onto the dying embers of their makeshift barbeques as they departed each house in the morning. It was part of his departure process. Kali still planned to stop at each place they had stayed on their return trip to retrieve the clothes she had left behind. Maybe Lev had a full wardrobe back at Ivy, but this was all she had accumulated in her short time here.

They packed their bags, refilled their gallon water containers, and walked while eating some of the dried foods that they were both getting tired of eating. Lev entertained her with his take on her approach to dealing with the two teenagers who had shown up. Again, he insisted she never approach armed strangers. She laughed at him. He also asked her if she knew how to properly hold a gun, noting she had waved the gun around like a drunken cheerleader twirling a baton. She assured him she was an excellent shot and skilled in the use of firearms and other things.

He stopped walking and handed her his gun and said, "Show me."

"What should I shoot?" she asked him, looking around. While he was looking around for something for her to shoot, she said, "There. That bird."

He turned to look where she was pointing and saw a black bird sitting on a branch in a tree quite a distance away. Lev dismissed the bird as a good option. "That's too small and too far," he said, dismissing her suggestion.

She was still wearing her backpack when he unzipped it and pulled out the mostly eaten jar of berry preserves and ran up ahead of her and placed it on a car that was sideways in the overgrown grassy median. He came back to her and said, "Ok. Shoot that."

"That's too easy and it's also food. How will you eat your delicious hardtack if I shoot the last of the berries?"

She was smiling and he said, "I'm going to die of starvation before I take another bite of hardtack. That's far away. If you hit that from here, I'll be impressed."

"It's not even a moving target, man," she grumbled at him.

"Are you really that good?" he asked, suddenly not doubting her as much as he had initially.

"Yep. I'm amazing," she said and rubbed her hand up his chest. He raised his eyebrows and agreed with that fact, but told her to back up as far as she thought she should to make it a challenge. He figured if they wasted a couple of bullets, it was still worth the little bit of fun they were having.

"Ok," she said, and started running down the street away from him and the preserves all of a sudden. He waited for her to stop and when she did, she was a fair distance away from what she was aiming for. She motioned for him to join her and he jogged up to her.

"I don't like the way it feels to shoot past you like that," she said, scowling at him.

He had his hands on his hips and squinted to see the jar he had placed on the car.

"I'm ready. You ready?" she asked him.

"Yeah," he said, and she shot instantly, and he saw and heard the jar explode from the impact of the bullet.

He yelled out that she was an amazing shot, and she suddenly turned away from him and shot a bird flying high in the air past them. He grabbed his chest with one hand and said, "Holy shit, Kali! You're a fucking awesome shot!"

She smiled and blew on the tip of the gun and said, "I know," and handed it back to him.

"You want to keep it on you?" he asked her seriously.

"No. If someone fucks with us, I'll kill them with my bare hands," she said, still smiling.

"You looked like the gun was too heavy for you the way you waved it around at Trent and Olivia this morning. I mean, you really looked dangerous but dangerous because you didn't know how to handle a gun."

"That's how you make people think you can't take care of yourself," she explained to him with a sly look on her face.

"You had me fucking convinced," he said, impressed by her skills at shooting and deception.

"I forgot to tell you I can shoot after they left. You know. Coffee, then sex. It slipped my mind."

"Fair enough," he agreed and kissed her as he put his gun back into his belt. "Did you do range shooting growing up?" he asked as they continued walking.

"Yeah. My dad was really into it. I did archery a lot, too. We did spearfishing around the world. Yeah. I grew up doing all of that stuff. Gave me really good hand-eye coordination."

"Damn, you're full of surprises. I like it. It's fucking sexy," he said as they walked past their destroyed jar of berry preserves.

"The shooting or the surprises?"

"Jesus, both," he admitted, putting his arm around her shoulder while they walked. She never had to ask him to slow down anymore.

He always walked at her pace.

The Haircut and the Kiln Shop

After walking for eight hours, they entered a small town with a large highway running straight through the middle of it. That road was intersected by an old-time main street lined with brick storefronts for one continuous mile. Many of the shops were connected one to the other, and when one had caught fire, the ones connected to it also burned. They walked down the main street looking for a park bench or a table and chair where they could sit and rest and have a bite to eat because Lev had said he was hungry, and Kali said that she could use a break.

As they walked past a hair salon that had survived all the years somewhat intact, Lev caught his reflection in the dirty window and said, "Let's stop in here so I can get cleaned up. Bolin's been making fun of me anyway. Said I look like shit. Did I tell you my mother was a hairdresser?" he asked Kali.

"No, you didn't mention that. Were you always neatly trimmed having a stylist for a mom?" she asked him.

"Yeah, until the world ended, I always shaved and kept my hair short. It was so lame that when I was in high school, my mother would tell me I could wait longer between cuts," he laughed.

"Oh, to have a picture of you back then."

"I was really into looking like a naval officer. You know, all the military in San Diego? I was really tall as a teen and built even in high school. I thought looking like I was in the navy would help me get into bars."

"Did it?"

"Yeah, sometimes, but my friends couldn't get in, so it wasn't worth it. Where it really helped was purchasing alcohol. I had no trouble buying beer for myself and my friends until one of my friends got really drunk and his parents complained at a town meeting that the local businesses weren't checking their precious darlings for legit ID during alcohol transactions."

"Those bastards," Kali said, shaking her head and laughing at him as they entered the salon.

The salon was full of people who had died nearly two decades ago, but there were two empty salon chairs and Lev sat in one. He took scissors from the counter and began to trim his beard, removing the length right up to his skin. Kali walked by and said, "Gonna feel like I'm kissing a new guy."

"The old guy will be back in a few weeks," he said to her smiling as he got up to get a closer look at himself in the mirror in order to cut the hair growing closer to his ears. When he finished trimming his facial hair he began cutting the hair all around his head and Kali was impressed by his skills.

"You must have gotten that from your mom," she said, looking him over adding, "It even looks good back here."

"I'm done," he said, brushing himself off. "Let's take some of these scissors back with us," he said, getting up from the salon chair to grab a few more from the other work stations.

"Ok. Then we can go get the tech," Kali said as she unzipped her backpack and added the scissors he'd collected.

"Is the tech here, Kali?" he asked her, sounding confused.

"Yeah, I hid it in the kiln shop down the street from here. I put it in a kiln so it would be safe."

He stared at her. "What are we doing cutting my hair if the tech is here?" he asked her quietly.

"You wanted to stop in here. It was on the way," she said, shrugging.

"Hey. Come here," he said, taking her arm and sitting back down in the salon chair he'd just vacated. "Have a seat," he said, patting his lap. "I want to tell you something I've been thinking about."

She offered him a confused smile but sat on his lap. He wrapped both of his arms around her waist and sighed. He didn't want to make her mad.

"What?" she asked as she reached around his neck and continued to dust hair from his newly exposed neck.

He leaned forward and kissed her.

"Ok. Now tell me what's up."

He breathed in deeply and said, "I don't care if there isn't any tech. Bolin said you're probably going to hand me silverware and tell me it's time traveling tech. I don't care."

She laughed at that and said, "I can't believe I said I'd make this trip with him."

"He never would have survived the first day with you," Lev laughed. "He would have turned around and walked back to Ivy and yelled about how you walk too slow and he wasn't going to tolerate it."

They both laughed at that and Lev said, "Ok, ok. Seriously. I wanna say this to you. I don't care if there's no tech. Or if you're crazy. I like you, and It doesn't fucking matter to me if you have this fantasy in your head. I'm gonna be honest with you if you show me stuff that isn't technology, ok? I'll tell you it's not technology, but it won't mean I'm pissed off at you or whatever. I'm just going to be honest. When we get back to Ivy and, you know, some people will be annoyed about you not having tech we can use, I'll deal with them. I told you I haven't told you everything. You just remember the part about me liking you and not giving a shit if you brought us tech or not. Deal?" he asked her.

"Deal. And I'm glad you like me. I like you, too," she said, nodding.

He nodded back at her and held her hand as she got off of his lap from the elevated salon chair. They grabbed their backpacks and headed to the kiln shop.

Lev had made peace with the fact that Kali was crazy. He liked her brand of crazy. She made him feel more alive than he had in a long time. She was like gravity pulling him closer to her. He knew he didn't understand her yet, and he didn't care. He would in time. He couldn't resist her or deny his attraction to her. He felt committed to her. He was committed to her being. Not being something, but her existence. Fuck it. If she wanted to live in a fantasy world, fine. He wanted to let her be, and he wanted other people to let her fucking be. He liked her even when she was annoyed at him or challenged him. He was committed to her the way he was committed to Bolin, Aisha, and the others in his small post-apocalyptic family. None of them conformed to an expectation he had of them. He didn't have expectations of them. They just existed as they were. Add Kali to that list of people he was committed to. She didn't have to give him tech or even her affections. He was fucking committed to her because of whatever it was that happened during a life that drew you in and made you feel connected to another person.

They walked down the street and Lev heard Kali say, "There's the kiln shop!" She was excited, but he was nervous. He didn't want to say something that freaked her out. Ending her fantasy wasn't his goal, but he didn't want to lie to her. His apprehension grew as they drew closer to the shop and she, of all people, picked up her pace making him have to walk faster to keep up with her.

He followed her as she stepped over the low brick wall that used to contain a large glass window at the front of the shop. She was practically hopping over the long-dead bodies on the floor as she headed to the back of the shop and into a room lined with shelving that contained numerous finished and unfinished ceramic products. She walked briskly over to one of the three large kilns on the floor bypassing two smaller kilns. He looked at her as she swung around beaming with excitement and pointed to the kiln she was standing next to. "Lev! The tech is in here!" she said happily.

He noticed a lock on the kiln and walked over and lifted it. "I think we need a key," he said to her, smiling lightly.

"I put it over here. Hold on," she said as she dropped her backpack onto the floor. He watched her walk over to one of the tall shelves with ceramic products in various stages of having been fired. She reached for a broken cup that was along the back wall and brought it over to the kiln, placing it on top. Inside was a key. Lev could feel his heart start to race knowing that this was the last stop on this crazy adventure with her. "I put it in a broken cup because that way if someone came around looking to take a piece of pottery, they'd skip the broken cup."

"I still think you were taking a chance," he laughed lightly.

"I know. I was in a hurry. I didn't know what to do, if I'm being honest. It felt like a good plan, but maybe it wasn't." She was moving towards him and shooed him away from the lock now so that she could open it and open the kiln.

"I found the lock in that hardware store across the street. It's mostly burned down, but there were locks. It felt like it was meant to be."

He remembered sitting outside the tractor supply store with her the day she told him about Time and Time's preference for not using pronouns and reminded himself to be considerate of her fantasy when she revealed what she had locked inside the kiln. Clearly, she had gone to a lot of effort to create and maintain the fantasy. The apocalypse took its toll on people in different ways, he reminded himself.

She removed the lock and he could see that her hands were shaking. He didn't want her to open the kiln. She tossed the lock in back of her and he listened as it skidded across the floor while she opened the lid of the kiln. The broken ceramic cup fell to the floor as she lifted the lid, breaking for a final time.

Lev looked inside the kiln and turned to her. "There's one thing in here," he said quietly.

She was beaming and told him in an excited voice, "It's called an optical. Go ahead and get it for me. I'll show you what it does."

Lev was silent as he looked away from her and reached inside the kiln to get the item. He leaned over and picked it up then stood back up and handed it to her, looking at her face kindly. "Kali, it's ok," he said calmly as he touched her arm.

She nodded and smiled at him. "I know it is. You ready? Watch my finger," she said as she moved her finger over what resembled a touch screen that suddenly lit up. "Look inside the kiln, Lev."

He turned and looked inside the kiln as she requested and then turned back to look at her before looking back inside the kiln again. He grabbed the edge of the kiln with both hands to steady himself and said quietly, "Kali. You brought us tech from The Benefactor."

He grabbed her and lifted her off her feet and held onto her in a tight, silent embrace. He was hugging her and kissing her, and he suddenly huffed a deep breath of air out of his lungs and pressed his forehead against hers and put his head down with his eyes closed. She was still suspended by his embrace with her arms wrapped around his neck, and she waited for him to say something. When he didn't, she asked, "Lev, are you ok?"

"Yeah," he said. But she heard his voice crack.

"It's exciting. The tech is real. I know your scientists have been waiting a long time to get help from us."

He still hadn't moved his head to look up at her. "I'm so glad the tech is real. But, it's not just that the tech is real, Kali. It's that you're real, too. You're that good kind of crazy," he laughed, finally looking at her face.

"I told you so!" she laughed with him.

He put her down on the floor and wiped away the few tears that had escaped. "I guess you're really being chased. I'm sorry I gave you a hard time about wearing your fucking shoes to bed and being ready to fight and run. Oh, Jesus. And I guess this means Time doesn't use any pronouns?" He looked startled and shook his head. "Time isn't human. That's weird. Holy shit. I need a minute to process some of this information before my head explodes. Oh...." he said, looking at her with concern mixed with visceral anger. "This means you've been a hostage, and the person who kept you was, quote, "the evil fucking villain." You're scared. You're not crazy. This isn't good."

"Yeah. All that, and more. More will come to you. I told you it's abstract until you believe. I know you needed proof. It's ok. And you know, being honest here, I'm definitely on the crazy spectrum. Don't discount that just because you believe me now. I can't pretend to be sane for you," she said, smiling happily and touching his arm.

"Can I hug you some more?" he asked her.

"You can hug me all you want," she said, wrapping her arms around his waist as he wrapped his arms around her shoulders. His head was resting on top of her mess of hair, and he was talking aloud about the things she had done and said while he had not believed she was who she claimed to be. "And the shampoo and conditioner came from Australia, and it's not expired. That's weird to consider, too. Some of the tech will send a person to Hell, a lightning storm is the safest place to be, you're not afraid to die, you're afraid of being captured and being tortured forever. I'm sorry I didn't believe you. Was I too rude?" he asked, looking at her with concern about how he'd treated her.

"No, you weren't too rude. You were just confused. Who's The Benefactor and what's the quote about the evil fucking villain from?" she asked him.

"I'm pretty certain it was your Friend, not Time, who came here and spoke to the Research Team the day of the extinction event. They wrote down what he said. He referred to the guy who killed nearly everyone on the planet as an evil fucking villain. There's more, but you'll see. We refer to him as The Benefactor because he built Ivy, left a ton of useful supplies, and admonished everyone not to use his name. Out of context it's difficult to explain. See? I can be confusing, too," he added with a smile.

"The Benefactor, huh?" Kali asked, smiling.

"You like the doors and windows open, and you want to know escape routes. You must have felt alone being the only one who knew."

"It kinda sucked, but I felt like you were trying, so I didn't feel completely alone. I had the mission and some hope," she said reassuringly.

"Well, I apologize for how we treated you at Ivy. Jesus, I'd be really mad at myself right now if I hadn't let you sleep on my couch that first night. I was so confident and arrogant, you know, believing I knew how to protect you. How did you put up with me?"

"I did argue with you on my own behalf." She reminded him.

Lev laughed and agreed that she certainly hadn't abandoned her own best interests no matter how much he had wanted her to trust him.

"Let's get this tech back to Ivy and see if I can explain to the scientists, I mean, the Research Team, how to use it. You know, I'm pretty nervous about someone being an asshole with the tech. I was told there was a small team of 11 people and I counted 20 people in the room at my meeting."

Lev grimaced. "Yeah, there are more than that even. A lot more, actually."

"Makes me worried someone won't be listening when I tell them about the tech and what each piece does. Some of it has really awful potential for misuse. I could bring it in and put it on the table and someone could have attitude and touch something that--"

"Sends us to Hell?" Lev offered,

"Yeah. And that's no joke. Game over," she said gravely.

She looked really concerned and Lev told her, "The only thing I can say to you right now is that I believe you and I trust your advice regarding the tech. I'm going to be an asset to you and your mission, which includes making sure you're listened to. You can trust me. Ok?"

"Ok. Until everyone knows what I know, I worry that a mistake will be made and his army shows up and we're all.... not dead. We're all locked in time cells and tortured forever." She looked at him. "You can't imagine," she said, shaking her head.

"I get it. Someone blinks too loud, I'll make them repeat what you told them to prove to you they heard you the first time. We'll take it slow. Make sure everyone's clear."

"You sure they'll listen to you? It's hard to manage a lot of people."

He could see she was still worried. "I'm Head of Security and I've kept them safe for a long time. They'll listen to me," he said, trying to reassure her.

"So how many people?".

"Around 80," he said, looking down at her face with an apologetic smile.

"Oh, my God!" She laughed. "I'm not a public speaker. I'll think about what I have to tell them on the walk back to Ivy. Jesus. Fucking hell," she muttered. She tipped her head and added, "Well, my Friend would be happy to hear more people joined. That was the hope."

"Do we have to put this tech in one of our backpacks?" he asked her as they stood over the open kiln looking at the tech together.

"No. I have my optical now. I can recall the tech whenever I want to. I'll hide it again," she said as she placed her finger near the top of the optical. The tech disappeared, and Lev shook his head in amazement.

"Is that a computer screen? It looks like it's moving weirdly."

"It's an energy field that's been given a formula to make it fit inside this frame. You can put the energy of an optical into anything with closed edges. This used to be a magnifying glass. One of our techs made it for me a long time ago.

"How does it work? Where did the tech go?"

"The optical hides what the operator wants hidden in the past. I'm this optical's operator. Only one person can control an optical. A thought neuro synthesizer reads the mind of the operator. I don't have to place my finger near the screen, but it helps me to focus. Intention is important when you're communicating with the tech in an optical. I'm the only person who can recall what's hidden on my optical. I can't be forced to hand over what I've hidden. My optical will know if I'm under duress or if I've been tortured to reveal what I've hidden on it. You can't break it and release what I've hidden, either. The energy exists even if the frame breaks. I can carry it with me, get it a new holder if my frame breaks. Well, I wouldn't know the formula to make it fit in a new space. But I could keep it in a box or something. All my secrets would still be hidden by it. It would still be usable even if it wouldn't be as easy to walk around with."

Lev listened to her and tried to keep up with what she was telling him. "So, I can't force you to give up the tech the optical hid?"

"No. The optical will know my decision to reveal what I wanted hidden is a result of my being threatened. It'll let me die rather than give up what I've hidden."

"Then why didn't you bring it to Ivy in the first place?"

"The optical can be stolen from me. People steal opticals. If you can't get what someone else hid, you can steal the optical from them and prevent them from getting what they hid that way. If I can't have it, you can't have it either, you know?"

"I see."

"I could have been robbed. I didn't know what to expect on my walk to Ivy. I've never been here before. My Friend and I thought it would be best if I made sure the scientists were still there before I brought in the tech. We've never done this before. It took years just to gather the tech and the information in the recipe book. Can you imagine how awful it would have been if I'd gotten robbed when I was walking to Ivy? All this for nothing? All these years gathering tech for Ivy's scientists would have been for nothing."

"I think you did an amazing job," Lev said, sounding very impressed.

"Why don't you have more experience using the other technology you brought us? Why would you be the person to bring tech to us if you've never actually used it?" he asked her. She turned to look at him and answer, but he felt like he had been accusatory and added, "That sounded like the question you were asked at the meeting with the RT. I'm not saying you're incompetent, and I get the electrician analogy, I'm just wondering why you. Why not someone who could help us learn more about this tech we're being given. Ugh. No matter how I try to phrase that, it's gonna sound like I don't fucking appreciate your role in getting the tech here," he said, shaking his head.

"No. It's ok. You're not being a condescending asshole like that other guy was. I get it. I've told you since the first day I'm not a scientist, or a math person, or an IT person. It must seem nuts that they would have me go, but really, I'm very good at some things. My friends had faith in me to complete the mission. You'll see. I have a great memory when I'm not forgetting shit. And I'm pretty brave even when I'm scared. Oh, and I'm trustworthy except when I have to lie. And I can keep a secret. There's not really an exception to that one. Can't even torture a secret out of me. It's been tried," she said, raising her eyebrows at him. "And I don't get discouraged easily, which is obvious, right? I'm pretty tough, in my opinion."

Lev realized she could keep going and smiled at her. "I don't need to be convinced."

"Our band of traitors is small. We lost our last tech awhile back. We didn't have one to send you."

Lev looked at her and frowned. "Well, what about you? I'm sure you're one of a kind. Are they concerned about losing you?"

Kali looked at him and tipped her head offering him a small, reassuring smile. "Yeah, they're my friends. There were reasons that my going made the most sense. Plus, I wanted to go. No one made me go. They would be really upset if I died, but they'd also be happy for me. You know? To finally be dead. At least for a little while."

Lev looked at her and closed his eyes, shaking his head. "This is an unfinished conversation. Let's find a place to stay for the night." He added, "I need a drink."

"Then let's go get you one," Kali said, smiling at him.

He looked at her and said, "I'll probably also need you, so maybe you have water?" And then laughed when she said in a loud, bored tone, "It's about the quantity, Lev. I'm having a fucking drink with you," while zipping up her backpack with the optical inside.

They walked around looking for alcohol and a habitable place to sleep for the night deciding not to bother with any homes that had bodies in them. Finding a structurally sound home with no dead bodies in it that Kali approved of took a while, but they finally found a clean single story home and got themselves set up inside with candles and a DIY barbeque compliments of Lev. He made quinoa with beans and some of the tomatoes for their dinner. He drank whisky straight from the bottle he'd found. Kali poured herself a shot of Lev's whisky and they toasted their success at finally reaching the hidden tech, Kali not being as insane as Lev had feared, or sane with caveats as she described herself, and the excellent dinner Lev had prepared for them. They went to bed after Kali started kissing Lev's neck, enjoying greater access to him since his haircut earlier in the day. Lev went down on Kali until she came and then slid himself inside her and fucked her and kissed her until he came. Alcohol did not negatively impact Lev's ability to perform or have an orgasm.

He laid in bed awake for a little while after Kali had fallen asleep and considered the man he had become since that day driving down the highway to get Yuna from the airport. He was different now in a lot of ways, but he liked himself. He wondered if Kali would like him, too, if she knew him better. He considered himself in the context of the post-apocalyptic world. He didn't have regrets. He didn't kill people for fun. He killed those who had to be killed. People who couldn't play a part in the plan. He just didn't care after he had killed them. He killed to survive. He killed to end suffering. He killed bad people. Was he occasionally wrong and discovered that after the fact? Yeah. It happened from time to time. He never tortured people. That was disgusting to him. If a person needed killing, he killed them. Even incredibly shitty people got killed as quickly as possible. He didn't get off on killing. Killing was a part of a workday in the post-apocalypse office to him. He never raped anyone. He killed people who raped others. He had a code. He didn't explain or justify his code to anyone. He didn't care if others didn't understand what his code was. It was up to people who interacted with him to figure it out. Yeah, if he went back to Ivy and Trent or Olivia had fucked up his instructions, he'd kill whoever fucked up. He was their commanding officer. He had told them what to do. If a person couldn't be reliable, that person had to go.

With a few exceptions. Kali was one exception. Kali could fuck up. He didn't care. He trusted her. Her fuck ups would be well-intentioned. Or a result of her inability to stay focused. Or some other reason that he couldn't imagine right now. Fuck anyone who demanded he explain why Kali was off the killing field. He'd kill anyone who asked him to defend his stance in regards to Kali. He'd have to. That person would probably be a threat to Kali. Can't have that. No. Just the thought of someone out there willing to hurt her, or expecting him to hurt her, made him angry even while lying in bed with her safe next to him. He looked down at her. She was curled up on her right side wedged perfectly under his left arm and pressed against him. She was dressed and wearing shoes. So was he. Even if he didn't understand what she was doing, she'd be safe. He knew her intentions now, and he trusted them. He trusted her.

Lev was asleep on his back tonight. She was lying on her right side looking at him in the dark, watching him breathe. His right arm was bent up onto his chest with the palm of his hand resting over his heart. The other was flung somewhere above her head. She was lying against his side, which should have been close enough for her, but it wasn't. She ran her left hand across his stomach and wrapped him into her one-armed hug as she watched his chest rise and fall with his deep breathing.

He stirred and asked, "What's wrong?" She smiled at his lightning quick reaction.

"I'm hugging you," she said quietly.

"Mmmm," he said as he slid his hand from his heart and put it on her arm. She felt his other arm slide down around the back of her head and shoulders and felt him pull her tighter against his body. He fell back to sleep quickly, and Kali decided she wasn't confident in the scientists she had met at Ivy. She watched him breathe until she fell asleep again.

Day 5

They woke early and decided to walk back to the farm house. The water bowls would still be there for them to use for bathing, and they could fill their containers to have drinking water for the walk back to Ivy. The sky had cleared considerably since the storm and the day was starting out warmer than usual.

Lev had them stop outside a considerably dilapidated music shop as they departed the small town and went inside to look for guitar strings for Bolin.

"I took what I saw. I don't know what he needs," Lev said to her, as he came back out onto the sidewalk where she had waited for him.

"I know about guitars and strings," she said helpfully.

"The way you know about guns?" he asked her, hoping for a 'hell yeah.'

"Oh, yeah. I play."

"Well, you want to go back inside with me and make sure I didn't miss anything he might need?"

Kali stepped over the low brick wall saying, "Yeah, maybe I'll spot something. I want to find a way to make Bolin like me even if he still wants to shoot me," she laughed.

Lev followed Kali around the shop and she gave him a few items that she thought a guitar enthusiast might need. They went into a back room after Kali asked Lev to kick down a stuck door. Inside, they found some inventory that had not made its way to the storefront before the extinction event.

When Lev saw her raise her eyebrows and drop open her mouth, he asked, "What did you find?"

She turned to him holding a box that was a little bigger than a shoe box. "Remember when he said to me 'everything expires' about my shampoo? Well, I sure hope guitar strings don't expire," she said as she shook the box gleefully.

"The whole box?" Lev asked, stunned.

"Yeah, and these boxes, too! We need to bring back all three of them. They're for different guitars. I don't know what he has."

"This is great, babe!" Lev laughed. "I'll carry them in the duffle bag," he said leaning down to unhook it from his backpack. He put the three boxes of strings into the duffle bag and said, "If the strings are any good, we'll all win. He's a fucking excellent musician. Bastard can sing, too." He zipped up the duffle bag and attached it to the top of his backpack and they headed back on their way to the farm house.

While they walked, they didn't talk much about the tech or what the various pieces she had brought for the research team did because Kali said she didn't want to explain everything once to him and then again to the team. She explained that she had been working on a script in her head for describing the tech to the Research Team. She said she didn't want to mess up and miss important details. He agreed that made sense and said he'd rather learn about the tech at the same time it was in front of him anyway.

"Are you going to be there, too?" she asked him, sounding surprised.

"Yeah, I told you, Bolin and I are informed about all things regarding the work of the RT. That's what we call the Research Team. Like I said yesterday, I'll make sure everyone's paying attention to you when you discuss what the tech does. What you need them to know." He asked her if she would elaborate on the piece of tech that she said would send a person to Hell, though, because he wondered if she meant actual Hell as in Heaven and Hell.

"I feel like anything's possible these days," he said, looking worried.

She offered that the tech took a person straight to their prison, which was called Hell, where a prisoner had no chance for escape. He considered her apprehension over being taken to a jail cell her first day at Ivy and wondered if she had been in the prison herself. He didn't ask. It wasn't that he had to struggle not to satisfy his curiosity so much as he had enough patience to wait for her to reveal what she wanted him to know. He had confidence that she would discuss all of this with the RT. She wasn't withholding information from him so much as waiting to present it thoroughly and accurately. She would be discussing things that she didn't specialize in and things that were upsetting to her. He imagined that would be difficult for anyone.

They arrived at the farm house and Kali decided she would clean up first while Lev got a fire going in the firepit on the back patio. Pieces of the furniture Kali had broken down the other morning were still lying about nearby, so Lev calculated he would need another chair and some books to get the fire going. He went inside and checked through the books he found in order to make sure there wasn't one he needed to add to his own collection. With an armful of books to burn stacked on a wooden chair he planned to break down, he walked out as Kali stood off to the side of the patio cleaning her body with the water that had been collected in the large containers Lev had brought out from the garage and barn before the rainstorm. She was using their dwindling bar of soap to clean her hair and neck and scooped a cup of water from the container to rinse the soap away. He liked watching her.

Lev placed the books in the firepit and smashed the chair along the side of the bricks, breaking it down quickly. He added the parts of the chair he had broken to the remains of the chair Kali had broken down and stacked the pieces to the side of the firepit while adding a few on top of the books. Kali walked over as he lit a match to start the fire, and she picked up a pair of clean pants she had left on one of the chairs they'd left by the firepit the previous morning.

As flames began to catch on the edges of some of the books, she suddenly reached into the fire exclaiming, "Lev, you found it! I'm going to win the bet with Bautista!" He watched as she used her fingers to dust off the darkened edges of paper that he had just lit on fire.

"What?" He laughed. "Were you making bets with your guards while I was gone?"

"Friendly wagers," she said as she held up the only slightly burned copy of the book about the rabbits. "And I rescued it from being burned. Totally enhances the story of finding it," she said, smiling as she put the book down on her chair and buttoned her pants.

Lev stood up and put his hand on her bare shoulder and kissed the top of her wet head laughing at her. "Glad you're going to win, but it sounds like he wins, too, because he gets a book," he said as he went inside to get a pot and the food he was going to make for them.

"I know! That's what made it fun!"

Kali pulled a clean shirt she had found inside the house over her head and sat down in the chair and opened the book to the place she had left off while at Ivy. She read while Lev put their food into a pot and added water and then the lid. She read while he cleaned himself up and found clean clothes to sleep in beside her during the night. She read until he offered her a bowl of quinoa, tomatoes, and the last of their beans. He sat down beside her in his chair and put his feet up on the edge of the brick firepit so that his shoe touched hers. She leaned over to his arm and kissed his skin where the sleeve on the t-shirt he was wearing ended.

"Thanks for dinner. It's good," she said.

They had sex in new positions, and Kali touched him in ways and places that Yuna never had. He and Yuna had been much younger than he and Kali were now. He knew Kali likely had a number of sexual experiences that went beyond the average person's experiences. The scars on her body told him she had been kept by a man who was a sadist, but she only demonstrated an enthusiasm for consensual exploration of his body and a desire to be touched in ways that were erotic and sensual not degrading or painful. She never so much as hinted at the existence of the scars that covered her body. It was as if they were invisible to her, or maybe she simply believed she didn't owe anyone an explanation. Frankly, he believed she didn't owe him any information or explanations about her scars or her sexual history. What was done, was done. She was in control of how she wanted to deal with her personal history. Her sexual history and how she got the scars was not his fucking business unless she wanted to make it his business. On the other hand, if he even suspected he was near the person or persons who had subjected her to torture, he'd kill first and confirm later. There was a lot wrapped up in that fact, but he decided he could live with any outcomes in the pursuit of killing those who had participated, even peripherally, in hurting her.

Lev never asked her about her scars. He never avoided touching them with his hands or his mouth. He laid his body against them, and wrapped his arms around them, and looked right past them when he looked at her while she was naked. He saw her, who she was. She knew he saw the scars, too. They were part of her body now and for the rest of this lifetime. But he was turned on by her regardless of what had been done to her skin. The scars didn't turn him on as they did the man who had put them there. She didn't wish she could hide herself or her scars from Lev, but she adored him even more because he had never asked her about them. She didn't put the scars on her body. She owed no one an explanation for them. She was happy she could exist just as she was without offering explanations and hoping in some pathetic way to be accepted. Fuck that. His gaze made her feel sexy and desired. She felt like she told him all this by never saying any of it out loud.

Day 6

"We're going to get back to Ivy a lot sooner than I thought we might," Lev said to Kali as they left the farmhouse and walked down the long driveway to the beige rocks and fallen mailbox.

"I'm excited to show you what the tech does, but I'm concerned the Research Team, I mean the RT, thinks I'm not an important part of their process for understanding how the tech works," she said.

He heard her and responded reassuringly. "I'll make sure they listen to you." But he was distracted by other thoughts. He had told Dave to have Aisha arrive eight days from the day they left and calculated if his and Kali's return would coincide with Aisha's arrival. He'd try to drag out the last day of walking to give Aisha time to arrive. He said nothing to Kali. It wasn't a lie or a lie of omission. It was necessary. It felt necessary, anyway. This wasn't the time to explain to her what was going on.

There were no clouds in the sky, and the air was uncomfortably hot, but they had plenty of drinking water from what they had collected at the farm house during the rainstorm. Lev had boiled it all and refilled their containers. They were out of the instant coffee now, and for breakfast, Lev had made them two cups of stale tea to have with the remains of jerky and dried fruits. Kali had some hardtack telling him to have her jerky. He thanked her for that and took her up on the offer.

They arrived at the two story house with a lot of daylight hours remaining in the day. They had walked about 20 miles and the remaining daylight gave them time to look for some edible food products in the nearby homes. They still had a small amount of jarred tomatoes from Ivy, so Lev went to find sealed pasta. There were plenty of cardboard boxes of pasta, but Lev had strict food consumption rules and would only risk 17 year old pasta sealed in plastic. He wasn't a fan of getting sick from expired food. He said he'd rather go hungry for a couple of days than risk food poisoning, but Kali watched as he continued to search with determination for food entering one home after another in the small development. He definitely wasn't going to go hungry without putting up an effort to find food. She suspected he was close to going into the fields and hunting unsuspecting animals. Luckily for everyone, he found dried pasta sealed in plastic bags that he felt was safe for them to consume.

After they ate their pasta, they poured him a drink and her a shot and toasted him for finding them a good meal and then talked about the music they missed. Kali learned that his parents were both immigrants who brought their musical interests into the home they had raised him in, so he had been exposed to the Indian music his father loved to listen to and the Russian music his mother preferred. His musical tastes were much more modern and mainstream at the time of the extinction event, but he had grown up particularly interested in the hippie music of the 60s and 70s.

Kali asked him if he was a professorially clean shaven, stoner surfer as a teen and he laughed and said, "Oh my god. I was. I was high all the time, but especially on the weekends." She was laughing and asked how his parents responded to their California stoner son with the influence of so many cultural backgrounds in one house.

"They were both incredibly easy going. My mom was so cool. She'd tell me to call if I needed a ride home. She'd pick me and my friends up from the beach or from where ever, and we'd be laughing our asses off, high as fuck and she'd take us to the In-N-Out drive thru and buy us food and sober up my friends before sending them home."

"Aww, I wish I had met your mom," Kali said thoroughly enamored with her without having met her.

"Yeah, she was great. And my dad... This is... don't tell Bolin this," he said. "My dad and Bolin, so many fucking similarities. I totally got Bolin the first time I met him. My dad was a physics professor in India before he moved to America to be with my mom. He ended up studying philosophy in the states, on the east coast, and then teaching philosophy courses at SDSU."

"How's that like Bolin? Was Bolin a philosophy professor?" Kali asked him.

Lev raised his eyebrows and smiled at her. "You notice anything about Bolin? Like he might be a little bit on the spectrum?" he asked.

She laughed. "Yeah, absolutely. I noticed. Not out on the field when he wanted to shoot me, but once you two started interrogating me. Actually, to be honest, I was sure I liked him before I was sure I liked you."

Lev laughed out loud at that and said, "Yeah, so, he reminds me of my dad. My dad had a diagnosis and everything. I don't know if Bolin does. I never asked him, but I know he and my dad are probably shoulder to shoulder on the same spot on the spectrum. We've been friends for years. I think of him as family." He wanted to tell her about Bolin. He wanted her to know that Bolin was important to him.

"Can I still gloat about finding him the guitar strings?" Kali asked Lev.

"Yeah. Even if they're rusty, he's still going to be impressed you did that," Lev said, kissing her.

"You know," she said to him waving her hand around him, "I see your dad here, but where's your mom?"

Lev smiled and held up his glass of vodka while raising his eyebrows and saying, "За наших мам! To our mothers!" before taking a large sip from his glass and kissing her.

"Oooh. I see it now!" Kali laughed.

Lev didn't ask her to sleep upstairs in the two story house. He knew from the first time they had slept there, she wouldn't. Now he knew why. Sort of. You can survive if you jump out of a second story window. She had said that about Dorm 17. He didn't fully understand, but he knew it mattered. He went upstairs and dragged a queen mattress from the master bedroom down the stairs and into the living room. He pushed the coffee table away from the couch with his foot and positioned the head of the bed on the floor against the couch. The twin mattress Kali had slept on last time remained where it had been since the night she had slept on it.

He sat on the queen mattress with his back against the couch sipping his second glass of vodka watching Kali as she stood a few feet away by the coffee table removing her clothes slowly while looking at him. He thought she was beautiful with her hair all big and full with large untamed loose curls framing her face. When she walked over to him, he lifted up his glass and handed it to her silently. She took it from him and turned to place it on the coffee table along with her own glass and the bottle of vodka they had been drinking from. He stood up and got off of the mattress standing on the floor beside her where he took off his clothes while she watched him.

They laid down on the mattress with Kali under him while they kissed and ran their hands over each other's bodies. Before they had sex, Lev told her how he liked to open his eyes and watch her when she came. She told him that tonight she was going to watch him while he fucked her and made her cum. He immediately responded to that by sliding himself inside her, kissing her neck, and telling her he wanted her to watch him. As they fucked, and she neared her orgasm and called out his name, he told her gruffly, "Watch me make you cum, Kali. See how much I want to make you cum."

Afterwards, they sat on the mattress with their backs leaning against the front of the couch. They were dressed again and had their shoes on. Lev had filled both of their glasses with the remaining vodka, not holding back as he filled Kali's glass since they had already had sex. Kali was smiling as he stroked the back of her neck under her hair and she confessed that she might have had to close her eyes a couple of times while she had an orgasm. Lev smiled and said, "I know. I saw you," while he kept playing with the hair on the back of her neck.

Lev had something on his mind and wanted to talk to her, but he didn't want to ruin the relaxed mood they found themselves in. The candles around the living room cast a warm glow on them and their comfortable surroundings in the messy room. The coffee table was askew to the right of the queen mattress, and the brown leather of the large couch caught the glow of the candlelight warming the look of the room. The twin mattress Kali had slept on the first time they had stayed in the house remained to their left under one of the open windows, and the candlelight reflected off of the glass in the upper window.

Kali read the look on his face as he looked at her and asked, "What? Just ask already. I've seen that look on and off for a couple of days now." When he looked away from her, she added, "Hold on. Obviously I need to be less sober for whatever's got you looking like that," and took a sip of vodka from her glass.

Lev smiled at her and said, "Me, too," lifting his glass and taking a large swallow. He looked at her and asked, "Why aren't we fucking with our shoes on? The lightning storm. That makes sense now. But all the other times we've been together, we're undressed. Is it that you decide to take a chance? Because, honestly, I don't ever feel like we rush to get through being together. I feel like we take our time, so I'm not complaining at all. I wonder, sometimes, if I should hurry, though."

She was looking at his face while he spoke and said, "It's annoying to want to live a little. To enjoy being alive for a change." She looked at him and held up her glass of vodka and took another large sip.

That was the first time she had ever mentioned wanting to live and he felt it like a shockwave going through his body when she spoke the words. She had spoken so casually about dying since the day she had walked up to Ivy. To want to live, even a little, was an improvement he wanted to encourage.

He consciously tried not to overwhelm her and have her shut down and asked, "You decide not to worry? And that works?"

"Sort of," she said, turning away from him to look across the room at nothing in particular.

He looked at the side of her face with the candle light casting a soft, bouncing yellow light on her cheek and tried to access his best calming voice as he felt the warmth of the alcohol he'd been consuming catching up with him. "You wanna tell me what "sort of" means? I'm not saying you have to. Just asking so I understand."

She still wasn't looking at him when she said, "I'm not really sure I want to tell you."

He let a small laugh escape at that and said, "Jesus, Kali. What's left that we can't say or do to each other? For instance, you should know I'm starting to feel this," he said as he held up his almost empty glass of vodka. "I've got my shoes on, but I'm wondering if I can finish this or if I should put it down now. You seem to know when we can let go. Can I know the secret?" he asked, smiling at her.

She turned back to face him and smiled saying, "Go ahead. I've got you."

"Is this the "Sort of" you mentioned?" he asked her as he finished his drink and placed his empty glass on the floor next to the mattress.

She closed her eyes and tipped her head back against his shoulder and looked up at his face and said, "Ok. I'm going to tell you. You don't have to promise not to be mad. Be as mad as you want to be."

He laughed at her. "Well, fucking awesome."

She looked at him and shrugged saying, "Except for the time we were together during the lightning storm, I make sure I have some way I can kill you nearby before we begin."

He looked at her and worked to maintain a blank expression as he gently took her glass of vodka from her hand and took a large sip. "There's more to that, right?" he asked her with a surprised look on his face, nodding his head.

"Ok, I want to think of a better way to say it, but I can't. If they show up when we're unprepared, I'm going to kill you. Quickly, so don't worry. Hopefully, I'll be able to kill myself, too."

She watched him consider what she was saying and he asked, "So, tonight? What was the plan for the murder/suicide you had planned?"

"I hid a knife under the couch cushion," she said.

"This couch has a potential murder weapon hidden in it?" he asked, flicking his head to the side.

She nodded, saying, "Yeah."

He closed his eyes and mouthed, "What the fuck?" silently and shook his head back and forth rapidly before opening his eyes and taking a deep breath and raising his eyebrows offering her a reassuring smile. "You planned to kill me to keep me from being captured and tortured, right?" he asked her.

"Yeah. I don't want to kill you, but I will."

"How about showing me where this instrument of death is hidden?" he asked, leaning to the side and reaching to put the glass of vodka he'd taken from her on the coffee table.

Kali turned around onto her knees and lifted the edge of the couch cushion where they had been leaning their backs and pulled out a large kitchen knife she had placed there earlier when he was doing something else, unaware of her potential plans for him. "Just in case," she said as he put out his hand to take the knife from her. "I want to put it back under the cushion for the night. I might have to kill you if they come for me when we're sleeping. It's not just for when we're having sex," she said in a serious tone.

"Yeah. Sure," he said with his hand still waiting for her to hand him the knife.

She handed it to him and watched as he felt the weight and nodded his head. He handed it back to her saying, "That was a good choice. Nice weight to it. Might not be great for stabbing, though," he added with a smirk.

"I planned to cut your throat. Hopefully behead you," she said as she replaced the knife under the cushion.

He watched as she adjusted the handle so that she could reach up and grab it quickly if she needed to. "The knife I hid last time we were here is on the other side of the twin mattress," she offered. "That one was smaller. I meant to cut my wrists with it. I wasn't going to kill you then. I didn't know how much I liked you. Hopefully, they'd have just killed you. I think they'll think you're worthless and let you die. It's just me they're gonna want."

Lev laughed involuntarily as he reached for Kali's glass of vodka from the coffee table and took another sip. He held out the glass to her and offered her a sip which she accepted. As she took the glass from him he asked, "So, there's a knife on the side of the twin?"

He was crawling off of the queen mattress and making his way over to the twin as she said, "Yep. Down against the wall. Not under the mattress."

Lev sat on the twin mattress and felt down the side against the wall with his hand and pulled out a knife that was smaller than the one hidden under the couch cushion. He put his head down and laughed a little and looked up holding the smaller knife in front of him telling her, "Babe, I really appreciate how I never know what the fuck you're up to, but I'm thinking here, and I know I'm lit up right now, but I'm wondering how I'm supposed to get you back if you get captured and I'm dead."

He put the smaller knife down along the side of the twin against the wall again and got up and stumbled back across the queen mattress to sit back down next to her. Kali waited for him to sit back down beside her and smiled at him while offering him the last of the vodka in her glass.

"You already rescued me, Lev," she said.

"No. Not until I kill that fucking guy," he said coldly as he finished their shared drink.

Day 7

Kali woke up before Lev and left him to sleep more while she got ready to walk to the white house. They would pass the field of cosmos on their way and she wanted to find a bottle she could add a little water to in order to carry some flowers back to Ivy with her. She brushed her teeth with the baking soda and went outside to feel the cool morning air. The two dining room chairs remained outside alongside the barbeque Lev had dragged over to the driveway days earlier. She sat on one of the chairs and looked up at the sky, which was gaining sunlight slowly, and tried to think of nothing but the possibility of enjoying being alive.

Lev slept in late after having become legitimately drunk the night before. After the vodka was gone, he'd opened a bottle of gin he had planned to take with them to the white house and toasted Kali and her relentless efforts to see that he was properly murdered and not tortured by an evil, futuristic asshole. She had joined him in a few sips of gin, but shuddered at the taste, making him laugh.

He slurred as he assured her he wasn't an alcoholic and explained to her that at Ivy, he rarely drank because he was on duty 24/7. He told her how he would occasionally enjoy one of James' homemade wines or beers along with him, but mostly, he remained ready to address problems and work. She asked him who James was, having heard Ju speak his name as the maker of their soap, but he said, "He's a friend. You'll meet him soon enough. We'll drink his potato vodka together someday."

That answer satisfied both of them for the time being. Before they fell asleep, he made her promise not to tell anyone he could loosen up and have a good time, and she swore to keep his secret. No one would find out from her that Lev had a fun side.

Kali smiled at him when he finally stumbled out to the driveway and sat down hard on the vacant wooden chair.

"What time do you think it is?" he asked her, unable to maintain a gaze at the rising sun to gauge for himself. "Ugh. My fucking head. I can't look at the sun," he said, squeezing his eyes closed.

Kali watched him rub his eyes and got up saying, "We're doomed. I don't have the apocalypse skills you do. I'll go look for some ibuprofen."

"There's some in the first aid kit in my backpack," he offered as she ran her hand along his shoulders while walking by him.

"I'll be back with that and some water."

"I need food!" he shouted to her.

She laughed.

When Kali returned to him a few minutes later, she handed him the ibuprofen and a cup of water. She walked back inside and grabbed a pot and poured water and the rest of the dried pasta into it and grabbed another dining room chair. Outside, she had Lev break apart the chair on the driveway and she got the flame in the barbeque going under the pot with the water and pasta. Lev ate the food they had planned to save for dinner and promised he'd find them something else along the way. She assured him she could wait for her next meal until they got back to Ivy, but he scoffed and said he couldn't.

With the sun high in the sky, they ate the last of the peanuts on the walk to the white house. They walked along the road where Kali had turned to him and told him to go back to Ivy because he didn't believe her about Time.

Lev said, "I didn't think you were a liar. I thought you were fucking insane. It was depressing," he said absently as they kept walking.

She looked up at him and smiled. "I really wanted you to go back to Ivy and let me go get the tech myself. I was so mad at you."

At the field of cosmos, Kali picked a small bunch and put them in the water bottle she had found at the two story house. Lev held the bottle for her while she pushed the slim stems of the cosmos into the bottle. "I think you can fit a few more in," he said, encouraging her to get as many as the bottle could hold.

Lev was mostly recovered from his hangover by the late afternoon, and ran inside several homes they passed along the way to the white house, checking for anything he knew was safe for them to eat. He found two packages of dried pasta in plastic bags in one house and an unopened bottle of soy sauce in another.

"Soy sauce and spaghetti?" Kali asked, making a face.

"It's linguini, and don't question the chef. We both know I'm the better cook in this relationship," he said in mock defensiveness while she shook her head at him, cringing at the meal he was suggesting.

As the white house loomed ahead of them, Lev told her, "I saw you shirtless for a second the morning we left here. I didn't mean to. I looked away quickly. Then you came into the kitchen and handed me the knife and the pants." He laughed. "For a moment I thought you knew and were pissed off at me, but really, the open doors? Makes it difficult not to accidentally see you sometimes. Did you see me see you?" he asked her.

"I didn't, but it's fine. I'm used to not having any privacy," she said reassuringly.

"At Ivy, I want you to have more privacy. Except with me. If that's cool," he said to her.

"I don't want to be in a closed room."

He thought about it for a minute and said, "I'm asking you if you want to stay together in one room. Us. Or do you need your own room? I don't know what you want or what you need. You can have what you want. I'll get you what you want. Hell, you can go to Campus if you want, but I have to stay at Ivy. What I'm picturing is the two of us in our own room in our own bed every night. You can think about it and let me know. Take as much time as you need."

They stopped walking at the end of the driveway and Kali stepped closer to him and said, "I didn't even think this was a conversation we were going to have. I just assumed you knew you were stuck with me." She smiled up at him as she wrapped her arms around him.

"Yeah?" he asked her, putting his arms around her waist.

"Yeah, but, I have to tell you, I can't be on the second floor. It's really hard on my nerves. And I can't close the bathroom door all the way. And I need the window open."

"It's gonna get cold in the winter," he said, smiling at her.

"We'll keep each other warm," she said as he leaned in to kiss her.

They headed around back to the hand water pump to bathe before going inside and Kali said, "I don't want to close the door to the room either."

He looked thoughtful as he removed his backpack and the duffle bag and then said, "Well, I don't want an audience when we're fucking. First floor has a dead end hallway with a storage room. How about that? No neighbors but the hallway offers only one escape route the same as when you were in Dorm 17. The window is a first floor jump, though," he said, raising his eyebrows and nodding as he removed his shirt.

"That sounds pretty good," she said as she walked her backpack with the optical to the deck and placed it and her bottle of cosmos against the wall of the house.

She removed her shoes on the deck and walked over to him where he stood naked using water from the pump to clean sweat off of his face. "Baby, get naked," he said as he reached down to pull her shirt up over her head.

Lev had gone into the white house to get them a bowl, some towels, and wash cloths while she grabbed the last of the soap from his backpack. They took their time cleaning themselves and each other, and their foreplay ended with them each having orgasms as they each took the time to pleasure the other. They gathered their backpacks, shoes, and Kali's flowers, leaving their dirty clothes and the other items outside and found clean clothes to nap in. They put on their shoes and Lev put one of his guns on the night table on his side of the bed and gave Kali the other for her side of the bed. They fell asleep holding each other in the bed Lev had slept on alone only a week earlier.

When they woke up, they laid on the bed for a little while and Lev asked her, "Did you have a knife in here when you went to sleep on the floor?"

"Yeah, I got it when I went to use the bathroom."

"Did you really have to use the bathroom?"

"Yeah, but I would have lied to you and said I had to if I didn't have to. You know... Lie to survive. But I did actually have to use the bathroom. So, I didn't have to lie."

"Where was the knife? Under the pillow?" he asked her.

"While I was asleep it was, but in the morning, I put it back in the kitchen so you wouldn't accidentally step on it and get hurt."

He rolled on top of her and smiled saying, "You're so fucking thoughtful, you know that? And so fucking sexy, too."

They began to kiss and eventually undressed again. Kali spread her legs apart to invite him inside of her and Lev accepted her invitation.

Lev prepared their dinner of linguini and ate his with soy sauce while Kali declined, preferring hers plain. He didn't drink any alcohol, declaring loudly that his days of debauchery had come to an end and then assured Kali more quietly that that did not include his appetite for her. "I'm gonna want to continue to indulge in you," he said, taking her hand and kissing it as they sat together outside near his DIY barbeque drinking hot, stale tea sweetened with honey.

When they went inside to go to bed, Lev placed several weapons around the room for Kali and told her it would probably be best if she let him help her kill any would-be assailants before resorting to killing him.

She looked at him in the candle-lit room and said, "I can't let you be tortured."

He climbed onto the bed and laid down beside her, both of them fully clothed, and said, "God damn, I hope we get another lightning storm soon," while he moved her hair away from her face.

Day 8

Lev woke before Kali and laid in bed beside her considering Aisha's arrival. He had told Dave to have her arrive at Ivy today. He was an idiot for not specifying a time of day. Would she be there this morning, afternoon, night? Aisha was reliable. From the day he had met her in the fast food restaurant, Aisha had only ever displayed an ability to think critically in a crisis and recover quickly using her gift of resilience. Before he had moved to Ivy, he had told her his plan and she helped him refine it. It was their plan. Today was the day. After all these years, it was satisfying to finally shake up what was going on at Ivy. Who could have ever predicted The Benefactor would send someone like Kali. He had always assumed The Benefactor, himself, would reappear. It was going to be fine. He had an idea about how best to deal with Kali.

He tried to get out of bed quietly to go make them pasta and some tea for breakfast, but Kali woke up with her usual efficiency. She opened her eyes and looked at him and was instantly oriented. It was impressive actually, he thought. She probably could murder him quickly if her assailants showed up, even before he knew what was happening. The room was still dark and Lev whispered to her that she could go back to sleep. She moved herself onto the spot on the bed he was vacating and appeared to fall back to sleep as he left the room quickly.

Lev had made them tea and the rest of the pasta before going in to wake Kali. This was the first time he had had to wake her. She was usually up before he was, but when she overslept him, she woke up on her own. It would help if they left later in the morning so that they could give Aisha and her crew time to arrive, so he wasn't bothered by her sleeping in.

He laid down on the bed in back of her and wrapped one arm over the top of her head on the pillow and the other around her while kissing the side of her sleepy face.

"Hey, you want to stay here an extra night?" he asked her, not entirely joking.

She placed her arm over his and said sleepily, "No. I like food. I want to get back and have food. Lots of food."

"There's some stuff I have to take care of when we get back to Ivy," he said, and Kali responded, "Man, are you gonna give me a business speech already? I'm enjoying not thinking." She turned over to face him with her eyes still closed, and pressed her head against his chest and put one arm around him, pulling herself as close as possible to him.

He stroked her messy hair and said to her, "I would stay here in this house with you forever, but I know we won't have peace until we get that asshole. What I was going to say is that the person in charge of Campus will be at Ivy at some point today. I'm going to need to have a meeting with her. Take care of some things. Her name is Aisha. I'll be gone for a little while. I'll need you to stay put. Maybe I can send Bolin to check in with you if I'm not able to."

"Will I be in your room again? I thought we'd have a meeting about the tech right away," she said unhappily.

"No, tomorrow. Early tomorrow. I have Campus stuff to take care of."

"How do you know that if we've been gone for a week?" she asked him.

"I asked for Aisha to be at Ivy around the time we would return. I asked her to be there on the eighth day. This is that day."

"Will I wait in your room?" she asked him again.

"Our room. We'll see. Maybe Bolin can take you to his place."

"He's in the room with the green door at the end of the halls. I remember," she said.

"Better than that. He has a place with his family over by the gardens."

"That sounds nice."

"It is. I'm hoping you can wait for me there," he said, silently preparing himself to get through the rest of the day.

They ate and went and cleaned up at the pump out back before packing up. Kali grabbed her cosmos, and Lev made sure the doors and windows of the white house were closed. He even cleaned up making sure all of the food, old and new, was out of the house as they left. "This will be our vacation home," Lev told her when she looked at him quizzically.

"Babe, you got us a vacation home?" she asked happily.

"I did. It's even got water," he said, smiling proudly.

Lev was fairly certain they were less than 15 miles from Ivy.

"We didn't walk a full 20 the first day," he said raising his eyebrows at her.

"Oh, yes. That's how we found our vacation house. You're welcome," she said as they headed out.

"I want to stop by the apartment behind the gas station and grab a bunch of clothes from there because the person who lived there was my size," she reminded him.

"We can do that. We have time. No need to rush today. We'll be back by the early afternoon."

The Kids

They were a few hours into their walk when Kali saw the gas station up ahead. She went to tell Lev, but he stopped walking and appeared to be looking at something else.

"I think I see some kids," he said, sounding concerned.

"Kids aren't scary," Kali said.

"No, but their parents sometimes are," he said, frowning.

He knelt down and opened his backpack and handed her his second gun. He took Olivia's gun and added it to his pocket and added Trent's knife to his boot.

"Here. Take the knife Bolin sent us with. It's sharper than Trent's knife," he told her. He tossed his backpack and the duffle bag into the tall grass on the side of the road and looked at her with her backpack and the optical inside and frowned.

"I don't even know what's the best plan for what you're carrying. Back pocket?" he asked.

"I guess so. This makes me nervous. This is why I didn't travel alone with it."

She knelt to the ground and opened her backpack while Lev continued to scan the horizon looking for potentially hostile parents of the two kids up ahead of them near the gas station. She quickly slipped her optical into her left back pocket and put the knife Lev had given her into her right back pocket. She left her flowers and her backpack in the road further away from where Lev had tossed his belongings.

"Hopefully any thieves will steal my stuff and not look for more thinking we left everything right in the street."

"Maybe," Lev said. He was busy looking around for anyone who might be lurking about near them.

Lev looked at Kali and said, "I've got to tell you something really quick just in case I haven't already been crystal clear with you. I kill people. A lot of people. I'm not opposed to killing those two kids. If something's fucking wrong, I'm going to start killing people. If you're not cool with that, stay in the grass near my pack."

"No, I'm fine with that."

"I'm serious. I wanted to tell you sooner. I make jokes about it sometimes, but the truth is, I murder a lot. I don't do it for the kicks. It's how I've survived this long."

"Let's go, Lev," she said and started walking ahead of him.

Lev's height and size made it impossible for them to sneak up on the two kids, so they walked up to them until they were noticed by them. As they approached, it became obvious that the smaller child was considerably younger than the older child.

"Hi!" Kali called out, waving a friendly hello at them.

Lev recalled how Kali had dealt with Trent and Olivia and realized he had no idea who he was working with during this confrontation. He liked working with people on his team who he had trained. He liked working with Bolin who he knew. He liked knowing what to expect. With Kali, he had no idea how she was going to proceed. He knew she could shoot. That was good.

The two kids stood in the middle of the road in front of small toy cars they had been playing with.

"Hey you guys. How's it going?" she asked the two children as they came up to them. The smaller child looked in shock. Not shock because of the arrival of Lev and Kali, but he looked distant as if he was already checked out before they had arrived. Kali turned her attention to the older kid.

"I'm Kali. What's your name?" she asked him in a soothing and friendly voice.

"I'm Renny. This is Ace. Who are you?" he asked Lev, looking up at him.

"I'm Lev. Nice to meet you, Renny. Ace," Lev said in a tone far less friendly than the one Kali was employing. "You got any parents with you, or are you alone out here?" Lev asked Renny.

"Yeah, back there in the gas station," Renny said, pointing to the right but not taking his eyes off of Lev.

"They're not my parents," Ace said quietly.

"Oh, boy," Lev muttered as he breathed a deeply defeated sigh.

"Where are your parents?" Kali asked Ace.

"Those guys--"

"He's tired," Renny said, interrupting him.

"No he's not," said Lev, staring at Renny.

Kali shook her head suddenly. "Renny? You need some help? We're good guys. We kill bad guys. You need some help? Man, I've got you. Tell me," she said, adding, "Ace, you wanna take my hand, kid?"

Lev continued to stare at Renny but could see Ace slowly leave his side and take Kali's outstretched hand.

"Ace, get behind me," Kali told him.

"Renny, are you a bad guy?" Lev asked him.

"I don't want to be," Renny said quietly in a voice that sounded haunted.

Lev shook his head. "Who are the adults?" he asked him.

"Dan and Pat," Renny said with wide eyes.

"They both men?" asked Lev.

"Yeah," Renny said.

"How old are you?" Lev asked him.

"I think I'm 13. I'm not sure," he said.

How long you been with Dan and Pat?" Lev asked him.

Renny stared at him and didn't answer.

"How long?" Lev asked him again.

"I can remember five summers now."

"They kill your parents?" Lev asked him.

"Yeah."

"Any other adults or kids in this group you're traveling with?" Lev asked him.

"Danny is a kid that's a little older than me and that's it."

Lev sighed. "Renny, when'd they take Ace?" Lev asked him.

"Yesterday," he said.

"Any of you hurt him yet?"

"No. They want me and Danny to first," he said and started to cry.

"I understand," said Lev.

"Hey, Renny. Where's Danny?" Kali asked him softly.

"He's drawing under that tree. On the other side." Renny pointed to a group of trees in the distance to the left of where they were all standing in the street.

Kali nodded while looking over at the trees. "Ok, take us to meet Danny. We'll help you guys out of this mess," she said reassuringly.

"Really?" asked Renny suddenly crying harder. "I really don't want to be here tonight," he said with his shoulders starting to heave up and down as he cried.

He was wiping away tears with his dirty fingers and Kali said, "Renny, you gotta help us help you. Cry later. Get us to Danny so we can help."

Lev watched as Renny composed himself and started walking in the direction of the trees to find Danny. Lev walked but kept his eyes on the gas station hoping to catch a glimpse of Dan and Pat.

Ace followed behind Kali, and they saw the older boy sitting under the tree with a drawing pad and a pencil sketching the landscape. He was deep in his thoughts and didn't hear the four of them approach through the soft grass. Renny looked at Kali and she nodded her head at him to encourage him to get Danny's attention.

"Danny?" he said.

Danny turned around and suddenly jumped up, dropping his paper and pencil. "What the fuck, Ren?" he asked him while staring at Lev and Kali and then back at Lev again.

"They're here to help us," Renny said, and Lev could hear him try to make their assistance sound appealing. Lev knew it was too late for Danny. He was more than a couple of years older than Renny. He felt Kali move slightly alongside him and thought maybe she was attending to Ace who was absolutely silent behind them.

"Fuck you, Ren! You're gonna get beat to hell tonight for this!" Danny said, shaking his head with a face full of rage.

"They can help us. Look at this guy!" he said, referring to Lev's size. "I don't want to be here tonight!" He pleaded with the other abused child, "Let's go with them!"

Danny bent down and picked up his drawing pad and searched for a moment for his pencil. "You're fucking dead!" he said to Renny as he stood up glaring at him.

The knife landed deep in the center of Danny's forehead and Renny gasped and closed the short distance between himself and Danny as Danny's legs crumpled beneath him and he fell to his knees and then to his side. Lev was startled but turned to Kali as he recognized the handle of the knife as the one Bolin had packed for him.

Kali was staring at the scene and walked ahead to Renny who had dropped to his knees alongside Danny, saying, "He wasn't a bad guy, Renny, but he couldn't be saved. He was too old. Dan and Pat hurt him too badly. He wasn't ok." She was trying to pull Renny up from the ground and turned to Lev and asked him to make him stand up. Lev looked at Ace and said, "Stay there kid." He stepped up alongside Renny and pulled him up by his arm as Kali stuck her foot on Danny's neck and pulled the knife out of his forehead. Lev watched as she wiped the blade on Danny's shirt and stood up and put the knife back into her back pocket.

She walked towards Renny and he leaned closer to Lev for protection. She got right up next to Renny and rubbed his upper arm saying, "Hey, Danny was too far gone. Dan and Pat fucked him up too much for him to ever be ok. You're ok. You *want* help. Danny didn't want help. You get it?" she asked him sternly.

"He was my friend," Renny said quietly.

"He was going to live a whole life abusing people the same way you and he have been abused. You understand that?" she asked him. "Say, yeah, Renny. I need to hear you say, yeah," she said authoritatively.

Renny whispered a quiet, "Yeah" to Kali while still leaning his back against Lev.

"Ok, Lev. Renny gets it," she said, looking up at Lev. Lev shook his head no at her in very small movements above Renny's head indicating he did not agree.

"That's right. We can save Renny and Ace," she said in a reassuring tone. "Renny, I know Danny was your friend. Would you like to keep his drawings so you can remember him?" she suddenly asked Renny in a soothing tone.

Renny was still in shock after watching Danny be killed in front of him, but he nodded his head.

"Ok, you get the drawing pad he was using and when we get back to our place, you can hang his art work up in your new room. I'm sorry it had to be this way, but there aren't any psychiatry appointments available in the post-apocalyptic world, you know?" she said as he walked away from Lev and to the sketch pad lying on the ground next to Danny's body.

Lev went to shake his head no more intensely at Kali's suggestion they bring Renny back to Ivy when he watched her quickly take out her gun and shoot him in the back of the head as he leaned forward to pick up Danny's sketch pad. His body crumpled forward onto the pad and the two boys laid there dead together after a lifetime of shared horror. Kali looked up at Lev. "I knew he was too far gone. I just wanted him to have a nice thought before he died," she said and walked towards Ace. "I'm sure they heard the gunshot," she added

They walked away from the tree and towards the back of the gas station. The back of the gas station contained a large paved parking lot with lots of grasses and plants sprouting up through the cracks. At the far end of the paved lot was a medium sized barn. Trees lined the paved driveway that led from the front of the gas station, to the small apartment in back, and to the back lot, and the barn.

Lev knelt beside Ace and told him to run to the tree closest to the barn and sit under it and wait for him to come back to get him. He didn't treat Ace like a child. He said, "Ace, listen, man. We're gonna go kill those fuckers that killed your parents now. Kali had to kill those kids. They were messed up. You understand?"

Ace nodded and said, "Renny was nice, but he told me they were going to hurt me."

Lev nodded. "Yeah, kid. They were going to. But they didn't get a chance to. I'm going to go kill Dan and Pat so they can't hurt anyone else ever again. Sit under the tree and wait for me. Don't leave the tree because I won't look for you. You'll be alone and some other bad guys will get you. Now run to the tree."

"Ok!" Ace said, and ran to the tree.

"Is he bait?" asked Kali.

"What? No! I just wanted him to be where I could find him after we take care of this!" Lev said, completely startled by her question. "Bait!? What the fuck are you thinking?" he asked her, shocked.

"You know, Dan and Pat will see him running and come out to get him. Why is that so shocking?"

"Because you think I'd use a kid as bait!" he said still sounding shocked and insulted.

She rolled her eyes at him and said, "Jesus. It's war. Use me as bait if you want to," and started walking.

"I will if we agree that's a good plan!" he said, still shocked.

Kali stopped walking, and Lev noticed the man come up the tree lined parking lot walking towards Ace as he approached the tree he was supposed to sit under. When Ace noticed the man, he hesitated and suddenly turned and started running back towards Kali and Lev.

"See?! That's why you don't use kids as bait!" Lev said, pulling out his gun to shoot the adult in the distance.

"Let me," Kali said.

Lev lowered his gun. "Be my guest," he said, exasperation still evident in his tone.

He wondered if she would wait for Ace to get back to them, remembering how she refused to shoot past him when she shot their jar of berry preserves while showing him her skills as a marksperson.

He watched her take aim, and then he looked towards Ace who was fast approaching them. He noticed that the man was now aware of their presence.

He looked at Kali and said calmly, "He sees us."

"I see him seeing us," she said and fired.

Lev watched the man and said, "Oh, shit! You missed!"

"I didn't miss. I got him in the nuts," she said, smiling.

"Hey, what?" he asked her as Ace finally reached them and grabbed onto Lev's leg tightly, yelling, "That's Pat! That's one of them!"

"I know. I'm getting him," Kali said to Ace as she walked forward, leaving Lev to deal with the frightened child.

"Did you miss him on purpose?" he asked her as he caught up to her. She didn't answer right away and he said, "Ace, run to that fucking tree. We're getting the bad guys. If you hear shooting, stay on the ground near the tree." Ace ran to the tree again and this time, Kali and Lev followed across the parking lot as they made their way to the injured man lying on the ground.

"I didn't miss. I shot him where I wanted to shoot him," she said as she marched forward towards the man writhing in agony on the ground.

"Hey, shoot to kill," he said with concern, looking over at her quickly as they walked up to the injured man.

"He tortured kids. He made torture their lives. He made me kill kids to end their torture. He should suffer!" she said angrily, not looking at Lev.

"Ok. We still have another fucking guy out here somewhere who may or may not be aiming at us as we discuss this. So, let's drop the revenge shooting and shoot to kill these fuckers. Be done. Get back to Ivy."

They were almost up to the man now, and Kali suddenly pulled out the knife she had used to kill Danny and flung it hard into the man's two hands as they held the bullet wound to his groin area. The force of the knife impaled his hands to his groin, and he screamed in pain and terror.

"Shouldn't hurt kids," she said to him, shaking her head and using a scolding tone. "I had to kill your victims. You can't torture them anymore," she said as she walked up to him and suddenly stomped on the handle of the knife driving it deeper into him.

Lev was holding his gun and suddenly fired a bullet into the man's head.

Kali turned to him and yelled, "Why'd you do that?!" She was furious with Lev for killing the man.

"You can't torture people, Kali," he said, stepping up to her.

"You kill people to save them, Lev!" she shouted at him in a rage he didn't expect. She was beside herself with rage and kept screaming at him, "You kill people to save them!"

When he tried to calm her down by gently touching her arm, she screamed as if he'd hurt her and yelled, "Don't touch me!" and turned away and began running through the empty lot down the long driveway headed towards the front of the gas station.

They both noticed Ace suddenly stand up and jump up and down pointing towards the open barn doors, and Lev watched as Kali turned instantly and began running with speed towards the open doors of the barn.

Lev muttered, "Oh, shit!" and took off after her.

He entered the barn as she was taking aim at the man ahead of her and watched as she shot him between the legs, as well. He fell to the ground screaming in pain, and Kali ran towards him and sat down on top of him straddling him with his two hands holding his wounded crotch. She had him pinned underneath her with his arms of no use as she sat on them. Lev watched her straddling the man and tried to tell her to stop doing what she was clearly intent on doing.

"Get off of him and let me finish him!" he yelled to her as he ran towards them.

He tried to speak to her sternly hoping his tone would motivate her to listen to him. It was no use. Her face was contorted in a rage, and as he ran up to them, she suddenly reached into the man's left eye socket and pulled out his eyeball as he screamed in horror at what was being done to him. The sight caused Lev to stumble and he caught himself and righted his body while watching her punch her fist, full of the man's eye, into his own mouth. The man's mouth was open as he screamed and her fist made its way deep against the back of the his throat and she screamed at him, "Hey, I had to kill those kids you sick fuck!"

"Kali, you're torturing him!" Lev was searching for words as he watched Kali unleash her fury on the prone man.

"I'm going to *kill him,* too. This is me being *nice,*" she said viciously as she stared into the man's one remaining eye with her fist still wedged down the throat of his open mouth.

Lev watched as the man's legs began to kick on the ground and said, "We'll put a bullet in his head and leave with the kid. Ok? Let's go. Come on." He walked up beside her where she remained straddling the man under her, not showing any indication that she had heard what he'd said to her. Lev watched as she suddenly pulled her fist from his mouth and immediately dug her bloody fingers into his other eye socket and ripped out his second eye, shoving it violently down his throat. He could see that her hand was shredded from forcing her fist past his teeth, but she didn't seem to notice or care. She was screaming at the man, calling him a fucking animal, and telling him he deserved to feel the same pain he had inflicted on the kids he had tortured.

Lev knelt down beside her as the man convulsed, unable to breathe with her fist lodged in his throat. "Kali, can you hear me?!" he asked her loudly. "Kali, he's as good as dead! What you're doing is torturing him! Let me kill him!" he said to her sternly.

She turned to him and yelled angrily at him, "*No!* He's getting what he deserves!" and suddenly pulled her fist out from the man's mouth and punched his mutilated face with both fists several times before getting up and standing on the opposite side of his body from where Lev was now standing.

"I'm going to put a bullet in him," Lev told her.

"I said no!" she yelled angrily.

"I don't believe in torture, Kali."

"Oh, you don't?!" she asked, scoffing at him. "I already know you don't believe in torture, that's why you're not afraid enough, but, torture isn't Santa Claus. It exists, Lev!" she said as she stomped on the man's neck. "You're lucky! You get to die!" she suddenly screamed at the man.

Lev stepped over the man's body and grabbed Kali by both of her arms and said sternly, "Kali, look at him. He's dead now. I heard his neck snap when you stomped on it."

She looked up at Lev and sighed deeply, and he watched her shoulders lower as she relaxed. "He didn't deserve such an easy death after what he did to those kids," she said to Lev in a much calmer tone.

Lev wanted to get out of the barn and get her as far away from the man's dead body as quickly as possible. "Let's go pour some water on your hands and maybe wrap up the right one. It's pretty fucked up," he said, trying to coax her out of the barn.

"I should cut off his head," Kali said, turning to go back and do just that.

"Let's go," Lev said firmly, using his hand on her back to direct her outside.

Once outside, Lev could see Ace still sitting under the tree where he had told him to wait for him. He had Kali hold out her hands so he could look at the damage she had done to herself. He could see deep grooves from her fingers to her lower wrists where the man's teeth had shredded her skin. He needed to get her back to Doc. Water and a ripped cloth weren't going to be enough.

"Hey, Kali?" he asked her.

"Yeah?" she asked in a normal voice.

"Are you with me now?" he asked her, looking at her face as he slowly lowered her torn hands.

"I've been with you the whole time," she said to him, shaking her head, perplexed by his comment.

"No, I don't think so. I think you kind of freaked the fuck out in there. I... I didn't expect it, but maybe I should have." Lev wasn't looking at her as he spoke. He sounded confused.

"Expect what, Lev?" she asked, scowling at him.

"Hey! I'm freaked the fuck out right now, myself, if you don't mind!" he said in exasperation, looking at her now. "I just watched you kill two kids, and I get it, I totally get it. They were too fucked up after what was done to them to risk taking back or letting them loose. What you said about there being no psychiatry appointments in the apocalypse, I hear that. I don't disagree with killing them. You did it quickly, too. That was good. But the two men? Kali, you tortured the fucking hell out of them. The second guy... I think you should have let me shoot him and end it." He sighed and stopped talking. He didn't know what to say, and he couldn't think of how he would bandage her hands. Everything they had was dirty.

"I already told you, Lev, if anyone fucks with us, I'll kill them with my bare hands. Well, they fucked with kids, and they threatened to fuck with us. You're only pissed off because you think I'm a fucking disposable, helpless, insane person sent from the future. You think I only have tech to deliver, like I'm the postal service, and you want to know why the hell they'd send stupid, little, not-a-scientist Kali to help the brilliant Research Team. I told you. I'm not afraid." She wrenched her hand away from him and said, "I'm not a child, Lev. I can take care of myself, and I can protect myself. I can fight. And you're upset because you expected less from me."

"That doesn't feel true," he said, looking at her, shaking his head. "I don't think any of that bullshit about you. I'm concerned because I haven't seen that side of you, where, you know, you seemed to really enjoy making that guy suffer."

"I did!" Kali snarled at him. "But I still killed him. See the difference?" she asked him and began to walk away from him.

He ran in front of her, and she stopped. "I'm not going to touch you, but I want you to stay and listen. We're not finished here."

She stared silently at him, so he continued. "I don't think you're stupid. I know you can do a lot of things I'm not aware of yet. For instance, I didn't know you could shoot a gun. I knew you could when you showed me the other morning. I don't think your friends sent you to us because you're disposable or acting as a time traveling postal worker. I think you might be hiding some of what you can do from me, though. I'm guessing you have reasons. Killing, like what you did in there, is different. I know torture exists." He stepped up closer to her, nodding his head in the affirmative. His voice was much softer now while he tried to reason with her. "Listen. I know torture exists. I know it's what they're using where you're from. I know that's what they used on you. We don't do that here. It's what separates us from them. Ok? Can you understand that? I need you to. We kill people here for reasons that make sense to us. I'm a straight up murderer, Kali, but we don't torture."

"I killed him," she said flatly.

"Not before you fucking tortured the hell out of him."

"He deserved it."

"Yeah, he did. He really did. But I want to ask you if you can please not do that anymore."

"He deserved it," she said, sounding confused.

"Yeah," Lev said again, suddenly aware of something else that needed to be said. "And you didn't deserve to be tortured."

She looked up at him, and her shoulders dropped from their defensive position up by her ears. He leaned forward and kissed her forehead while wrapping his arms around her. He felt her arms wrap lightly around him and he asked her, "Are we good?"

"I'm trying," she said quietly.

Lev called Ace over to them, and they walked back to the main road to retrieve their backpacks and Kali's cosmos. Kali put her optical back inside her backpack. Ace asked Lev if he could keep the two small toy cars he and Renny had been playing with, and Lev told him to put one in each pocket and leave them there until they got back to Ivy. Ace did as he was instructed, and they waited for Kali who had remembered that she wanted to look for more pants and shirts in the small apartment. When Kali returned, she was carrying a cloth bag by the handle stuffed with clothes in one hand and picked up her cosmos to carry them in the other. Lev made her give him the bag of clothes so that he could carry it. It was light, but the condition of her hands bothered him. Her right hand was really cut up, and he used the last of his water to try and rinse away some of what was on it. He recalled the little boy in the field all those years ago and his eye that had been torn by the barbed wire. Lev's arms still bore several white scars from the tears in his skin that he had received that day trying to untangle the small child. He felt the weight of those memories now while walking with the small boy named Ace, Kali with her hands covered in jagged tears, and the dried leftovers of two eyes she'd ripped from the skull of a pedophile.

They had no water left, and he wanted to get her back to Doc and get her some antibiotics and maybe a few stitches if necessary. He felt like he was walking in a daze and just wanted desperately to get back to Ivy. He kept forgetting Aisha would be there and that the plan was in motion. The day was not turning out like he had expected it to. Ace walked without any complaints at all, but they did have to walk at a pace even slower than the one Kali normally required.

Back at Ivy

When they caught the first glimpse of Ivy, Kali pointed it out to Ace and he asked her if it was a city. She told him it was a community of nice people who wouldn't hurt him. He asked her if she was the person who killed all the bad guys and she said, "I try, kid. I try. But there are a lot of bad guys."

Lev realized he had been very quiet the entire rest of the way back to Ivy and asked Ace to let him talk to Kali privately for a moment. Ace walked over to the side of the road and sat in the grass picking at the blades and waving them like swords while Lev said, "I know I've been quiet. I've got a lot on my mind. I'll take you to Doc, and get Ace put someplace where someone else can play parent with him, and I'll get us lunch. We can eat in our room after Doc cleans up your hands. I'll deal with Aisha after that. Sound good?" he asked her.

"Yeah," she said and went to place her hand on his chest. She stopped and said, "Actually, this hurts too much to touch you right now. I have to tell you something. It might piss you off," she said, looking up at him.

"Tell me," he said wearily, running his hand down from her shoulder over her arm.

"I'm really uncomfortable bringing the tech inside with those Research Team members I met. When we left here, no one even believed me, and they all, including you, thought I was crazy, which I don't entirely dispute, but I'm concerned they'll be dismissive of what I'm supposed to tell them about the tech. They won't listen to me. I do know important things. They don't understand how cruel their enemy is. Worse, they don't understand how powerful he is and what he's planning. Now you say Campus people are here, too. And also, I think you think less of me because I killed those men. I mean, tortured those men. Which to me feels like even you don't understand how bad things really are."

"What are you saying, Kali?" he asked her, looking into her eyes.

"I'm saying I feel alone right now. I feel entirely responsible for the tech, and when I felt like you understood how serious this was, I didn't feel alone. Now, I feel alone. My friends could be captured and tortured forever. This tech is dangerous. People who don't believe me, or think I'm stupid, or think shooting pedophiles in the nuts is unwarranted torture, make me think I need to be sure I'm giving this tech to the right people. I'm in a war. I've been a prisoner of war for a lot longer than you know. I'm a traitor to a King. I'm a soldier in a traitor's army, Lev. But I'm not your soldier."

"Where's the optical, Kali?" he asked her quietly.

"I hid it," she said.

"This fucking day," he muttered as he bent his head towards his feet and sighed while letting go of her arm.

She was looking at him as he processed what she had told him.

"I listened to every word you just said, and I'm not going to argue any of your points except for one. There are other points you made that I don't agree with, but this one bothered me, ok?" he said, nodding his head. "You are not alone. I'm with you. I'm going to have to go in there and tell them you decided to hide access to the tech again, but that you have valid reasons and concerns. I'll work it out. You and I will talk about this later. Let's stick with the two pressing items on our agenda before getting to anything else. You need to be seen at medical, and we both need food and water. Are you saying you don't trust me?" he suddenly asked her.

"I'm saying I feel like you're not with me since I killed and lightly tortured those guys."

"I do want to talk to you about that some more. Later. Not now. Not today. Come on, let's get this day over with," he said to her and started walking down the long dirt road leading into Ivy.

"Come on, Ace," he said, and Ace hopped up and ran over to them following behind them.

The crows alerted the ground duty that people were approaching, and a signal was sent out that it looked like Lev arriving with Kali and a kid. Lev raised an arm and waved at about the point he knew from experience was close enough for the crows to identify him with their binoculars. Bolin's team was on duty with Dave's team heading in to replace them. Lev was hoping to catch Bolin but was told by a security team member that he was out in the back field repairing fencing around one of the greenhouses. Lev decided Kali getting to medical was his priority. He'd drag Ace around with him until someone volunteered to take him on.

Kali felt dejected and uncertain about how things were going to proceed now that Lev knew she'd hidden their access to the tech again. He seemed to understand her reasons, but he also rejected her assertion that she was alone. She felt alone. She felt like the people she had been sent to bring the tech to didn't understand their enemy. She followed Lev inside the gate and didn't doubt her best instincts. She had needed to hide the optical. She needed to speak with them and make them understand how dangerous the tech could be if mishandled. The Research Team, and even Lev, needed to know that the tech was dangerous before they could have access to it. She had to tell them what Bas and his army were like. They needed to be more motivated to fight Bas and his army. They needed to know what he could do to them. They needed to know death wasn't the worst thing that could happen to a person. She shuddered. These people were soft and uninformed. Lev seemed to understand more than the others, but he couldn't have any doubts. They had no idea how cruel Bas was. Worse, they had no idea what he was planning to do.

They walked through the confusing maze of corridors with Lev leading the way to medical which he told Kali was located on the first floor despite the stairs they found themselves ascending and descending. The residents of Ivy they passed in the hallways seemed to want to give Lev a wide berth as he had clearly just returned from his mission. No one wanted to get in his way by attempting to be social, fearing he had important business to attend to. Business, like walking into Ivy with a small child in tow. Kali noticed that raised more than a few eyebrows. The community lie was enhanced by the full duffle bag on top of his backpack. No one knew the duffle bag contained three large boxes of guitar strings for Bolin and other random items a musician might appreciate.

They finally arrived at medical, and Lev led them into the large open room. Numerous available beds lined both walls, and four large windows looked out on the expansive property. Kali saw only one potential patient speaking with an attendant as Lev led them back to an office where a slight woman with short dark brown hair with a lot of grey throughout was sitting at a table eating a salad.

"Lev!" she said loudly through her mouthful of food and got up and walked over to the three of them.

"Hey Doc. I've got a patient for you," he said.

Kali watched as she looked down at Ace and asked Lev, "This little guy?"

"No. The kid is doing great. This is Kali. She's the one who needs some help."

The woman Lev called Doc stepped closer to Kali and smiled kindly asking, "What's up, Kali?" Kali held up her hands without saying anything, letting her hands speak for themselves. "Jesus, woman! Did you wrestle a bear?" Doc asked not trying to cover up her shock at the condition of Kali's hands.

"No. I ripped the eyes out of a pedo and made him eat them... before I killed him, which caused some tension between myself and my traveling companion. The older one. The kid didn't care."

Lev frowned at her from behind Doc and said with a hint of exhaustion, "Hey, the hands first. The rest later. Come on."

Doc didn't acknowledge Lev's comment, focusing her attention on Kali's overall condition. She looked at Ace and said, "Can you take the big guy here over to that bench and hang out with him a for a bit while I check Kali?"

Lev started walking and said, "Ace. Follow me," and walked with him over to the bench. He stopped the attendant and Kali heard him say, "We need water. Her, too," and assumed he was pointing at her.

"Call me Santi, Kali. Only my big brother over there calls me Doc. So, I'm looking at you and I think I need you to get into some clean clothes, definitely a quick shower, before I can deal with your hands."

"Can't you just pour something on them and wrap them up?" Kali asked her.

"No, because you'll go back to your room and need a shower with newly bandaged hands and I'll be wrapping them again in an hour. The shower's back there. It's private. I'll grab you some clean clothes. Did you really rip the eyes out of some guy and make him eat them?" she asked her.

"Yeah. He was raping kids. We saved that one, though," she said, nodding towards Ace and Lev.

"What's all this?" Santi asked, waving her hands around Kali's pants at the blood and dirt.

"I shot him in the balls and sat on him," Kali said with a shrug.

"Alright. All these clothes have to go. Go back there. Pick a shower curtain. They're all empty. No one's back there. I'll bring you some clothes and a towel." Santi turned to go get the items Kali would need, and Kali dropped her backpack on the floor and walked over to the showers in the side room. She stood in front of the row of curtained shower stalls and removed her shirt and pants as Santi came into the area.

"Oh, Kali. You can have more privacy if you want by going behind a curtain. The space is large enough and has a bench to place your dry clothes. I'll help you." Santi grabbed a shower curtain and opened it up and tipped her head to show Kali the space behind the curtain. "I'll put the clean clothes here so you don't get them dirty with those hands. Soap's here, and I left you a washcloth there on the bench," Santi said as she closed the curtain. "Come out when you're dressed. Be gentle with your hands. I just need you to rinse those." She walked back out to the open medical room and motioned for Lev to follow her into her office. When Ace tried to follow him, she shook her head no, and Lev told Ace to stay put and drink his water.

"Lev, she's been abused. A lot."

"I know." He nodded.

"No, I mean a lot. Not just what you can see on her arms. All over. It's bad."

"Santi, I've seen the scars. All of them. I know," he said gently, appreciative of her concern. He never used her name and, in doing so, she believed he was fully aware of what she was telling him.

"You're together? It's none of my business, I know, but I saw her and I'm asking because... What I saw... You're my friend. She's my patient. I'm asking my friend if he knows there's a lot of physical damage there that probably, no, definitely speaks to emotional damage," she said.

"I know. We're good."

"Alright." She took a deep breath in then exhaled quickly.

"I don't want to tell you what to do as a doctor, but my advice would be to not mention the scars. I think she'd find it confrontational," he said, nodding his head at her.

"Don't acknowledge them. That's how you think she copes?" she asked him.

"Yeah."

"Alright. Not a word. They're all healed anyway," she said, nodding in agreement. Santi looked at Lev and said, "I want to say I've seen worse, but I haven't. Alright. I want to get back to what she came in here for. I'll take care of her hands. Might take some time. Are you and Ace going to wait?" she asked him.

"No, but, I'll be back. I need to get rid of the kid and our bags." He leaned down to pick up Kali's backpack off of the floor and looked around for her bottle of cosmos. He noticed them by Ace's feet and said, "Hey, Ace. Grab Kali's flowers for me." He turned to Santi and said, "Tell her I'm taking her backpack and the rest to our room. I'm going to go grab us some food. I need to get a couple of guards for her, too. Then I'll be back."

"I'll tell her to wait for you. Should I offer her a sedative?"

"No. She's got issues with being sedated," he said grimly.

Santi shook her head. "Jesus. Understood."

Lev walked back to Ace, and Santi watched him leave with the child. She knew most people feared him and considered him a murderer, but he wasn't a murderer. He was a killer. There was a difference most people didn't bother to appreciate. Not even Lev. Santi appreciated the difference. He had saved her life 15 years earlier from a man who had decided to make her his own in a world that no longer offered help to people who were weaker than the aggressors who roamed unchecked. Lev checked them when he found them. When she had referred to Lev as her big brother to Kali, she meant it. Lev was her big brother. He brought her to

Campus after he killed the man who was holding her against her will, and she had been safe ever since. She knew it was in part because she had skills he wanted for his community, but they were long beyond that. They were family. He clearly liked Kali. Hell, she liked Kali after hearing how she injured her hands and also how she gently antagonized 'her traveling companion. The older one.' Most people were afraid to walk past Lev. To her, it seemed like Kali could tell him to get out of her way, and he would.

Santi and Kali

Kali walked over to Santi wearing the clean clothes she had given her. Santi had given her a soft, long-sleeved, grey shirt and loose fitting blue cotton pajama pants with a drawstring waist.

"Where's my backpack? Where's Lev? He had my bag with clean clothes. Do I have to return these clothes to you? They're so soft. Can I keep them?" Kali asked Santi all at once.

"Take a seat in this chair and I'll take a look at those hands and answer your questions," Santi said. She had set up a tray with items she believed would help her clean Kali's wounds. "You did a great job cleaning out the cuts. Are they from the man's teeth?" she asked Kali.

"Yeah. Where's my stuff? Where's Lev?"

Santi busied herself with examining Kali's hands to see if any wounds would benefit from being stitched. "Lev said to tell you he took your bags to your room, and he's going to find someone to take Ace. He's going to get you two some food. Apparently, you haven't eaten much the last couple of days, huh?" she said, looking up at Kali. "This water's for you, by the way," she said, nodding to the glass of water on the tray table. "He'll be back in a bit. He said you need guards, so he's finding them, as well."

"Why do I still need guards?" Kali asked, shaking her head.

"I don't know. I wouldn't think too much about it. Lev's always on duty. He'd place a guard outside everyone's door if we had enough people," Santi said, noticing that Kali was getting agitated. She stopped cleaning Kali's wounds and looked at her, saying in a friendly tone, "He's coming back. All of those things take a little time. It's just the two of us in here. Slow day in the medical office." She smiled at Kali, hoping to ease her concerns.

"You're nice enough, but I don't want to stay here. I want to go back to Lev's room now," she said, starting to pull her hand away from Santi.

Santi had treated difficult patients before and realized Kali was upset about more than just her hands or Lev going to get them food. She knew it was important to calm Kali down now before she became more agitated.

"Kali, Lev's putting your bags in his room. He's looking for someone else to take Ace, and he's getting you two some food. He'll be back."

"You said he's getting guards, too."

"He mentioned getting guards, yes."

"I don't need guards anymore. We just spent more than a week walking out there. Why would I need guards?"

"He must have his reasons. I really wouldn't worry about it. Ask him when he gets back. I have to do a couple of stitches here. Do you want a pain reliever now? It won't work while I'm stitching you, but it will begin to work after I'm finished?"

"No. I don't want anything that will make me sleepy," Kali said, revealing her discomfort for the suggestion.

"Not a sedative, but something to ease the pain. These hands must hurt a lot," Santi said reassuringly.

"No."

"Alright. I'm going to pour the antiseptic on both of your hands now. Place them here. It's going to sting. Ready?" she asked her.

"Yeah," said Kali and Santi poured the solution on Kali's wounds. "Fucking ow! Fuck. Bitch. Not you. The stuff you poured on me," Kali said through gritted teeth.

Santi laughed and said, "Either way, I've been called worse by patients. I'll stitch the larger wounds to help the skin mend."

Kali watched as Santi stitched some of the larger wounds and then wrapped her hands in clean bandages. She told her to come see her the next day so she could check for infection. Lev still hadn't returned, and Kali was getting more agitated.

"Kali, you can choose a bed and try to take a nap while you wait for Lev to return," she offered.

Kali declined and remained in the chair staring at the door waiting for Lev to come back and get her out of the nice doctor's hospital.

Lev, Ace, and Heather

Lev walked with Ace to his and Kali's room. He wanted to think of it that way all the time. No more thinking of it as his room. He saw the plastic bin with clean laundry, including sheets, at the door and was happy the guards had taken care of that for him. He wouldn't have had clean sheets to put on their bed tonight without that help. He told Ace to wait in the hallway and used his foot to push the bin of clean laundry into the room. He dropped their bags on the floor and got Kali's bottle of cosmos Ace had been carrying, and took them into their room, and put them on the table. He closed the door telling Ace to follow him.

The kid had stamina. He didn't complain. He wasn't too bad for a kid, Lev thought to himself. He was looking at the faces of people he passed in the hallways trying to find someone available and friendly enough to take him. He kept his eyes out for Dave and Aisha or a member of her crew, but didn't come across any of them. He headed to the cafeteria hoping to order himself and Kali food as well as find a babysitter for Ace who would see to it that he was also fed. As he went around one of the corners, he found himself facing Heather.

"Lev! I heard you were back. I've been running around trying to find you. How did it go? Who's this?" she asked, looking down at Ace.

"It went really well. There's tech. It's real."

Heather's face beamed and she couldn't contain her excitement saying, "I knew it. I knew it. I felt it in my soul this woman was for real. We have to have a meeting immediately. Where is she? Where's the technology?"

"Ok, that's where this all begins to take a turn down a dark alley."

"Where is she? Did she leave and take the technology?" Heather asked him, looking horrified.

"What? No. She…. She didn't take the technology, but she's got a lot of valid concerns about the team. She's afraid the technology will be mishandled. She hid it again on the way back here. She wants to talk to the team."

"She killed everybody all by herself," Ace suddenly said.

"What?" Heather asked, looking down at Ace.

"She killed Renny and Danny and then she killed Dan and Pat. A lot," he said to Heather.

Lev corrected Ace. "Technically, I killed that first guy when I shot him in the head."

"She was really killing him. You made her stop," said Ace, shaking his head disapprovingly at Lev.

Lev frowned at Ace.

"She killed four people?" Heather asked, stunned.

"She's a really good killer," Ace said.

"Ace, be quiet," Lev said.

"The tech is real. She's unstable, though?" asked Heather.

Lev sighed. "I just spent more than a week with her. She's stable enough. Just like the rest of us. But she's got some concerns. We'll get the tech back. We just need to listen to her."

"Lev, she rambles and doesn't make sense. Maybe this is a game to her," Heather said, frustrated with him, as he shook his head no at her.

"No, Heather. She's in charge. She makes sense. She believes the team doesn't respect her. That's a problem. Tomorrow, we'll have a meeting and listen to her. We'll get the tech back. Right now, I need to get this kid to a fucking daycare center and get some food. We've barely eaten in two days."

"Well, why can't we have the meeting today?" asked Heather. "Eat your meals and make her give us the tech."

Lev scoffed at Heather. "You… You can't make her give you the tech. You know what? She's right. You're not ready to listen to her. You're not even listening to me right now which is becoming a really big problem in my mind. Now, I'm giving you Ace. Ace, go with Heather. She'll find you nice people to hang out with. I'm going to go get myself and Kali some food, and I'm going to go get her from medical."

"Is she injured?" asked Heather.

"Yeah, her hands are broken from killing people!" Ace said enthusiastically.

Lev closed his eyes and pursed his lips. "Ace, stop. I'm going to have some food, get some guards on Kali, and then I'll meet everyone in MR1 to personally tell all of you that we're going to have a meeting tomorrow. I'm not going to talk about the tech with the team until Kali is there."

"She's hidden technology The Benefactor sent for us to have. You claim she's safe and stable enough, but she killed four people, and you need to put some guards on her?" Heather asked with a tone of irritation.

"Watch it," he said and headed to the cafeteria leaving Ace with her. "MR 1 in one hour!" he yelled as he turned a corner.

Heather

Heather told Ace to follow her and knocked on the first door she came to. When no one answered, she knocked on the next door in the hallway. A man named Louis opened the door and looked at her. He recognized her as a member of the RT, and it confused him that she would be at his door.

"Are you off duty right now?"

"Yeah, but I was just going to do my farm work."

"This is Ace. He needs a babysitter. Take Ace with you."

She walked away and heard Louis ask Ace, "You want to work in the garden or with the animals?"

"Animals," Ace said.

Heather opened the side door and walked over to where Bolin was still fixing the portion of fence around the greenhouse that had recently fallen. She had spoken to him earlier when looking for Lev after she'd heard he'd returned.

"Bolin, I found Lev. The technology is real. Kali killed four people, and hid the technology ,and is refusing to divulge where she's hidden it. She's out of control. She's in medical, but we have to put her in a cage and get her to reveal where she's hidden the technology that was meant for the RT. This is an immediate need. We'll need at least two others to help us get her into the cages. Even injured, she's dangerous."

"You spoke to Lev?" Bolin asked, shaking his head and frowning over the news Heather was telling him.

"Yes. We need to get her from medical, and put her in a cage, and get her to tell us where she's hidden the technology. Right now."

Bolin turned and called two of his engineering team members over and said, "Follow me. We have to transport a prisoner."

Heather ran towards medical, and the three men ran in back of her.

Kali and the Cages

Santi was doing her best to soothe Kali's anxiety. She assured her that Lev would be back with food and would take her to his room or someplace else to eat their meal. Her hands were stitched and neatly bandaged, and Santi offered to brush her still damp hair with her own hairbrush to help distract her. Kali insisted she could brush her own damn hair, and then quickly realized her hands hurt too much to accomplish the simple task. She relented and handed Santi the hairbrush.

Santi had just finished brushing Kali's hair when Heather appeared in the doorway of her medical room. She had three dirty men with her, and Santi thought one of them might have been injured working in the yard or gardens.

"Is everything alright? Is one of you injured?" she asked as she walked towards them looking for signs of injury.

Heather responded saying, "No. Lev sent us to get Kali."

Kali was looking at them and recognized Bolin and smiled at him while offering him a small wave with a bandaged hand.

He looked at her with concern on his face asking Santi, "Is she ok?"

"She'll be fine. Her injuries aren't fabulous, but she'll recover. Lev sent you to get her?" Santi asked him to confirm with him specifically the request by Lev to release Kali to them.

"Heather spoke with him," he said reassuringly.

"Are we going to your place?" Kali asked Bolin, sounding hopeful. Lev had told her Bolin's family had a place near the gardens. Maybe Bolin was dirty because he had been working in the gardens. Before Bolin could answer, she asked, "Are these my guards?" She decided she would be agreeable if Lev thought she still needed guards.

Santi was still concerned about releasing Kali to them, but she trusted Bolin and tried to confirm with him personally what she should do. "Lev told me he was going to come back for her. I told him I'd keep her here until he got back. Is this ok?" she asked him, furrowing her brow.

Bolin didn't respond. Instead, he looked over at Heather and she told Santi, "Lev asked us to come get her from medical."

"Alright," Santi said, still unhappy about the three dirty men taking off with Kali after she had just gotten her cleaned up and bandaged.

Kali walked towards Bolin, eager to leave. As they left, Santi heard Heather ask Kali, "How did you injure your hands, Kali?"

"I killed some people on the way back here," she said and followed the men she believed were her guards sent by Lev.

Heather looked at Bolin and nodded, raising her eyebrows at him. Bolin grimaced. He had kind of liked her last week. She had seemed a little crazy, but mostly harmless. Killing wasn't a problem unless she had crossed the line. If Lev wanted her in a cage, she had crossed the line. He wanted to get Kali into a cage and go find out from Lev what had happened. Last week he had thought that maybe Lev liked her more than he was letting on. He had told James, "I think Lev might have finally found someone who can make him laugh." And James had said, "Will there be a wedding? I'm making vodka for it." And Bolin had said, "Don't wait on Lev. I like vodka. Make vodka anyway."

Kali followed in the space between the two men in front of her and Heather and Bolin in back of her. As they walked she began to notice there were no windows and the hallway began to resemble the hallway her previous guards and Ju had walked her down when she had gone to the meeting with the Research Team. At the bottom of two short staircases, Kali saw a large door with a coded entry at the end of the very short hallway. Although it was similar, it clearly wasn't the same door she had passed through a week ago.

As she waited for one of the men who she believed to be a guard to punch in the code, she turned around to Bolin and asked, "We're going to your place with the garden, right?" He frowned and didn't answer her. "Are we going to a meeting?" she asked him as one of the men told her to walk through the doors. She ignored him and asked Bolin, "Is Lev inside? Where's Lev? I don't like the basement. I don't know how to get out."

Bolin sighed and said patiently, "Kali, Lev said you killed four people and you hid what you were sent to bring the team. That you refuse to give over what you brought to the team." He avoided using the word technology because the two men were close enough to hear their conversation.

"Where are you taking me?" she asked him, still not sure that the answer would be upsetting.

Heather suddenly spoke up and said tersely, "You're going into a cage until you agree to tell us where you hid what we need."

"What? The cages? No. Lev said I wouldn't go to jail or the cages."

Heather responded sharply with a condescending tone, "The cages are our jails. You two. Take her inside."

Whatever reaction Heather, Bolin, or the two men were expecting from Kali, nothing prepared them for what happened next. Realizing that she was about to be put into a cage in the windowless basement of the facility, she began to fight with her damaged hands as well as every other part of her body. Before they managed to control her, she had bitten each of them multiple times, kicked them all repeatedly, ripped hair from Heather's head, and wrapped both of her arms around one man's neck and tried to strangle him before Bolin managed to remove her. Heather had bite marks on her hands and her scalp was bleeding from having a large handful of hair pulled out. Kali still had strands of Heather's hair in her damaged right hand as she swung and connected hard with the mouth of one of the men. Bolin had to intervene to stop the man from retaliating against Kali for the punch to his face. When the man went to strike Kali back, Bolin kicked one of his legs out from under him, making him fall to his knees. Kali took that as an opportunity to kick the man in the mouth, fully dislodging the teeth she had loosened when she had punched him. The other man knocked her to the ground and sat on top of her as Bolin shouted at all of them to restrain her, not assault her.

When Kali saw the malice in the eyes of the man whose teeth she had knocked out, she laughed loudly at him and shouted at him venomously, "Yeah, you wanna kill me? You'd better before I kill you first." Heather hid behind Bolin telling him, "You see?" Aside from the physical assault she initiated against the four of them, was the harrowing experience of the verbal assault she launched. It wasn't the course language or threats. It was the screams. She screamed in a terror that came from her soul that Bolin would later tell James, shook him inside as he tried to get her under control.

Bolin opened the door to the fourth basement prison ward using a code which unlocked the large door. There were no hallways or meeting rooms in the prison ward. It was a vast open space with floor to ceiling barred prison cages in rows separated by 10 feet of space on each side of every cage. Each cage had a small cot and a toilet and nothing else inside. A desk with a chair was located just inside the large door. A short row of locked cabinets lined half of the length of the right wall.

It took all three men to force Kali into a cage and lock the door behind her. Once inside, she continued to scream in terror, mixed with rage, to be released, while the three men talked about what they should do next. Heather approached the cage and yelled angrily at Kali to turn over what she had brought them, but Kali only screamed that they would all get taken to torture for eternity.

Bolin noticed Trent and Olivia in two of the other cages watching them as he told Heather he would be the one to remain with Kali. He told the more severely injured man who had accompanied Kali to the cages to go to medical. He told the other man who had accompanied Kali to the cages to walk the teenagers to guest quarters, lock them in separate rooms, find two guards for them, and then clean up the fencing project for the night.

Heather was sitting on the edge of the desk with her head down, lost in her own thoughts, as Olivia and Trent were led past her. In the backdrop of Kali's screams, Olivia suddenly stopped walking and turned to face Heather and said warningly, "My commander is going to be angry at you for hurting her." Trent shook his head and said, "Shhh," to Olivia as the man from Bolin's fence project led them out of the prison ward to their secure guest rooms. Bolin heard what Olivia said to Heather and walked angrily up to her and told her he needed to speak with Lev about what was going on with Kali. Heather shook her head at Bolin and responded with authority, "Lev's busy. We're having a team meeting in a few minutes. I have to get up there. I'll tell him you want to speak to him when we're finished, not before."

She walked past Bolin and went up to the cage where Kali was still screaming in wild-eyed terror and roaming the barred cage she was locked in. Heather shouted loudly at her, "Just tell us where you hid the tech. It's our tech. It's not yours. It was sent to us. You were supposed to deliver it to us. Tell us where it is and I'll release you." But Kali couldn't hear her.

Bolin saw terror and even madness in her eyes. He shouted to Heather, "Kali isn't there, Heather! Look at her!" The woman with the easy smile who spoke in confusing circles wasn't there, and the fact that Heather was oblivious to that fact frustrated Bolin. Heather walked away from the cage back to Bolin and he said firmly, "This is wrong. She's being tortured. Look at her. She can't be in there. She told us she didn't want to be in a jail cell the first day she came up here. Lev told her he wouldn't put her in one. I want to see Lev now. He needs to see this. It isn't right, Heather."

Heather turned to Bolin and said, "Follow your orders, Bolin. Wasn't it you who told us we're in a war and we're not tough enough? You were right. We need that tech. She hid it. She can come out when she tells us where to find it. We'll wait her out. I'll tell you when she can be released." She walked to the door and punched in the code to open it and left Bolin with Kali.

Lev and Doc

Santi was confused as Heather, a dirty and sweaty Bolin, and the two dirt and sweat covered men left with Kali. She had asked Bolin twice to confirm Lev told them to come collect Kali. There was nothing more she could do. She would check on Kali and her hands tomorrow. She was cleaning up Kali's dirty clothes from the floor in the shower room when she heard Lev calling for her and Kali. A feeling of dread washed over her, and she walked out into the larger room and looked at him with concern.

"What are you doing here looking for Kali?" she asked him. In all her years of knowing him, she had never seen him go off balance so quickly and so completely.

"Where's Kali?" he asked her in a voice just barely above a whisper.

"Heather, Bolin, Denton, and Ramish, guards, I guess, came in here and said you told them to get Kali. I checked with Bolin twice. Heather told me directly you told her to come get Kali."

Santi watched as Lev put the tray of food he'd been carrying down on a bed and asked her, "Did you see which way they went?"

"No. But Kali asked Bolin if they were going to his house."

"That bitch took her to the cages. She's going to lose her mind." He turned and ran out of the room, and she stood motionless in his absence as she absorbed the fear her fearless, rage-filled friend of 15 years had just shown her he was capable of feeling.

Bolin and Kali in the Prison Ward

Bolin tried to make sense of his orders. He had no interest in hurting Kali. He didn't know why she had killed four people. Maybe she had good reasons. Lev didn't tell him to put Kali in a cage, Heather gave him the order. She implied Lev agreed. Lev was Head of Security, but Heather was the Leader of Ivy. She told him Kali had to be put in a cage and Lev was aware. Lev didn't torture people. This was torture. Maybe Lev didn't know. He needed to know. Bolin was trying to calm Kali down, but her eyes weren't focused on things that were there. Nothing that Bolin could see, anyway. He tried to soothe her with his voice and calming words, telling her that he was going to stay with her and that he'd sent for Lev. But when she did face him, he saw madness in her eyes that was the result of sheer terror. She grabbed the bars and frantically begged him to let her out. He felt it was wrong to keep her in the cage, but he had orders from Heather and Lev was aware.

When he and Lev had taken Ivy back from Moira, Lev had told him Ivy would have structure now and a chain of command. He told Bolin to follow orders and Ivy wouldn't go through the kind of bullshit they went through with Moira a second time. He couldn't ignore orders. Kali was physically safe. Lev would be here soon and see this wasn't right and tell Heather to reverse the order. Heather said the tech was real and they needed to get it from her. They could put her back in Dorm 17 with two guards. She would calm down there. They had rules in place meant to ensure Ivy was run properly. Without rules, they were back to chaos.

He offered to get Kali a blanket and suggested she could lie down and sleep. She didn't acknowledge his offer. When he went to get her a blanket from the locked cabinet along the wall, he turned around to see she had removed her shirt and was standing on the cot, tying one of the long sleeves to the top side of her cage. He realized she was going to hang herself, but seeing the scars on her body caused him to hesitate for a second as he gasped at the damage done to her.

He was trying to get the key to the cage into the lock so that he could stop her from hanging herself before she managed to successfully tie her second long sleeve around her neck. He made it into the cage just as she jumped off the bed. Bolin yelled at her to stop and grabbed her body as she kicked him and tried to snap her own neck by lurching her body about. He held onto her as he climbed on the bed and created slack in the shirt-rope she had created and untied the knot on the cage bars while she kicked and screamed at him. When he tried to get her back onto the floor, she snapped her head back on purpose and he felt her break his nose.

The cage door was open and she went to run to it, but he grabbed her around the waist and threw her down on the cot before turning to run out the open cage door himself. He struggled to keep it closed as she pulled on it and he worked a key inside and locked it.

Her shirt was in his hand as he stood bent at the waist panting in front of the locked cage door imploring her to calm down. Blood was running from his nose onto the floor, and he stood up with his hands on his hips panting from the effort to prevent her from hanging herself. He had been out of the cage for only a couple of seconds when he felt hands on his back that shoved him aside and sent him against the wall on the right side of the room. He looked over at Kali and saw a look of recognition and then pain flash across her face as she stopped screaming and stood with her bandaged hands against the bars of the cage door. He saw that she was looking up at Lev.

"Bolin let her out!" he yelled while staring at Kali and putting his hands on the bars near hers.

Kali started screaming at him in a rage. "You told them to lock me up! You put me in a cell! You lied to me! You locked me in a cage! You told them to lock me up!"

Lev turned to look at Bolin as he leaned disoriented against the wall, bleeding heavily from his broken nose, and shouted at him to let Kali out.

Bolin shook his head and said apologetically, "Heather gave me orders. She said that you agreed with the orders to lock her up."

"She lied. Give me the fucking keys."

Lev was charging him now and Bolin said, "She gave me orders. You told me to follow orders or this whole thing breaks down. I'm following orders."

Lev looked at Bolin and appealed to him in a gentler voice, "Then let me in. She can't be in there alone. She's terrified."

Lev didn't wait for Bolin to pass him the keys. "What the fuck are you hesitating for? I'm Head of Security, man!" he said as he lunged at Bolin and took the keys from him. He quickly opened the cage door where Kali continued to scream at him that he was a liar and had tricked her.

Lev was in the cage now with both of his hands up in front of him shouting loudly over Kali's accusations. "Hey! Hey! I didn't put you in here. I didn't tell anyone to put you in here!"

Bolin said, "She just tried to hang herself with her shirt. I got her down."

Lev appeared to have heard Bolin and kept talking to her as he advanced slowly towards her where she stood in the center of the cage now. "Hey, baby. What the fuck? Hanging yourself? That why your neck is red? I'm not mad, but you can't be killing yourself without at least giving me a chance to rescue you, right? We talked about that."

Bolin watched as Lev moved very slowly towards her with his hands up in front of him and Kali stood like an animal ready to attack him.

Lev told her, "I've got the keys now. The door is open. I won't close it."

She screamed at him saying, "You locked me up! I won't even have a chance! I'll be captured and tortured! You're the fucking worst, Lev!"

Lev was closer to her now and Bolin said, "Be careful, man. She's stronger than she looks." He remained by the cage door ready to close it and hold it closed if Kali made her way to it around Lev.

Lev's voice was reassuring and quieter now as he said, "I didn't lock you up. I swear I wouldn't fucking do that to you."

Kali continued to scream her words and shouted, "You locked me in here because you didn't like the way I killed those people today! You only want the tech I brought! You don't care about me! You used me! You made me think you were coming back and told your friends to lock me up!"

Lev continued to respond to her calmly and said, "Baby, I was coming back. I brought us food. Doc told me they took you. I didn't know. I swear I didn't know. I ran all the fucking way here."

But Kali was listening to him, too, and screamed, "You're a liar! I'm not releasing the tech to you or Ivy! Fuck you! Fuck Ivy! Ivy is a lost cause! I'm not helping you! I'm not gonna be captured! You will and you'll see! You all fucking deserve what happens to you!"

Bolin caught a glimpse of the gun on Lev's belt and groaned, "Oh, shit." He didn't know how he could warn Lev without Kali taking advantage of the information. He listened as Lev continued to try and calm her down saying, "I ran here as soon as I found out. I would never send you to a cage. Bolin says you tried to hang yourself. You can't do that. Wait for me. Give me a goddamn chance." He was walking closer to Kali, and Kali was standing still, not walking away from Lev.

Bolin felt he had to warn him and said, "Lev, she's not letting you get close for any good reason."

Lev said, "Shut up, man. Kali. It's me. I didn't lie to you. You can hide the tech. I don't even care anymore."

She squinted her eyes and screamed, "I risked torture and my friends to come here! None of you fucking care!" She suddenly turned to glare at Bolin where he still stood by the open cage door.

Bolin watched as Lev did exactly what she wanted him to do. He walked closer and put his hands gently on her shoulders, believing he was calming her down, and she looked away from Bolin and up at Lev and grabbed for his gun as Bolin shouted, "Your gun!"

Lev didn't make any attempt to move. He looked at her as she took his gun and remained standing with his hands still on her shoulders as she aimed it at his head. Bolin watched, horrified, and said imploringly, "Don't shoot him, Kali. Don't shoot him."

Lev hadn't moved even when Bolin had shouted at him that Kali was going to go for his weapon. He didn't move now as Kali had the gun aimed at his head.

He stood there and looked down at her and said, "She's not going to shoot me, Bolin. Right, baby?" he asked her with a small nod.

Bolin said, "Kali. Please put the gun down," and watched as the two of them stood completely still, staring at each other, while Kali held a steady hand with the gun aimed at Lev's head with a stony expression on her face.

Lev said quietly, so that Bolin could just hear what he was saying, "I'm not good enough to kill. She's going to shoot herself and leave me to be captured and tortured." And Kali began to slowly turn the gun towards her head while still staring stonily at Lev's face.

Lev stood perfectly still, but as she went to reposition the gun at her own head, he quickly and quietly asked her, "Where's the safest place to be when he's in charge?"

Bolin was hardly breathing as he watched their standoff and was mentally preparing himself for Kali to shoot herself in the head.

He listened and watched as Lev quickly stepped his body right up against hers and asked her again, "Baby, where's the safest place to be?"

Kali suddenly blinked twice as she stared, emotionless, at Lev.

"Where, Kali?" Lev persisted gently as he leaned his face towards hers and kissed her forehead softly.

She had the gun to her head now, but Lev ignored it. He brought his hands up to her face, through her hair near her ears and told her, "You were so beautiful that night on the rocks. Confusing? Yeah. And I thought you were fucking crazy, but I thought you were beautiful, too," he said with a small smile while nodding his head slightly at her.

Kali continued to look at Lev without making a move or a sound. She kept the gun at the side of her head but suddenly said in a completely normal voice, "A lightning storm."

Lev nodded and told her, "That's right, baby. And I'm the fucking lightning." Then he leaned over and kissed her mouth even as she kept the gun aimed against her head.

As Lev stood up from their kiss, Kali said unhappily, "You're not lightning. You won't even kill me."

Bolin listened as Lev gently insisted, "Oh, yes I fucking will. I'll kill you. I'll absolutely kill you. I'm your own personal lightning bolt." He reached down around her waist and picked her up and kissed her harder.

Bolin watched as she finally lowered the gun from the side of her head and held onto it loosely as she wrapped her arms around Lev's shoulders and kissed him back. "Holy shit, you two. Are we ok, now?" Bolin asked in exasperation at the result of the standoff. As Lev put Kali's feet back down on the floor, and turned his head to speak to Bolin, he noticed Kali stayed pressed against Lev with her arms wrapped tightly around him with the gun dangling in her hand and her face buried against his chest.

"She's not ok. Not even a little. She needs to get the hell out of here, man," he said to Bolin.

Bolin was explaining to Lev his reluctance to immediately release Kali. "Heather will be back soon. She's the leader of Ivy. She gave me orders. I want to let Kali out, but you remember how it was. We agreed to create a hierarchy. You told me to follow Heather's orders. Right now, I'm following your orders by following Heather's. If I don't follow Heather's orders, I'm not following your orders.
If you want to get rid of Heather, I'll support that. You know I will. At least, I think you know I will. What I saw her do with Kali was fucked up. She involved Santi, too. Don't blame Santi. Santi was worried about handing Kali over to me and Heather. Heather ordered me to lock Kali in the cages. Said she was dangerous. I thought it was a security issue because she used your name. For me, that's a bigger problem than me saying I don't think Heather should be the leader at Ivy anymore.

"Maybe the tech Kali brought us went to Heather's head. She was screaming at Kali, I didn't even know Heather could scream, but she was screaming at Kali that the tech wasn't hers. She said it belonged to the Research Team. She told Kali she was only meant to deliver it and that she'd be locked up until she told them where the tech was hidden."

Kali and Lev were sitting side by side on the cot in the cage with Lev's hand resting on the cot behind her back. Kali was leaning the side of her body against Lev's for the proximity more than for the support. She still held Lev's gun in her right hand and looked like she was ready to fight if necessary. Her hands had bled through the bandages Santi had wrapped them in earlier.

As Bolin repeated Heather's comments to Kali, Lev felt his blood boil with rage and he turned to Kali and said, "You were right. I was going to do it your way, anyway, but you were right about the arrogance of the Research Team."

"I'm not a delivery service," Kali said angrily.

"No. You're not," Lev agreed.

"I have to tell you something else," Bolin said to Lev with a serious tone in his voice.

"Great. What?" sighed Lev, looking at his friend.

Bolin put his hands on his hips, and went to speak but suddenly turned around as he heard the security door being accessed. Looking around Bolin's body where he stood just outside the cage, Lev could see Aisha through the textured glass outside the entrance to the prison ward.

She was looking through the glass at them as she entered the code and quickly opened the door saying, "Lev! I've been looking all over for you. Are you... Why are you in a cage?" she asked, also noting that the cage door was actually open. She scowled and looked over at Bolin. "What's going on? Why is Lev in a cage? Is this Kali?" she asked, pointing at her.

She suddenly noticed Bolin's nose was broken and he had black eyes forming as well as a bite mark on his hand and scratches on his arms and neck. Bolin went to speak to Aisha, but she held up a hand to him and shook her head saying, "Wait. No," and looked back at Lev. Lev was sitting inside the open cage alongside Kali with an arm around her while she held his gun. Kali was still shirtless and Aisha noted the scars she could see on her torso and arms. Her hands were bandaged but looked like they needed rebandaging, and she had a terrible red ring around her neck as if she'd been strangled. Lev didn't look physically injured, but he looked dirty, exhausted, and miserable.

"I don't know what the hell I just walked into, but someone needs to explain it to me right now. This is too much," Aisha said impatiently. Neither man spoke before she suddenly asked, "What is this?" as she noticed a crumpled shirt on the top of the cabinets that lined the wall. She walked past Bolin and grabbed it. She shook it out and nodded her head as she confirmed to herself it must be the shirt Kali had been wearing at one point.

"Is this your shirt?" she asked Kali as she walked past Bolin again and entered the cage to hand it to her.

Kali said, "Oh, yeah. There it is. Thank you," and took it from Aisha.

The arms were noticeably stretched out and Aisha closed her eyes briefly and shook her head as she heard Bolin say, "Kali tried to hang herself with her shirt. I had to take it away."

She turned to him and said, "Well, she looks fine now. You could have given it back already." She turned to Lev. "Let's get out of here. Heather's pulling some bullshit in the other basement in a meeting she's locked everyone from Campus out of. She only let the original Ivy RT inside. You should see Dave. He's so pissed off. We're all just waiting for you."

"I'm staying here until Bolin gets orders from Heather to release Kali," he said.

Aisha looked at Bolin. "Heather gave you orders?"

"Yes. But I've already told Lev that I'm ready to participate in a coup as soon as she releases Kali."

Aisha smiled and let out a small laugh at that and tipped her head while looking over at Lev, "Seriously?"

"Seriously," Lev said.

"Can I go fix this?" she asked him with furious confidence.

"Please, do," said Lev.

Aisha looked at Kali who had gotten her shirt back on and was fumbling with the stretched sleeves. She said, "I heard you brought us technology to help us fight the son of a bitch who killed everyone including my mother."

Kali looked up at Aisha and nodded, asking, "Yeah. Are you mad I hid it again, too?"

"Not even a little. You did the right thing. I'm going to get you out of here. I'll be right back," she said and walked quickly out of the cage and left the prison ward.

"That was Aisha," Lev said to her.

"I think she's an asset," Kali said absently while trying to get his gun through the opening of her sleeve.

Lev laughed a quick, "Yeah."

"What was the something else you wanted to tell me?" Lev asked.

"Denton and Ramish accompanied Kali here. There was a fight. It was bad. Kali, Do you mind me talking about this in front of you? I can tell Lev later if you prefer," he asked her.

"It's fine. I tell him a lot of crazy stuff. I don't even know what you're going to tell him right now," she said, resting her head on Lev's upper arm.

"Denton and Kali went at it. He wasn't restraining her. I had to stop him from attacking her. He lost more than a few teeth."

"You knocked his teeth out?" Lev asked him approvingly.

"No, I did. I kicked them out after I loosened them with my fist," Kali said.

Lev looked down at the top of her head resting on his arm. "He attacked you?" he asked her.

"I'm gonna kill him," she said as a matter of fact. "I won't torture him," she reassured Lev, looking up at him.

Lev looked at Bolin and rolled his eyes saying, "More information, please."

"Denton crossed the line. I was forced to stop him. I don't see how it's not going to be a problem. If you saw how he looked at her... And then how she looked at him. What she said to him. You know what I mean? I know what I think needs to be done."

Lev nodded at Bolin and said, "Thanks for telling me."

Kali said, "That's ok you guys. I want him to find me."

But Bolin saw darkness in Lev's eyes while Kali leaned her head against his arm oblivious to the fury Lev felt swelling inside him at the thought of Denton having it out for Kali. He had had to tell him. He knew Lev wouldn't let anyone breathe who was a threat to James or Meabh. He looked at Lev now and knew Kali's well-being had to be considered from now on.

Lev told Bolin about the walk to get the tech while they waited for Aisha to return hoping the familiarity of the events would soothe Kali who sat leaning against him quietly holding his gun. After some time, Aisha's face was visible behind the glass of the closed prison door again. Bolin and Lev stood up and Kali quickly grabbed a hold of a belt loop on the back of Lev's pants as she stood up alongside him in the cage.

Aisha and Dave walked in with a battered Heather between them, and Kali held up Lev's gun and aimed it at her through the cage bars. Lev was staring at Heather as he told Kali, "You've got new grudges. I've got new ones and old ones. Mind if I take care of this?" He could see Kali's arm out of the corner of his eye as she passed the gun across her body over to him as he stood on her left side. He took it from her and said, "Thanks, babe."

Heather had clearly just been roughed up by the look of her. She was bleeding from her nose and mouth, and she was staggering between Aisha and Dave as they walked her into the prison ward. Aisha spoke first saying, "Bolin, Heather has something to tell you. Go ahead, Heather." She stepped aside to allow Heather to move in front of her and stood by Dave's side. Bolin was silent as he stared at Heather, waiting to hear what she had to say.

"Bolin, release Kali."

Bolin turned to Kali and said with relief, "Come on, get out of there, Kali."

Heather was staring at Lev with wide eyes full of terror. He glared at her with eyes full of rage as he put his hand on Kali's back and gently directed her out of the cage letting her leave first. "Give me a minute here, and I'll get you to our room and get you food like I said I would," he said to Kali. She looked up at him and nodded.

Lev looked back at Heather and asked her, "Did you tell Bolin, Santi, and Kali that I wanted Kali put in a cage?"

Heather was visibly shaking but she answered quickly in a voice that quivered in fear. "I did."

"Use more words. Explain to Kali why you told her I was responsible for torturing her."

"I... I.. heard she had killed four people..."

Lev shook his head and laughed in a disgusted tone saying, "Nobody here gives a shit about Kali killing four people. It's fucking impressive, and we all know it. Tell her why you told her I was responsible for torturing her."

Heather's head was shaking on her shoulders now and her voice quivered as she said, "I heard you hid the technology you were supposed to deliver to us. I wanted you to give us our technology. Lev said to wait until tomorrow and we'd have a meeting and let you talk to the team..." Heather suddenly looked defiant and held her head up higher and spoke louder saying to Kali, "But you, you're not a good messenger. You think this is a game. You like the attention! Dragging Lev off to get the technology and then hiding it again. It's not yours to keep. We've been waiting for 17 years for his help. You have no right to keep it from--"

Heather was still speaking when Kali said, "17 years, huh? Wow, that's a long time to wait. I'll bet you think that was torture. Waiting here at Ivy where this guy doesn't even approve of torture," Kali said as she pointed at Lev. She took a step closer to Heather who took a step backwards, and continued. "Here's a story for you. One time, I got caught trying to memorize the equations for Rewinds. I was two years into catching glimpses of the symbols and helping my Friend record them for Ivy. I was sent to a time cell and tortured for five fucking years because the guy who killed everyone else in the world won't just kill me even when I get caught, dead to fucking rights, being a traitor to him. Even when I wouldn't tell him who I was working for, he wouldn't fucking kill me! But he killed some of his own people and sent a bunch he suspected of helping me to torture. That was funny, actually. They were all innocent of helping me. They weren't innocent of being loyal to him, though, so fuck 'em! Anyway, when I was released, I found another way to get the remaining information to make Rewinds even though he had me watched constantly. And guess what? I brought you a Rewind. Not only are you gonna have a Rewind, you're gonna have the ability to make more because I memorized formulas, or algorithms, or symbols, or whatever the fuck they are that I don't even understand. I got you a working fucking Rewind, you shitty bitch. I got you the recipe to make more." Kali finished and turned to Lev and stepped back alongside him.

Lev heard Kali casually say she had been put in a time prison and tortured for five years and was having a difficult time recovering from the statement he knew was true the minute she said it. She didn't exaggerate. She wouldn't lie about torture to shame Heather. She had told him as they had approached Ivy this afternoon that she was a soldier and felt people didn't respect her or her efforts. He had thought her efforts were just in bringing them the technology. That was more than enough in his opinion. Now he understood that she didn't want all of her espionage efforts and her time spent in torture time prisons to go to waste on people who didn't value what they were being presented with. She really was a soldier. Even with soft hands and blisters on her feet.

"Jesus Christ," he muttered, looking at no one. He made an effort to compose himself and looked back at Heather. "Tell Bolin who's in charge at Ivy," he said to her.

Heather turned to Bolin and said, "Lev's in charge."

"Tell Bolin how long I've been in charge at Ivy."

"Since the day Campus killed Moira and her people."

"Bol, you good?" he asked him.

Bolin looked stunned. He said, "You've always been the boss at Ivy?"

"Yeah, man. You were always following my orders by following Heather's orders... until today. Today was all Heather. No coup necessary. By the way, you've always been my second here. I always told you that. Yeah?"

"Yes. Does this mean I could have released Kali sooner?"

"Yeah, man, but also, you couldn't. I set us up for that one. You were following orders."

Bolin looked at Kali and said, "I would have let you out sooner."

Kali believed Bolin, but also appreciated his commitment to being a loyal soldier. "Thanks for not letting me kill myself," she said, smiling at him.

"Bol, about the coup you were willing to be a part of earlier, Heather was the one actually staging a coup by undermining my authority and holding a meeting and locking out my team."

"Your team? Are you a member of the RT?" asked Bolin.

"Yeah, so, we have more to talk about, but Kali needs to eat. When we're done here, I'm gonna need you to get James and meet us at our room. We'll go to a meeting with the RT from there."

He turned his attention to Aisha and Dave and said, "I want the combined Ivy RT there. Who can you put on Heather until the meeting?" he asked Aisha.

"Oh, I'm going to personally sit in the meeting room with her and wait for you. I've got my team. They'll wait with me. She won't be making any more moves today."

Dave said, "I'll make sure the locals get to the meeting. Are you ready for all Campus RTs tomorrow, then? Want me to send someone to let them know? Time for arrival?" asked Dave.

Lev asked Aisha, "You spare someone for that?"

"Yeah, send Gemma. She already asked me if she could go."

Lev told Dave, "Find Gemma. She can head out now. Orders for all Campus RT members are to leave at sunrise. Go straight to MR4 when they arrive."

"How many of your team came here with you?" he asked Aisha.

"Eight, minus Gemma," she said.

"Can you spare two more to act as guards on Kali at our room until we're finished? I don't want anyone on her that I don't trust while we do the transition."

"You got it. Kali, I'll send you people I would have guard my own son," she said to assure her.

"Ok," said Kali with a friendly smile.

Heather had been silent while listening to the arrangements being made right in front of her without her contribution and suddenly said, "You can't kill me, Lev. I know too much. I know things others don't. Even if you have a separate team at Campus, which apparently you do and have been keeping a secret from me, I don't believe you found someone in my field walking around out there in this burned down world. You need me. Let's put this behind us. You're the boss. You always have been. Keep me in a cage, and I'll do my part from there. I want to be a part of this. You can't kill me. Your mother and I were friends," she said adamantly.

"You were friends with Lev's mother?" asked Bolin with a look of confusion. "Was she your hairdresser?" he added.

Heather looked at Bolin with confusion and said, "Hairdresser? No. Here's a fact for you Bolin, since you like facts so much."

Lev felt the insult Heather directed at Bolin was also meant to further piss him off and deliberately let it slide so as not to give her any satisfaction.

"Lev's mother was the most brilliant academic in any room of academics. Her work in understanding time, combined with her work in various quantum theory fields, left her with a very small professional cohort she could work with and an even smaller friend group. I was one of her friends and she was my professional mentor. I've continued to explore the foundations of her work since the day The Benefactor gave us our instructions. Lev, tell them. I'm valuable to the RT!" she said proudly.

Lev was staring down at her face with contempt as she spoke.

"Lev?" asked Bolin.

Aisha stood silently next to Dave looking increasingly annoyed while Dave rolled his eyes and sighed loudly.

"She was probably both," Kali said to Bolin, offering him a reassuring nod. Lev had told her his mother was a hairdresser, so she must have been a hairdresser, too, she told herself.

"Yeah. She was both," he said to Bolin, confirming Kali's assumption.

Aisha spoke to Bolin saying, "Some of the things we decided not to tell you were to keep the research protected. You'll see, Bolin. Some information needed to be compartmentalized in case someone working for the guy who did this to the world showed up. We didn't want to lose everyone if attacked. But we got Kali instead of the guy who destroyed the world. The Benefactor got in touch with us again. He sent the help he said would take some time to get to us. We need to get to work now. Lev's mom was both. Lev is… Well, he's his mother's son," she raised her eyebrows at Bolin.

Bolin looked at Lev and asked, "Is Aisha saying you're smart?"

"Yeah! I am! Say it like it might be a possibility, why don't you? Jesus," he laughed.

Bolin raised a hand and shook his head with a look of incredulity but remained silent, staring at Lev.

Lev scoffed at him and said, "Go get James and bring him to our room. Bring food, too. Everything will get sorted out at the meeting, or at least begin to be sorted out. It's gonna take a few meetings probably. Aisha, Dave. I'll be down in about 45 minutes. Anything else?" he asked them.

"Tell your people not to kill me," Heather said haughtily.

Lev stared down at her while he said, "Aisha, Dave, Bolin…. Don't kill Heather."

He turned to Kali and said, "The code for this door is 837479."

They walked over to the door, and Kali punched in the code and pulled open the heavy door with her bandaged hand and the others heard Lev tell her, "To get out of here, you go up these stairs and turn right…"

Today, she would learn about the exits in the basements.

Kali Meets James

He started to close the door out of habit, then remembered to leave it open and turned around to look at her as she stood in the middle of the room.

"There are a few things we need to talk about, but not right now. When I get back," he was nodding as he said this to her.

"Are you stuffing me in another room to go do your man business? Because I'm getting tired of this routine," she asked, challenging his intention for her.

His expression became one of exasperation as he shook his head and raised his hands up by the sides of his head saying, "Are you kidding me?! Look at your hands. You bled through your bandages. I'll send Doc down here to fix them. And neither of us has eaten. I'm starving. You have to be, too. It's not 'man business' I'm doing. Jesus, Kali. I'm taking over the facility. Merging Campus with Ivy. It's gonna take a minute to do that. I told you this morning there'd be a few things I had to take care of with Aisha. This is one of the things I was talking about."

She was watching him and closed her eyes and shook her head slightly, obviously annoyed as he continued to lecture her.

"Come here," he said not waiting for her to come to him and walked up to her wrapping his arms around her. He felt her arms wrap around him as she turned her head and laid her cheek against his chest, and he said, "I wanted to have you wait at Bolin's house. I was looking for Aisha after I left you with Doc. I wanted Campus people to be your guards in case anyone loyal to Heather and the Ivy structure that never even existed decided to fuck around and play hero for that bitch. I've gotta take care of the transition with the combined Research Team first. It's not 'man business.' That was really insulting. I'm not that guy," he said, still annoyed about the accusation.

They lingered in their embrace and Kali said, "You know, it's a lot easier if you explain things to me rather than leaving me to figure out what's going on by myself."

"Yeah, I saw how you figured out things in the cage," Lev said, pulling away from her and looking at her face as she turned to look up at him.

She rolled her eyes at him and shook her head quickly. "I thought you didn't like me anymore… or ever, actually. That you'd been playing me for what I brought to Ivy. It felt awful." She turned her head to look down at the floor for a quick second then turned her face back up to look at his, determined not to be shamed for her errors in understanding what was going on.

"I didn't know you weren't just Ivy's Head of Security. I didn't know what your plans were or that you were part of the Research Team. That's a discussion to have later, too, huh? Your mom? Guess you got two things from her. I only knew what you told me. I didn't have all the information," she said defensively.

"I also told you I like you. We need to trust each other. I trust you. I swear to God, Kali, you could personally hand me over to the guy who broke the world and have me locked up in some time torture chamber and I wouldn't doubt you were working to get me out no matter how long it took you. You need to know that, even if I stood there next to Heather and looked at you like a stranger, and ordered you locked in a cage, that I would have a reason, and I'd be back for you. If you're not able to do that now, I guess I'll wait until you are. I'll keep reminding you that you can trust me if that's gonna help you get there."

Kali quickly leaned herself against him and wrapped her arms around him tightly. "Ok, but that would be really hard. Is it ok if I still legitimately freak out even if I'm also trusting you? Because I'll freak out if I'm locked up. That's not about you."

Lev grimaced at what she was telling him and hugged her tightly back and said, "Yeah. Of course. Can you... Can you not hang yourself, though? Or kill yourself in any way? I'm not going to itemize the different ways. I might miss one and you'll think it's not on the list of ways I don't want you to kill yourself," he said without a hint of humor.

She continued to hug him and asked without accusation, "You'd rather I go to torture?"

"No, baby. I'd rather have a chance to get to you before you're put in to some futuristic torture machine."

"You said you'd kill me," she reminded him.

"Ok. Ok. You're misunderstanding me. I will kill you. Don't doubt that. What I mean is, if you're going to be tortured in a... What are they called?" he asked her.

"There's lots of torture methods with different names," she said as she continued to hug him with her eyes closed.

"If you're gonna be dragged off for torture in some diabolical torture contraption, I'll kill you. That's not a problem at all. You kill you if I'm not able to kill you. We both do whatever's necessary to stop you from being taken to more torture. But, today was a different situation. If you can wait for me, maybe do that. Maybe wait," he said quietly, adding, "There's a distinction, Don't you see it?" he asked her as he slowly stroked her back. "This is complicated. But I don't want you to be tortured, so let's agree killing you is approved for those situations."

He began to doubt what he was negotiating with her. He looked down at her head against his chest as she told him, "I'm always afraid they'll find me and show up and take me back. Even right now. But maybe the torture device today was in my mind. Memories and fear. It's so real in here. I'll try to remember that next time."

"Jesus, Kali. I don't know if it's really any different for you anymore. Let's talk about this more later and you tell me what the hell to do. I'm probably just a selfish fucking idiot. I don't want to lose you, and I think I'm going to rescue you from things I can't even imagine. You don't have to agree with any of this."

"I like when you give me hope. I forgot what it feels like to have hope," she said as she looked up at him and said, "I'm thinking about kissing you."

He smiled as he leaned down and they kissed slowly for a few minutes before they heard angry voices and footsteps approach their open door. Lev pulled away from their kiss while pressing his forehead against hers and smiled at her telling her, "This guy knows everything Bolin knows. He's one of us."

Kali nodded and looked intrigued.

The voices in the hallway stopped arguing, and James suddenly appeared in the doorway.

"Hi. I'm here to finally meet our new friend," he said with a big smile and eyes focused on Kali as she stepped away from Lev.

He walked into the room and extended a long arm towards her saying, "I'm James. You must be Kali."

Kali took his hand with just the tips of her fingers and barely touched his hand as her own hand was very sore. She saw that his other arm was in a sling and bandaged thoroughly and then noticed a concerned Bolin now filling in the empty space provided by the open door behind James. He was still wearing his dirt and sweat covered clothes that now had blood from his nose added to them. His broken nose had been wiped with cloth or his own hand, but not properly washed yet. Bolin was filthy compared to James' clean appearance.

James was tall like Lev and had thick wavy red hair with some grey scattered throughout. His hair was untamed and surrounded his head like a flaming halo. He also had a face full of thick red hair that didn't manage to conceal his smile.

"Are you the soap maker?" Kali asked him.

"Yes, I make the soaps we use here," he said, looking at her intently but still smiling. "I hear we're gonna hang out together while these two guys take care of some business," James said, flicking his head towards the door where Bolin remained.

Lev said, "Just stay in the room until I get back. You're not a prisoner. It's not guy business, James," he said, still not over Kali's earlier comment. "I just want to ensure a smooth transition. Aisha's got two of her guards coming up here now."

Bolin looked agitated and asked Lev, "Can I talk to you privately?"

Lev walked to him in the doorway saying, "Yeah, what's up?"

They disappeared from the doorway and James looked down at Kali and rolled his eyes while shaking his head and said, "He thinks you're dangerous. He likes you, but he still thinks you're dangerous. Told me what you did, too. You might be a little dangerous, eh?" he said, raising his eyebrows and smiling brightly at her. "Now we both have to get used to our new faces," he smiled while pointing to his own nose which had clearly been broken recently but was much further along in the healing process than Bolin's newly broken nose.

Kali said, "To be fair, he was trying to save my life. I didn't have a choice. Well, I believed I didn't have a choice. Lev was just explaining to me that killing myself isn't always the best option," she said trailing off while considering how she had ended up breaking Bolin's nose. She shrugged adding, "I was pissed off before, but It's fine that he stopped me."

James was amused by her and laughed and said, "Bolin warned me that you don't always make sense even when you're making sense. Away with the fairies, right? Guess I'll figure out what you just said later."

Bolin and Lev walked into the room and Lev said, "We have to meet with the combined Ivy RT. I don't know what else will come up. Don't know when I'll be back, but I'll be back," he said reassuringly to Kali. He stepped up to her and leaned down and kissed her saying, "Be nice to James. I like him, too."

Kali looked at him and nodded that she understood what he meant.

Bolin stepped out of the way as Lev left the room and told Kali, "He's got three broken ribs and a broken arm. He's here to be good company, not fight."

James frowned and said, "For God's sake, I can still fight! It takes more than some broken bones to keep me down. You know, it's very patronizing to be called good company under the circumstances. Maybe I'm shit company?" He turned to Kali and whispered, "I'm not. I'm very good company." And Kali watched as Bolin touched the shoulder of James' broken arm gently as he looked away from him and silently walked out of the room. James looked down at Kali and said, "One minute," before springing out of the door and to the right. She heard the two of them speak for a bit and then James reappeared smiling at her again.

"Aisha's people are here. One of them is carrying food for us. I heard you were hungry. Had them send us up a really fine meal," he said proudly as the guard appeared in the doorway and walked their food and drink to the small table placing all alongside Kali's bottle of cosmos before departing to stand outside the open door.

Kali walked to Lev's table to take a seat and asked James, "Are you and Bolin a couple?"

"That we are! My dear, sweet husband with the appalling savior complex. Someone was bound to break his nose, you know. It just happened to be you." He smiled at her while taking his seat across from her. As he removed the two drinking mugs from their bowl of food and poured them each some water he asked, "Are you and Lev a couple, then?"

"We're something," she said, taking the cup of water he was offering her.

"Well, my husband and your something are apocalypse brothers so that makes us as good as family in these times. I may have a bunch of broken ribs and a broken arm, Kali, but I'm someone you can count on. Let's raise a glass to our new little family," he said, as he moved his water cup to the center of the table between them.

Kali looked at him and said wistfully, "I'm sure you're a nice family."

"I promise you, we're not perfect, but we're loyal," he said adding, "That's the toast. Cheers!" and clinked her mug against his then took a sip of his water, encouraging her to seal their toast with a sip from her own mug.

She obliged his enthusiasm for tradition, then placed her mug on the table to reach into the bowl of food saying, "Well, Lev and I haven't determined our actual status. Like I said, we're something."

James looked at her with a smile and said, "Yeh, deirfiúr chleamhnais." He picked up a potato from the large bowl they were sharing telling Kali, "I distill excellent vodka from these potatoes."

"Lev likes vodka," she said with a smile.

"I've heard that," James said, smiling back at her while they ate.

Bolin and Lev

"He'll be fine. Kali probably isn't going to hurt him. I want to say I'm one hundred percent sure of it, but with Kali, uh… More like ninety-two percent sure she won't hurt him. I'm positive she won't kill him, though. Unless she has to, which you're going to find out is really not meant to be a criminal act. Only if it's necessary." He glanced over at Bolin who was walking beside him silently as they left Doc and headed to the meeting. Doc had Bolin clean himself up in a quick shower and gave him a clean shirt after trying to set his nose quickly. "Not my best work," she had muttered, annoyed at how the two of them were rushing her. She was going to head up to rebandage Kali's hands next.

As they walked, Bolin said to Lev, "I like her. I'm putting the pieces together slowly. I saw the scars. I realize now that she wasn't going to kill you. She didn't kill Heather when she could have. All of this at once, you, Heather, a secret Research Team….the tech is real and Kali's a time traveler, and on our side even if she killed four people today… Who were they? It's a lot to make sense of all at once. And why didn't you try to stop her from killing herself? Did you let her take your gun?"

"Yeah, that sucked. I had to let her. If I'd tried to stop her, she would have kept trying until she succeeded. She wanted to die. She had to want to live. She told me she felt alone before we got back to Ivy. I heard her say the words, but I didn't listen to what she was telling me. In the cage, believing Heather...she was done. She wanted out of what she believed was a failed mission."

"That stuff about killing her--"

"Yeah. I know how it sounds. You and James can stick around in our room after the meeting, and you can ask us anything you still need to have clarified. I mean, I'll clarify. Kali's still a little unintentionally confusing. I think she's speaking a different language sometimes, but then I realize she's speaking through different experiences."

"Yes. And also, you walked out of here a week ago with her and came back *with* her," Bolin said with a smile adding, "Just so you know, I knew it. I told James before you even left," he laughed.

"Well, I didn't see it until I suddenly did," Lev said.

"That's because you weren't looking," said Bolin.

They were approaching the open, broken down, meeting room door and Lev muttered, "I should have gotten something to eat first. I'm fucking starving."

"When James heard Kali needed food, he figured you did, too, and ordered the kitchen to send down whatever was immediately available for the entire team. Kali's was a special order." Bolin laughed, adding, "He wanted to make a good first impression on her. I told him it wasn't going to prevent her from kicking his ass."

They both laughed and took a second to compose themselves in the empty hallway before walking into the meeting room. It felt good to break up the tension they both felt inside and enter the meeting as the friends they were.

Lev Sets the Ivy RT Straight

Lev stood in the doorway and told Angelo to finish removing the door which had been kicked in by Dave when Heather had held her exclusive meeting with Ivy RT members earlier. In the center of the long conference table were three plastic bins, and five pitchers of water. One bin held plates and ceramic mugs, while the two other bins contained an assortment of foods. Lev was happy to see the food was already there. Ivy's nine RT members were present along with Campus's nine RT members. Maren, Wong, and Carter were also seated. Everyone was assembled around the table in chairs except for Aisha and Heather. Aisha and Heather occupied chairs placed against the wall on the right-side of the room. Aisha's remaining team of five Campus security guards were standing against the four walls of the room including one standing on each side of Heather and separating her from Aisha.

"Aisha, come take Heather's seat beside mine," Lev said to her as he walked in and surveyed the room.

"Dave take the seat by Heather. I need food. If anyone else does, too, get some now. Heather, fuck you. Starve," he said as he walked around to the center side of the conference table and reached for a plate to pile food onto. No member of Aisha's guard made a move towards the food or drink. They remained ready to kill anyone from Ivy who posed a threat to a member of Campus.

Bolin sat in the chair to the left of Lev as he always did and waited until others had taken their food. Some members of Ivy's original research team sat quietly and did not reach for food or water, and Lev didn't bother to encourage them. The time for polite protocols had ended. Ivy was going to be under demonstrably new management from here on in. To hell with the polite protocols. They had created a team of spoiled elites at Ivy who couldn't comprehend the true nature of their situation.

To some extent, It had served Lev and the research to keep the Ivy RT separated from the realities outside of Ivy because the Ivy RT brought different approaches to their research through their limited perspectives. His team at Campus was grittier, had seen the world, felt more fear of their unknown enemy, so they sought a different kind of hope rather than relying solely on the words of The Benefactor. Contributions from the Ivy RT and the Campus RT did not always resemble each other. Motivations diverged, and spurred unique, creative ideas on each team. Value had been added to the cumulative research from both sides by maintaining different perspectives.

When Lev had brought nine members of his Campus RT team into the Ivy RT, he had his nine Campus RT members lie and say they were the only RT at Campus. They weren't. Campus's RT was sizable. Lev had been gathering skilled RT members for Campus during the years before he had moved to Ivy, before he knew what was going on at Ivy. He had his nine take the work Ivy was doing back to Campus to work on a separate RT at Campus created just for collaborative efforts. Unique perspectives. In all, Campus had three separate RTs: A nine member team at Ivy, a 16 member collaborative team at Campus, and the larger 43 member RT that had access to all research and broader powers to diverge and create teams as they saw fit.

Lev was the head of all Campus RTs overseeing all research and development as well as being an active and contributing member. When he had taken over Ivy, he became head of their RT, as well. Heather was reduced to a figurehead for the Ivy community. Ivy's RT was in the dark about all except what went on at Ivy. They knew Lev was in charge. All Campus RTs knew Ivy was in the dark. The secret collaborations had created unique advances to the research on both sides. The work at Campus had produced excellent results. The Campus RTs were far ahead of Ivy's RT.

Lev kept Ivy's RT in the dark and moved from Campus to Ivy's community years earlier because he wanted to be the person in charge at Ivy when and if The Benefactor ever reappeared. He wanted to be a soldier in The Benefactor's army. He wanted to work for this man, serve him. He wanted to show The Benefactor that he was a leader with vision. No one in Ivy's RT was a leader. Heather wasn't a leader. He saw that the day Bolin took him to meet the environmentalists, as they had once called themselves. They were 10 academics adrift in a sea of personally competitive narcissism, and they were incapable of organizing effectively to produce the research The Benefactor needed from them in order to defeat their enemy. They were about to be wiped out by a small religious cult. Despite those facts, they were arrogant in their assumption that they were anointed and special because a terrified, confused, angry, and amazingly resourceful 25 year old had gathered them together and implored them to help him by providing them with the research facility at Ivy.

The Benefactor had assembled 11 God complexes who spent their time getting little done except preening and posturing. They were failing the mission initiated by The Benefactor. They served themselves, their own egos, more than they served The Benefactor. Lev didn't create the original Campus RT to serve The Benefactor, he hadn't even known about The Benefactor back then, but everything else after he learned of the man, he did to serve him. Lev helped right Ivy's sinking ship that day he wiped out Moira and her cult. He read the words of The Benefactor and told Heather and her team he was taking over and going to provide them with needed leadership, or he'd kill them all. He got them to focus and produce research that had actually led to advancements they could build on at Ivy and at Campus. Today, he was going to finish the job. The Benefactor had sent Kali. She hadn't confirmed his identity, but he was sure her Friend was the same man. He was ready to serve the man he believed was capable of taking down their shared enemy.

Lev noticed Genji, Niels, and Jessica get up to get themselves food and water. Angelo removed the broken meeting room door and walked over and grabbed a plate and a mug, both of which he filled before taking his seat. Lev also noticed Margie, Sathindar, Charles, and Jim remained seated. None of them got up to get food or water. Heather must have done some real damage during the time she had them locked in their private meeting with her earlier. He grabbed handfuls of food onto his plate and walked back to his seat quickly. He wanted to be finished eating before everyone had taken their seats again.

"Let's go," Lev said as he finished eating enough food to beat back the hunger pangs of too much activity and too little food for the past few days. He had Bolin pass him a pitcher of water as he got up to get himself food last. Aisha poured herself more water after Lev filled his cup and she passed the pitcher over to Dave who drank from it directly then put it on the floor alongside his chair. The last person standing was Bolin, but only by a few seconds. He was quick to gather his food and water. His hands and arms showed the battle scars he'd earned fighting with Kali earlier, and his face was swelling painfully around his broken nose. Doc had given him some pain relievers, but nothing strong enough to completely control the pain he must be in.

Once Bolin was seated, Lev spoke up. "Looks like Jim, Charles, Margie, and Sathindar are not hungry. That, or they're staging a hunger strike because of what's going on right now. Which is it, Margie?" he asked her. She looked at him and didn't answer. "Answer, or I'll kill you right now," he said, bored.

"Heather said Kali brought us tech but that she refuses to give it to us, and you've lost your mind on some power trip, and you're going to get us all killed," she said with a small, scared voice.

"Hm," said Lev. "Charles, go," Lev said, looking at him.

"Like Margie said, only I want to add that Heather told us Kali killed a bunch of people before she hid the tech. I really don't know what the fuck is going on, man. I'm just not fucking hungry right now. I'm not choosing a side until I have all the information."

"Ok. Jim," Lev said as he picked up his water and took a sip.

"I don't hear you disputing that Kali brought us tech or that she hid it from us. We all saw Dave, some Campus's RT members, and Aisha's people kick in the door and knock the crap out of Heather before taking her out of here. Then we were made to wait here with Aisha's people and a few members of the Campus RT who looked like they would kill us if we scratched an itch. I don't even know what I'm allowed to say right now. We've got Aisha's people here, and Bolin. I'm not sure I can add more right now."

"Go ahead. All clearance protocols are abandoned for the purpose of setting shit straight during this meeting," Lev said to Jim.

"No, really, Lev. I'm not sure what's ok to say."

Lev rolled his eyes and said, "Bolin knows I'm in charge of Ivy and that I have been since I got here. He knows I'm part of the RT. Actually, he currently knows more than you do. Aisha's guards are informed. Feel free to abandon clearance."

Jim looked over at Bolin and said, "I don't even know who beat the hell out of Bolin. Did you?" he asked, looking at Lev.

Bolin laughed a little and shook his head no while he carefully chewed small pieces of his food.

Lev looked at Bolin and let out a small laugh saying, "No. Kali did that to him."

Bolin added, "She's the one you should all be afraid to piss off."

Jim wasn't smiling. "Why did our order break down? This wasn't supposed to happen after you took over Ivy," he said, sounding shocked at the situation they were in.

"Are you finished?" Lev asked him.

"Yeah," he said, shaking his head and looking down at the conference table.

"Sathindar, bring it home, man." Lev said to him.

"Everything they said, and I want to add that Margie and I just spent three weeks on the road with Heather. She was--"

Margie surprised Lev by speaking up suddenly. "Excuse me, but Sathindar, I don't want to be pulled into your explanations. Leave me out of whatever you're going to say," she said, looking at him with concern. She turned her attention to Lev and said, "I'm not looking to get killed over what's going on between you and Heather. I've been working under your command for years now. I wasn't out on a three week road trip with Heather and suddenly returned looking to overthrow your leadership," she said adamantly.

Lev sat back in his chair and took another sip from his mug of water saying, "Got it, Margie. Sathindar, rephrase your explanation to exclude Margie."

Sathindar looked shocked at having been turned on by Margie and having to reconsider his response to Lev. "I... I felt that Heather was very ambitious in regards to finding usable technology for the RT during our trip. I know you were angry with her, Margie, and myself when you sent us out to Norfolk, but I felt we did a really good job getting the materials you requested. I felt like the team was working well. I thought Heather was showing good leadership. I'm confused by what she told us today."

"What exactly did she tell you?" Lev asked him.

"That Kali brought us tech from The Benefactor. That she hid the tech and refused to hand it over to us. That you were letting Kali control the situation which she said meant you had lost control of Kali and the tech meant for us. That Kali had killed multiple people in front of a young child. She said Kali had one job but was refusing to complete the job she was sent to do because she liked the attention we were giving her here at Ivy."

Lev's facial features darkened at the description of Kali as a vapid attention seeker. He looked across the room at the faces of the people around the table and remained quiet for a minute while he contemplated how he would respond. No one said a word. No one ate. No one drank.

Finally he said, "I'm going to disabuse you of the misinformation you were served earlier by Heather. Kali brought us technology. I've seen some of it. It's way beyond what we're capable of creating with what we know. We're in big fucking trouble if we don't get our shit together as soon as possible. We've probably wasted most of the past 17 years fucking around only half understanding what's going on. Now Heather's wasted time locking Kali up and staging a little coup attempt." He sighed and leaned forward onto his bent arms on the conference room table.

"Kali brought us the tech, but she isn't a messenger. She's a soldier. She doesn't answer to me. She answers to her Friend, as she calls him. I'm convinced her Friend is The Benefactor. Don't look at me and think that I'm in control of Kali. I'm not her commanding officer. She told me as much. I told you all last week, she's not afraid of me. She looks harmless, but she's not." He tipped his head towards Bolin and looked at him.

Bolin said, "She's the toughest soldier in either community right now. We're all safer at Ivy than at Campus because she's here with us," he laughed and started eating again.

"Does that make her a threat to each of us? To the communities? No. I don't think so. Theoretically, she's on our side. But are we on her side? The Benefactor's side? I think we're a bigger threat to her well-being than she is to ours. Guess what? So does she. Are you on Kali's side, Sathindar? Jim? Charles? Margie? Any of you? Are you beginning to understand who she is? Do you want to feed your own egos by insisting Kali come over to your side? Her side is where you want to be.

"All of you from Ivy, listen to me. Her hands are softer than yours. But it's not because she's been hiding in towers and deemed essential. She was a prisoner. Her hands are soft, but she's lethal as hell. That's not a fucking exaggeration, either. She's a soldier, a warrior, a spy, and doesn't dispute it when she's called crazy. I watched her kill four people today. She was in a zone, man. She doesn't know math or science in any academic capacity that would be useful to our RTs. I watched her count hours on her fingers to win a fight with me. But I also know that the tech she brought us is so far out of our comprehension of math and science as we understand it right now, that it would be useless to us if she hadn't done more than bring us the tech. That would have been enough for me to be impressed with her efforts, though.

"I don't know what Heather's problem is when she bitches that Kali's a delivery service. It was a big fucking deal just to get the tech to us. She had to escape her captor, and then walk here alone and approach our 'Probably gonna shoot you first and ask questions later' community, but that's what she did. She landed here with half a sandwich and a bag of time-traveling technology and rolled up on us a week later after having hid the tech, very well, by the way, holding a handful of flowers, and then laughed at Bolin when he threatened to shoot her."

"Mm-hmm," agreed Bolin through a mouthful of food.

Lev sighed and leaned back in his chair again. "But Kali's done more than deliver tech to us. She spent years secretly gathering information about how to create the physical tech, and more importantly, how to get it to work. She committed espionage against the man who killed nearly 7 billion people in a split second one day in May 17 years ago.

"She got caught, too. Yeah. The guy who killed 7 billion people and can fuck with time, is the same guy who's been keeping her a prisoner. He had her tortured for five years trying to get her to turn on the people she works with. Probably The Benefactor, and don't forget us. She could have told him she was getting tech for some dickheads over at Ivy and spared herself years of torture, but she didn't. And apparently, the mass murderer who killed 7 billion people, won't kill her. Frankly, she finds it exasperating that he won't kill her. So, to suggest Kali is an attention seeker...." Again, Lev felt disgust rise up in him at the description. He shook his head and didn't make eye contact with anyone for a moment while he considered the arrogance of some of the people in the room.

His eyes scanned the faces before him and he said, "Heather wasn't going to listen to Kali if she'd brought the tech in to us today. Some of you here wouldn't have listened to her, either, because you don't respect her. She's not an Ivy RT member chosen by The Benefactor. She doesn't have math or science skills to impress you with. And yet, she's an invaluable part of our team."

Lev gave the people in the room time to absorb what he had just told them. After a couple of minutes he continued. "She killed two pedophiles this afternoon after killing two of their older victims, who were still children, but were too far gone. She rescued the little kid we came in with today. And she told me she wanted to talk with all of you so that you understood the mission and how dangerous the technology she brought us is. She doesn't trust you. She said you don't respect her or her efforts. I told her I understood and that we'd have a meeting tomorrow and make sure everyone was on the same page before she presented the RT with the technology she risked her life to gather and bring to Ivy. Does that sound like I lost control of the situation, or that I was going to get us all killed?" He looked at the faces around the table again and let the accurate information he was presenting confront the lies Heather had filled their heads with earlier.

"When I ran into Heather after Kali and I had returned, I told her we would have a meeting today and I would inform all of you that we'd have a meeting early tomorrow and listen to Kali because Kali had concerns and felt she needed to talk with the RT first before bringing in the tech. And, by the way, she's not handing the tech over to you like gifts. She knows how to use these items. The tech isn't yours. You didn't risk your lives to obtain the tech. Kali remains an asset to the understanding of the tech even when she walks it into this room and it leaves her hands.

"What happened today was Heather enlisted Bolin and two others in a coup. She lied to Bolin, Denton, Ramish, and Doc and took Kali from medical after I told Doc to keep her there until I returned for her. She told all of them that I had consented to having Kali locked up in a cage. I did not. The single biggest threat we were all under today was when Heather ordered Kali locked in a cage, and Kali, who has a time-traveling mass murderer and his army after her, lost her fucking mind and tried several times to kill herself fearing being locked in the cage made her a sitting target for capture and years more of torture. Imagine if she'd killed herself. We wouldn't have been able to find the tech or the recipe book she referred to last week. Wanna know why we wouldn't have been able to find it? Well, I'll tell you. The tech is hidden by something called an optical which displaces it from the current time. Yeah. It's hidden outside of current time. It's all in the past right now as I explain this to you. And it's got some insane safety features connected to her mind. She showed me how it works. You won't believe this shit." Lev laughed and rubbed his face before he could compose himself.

"Now, I believe Kali still wants to work with us, but I'm not positive at this point. I blame one person in particular for the breakdown of Kali's trust in us to behave responsibly with the technology she's brought us. That's Heather. I'm also pissed off at all Ivy RT members for being assholes who didn't open the door to Heather's private meeting earlier. Not one of you stood up to her. And every single one of you knows I'm in charge." Lev looked up towards the ceiling for a moment and then back at the RT and added, "Yeah. That's a problem, because I know she wasn't holding you by force.

"Finally, to be completely honest, I planned to end this 'Heather at the Helm' fantasy for the rest of the Ivy community today or, more likely, tomorrow, anyway. That's why Aisha and her team are here. This was planned years ago. Deal with the deception. The woods surrounding Ivy are loaded with Campus soldiers already in case you think you want out. Our dual communities are like the Hotel California. I trust you're all old enough to get the reference. This is war. You're soldiers. Desertion will not be tolerated. Conscientious objectors will be shot. Fuck your conscience. You can't object to being on the right side. Just means you're on the wrong side.

"My entire Campus RT will be here shortly. Ivy, you'll finally be able to meet the gang. Oh, about that, some of you here are under the delusion that you're irreplaceable, essential. You're not. Campus has two separate RTs. There are 59 members between the two teams, plus the Campus RT, including the Tech team, of 11 here, and finally, me. Maren, do you want to be considered Ivy or Campus?" he suddenly asked her.

"Campus, please!" she said loudly.

"Plus the 12 here," Lev corrected himself. "Ivy, your numbers were 11 and you've been successful some of the time. Lots of great minds assembled by The Benefactor. We moved objects through space through our collaborations, invented new maths. You're all brilliant. But you're not a protected class. Cancer got Christo, suicide got Irena, and a bullet got Heather."

Dave stood up and shot Heather in the head and sat back down as her body slumped backwards and then sideways and she fell from the chair she'd been sitting in while silently listening to Lev.

"Thank you, Dave," Lev said while staring at the faces around the conference table. Aisha's guards who had been standing near Heather walked towards the doorless exit of the meeting room in case anyone decided they wanted to leave the room. Lev continued. "Ivy started with 11 and is now down to eight members. I want to stress how very self-deluding it would be for any Ivy RT member to continue to believe they are a member of a protected class. Heather tried to make the case to me earlier that she was far too brilliant to kill. She reminded me that she had been a friend and a colleague of my mother's long ago. None of that would have helped us find the tech Kali has hidden from us if she had successfully killed herself after being caged by Heather. Oh, might want to thank Bolin at some point after the meeting. He got the injuries you see now when he stopped Kali from committing suicide. He did that before he knew what we'd lose if we lost Kali."

Bolin raised his water mug to the combined team, and then took a sip.

"For years, I wasn't sure who would show up at Ivy, either The Benefactor or the asshole who destroyed the world. It was important not to put all of our smart eggs into one basket in case the asshole showed up and wiped out Ivy. The hope was he'd be unaware of the threat Campus, just five miles away, posed. The work could continue. But I wanted to be here no matter who showed up. Now that The Benefactor has made his second contact with Ivy and provided us with technology he feels we need in order to assist him, it's time to merge our two communities and prepare ourselves to be ready to serve in the fight against our enemy. We are one RT moving forward. This is all or nothing now."

Lev continued. "We need a reset. Heather is gone, so Dave is now in charge of the remaining members of Ivy. Dave, what is the first order you want to give your new team?" Lev asked him.

Dave was stretched out casually in his chair next to Heather's body which was on the floor beside him. He held the pitcher of water in one hand on his lap and looked completely relaxed like he was at a beach bonfire with his closest friends. "I'm gonna say... Clean up this dead body. Get this bitch out of here."

"That's an excellent first order, Dave. I have faith in you to cure what ails the eight remaining members of Ivy's RT. You all see Aisha sitting next to me. Aisha shares all authority with me. Aisha is not Heather. An order from Aisha is an order from me and vice versa. All Campus community members are already informed about what's going on here. The entire Campus community has always known what's going on. Only Ivy was unaware. If there are any hostilities discovered at Ivy, they will be dealt with immediately. You eight either assimilate or you'll be removed. You are currently the only Ivy residents who know what is going on. Tomorrow, things will change, so keep it to yourselves overnight. Any questions?"

Lev was surprised by the sight of Maren raising her hand.

"What?"

Maren looked wary, but spoke loudly and clearly despite her fears. "I've worked with Oscar and Shoshi for two years, training them to be techs. Oscar's been assigned to the farms working under James for years, so you can check with James, but I think he'd be a trustworthy asset to this three person tech team. I'm bringing this up because we have new tech coming in on top of the tech Kali's bringing in, so I'm wondering if three of us, with..." Maren waved her hands indicating that more RT members would be in the room tomorrow. "It sounds like there's gonna be a lot of RT groups with tech needs. They might need more from us than we can get to in a timely way. Plus, I don't mean to ignore Shoshi. She's great. She works in the cafeteria. James would know her, too. She's been there for years. I never had a problem with either of them in the two years I was training them. They might be worth bringing in. But I don't know. I'm just putting it out there," she concluded, looking a little nervous, but also certain that she had had to tell Lev what she was thinking.

"Bolin, can you check with James and get his opinion on Oscar and Shoshi in time for tomorrow's meeting?" he asked him, still staring at Maren.

"Yes. What would you like me to do if he approves of them?"

"Find a second and knock on their doors and tell them they're on the team with full clearance. Same rules apply. Community members will know more in the coming days, but we still need responsible RT members who can practice discretion with the work we'll be doing in the labs. I trust you'll know if they're up to the task. Kill them on the spot if you feel they don't get it."

"Yes. Done."

Lev looked at the entire team, "No mention of this to either of them tonight. You see either of them here tomorrow morning, you'll know James approved of their character and they accepted the responsibility we offered them. Thank you, Maren. I agree. We need a robust tech team to work with the RT. Anyone else?" asked Lev.

Lev, Aisha, Dave, and Bolin

After Maren spoke, no one else had questions. Lev told Aisha's guards to remain with the eight remaining members of Ivy's RT while the Campus RT was dismissed. Lev watched as Maren left with the Campus RT and was glad she had publicly aligned herself with Campus. She was a natural soldier and he trusted her commitment to the research mission. It wouldn't have been right to force her to be a member of the Ivy RT. He told the Campus guards to have the Ivy RT sit in silence and wait for Dave to return while he took him, Aisha, and Bolin to the meeting room next door.

The four of them sat down at the conference table in the meeting room and Lev asked, "Questions?"

"Can I kill any Ivy RT members who I believe need to be killed? Or do you want me to cage them and wait for you?" asked Dave.

"I wanna say yeah to the killing, but my concern is that The Benefactor wants these people for other reasons. Heather was a traitor from the start, and then today, undermining the chain of command, lying, basically kidnapping Kali, she could have cost us Kali and the tech he sent us. She had to go. Genji's brilliant, but she'll be the first to tell you that fact. She has a really difficult time working with others. I can't imagine how she'll respond to being tossed into a room with 59 new researchers. I expect a fucking nightmare of narcissistic competition coming from her for a while. I think Niels is brilliant, but we've got great Campus people who can make up for his loss. You know the Ivy team as well as I do. They've all got perfectly acceptable replacements who are already committed to the mission and are working a lot harder than Ivy RT members ever have. Ivy RT members need to be fully committed to the mission or they're a liability. No explaining it to them. No more time for that. The cage for now," Lev told him.

"I'm still playing catch-up with a lot of this information," Bolin interjected. "I know both of you," he said looking at Dave and Aisha, "but I know Aisha's relationship to the situation far better than I understand yours, Dave. I thought you were the Campus RT astrophysicist, but I want to clarify your leadership position now so that I can interact with you respectful of your role and authority."

Dave was glad Bolin was finally informed. He had told Lev he would be happy to give Bolin a private tour of what was going on at Campus years ago, but Lev felt that keeping Bolin in the dark offered Bolin and James a less complicated lifestyle while they raised their young daughter. Bolin and James were intricately involved in numerous community aspects of the successful running of Ivy and were the only family at Ivy with a child. The day Bolin had approached him for help in removing Moira and her cult, he had told him specifically that his primary interest was in raising his daughter with James in the best environment he could secure for her. He said he didn't want a leadership role once Moira was removed. Lev wanted to honor Bolin's wishes for as long as possible, even as he did ask him to lead a small security detail in addition to his engineering and infrastructure maintenance duties. Bolin enjoyed using his military training and academic skills in both capacities. That was a comfortable fit for Bolin and the life he wanted with his family.

Dave explained all of this to Bolin now, and assured him, "We're in comparable leadership positions, man. You've always been plenty respectful of me. No need to change a thing. I'm glad you're informed. Let me know if you, include James if he's interested, want to talk more about what's been going on over at Campus with the RTs. You two might wanna know what we've been doing to secure a future for all of us, especially the kids."

Bolin was extremely grateful to find Dave was motivated by commitment to Lev, the mission, and the future, and said once things settled down, he would appreciate learning more from him about what had been going on over the years with the Campus RT. He asked Dave, "How did you find Campus?"

Lev responded instead. "I found Dave. I had his contact information and walked to his house with Aisha and Bob in the early days."

"Yeah, we did that," Aisha agreed. "But he wasn't home, so Lev dragged us 25 more miles to where he worked because he was convinced Dave would have gone to work in his office during the end of the world. The craziest part of that story is that we found Dave in his office with two others that are still with us on the Campus RT now."

Lev was nodding and said, "Dave was my first boss post university."

"Almost your first boss." Dave corrected him with a laugh.

Lev nodded. "After graduating, I was hired as a civilian to work on a project with the U.S. Naval Research Laboratory which was coordinating with Fermilab, two university research labs, and two international research labs. They were working together to improve their understanding of time based on some recent discoveries that had led to some new theories. Dave conducted two interviews with me. I really wanted that job. Back then I thought working to understand time and space was fun," Lev scoffed.

"I conducted the second interview just to make him want it more. Didn't know if he'd be a cocky bastard if we begged him to join us," Dave laughed, adding, "I knew who he was already. We all did. I couldn't believe we were going to get him on our team. Too bad the son of a bitch who figured out how to manipulate time turned out to be a psychopath and not a decent human being."

"Oh, so you were a naval officer, too? Wait, were you onto the possibility of this happening already?" Bolin asked in astonishment.

"It's hard to say. We were beginning to understand some things about time, but it was all theoretical, some straight up science fiction madness. Then..." Dave raised his eyebrows and looked at Bolin and made a hand motion to indicate something blowing up.

Bolin turned to Lev and said jokingly, "I still can't believe you're not as dumb as you look," and they all laughed.

"So, astrophysicist?" Bolin asked Lev and Dave, pointing at them.

Dave said, "I had moved into plasma physics from astrophysics a few years earlier. They were really overlapping studies. But I began my journey in physics as a young academic and spent time looking behind many of the curtains. I was working on a team with members from three organizations already, contributing what I had to offer and learning more about astroparticle physics for a year when I interviewed Lev."

Bolin looked at Lev for a response.

"Yeah, all that and theoretical astrophysics, unique interactions involving gravity of dark matter and dark energy when combined with time and space, negative matter. I started with math, couldn't give up physics, but got taken in by quantum mechanics. I know math and physics are independent in a lot of ways, but when you find a barrier, it's usually something you can go over, around, under, or through, right? Then you can see more clearly. That's fun."

Dave shook his head and said, "Yeah, that last bit. He already had the team's attention, but then he wrote a paper that was published in some international strategic foresight journal... Everyone on my team was sending texts at the same time to see about grabbing you before some other organization got hold of you. I flew up and met him before his classes the next morning. Told him to come interview with me and my team for an exciting new position," Dave laughed at the memory, "Yeah, there's not a name yet for what you were on to. Lev looked behind more curtains in his short time than I did in 20 years because he could imagine all of the curtains. You have to have an open and creative mind for this work."

Bolin suddenly asked them, "Don't you think it's weird that you and Dave would both survive? It can't be a coincidence."

"Well, " Lev said, "The Benefactor arranged to have 11 brilliant researchers assembled for his plan. How do you suppose he coordinated that?"

Bolin looked at him and asked him flatly, "Are you suggesting some of the team at Campus was organized, too. Some were saved purposefully. Like the RT at Ivy. Do you think you and Dave were spared by The Benefactor?"

Lev looked at all three of them and said, "Maybe The Benefactor, or someone else. And I'm sure Kali already told me."

"Who?" They all asked him.

"I really need to wrap my head around it some more before I talk about it out loud. I don't have enough information. It's fucking insane. I don't understand it enough yet. Kali should tell us just so I'm sure we're all hearing the same thing."

"If you're freaked out by it, it's gotta be wild," Dave said, looking wary.

"Yeah, she told me on the second day of walking to get the tech. We ended up having a fight, and she told me to go back to Ivy to pout." Lev laughed at the memory. "But, like everything else she says that sounds too confusing at first to be real … "

Lev looked at Bolin. "I know you're passionate about Ivy's community being prepared for battle, but Campus already has an organized military that's really well-prepared for ground battles in case the psychopath shows up."

Bolin laughed, "So it wasn't that you had Campus ready to defend against the occasional band of raiders or travelers? You guys were really preparing this entire time to fight the guy who took out humanity? I did wonder why you felt Campus had to be so militarized. It makes sense now."

"I wanted us to be prepared for anything. Listening to Kali this week, I think what we need, which we don't have, are people capable of conducting covert intelligence. You heard Kali down in the cages today. We lack people trained in espionage. I think we need to look into that, get a team prepared and ready to work with Kali's people. Would you consider leading this team?"

"Yes. Can I solicit recruits from Campus as well as Ivy?" he asked Lev.

"Yeah. Work with Suijin and Nova. They're the lead commanders of the Campus military units and know all the members well. They can help you narrow down potential recruits quickly. Don't hesitate to come to me or Aisha with what you need. Can you maintain your security detail, Team 1, if you take this on?" he asked him.

"Yes, I believe so. Let's get it going, and I'll tell you if I need to find a replacement. Anna's my second on Team 1 now. If it came to it, I already know I'd suggest she take over if I couldn't handle both roles."

"Perfect," said Lev.

He turned to Aisha. "You need anything?"

She shook her head and said, "I'm fine. Campus is ready. We've prepared for today for a long time. I'm wondering if Ivy needs anything from Campus, though. Specifically James. He's gonna have 59 new mouths to feed in the morning. I want to bring supplies for that at the very least. Do you have enough bedding? Dishes? What does Ivy need to suddenly house 59 people? I suspect they'll be here for at least a few days while Kali goes over the tech and tells us who the fuck did this to the world and what the hell we can do to stop him. You said it's a him. Did she tell you who he is?"

"She hasn't said, exactly. I'm not pushing her for details. You know, she has her own rhythm for communication. I think it's tied into her feelings of personal safety. But yeah, good call. I didn't think of that. We can cover everyone tomorrow for the day, and hopefully, we'll get a sense of how long they'll be here. We'll send for supplies from Campus, if we're gonna need them, after we get a feel for things after tomorrow's meeting.

"Sounds good. As for tomorrow, when we have all of the RTs, what's the plan?" she asked.

Lev looked at Aisha and Dave and pointed at them saying, "You two hold the morning meeting. I'm not going to be there. I'd have to bring Kali, and she... Well, sitting through a recap of today's events would just bore her and she'd get pissed off and leave because we were wasting time. I'm sure she'll get pissed off about something and leave, anyway," Lev laughed. "Everyone else must be there to get them all up to speed at the same time. Tell them what was said and done at the meeting today. Cover everything. Nothing's off limits as long as it's what we already discussed. Shut down any guesswork. Insist on facts. What we know. Tell them who Kali is. I don't imagine anyone from Campus will display the kind of outright hostile disrespect for her that Heather demonstrated today, and I want to believe all Campus RT members have their egos in check, but just in case, and for the benefit of the slow learners at Ivy, reiterate who the hell Kali is to our mission. We'll need to use MR4 to fit everyone. Kali and I will come in after the morning meeting. Bolin, you're at all meetings from now on," he said with a nod.
"Yes."
Dave pointed at Bolin. "Bol, I've got clearance. I'll be your second for Oscar and Shoshi early tomorrow. Meet at Shoshi's room first?"
Bolin responded, "Yes. 5am gives us time to dispose of bodies, or if they're agreeable, get an early breakfast."
Dave nodded.

The three of them looked at Lev, but Aisha was the only one willing to ask the question.
"So, you and Kali, huh?" She smiled and raised her eyebrows at Lev.
Bolin also smiled despite the pain from his broken nose and winced.
Dave put up his hands and shrugged saying, "She's a whole lot of interesting. Gonna take a long time to read that book."
"That's right," said Lev not hiding his own smile.
"I know everything you said about her in there is true," said Aisha.
Dave and Bolin agreed with her.
"Continuing Dave's metaphor, I think I've only read the first paragraph of a very long book. You heard the stuff about how she's been tortured, but don't treat her like she's fragile. It just means, watch out. She's gonna say and do things that will either unsettle your nerves or get on them, but her motivations are good... I mean, through her filter of what good is," Lev said, waving a hand absently through the air.
Bolin added, "She's not fragile. She didn't hesitate to take on me, Heather, Denton and Ramish in the hallway. We could have lost, too. We were lucky her hands were already injured before she came after us."

Lev nodded and said, "If she'd had a weapon, you would have lost. I've seen her use several now. Probably the best marksperson I've ever seen. She rattled me a bit today with the pedophiles she killed. In a zone, man."

"Mmm. I've met people like that. They don't usually give you a second chance. I hope Ivy's RT and Heather didn't make her turn on the idea of assisting us," said Dave.

"If she and I hadn't found a connection while we were out getting the tech, I would say that would be a bigger possibility. Then again, I could go back to our room tonight and she could be gone. But it just so happens that she and I have a connection that means something to each of us. I think she's going to come through for us despite what she was put through today. It's up to her, though. Like I said in the meeting, she's a soldier, and I'm not her commander. She's answering to someone else. She's making decisions based on how best to complete her mission. Everyone needs to get on her side. She's been trying to help us based on her orders.

"I think we're finished here now that we've touched on my personal life," Lev said. "Any questions?"

Aisha, Dave, and Bolin said no.

"Have those fuckers clean the dishes we dirtied, too. If Jim even hints that he shouldn't have to wash a fucking dish because he didn't eat, you know he can't learn. Put him in a cage," Lev said in disgust.

"Happily," said Dave as they all got up and headed back to MR1 and the Ivy RT.

Lev walked into MR1 and saw Aisha's guards and the eight members of the demoralized Ivy RT.

Aisha turned to Lev and said, "I don't trust them on their own overnight. Not after today. Locking us out and not one of them getting up to let us in, like you said."

"What do you want to do?" Lev asked her.

"I want them to sleep here tonight with my guards on them. I don't want to lose any sleep over these people, imagining them fucking around while the rest of us try to sleep. Dave and I have a lot to do very early tomorrow. Dave, you want to get some sleep tonight?" she asked him.

"That, I do," he said, staring with contempt at the small team he had to reform or cage.

"So, it's decided, then?" asked Lev.

Dave nodded at Lev and addressed the Ivy RT loudly, "Yeah. Ivy RT you're to clean up the mess Heather left behind. Then you will clear the dishes and food from the room bringing all to the cafeteria where you will show me you remember how to wash dishes. Probably been 17 years for some of you spoiled assholes. You will return here and spend the night on the floor. No comfortable chairs." He turned to Lev, "Might I suggest you change the combination on the locks when you leave here?"

"That you may," said Lev.

Dave turned back to the Ivy RT. "Your freedoms will be restricted until you demonstrate you plan to use any freedoms you are afforded to assist in accomplishing goals that will secure us success in our mission to defeat our enemy. Or you can die. I can do that for anyone at any time. Just ask. You don't have to piss me off first," he said.

Ivy RT members remained silent, and Aisha spoke to her guards, "I know it's been a long day for you. You can do three on, two off and catch some sleep that way. Jenna and Harry are at Lev's now, but if they come back, work it out so you can all get some rest. Please assist Dave in any way including forcefully subduing anyone who poses a threat. I'll have a team replace you early tomorrow. I'll bring your relief, myself, when they arrive after sunrise. You'll have off until lunch. I'll go get you some food and bring it down to you after I leave here."

Lev admired Aisha's professional courtesy. She was always very good to the people who worked for her. She had killed a lot of people in order to surround herself with a smart and loyal crew. She had no tolerance for people she didn't completely trust to listen to her. She rewarded her people with praise, but also with thoughtful and considerate leadership. Working for Aisha was a highly regarded position. She had never experienced a defection in loyalty from anyone on her team.

"Bol, you wanna walk with me to get James?" Lev asked.

"Yes. Let's change the codes first, though. I'll get the door at this end. Meet back at yours," he said.

They did that and informed Dave, Aisha, and the guards of the changes before heading upstairs to see if James had survived keeping Kali company.

Kali and James

James was very nice. Kali liked him right away. Lev hadn't needed to tell her he liked him. Bolin hadn't needed to ask her not to hurt him. She listened to him talk about how he and Bolin had met all those years ago in Philadelphia. He told her the reasons why he chose to make meals for strangers with the food he had available to him at his uncle's restaurant. He told her he didn't believe he would survive. He wasn't familiar with the area surrounding the city because he had spent most of his summers working in the restaurant and exploring only the city.

She watched as his face still lit up and his eyes took on a faraway look as he reminisced about the first night Bolin showed up outside the restaurant. He had liked Bolin right away, but Bolin had assumed he was with Maria. James laughed at that memory. The way he told the story made her laugh. When he told her about Bolin playing his guitar for the dinner guests, she listened until the end of the story and had a new affection for the man who had seriously threatened to kill her the first time he spoke to her.

She told James, "I was told he's an excellent musician. You reminded me that Lev and I found something for him when we went to get the tech!" Either her excitement was infectious or she and James just simply shared similar expressive enthusiasms, it didn't matter which, they both bounded over to the couch as she told him she had to show him what she brought back for Bolin. She picked up the full looking duffel bag and brought it to the coffee table.

"It looks heavy, but it's not. Do you want to guess what's inside?" she asked excitedly.

"Tell me how you got it, and I'll try to guess before you show me," he said, enjoying the suspense and wanting to prolong it.

She told James about her first day at Ivy when Bolin had gone through the contents of her backpack and discovered her shampoo and conditioner. How he had told her it was expired, but it wasn't, because she really did get it from a recent trip to Australia. James had her stop at that part and told her he needed a minute to catch up with the reality of time travel.

He asked, "Does Lev keep any alcohol in this room?"

"I don't think so. He's on duty a lot and needs to be boring. I mean alert."

James laughed and said, "Well, do you want to have a drink with me, then?"

"Hell, yeah! Today has sucked so bad, man! What can we have?" she asked him enthusiastically.

"I make all the adult beverages here, but I can only recommend the sugar shine tonight. It's the easiest for someone to run over and get for us. There's better stuff, for sure, and we'll have that together another time, but anyone can grab the sugar shine."

"Let's have that sugar shine, then!" Kali said with an encouraging nod.

"Let's wait to open the bag until we have our drinks," said James.

Kali could tell he liked to toast moments and was happy to wait.

James asked Aisha's guards to get them the alcohol, but they said they were on duty and had to wait for someone to pass by them and ask that person to run his non-essential errand.

James scoffed at the insinuation that his and Kali's need for alcohol was not essential and immediately started calling out for anyone within earshot to respond to him. He shouted loudly down the hallway for anyone willing to run an errand for him several times and the guards stood by silently watching him and wondering if they should put a stop to his efforts. Kali couldn't stop laughing at his commitment to get them their drinks.

Santi appeared and told James she could hear him across the building. That only outraged him as he demanded to know why his cries for assistance were being ignored by the community. He then asked her nicely to go get them the sugar shine, but she looked at Kali and asked him, "Will that be alright with Lev?"

Kali's eyes shot wide open and her mouth dropped. "Oh, no! Lev is not my keeper. I'm old enough to drink. I killed pedos today and beat up three grown men. Sorry, James. One of them was Bolin. I still have Heather's blood under my fingernails and that asshole Denton's teeth in my shoes. There's more. I could go on. I want a fucking drink!" She laughed.

"You know what?" Santi said, putting down her medical kit, "I apologize for suggesting Lev needed to approve your request for a drink or even lots of drinks if you so desire. If your hands can wait ten more minutes, I'll go get the shine, myself."

Kali assured Santi her hands could wait a bit longer, and James told her where to find the sugar shine. He admonished her to bring enough the first time or risk being sent back out on a second mission. Kali told her she hoped she would join them and to bring back enough for three. James said he was large enough to count for two people and upped the amount Santi should bring back to them. Santi reminded them she was a small person who would carry back what she could.

While they waited for Santi to return, Kali answered James' questions regarding the events of the day, and he sat mesmerized by her accounts with the children, the pedophiles, the fight with Heather, Bolin, Denton, and Ramish, and her time in the cage. He asked if she knew where Ace had ended up, but she said Lev had him last she saw him.

Santi appeared again and they rinsed one of the dirty canteens for her to use for her drinks. James filled her canteen telling her to drink it all with them or bring it back to her room. They all laughed as James filled his and Kali's mugs to the rim with the shine. James raised his mug, spilling some on Lev's floor saying, "May your troubles be less, and your blessings be more. And nothing but happiness come through your door!" Their drink holders met between them and they each took a large sip of the sugar shine James had made.

"Holy hell!" Kali coughed and struggled to catch her breath.

"Ah, have more. It gets easier that way!" James laughed as he patted her on the back.

Santi's eyes were watering and she struggled to say, "It's true. It does get easier. I've done this with him before."

They all laughed and Santi put down her drink so that she could tend to Kali's wounds a second time before she got too drunk. James marveled at the injuries on her right hand and had Kali confirm they were the result of teeth. He drank more of his shine and told her she did indeed earn her drinks. He held her mug of shine up to her mouth so she could drink while Santi re-stitched her wounds.

Santi made quick work of taking care of Kali's hands, and the three of them toasted the mystery present for Bolin contained in the duffle bag. Kali started from the beginning again to include Santi in the suspense but left out the part about time traveling and Australia. She told them about the music store and how Lev came out with only a handful of undamaged items for his effort. She stopped and looked at them and said, "Even drunk, which I am getting….. What the fuck is the alcohol content of this?" she asked James in a shocked tone. James shrugged and shook his head while he took a large sip from his mug, so she continued. "I forgot what I was about to say. Anyway, I'll give you a hint. What I found was in the stock room. It's all still in boxes. So this is the shape of three boxes," she explained. "See, I went into the store with Lev and rummaged around and I had him kick down a door where I found.....". She waited for one of them to guess.

"Well, he's going to appreciate anything you found for his guitars and then brought back to him. Lev carried this for four days?" he asked her.

"Yeah. It's bulky, but really light. I hope it's going to be worth it."

"Well, Bol's really going to be touched. I mean that. So, I'm looking and I'm trying to guess. It's too big to be strings unless it's boxes of strings. Can you imagine if it's strings and they're not rusty?" asked James, finishing what was in his cup.

"Santi shook her head. "I'm terrible at guessing when I'm sober. And I already know less than when I walked in here. Someone's going to have to help me back to my room."

Kali was smiling at both of them and said, "We didn't check that they're in good condition. We left them in the boxes and kept the boxes closed hoping not to damage them."

James looked at her and tipped his head. "Are you telling me it's strings? Did you find entire boxes of strings for my husband?" he asked her.

Kali's face lit up and she said, "Yes! But they might be damaged. We won't know until he opens them. I really wanna open them so badly."

James put his drink down and unzipped the bag and looked at the three boxes of various strings reading aloud the descriptions on the sides. "These will work. And look. These are different ones. He hasn't had these in years. Oh, he's going to like these!" He also noticed the assortment of other items inside the bag that she and Lev had taken. "Oh, come here. Let me give you a hug for this," he said affectionately and wrapped his one arm around her shoulders. "Bolin's going to appreciate this even if the strings didn't make it."

Santi raised her canteen between the three of them. "To Kali! Killing pedos and bringing the music back. You're making this shitty world a better place," she said.

"Here, here!" cried James. And the three of them clinked their drink containers together before taking large sips of their sugar shine.

"This does get easier to drink," said Kali, nodding her head at James.

"Now you're at the point of no return," he laughed.

Santi shook her canteen and said she was low, but couldn't possibly manage to put more in herself. James assured her he could do it and spilled some on Lev's coffee table just missing the duffle bag.

Kali laughed and moved the duffle bag aside and said, "Lev said if the strings aren't rusty, we'll all win because Bolin is an excellent player and can sing, too."

"That he can. And I don't get to hear him nearly enough lately," said James, smiling kindly at her.

The three of them continued to drink, and get drunker, and toast various things such as their hope that the strings would not be rusty and that Bolin would play for them soon, and dead pedos, and Kali surviving her suicide attempt, and Bolin for saving her, and Santi for stitching her up twice, and James for alcohol and good company, and Lev for overlooking the fact that Kali was probably crazy and going to hand him silverware but headed out on an adventure with her anyway. Santi slurred while asking them, "Silverware? What?" and they laughed at her saying they'd explain later.

Eventually, Santi said she had to leave, but not before James refilled her canteen for the road or "hallways" as Santi corrected him. Although she had stated she would need assistance returning to her room an hour earlier, as she left, she assured them she was fine and could get back without assistance. James shook his head laughing hard at her as she bumped into the door frame on her way out and Kali stood up to help her and then forgot why she was standing up.

"Where was I going, James?" she asked him, laughing.

"Why are you standing up?" he asked her, laughing at her.

"I'm going to eat," she said as she staggered over to the table and looked at the remnants in their shared meal bowl.

James stood up and told her he'd be more steady if he could use both arms to balance himself, so she went back to help him walk to the table. They sat down in their chairs and finished the food they had not finished earlier, and James brought the empty food dishes out to the hallway but kept the pitcher of water telling her, "Oooh, we're gonna need this later!" while laughing knowingly.

Kali took a pink cosmos from her bottle of cosmos and put it haphazardly behind her ear through her disheveled hair. Lev's mattress was bare, and the clean laundry was still in the bins, but neither of them wanted to make the bed. They refilled their mugs and sat down together on the bare mattress with their backs against the wall at the head of the bed hoping the new position would be more comfortable for James' ribs. Kali finished her drink and had James put her cup on the floor, and James got up and refilled his cup again before shuffling back to the bed sitting up next to her while they talked. They were both sufficiently drunk by the time James put his cup on the floor, and they laid down next to each other where they talked some more before falling asleep laughing about how Lev got stung multiple times getting James his bees.

Lev and Bolin /Kali and James

Lev and Bolin were heading back to check in on Kali and James after the meeting. Bolin told Lev that he thought Denton should be taken care of immediately, rather than letting him become informed about Kali the following day through the Community News awareness effort which would describe what had ultimately happened with Heather. Lev agreed. He said he would take care of it before going to bed. Bolin offered to help, and Lev accepted the offer. They wouldn't hide their act. They would kill him immediately and take his body to the burn pit. People would see them. They didn't have to explain themselves. It was a non-issue unless Denton fought back. That's why it had to be quick. No other reason.

As they approached his and Kali's room, Lev noticed that the door was not open all the way and scowled at Aisha's guards.

"Orders were to leave this door wide open. Did Kali adjust this door?" he asked them.

One of the guards spoke up and said, "No, but it seemed appropriate to close the door a little. To give them some privacy," he said uncomfortably.

"What the fuck does that mean?" asked Lev with a laugh. He turned away from the guards and slowly pushed the door open all the way. The room was illuminated. All the lights were on, even the bathroom light. Lev could see the two of them on the bed with James on the edge and Kali on the side closer to the wall under the open window. Their faces were leaning towards each other as if they were talking to one another. Kali had her re-bandaged right hand on James' stomach. Lev surveyed the scene. He saw a large, empty glass bottle on the dining table. Looked like a sugar shine jug to him.

He turned to Bolin and whispered, "Is that sugar shine?"

Bolin stepped forward and looked into the room. He laughed as quietly as he could at the scene. The two of them pointed at the fallen mugs at the side of the bed and listened to James snoring. They struggled to laugh quietly and not wake Kali and James.

"Yes. That's his sugar shine and his sugar snoring. My husband got your girlfriend wasted!" he said laughing and turned around into the hallway to laugh harder.

"Wait, wait. Come here! Look. There're three fucking bottles and two are empty and the third one is almost empty!" Lev whispered to Bolin while laughing.

Bolin said, "This might be a medical emergency. We should call Santi." Which made them both laugh harder.

One of the guards spoke up saying, "Santi was here earlier, and when she left, she had a canteen full of what they were drinking. We were a little concerned about her, but she said she was fine. We heard her talking to someone after she went around the corner. We're pretty sure that person walked her to where she needed to go."

Lev and Bolin were beside themselves laughing at what they had returned to. The two of them had each been so worried about their partners when they left them together. Bolin worried that Kali would hurt James, and Lev worried that Kali would hurt James. Returning to find them in this state was an enormous relief for both of them.

Lev pushed the door all the way open revealing for all who walked past the room, the scene inside. He motioned for the two guards to walk away from the door a bit and follow him so he could speak to them without waking Kali or James.

Bolin followed and Lev said, "Never close the door on her. Door stays open unless she decides otherwise. What the fuck did you mean you closed the door to "give them some privacy?" Lev asked, looking outraged.

326

"Yes. Tell me what you meant by that, as well," Bolin asked. "I'm wondering if you really thought my husband was cheating on me with a woman," he laughed.

Lev laughed, too. It took them a minute to compose themselves and Lev struggled to say, "Wait. Jesus, Bolin, I keep forgetting I'm a little annoyed. Stop laughing, man." He composed himself and said to Aisha's guards, "Ok. I appreciate… No, I don't. I don't appreciate you giving them some privacy because you thought they were doing something they shouldn't be doing. That's bullshit. You want to give them privacy? Leave the door wide open and block the view into the room using your bodies. That was really your only option."

Lev turned to Bolin. "Want to go take care of some business now?" he asked him.

"Yes. Let's do that, and then come back and drink what they didn't and see if we can wake them up."

The two of them kept laughing as they walked down the hallway to go find Denton and kill him.

Lev, Bolin, and Denton

Lev and Bolin found Denton, and Lev shot him in the head in the open doorway of his room. It was a first floor room, and Lev considered if Kali might prefer Denton's newly available room to the storage room on the first floor. He would ask for her opinion. He told Bolin about his need to find a room Kali could feel comfortable in, telling him that she needed escape routes and doors and windows open. He explained that continuing to have sex with her was a major priority for him now that they were back. Bolin understood and asked if he might consider letting him build them a house. Lev was surprised at the offer. He hadn't considered that as a possible option. He really liked the idea and asked Bolin to consider it more since he, himself, lacked a vision for the project.

They wrapped up Denton's body in his bed sheets, and they both wiped down the area behind the gunshot blast to Denton's head. Finally, they piled up the bloody laundry on top of Denton's body.

Lev told Bolin about the white house he and Kali had stayed at. He told him about the hand water pump and asked Bolin how they could determine whether or not the water was safe to drink or cook with. Bolin told Lev he would get back to him about the water testing. Lev told Bolin that if they succeeded in killing Kali's tormentor, he wanted to take her back to the white house and live there until they died. Bolin told Lev he wanted to see this house that had inspired him so much to finally want to live. Lev told him it wasn't just the house, but also the landscape surrounding it, the hand water pump in back, and the morning coffee he had with Kali in the driveway. It was the thought of living there peacefully with her.

They tossed Denton's body into the burn pit and lit him up.

"Let's go get a drink," Bolin said to Lev.

"I can't believe it hasn't been 24 hours since I woke up this morning," Lev told Bolin as they walked back to their inebriated partners.

Lev and Bolin

Lev picked up the two mugs off the floor by the side of his bed. He handed one to Bolin with a quiet laugh and they sat on the couch together. Bolin filled each of their mugs with the sugar shine still remaining in the third bottle.

"Let's toast several things," Lev said to Bolin.

"What would you like to toast first?" Bolin asked him.

"Man, thank you for saving Kali when she tried to hang herself today. I can't even... If you knew. I want you to understand what she's been through. I don't even know, though. We'll get to it eventually. But thank you," Lev said, beginning to lower his mug.

Bolin tapped his mug against Lev's and said, "I saw her body. I've been around people who survived war. That was different. I don't blame her for my broken nose or all this other bullshit. When she screamed... She was terrified. I'll never forget it. I don't think you know all that's going on with her," he said pointedly.

"I know I don't," Lev said, and they took big sips from their mugs.

Bolin looked at Lev. "It's been awhile. If you like her, I'm all in. Like family. Let me know," he said, raising his mug to Lev.

"I like her."

They clinked their mugs and emptied them.

Bolin refilled their mugs with the last of the alcohol from the bottle. Lev looked at Bolin.

"It's going to get bad. The guy who killed everyone, he was a boogeyman for a long time. But he's real. And he's worse than we can imagine. You in for the long-haul?" he asked Bolin.

"Yes. You know I am," Bolin said as they clinked mugs and took sips.

"One more," Bolin said, looking at Lev.

"You take it," Lev told him.

"I'm all in. James is all in. You never hold back from me again. You tell me what you need. I'm there."

Lev looked at him and said, "You can take James and Meabh and leave if you want to. I'd understand."

"Never," Bolin said firmly.

Lev held up his mug and said, "Brothers."

"Brothers." Bolin agreed and clinked his mug against Lev's.

They each finished their drinks and Bolin stood up and laughed asking, "How the hell am I going to get my husband home?"

Lev laughed and put down his empty mug on the coffee table and said, "It would help if he was smaller than you, but you got yourself an Irish giant instead of a leprechaun, and I really can't tell you how to get him home. Let's see if we can wake him up enough. If we can't, we'll think of something else. We can leave them there and I can sleep on the couch?"

Bolin shook his head laughing quietly. "We'll get him out of here someway," Bolin said with determination.

Lev nodded. "Oh, we have the guards. They can help," Lev said as Bolin tried to gently wake James.

Lev and Kali

Lev laid down on the bare mattress next to Kali and looked at her sleeping face. All of the lights in the room were off now, but the light coming in from the hallway through the open door provided enough light for Lev to admire her. He removed the wilted cosmos from her hair, placing it on the floor in back of him, and gently moved her messy hair back and away from her closed eyes and stared at her while she continued to sleep. Normally, she'd have opened her eyes by now and been fully oriented. But, he smiled, this was not a normal sleep. She was probably passed out. She and James had gotten pretty drunk on his distilled home brew. He tried to suppress a laugh that wanted to escape as he remembered the moment he saw the two of them passed out together on the bed.

Kali stirred and slowly opened her eyes and looked at him.

"Lev? Is that you?" she asked sleepily.

"Yeah, baby. Looks like you and James had some fun tonight, huh?" he asked her with a little laugh.

She closed her eyes and said, "I got so drunk. I'm still drunk. I like James. He's so nice." Lev leaned over and kissed her lips. She was too drunk and sleepy to kiss him back, and he smiled at her even though her eyes were closed.

"Did you kiss me?" she asked him.

"Yeah."

"I missed it. Do it again."

He laughed and leaned back towards her and said, "Ok. Here's your kiss. You ready?"

"Yeah," she said with her eyes still closed.

He kissed her slowly until he felt her kiss him back. He moved away from her and laughed a little and asked, "Was that better?"

"Yeah," she said.

And he watched her fall back to sleep.

Bolin and James

Bolin walked James back to their house across the grounds of a late night Ivy, illuminated poorly by the light of a small crescent moon. James was still completely drunk and walked holding onto Bolin's right arm with his one good arm talking to him about his evening with the "lovely Kali." He told Bolin, "You told the lovely Kali that her shampoo expired! It didn't. She's a time traveler, Bol. I can't believe you were worried about her hurting me. She likes you. She got you a present. I'm not supposed to tell you. I can't tell you what it is. Don't ask me. I won't tell you."

"What did Kali get me?" Bolin asked, laughing at him.

"Normally, I'd tell you because you're my favorite person, and it's gonna make you happy, but I like her. And I told her I wouldn't. Stop asking me. It's a surprise. Let's have a drink when we get home and toast our lovely Kali. You know, she wants to see my bees. I'm going to show her my bees. Are we having a drink then?" he asked Bolin.

"Yes. What would you like to have?" Bolin asked him, still amused by the state of his husband.

He had been deeply concerned when he left James with Kali. Concerned that Kali would hurt him. He understood now that Kali was in a state of constant reaction to fear and past traumas. He knew about PTSD. He had seen it in others during his time in the military. Kali had it bad. They all took risks waking up each day in this post civilized world. He was grateful that James had made a connection with her. James always seemed friendly and open to others, but he was a discerning man. Sometimes, he would privately tell Bolin, "I don't like…." and Bolin knew to listen to James. He told Bolin that he picked up vibes from people. He said it was all the time he spent working the earth and tending to animals. He felt he could quickly and accurately assess the nature of a person upon meeting them. He ignored flaws, but focused instead on the deeper nature of people. Bolin had never known him to be wrong. James had liked Lev and told Bolin he could be trusted in the early times knowing him. Tonight, he seemed enamored with Kali. Drunk or not, Bolin trusted James' assessment of her. Lev also liked her. He also liked her, but he didn't always trust his own instincts when it came to people. Heather had fooled him. He had never liked Heather, but he never would have guessed she could be so deliberately cruel. Kali may have beaten the living hell out of him earlier, but he understood why now. Even at the time she was attacking him, he felt he saw her for what she truly was- a terrified person who had already suffered too much and was trying desperately to avoid more pain. Heather had tried to leverage Kali's obvious traumas to her own advantage.

"Would you like to have some of your Irish whisky, sweetheart?" Bolin asked him.

"To toast the lovely Kali?" James asked him in a serious tone.

"Yes," Bolin said.

James stopped walking and leaned over and kissed Bolin. "You understand what I'm saying."

"Yes." Bolin smiled at him

The Irish whisky was only for special occasions. They went home, and James and Bolin toasted the lovely Kali coming into their lives.

Kali Wakes Up

Kali woke up and immediately didn't feel like herself. She saw Lev sleeping next to her and remembered drinking with James. When did Lev get back? Where were they? Oh, Lev's room. She rolled over onto her back and sat up. She quietly got off of the bed and walked into the bathroom managing not to wake Lev. It was nice to be in his room and not be a stranger as she had been before their walk to the tech. She brushed her teeth with his toothbrush and used the running water to clean her face. She looked at herself in the dirty mirror and could see the red wound around her neck.

The water on her face wasn't enough to shake off the hangover, so she removed her clothes and didn't consider the doors to the room and the bathroom were both open. She didn't care. She walked into the shower and let the warm water run over her but tried to avoid her bandaged hands. Her eyes were closed and the water was running over her head when she heard Lev's voice.

"Using the bathroom. How are you feeling this morning?"

She sighed and said, "Please help me."

"I'll get us some breakfast," he offered helpfully.

He walked into the shower, grabbed her in an embrace, and kissed her forehead. She couldn't open her eyes, but she could feel that he was dressed and imagined he was getting wet and he didn't care. Her body relaxed against his.

"Mmmm...I'm feeling better now," she said with her eyes still closed, hugging him.

She heard him laugh a commiserating laugh as he rubbed her back gently under the running water telling her, "I've been where you're at after a night drinking with James. I'll be back with some food and something for the headache you're about to have."

"James is awesome, but also the devil," she said as he left the shower.

"We all know that!" Lev laughed.

Lev returned with hot chicory and a large bowl of breakfast for them. He looked in his backpack, pulled out the first aid kit, and put some ibuprofen next to Kali's mug on the table. It was still dark outside, and Kali felt that the light coming in from the hallway was enough.

"You finally left me in your room without a guard," she said, smiling lightly as she took the ibuprofen.

"Our room. I did. Sent them on their way last night after I returned. We've almost got privacy," he said as he tipped his head towards their open door. Kali looked over at the window above the bed.

"First floor would help alleviate my anxiety."

He nodded. "Yeah, I'm going to make that happen tonight. That's done."

He told her about the night before with the guards who had wanted to protect her and James' privacy and she laughed along with him at his description of his and Bolin's reaction despite the pain it caused in her head.

"My brain is dried out," she told Lev as she grimaced and rested her head in one hand.

He poured her some more water and told her, "Careful drinking any kind of shine with James. He's Irish. He's a maniac. He's probably outside right now plowing a field and doing one-armed pushups. His whisky and his brandy are easier on a person. But any shine is gonna destroy a normal person. Too bad it's so fun to drink!" he laughed adding, "His wines are all excellent, too. Plus, once a year he makes a bunch of vodka. That's my personal favorite. I heard Doc joined you two."

Kali squinted and said, "Yeah, she did. She actually went and got us the alcohol."

Kali laughed remembering how they cajoled Santi into getting them as much as she could carry. She laughed as she told Lev how James had stood in the hallway yelling for someone to go get them drinks before Santi arrived.

Lev was laughing and said, "I can't believe that went on when you were all still sober."

"She got so drunk!" Kali said, laughing and telling Lev about their conversations. She also told him she really wanted to see the bees he'd given James.

Kali suddenly looked sad and Lev didn't like to see her look that way. He reached out and touched her arm and asked, "What is it?"

"I like your friends."

"Obviously, they like you, too," he said with a reassuring smile. "Come here," he said, pushing back his chair and patting his leg.

She got up and went over and sat on his lap and leaned into his hairy cheek while wrapping her arms around the top of his shoulders.

He wrapped her up in his arms and said, "We have a big fucking day again today. You tell me when you need a break. Ok?"

"Ok."

He kissed her cheek. "Heather's gone. So is Denton, the guy whose teeth you knocked out yesterday. Ivy's RT is being straightened out by my good friend, Dave. He was with Aisha yesterday. You saw him. You don't have to worry. I told you I'd take care of things. I'm taking care of things. You tell me what else you need, and I'll get you whatever it is."

She looked down at him and moved towards his neck where she kissed him for some time while he made his neck more available to her and encouraged her to continue. Eventually, she made her way over to his mouth where they both kissed each other softly. While they kissed, she ran her hand down his chest slowly and sighed telling him, "I need a first floor room with several escape routes." He made growling noises and laughed and hugged her tighter, kissing her neck as she laughed.

Olivia and Trent

Bolin knocked on Lev's open door. He could see Kali was on Lev's lap and that they were laughing together. They turned and looked at the doorway and Lev asked, "What's up?" and waved for him to come inside the room. "Have a seat in the dark with us," he said, pointing to Kali's empty chair.

"I need the apocalypse coffee, though," Kali said, reaching for it across the table past her cosmos.

Bolin looked at her. "No more drinking with or sleeping with my husband. You two together are a community scandal waiting to happen," he said to her, smiling.

"Well, we're going to go visit his bees together. We'll try to stay out of trouble, but I can't guarantee trouble won't find us."

"He went back to sleep after I woke him up this morning. You look showered and ready for the day. That means you won, Kali. You drank James under a table. He's met his match."

"Honestly, I feel like hell. I'm probably going to need a nap today," she laughed as she leaned into Lev who was reaching for his chicory.

Bolin nodded and said to Lev, "Two things. James approved Oscar and Shoshi. I'm meeting Dave to knock on their doors after I leave here."

"Good to know."

"Also, you sent me Oliva and Trent."

"Yeah. Promising kids. Did they follow instructions or do I have to kill them?"

"Oh, no. They followed instructions perfectly until Olivia was released from the cages and confronted Heather about locking up Kali. She was being walked past Heather by Ramish, and she stopped and told Heather to her face that her commander was going to be mad that Kali had been mistreated or something just like that. It was a threat. She's got a warrior spirit."

"I like it. I liked her the day we met them," Lev said, looking at Kali.

She nodded in agreement.

"How's Trent?" Lev asked.

"Trent's all about following orders. I want him trained and put into a security team. He's so eager to do what he's told. Completely trainable, but he's a follower. Also, they say they can both ride really well. They're apocalypse babies. They grew up riding horses. Olivia's got an independent streak but also demonstrated a spirit of loyalty. She takes it seriously that you're her commander. She watched us handle Kali, must have identified Heather as the boss, and wasn't afraid to approach Heather to tell her off. She didn't care who Heather was. She was loyal to you. I heard Trent shush her. He's not as independent as Olivia. I want to get them out of guest quarters today and assigned to separate duty sections and farm. Dave's putting him on Team 3 for a couple of weeks for his training. Team 3's getting the new people from Campus tomorrow. They're already trained, but they can all learn what works for Ivy together. We're also getting 20 new people from Campus for the new security Team 5. Trent's coming onboard at a busy time, but it will also help him learn a lot. He can start farming today and earning his keep, too.

"I want to send Olivia to Campus for an interview with Nova this afternoon. I want to see what trainers over there think of her. I want her to go straight into farm, too, but I want to confirm with Campus military leadership that she has an aptitude for more interpersonal military missions."

"You're thinking of espionage and working with the opposition? The first member of your Team?" asked Lev.

"Yes." Bolin looked at Kali. "We discussed a need to train a team for working with your people. Shared human resources. I think Olivia demonstrated she might be a good candidate for that type of cooperative work between your people and ours. She would need to be physically strong, too, but I think she's got the mental and emotional aptitude for getting inside and working interpersonally in ways that would be really helpful."

Kali looked at him and was clearly concerned.

"What is it? Do your people not want to work with ours in the way I'm suggesting?" he asked her.

Kali looked over at Lev and then again at Bolin. "It's not that. My Friend would like to have more spies. It's that so many are caught and sent to torture. Some have been in torture for a very long time. Spying for the opposition is a serious crime with merciless penalties. The spies that come from there understand that world better. They know what it is they're risking. They volunteer anyway. Olivia's from here and so young. She said she's turning 17. I was 19 when I was kidnapped."

Kali felt Lev stop breathing for a second and turned to him, placing the palm of her hand on his chest. "It's fine. It's just a detail at this point," she said reassuringly.

He frowned at her and shook his head. "We're the same age. I was 26 when the world ended," he said, sounding confused.

"It started years before that day, and it started long before he took me," she explained.

"You were a baby," Lev said, sounding angry.

"So's Olivia. And she's not from there. I'm not saying she shouldn't train to be a spy. I'm saying you two don't know what exactly that would mean in their world. It's not the same over there. Her training, the training you think people like me or people like Olivia would need to be successful, it's not what you would consider. I know my Friend can always use more spies. But I can tell you what will help spies to be successful. It's not muscles, Bolin. Olivia doesn't have to be physically strong to be a spy. Spies need to be mentally and emotionally strong. Getting caught doesn't end in a firing squad. Olivia and others would need to know exactly who they were dealing with. They'd have to still want the job even knowing what could happen to them. If they didn't know in advance, they would break. It's too much. You have to want it."

Lev didn't like what he was hearing and asked her, "You said when '*he*' took you. Did your Friend kidnap you to be a spy for the opposition?" He had never doubted the man he intended to serve until this moment and he needed to know. He suddenly hoped Kali's Friend and The Benefactor were two different people.

"What?" she asked him quizzically. She shook her head no, while frowning and responding emphatically, "No. No, never. My Friend was there the night I was brought in. We were in the hospital together. Briefly. My Friend heard me fighting the staff from behind a curtain. It took a while for my Friend to be able to find me after that night, but when my Friend found me... I'm not using pronouns...I was told right away who my Friend was."

"Who did your Friend say he/she was?" asked Lev.

"The leader of the opposition."

"Just like that?" asked Bolin. "He/she didn't even know you. Wasn't your Friend afraid you'd turn him/her in?"

"My Friend's entire family had just been killed. All avoided torture, thankfully. Well, except one. I think my Friend needed a lifeline just as much as I did. I had been kidnapped into their world, and everyone my Friend knew and cared about was either dead, thankfully, or put into torture. Some are still there, by the way. The opposition was destroyed. We became each other's tethers. We were all each other had for a little while. My friend had to rebuild the opposition all over again. I was 19 years old and my Friend was 18 years old."

"Kali, The Benefactor said he was 25 years old. I know you're reluctant to confirm your Friend and The Benefactor are the same person, but did you help set up Ivy?"

"I knew about the plans, but I wasn't available to do much until later. I definitely wasn't a part of the architecture crew," she said with a smile, raising her eyebrows. "If you want to prepare spies, you need to prepare spies for their world. This world isn't as cruel. I think you need to accurately and honestly prepare spies to withstand what will happen to them if they're caught. Olivia can do it if she wants to, but she needs all the information. No one should be put over there and not know what they're capable of doing to your body and your mind. What I'm saying is, if you would like, I can help you to train spies. Truth is, most people wouldn't be up for the job once they heard what happens if they're captured. You can't make anyone do that. You shouldn't. They'll break and tell Bas all about you and all about your Benefactor."

"Baby, did you just tell us the name of the man who killed everyone?" Lev asked her.

"Yeah."

"On purpose? Or do you want us to keep it a secret?" he asked her with a nod towards Bolin.

"I told you on purpose. He doesn't need or deserve protection," she said confidently.

Bolin looked over at Lev and caught his eye. "Do I ask you for approval in enlisting Kali in training spies?"

"No. Ask Kali," Lev said, still stunned at what she had just told them. He had a name.

"You want to be a consultant?" Bolin asked her with a hopeful expression. "Sure," she said, sipping her chicory with her bandaged hand.

Kali and Lev

Bolin left to meet up with Dave and extend invitations to Oscar and Shoshi to join the Tech Team and accept clearance rules or die. He was in a hurry because he and Dave also had to attend the early morning meeting with the entire soon-to-arrive Campus RT. Lev sat there with Kali on his lap with both arms around her waist.

"You don't seem alright," she said to him, running her bandaged right hand up over his shoulder and around his back where it interlocked with her left.

He looked at her and said, "I'm... not. I thought for a minute that your Friend, who, being honest, I believe is The Benefactor, kidnapped you and made you spy for the opposition. That thought was a gut punch. No. Worse than that. I've never doubted The Benefactor for one second in all these years. Then, I did for a second, and it felt like forever."

Kali shook her head at Lev and said, "My Friend would never hurt me or make me do something I didn't want to do."

She reached over and pulled a pink cosmos from her supply of flowers and placed it through her hair, resting it above her ear. With her flower behind her ear, she looked like she was considering something as she looked over at Lev.

She leaned closer to him and whispered in his ear, "Don't doubt your Benefactor," and then sat back up and looked at him.

He nodded once at her.

The Combined Research Teams Meet

Including Lev, and Dave, there were 80 RT members present. Aisha and Bolin were also seated. Dave and Aisha had fully informed the combined RT about the events of the previous day earlier in the morning and had then taken a breakfast break in the cafeteria with the members of the Campus RT while waiting for Lev and Kali to join them. As a declared member of Campus, Maren joined the Campus RT for breakfast. Ivy's RT was forced to remain in the meeting room with Aisha's guards. Ivy's RT did not eat. They were tired from sleeping poorly on the floor overnight and hungry. Lev didn't care. Lev asked Dave and Aisha, "Everyone caught up?" Both nodded at him and he looked over at the two new faces of Oscar and Shoshi who were now officially members of their Tech Team. "Oscar, Shoshi. Glad you decided to join us. You were each recommended by Maren as having skills the RT could rely on," Lev said, acknowledging them and giving Maren credit for expanding the Tech Team.

Kali thought to herself how happy her Friend would be to know how many people were present and working for the opposition. At the same time, she was overwhelmed at having to communicate clearly and concisely to such a large group.

She felt she had failed in that regard when she had spoken to the much smaller Ivy RT a week ago. She was determined to do better with this group. Lev was touching her arm as she was lost in her own thoughts. She looked at him, and he looked like he had just asked her a question she had missed.

"What?" she asked him.

"I want to bring something up that might piss you off. Ok?"

She frowned. "Well, that sounds like it's gonna suck."

"I won't reveal any secrets. I'll dance around them."

"Fine," she said, looking apprehensive despite his assurances.

Lev looked back at the people assembled for the meeting and said, "Raise your hand if you know the name of The Benefactor."

Everyone in the room raised their hand. Lev looked at Kali who was looking around the table at all the raised hands and he saw a look of concern cloud her face.

"Kali. He told the original 11 at Ivy his name. I learned it when I came here. I told my RTs. Do you want to keep using aliases for him?"

She looked at him and said nothing.

"We can. I just want to confirm to the RTs that The Benefactor and your Friend are actually the same man. I know you've been avoiding using his pronouns, but I think it would help to either confirm this is the same person and settle on a preferred alias for him without ever uttering his name, or we can start using his name. What do you want to do?"

Kali was looking at Lev as he spoke and suddenly looked absolutely pissed off.

Shit, he thought to himself.

"I thought only Ivy RT members and your handful of Campus RT members working with Ivy knew The Benefactor's name. Maybe you and a few others. I thought if you had more research people at Campus, maybe I'd just kill the Ivy people who know The Benefactor's name because they've already demonstrated they can't keep a fucking secret just by telling you. You threatened them with death, right? And they broke and told you?"

Lev nodded at her with a blank expression trying to counter her growing anger. "Death was implied," he said.

It didn't help. Kali was pissed off.

"That's so weak! Who cares about dying?!" Kali had stood up halfway through speaking and was now speaking loudly at Lev.

He stood up and said calmly, "I understand why you thought that was one way you could handle this. It makes a certain amount of sense." He didn't look around the room to see who was startled by her revelation of potential premeditated murder. Fuck them. Also, she was right. He was concerned because he could see she was getting extremely agitated.

"It makes a lot of fucking sense!" she said loudly. Kali glared across the faces of the RT members in the room asking Lev, "Are you sure all of these people know the name of The Benefactor and can be captured and tortured and reveal the name?"

"Yeah, and If they reveal the name of The Benefactor, I feel almost certain it's gonna be the name of your Friend. What if by not confirming his name to them now, someone here continues to doubt that you were sent here by him?"

"Even with the technology I brought?" asked Kali angrily.

"He built them this facility and they gave up his name," he reminded her gently.

"Why are they still alive?!" she shouted in frustration.

"The Benefactor assembled the team at Ivy," Lev said calmly. Her back was to him now and he noticed she was sizing up the various members of the RT in her fury. He asked her to look at him.

She turned around and he could see she was deciding what to do. He tried to focus her attention on reasonable choices she could make rather than killing everyone in the room who knew her Friend's name.

"You have choices that don't involve killing everyone. Yeah? They know his name. Did you promise to keep his name a secret, or are you not saying it because you believe this is the best way to protect him?"

Kali was beside herself and began to rage at Lev in front of the entire RT. "I didn't want anyone to know the name so if they got captured, it couldn't be tortured out of them. You see?! Maybe they could just die. They might get tortured anyway, but they wouldn't be able to reveal the name! But if the army comes here, they'll know this group of people know the name. These people aren't in danger of being tortured are they? They'll just say the name and accept working for the wrong side just to live stupid little lives forever!

"Why did Ivy tell you the name of The Benefactor? You didn't torture it out of them. You just threatened to kill them! I don't want my Friend's identity revealed. These people would rather lose the war and give up The Benefactor's name than be tortured! They don't serve your Benefactor! They serve the guy who destroyed the world!"

Lev had no interest in lying to her. He said, "I think right now, just the threat of death would be enough for some of these people to reveal his name. Torture wouldn't even be necessary. His name can be tortured out of Ivy's RT for certain. Learning about what goes on where you're from... I don't know, maybe his name could be tortured out of some of my RT members from Campus."

Kali gasped. "What?! Not you!" she shouted at him.

Lev shook his head and said, "Not me."

Kali shook her head saying passionately, "Not me!"

Lev nodded in agreement saying, "Not you."

Kali turned to the faces around the table and scanned them all slowly and then glared at Dave. "You're Dave?"

"I am."

Her voice lowered and she asked him coldly, "Why aren't they all dead?"

"Some will be soon enough," he said in a calm voice, adding a reassuring nod.

She turned to Lev, "You surrounded yourself with *mostly* loyal people at Campus? Because Ivy thoroughly sucks!"

Lev nodded saying calmly, "Yeah, I think I've managed to surround myself with loyal people. I need my RT fully informed about what they're up against, the use of torture by our enemy, and the man whose identity they have to protect. I think putting it all out there will help. You told me this morning that people who work for The Benefactor need to know the danger they're in. Campus RT members need to know, too. I agree with you about Ivy. Dave's working on them. He's going to weed out the ones who don't get it. Honestly, The Benefactor has been in danger of having his identity revealed ever since he told the original 11 at Ivy his name. Every one of them would have folded every day since. But I trust my people to hear the truth and still want to be here no matter the cost."

"I need some air," she said, shoving her chair away from her and leaving the room.

"Fuck," muttered Lev as he remained standing.

Dave and Kali

"Lev, can I go try to talk to her?" Dave asked quickly before she could get too far from the meeting room.

"Yeah."

Dave jogged out of the room.

Dave had been 45 years old when he'd interviewed Lev for the job at the research laboratory. He was now 62. He had spent 20 years in the navy and had a trim and fit body for a man his age. He worked at it. His long white hair was pulled back into a tidy ponytail and he kept his facial hair trimmed neatly, but still a decent length. He had been a young widow that day in May. They hadn't had kids. Neither had wanted children. They were both more enamored with their careers and the contributions they wanted to make to science. She had been the one and only for him, and her cancer diagnosis had come as a surprise, but her end had come swiftly. He threw himself into his work for the two years after her passing and was passionate about living his best life until his own eventual end. The younger Lev had come into his professional life at the same time he had developed an interest in having a younger person to mentor. Frankly, the younger scientists were often welcomed for their new ideas and unabashed enthusiasm for the fields they were entering. Dave was excited about working with Lev. He already had a reputation as a person who had the potential to shake things up. He had hoped the feelings would be mutual. But then the world ended suddenly.

When Lev showed up at his office that afternoon with Aisha and Bob, he knew he was in the presence of a man he was meant to align with. If he'd had a son, he'd have wanted him to be just like Lev. Lev, Aisha, and Bob spent a year living in the research facility with Dave, Hans, and Cheri. They organized their ideas about what they believed had caused the extinction event. Their theories ranged from simplistic to complete science fiction.

Dave knew plenty well working in science to never discount science fiction. Lev was convinced something had happened to time, itself. They had argued with him from their understanding of time, but Lev had other theories. He couldn't prove any of the wild theories he had, but, one day, they woke up and he was gone. He'd left a note for them. He was going to the nearest nuclear reactor. He was fucking crazy. For months he had asked them why the reactors weren't melting down. Aisha immediately walked out and headed towards the reactor Lev was headed to to try to catch up with him and stop him. Bob said he had to follow her and left. Dave turned to Hans and Cheri and said, "I'm not gonna be the bitch that didn't follow him," and left. In the end, they all caught up with Lev before he got too close to the presumed fallout zone.

Lev insisted that the nuclear power plant they were approaching would be safe because the extinction event had been planned by someone who had manipulated time and had controlled time to shut down the reactor safely. Not just this one reactor, either. All of them. That person would have controlled fallout to keep the world habitable. But a safely controlled shutdown of a nuclear reactor wasn't what they found that day. What they found was that the nuclear reactor site had simply vanished. It no longer existed. They walked to the location of a second nuclear reactor site in Virginia. They couldn't find it where it was supposed to be. Cheri was originally from Pennsylvania and knew exactly where a third nuclear power plant was that they could walk to in order to further test Lev's suspicions. It took them three weeks to walk there and back, but by the time they'd returned to Dave's office in D.C., they had a plan. They had visited three nuclear power plants that no longer existed. Couldn't be found. They packed up all of the research they could carry and left.

Even a scientist can sometimes stop and consider spooky shit they can't explain. Einstein didn't have all the answers, but he noticed some weird shit that was worth pointing at and considering, suggesting it might take some time to figure out answers. Lev could wait for answers as long as he was figuring out the questions. Where were the nuclear power plants? That was a question they all now had to consider. They packed up their lab in DC and headed to UVA on foot. Their group of six was led by Lev from that day on. Lev was looking for the son of a bitch who had broken the world. He insisted the extinction was intentional. He swore it was a person who had orchestrated the extinction. But how? According to Lev, the manipulation of time and space was involved.

Dave saw Kali looking confused in the crowded cafeteria and approached her.

"Hey. Dave. We haven't been properly introduced," he offered in a bored tone.

"I'm really angry right now, Dave. Furious. I need to get outside. I don't know my way around here. Where the hell is the exit?"

"Follow me." He led Kali outside and headed over to the horse corral.

"I don't like horses," she said.

"Then fuck those horses," Dave said and veered off towards the gardens. "You like vegetables?"

"Yeah. I do, actually," she said with a laugh.

Dave could see why Lev was attracted to her. She was without self-conceit about how she projected herself to others, and she was innocently amusing without making an effort. She wasn't trying to be anyone other than herself, and she was unapologetic about who she was. She was entirely herself, and he imagined she'd inadvertently reminded Lev of things about himself that he'd forgotten or forsaken in order to survive.

They leaned against the wooden fence around the garden and stood looking at the field of thriving summer vegetables and fruits.

"I'm not gonna play games with you. You're not wrong. The Ivy RT members are spoiled assholes who sold out The Benefactor the minute Lev walked into the room. He didn't even have to threaten to kill them. Heather gave him up first. I killed her yesterday on Lev's order.

"When Lev read the words of The Benefactor that day, he asked me what I thought about Heather giving up his name the way she did. I knew he had his own thoughts, so I asked him to tell me what he was thinking first. He said anyone who would give up the name of The Benefactor was a threat to him and could undermine the research work that needed to be done. I agreed.

"Lev moved to Ivy from Campus for several reasons. He wanted to keep Ivy's poison contained while also remaining where he believed The Benefactor would show up again one day. He kept Ivy's RT separate and uninformed about the other RTs to keep their toxic delusions of grandeur away from the research and the rest of the people serving The Benefactor. Yeah, Campus's RTs serve the Benefactor under Lev's command. Lev has killed a lot of people in pursuit of an RT that would protect the identity of The Benefactor. He's killed brilliant scientists who he doubted were committed to protecting his identity. His RT all know The Benefactor's name, and he trusts them. His RT is solid.

"I can't get into that man's head, but I've been hanging around his thoughts for nearly two decades. I can promise you this, he's been a soldier for The Benefactor since the day he learned his name. We all are. I know Ivy is bullshit. But here's what I think is going on. Listening to Lev over the years, I think he's conflicted because The

Benefactor chose those 11 scientists. By himself, he'd have killed them all long ago. But he doesn't know if they're important to ... his commander. I'm laying it out there for you. Do you know? Do you have an answer to that? Look at me, Kali."

Kali turned towards Dave and looked at him. She was far less angry now.

"What would Lev's commander have Lev do about Ivy? I think you know the man. Lev doesn't know what he would want him to do."

"Kill them all."

"That's not a problem."

"I think I'll stay out here for a little longer. I need to be less angry."

"Understood. Take your time."

They both stood leaning on the fence a bit longer and Kali turned to Dave.

"What?" she asked him.

He sighed and said, "I heard you in there. I heard you in the prison ward yesterday. Lev knew before any of us did. I guess you can imagine what it's like to be the only person who knows something before others know. He knew. He believed for years. A lot of people believed in Lev, but he fucking knew. Some of us are grappling with that now that you're here. Give us a chance. I know those people. Some of us have been following Lev for nearly two decades. We answer to him. We all know he's been waiting for The Benefactor. We wouldn't give up his name any more than we'd give up Lev's. You understand that?"

"I do."

"I'll tell Lev you're doing alright. Can I tell him you'll be back soon?"

"Yeah."

Kali watched Dave walk away.

Dave walked into the meeting room and looked at Lev. He motioned for Lev to follow him into the hallway.

"She's ok. She's gonna be back in a bit. It's obvious she knows The Benefactor and can speak on his behalf. Ivy is an amazing facility. The team is a bunch of assholes, but they contributed to some brilliant outcomes. We've moved objects across space, moved living things through time even if they died on route, Lev. They helped make that happen. But they're shitty, weak, spoiled people who are a danger to The Benefactor's life and the mission.

"About Ivy's RT, I asked her what he would have us do. Her words, '*Kill them all.*' She didn't hesitate when I asked her. She's not conflicted the way you are. This is an all or nothing effort here. Letting them live? Not gonna work. Kill those fuckers. They served their purpose. That was my take away. The Benefactor sent us his contact. She's here. Game on, man. You're ready for this. Scrub his remaining team of 11. You got blood from that stone already. Let's show our boss what we're made of."

Lev nodded.

Kali stood outside the locked basement door. She'd already punched in the code Lev had given her twice. He had made sure she had the code so she could escape the windowless basement ward. Each time she entered the code, the door wouldn't open for her. She walked back into the cafeteria.

"Hi. I need someone to get me into the basement. I must have forgotten the code," she said. The manager asked her for her name. She didn't give it to her. "I need to get into the basement. I'm in a meeting with Lev," she said.

The manager looked at her warily. "Who the hell are you?" she asked without being rude.

Kali could hear her confusion. "Is James around?" she asked.

"I can get James," the manager said and walked away from her.

Kali figured the cafeteria manager was happy to pass her off onto James. She waited and eventually she watched as James and Ace approached her from across the cafeteria.

"Hey, you! Look who I found eating breakfast this morning. He told me he was looking for you and Lev."

"Hi, Kali. Are you killing bad guys today?" Ace asked her enthusiastically.

"I'm trying to," she said, smiling back at him.

"They lock you out of the meeting?" James asked her as he punched in the code to the door.

"I don't know. I used the code Lev gave me to get out, but I can't get back in now."

"I know they changed the interior codes last night after they locked up Ivy's RT. Lev must have given you the code to get out, but not back in. Check with Lev, maybe we can have some drinks tonight if you two aren't busy. You, me, Lev, and Bol. We'll raise a glass. Check out those strings."

"As long as it's not your sugar shine again. I'm brain damaged from that!" she said with a concerned look on her face.

He threw his head back and laughed saying, "Me, too! No, we'll have some carrot wine. That's basically a salad. Healthy, even."

"That doesn't sound true!" she laughed as she headed back to the meeting with a wave to Ace.

Waiting for Kali to Return

"Why do we allow ourselves to be threatened by her? She's clearly unstable. Sure, she has our technology. I get that she's from the future, but she's threatening to kill us all and Lev, you're negotiating with her!" said Jessica.

"Jesus Christ almighty," Dave muttered quietly as he walked back to his seat next to Aisha.

"What? She's unstable. She's threatening to kill us for knowing the name of The Benefactor. We've known it for 17 years," insisted Jessica.

"Yeah, and you gave it up to Lev the minute he walked in here," Dave said, shrugging as he made himself comfortable in the chair next to Aisha's.

Bolin raised his hand politely and cleared his throat before speaking. "Aside from the fact that Kali's correct, she's the only one who knows where the tech The Benefactor sent us is hidden, and she--"

Jim suddenly spoke up interrupting Bolin saying aggressively, "So, we get the tech from her and then cage her. Heather wasn't wrong."

Aisha made an audible noise and stood up suddenly. She glared at Jim in shock and said loudly, "You did *not* just say that, Jim!"

Bolin shook his head and laughed derisively at Jim. "Ok, aside from the fact that she's correct and she's the only one who knows where the tech is hidden, and she also knows how to work it, then there's the fact that I like her," he said coldly, staring at Jim with hate in his eyes for the man.

"You like her enough to excuse her threat to murder people you've lived with for a decade?" asked Jim in a condescending tone.

"Fuck you, Jim," said Bolin still glaring at him. He'd always found Jim to be insufferable.

A Campus RT member most called Ordonez spoke up saying, "Jim, you're not making a good case for your survival. You realize that, right?"

"No, Isla, I feel like this is getting ridiculous. We need to keep it simple. Give us the tech. This woman is crazy. She's got a flower in her hair while she's talking about killing us. We'll figure it out without her. There are 80 or so of us and one of her. Guaranteed, she doesn't know how the tech even works. I spent my whole life working on this shit. I don't need crazy polluting the air."

Some people gasped at Jim's speech and looked away not wanting any part of it.

But Sathindar said, "I agree with Jim. This has gotten out of control. This woman showed up a week ago. I get it. She's from the future, but she's clearly not equipped to help us understand the technology she brought us. What field does she specialize in? She's talking about murdering us and Lev's letting her. Lev! She showed up a week ago. We all know The Benefactor's name. She can't murder us all. She'd get one of us, maybe two if she was lucky."

Lev sat silently listening to the conversations. If he could, he'd kill the rest of the Ivy RT right now. But, in reality, they would have to be taken care of more methodically and with a touch of politics. Plus, letting Ivy's RT spew gave Campus RT members an opportunity to see how far gone Ivy's RT truly was. No one at Campus spoke to Lev this way. Even posturing in such a manner had led to the deaths of some truly brilliant people. But this was war. Lev was their leader. He didn't serve himself. He worked for The Benefactor. Lev didn't need permission to kill them, but he liked the idea of letting Ivy's RT members hang themselves.

"Dave? Please take Jim to a cage. I can't stand him anymore," Lev said.

"Got it."

"Aisha, please take Jessica to a cage," Lev said quietly.

"Done," said Aisha getting up.

Lev heard Aisha respond to a quiet comment made by Jessica.

"Oh, you don't want to go to a cage? I can't make you go?" Aisha was saying. "That's fine. I won't take you. My guards will." Aisha walked out of the meeting room and came back with her guards who had been waiting in the meeting room next door. "Jessica, meet my guards. Two will be taking you to the cages. Six will remain here to deal with bullshit."

Aisha sat down as Jessica was led out of the room. She resisted by slapping one of the guards in the face. The guard punched her in the stomach and she fell forward from the blow, still yelling at the collected RT that Lev was on a power trip and not honoring the wishes of The Benefactor.

"No one gives a shit, Jessica," said Aisha with a bored wave of her hand.

Lev said calmly, "Let's get some work done while we wait for our time traveler to return. Every RT member will have to become a trained soldier. We cannot run and hide in the towers any longer. There are about 80 of us. I know everyone from the Campus RT is already highly skilled in combat training and how to defend Campus. We need to get you familiar with the Ivy facility and available resources here. I can imagine scenarios where you may have to fight, defend the labs, the work we're doing. Anyone have a problem becoming a part of the RT military?"

Sathindar raised his hand.

"Sathindar, I already anticipated you would insist you couldn't become a soldier. I'm going to give you 24 hours to reconsider your understanding of the situation you find yourself in."

Sathindar shook his head vigorously. Lev glared at him and said nothing. Silence filled the room as Lev continued to glare at Sathindar, waiting for him to speak.

"Lev, war goes against my personal beliefs. I cannot submit to training which would lead me to killing another."

"Ok," said Lev, shrugging and shaking his head.

"Aisha, you want to take him or do you have two more guards to spare?"

Aisha waved over two of her guards. "Take the hippie to the cages. Make sure Dave gets back here quickly. Take over for him so he can be here. Then hurry back because I'm not sure we're finished here."

Genji raised her hand.

"Go." Lev nodded.

"I was part of the team that discovered how to move inanimate objects across space. It's all about formulas. I can do this. Cage me later if you want to, but let me see what Kali brought us. I really feel that I'm missing something, and if I'm shown what I'm missing, I'll get it. I'll get it all. I'm just missing a piece to the puzzle."

"What you're missing is the point. It's about not revealing the identity of The Benefactor despite being tortured. We could all be captured and put into one of their torture devices, but The Benefactor must remain anonymous and elusive to the man who pushed the button on the extinction event. That's how the fight continues." He looked at Genji, bored after years of exposure to her arrogant form of self-confidence. "Are you willing to die, Genji? I am. Kali is. I actually have it on good authority that dying is the preferred option. It's the torture that's problematic. And they really like to use torture over there. I'm willing to be tortured. I know Kali is. She already has been. Aisha, you willing to die? Be tortured forever and not reveal the name of The Benefactor?"

"Get the bastard who broke the world? Yeah, Lev. I'm all in. Torture me for fucking eternity."

Lev turned to Margie, Charles, Niels, and Angelo.

"Awfully quiet over there," he said coldly.

Kali walked into the room and took her seat.

"Hi," she said to Lev with a friendly smile.

"Hi. You good?" he asked her.

"Yeah. Where's Dave?"

"Escorting Jim to a cage."

"Three from Ivy are gone?"

"Yeah. They were being rude."

"These ones weren't being rude?" she asked him.

"They've decided silence is their best option for now. Margie, I have a question for you. Why didn't you open the door and leave the room when Heather held her private meeting with Ivy yesterday?"

"I trusted Heather. I worked for her for years before you came here."

"Ok. Charles. Same question."

"Sometimes, in my opinion, you're unhinged. Killing people for stupid shit. Heather said the technology Kali brought is real, but that you'd lost control of her and the tech. She reminded us that The Benefactor chose us, not you. He sent the tech to us, not you. She said this was our moment."

"Oh, so she was going to take over, then?" Lev asked with a look of surprise on his face. "What was supposed to happen to me?" he asked with a laugh.

"You were going to be sent back to Campus with the Campus RT you've had us working with at Ivy. We weren't going to work with you anymore."

"Niels?"

"What Charles said. All of it. I liked the part about getting rid of you. Letting us work with our new tech."

Lev waved his left hand across the sea of Campus RT members listening to Niels. "You thought nine Ivy RT members could handle Kali's future tech on their own without any assistance? No help from Kali in understanding the technology? No help from the Ivy/Campus RT you've been working with all these years? What about the 59 Campus RT members?"

"I didn't even know you had these extra teams. But yeah, I have confidence in the Ivy team. The Benefactor chose us. He didn't choose them. You did. The

Benefactor sent *us* Kali. We weren't going to get rid of her."

Lev's entire demeanor became palpably frightening to everyone in the room as he leaned forward and asked viciously, "You planned to keep Kali as a hostage? Forcing her to help you figure out the tech?"

Niels lost the arrogant tone he had been using initially and suddenly looked nervous as he pointed at Kali and said, "The Benefactor sent her to us, not to you."

"So you all agreed to a plan that would deprive Kali of her freedom? Were you going to keep her in a cage?"

"Oh, I wouldn't have lasted a day in there," Kali said as she used her index finger to swipe back and forth in front of the red strangulation line still visible around her neck.

Before Lev could continue, Angelo interrupted saying, "I didn't agree to that plan. I told everyone that Kali shouldn't be kept in a cage."

Lev seethed as he turned to Angelo. "Ok, Angelo. Got anything new to add?"

"After they all agreed to keep Kali in a cage, I got up to leave. Heather said if I left, I'd never get to see what The Benefactor sent us. I made a choice. I wanted to see what he sent us. If I had known you had all these other researchers working over at Campus, I'd have left. I'm sure with a research team of this size, Campus would have fought back and taken Kali and the tech back to Campus, anyway. We'd have had nothing."

"So, you're opportunistic, not loyal. Under the circumstances, that's kinda worse when you think about it," Lev said in disgust.

Dave walked in and asked, "What did I miss?"

"Some confessions," said Aisha, shaking her head at him with a furious expression.

"More need to go to the cages?" he asked Lev, stopping himself from taking his seat and glaring at the remaining Ivy RT members.

"No. Have a seat," said Lev. "I want to ask Kali if she's decided what she wants to do about this room full of people knowing the identity of The Benefactor. You have anything you want to say to us?" he asked her not knowing what she would say, but having faith in her decisions.

"Yes, but send Aisha's guards away."

Aisha waved at her remaining guards and they left the room, closing the door. Lev got up and opened the door and nodded to Kali as he walked back to his seat.

Kali stood up slowly from her seat and took a deep breath and spoke slowly, wanting to choose her words wisely rather than emotionally.

"My Friend is loyal and caring and *he* wants to save humanity from a man named Bas. Bas killed everyone in my Friend's family. He imprisoned my Friend's extended family in endless torture where time moves differently. Some have been in torture for hundreds of years. Yeah, they can do that to your body and mind. My

Friend has never given up the fight against Bas. He has rescued me from torture many times. He's made my time spent in torture bearable to the extent that he could.

"I have watched him cry and scream in horror and helplessness at the torture imprisonment of those who have been caught working as traitors for him in the fight against Bas. He carries enormous guilt for each one. He's been broken so many times, but he always gets back up and he has never stopped having faith in the people he assembled at Ivy to help us win the war against Bas.

"I can't believe he trusted some of you. You're disappointments. Not worthy of being asked to help in our fight. He told me he hoped others would have joined the team at Ivy, but he wasn't sure if any of you would be alive let alone joined by others. I'm listening to Ivy people say they wanted to shut out Campus RTs yesterday believing they had an exclusive right to the tech I brought here. That's not what my Friend envisioned. I want to tell him that more joined in the fight against Bas. Better people than he originally assembled.

"Some of you sitting here are outright threats to the mission. I told you last time I spoke here that I am concerned. Where I'm from, many have been captured and tortured in an effort to get them to reveal his identity to Bas. None have ever broken despite torment you can't imagine. If you only knew what you were fighting against, you would understand how that's possible. I believe billions of people, dead in an instant, has become an abstraction to some of you. Some people here already broke and revealed his name when threatened with death. You're pathetic. You are the first people I have known to work for him, who I don't trust to protect his identity. You don't understand what you're up against.

"If you weren't sure who you were serving in the fight against Bas, I'll tell you now. Your Benefactor's name, my Friend's name, is Rollo Vespry," she said, her voice strong and sure.

Emotions overcame the room, and some people cried quietly while others sat in stunned silence. Some people covered their faces with their hands and she heard some issue a quiet thank you to her. She sat down and glared at the remaining five Ivy RT members.

She turned to the Campus RTs, pointed at the five Ivy RT members and said, "These people are weak, and they're going to give Rollo up to a psychopath to spare themselves death or torture. They'll get Rollo sent to torture forever. He told them not to reveal his name. They did it anyway. That makes them traitors. They're on Bas's side!" she said loudly in a tone of confident condemnation.

"We'll make sure Campus RTs are secure," Lev said.

"I could torture them for one minute and they'd break!" Kali said with earned confidence.

"Kali--"

"They hear torture and they think it's pulling out teeth. It's not that over there. Torture can last for hundreds of years. More, even. Forever." She leaned back in her chair, scowling.

"You're gonna have a chance to tell us about it. We're going to know. We'll be ready." Lev assured her calmly.

Lev spoke up with authority addressing the entire RT. "I hope the confirmation of Rollo Vespry's name has had a positive impact on your commitment to our mission. For the time being, no one outside of the RTs and this present leadership will know his name. We'll continue to use the alias 'The Benefactor' when Campus and Ivy community members are nearby. However, we will inform both communities about what the RT is working on. That's not going to be a secret any longer. We need every team member to be highly motivated to get to work once Kali brings in the tech. Kali is not a scientist. She was chosen for this mission by Vespry because she has other skills which he knew would help her get the tech to us. One man, Bas, killed 7 billion people, and another man, Rollo Vespry, is counting on us to help defeat that man. In case it wasn't clear, you are currently a citizen of Bas's Kingdom. By being a part of this RT, you serve Rollo Vespry. You are all traitors to Bas. Get your heads in the war we're fighting."

Lev leaned back in his chair.

"Margie, Genji, Charles, Niels, and Angelo, you are all guilty of being traitors to Rollo Vespry and participating in a coup against my leadership. You're each sentenced to death immediately."

As the convicted members of Ivy's once illustrious RT gasped and began to protest the sentence Lev passed on them, Lev turned to Dave asking, "Head of Security, what do you need to assist you in carrying out the sentences of these convicted traitors?

"Maybe one of Aisha's guards can go get Team 4 to assist me in carrying out the executions of the traitors who sought to overthrow the leadership of their former security team leader?"

Aisha laughed. "I like that, Dave. I'll send Steph out for you." She left the room to send her guard to collect Team 4.

Some members of the Campus RT stood up and walked over to Ivy's protesting RT members and silently dared them to continue to be disruptive. Crying was ignored, but when Genji began to shout at Lev and demanded Campus RT members stop him, she was punched in the face by a Campus RT member who shook his head in disgust at her as she stared at him in shock with blood running down her chin.

"Are the three in the cages guilty of treason and participation in a coup against your leadership, as well?" asked Dave with a smile.

"Yes, they are," laughed Lev.

"Same sentence?"

"Yes." Lev nodded once, smiling.

Bolin spoke up. "Dave, may I participate in the execution of the traitors?"

"Absolutely! What are you thinking? Hands on? Whatever you want," he asked Bolin.

"Would it be alright with you if Team 1 collected the traitors in the cages and brought them out to you to receive their sentences?"

Dave nodded adding, "Meet us at the burn pit. We'll take care of these assholes all at once. Let me know how you'd like it to be done, man."

Bolin nodded once saying, "I have a preference."

"Dead's my preference. You decide how," Dave said coldly.

"Does anyone else have something they need to bring up, or are we finished here?" Lev asked the team, as Aisha returned. When no one said anything, he said, "Kali and I are going to go get the tech now. We'll be back later, and we'll have another meeting. Stay close. Be available for the regroup. We need to get moving sooner rather than later. What's discussed in this room will be revealed to the community members of Campus and Ivy through predetermined leadership who will be informed sometime tomorrow. Vespry's name is the only secret that remains. Only the people in this room will know his name.

"Dave, Bolin, inform the security team leadership right away. Start with the two that are going to facilitate the executions. Our security needs to be informed in order to fight if Bas and his soldiers show up. Tell them not to share what you tell them with the community today. That'll happen tomorrow. Aisha, tell your guards, and also do a quick couple of Community News speeches in the cafeteria so the community knows leadership is intact and will address facts more fully tomorrow. We'll have a meeting with selected leadership tomorrow who will then fully inform community members so we can get the word out quickly and hopefully with a decent amount of accuracy. Then everyone can talk and try to make sense of their new reality."

Lev turned to Kali. "Let's go."

She stood up and walked out of the meeting room with Lev and he asked her quietly, "Hundreds of years in a torture chamber?"

"Yeah."

"That's a lot more than the five years I heard you reference outside the cage yesterday. Were you tortured for hundreds of years?"

She said nothing, and he didn't ask again as they walked to their room to get ready to get the tech she had hidden a second time.

Kali heard Lev ask the question, but she didn't want to answer him. She was glad that he dropped it and didn't insist on getting an answer. She felt him gently take her arm and looked over at him. He was heading down a different hallway that didn't lead to his room on the second floor.

"Follow me. You're in a daze today, woman. Heading down hallways without me," he said to her.

"I'm hungover, remember?" she said, smiling while shaking her head with a confused look on her face. "But I know this isn't the way to your room."

"Our room. I know. I want to show you the storage room on the first floor at the end of the hallway. Remember, I told you about it? You can consider it. Let me know if you approve. We can sleep there tonight if you want to try it out. I want to be alone with you tonight, so let's sleep there even if you don't want to make it permanent," he said, raising his eyebrows at her.

"Let's see this room."

Lev stopped walking and grabbed her hand.

"Hey. Thank you for being patient with me today. I'm trying to do the right thing."

Kali nodded and offered him a small smile saying, "I like Dave."

"Dave is like a wise old grandpa with no filter and anger issues. I'm glad you like him," he said with a smile and a nod as they started walking again.

She held onto his hand as he led her to the room he wanted her to consider.

Similar to Dorm 17, the room being used for storage was located at the end of an odd hallway with a door across from it. "Again, what's in this room across from the room you want me to consider? Another dorm?" she asked him.

"No. There are random doors throughout the place. The door across from Dorm 17 also opens to a cinder block wall. Look." Lev opened the unlocked door. Kali looked at the cinder blocks and looked at Lev.

She shook her head. "My Friend, I mean Rollo, designed this place, you know." She put her hand on the open door and slowly closed it telling Lev, "Let's see the storage room."

He opened the door to the room, and Kali could see that the room was exactly like Dorm 17, only it was full of old technology. Old cell phones, computers, keyboards, game controllers, remotes, televisions, and more. All neatly stored on floor to ceiling shelving and labeled.

"This is the most well-organized storage room I've ever seen."

"We have a team that's in charge of organizing things we collect. We could keep it all down in the third basement, that's where storage was when I got to Ivy, but I was concerned about keeping it all in one place. Didn't want to lose it all in a single incident, so I had it separated into areas throughout the building. We can move all of this tech out and move us in easily," he said, looking down at her.

She walked toward the wall where the window was visible between the shelving. The shelving was arranged in stacks the way a library would arrange bookshelves. Looking outside, she could see across the entire grounds of Ivy looking east.

"Is that where James and Bolin live?" she asked him. Off in the distance, up against the forest, she could see a small house on the other side of the gardens.

"Yeah."

"The property stretches pretty far across to that wooded area. Bolin must have had a hell of a time getting James home last night," she said, laughing back at Lev who was making his way towards her through the narrow shelving space. He agreed as he walked his body up against her back and wrapped his arms around her waist pulling her towards him.

She put her bandaged hands on his forearms and leaned herself against him as she spoke. "I could jump out this window to escape, and from here to the woods there are a lot of places to hide and die," she mused.

"Mmm-hmm," agreed Lev. The gardens, the barns, the windmills, the water tower, the farm equipment, the horse corral. Kali was right. A lot stood between the window and the woods.

"We're on the ground floor. The hallway ends, but from the outside it appears connected to the rest of the building," she said as they walked back towards the door.

"Yeah, and down the two short flights of stairs that led up here, which someday, ask Vespry why? Why he designed the place the way he did. No one here can figure it out," he said, looking confused, "...down the stairs is an exit to the outside. I don't know how much it would help you, but it's there. And come look here," Lev took her to the hallway outside the open doorway of the room. "See? There's the exit door to the right. The third door on the left, that's where my former security team musters and rests. Turned the team over to Williams permanently last night. The first two doors have rooms with gear for the team. 20 guards are in and out of there throughout the day, you know, except when they're on duty. But armed guards are often nearby. They have their own rooms, too, but people are in and out of there day and night. The door beyond the exit door is their exercise room. People are always in there working out. That's where I have my membership," he said, smiling. "There're always people near this storage room, but no one needs to walk up these two half flights of stairs to come into this corner. It can be our corner. You can leave the door open. I'll put up a stop sign at the bottom of the stairs and put a bell out that people can ring when they want to come up to our door."

Kali laughed at the idea of a bell.

Lev continued. "No one would have to come up the stairs. I'll kill them." He smiled then nodded his head and shrugged at her, indicating he might actually do that.

She smiled back at him and shook her head. "Maybe don't kill potential visitors. This room is perfect."

He looked down at her and put his arms around her asking, "So, I'm getting some of this tonight?"

"Oh, you're getting all of this tonight," she assured him as he kissed her.

"I've gotta find someone to clear this room out while we're gone today. I'll carry our mattress down. We can sleep on that on the floor tonight. Move the rest tomorrow."

"You're so efficient," she said in mock wonder at him as they hugged and kissed.

"Yeah, I'm that, too," he said as he ran his hands down over her ass.

The Hidden Tech

It was mid-morning, still very early in the day, when Lev and Kali got back to their room. Kali sat on the couch, and Lev stood by the bathroom door and snapped his fingers at her.

"Come on. We have to go," he said impatiently.

Kali stood up and rolled her eyes at him. She walked over to her backpack, which remained near the duffle bag with Bolin's boxes of guitar strings, and picked it up.

"My optical's in here," she said.

"What the hell?" What?" You're fucking with me," he said, tipping his head, clearly not believing her optical had been with them the entire time.

Kali bounced the backpack up and down in her hand. "Yeah. It's here. It just responded to me. Not like I could leave it out behind a tree or something. I had it chained up in a kiln. Remember?"

"You said you hid your optical. How is it hidden?"

Kali nodded and opened the backpack and took out her optical. "It was cloaked inside my backpack the same way it was cloaked inside the kiln. I'll show you what I mean. She put her optical near her backpack and the backpack disappeared. "The backpack's hidden in the past now." She put her finger near the energy in the optical and her backpack reappeared. "That's pretty standard use of an optical. Hide stuff you own, your own research, etc. with your visible optical.

"But spies use opticals, too. When you're trying to steal stuff with an optical, you use the cloaking formula. If people see you walking into a research lab with an optical, they're gonna know you're looking to steal stuff, or return stuff you stole previously. So, you do this..." The optical disappeared from Kali's hand. She stepped next to the small table that still contained their breakfast dishes from earlier in the morning and Lev watched one of the mugs disappear.

"The mug is in the past. Pretend it was a document with the formula for creating tech that allows you to time shadow suspects. You hide it in the past and then reveal it at home, read it, make copies of it, whatever, and then return it to the past and go back to the place you stole it from. Maybe put it on the floor, so they think a breeze blew it there. Whatever."

Lev nodded in amazement as she explained the capabilities of her optical.

Kali held out her empty hand and her optical reappeared. She put her finger near the optical's energy, and the mug returned to the table.

"The cloaking device is great for stealing shit, but it's also an excellent way to lose your optical. It's difficult to feel it when it's cloaked. You have to know where it is and you have to be close enough to it that it'll respond to your command to reveal itself like it did when it was inside my backpack just now. You know, become solid again. I uncloaked it when I stood next to the kiln before I unlocked it.

"I cloaked it inside my backpack because I didn't trust the Research Team. If they were going to screw everything up and have Bas and his army show up, I already didn't want to get caught, I'd rather die, but I really didn't want to get caught with my optical. Bas doesn't even suspect I have an optical. It's one thing if I escaped the Kingdom and got caught and brought back for running away. It's another thing entirely if I get caught at a research facility with an optical. Cloaking seemed like a necessary risk management decision.

"It's possible that I could have lost track of it. I'd have lost everything I've got hidden on it, too, including all the tech I brought Ivy. It was really scary when you took my backpack from medical. Santi told me you took our stuff to your room.

"Our room."

"Our room. I was so anxious waiting for you to come back to get me. I wanted to talk to you and make sure we were... That you understood why I was worried about the RT."

Lev walked over to Kali and took her hand. "Let's sit down."

Kali kept talking to him as he led her to the couch where they sat down as Lev listened to her.

"Cloaked opticals get lost really easily. I decided it was a risk I needed to take because I didn't trust those people. The other stuff with Heather came later after I had already decided to cloak it. I was glad I'd cloaked it. I was going to die and you guys wouldn't get the tech."

"We're good now, though, right? Do you need to talk more about it?" he asked her as he kissed her temple.

"No. I just want you to know why I hid my optical. I'd rather lose it and everything on it than be caught by Bas with it. If Bas ever got what's on my optical, Rollo would be caught, too."

"But you're the operator. Can Bas get inside an optical?"

"Oh, he's trying to break into opticals!" she said passionately, nodding and looking at Lev with a very concerned expression.

"I understand now. I trusted you without you telling me, though. I want you to know that. What Niels said... That was fucked up. Again, just to be clear, I'd have come for you and killed them all. Ok?"

"Yeah."

"That's a 'try to wait for me' situation. Something I couldn't have thought of happening." He nodded while looking at her for confirmation of her understanding. "I'll come for you wherever you are."

"Ok." Kali smiled at him and stroked the side of his bearded cheek affectionately. "Can we hang out for a little while before we go back to show them the tech?" she asked him.

"Yeah, it's gonna take Dave and Bolin some time to kill Ivy, anyway," he said as put his hand on her upper back and played with the hair on the back of her neck.

"Wanna make out?" she asked him as they leaned their faces closer together.

"Hell, yeah," Lev growled and pulled her onto his lap.

They kissed for a minute before he suddenly pulled away and told her he needed to find someone to clear out the storage room downstairs. "I'll be right back."

Kali waved him off and laid down on the couch and quickly fell asleep still working James' sugar shine out of her system.

Lev found someone to initiate the clearing out of the storage room. He was assured the room would be cleared and thoroughly cleaned by the late afternoon. He hadn't been gone long when he came back to their room to find Kali asleep on the couch. He laid down alongside her, waking her as he worked his way slightly under her. "Get up here or one of us is gonna roll off onto the floor," he said.

She found a comfortable spot up on his left side and they kissed in between talking about some of the things they had delayed talking about over the past 24 hours.

"You're gonna kill me?"

"Yeah. I will. Don't worry about that ever. No one's taking you to torture if I can kill you first. Were you in torture for hundreds of years?"

"Yeah. I don't want to talk about that right now."

"Ok. Can we later? I'll drop it if you want me to. I'm not asking for details, just wondering how long. Also, can you wait for me if future torture isn't an issue?"

"Yes, to both. I get the difference. I'll try not to torture people I kill even if they really suck and deserve a little torture."

"I appreciate that. I realize this isn't easy for you. I'm sure you'll get better at it, too."

"Maybe. I can only promise that I'll try. Can I have my own gun and a knife instead of borrowing yours?"

"Yeah. Of course. You want separate weapons for when we're asleep? So you can kill me? Keep them around our bed?"

"Yeah, that would be nice."

"Ok. I'll have Dave take you to the armory and you can choose what you need."

"Thank you. What was your mother's name?"

"Marina Patel. Do you still feel alone?"

"No. I don't. I've heard your mother's name. I have to tell you about Rewinds."

"What? Ok. Wait, what?"

"A Rewind can bring a dead person back to life up to 15 seconds after they've died. So, when you kill me, you have to keep the person with the Rewind away from me. It helps if you decapitate the dead person and throw the head as far away as possible. Doing that takes up some of the 15 seconds because the head has to be close to the body in order for the Rewind to work. Does this make sense?"

"Jesus."

"If you rewind someone who's dead and they got their leg chopped off, and the leg was tossed, they can still be rewound. But they won't have their leg. But you can't rewind without a head. So, one option is to chop off my head and throw it to prevent a successful rewind. There's a 15/15 rule, too. Rewinds need to be completed within 15 seconds of death, but also, they heal all wounds that occurred 15 minutes prior to death."

"Hold on. I'm working it out. How were you going to kill yourself when we were walking? You only had a knife. If you'd slit your wrists, they could rewind you."

"Yeah, but I always slept near an open window. I was going to run and hide. I always looked around outside to find places to hide. Slit my wrists first and run and hide. Hopefully be dead for just over 15 seconds before they could locate me and rewind me."

"I see. That was a good plan. That's how you found the water pump? Looking for a place to run and hide and die?"

"Yeah. Exactly."

"Can you really not cook, or do you just not like to cook?"

"Man, I cannot cook. I never learned how. My father and I ate out almost exclusively after my mother died."

"Speaking of mothers, where did you hear my mother's name?"

"Time told me about her."

"Kali--"

"That's a really big conversation. We should plan for it for another time."

"Ok. But I'm going to be distracted by that, so how do I do anything else until we talk about that?"

"Yesterday, when Heather talked about your mother, I wondered if Marina Patel could be your mother because Marina is a Russian name and Patel, well... It just suddenly occurred to me that maybe she was your mother. We had a lot to do yesterday. And so far today, as well."

"Time knew my mother?"

"Yeah."

"Did you?"

"No. Time and your mother were friends years ago. Before you would have been born. It's possible that some of the formulas in the recipe book are hers."

"Kali, for real, I'm feeling overwhelmed right now."

"Please don't be. I'll tell you what Time told me after our meeting. It's mostly the story of a friendship."

"A friendship between Time and my mother?"

"Yeah. It's a nice story."

Lev rolled onto his side, and Kali was pressed between him and the back of the couch.

"Do you think I'm here by accident, or luck, or by design?"

"Just now, when you told me your mom's name, I thought by some design

Time was going for. But I don't know. Time didn't tell me anything about you. Design seems very likely, though. For other reasons, too. Probably design. Just so you know, Time can't control outcomes. Time's designs are very loose with a lot of hope that things will work out."

"What about me and you?"

"Time can't control outcomes or feelings. Time's not like that. You don't have to like me."

Lev kissed her. "Hey, I do. I was just checking."

"And Time didn't tell me about you."

Lev kissed her again.

"And I wanted to come here."

Lev kissed her again. "Ok. You and I might be an accident or luck," he said.

They kept kissing until they both fell asleep without meaning to.

Before the Second Meeting of the Day with the RT

Kali woke up and looked at Lev's sleeping face. He looked so peaceful and sweet to her. She thought of the unflattering remarks made by the Ivy RT about him earlier in the morning. They really were assholes. So he killed people? Big fucking deal. They had no concept of what it must have taken for Lev to find and assemble 71 scientists to do research into what had happened. Dave described Lev as loyal to Rollo. She cared for very few people, but Rollo was one of them. Actually, until she had met Lev, Rollo was the only person she cared about. Time wasn't a person.

She and Rollo had been through a lot together. Just two average young adults when they had met. Neither was special in any measurable way. But they were both emotionally strong and resilient. Resiliency was an underappreciated strength in a stable world. She and Rollo could plan ahead strategically. Him more than her. Both of them were managed risk takers.

He was older than her now. Bas had punished him by accelerating his age. He estimated he was in his mid 50s. Bas was still 28. He had told Kali he was going to stop her from aging when she turned 45. She would be 45 forever. Didn't matter how old her soul was after the time spent in torture and Time. He was an idiot. An idiot psychopath. He wasn't even interesting or clever. He was a fucking idiot with some math skills who got lucky. Lev was loyal to Rollo. He had planned so much out in order to be an asset to him. She wished she could tell Rollo about Lev. He would really like him. She looked at him as he slept. She really liked him.

She ran the fingers of her less bandaged left hand gently through the hair on the side of his head.

"Hey, wake up," she said quietly.

He stirred and grabbed her tighter as his mind cleared the dreams and he could focus on her face. "I fell asleep," he said, closing his eyes again after having identified her.

"You did. I did, too," she said quietly.

"What time is it?" he asked her sleepily.

"I can't read an apocalypse clock," she reminded him as she ran her hand down his back.

He leaned into her and kissed her, running his right hand down her side and up again to the back of her head. "I want you," he said between kisses.

"I want you, too," she told him.

They were kissing and he was pulling her against him and he said, "You'd agree to fuck right here with the door open, wouldn't you?"

"Well, I think there's a possibility we could be discreet," she said optimistically.

He smiled and laughed. "Ughhh, God. No. I want to. But no. Tonight in our new room. Yeah. Over and over."

He moved her under his body and positioned himself on top of her between her legs. They kissed for a few minutes and Lev moved himself back and forth on top of her pushing his erection against her while she pulled him down onto her.

"Fuck. I gotta stop," he groaned, moving off of her.

He sat up and rubbed his face with both of his hands and turned to look over at her as she slowly sat up beside him.

"You're so fucking hot," he said and kissed her cheek.

"Right now I'm annoyingly hot and frustrated," she said, scoffing at his compliment with a small smile.

Lev got up and looked out the window. "It's before noon. Wait. I just remembered the thing about Time and my mom." He appeared to shake off the thought and said, "We have to get ourselves together and bring the tech down to the RTs."

"Babe, can we eat first?" she asked him as she stood up and stretched her body to work out the residual sleepiness that lingered.

"Yeah. Let's do that. I'm hungry, too. I'll find someone in the hallway to get us food. I'll get a shower, too." He walked out of the room and came back saying, "Fuck it. I'll walk down and order it and have it sent up. Oh, wait. Hey, Ramon, you busy? I need a favor...." Lev came back into the room and said, "Shower now. How can you stand me? I'm filthy?"

"I like you spicy," she said as he walked by her.

Lev laughed and disagreed saying, "No, it's not right. Out in a few."

Kali went and drank some of the cold chicory from earlier in the morning. Lev's shower was quick, and he walked out naked and headed to his closet to get clean clothes.

She looked at him with raised eyebrows. "But we can't have sex?"

"No. It's different," he said, in a mock authoritative tone.

Kali squinted at him saying, "Ok. If you say so. Nice ass."

"I know," he said as he quickly got dressed.

He walked over to her as he put on his clean shirt and kissed her. "I'm gonna give the delivery person the breakfast dishes. I've got to remember to tell James his kitchen crew has been really great while he's been recovering."

"Speaking of James…." Kali told him about being locked out of the basement ward earlier and how James and Ace had shown up and gotten her back inside.

"I was worried you weren't coming back."

"I was trying. Anyway, James was talking about him and Bolin stopping by tonight with wine. I thought it would be a good time to give Bolin his strings."

"Sure, but… You know…? I want you."

"I want you, too. I'll taste his wine. Not an issue."

"I don't understand. Why don't you get all horny when you're drunk?"

"I do! It's just impossible to have an orgasm for some reason. So fucking frustrating. I don't like to set myself up for not finishing."

Lev laughed and grimaced at the same time saying, "Yeah, that's not good."

"No. It's bullshit. I know my limits," she agreed while also assuring him she fully intended to have sex with him.

Their food arrived quickly, and they ate at the small table.

"Did you hear gunshots yet?" he asked her.

"No."

"They should have done it by now. Maybe they cut their throats," he suggested.

"Oh, that's an option?" she asked, surprised.

"Yeah. Borders on torture. I can't lie. Bullet to the head is quicker."

"Lev, fuck them. People I know are in torture right now. Hundreds of years of it, too. I'm sure they'd rather have their throats cut. And still they won't break and tell Bas that Rollo is the leader of the opposition. You should know, Rollo works as Bas's main advisor. They're with each other every day. Bas has been searching for the leader of the opposition for decades and, the whole time, he's been standing right there next to him."

Lev looked startled. "Well, fuck. Really?"

"Yeah, and… You know what I am to Bas, right?" she asked, looking concerned.

"Yeah, baby. I know. You don't have to say it."

Kali moved her head involuntarily in what looked like a twitch. She said nothing and stared across the room not looking at him.

Lev reached across the table and grabbed her arm saying, "Hey. Stop. It's ok. Don't think about it."

She closed her eyes and lifted her chin a little and Lev watched her breathe, trying to calm herself down.

"I'm fine," she said, opening her eyes.

"Can you finish what you were going to say, or no?" he asked her.

Kali turned to face Lev, telling him with authority, "Rollo is right there every day with Bas, and so am I. He might have figured out how to control Time, and destroy civilization, and make himself immortal, but he's a fucking idiot clown. Too stupid to see the two people he keeps near him night and day are his worst enemies."

"He's immortal?" Lev looked overwhelmed at the thought.

"What's the point of controlling a being like Time if you're not going to make yourself immortal?" Kali laughed. "I mean, his lifespan is endless. But he can be killed. He stopped aging at the age of 28. He's healthy. He's not going to die of some disease. He can die from a bullet, though. He can die plenty of ways."

Lev looked at Kali with a serious expression and put his hand on hers. "Listen, I'm not ignoring what you just told me and what just happened. I'm trying to… not be the reason you keep thinking about it. I'm only saying this so you know I'm not ignoring what just happened. There's nothing about what you've been forced to do that changes how I feel about you. If you tell me nothing, or if you tell me everything, not gonna change how I see you, and how I feel about you. I don't need protection from your personal narrative. I'm not waiting for you to tell me anything. I'm not opposed to hearing it all. I've never had a conversation like this. If I'm fucking it up, let me know."

Kali smiled at him. "You're not fucking it up," she said quietly.

"You want to tell me how you two have been successful?" he asked optimistically in an effort to change the conversation.

"Yeah! Rollo and I aligned with his enemy. That took so long. She didn't trust us. There were three of them who started this. One was Bas, the other was a woman named Pele, and the third person was Pele's brother, Jorge. Pele and Jorge broke away from Bas when he decided to kill everyone, but Jorge got captured. Now, Pele is trying to take down Bas and rescue her brother. Shit like this makes me think the stories of the Greek gods are actually true accounts of actual events. So much myth-making going on with these three."

Lev was silent. He was confused and considered what to say. "You and Vespry aligned with Pele?"

"Yeah. For the longest time, she thought Rollo was fucking around with her about wanting to take down Bas, but finally, she came around. I don't know what he did to finally convince her we were really traitors to Bas. But she came around in a big way suddenly. She controls 33 percent of Time."

"What?" asked Lev.

"Bas got Jorge's 33 percent. Made him so fucking powerful."

"Kali, I can't keep up."

"It's a lot. But, you asked about mine and Rollo's successes and getting Pele to trust us was huge. Game changer, man."

"You and Rollo? You keep saying you and Rollo. How big is the opposition?"

Kali stared at Lev and grimaced. "It's small."

"How small?"

"It's bad over there, Lev."

He tipped his head and looked at her. "How small?"

"Starting with the good news... With Pele's army we're a million strong."

Lev waited. "Kali, how small?"

Kali laughed and said, "Oh, fuck." She sighed and looked at Lev with a big nervous smile.

Lev waited.

"Ok, so twice now, the opposition has been wiped out. Imprisoned in time cells and some were killed. There's probably a hundred of them being tortured right now. They count. They're not dead. They're keeping Rollo's identity secret. They're part of the opposition. Don't discount them. No one knows about me. I'm a secret. Only Rollo knows about me. Pele probably doesn't even know who I am. She's only dealt with Rollo, but maybe she knows. Wait. Time knows about me. But, not even the captured know about me. All these fucking people here know about me, but no one knows my real name. We worked hard and got our numbers up again. So, we're at 17 people in Bas's Kingdom."

"Oh, my fucking God," Lev said quietly, sitting back in his chair suddenly.

"That number doesn't even include Time," Kali said, sounding positive.

"Jesus! Time's counted as one of the opposition?" Lev asked.

"Yeah. Time does what Time can under the circumstances. I think it's safe to say, you didn't find all of your research scientists just accidently left alive locally after Bas intended to end most everyone. Just like the Ivy 11. I can't confirm my suspicion, but I'm still 100 percent positive that Time excluded your Campus RT members from Bas's extinction and hoped, just fucking hoped, you'd all find each other. Design, you know? Thank goodness you were looking, Lev. Time must have looked at the strands of Marina Patel's son. You'd all still be scattered in the wind if a leader like you hadn't come along thinking about getting everyone together to figure out what was going on. Still, it was up to you. Time can't control outcomes, but Time's an excellent team player in the opposition."

Lev threw his head back and laughed loudly and sat up looking at Kali, stunned.

"17 people, plus Time?! You really are crazy! And baby, I mean that in the nicest possible way. You're fucking nuts!" he laughed loudly and took her hand.

"I know!" she laughed with him..

"How have you stayed a secret?" he asked as he shook his head at her, still laughing.

"Rollo's always been adamant about keeping my role in the opposition secret. He's killed loyal people who've figured me out. He won't have it. I don't really understand what's motivating him to keep me a secret, but he's killed good people we probably needed. Everyone in torture has gone in knowing Rollo's name. None have gone in knowing mine. But Rollo would go to torture forever and not reveal my name.

"Whenever I get caught doing something, Bas just assumes I was trying to escape or I'm trying to win favor with the opposition. He doesn't think I'm smart enough to be part of a group working to get rid of him."

"The obvious question would be--"

Kali interrupted Lev. "No. It's not like that between us. We're family. There's not an emotion to describe what we are to each other. He's my family."

Lev stopped laughing and looked at her. "Will you be *my* family?" He dragged his chair beside hers at the table and said, "I want that. Do you?"

Someone came to the door before Kali could respond.

Dave and Lev

"Knock, knock," Dave said as he stood in the open doorway.

"Hey, what's up?" Lev asked him, getting up and walking over to him.

"It's all done. Traitors went down all at once."

"Nice. I didn't hear gunshots."

"Our man Bolin wasn't in the mood for the ease of a bullet. Seems he was more than a little pissed off about their plan to get rid of you, and equally pissed off about some of the plans they had for Kali. Hey, Kali," Dave said with a nod of his head in her direction. "Bolin wanted their throats cut. He personally cut Jim's throat. Wind's blowing away from the building, so the burn smoke isn't reminding everyone what happened earlier. Aisha's having Community News spoken at each meal. Lunch crowd's getting the first edition from her as we speak, dinner will get the second. Community will know by tonight who's in charge and that the Ivy RT has been executed for treason against you. Anyone who tries to flee will meet Campus patrols in the woods. No one at Ivy's been warned. The Campus patrol in the woods is waiting for runners. Let them run. Weed out the people that aren't loyal."

"Agreed. Thanks for talking with Kali earlier. Whatever you said to her, helped a lot."

"Yeah. You two already go get the hidden tech?"

"Wasn't necessary after all. She used a feature on the tech she's using to hide the tech she brought us, to hide the hiding tech. Now I sound confusing like her. Anyway, turns out, it was here all along. Wait until you see this stuff. She's also been telling me about Vespry and Bas, among other things." He shook his head and said, "We're gonna need to be really prepared and equally clever because we're seriously outnumbered."

"Should we be worried?" asked Dave, frowning.

"Yeah. This guy's way ahead of us."

Lev's expression was hard and Dave said, "Alright then."

Lev and Dave discussed who should attend the leadership meeting the following day and agreed on a list of people from Campus and Ivy who should disseminate the information about Bas and the fight they were all in against him.

After nearly 20 years, the survivors of Bas's extinction event were finally going to learn his name and his intentions for them. They wanted to choose calm, articulate leaders who could impart the information to the community clearly.

"I want to ask you to be an RT leader, but I don't know if you want to take that on along with Head of Security," Lev said to Dave after they'd decided who would attend the leadership meeting.

"I want that role." Dave nodded.

Lev said, "After that bullshit with Ivy, I don't want another insular group that develops its own agenda and has its own talking points."

Dave nodded in agreement and said, "Yeah, that's a good idea. We need to get about 700 community members informed about what's going on here. No more secrets. Two communities, one mission. We killed fifty percent of the people who came into Campus for a reason. We have excellent people we can trust."

Lev agreed. "The Campus community already has a much bigger foundation to build on. Getting the Ivy community up to speed with reality might pose the bigger problem but there are less than 200 community members here." Lev's face darkened and he added, "We'll, start killing again if we have to. We don't have time for bullshit. We have to get to work."

"Agreed," said Dave without a hint of reservation.

"Downstairs in 10 minutes?" Lev asked.

"Yeah."

Time, the Tech, and the RTs

It was still early in the afternoon when Lev and Kali returned to the meeting room containing the RT Lev had assembled over the years. There were 74 RT members left including Dave and Lev. Aisha and Bolin were also present. The room had been quiet when they'd entered and remained quiet as they took their seats. Lev asked Dave and Aisha, "Everyone here, ready?" Both nodded at him and he scanned the faces of his new RT minus Ivy RT members. It was a relief to have them gone.

"Let's start. Whenever you're ready," he said, looking at Kali.

Kali turned in her chair to face the RT. "Before I explain the tech I brought you, I think it'll help to explain to you about my friend Time. You're all familiar with time as you understand it because of what you do, but there's another type of time. The Time I know is a Time that controls the lifespans of all living organisms Time is observing. That Time is a sentient being from a race of beings that inhabit the Universe. They live symbiotically with other living beings they encounter. They're born, they live, they die. They live a long time, but they're not immortal, because they have a lifespan, too. This is the Time I'm friends with.

"Bas is powerful because he took control of the Time on Earth. He bound Time and caused the extinction event. Rollo Vespry and I are working with Time to help free Time and get rid of Bas. Also, this is just a personal quirk of Time, but Time doesn't like to be referred to with pronouns. Unless I'm telling you about the species, I'm going to avoid using pronouns as best I can. Even though Time is bound, Time is still here with us, and I want to be respectful of Time's preferences. You should be, too."

Kali looked at the RT and then continued. "Earth has a member of the Time species because Earth has living organisms. Even before humans came along, Time was here on Earth assigning lifespans to the living organisms on this planet, helping life to evolve. Even one tiny living organism on a planet or a moon, or whatever, is enough for a member of the Time species to arrive and assist and nurture life to evolve. The species is peaceful and kind. They're like scientists, similar to all of you, except a lot more benevolent. They don't have an army, they don't wage wars. They're friendly, supportive, curious, inquisitive, helpful observers of life in the Universe. Their purpose is to help life in the Universe evolve in positive ways.

"As far as I've been told, all life in the Universe has a lifespan dictated by a member of the Time species. Trees, plankton, bacteria, don't ask me about viruses, people, cats, you know, all living things on Earth and in the Universe. Sometimes Time see that it would benefit the evolution of a species to have a shorter lifespan. Other times, a longer lifespan is deemed best. Sometimes it's something in the environment that Time uses to determine the lifespan of an organism. Time doesn't kill people in a murderous way, but Time did put an expiration date on us. But this isn't just about your physical body that you see.

"Think of Time as a part of the process of evolution for both your body and your mind. Your body is important here, and it can evolve in positive ways, but your consciousness is really who you are, not the body you currently inhabit. If people lived here forever after they were born, would they be better off? We used to have a longer lifespan, and Time told me people weren't better off for it. Our bodies lasted longer, but our minds wanted something else we couldn't get here. And now I'm gonna tell you about that something else."

Kali looked at the Research Team and took a breath. "After you die, your consciousness moves on to where it can continue to evolve. Where we move on to, there's another type of Time. I call it Death Time, but feel free to come up with a better name for them. I'm not very creative that way. It's a scary name, but don't think of Death Time as scary. Our Time told me that Death Time deal with destructive consciousnesses of species like ours throughout the Universe. Higher-level thinking organisms with extended consciousnesses sometimes have to be dealt with. Plants, animals, bacteria, shit like that doesn't factor in here. Think of intentional actions that are destructive like you'd expect from a sociopath or a psychopath.

"In the case of humans on earth, this would be bad people who don't have empathy or kindness. Time says they don't evolve properly. Their consciousnesses are incapable of evolving in a positive way. When they die, they move on to where Death Time deals with them. And when I asked Time to be more specific about how

Death Time deals with destructive higher-level thinking consciousnesses, Time didn't elaborate. Time just assured me they're no longer a problem. So, when I told you Time doesn't get pissed off at us and murder us for being assholes, I'm not exactly sure about the nature of the Death Time we'll be meeting after we die. I'm not afraid, though.

"Here's the thing, Bas doesn't know about Death Time. That's an advantage we have. He already doesn't want to die here because he likes living here and wants to keep his power here, but if he learned about Death Time, I know he'd try even harder to accomplish the goals he's working on now. Any questions?" Kali asked.

Everyone in the room except Lev and Dave raised a hand, and Kali sighed loudly.

Kali turned to Bolin. "What's your question?" she asked him.

"How did this, Bas killing everyone happen? Can't Time see into the future?"

"Did anyone else have this question?" asked Kali.

Again, everyone in the room raised a hand except Lev and Dave, and Kali said, "Alright. No member of the Time species can see into the future. I don't know about Death Time. What Time can do is split a second, I guess forever, if Time lived forever, and make predictions based on potential outcomes. Makes it seem like Time can tell the future, but Time cannot. Think of people who are really good at chess, but apply that to a consciousness as big as Time's.

"I'll give you an example. You're all alive here. Think of all the people who died when Bas ended their lifespans. He actually meant to kill everyone. Time convinced him that the environment would recover more quickly if he left some survivors. Said the human species would be stronger with more diversity, too. He allowed a small number of survivors, thinking he could cull from them later, but he got pissed off one day and ordered a second wave of extinctions which you probably didn't even notice because you lost so many in the first wave.

"But here you are. How did all of you, who just happen to be scientists, people who could potentially help to free Time and get rid of Bas, survive his extinction events? Only the people in locked spaces were completely safe. More about that later. Remind me if I forget," she said looking at Lev.

He nodded.

"I'm gonna use common sense here, not math, and say there's a 100% likelihood that Time was involved in preventing Bas from killing you and hoping like hell you'd find each other. Same with Rollo's 11 at Ivy. I know for a fact that he had a list of names and worked with Time to keep them from Bas's extinction. Doesn't mean you couldn't die accidently, or some other way. Just meant Bas didn't get you first.

"Seeing all of you here, I'm 100% common sense positive Time saved you and hoped for the best after reviewing potential outcomes by splitting a second. Each of you should consider that you were personally chosen by Time to help in this fight. Especially when I show you some of this tech I brought for you and you feel tempted to fuck off into the past or tap into your own megalomania like Bas did. Just stay cool. You were chosen to help not add to the problems we already have. You don't want to meet Death Time on bad terms," she said, shaking her head in exasperation.

"Here's another example for you. Rollo was contacted by Time to work with Time when he was 16 years old. Time told Rollo that after looking at all the possible strands of potential partners, the one where Time worked with Rollo had the best chance for success. You hear what I'm saying? It's a chance. Not a guaranteed outcome. We have to fight for it. Rollo agreed to work with Time all those years ago on the chance that he could help get rid of Bas. You're all part of that chance that we have. So far, Bas is kicking our asses. We really need to rally.

"Here's another example for you. I had the best likelihood of surviving bringing you the tech we wanted you to have. Time said I might die, but my chances for success were better than Rollo's. No outcome Time saw where Rollo brought you the tech himself, led to success. He died in every possible outcome. You never got the Tech. None of us knows the future, though. Rollo could have survived. He could have made a decision that saved himself, or someone here could have made a choice Time couldn't predict. Bolin could have *shot* me when I walked up here that morning. He *wanted* to. Time didn't know if he would or not," she said adamantly, and turned and smiled at Bolin.

Bolin raised his eyebrows and said nothing.

"I need to clear something up with you all. I've heard some comments about the future, but I'm not from the future. I'm from the present. A locked present, but lowercase time still moves the same there. As far as I know, there's no way to travel to the future using what Time knows. Bas doesn't travel to the future. He can't. The past, though, that's accessible. Think of the past as a shadow, though. You have the past and the present, that's it. Some of you might have heard that I've been locked in torture for years, and it's true. I have been. That's not going to the future. That's a torture device that uses formulas to alter your experience of time. The kind of time you know, not the species Time. Your consciousness feels every second of it.

"I was locked in torture for five years one time, but when I was released, only a few hours had passed. I could have been in torture for one minute and experienced five years, but Bas told them to leave me in for a few hours while he took a nap, got a shower, had some dinner, you know. My mind was five years older, but my body wasn't, and he had had a nap and something to eat and was ready to punish me personally for something I felt like I'd done five years earlier. It really fucks with you. But, there's no access to the future using any formula known to Time as far as I know. I don't think Time's holding out on us. The present is as far as Time goes, too."

Kali stopped talking, giving the RT time to digest what she'd told them.

"Any questions, now?" she asked, and everyone raised a hand except Lev and Dave.

"Aisha? What do you want to know?" Kali asked her.

"How did Bas kill people using Time?"

"Bas bound Time using formulas the same way we'd use chains on a person to bind them. He captured parts of Time's consciousness because Time doesn't have a physical body like ours. Time's consciousness is huge though. Some of Time is still free, but important aspects of Time are bound. Bas is exploiting Time's abilities. He used the formula for human lifespans to suddenly end the lives of all the people he killed during that first extinction event. He only targeted humans. He could have killed all the trees if he had wanted to. All the mosquitoes. It's just formulas. Math and physics. Math you don't know yet, physics you don't know, but I've brought most all of it to you in the recipe book.

"He used Time's formulas to establish a personal lifespan to make himself immortal. He has an endless lifespan right now, so it's not immortality like a truly immortal being. Time isn't even immortal. He stopped his aging process at the age of 28, but he's in his 70s. He's healthy. His cells aren't creating cancer. He can be killed, though. But there's tech that can help him avoid death. He's actually been killed a few times. But he's got tech they created called a Rewind that brings him back. I brought you one. I'll explain how it works when I show it to you. Did I answer your question, Aisha?" Kali asked her.

"So, Bas doesn't even need Time to change the lifespans of people anymore because he knows Time's formulas?" Aisha asked, looking confused.

"Yeah. Anything he figures out, he can make happen without Time's assistance. He's fucking persistent. When I met the Ivy RT, I was really upset because they didn't have the same fire Bas and his team have. It's a fucking cult over there. He's insane and they fucking love him. They'd die for him. They do die for him. I mean, you've seen what this guy is capable of right outside this room. They're also doing things Time would never dream of now that they understand the physics and math used by Time. I want to tell you some more things. Did I answer your question, though?"

"Yeah, but you also said you brought us tech that can rewind a dead person," Aisha said with a shocked expression on her face.

The rest of the RT agreed with Aisha.

Several people raised their hands to speak, but Kali said, "You know what? I thought of some important stuff you need to know when I told you Bas's people are working on things Time doesn't even do. I wanna tell you some of that first before you ask more questions. I'll tell you about the Rewinds when I show you the one I brought you.

"I told you Bas can torture you for extended periods of time with his formulas and that your mind ages, but your body doesn't, but you should know he can also age your body. Rollo used to be a year younger than me, but he's about 15 years older than me now. Bas aged his physical body to punish him one time. That's not something Time can do. That's not something Time would do because it goes against natural evolution processes. Time isn't about that at all. Bas figured that out.

He's building on what he's learned.

"When you guys get this tech from me and open the recipe book and start looking at the new math, the new physics, the discoveries they've made, you can't sit and contemplate it for years and find out, you know….Why? What does this mean for us, for our religious beliefs, for the environment? You know? Fuck all that. You just have to accept it and move forward immediately. You're gonna see where they're at. See what they're working on. You'll see what they know, what they can do with what they know, what they want to know, and why they want to know it. Trust me, they have no good intentions. There's no time for distractions. The last few pages in the recipe book are things they're working on now. Rollo made you a list.

"The first thing on the list he made you has to do with consciousness. This is really important and very scary. First of all, you have to know that consciousness is a state of matter."

Kali sat back in her chair and scowled as the RT all started to talk quietly about her statement.

"See, this is what I meant when I told you to accept shit and move on quickly. Just accept it. You actually have recipes in the book for this because some of the tech I brought you plugs right the fuck into your consciousness, and some of it's for traveling. You ready now?" She looked around the room at the RT to assess their readiness, but everyone had gone silent the moment she had begun to scold them, so she sat back up and started again.

"You can't move things through time or space without moving the consciousness, too. It's separate and requires a separate universal formula. The formula is the same for every person, but you gotta account for that in the formulas. If you don't, the person will die. You'll move the physical body, but not the consciousness. Travel tech depends on you accepting what I just told you.

"That being said, understand this, consciousness can't be destroyed. Death here on earth transforms it. Remember Death Time plays a role in dealing with the bad consciousnesses that move on from here, and I trust Time when Time says bad consciousnesses are taken care of by Death Time, but for regular people, even after death, we're each still the operator of our own consciousness. That consciousness lives in the present of a new place that's appropriate for the transformed version of you.

"Some of the tech you'll create will be tied to the unique consciousness of its personal operator. Operator tech is different from traveling tech. That's important. That means some secrets can die with an operator. Information you don't want Bas to get ahold of. Even after death, you're still the operator of the information on operator tech.

"Bas is working on being able to access and control your consciousness in this life. That's not good. But here's something worse. Bas is trying to access the consciousnesses of people who have died. People who serve him? He already knows their secrets. They took nothing to the grave with them that he doesn't already know. He wants the secrets of people who oppose him. Discoveries they've hidden from him to keep power from him. I'll read you what Rollo wants you to know."

Kali reached into the backpack she'd brought to the meeting and pulled out the recipe book. "This is the recipe book. We call it a recipe book, not just because we think we're funny, but calling it that meant we didn't draw suspicion to our conversations. See, Rollo likes to cook. He pretended he was teaching me how to cook, but he wasn't. He'd come over in the evenings and Bas would be doing whatever bullshit he was doing, and Rollo and I could build on these so-called recipes with intel we and others had gathered while Rollo cooked an actual meal and I pretended to learn how to cook. Bas let us hang out in the kitchen for hours cooking, never once looking at our recipe book."

If Kali had been looking up and not flipping through the recipe book, she would have seen Dave catch Lev's attention and close his eyes and mouth an exasperated, "What?!" and then seen Lev who mouthed back, "I know!" with a silent, nervous laugh.

Kali turned to the back of the book.

"This page is titled, 'Some of the Things Bas is Working on Right Now.' There are 29 very scary things he's working on. Here's the first one. One. Is consciousness from the past able to be captured if you can find it in its present? Can the past be changed if you control a present consciousness alive or after death?"

Kali looked at them with a stony expression. "Let me tell you what this means. Currently, no attempts to change the past have worked. I told you travel to the past is possible. I've done it thousands of times as Bas's hostage. But when you visit the past, you're visiting a time that no longer fully exists. It exists in …. I don't know…The creative consciousness of the Universe, is maybe the way to describe how the past exists. I call it a shadow. But the people you see in the past, their consciousnesses have all moved on to their current present.

"Here's a fact. You can't go back in time and kill baby Bas in his crib. He exists. His consciousness is here in the present. You can't go back in time and find your dead friends and bring them back here. Those people are already dead. The dead live, actually live, in their new present.

"But you can order a meal in the past. You can talk to people. You can get your hair done. Lots of things. It's just different. The present, no matter where you experience it, is different from the past. Time told me the present of the dead keeps time with our present. We're all still alive. Just alive differently in different places.

"Bas wants to find the consciousnesses of the dead in their new present to see if he can change the past, among other things. He's experimenting on Jorge's people who are alive now. I know I've gotta tell you about Jorge. In a minute, because the point I'm trying to make is important. Bas is trying to control present consciousness and bring it back to the past to change things he wants changed. If he figures that out, he's going after the consciousnesses of the dead in their present.

"The scientist who discovered Time and made contact with Time first, was named Marina Patel."

There was some quiet talking among the RT and Dave and Aisha looked over at Lev.

"Yeah, that's my mom she's talking about. I just learned about this. I'm just as surprised," he said to them all, confirming the chatter.

Kali continued. "Bas, and two others named Pele and Jorge discovered the work of Marina Patel long after she'd left... science. There's a lot of information in between, but to make my point about consciousness and Bas's intentions, he's gone back in time and tried to kill Marina Patel, Pele, and Jorge a bunch of times. He has his reasons. All those reasons amount to him becoming even more powerful in the present. But no matter how many times he went to the past and killed them, they never died. Their consciousnesses exist in the present. There's no grandfather paradox. The Universe is creative and restores what was and maintains the present. Marina Patel is deceased and alive in the afterlife present, Pele is alive in this present, and Jorge is alive in torture in this present.

"If Bas can figure out how to capture present consciousness, alive or dead, he's gonna be able to control two present worlds. I guess he'll eventually be able to control the past, too. I'm not sure if the Universe will be able to restore what he changes in the past at that point. In any case, he'll probably be able to bind people like Marina Patel and force her to work for him even in her present. The present where she currently lives now, now that she's deceased from this world."

Kali looked at Lev. They all did.

"I'm ready for a break," Lev said, getting up from his seat. He looked at Kali. "Come with me," he said flatly. "Aisha, give me 10... fucking 20 minutes," he said as he grabbed Kali's hand and walked out the door with her.

Lev and Kali and Consciousness

Lev walked silently with Kali into the meeting room down the hall and shut the door.

Kali looked at the closed door and Lev said, "I wasn't thinking. Let's go outside."

They left the room and walked through the halls and cafeteria quickly and sat next to each other on a bench at a picnic table outside. Lev shook his head and didn't look at her.

"You mad?" she asked him unapologetically.

"At you? No. For what? Telling me what's going on? You're not doing it. You're not killing my mother in the past and hunting for her in the afterlife. Jesus fuck that's fucking nuts," he said. "I don't even know what the fuck to do with that information!" he said, throwing up his arms and beginning to yell.

"What you do with that information is what you have been doing for years. Find a way to kill Bas. Figure this out. I can't. Maybe I brought you something that can help you stop him. Look what you've done already. You have a team. You're their leader. I believe in you. You can--"

"You believe in me?" he asked her, turning to look at her.

"Yeah, I do. Even if you fail. I know you're trying just like I am. I could have failed to bring you this tech. We wouldn't even be having this conversation. You guys could have shot me that morning. Even Time didn't know if I'd make it here. We're all doing the best we can."

"I don't like the fail part." He laughed.

"Me, either. Hopefully you won't. But there are no guarantees. It only matters that we're doing our best. Ivy's RT wasn't up to this task. Hopefully, we are. You say your RT inside is, too."

Lev was quiet.

Kali turned to him and bent her arm around his. "Bas wants to go to the past with the present consciousness of the deceased and see if he can kill or capture and torture people from earlier vantage points."

"Give me a minute to figure out what that means," he said, looking away from her. Kali waited and gave him the time he needed to consider what she had said.

"Bring back the consciousness of a deceased person like my mother, be able to abduct her or control her from a younger age?" he asked.

"Yeah, Lev. I don't know what that would mean. He's an insane and cruel person with insane and cruel ideas. Currently, you can't change the present by fucking with the past. Like I said, there's no grandfather paradox at play. He hasn't been able to change a damn thing in any meaningful way. He can't even go to the past to spy on the opposition. It would alter too much that presently exists. When he's tried, he's been prevented. But he's trying to figure it out. Then he'd see what Rollo and I have been doing! I don't know what he could do with the past. Maybe he could make it so you don't exist. I don't know if the Universe would stop him. You have a consciousness. You're here. I don't know if you can be erased by Bas. Right now, my understanding is that only Death Time can do that to a consciousness. I just know Bas is working on bringing the consciousnesses of the living and the dead back to the past. That's something he wants to do.

"I'm fairly positive he can fuck with the afterlife and the deceased if he figures out how to get ahold of their consciousnesses in their present. That I'm sure about. Time said the deceased are in the present. Not the past. Not the future. So, that's bad. He can get to them if he can figure out how. And he's trying. He wants to rule the living consciousnesses of the dead. Two worlds. Ruining this one wasn't enough for him. But I'm not sure what he can do with the past. I don't want to find out. He needs to be stopped."

"Alright. So we only have to worry about the deceased in their present and the living in this present for now. He definitely can't fuck with the past and change the present?" Lev asked her.

"Small changes. You can go back in time and give your five year old self an ice cream cone. You can try lots of smaller things, and from what I've heard, the

Universe lets those things happen. But the killing, the stopping yourself from being paralyzed, even your dog from getting hit by a car... transformational things that alter who you, or someone else becomes in the present, those things are never successful. That's why he hasn't figured out who the members of the opposition are. I don't know if Bas can be successful in the past, but I know he's working on it. I'm also convinced he can figure out how to get to the deceased in their present. I know some of the dead, too. I'm afraid for them. I want to go there and warn them. Maybe hide with them," she said, looking at Lev.

"Yeah. And all of us. We're all going to be dead someday. I'd like some peace in the afterlife," he said.

"He'll never leave me alone. I don't know what it's like over there, but maybe I could get a head start," Kali said in a haunted tone that unsettled Lev.

He took his arm from hers and turned to her, putting both of his arms around her.

"I'm going to do everything I can to figure out how to stop him and get him sent over to Death Time. I'm more motivated to stop him than he is to do whatever the fuck he's trying to do," he said, looking at her.

"Ok," Kali said.

But Lev saw the fear in her eyes and realized he'd underestimated the ambitions of the enemy.

A Day Trip Away

Lev figured they had a few more minutes to spare until they should head back into the meeting and wanted to get Kali's mind off of the conversation they'd just been having after seeing how frightened it had made her. She might not be ready to start talking to the RT again, otherwise.

"You asked me to remind you about something... locked spaces. You gonna talk about that next?" he asked her, hoping that locked spaces were a less emotionally charged topic for her to cover.

"Yeah, I guess we can move on to that."

"Yeah, what's it about? Want to give me a head start?" he asked her, hoping he was helping to orient her to the new topic.

"It's something that all Time can do that Bas figured out how to do right at the beginning. It's supposed to help Time with encouraging evolution, but Bas used it to hide himself so that he could consolidate his power, build his Kingdom. Time can bend space around places. Bas doesn't need Time to accomplish this. So, Bas's Kingdom.... It's hidden. He's got space bent around his entire Kingdom and it's locked. You can't see it. If you walk up to it, your perception will tell you you're walking in a straight line, but you're really walking around a huge curve in space around the place he's hidden using Time's formulas. You won't feel it or notice it. If you can locate a hidden space, dropping bombs on it forever won't penetrate the space. There's currently no technology that can discover a hidden space or detect an anomaly that might indicate hidden space is present. Finding hidden spaces isn't nearly as important as discovering how to unlock Bas's Kingdom. When I escaped the walls of Bas's Kingdom to come find Ivy, it only took me about five hours to ride from Bas's mansion to where I hid the tech."

Lev suddenly shook his head and inhaled deeply while abruptly getting up from the bench they were sitting on. He started to walk away, but turned around and sat back down next to Kali. He looked at her with shock on his face and alarm in his voice asking her loudly, "You've been five hours from here all this time?! Five hours from me?!"

Kali shook her head no. "You forgot to add the distance I had to walk here, too. That would add some time."

Lev leaned his head forward towards the picnic table with his eyes closed and grabbed Kali's hand.

Kali let him pull her closer and put her other hand on top of the one he was using to hold her hand. "Lev--"

"I need a minute," he said quietly, but he didn't wait a minute. He sat up and looked at her in disbelief. "This motherfucker is a day's drive from here?" he asked her.

"Yeah," she said, nodding at him. "The whole walk to get the tech, we were just getting closer to him. It had me a little on edge, to be honest," she said.

Lev turned his body towards hers. "Come here," he said, pulling her closer, burying his head in her hair next to her face.

Kali hugged Lev and said, "You need to figure out how to unlock his Kingdom. Pele can't get in even after years of trying. Maybe you and your team can figure it out."

Lev kept hugging her and said, "Babe, I can't talk business right now. I just need to hug the fucking hell out of you and process what I just learned. For fuck's sake. Give me a fucking minute."

Kali started to laugh and Lev joined her in laughing while pulling away from her and holding her face in both of his hands.

"You keep rattling me with crazy information you have. Is there an end? Because I'm afraid of what's next," he asked her seriously.

Kali looked at Lev with a very sympathetic expression while he held her face and said, "It's still early. It might get crazier."

Lev smiled and nodded and said, "Fine. Let's get to it then. You said hidden spaces can't be discovered. Do you know the coordinates for his Kingdom in case you get taken? I want to be able to try to find you at least," he said to her.

"Yeah. First he hid Wayne National Forest in Ohio, but just before the extinction event, the whole state of Ohio. He spared a couple million people in Ohio randomly. They became his cult. He had a city built in Wayne National Forest, though. That's where his mansion is. And his government," she explained.

Lev stared at her and opened his mouth to speak, but then closed it again.

They looked at each other and Kali went to speak, but he shook his head no and closed his eyes and inhaled deeply.

"Babe. I'm gonna find that asshole and I'm gonna kill him for you. I'm gonna get Pele inside. I'm gonna do whatever it takes. Do you hear me?"

Kali nodded.

"I mean it. Whatever it takes. I'm gonna kill this son of a bitch. Can you deal with me having this as my fucking mission? It's gonna be my obsession," he said to her.

"Yeah. I'll help you," she said.

Lev sat up straight and turned to look at her. "I pictured you being kept in Australia. I guess because of the shampoo. I thought you were gonna say Bas's Kingdom is in Australia, and I was gonna have to build a fucking boat to come find you if he took you," he said, shaking his head in wonder.

Kali smiled and shook her head. "No nautical skills required. But, we were in that hotel in Australia the night I headed here."

"How'd you get from Australia to Ohio without him catching you?" Lev asked her, but he suddenly looked over her shoulder and said, "Hold on, baby. Hey, what's up?"

Dave was walking up to them and nodded at Kali. "Aisha wants to know if you need more time. Everyone's got questions," he said in his usual casual tone.

Lev looked at Kali and then back at Dave and said, "Yeah, Kali's telling me something pretty interesting right now. Why don't I hear the rest of this first, then we'll head back in. Maybe organize the questions the team has before we get back. Make it easier. Remind them to leave the science to us. Ten minutes enough?" he asked Kali.

"Yeah."

"Another ten. It has to do with the nuclear power plants," he said to Dave.

"There're no nuclear power plants in this story," she said with certainty.

Lev was looking at her and then up at Dave, so Kali turned to look at Dave, as well. She watched as the left side of Dave's mouth suddenly curved upwards in the unaccustomed shape of a smile.

"Is that so?" Dave asked Lev, raising his eyebrows.

"Yeah, man."

"Ok. See you inside in ten. Gives me a chance to get a cup of whatevercoffee," he said as he turned to leave.

Dave listened as Kali said to Lev, "I mean, yeah they're hidden, that's why the planet isn't a nuclear wasteland, but my story isn't about that exactly."

"I know, but it's related," Dave heard Lev say as he pulled open the door to the cafeteria.

"Tell me the rest. I'll tell you how it relates to what I said to Dave afterwards."

"Ok. So, we were in Australia in the past and he brought me back to Ohio.

Getting me back here required sacrifice," she said with a hint of pride.

"What'd you have to do?" he asked her warily as he reached for her hand.

"I didn't make the sacrifice. 22 people from our group did. We'd worked on the plan for the better part of a year. While Bas and I were in Australia, the 22 kidnapped top members of Bas's research team from their own locked lab and then executed all 12 of them by decapitating them and throwing them through a blown out window of the 24th floor lab. On top of everything else we accomplished that night, Bas's research team took a huge hit."

Lev agreed saying, "We'd be devastated if we lost 12 RT members in a day."

"Mmm-hmm. We were hoping we could slow down their progress. So, Rollo was home and contacted Bas and told him what happened. They agreed that Bas needed to get back right away. It was too catastrophic for him to not come back. I acted all bored by the drama and asked if I could stay in Australia with his security team because I'd just be in the way over there anyway and then he'd have to include killing me and rewinding me on his to-do list. He told me if what Rollo had just told him was accurate, he was gonna want to work out some anger on me, so I had to come back with him."

"I'm gonna kill him," Lev said in hostile frustration.

"I couldn't have done my part if he'd let me stay in Australia. I needed to go back. I only acted like I wanted to stay in Australia. He's kind of easy to manipulate once you know how childish he truly is," Kali said with disgust.

Lev nodded his head silently. He asked her, "So, that's part of why the opposition to Bas has only 17 members? 22 people went to torture to get you here?"

Kali squinted and shook her head no at him saying, "Yeah, but also no. They didn't go to torture. They shot themselves in their heads at the opening of the blasted out window and fell 24 floors to their own deaths. They couldn't be rewound in time. That was the plan. They got to die. That was good. For now, they live in the other present without Bas. I'm sure Bas put lots of his own people into torture for what went down. Honestly, I hope Rollo's ok. I wish I knew."

"How'd you get yourself to Front Royal?" Lev prodded gently, encouraging her to continue the story.

"This was the first time we worked with Pele. She immediately sent a message to Bas saying her first round of spies died willingly and her second round were coming for him personally. He freaked out thinking the 22 were working for Pele and stopped considering it was an inside job. You know? Which it was, except Pele was in on it now that she's working with us. He was really distracted thinking it was all Pele. I was told to stay at home. He went to work with his scientists to investigate how Pele could have broken his lock and gotten people inside, and Rollo was really playing his part, too. Totally improvising. There's a lot of improvisation that goes on in even our best plans," Kali said.

"Yeah, I'm getting that," Lev said, nodding.

"Rollo was covered in blood from personally helping clean up all the bodies.

He had a hundred possible suspects rounded up and sent to cells, waiting to be interrogated. He arrested top people in Bas's administration, powerful people. He summoned all the tech and science people to immediately start looking for traces of Pele in the system. He had all the family members of the traitors rounded up and waiting in cells. Everyone wanted Bas to be calm, so they were telling him how Rollo was on it and not missing a step trying to find more spies who might be working for Pele. Rollo was acting tired from all that he'd been doing and he purposely tripped and fell down a few stairs when he was walking next to Bas telling him what he knew so far. He played it really dramatically. Like he was so worried about Bas and the news of Pele possibly finding a way inside. He was a theater kid, but his parents taking him to Bas's Kingdom ruined that for him. He loves having an opportunity to act," she explained to Lev.

"He told me Bas turned to him and put his Kingly hand on his shoulder and thanked him for all he had done so far and told him to go home, clean up, get some food, and some rest. Meet back in the morning."

Kali laughed out loud at that, and Lev laughed mildly saying with a noticeable hint of concern in his voice, "I'm really glad you two have survived, but between the recipe book and now this, I don't know how you've managed it."

"Babe, I keep telling you. Bas is an idiot. He's just a lucky fucking idiot Clown King. He shouldn't be this powerful," she said, sounding disgusted.

"Well, this doesn't get you into a car and traveling to the kiln shop, yet," he said, trying to encourage her to keep telling him the story.

"Fine. When the 22 had executed Bas's scientists, they had an extra, limited travel passport on them I'd stolen a couple years ago using my optical. They removed the passport of the director because she's known to travel in and out of the Kingdom all the time, and it would have the Kingdom lock codes. They removed her passport from her wrist, put the one I had gotten them on her wrist, and the team leader of the 22 hid her passport in his pocket. The passport I had stolen didn't have the Kingdom lock codes, you see? So, when Rollo was dragging dead bodies around, he dug into the pocket of the opposition team leader and got the director's passport. Babe, it has the code to the lock on Bas's Kingdom! Rollo says it's going to be ungodly encrypted, though. So, we--"

Lev lowered his head a bit and closed his eyes laughing, and interrupted her shouting, "Kali! This is the stuff you mention at the beginning of a story!" He grabbed her shoulders, adding, "Baby, do you have that tech with you? Do you have a passport, or whatever it's called?"

"Yeah, of course I do. How do you think I got outside the Kingdom?!" she said, smiling broadly at him.

"Oh, my God!" Lev looked at her and laughed hard, saying, "The way you tell stories….You're driving me crazy. Just to be clear, because I'm afraid I'm not hearing this great news right… You brought tech that contains the lock code for that fucker's hidden Kingdom?"

"Yeah! No other way to get in or out! Do you want me to finish the story?"

she asked, laughing.

"Please, do," he said still laughing and putting his arm around her for a quick hug before he moved back to stare smiling at her as she finished her story.

"I was going to tell the RT when we went back in, just so you know."

Lev was looking at her with a big smile and shaking his head. "I'm going to figure out his fucking lock code, and I'm going to have a way to find you if you get taken."

Kali nodded and said, "I'll try to wait for you if it happens. I'll try harder than I would have, you know, two weeks ago."

Lev wasn't laughing when he said to her in a serious tone, "Ok. I appreciate that."

Kali continued, "Two years ago, Rollo got himself an electric motorcycle saying he might be able to get out and get to Ivy on it someday. But when we started talking about this plan, me going to Ivy, he snuck his motorcycle over to Bas's garage and we hid it in back of some, you know, garage junk that accumulates. He did that about a week before the Australia trip. It wasn't there long. Bas has a driver. He never goes inside the garage, anyway.

"After Rollo pretended to fall down the stairs and Bas sent him home, he stopped by Bas's mansion on his way to his house and my guards ignored him as usual. He's always stopping by to see Bas or me, so no one questions it. He didn't even come inside, he just stood in the doorway and rambled everything that had happened and told me to go immediately as he handed me the passport."

Kali suddenly inhaled sharply and Lev asked, "You ok?"

"Yeah. I just worry about him. That was the last time I saw him. I emptied my luggage onto the bedroom floor, grabbed the rest of my sandwich, and walked my suitcase to the garage. The guards didn't care. They would never think to offer to help me do anything.

"I got my backpack that was hidden in the garage with my cloaked optical and sat on the motorcycle. Rollo had told me how to use a passport, said if I was sitting on the bike, it would travel with me just like the clothes I was wearing and my backpack. I did what he told me to do, and it fucking worked. I wasn't even sure I was doing it right. I'd never been allowed to use one. I travel by touching a traveler who has a passport. Anyway, it brought me outside of his Kingdom to the real world.

"You know, it was the first time I'd seen the real world since I was 19. He'd only ever taken me to the past. I knew he'd destroyed the world, but I hadn't seen it before, what, two weeks ago? It's really terrible. I drove the motorcycle to Front Royal, I hid my optical and burned the motorcycle. I could have made it so I traveled straight here, but we decided it would be safer for Ivy if I scrambled up my journey. Riding, walking. We don't know what's best. We're guessing some of this. All of this," she said.

Lev looked at her and sighed. "There was a lot of shocking information in that story, but the fact that you only just recently saw what he'd done to the world is right up there with the more obvious stuff. No wonder you don't have a lot of post apocalypse skills. I guess it makes sense. Everything you've said so far should have informed me that you honestly don't know how to navigate this world. You're doing really well, though. Also, you're amazing. Vespry gets a lot of credit from everyone because he set up Ivy, had this place built for us, and he deserves all the credit he gets. He's amazing. But you are, too. I can't believe how much you've done to take down Bas. I had thought you were a soldier in Vespry's army. You actually said that to me. But do you consider that you might be Rollo Vespry's equal? I think you are. Do you?"

"You sound like Rollo," she said, rolling her eyes at him.

Lev nodded and touched her hand asking, "Were hidden spaces used to hide nuclear power plants?"

"Yes, but Rollo said Bas contemplated letting them all melt down before Time told him it was a very shitty idea. Rollo said Bas ranted for weeks like a raging temper tantrum throwing toddler at having to lock each power plant. If he hadn't, I don't think you'd have survived as well. The planet would have suffered. He hid them all across the entire planet, but he can also unhide them. Pele's Kingdom is hidden and locked. She'd survive if he unlocked them today, Lev. He might decide to unlock them if he finds out about Ivy and Rollo's role in the opposition. Me, being here."

Lev stared at the horizon and contemplated what that meant. "Bolin should know this. His spies have to be ready to die, be tortured forever, to keep Bas from finding out about Ivy, Vespry, and you."

"Mmm-hmm," said Kali. "Are the nuclear power plants related because you--"

"I looked for some power plants. I dragged Dave, Aisha, Bob, Hans, and Cheri around Virginia and Pennsylvania looking for nuclear power plants that were no longer there. They thought I was crazy at first, but then they knew I wasn't."

"I know how that feels," said Kali with a small laugh.

"Yeah, you do," he laughed. "We've been trying to figure out what happened to the power plants for years. Now we know. We have a lot of research on it. I knew it was a person who did it. I was positive time and space were involved. I just didn't know how. I didn't figure out the formula. I didn't consider a sentient being like Time. I was hung up on conventional understandings of time... which really don't understand time all that well. Dave's probably struggling not to tell Aisha, Hans and Cheri right now." He looked at her and laughed mildly at his failures.

Kali looked disappointed and shook her head slowly. "We could never find the formula to hide space. We both tried. Rollo thought we could run away, escape somehow, and come here and lock Ivy. Be safe from Bas like Pele is, at least for this present, but we're just not that good with the science and math. We could only get you what we could find. I mean, Bas broke Jorge's lock. We'd have never managed to create a lock to keep him out. Pele must be really smart, too. It drives Bas crazy that he can't break her code."

It hit Lev that Kali and Rollo had been desperately trying to escape Bas in any way imaginable for decades. "You and Vespry...You're both amazing. You were both teenagers. I couldn't do what either of you have done," he said, fully meaning it.

Lev looked over across the field and saw Olivia walking to the stables with someone else.

"Speaking of spies, I see Olivia. She must be riding out to Campus for the assessment Bolin mentioned earlier. She's heading out late. Maybe she'll stay there tonight."

Lev stood up and called to them and waved them over. He sat down on the bench next to Kali and said, "The RT is going to have a shitload of science questions from their various fields. I think I have a lot of good information from you right now. Would it be alright with you if I went inside and talked to them for a while and told them what you've been telling me? The stuff about consciousness, death, locked spaces, the passport? Give you a break. Maybe let you assess Olivia for spy worthiness?"

"Am I doing a shit job talking to them?" Kali asked without being afraid of the answer.

"No. If that's how that sounded, get it out of your head. You're doing great. I think I'm guilty of underestimating you. I know I am. I'm gonna stop that," he said emphatically. "I just think they're gonna go all science nerds on you with the questions, and I think I'll know what they need to hear."

Kali smiled at him and moved closer to him touching his chest saying, "I'm not intimidated by science nerds. In fact, I'm really attracted to one in particular."

Lev smiled at her and grabbed her suddenly around her waist and pulled her to him as they laughed, and they kissed as Kali wrapped her arms around his neck.

"Baby, the passport gives me hope. I think we're gonna be ok," he said as he leaned his forehead against hers and spoke quietly to her.

"Ok," she said.

Lev turned as Olivia and her escort approached.

"Need some space," he told the escort who walked back to the horses.

"Bolin talk to you about why he's sending you to Campus?" he asked her

"He said he wants their military leader to interview me. He told me I'd be back later today or tomorrow morning and he'd meet with me. You're still my commander, right?" she asked Lev without any hint of intimidation.

"I am. Call me Lev, though."

Olivia turned to Kali and said, "Bolin told me the woman who put you in a cage was executed and that my... Lev is the leader of both communities. I wanted to help you fight that day, but I was still following my original orders. In the future, I'd like to be able to make a decision to fight."

Lev and Kali were both facing Olivia as she spoke and Lev turned to Kali and said enthusiastically, "Damn, I like her!"

Kali smiled at both of them and said, "I was really fucked up that day, but Bolin told me what you did. Thanks for having my back. Wanna hang out and talk a bit before you leave?"

Lev said, "Yeah, but don't tell her anything."

Kali laughed at him and said, "I know! I'm the consultant. I know my job!"

"Alright," he said as he stood up to go back to the meeting. "I don't know how long I'll be. Here, our room, or the cafeteria?" he asked her.

"Yeah, one of those three," she agreed.

"Take my seat," Lev said to Olivia as he headed back to the RT meeting.

Kali and Olivia

"Do you know what's going on?" asked Kali.

"No, but I listen and I hear things. Weird things."

"Lev isn't wrong about listening being an excellent skill. He applies it to following orders most of the time, but listening for information you're not supposed to have is an equally important skill."

"You know who did this to the world. You brought us something that can help us defeat that person. They're after you. Lev's trying to help you help us. You can be tortured for eternity. You said that to that woman when she locked you up. I believe you."

"I'm impressed."

"Am I wrong?" asked Olivia.

"No."

"I want to be useful," Olivia said, looking at her earnestly.

"Being useful comes at a cost."

"I listened to you scream in the hallway when you were fighting with them, and then when they dragged you in to be caged. I heard the cost," Olivia said soberly. "I see the cost, too," Olivia said, looking at Kali's arms.

"We'll talk more before any decisions are made. Do the Campus thing. Talk to Bolin. I'll talk to Bolin. Then I'll talk to you more directly. Don't feel like you have to do anything. No one's going to ask you to do this. You won't be made to do anything regarding this. I wouldn't allow it."

Olivia nodded that she understood.

"I have to tell Lev what you told me. Don't talk about what you told me to anyone. Definitely don't talk about me. Lev will kill you," she said, looking at Olivia and nodding her head.

"I understand."

"You should go now. I've never been to Campus. Let me know what it's like."

Olivia stood up and headed over to her escort who was waiting by their horses. "I will. And I'll find useful information for you, too," she said, smiling at Kali.

"Ok." Kali laughed.

Kali laid down on top of the picnic table in the warm late afternoon sunshine and fell asleep.

Lev was talking to her. He was sitting on a bench alongside the picnic table with his face perched above hers because of his height.

"What?" she asked while pushing herself up into a sitting position on top of the table.

"I asked if you're narcoleptic," he said, sounding like he was only half joking.

Kali laid back down and said, "Oh, did you wake me only to make fun of me? I'm going back to sleep," and closed her eyes.

Lev leaned forward and kissed her, and she smiled and opened her eyes.

"I'm not narcoleptic. I still have a hangover. I might be good now, though. How'd it go?" she asked him while getting off of the table top to sit beside him. She noticed the bowl of food on the table and motioned towards it inquisitively.

"Yeah, that's for us," he said, pulling it closer to her. "It went really well. We talked for three hours. We finally took a break. I think this is dinner."

Kali stood up and said, "You eat, I'll go figure out how to get us some drinks."

Lev's mouth was already full of food and he nodded approval and waved as she walked inside the cafeteria.

She returned with a pitcher of water and sat beside him straddling the bench and listened as he told her about the long meeting with the RT while they ate.

"We came up with a plan for after we each die. First, we'll try to find a Death Time really quickly. If we can't find one or get them to help us kill Bas here in this present, we're going to find my mother and all the other people who can help protect our consciousnesses from Bas. We're not just going to cross over and wait like fucking victims-to-be. I'm gonna be proactive. I'm still not working with Heather or anyone from Ivy, though," he said, shaking his head at her with certainty.

"You didn't need to be at the meeting. Better you got some sleep. You gave us so much information that needed to be discussed by the RT. They're all excited, horrified, terrified, and ready to hear more. No one was being an asshole. They have more questions now, but new ones. I figured you could come in and tell us more of what you want us to know and see if that resolves anything first. I told them about the optical, too. What you told me back in Front Royal and this morning. Was that enough?"

"Yeah, I want to add something about the way they work using consciousness, but it'll be quick," she said, rubbing her hand along his lower back slowly as they talked.

"I think my lower back is an erogenous zone," he said as he turned to look at her.

"You want me to stop?" she asked him in a tone indicating she would.

"Fuck, no. Just thought you should know. Keep it up," he said, nodding approval for her to continue touching him.

They finished eating and Kali told Lev about her conversation with Olivia.

"I think she's got natural talent, but she'd still need to be informed before deciding."

"Mm-hmm. Especially given what you told me earlier about that asshole potentially uncovering nuclear power plants that melted down nearly two decades ago with no intervention measures. Who knows what else he'd do? Also, I don't like that she knows that much about you. We really don't know her. She could cause you trouble. I'm beginning to understand Vespry's propensity for murdering people who knew who you were. I like her, but I'll kill her if she makes me worry about you," he said in an offhand, but decidedly serious, tone.

"I know. I figure she knows enough now that's problematic. Bolin can see if he can torture information out of her and see if she'll break rather than remain loyal."

Lev raised his eyebrows at her. "Ummm..."

"We can test her pain threshold, too." Kali mused.

"We're gonna need to talk about this..."

"It's not like you can read from a book and take a multiple choice test, Lev," she said, sounding surprised that he wasn't being supportive.

"Ok. I'm staying out of this. You can work this out with Bolin. Any problems, I'll kill her," he said, finishing the water remaining in the pitcher. "Ready to go inside?" he asked her.

"Yeah.

Back to the Meeting with the RTs

"I want to tell you a little about Bas and his cult. Along with the tech, the recipe book, and your skills, you need to be motivated because they are. I was already Bas's prisoner the day he pulled the trigger on the first extinction event, so I didn't see what it looked like when it happened, but I was told that the lives he targeted ended instantly. You should know, there was a huge celebration over his success. It went on for days while all the survivors here tried to make sense of what was happening. While all the trapped people, sick people, kids, and babies that survived died slow, horrible deaths. You should know he and his followers celebrated, so that you know the intentional cruelty of the people you're trying to stop. There's nothing redeemable about any of them.

"If you're alive today, Bas either missed you by accident, let you live for future healthy human diversity, or Time eliminated you from the formula on purpose using what power Time had to do that and conceal what Time had done."

Lev listened and thought of Prisha dropping raisins onto the floor from her stroller. He thought of the terrified little boy who ran straight into barbed wire and died in front of him as the older man snapped his neck to end his pain. He thought of all the children, the elderly, and animals trapped and helpless. He thought of Bob's son. He looked up at the RT and their silence told him they all had similar memories as they listened to Kali tell them Bas had celebrated for days at his success in killing so many people in an instant. He looked at Kali and was glad she was telling them exactly what they needed to hear. The mood in the room was dark. It needed to be.

Kali tells the RT about Pele and Jorge and Opticals

"Lev covered opticals, but I want to talk about how opticals are tied to the consciousness of their assigned operator. The recipe is in the book. The optical I brought is mine. It's got stuff that's hidden in the past. Currently, when the operator of an optical dies, the information and items hidden by the optical are hidden forever. In a positive use of accessing the consciousnesses of the deceased after death, say I died and my optical was eternally locked but it had information that could help Rollo? Rollo could contact my deceased consciousness in the other present and access what I had hidden on my optical with my agreement.

"Unfortunately, Bas could find my optical and find my deceased consciousness, and maybe he could figure out a way to override the protections on my optical. I don't know. I know there's plenty of stuff out there on opticals that's being hidden from Bas by both Pele and Jorge. I have stuff hidden on this optical that I don't want Bas to find. He doesn't know I have an optical.

"Unlocking opticals, whether the operator is in this present or the other present, is a goal of Bas's. It's on the list Rollo wrote for you in the recipe book. If I were to die, and Bas got into the other present and had a way to control our consciousnesses there, probably nothing on opticals could remain hidden. I've heard Bas talk about unlocking Jorge's opticals once he can control consciousness. Jorge's still alive in torture. Bas pulls him out once in a while and they test ways of breaking into his opticals. Like I said earlier, Bas really wants to figure out how to get into the driver seat of each person's consciousness. Inside, maybe he could override operators. I need you to consider how awful that would be.

"You also need to know about Pele and Jorge. Pele and Jorge are super important to everything. Bas gets all the attention, but they were right there with him from the beginning. There's a whole history, some of it I'm not even sure about. I'll tell you the accepted version of the history, but don't quote me. It's probably wrong in several places. Pele and Jorge are a brother and a sister, twins, who were friends or acquaintances with Bas when they were all at college. That part's correct. I don't know how they came across the information, but they discovered how to communicate with Time using research information they discovered from one of their former professors, Marina Patel.

"Here's the shortened version. Once the three of them learned Time was a sentient being, they made contact with Time and initiated a friendly dialogue. Time told me Time had reservations about interacting with them after the first contact because Time began to see strands of potential negative outcomes based on interactions with them. Time suggested they discontinue their communication. But Bas had other ideas.

"He encouraged Pele and Jorge to look at Marina Patel's math and her formulas and whatever that they were using to communicate with Time. I hate saying this, but Bas is fucking smart when it comes to this shit. His brain was meant for understanding how Time communicates and how Time works. He just doesn't have a soul meant for goodness. He's not smart enough or creative enough to have figured out what Marina Patel figured out on her own, but he's the kind of person who can piggyback onto the original ideas of others.

"Pele and Jorge didn't like what Bas was proposing. Specifically, he envisioned a world ruled by the three of them. Said they could be Gods. He still bitches about that today. Says Pele and Jorge could have had it all right along with him, but since they turned on him, they had to be made to pay.

"Anyway, he wanted to bind Time. Hold Time prisoner and force Time to teach him more about what he could do with Time's power. He quickly figured out how to hide space once he learned it was a possibility. Time was free at that point. Time didn't fight him or stop him. To be honest, I don't think Time realized what a threat Bas was until it was too late. Time's not an all-knowing God. Time's like us. Time makes mistakes. Less mistakes than we make, but still. Time kept relying on strands that indicated Bas was going to get frustrated and quit. But Time can't see the future or read minds. Time didn't expect Bas to be as committed, resourceful, or lucky as he turned out to be.

"He gathered a team of his own, like yours, and they kept running the formulas he was able to pull from Time. He bent the space around his own Kingdom, but he was still limited. He wanted to work with people he thought he could handle, you know, manipulate. He didn't want to fight someone like himself for his share of Time's knowledge and power. From what I understand, Pele and Jorge were normal people. He went back and forth negotiating with Pele and Jorge, finally coming to a divided arrangement with them. Pele and Jorge were each keeping some of Marina Patel's work from Bas in order to limit his forward momentum. Remember opticals. They're easy to create once you have the formulas. He needed that information they'd hidden from him. He couldn't conceive of it on his own. Even with his research crew working for him, he's not a patient person. He's greedy and demanding. He craves instant gratification of all his desires.

"According to Rollo, Pele and Jorge decided to go through with Bas's plan and join him in order to be two-thirds of the power over Time to his one-third of power. Bas had already tried to kill both of them at this point. They knew he was mean, but they also knew he was still willing to work with them if they came around to his vision. He had been chasing them relentlessly with his growing army full of cultish devotees. They realized it wouldn't be easy to stop him at that point. So, they decided they'd convince him they'd come around. They each bent space and time around their own Kingdoms and reluctantly brought in kidnapped people trying to convince Bas they were onboard. They would go through with binding Time with Bas because they were afraid he'd just find others to work with who would go through with the plan if they refused. You know, cruel people just like him. So, they did it.

"The three of them limited Time's ability to move freely using the combined research work of Marina Patel that they'd corrupted. Told Time what to do and forced Time to comply through formulas that denied Time free will. After they captured Time with Bas, proving they were all in, the plan had been to learn Bas's formulas and free Time by removing the binding formulas constraining Time.

"For just a few minutes, they each had equal power. But Bas immediately threw up codes that interfered with Pele and Jorge's access to Time. Pele and Jorge discovered Bas had been planning to turn on them the entire time. He locked them out of their access to Time. They still had plenty of skills and knowledge, but no direct access to Time to learn more. They'd been gone a while, you know? And Bas had been learning new shit with his researchers the whole time. So you see, this whole dialogue didn't happen overnight. Years passed between the time Pele and Jorge left Bas and then returned to work with him." Kali shrugged and looked around the room at the RT. "It was his insistence that scared the twins. He wasn't going to quit and he already figured out how to stop his aging. He had bent time and space around his own Kingdom that now had tens of thousands of people he had kidnapped with his army."

"Were you there then?" Lev asked her.

"Not yet. Rollo wasn't there yet, either, but his older brother was. His name was Mick. Mick had initially been enamored with Bas. You know how charming psychopaths can be? Yeah. Well, Mick had skills Bas wanted to work with. He was a really smart guy. Bas recruited science-savvy younger people from college campuses. Filled their heads with positive plans. All lies. Turned out, both of Mick's parents were also assets Bas wanted on his research team. So, Mick gets them all over to Bas's Kingdom and Rollo is just a little kid in the real world. His parents go back and forth from Bas's Kingdom to their home in Miami every night on some weird space travel commute until Mick tells Bas his younger brother is old enough to be brought in. Kids aren't allowed in Bas's Kingdom. He only imports people over the age of 15. Rollo was having none of it right from the first moment he met Bas.

"Mick was already getting nervous because he had become Bas's right hand man. He saw some unsettling shit. He sat in on conversations between Pele, Jorge, and Bas that didn't go well. Next thing Mick knew, he was leading an army into Jorge's Kingdom and he personally captured him. Jorge told Mick things about Bas's intentions and what he and Pele were trying to prevent. He didn't believe him at first because undoing all the lies you're fed isn't easy. But Mick kept the information from Jorge to himself. He didn't let Bas know he was concerned.

"Rollo was barely adjusting to life in Bas's Kingdom. He was working in the labs as a janitor late at night, no longer able to go to school with his friends in Miami, just trapped in this new weird world run by Bas. His family were strangers to him because he was hurt by the secrets they had kept from him. He had no control over anything anymore.

"This is what he told me happened. A voice spoke to him. He said he thought he was going crazy and that the voice was right there next to his ear speaking without breath. It was a brief conversation, but Time asked him for help and told him there were multiple strands that indicated they could defeat Bas if they worked together. However, there were also strands that said they could lose. Rollo told me he agreed right then to help Time. Fuck the chances they might lose. Said he even considered he'd gone crazy after everything, but he didn't care. He'd rather die fighting Bas even if the voice was an auditory hallucination rather than spend another day complying to the will of an actual psychopath."

"Rollo was 16 years old?" asked Lev.

"Mmm-hmm. He was 16."

"Same age as Olivia," said Bolin.

"Yeah. Not too young to help," said Kali. She continued. "With Jorge captured and put into torture, Pele decided to go to war with Bas. She needed an army and scientists, too. She did whatever it took, sometimes looking like a really bad person in the process. I heard she kidnapped a lot of people. Caused natural disasters by bending spaces that shouldn't be bent, and abducting people before they could be swept out to sea or lost in avalanches. She was trying to hide the abductions. She didn't want Bas to know she was planning to fight back with her own army. That was in the beginning. He knows now, though. She was locked out of Jorge's Kingdom and had only her third of the power over Time left but no actual access.

"Rollo has tried for so many years to work with her because she's super hell bent on winning the war against Bas, but she's never even acknowledged him until recently. Maybe she thought he was fucking with her because he's Bas's right hand man, or she hates him because his brother abducted her brother. Just recently, she decided to work with Rollo, though. It means we have her army to back us. They're a million strong. Her Kingdom has families and kids, but the million is her army. I don't know what her population total is. Bas has at least two million people in his Kingdom now. They're all 15 and older, so they're all considered adults. All two million are considered members of his army. They'd all die for him. He's like a God to his followers. I don't know if you can count Jorge's people. He's been in torture for decades, but who knows how time is moving inside his cell? Bas uses Jorge's people as slaves. Slaves of all kinds. It's really sick. I won't talk about it now, but he experiments on them, too. You know, present consciousnesses? He's got plenty to work with.

"Jorge's kingdom is only accessible by Bas and his army. Pele can't get in. The people inside can't get out. I've never been, but Rollo says it's hell on earth. I get the feeling they're not potential soldiers, but they might be. He's always ordering people to be taken from Jorge's Kingdom to serve people in his own Kingdom. They definitely have kids in Jorge's Kingdom. Keeps up the supply of slaves and maybe even future citizens of Bas's Kingdom. So, that's who Pele and Jorge are. Pele's an ally. Jorge's a prisoner. Are there any questions?" Kali asked.

Everyone in the room raised a hand, including Dave. Kali looked at Dave and smiled.

Dave intrigued her. She now knew he had been with Lev since the beginning, but she had also come to realize that, like Bolin, James, and Aisha, Dave was important to Lev. She could pick up on the closeness of their relationship in the way they spoke to one another and in the way Dave had spoken about Lev to her. She knew Lev would have had to approve Dave following her when she'd left the meeting with the Ivy RT. Lev wouldn't have let Dave follow her when she was upset if he didn't believe Dave could help her. Dave had helped her. Lev trusted Dave. She would trust Dave, too. Aside from that, she thought Dave was cool.

"Dave?" Kali asked.

"Hidden spaces. The three Kingdoms, the sites of hundreds of nuclear power plants that are presumably melting down as we speak, and what else? My understanding is Time hides spaces to nurture the evolution of living organisms. What's being nurtured by Time?" Dave tipped his head to his left at Kali as he finished asking his question and nodded.

Kali could see he was still thinking. His head was full of possibilities for the answer she was going to give him.

"As long as Time has been on earth, Time has hidden and locked societies, cultures, and more that doesn't even necessarily apply to human evolution. But human evolution is a big focus of Time. We possess higher-level consciousnesses. Time said that higher-level thinking organisms are essential to the Universe, but I don't know in what way. Death Time are interested in us, too. We're they're actual job. Like I said, they eliminate bad consciousnesses that don't evolve here. Time nurtures the evolution of our consciousnesses, and Death Time removes those that don't evolve properly.

"To answer your question, I know that there are two more continents on earth. Big ones, too. But Time hid them a long time ago. They're not just hidden, they've been locked by Time. They have entire civilizations that are thriving. They don't know the rest of the world as we know it exists. We don't know anything about them. Kind of like Ivy's RT didn't know about the two thriving Campus RTs."

Kali stopped speaking and let the information she had just given them penetrate their understanding of the world they lived in.

She looked at Dave.

"Locked by Time means they survived asshole's extinction event?" he asked her, leaning forward in his chair.

"Yeah," she said, nodding.

"There are cities? Thriving cities that don't know who Bas is?" he asked her.

"They know nothing about him, including that he's trying to unlock their spaces. Bas getting in... would be terrifying. I think it would mean he defeated Time," Kali said, nodding. Kali watched as Dave leaned back in his chair and looked away from everyone, choosing to look up at the ceiling where he closed his eyes and sighed.

"That's huge," Aisha said quietly, staring blankly at the table.

"Everything has been huge," Bolin said quietly.

Kali glanced at Lev. He looked lost in his own thoughts.

The room remained silent until Shoshi, one of the newest members of the tech team raised a hand and waited for permission to speak.

"What?" asked Lev.

"Kali, you said Time spoke to Rollo. Can Time help us get into a locked space? Maybe not Bas's space, but maybe a space it, I mean, Time has locked and knows the passcode to?"

"It's definitely possible. Time is actually here now with us. Time is part of the opposition to Bas. I used to hear Time more often, but Bas has Time so tightly bound now that communication is difficult. All I can suggest is that you listen for Time's help when you're working. You might not hear a fucking thing, but then again, you might. Time's voice is not your own voice. Time's voice is different. You won't be confused if you hear Time. You'll know what you're hearing is not your own thoughts.

"That's one of the reasons I got so mad about the egos of the Ivy RT. You can't have an ego and hear anyone else, let alone Time. Time might try to interact with you by guiding you. Sometimes it's more like, *'Consider this….'*

"Time doesn't have all the answers, you know? Time's just trying like the rest of us. Time's help is one of the biggest advantages we have over Bas. Consider Time part of this team. Time isn't trying to help Bas. Time is trying to stop him. Time knows you asked that question."

Kali turned to look at Dave. "Time also knows you asked your question."

Dave nodded almost imperceptibly in Kali's direction at that information.

"Any questions?" Kali asked them. Every member of the RT raised a hand. Kali rolled her eyes and Lev watched her as she did so. She looked annoyed and said, "Ok. You," she said pointing at an RT member.

"Can you contact Pele?"

"No, actually. I can't. And I think it's a problem. Rollo handled all communication with Pele. We weren't able to get you communication technology, and Rollo couldn't send you his, but…." Kali opened the recipe book and flipped through pages for a few seconds and then sighed and went back to the front of the book and started again going more slowly the second time.

"Ok. Found it. This is the recipe for how to make a communication device, but don't get too excited. We're missing some of the formula. It's the only incomplete recipe in the book. We have most of it. Hopefully, you can figure it out. The pages aren't numbered. I'll bend the corner," she said as she bent the corner of the page.

"I'd like to talk to Pele. I want to ask her if she knows if Rollo's ok. I've been asking Time, but I guess Time's having trouble talking," she said trailing off quietly.

"We'll get a team on that right away," Lev said to her reassuringly.

"Thanks."

Kali looked over at the RT and said, "Anything you need, Time is here with you working with you. Stay open. Time might be able to help fill in the missing information for the communication device. I don't know. I don't think Time would tell me straight up technical stuff. Time's really never told me formulas. More like, Time's directed me to opportunities to see them, so I can write them down. I'm more of a visual learner, apparently. I probably wouldn't know what the hell Time was saying if Time started whispering partial formulas to me with all this math and physics. Which, when I say that, I'm thinking, you all really need to learn this new stuff quickly in case Time does try to talk to you about it. See? Maybe Time told me to tell you that. Time didn't. I just thought of it myself," she laughed a little and sighed.

"You ready to move onto some tech?" Lev asked with a smile, shaking his head at her.

"Yeah, let's do that," she said, smiling at him.

Rewinds

Kali pulled what looked like a large black flashlight out from her backpack and held it up to the RT. It was about 12 inches long and had a clear, half dome sphere at the top.

"This is a Rewind. They don't have individual operators. Anyone can grab a Rewind and bring a person back from death. Rewinds have a 15/15 rule. You have 15 seconds to bring a person back from death or the person can't be rewound. The person can't be near death for a Rewind to work. The person has to be dead. The 15 seconds start at death. A doctor could bring you back if you were dead longer, but a Rewind is useless after 15 seconds.

"The other 15 is the amount of minutes back in time that you're healed of your injuries. So, if for 15 minutes you were tortured and had your legs chopped off... Wait, you'd die from that too quickly. You'd be dead before 15 minutes were up. You gotta do that last. If you had your fingers, ears, nose, genitals, and lips cut off. Then you were stabbed repeatedly all over your body and lit on fire, but you didn't die, *then* you got your legs chopped off and died then you got rewound, you'd come back whole. If you cut off a person's leg and left it near the body and let the person die, the person would come back whole. If you chopped a person's leg off and tossed it a couple feet away from the body, the person died, was rewound... The leg would not be attached. It must be near the body to be returned to a whole state. Within two feet, I think.

"So, if you're in a fight with enemies, a good plan is always to chop off something vital, such as their head, or a leg, and throw it far away. One, it delays the opportunity to meet the 15 second window for a successful rewind, and two, the essential body part might not make it back to the body. Bas's army will all have

Rewinds and try to keep their numbers up by rewinding fallen fighters. The head is obvious, even a successfully rewound person can't come back alive without their head. As for the leg, a successful rewind would mean your enemy would come back minus a leg. That would throw them in their physical battle against you. You'd have an advantage then. Questions?"

Kali chose an RT member who asked, "How many times can a person be rewound?"

"There's no limit. I've been rewound…. tens of thousands of times."

Lev shifted uncomfortably in his seat. Kali noticed but didn't turn to look at him.

"I'm sorry to hear that," the person who asked the question said quietly.

"Yeah. It sucked. You?"

"Does being rewound hurt?"

"No. It's just frustrating to be so close to death only to be dragged back alive and whole, ready to be tortured all over again for 15 minutes or whatever, could be a minute, before being killed again. It's an inhumane cycle. I just want to say, a Rewind in the hands of someone who is kind, is an amazing piece of technology. Little kids can be saved from accidents. Accident victims can be healed from all injuries instantly. Use your compassionate imaginations to realize the potential for good a Rewind presents.

"But, as usual, Bas got the technology and used it for the absolute worst fucking possible application. An endless torture device. Refusing to let people leave this world and die. Refusing to let people be reunited in the new present with their loved ones who had gone on before them. Exposing traitors to him, like all of you, and torture, kill, rewind, and repeat until you make a confession.

"It's like I said, you can't imagine what torture is over there. Use your imaginations for considering the ways in which a psychopath would use a Rewind. He's a professional sadist. All of you together here now brainstorming ideas he'd come up with would still miss a bunch of cruel ways he's already used Rewinds. You'd be embarrassed by the terrible ideas you could come up with, whereas, he's proud of the sick things he comes up with. The Rewind is a hands-on torture device. They have plenty of tech for torture. This is just one tool.

"Any more questions?"

The room was silent.

"Rewinds are good for ground battles. Rewind your dead on the field if you can get to them in 15 seconds." Kali turned to Bolin. "Send your spies in with Rewinds. They can torture information Ivy needs from Bas's people."

Bolin nodded without hesitation and looked committed to the idea instantly.

Lev said nothing.

Prison Darts

Kali pushed aside the Rewind that was still on the conference table and reached into her backpack and brought out a rectangular, four inch black box.

"This box contains prison darts. The tech in a prison dart takes you directly to a prison located outside of the Kingdom. There are no prison lock codes or Kingdom lock codes in a prison dart. Bas's prison is not located inside his Kingdom. I don't know where it is. Rollo's been. He told me it's an actual prison somewhere in America. It's hidden, but it's not locked. That's why the darts can transport you right to the prison. A prison dart will get you inside the prison, but you can't get out once you're inside. The prison is called Hell. They generally use these in battles and on citizens inside the Kingdom who are being arrested. Because the Kingdom lock code isn't on a PD, if you get hit with one inside the Kingdom, you go to a cell in a satellite prison in the city and a decision gets made about transferring you to Hell using a passport designed for that. A person who's been tagged with a PD outside the Kingdom, arrives in a cell in Hell's prison intake.

"In past battles with Pele and Jorge, I heard that Hell's intake cells would become so full of prisoners arriving on PDs that bodies would be crushed and the metal cell bars would swell against the force of the captured. Bodies would be torn apart being pushed against the cell bars. You were lucky if you were only suffocated. Those are fun war stories they like to tell over drinks in the winter and at summer barbeques.

"I didn't want to bring prison darts. They're not well designed and accidents happen even when skilled people use them. They generally contain the identification of the owner on them, but the owner isn't an operator in the sense of consciousness. So, if you go to battle and you dart an enemy, your captures are recorded. They know it was you who got the person. But anyone could use a PD. If someone's killed in battle, you can grab their PDs and use them. You might not get credit for your captures, but you could demand recognition.

"The heat from a gun is too hot for the prison bullets they've created so far, so PDs are for hand-to-hand combat. I'm sure they'll figure out a work-around to the heat issue for bullets some day. Rollo says he deactivated these so you can't accidently send yourself to Hell while you try to figure out how to make more with the recipe. However, the formula for Hell as a final destination is in the recipe book, so you can turn them back on.

"He thinks you can make more and use them to dispose of bodies if, for instance, Bas's army shows up here at Ivy. You can dart their soldiers and send them to Hell. Or, I'm thinking, if you're one of Bolin's spies, and you're in the Kingdom as a spy you can capture someone, torture them to death for information that will help Ivy, and then dart them sending them to the local Kingdom prison intake. No identification for the spy will be on the dart. It'll freak them out." Kali laughed. "They'll know spies are inside the Kingdom."

Kali continued to smile at the thought and looked at Bolin who nodded in agreement. She told him, "A spy can't leave a tortured body behind. They'd know the location at the time of the kill. They'd start asking who was in the area. You know?"

"Yes. I see," Bolin said in firm agreement with her.

Kali continued, "Inside the Kingdom, capture, torture with Rewinds, get useful information, kill. Dart the body and it arrives in the local prison intake. No tracker. No one would know who sent the body."

"I like that," Bolin said, nodding his head.

Kali nodded at him approvingly. "Me, too. I guess Rollo was right about sending these to Ivy. Also, you can program PDs to send people anywhere in the present. They don't go to the past. Think about this option. You program a PD to send someone you're battling to Ivy's cages. Right? That's the point of them from Bas's perspective. If Campus's military was equipped with PDs, and Bas's army showed up, they could eliminate Bas's numbers by darting people on the field, sending them to your own prison cells. Maybe this RT can figure out how to make prison bullets. That would be great."

"One downside to using PDs is, I don't even know where Hell is. I don't want one of us to get sent there accidently trying to figure out how to work them. Be careful working with them. They won't reveal Ivy, but if you're working in the lab here and you get stuck and get transported to Hell, you might reveal Ivy to spare yourself. I don't know you people," Kali said, sounding uncomfortable.

Forte Keys and Passports

"Forte Keys were the first technology used for citizens of Bas's kingdom to travel to the past. Bas used Forte Keys as rewards for loyal citizens or for rewards when someone did something well and he wanted to show citizens he could be generous. Forte Keys would be programmed to keep track of a traveler in case the traveler decided to run and get lost in the past. If you got a Forte vacation and you tried to run and hide, you were brought back and publicly executed for weeks, because, you know, Rewinds. Over and over again before you were finally thrown into torture, or, if you were lucky, they missed your 15 second rewind window and you got to die. That rarely happened because letting someone die, who Bas wanted tortured, led to your own public rewind cycle and eventual eternal torture. A day has 96 rewinds. I'm not good at math, but this is a fraction I know.

"Forte Keys are super easy to make. Some people figured out how to make them themselves and began to run away into the past with their homemade Forte Keys that didn't have trackers. Bas finally outlawed them and... I don't want to talk about what the punishment for being caught with one was. They broadcast a public announcement informing citizens in graphic detail. I'll just say, the streets were littered with Forte Keys, legal and illegal, about a minute after he passed the order for the punishment. People fucking dropped them where they stood. No one wanted to be caught with one. I got one, though." Kali smiled proudly looking around the room. She saw Dave close his eyes and mouth something that looked like, 'Oh, my God." She turned to Lev, still smiling, and he smiled and nodded at her approvingly.

"A couple weeks after they were outlawed, I saw one wedged between the sidewalk and the grass. I kept it hidden for years. I never got caught with it, either. It was the first piece of tech we got for Ivy. We decided to bring you my Forte Key because it's easy to make and you might learn from the more basic travel formulas running it.

"High ranking officials in the Kingdom use passports now. Citizens have nothing. No Forte Keys, no passports. Members of the army and the guard have day passes, though. They use them to get in and out of the Kingdom to go to Jorge's, escort Bas or me places we go, visit the past for shit Bas wants, like fast food... I'm not kidding, and for their days off. You can only be gone for 24 hours. Missing your return gets you 24 hours in torture. I didn't bring you a day pass because, supposedly, they're monitored. They have codes tying them to their operator and when the operator uses their day pass, the monitors know when you leave, where you went, and when you return. I brought you a passport, instead. I guess Lev already told you that. Those are exclusively for Bas's inner circle. They're unmonitored and can be used to go anywhere for any length of time. No one's ever abused the privilege of a passport. Except Rollo."

Lev sat forward saying, "Wait, so Rollo's passport has the Kingdom lock codes and he's unmonitored? That's how he's made contact with Pele?"

"Yeah."

"Has Pele used his passport to try and figure out Bas's lock codes?"

"Not that I've been told. We've only been working with her for a very short amount of time. Just a few weeks. But maybe, if he's been that daring. I know we're that desperate. He might have. Rollo is expected to be available to Bas every minute of every day. It took him years of kissing that psycho's ass to become this invaluable to him. It would be devastating to the opposition if Bas became suspicious of Rollo. Rollo's using his passport in the most effective way possible to the mission," Kali said without sounding defensive.

Lev nodded. "Could he use it to come here?" asked Lev.

"Yeah, as of three years ago, he became, I guess, second in command to Bas. He was for a few years before, too, but Bas still had him monitored back then. A monitor accused Rollo of a CAB offense, a Crime Against Bas, and thankfully, it was for something Bas had asked Rollo to go do, because Rollo was definitely committing CAB offenses!" Kali assured them all with a laugh.

"So the monitor got thrown into torture for making the accusation public because it disclosed something private in Bas's agenda, and Rollo came over that night and had drinks with Bas and told him that he'd be a better servant to him if he wasn't always having to worry that he was still standing in Mick's shadow. Like, if monitors and others knew Bas trusted him. Bas agreed and gave Rollo privileged autonomy, as he called it. Rollo has more autonomy than any other person living in in the Kingdom except Bas.

"The next day, Rollo stopped by and told me we were finally gonna be able to contact Pele and Ivy because his passport was unmonitored. Took us years to figure out how to contact her with his passport, though. It wasn't like Bas removed Rollo's monitors and Rollo could suddenly contact Pele in her locked Kingdom. It was fucking difficult to figure out how to get in contact with her. Then the bitch wouldn't talk to Rollo for the longest time! Honestly, it's been exhausting," Kali said, rolling her eyes at Lev.

"He would have been wasting an opportunity to gain an ally if he'd just run away to the past with you, or come here to Ivy because Pele has an actual army. The opposition is small. Rollo met with Pele in person? Could he have taken you to Pele's locked kingdom?"

"Yeah, he met with her in person, but that only happened a few weeks ago after Rollo begged her to work with us for the millionth time. We believed our plan to bring tech to Ivy was worth the risk. It's not about me or Rollo escaping Bas even though we sometimes forget that ourselves. We need to stop him from figuring out how to control consciousness. Even Pele only just learned what Bas is trying to do when Rollo finally got a chance to tell her. Rollo said she was horrified.

"Time agreed that sending me to Ivy could help us defeat Bas. Time doesn't have full length conversations with us anymore, but Time never said go to Pele. It was always, 'Ivy.' I didn't know if you'd all be here, or if I'd make it, but Time would have seen your RT. I trust Time's opinions. We all make mistakes, even Time, but we're trying not to."

"I don't think you're making mistakes. I think you're avoiding a lot of mistakes."

Kali nodded. "Rollo's an expert with passports. It's all there. Supposedly, passports aren't difficult to make. Not for the people in the labs, anyway. You can make them and travel in the present and the past. It's the Kingdom lock code that's a bitch. But Bas's Kingdom lock code is on the passport I brought you."

"Dave, Cheri, and I are going to be in charge of the team that works on the passport," Lev said to the RT.

"You should all know how incredibly enticing this technology is. Especially the easy to make Forte Key. Rollo and I didn't want to lie to you about the temptations. What if we didn't include a Forte Key with a super easy to make travel formula to get to the past to see your loved ones? You'd figure it out. Then you'd think we were manipulating you. Not telling you how awesome things could be, focusing only on how awful everything is. You have a right to know. We felt we had an obligation to be honest with you. This is another reason why I've been so worried about sharing the tech with you. It's extremely tempting to want to make a Forte Key and get the hell out of here and go live in the past. But, I've told you Bas's plans for the past, both presents, and his vision of the future. A Forte Key isn't going to save you from Bas if he controls the other present or figures out how to control your consciousness. I hope the truth prevents you from believing you can escape the present.

The End of the Meeting

"Is there anything else you wanted to tell us tonight?" Lev asked Kali.

"Not that I can think of right now. I'm sure I forgot to tell you stuff, though. Are there any questions?" Kali asked the RT. Every member of the RT raised a hand except Dave and Lev.

"How about this?" Lev interrupted, addressing the RT. "We have a lot to think about. You can all talk amongst yourselves, organize your questions, figure out what's a science or math heavy question, as opposed to a clarification you need to ask Kali. Distinguish between the two. Can we discuss your question as an RT and figure it out? Or is the question specifically for Kali based on what she knows. If you're unsure, discuss with the RT first. We'll meet tomorrow morning at 8am. That's going to be the only late start from here on in. We'll discuss a schedule tomorrow. 8am discuss first, then Kali will come back in. We've been at this all day. It's getting late. Do what you want tonight, but be focused and ready tomorrow."

Lev stood up and motioned for Kali and Bolin to follow him out of the room. Kali grabbed the backpack and the tech and walked between Lev and Bolin.

"James and Kali have arranged for a double date tonight. You up for it?" he asked Bolin.

Bolin closed his eyes and laughed quietly. "Yes, but I have to say, I'm overwhelmed. Let's focus on the alcohol I know my husband will be bringing. No work talk. Oh, and also, am I allowed to discuss any of this with James?" he asked.

Lev grabbed his heart, making a shocked face. "Uh, I expect James to be informed of all things. James has clearance right along with you. Jesus. You two need to know everything so you can protect my niece," he said, scowling at Bolin.

"What niece? You two have a child?" asked Kali, surprised.

Bolin nodded. "Meabh. She's with Aisha's husband the rest of this week. Too much going on for us to be good parents. Plus, James getting hurt last week. Santi said he would heal faster if he took time to rest."

"I can't wait to meet her someday," Kali said with sincerity that Bolin took extra notice of.

"We'll make a point of introducing you two," he said kindly.

"Alright, we'll see you two in a bit," Lev said as he and Kali headed towards their room. Kali looked up at Lev and went to speak but he said, "Let's talk in our room."

Kali nodded silently and kept pace with him as he walked quickly to their room.

Lev took the backpack from Kali and put it on the floor near the closet door.

"Couch," he said, pointing to the couch. When they were seated, he said, "I'm not just learning about the tech, Bas, Vespry, Time, different presents, and all that other shit while I'm sitting in there having a very official meeting about how to save two presents from a madman. I'm also learning about you. And I'm not able to take the time to address the things I'm learning about you while I'm the leader of this facility, the head of research, and the commander of this little army," he laughed lightly, turning to her and placing one of his large hands on her cheek.

Kali smiled and nodded, laughing lightly with him and said, "I know. I didn't look at you on purpose when I said there are 96 rewinds in a day. I understand how you feel, because I'm talking to all those people I don't even know, and I know they're learning about me at the same time you are. I don't like it that way, but I don't know how to make it different," she said, looking up at him with an expression that made him shake his head quickly.

"Babe, this couldn't happen any other way. I'm just saying, I wish I could be more responsive to what you're saying when you're saying it. What I'm learning about you. I was hanging on every word you said in the meeting. I didn't ignore anything you said even if I couldn't respond to what you told me about yourself and your experiences."

Kali's expression turned serious and she told him, "It's true. I *was* telling you. I was telling them, too, but I was talking to you."

Lev nodded. "I know. And I heard you."

They stared at each other in silence, each contemplating any number of things they wanted to address. Lev spoke first and Kali could hear his fury just below the surface of his question.

"Tens of thousands of times?"

"Mm-hm."

"I know Time doesn't know the future, but listen to me... I do. I'm gonna kill that son of a bitch. I am. That's the future, Kali," Lev said, nodding his head reassuringly at her. "I'm going to kill him. I'm going to ruin all of his fucking insane plans."

Kali smiled and nodded at that and leaned over to kiss Lev who quickly grabbed her into both of his arms and kissed her with a passion she wasn't expecting but that she wanted after the long day.

They were lying side-by-side on the couch still kissing when Lev pulled away from her and gently moved her hair away from her face saying, "Baby, I'm glad you and James arranged this couples thing tonight, but I want to talk to you later. Yeah?"

"Yeah," she said.

She had her hand up under the back of his shirt and was running her palm down his back and he closed his eyes and said, "I think you've turned my entire body into an erogenous zone."

Kali laughed and kissed him as he pulled her body firmly against his own while he returned her kisses laughing with her.

Bolin and James/Kali and Lev

James was standing in the doorway holding two wine bottles. "Hello, you two! I thought we could each share a bottle with our partner."

"Oh James, that's a good idea," Kali said happily.

"Is this your carrot wine?" asked Lev, looking at the color in the two bottles. "That it is!"

"This stuff's really good," Lev said, looking at Kali.

Bolin and James made their way inside and sat on Lev's couch. Lev grabbed both of his table chairs and put them opposite the couch on the other side of the coffee table. He and Kali sat in the chairs, and he pulled her chair up alongside his so they were touching. Lev put his feet up on the coffee table and Kali put her feet up over Lev's legs because her legs wouldn't reach the coffee table. He draped his arm over her legs immediately, acknowledging he wanted them there.

"So you know, we're having a meeting tomorrow at the education center at 3pm, James. I don't even know how many people, but you're welcome to sit in. It's stupid not to include you at this point."

"Bol was just telling me. I'll be there," he said in a serious tone. "On a lighter note, I want to make a toast. And don't pick on me for making toasts. I like them. They remind me of my heritage and people I miss," he said sternly.

"Be yourself, man!" Lev laughed at him while Bolin and Kali encouraged him.

"To strangers who become family. Bol, I'm so glad you didn't kill our Kali when she walked up to Ivy. Kali, I'm so happy you didn't kill my husband. Sweetie, I'm so glad you didn't let Kali kill herself. Lev, I'm so fucking happy you're in charge of Ivy because otherwise we'd all be in serious trouble without your leadership. And to me, for making wine to make this toast to and with the people I care about."

"That was fucking awesome, James," Kali said while Lev and Bolin agreed and clinked the two wine bottles over the top of the coffee table saying loudly, "Cheers!"

Lev and Kali passed their bottle of carrot wine between them and Kali issued a surprised statement of approval for the flavor of the wine.

"I didn't know what to expect. Is that raisins?" she asked.

"Yes, and honey. Always appreciate the bees!"

"Wow! That's really good!" she said.

Lev casually took the bottle from her. He was concerned about their after party affairs. Kali put her hand on Lev's lower back and rubbed him while he took a large sip of the wine. Bolin and James exchanged their bottle and Bolin agreed that the wine had aged nicely and was perfect.

Lev got up from his chair and walked around the table to get the duffle bag.

He placed it on the coffee table and took his seat next to Kali telling Bolin, "Hey, man. You remember when we had Kali in Dorm 17 and you went through her backpack?"

"Yes. The vibrator?"

Lev and Kali laughed and James looked confused and laughed saying, "Oh, shit, I missed that story. Catch me up later."

Lev laughed heartily along with Kali and said, "No, not her vibrator. I forgot about that. No. The hotel shampoo and conditioner from Australia."

"Yes. I remember. I thought they were expired, but she insisted they were not. They smelled really fresh. It was confusing at the time. I get it now." Bolin nodded and took a sip from the bottle of wine he was sharing with James.

Kali spoke up and said, "Well, you told me that everything expires. So, when Lev and I were returning from retrieving the tech, he noticed a music store on our way out of town. I waited outside and he went in and looked for stuff for you for your guitars and whatever."

"I did," said Lev, "but the place was a mess. Not much I saw that you'd like. So, I went back to Kali on the sidewalk and was ready to give up. But she said, 'Oh, I play guitar. I can help find stuff for Bolin. So I followed her back inside."

Kali picked up the story and added, "Lev had found pretty much every useful item he could. The store contents were mostly damaged. But I noticed a closed door in the back and asked Lev to kick it in."

"Which I did," Lev said proudly.

"Mm-hmm!" said Kali, adding, "In this storage room, there were boxes of inventory waiting to be put onto the store shelves. That's when I noticed boxes you'd need as a guitar player."

Lev nodded and added, "We took them all."

Kali laughed saying, "Open the duffle bag. See if they're expired."

Bolin passed the bottle of carrot wine to James and leaned forward and unzipped the duffle bag. Inside he found three boxes with different types of guitar strings.

"No. No, you did not find all of these boxes of unopened strings."

"Yeah, we did!" said Kali enthusiastically.

"And you carried them for how many days?"

"They're light, man. No worries," said Lev.

"How many days?" he asked again.

"Four days," said Kali. "Lev carried them."

"She wanted to," Lev laughed, adding, "Told me if they weren't rusty it would be fun to prove to you that not everything expires."

"Yeah, so this is a slightly passive aggressive gift," Kali laughed.

James had his hand and arm around Bolin's back shoulder and said enthusiastically, "Kali showed me these last night. We're dying to know if they're rusty. Come on and open a pack for us. It's fun either way."

Bolin ripped open one of the boxes that contained strings for acoustic guitars and looked at the numerous individual packages of strings inside. "This is really nice, you two."

"Damnit. Open a package so we can see if the strings are rusty," said Lev, unable to deal with the suspense.

Bolin ripped open a packet of acoustic guitar strings and pulled them out onto the palm of his hand. "Not rusty at all."

They all erupted into excited cheers, and Bolin high-fived Kali.

"Thanks, you two. This is such a great gift. I don't care if all the other packages are damaged or rusty. I can't believe you brought back tech from The Benefactor and guitar strings for me. That's fucking crazy," he said with a smile.

"I think we need to toast the clean strings," Kali said.

"I think I need to toast you," Bolin said.

"Oh?" asked Kali.

"I've been hanging around James for almost 20 years, and I'm still not good at making toasts, but I want to say, thank you, Kali. You showed up here willing to die over some tired looking flowers, plus, you confused Lev. I've never seen him so confused. The two of you went off for a week and came back with technology to help us kill a madman and guitar strings so that I can play guitar again. I'm so glad I didn't shoot you that morning. That's my toast."

They all laughed and agreed to the content of Bolin's toast, and clinked their bottles over the coffee table. James insisted it was a great toast and Bolin pulled out the other small items Lev had found for him.

"I needed new picks. And this strap is really nice. What's with the lesson books?" Bolin asked.

"For Meabh. So she can practice after you teach her," Lev said.

They all looked at Lev and told him how fucking nice he was.

James said, "That reminds me. I really like Ace."

"Yes. It's fine," Bolin said, lifting their bottle of carrot wine to him.

"What?"

"I know you want to keep Ace. We'll keep Ace. Meabh would like a little brother."

James took the bottle from Bolin and kissed him before taking a sip. "I don't have a toast for getting a new kid," he said.

Kali held up her and Lev's bottle and said, "Congratulations! It's a boy!" and they all cheered the new addition to the household of Bolin and James and drank the wine James had made.

Bolin said, "Thank you both for bringing us back a son."

"He'll need anti-God Parents. Will you two accept that responsibility?" asked James.

"Anti-God Parents is going to need an explanation for the uninitiated. But, yeah, I'll do it," Kali said.

"Lev knows. He and Santi are already Meabh's anti-God Parents," said Bolin.

"Our job is to let the kids know they don't need to rely on a God. Remind them to be self-reliant and consult themselves and their family regarding morals, ethics, fear, hope and all the rest you'd normally throw at the feet of an imaginary deity."

"I'm so down with that." Kali nodded enthusiastically, taking a sip of the wine and passing the bottle to Lev.

Lev told them how he and Kali were switching rooms. James had a broken arm and broken ribs, so Bolin asked if he could help them move their belongings downstairs. Lev was appreciative of the offer and said they'd need help the following day, but tonight, they just needed the mattress moved downstairs so that they could be together. Bolin helped Lev carry down the entire bed, not just the mattress, and Kali heard Bolin suggest they rope off the bottom stair to prevent people from walking up to the open door. James and Kali sat on the couch talking about the Ivy team being executed earlier in the day.

"They were traitors, James. I listened to them brag about their plans to take the tech I brought them and get rid of Lev. Some wanted to lock me up in the cages again. Make me help them. I can't even believe how crazy some of them sounded. Me. I thought someone else sounded crazy. Can you imagine?" She laughed.

"No. Bol told me he was enraged. That was his word. He told me he insisted they all die by having their throats cut rather than getting a bullet to the head because he wanted them to suffer. I wasn't surprised. Lev is family. No one goes after our family. I hope you realize that means you, too."

"I told you Lev and I were 'something' last night. Today, he asked me to be his family, but Dave knocked on the door. I don't know what he meant."

"Well, I think you should check with Lev about what that means to the two of you," James said and kissed her forehead.

Kali and Lev's Room

Lev was making their bed with the clean sheets. Kali put their toothbrushes, soap, baking soda, and towels in the bathroom. She watched as Lev put his knife under her pillow and smiled at how thoughtful he was.

"Everything's so clean," she said as she put the nearly empty bottle of wine on the floor near the open window and looked outside. Bolin and Lev had placed the bed to the left of the door rather than directly across from the door and under the window the way it had been placed in Lev's former room. The light from the abbreviated hallway didn't cast a bright glow on the left side of the room, and anyone who showed up at their door would have trouble seeing them if they were in bed.

"James said he's going to be right back with the "Do Not Enter" sign that's above the stable office. I can see him walking over here now. Hey, James!" Kali yelled out the window, waving.

"I'm going to go get the table and chairs, so we have them in the morning," Lev said as he left the room.

James approached the window and passed the sign through the window with his one good arm.

"This will keep people away from your open door," he said sounding hopeful.

"Thanks, man!"

"You two have enough wine?"

Kali bent down and picked up the bottle that was near her feet and showed it to him. "There's still some left!"

"No. That's not enough. I'll be right back," he said as he turned around.

"James!" she laughed.

"You can't stop me!" he yelled back at her.

Kali took the sign out to the hallway and placed it at the top of the stairs by leaning it sideways. She couldn't get it to stay upright and it fell and slapped loudly, falling flat against the cement floor as Lev approached carrying the two chairs.

"Use these tonight," he said, putting them next to each other at the top of the short staircase.

"Be right back," he said as he left to get the table. Kali stabilized the sign and waved at some Team 4 Security members who were leaving their gym. They walked over and introduced themselves to her.

"We heard Lev was moving in down here. You, too?"

"Yes. I'm Kali. The door will be open. Don't come up the stairs."

A couple of the team members nodded and smiled and asked if Lev was in the room.

"No, I'm behind you," he said with the table in his hands. "Williams tell you we'll be neighbors?" he asked them.

They confirmed Williams had informed them of Lev's new residence, and Lev corrected them saying, "Kali and I are going to live here. It's her place, too. No one comes up the stairs. This area..." he waved his hand at the shortened hallway, "this is our patio. Probably throw some chairs and a barbecue over there." He laughed.

The members of the security team laughed with him, relieved that he wasn't angry with them for stopping by to see what Kali was up to.

"Sir, we heard the news from Dave and Bolin that you're Head of Ivy now and Head of Research. We were told about the coup and Dave, our new Head of Security, told us some of what's going on before we executed the Ivy RT. It's pretty wild. Just want to say, speaking for all of us, because we were all talking about it....We're happy to serve you, Lev. We'll keep this community safe so the RTs can work and get that guy."

"I appreciate your commitment."

Another security team member spoke up. "Your residence will be protected and private. Someone's usually around. We'll keep an eye on your place. Does your door remain open all the time? Or only when someone's home?"

"Only when Kali's home. Might be closed if I'm in there by myself. Will be closed when neither of us are there."

The group nodded and told Kali and Lev to have a nice night as they walked off to their various places post workout.

Lev and Kali walked into their room and Lev set the table down. He put his arms around her waist and was about to speak to her when they heard James calling to them from the open window.

"Oh, this is gonna be a thing with you two, isn't it?" Lev asked her with a laugh.

"Probably," she laughed back as they both walked to the window to see James.

He was smiling and holding out a bottle of carrot wine telling Lev, "You needed more. Take care, you two. I have to get back home. Bolin's stringing his acoustic guitar right now. He's going to put on a private concert for me tonight. He promised to play me the song he played the first night we met."

"Jesus, James. Get home! Lucky bastard," Lev said with a laugh.

"Thanks for the wine!" Kali yelled to him as he walked away waving.

Lev and Kali get Married

Lev turned out the lights and walked over to the bed and sat down kicking off his shoes.

"I wanna talk to you," he said.

The light from the hallway cast a soft glow on the left side of the room and on them. Kali removed her shoes and walked over to him, removing her shirt. Lev took off his shirt before Kali finished removing her own and threw it on the floor. She was standing in front of him and he put his hands on her hips as she unhooked her bra and worked each of her arms out of it and let it fall to the floor. Lev reached up and put a hand on one of her breasts and stood up in front of her letting his hand move from her breast down over her stomach.

"Hmm, take these off," he said as his hand caught on the waistband of her pants. They both removed their pants and Lev sat back down on the edge of the bed. Kali sat beside him and said...

"Earlier, you asked me to be your family. Tell me what it means to you to be family with me."

"Baby, can I call myself your husband?"

"Yeah."

"Would you like to be my wife, or no? If you don't want to be my wife, tell me what you want to be called even if it's Kali. That's enough for me. You can be Kali and I can be your husband. Or I can call myself your husband and you can decide you want to be called my partner, or whatever. It's you. You decide for you."

"I'd like to be your wife."

"Can I refer to you that way?"

"Yeah. And I can call you my husband?"

"Yeah. That's how this family of ours will work."

"I really like our family."

"Me, too. I think having sex makes our status official."

"Let's make it official."

Kali looked up at him and he leaned over and kissed her while caressing her shoulder.

"You're beautiful," he whispered to her between their kisses. "I'm so happy I get to be your husband. You can always count on me, baby. I'll fuck up, but I'll be doing my best for you."

Kali smiled at that and kept kissing him. "I'll probably fuck up more than you will. I promise, I'm doing my best. I'm just so fucked up, man."

Lev laughed quietly and assured her he was ok with how fucked up she was. They kissed more and Lev ran his hands down her back. He kissed her neck and she whispered to him that she wanted to suck his cock. He moaned approval for her suggestion and kissed her mouth hard using his hands to pull her face closer to him.

"Gotta let me go, babe," she said as she moved away from his mouth and moved off of the bed onto the floor in front of him.

He watched her get onto the floor on her knees and opened his legs for her to move closer and she slid his penis into her mouth. "Mmm, fuck, Kali," he moaned quietly.

She used her tongue as she went up and down on him and felt his hands gently touch her shoulders, then the back of her neck, and work their way through her hair as she sucked on his cock. He ran his hands back down to her shoulders and moaned saying her name and encouraging her to keep going as he leaned back to get a better view of her while she was between his legs.

Eventually, he started swearing quietly and told her it was time to stop because he was close to cumming and didn't want to cum before they had a chance to do more together.

Kali got back up onto the bed beside him where he quickly turned her over onto her back saying, "Don't cum, baby. Let me know when you're ready," and put his face between her open legs. He used his tongue on the outside of her and his fingers inside her to massage her clit slowly and she moaned calling his name and asking him come back up and kiss her and fuck her. He kissed her body on his way back up to her mouth while he continued to massage her inside with his fingers. He kissed her like she asked him to, and asked her if she was sure she was ready so quickly, but she admitted she could go longer. He was amused at her protests for him to stay and fuck her anyway, telling her he'd be back but that he had to go back down on her and taste her some more.

"I'm so fucking hungry for you, baby," he said as he worked his way back down her body while she breathlessly said, "Ok, yeah. Actually, that feels really good."

He went back down on her and she put her hands through his hair as he sucked gently on her clitoris pulling on it and rubbing it with his tongue while using his fingers to rub her interior clit softly. He went slowly and took his time, listening to her encourage him as she became more excited. When she said she couldn't wait any longer, he brought his face up to hers and put his tongue in her mouth and let her taste herself while they kissed.

He moved on top of her pushing his erection against her and said, "Fuck, Kali. I want to be inside you now."

"Baby, get inside me, then," she said, and he pushed himself inside her and they fucked slowly for a while before their impending orgasms dictated they pick up the pace. He watched her face in the soft light coming in from the hallway and told her she was beautiful as she called out his name when they fucked harder and faster and came together.

They got dressed and put on their shoes afterwards and wrapped themselves up in each other's arms.

"Kali, I'm not exaggerating. I'm so happy you let me be your husband," he said as he kissed her temple.

She turned to him and kissed his lips with one hand on his cheek. "I have to tell you something."

"You probably don't have to," he said with a faint smile.

"I should, though."

"You can, of course, but I'll bet you'll find you didn't have to. But go ahead, because you seem worried. Tell me."

"Bas made me marry him when I was 19. I didn't have a choice."

"Then it doesn't count," he said as he kissed her and pulled her closer to him. Her body was rigid and he smiled kindly at her. "You need to realize I'm not threatened by that asshole. I really think I'm better than him," he smiled, while nodding.

Kali inhaled sharply and looked at him very upset.

Lev suddenly looked serious and grabbed her tightly, saying gently but firmly, "Listen. You and me- we want this. If he fucking kidnaps you again and you spend another 20 years there, I'm still here being your husband. You're there being my wife. That asshole can't change the truth. I'm your husband. You got that?"

"Yeah."

"That make sense to you?"

"Yeah."

"I don't fucking care what he believes. It's what we know that matters. You don't have two husbands."

Kali smiled and shook her head no.

"That's right, baby. You've got one husband- me. I've got one wife- you. I know you can be forced to do things. I'm not here to hold you accountable for shit you can't control. You need more words from me? Or can I kiss my wife?"

Kali nodded. "Kiss me, husband," she said.

And he did.

Kali is Lev's Wife

Kali woke up early and laid there looking at Lev as he slept. She remembered he was now her husband and smiled happily. She wanted to touch him and kiss him and do things that would wake him up, but she decided that wasn't in his best interests. He needed sleep. She laid next to him smiling at the man sleeping next to her. Not waking him up was incredibly difficult for her. She waited and watched him sleep. She was lying against the side of the bed that was pushed against the wall. She had a clear view of the open window on the other side of the room. The sky had been black when she'd first woken up, but was now a soft grey with the beginnings of light illuminating the early morning hours.

She heard some people moving about outside their room and figured it was people from Team 4 who had gone to the gym to work out. That suspicion was reinforced when she heard sounds through the open door of their room. People were in the exercise room down the hall lifting weights. It wasn't too loud. It would be easy to sleep through, but she was paying attention, so she could hear it.

The sun rose and the sky turned from black, to grey, to a weird yellow, and then to a light blue. Kali heard someone outside their door and was surprised that anyone would walk past the sign James had given her the night before. She gripped the knife under her pillow ready to kill Lev if necessary. The person outside their door was quick and she heard quiet footsteps down the stairs followed by some quiet talk further down the hallway. It wasn't Bas or his army. Must have been someone from Ivy. Maybe security Team 4 corrected the person and told them to leave. Kali decided that what she had heard was not a threat. She really wanted Dave to give her weapons today. Lev had given her his knife to kill him with. She released her grip on its handle and looked at her husband. She didn't want to kill him, but she would.

She realized she had to use the bathroom and worked her way off of the bed without waking Lev. She used the bathroom, brushed her teeth and was cleaning her body in a quick shower. She thought of the ways Lev had touched her the night before and closed her eyes feeling her body become aroused at the memories.

She heard a noise and looked up as Lev entered the bathroom smiling and said, "Hey, wife. I'm gonna brush my teeth, take a quick shower, and then let's go back to bed, ok?"

"It's like you read my mind," Kali said playfully as she walked out of the shower and grabbed her towel.

Lev was still brushing his teeth as he raised his eyebrows at her and flicked his head at her in the direction of their bed. He spit into the sink and said, "I'll be right there, huh?"

As she headed towards their bed, drying her hair and walking naked across the room, she called back to him smiling, "I'm going to get started without you!"

He looked at her and shook his head in amusement. "Oh, you.. I'll be right there!" he said laughing.

When he got back into bed with her a few minutes later, he asked, "You wait for me?"

"Mostly."

"Mmm, wanna show me what you were doing while you waited?"

"Mmm-hmm."

"Fuck, Kali..." he groaned deeply as he watched her touch herself. "Let me take over, baby."

He was breathing hard with his eyes closed and his forehead against hers while she whispered, "That was so fucking nice, Lev."

"Mm-hmm," he agreed, opening his eyes slowly to look at her and kissed her.

Kali ran her hand over his ass and felt his body leave her body as he rolled away from her onto his back.

She turned herself towards him, and he grabbed her up onto his side with his long arms.

"Give me a minute, and I'll go get us breakfast," he said as he kissed her. "Give me two minutes. I think I need three minutes," he laughed with his eyes closed again.

Lev finally said he'd go get them breakfast and bring in their chairs so they could eat at the table. They got dressed in their clothes from the day before, and Kali laid down on their bed on her stomach watching him as he sat next to her and put on his shoes.

"I'll be back with food," he announced like a warrior.

She laughed at him and watched him leave the doorway.

He came right back in and said, "Uh, yeah. Looks like Bolin and James were here earlier. Left us breakfast and a present for you."

"What?" she laughed and pushed herself up on her elbows and looked at him in back of her as he stood by the open door.

Lev disappeared again and came back carrying a full vase of cosmos which made Kali gasp.

"Right?" Lev said as he placed them under the window next to the two bottles of carrot wine. "This has to be Bolin. And this has to be James..." He disappeared from the doorway and reappeared a moment later with a full tray of breakfast. "There's more," Lev said. He returned with a carafe of hot chicory and mugs. "Hold on. There's more."

Kali laughed a gasping kind of laugh.

Lev disappeared and returned with honey and a small cup. "This is goat milk for the chicory. They went fucking nuts," he laughed.

"Well, we did get them guitar strings and a kid," Kali said, smiling.

"Yeah, that's true. We deserved this," laughed Lev. "Ok, I'll get our chairs." Kali heard Lev talking to someone in the hallway and he returned with the chairs. "Kartethe said it was Bolin and James."

Kali looked at Lev and furrowed her brow. "Do you think Bolin went all the way to the field of cosmos to get these for me?" she asked.

"Yeah. Unless he knows where there are more. I've never seen them around here. Nowhere between Ivy and Campus and that's five miles. He must have ridden a horse out early this morning."

Kali looked concerned. "This is a lot."

Lev placed the two chairs he was carrying next to the table full of food, and held out his hand to her where she was sitting on the bed. "Family does shit like this. Come on. Let's eat."

Kali walked over to her bouquet of cosmos under the window and removed a pink one. She trimmed the stem and placed it through her still damp hair behind her ear and sat down across from Lev. He asked her, "So, is Vespry my brother-in-law now? My uncle-in-law? Cousin? You said he's your family. What's he to me now?"

"He'd definitely be your brother-in-law. And so you know, I'm sure he'd really like you. I keep thinking how I wish I could introduce you to him."

"I hope to meet him when this is over. Celebrate with him and thank him for trying to help us. He risked a lot. He's still risking a lot every day."

"I killed Rollo once, but he wasn't mad."

"Ok. I'm really interested in that," Lev laughed while looking through the assortment of food.

Kali looked at Lev and asked, "Do you like dark comedy?"

"I do. I liked Python back in the day."

"This might be darker."

"Let's hear it," he smiled while handing her a piece of bacon. "James made us bacon!" he said with a big smile.

Kali goes Crazy and Kills Rollo

"There was a time when I went really crazy. Not all at once, like I suddenly woke up crazy. Rollo said it escalated over time. People were putting up with me for a while before it got totally out of hand. I kept trying to kill myself and everyone had to have Rewinds on hand. I wasn't even waiting for good opportunities to kill myself. I would just throw myself on a fire. Then someone would have to drag me out of the fire and shoot me in the head and someone else would have to rewind me."

"Wait, this is supposed to have comedy along with the dark," Lev said, looking concerned.

"I said it was darker. One time, Bas saw me looking out of a high window in a hotel we were staying at and he had us change rooms because he realized if I jumped, it would take too long for someone to get to the ground and rewind me, or I might have a gun and shoot myself in the head while I was falling...15 seconds can seem like a lot of time or not enough depending on the situation. Bas just thought he might not be able to rewind me at some point.

"He started being careful with me. Can you fucking imagine? It messed with my mind even more. So, we started having to stay on the lower floors of hotels, and I couldn't ride the skyrides, and my drinks were served in plastic cups, and child locks on car doors, and someone had to hold onto my arm on the streets so I didn't jump in front of traffic, and I could only have a plastic spoon when I needed silverware, and shit like that. Wouldn't even let me have a spork... But I gave them a reason for that one, actually." Kali laughed and told Lev, "See? You didn't laugh. This might be too dark for you."

Lev shook his head and said, "Ok, I'm getting into the groove. Was the spork thing real, though?"

"Yeah."

"Jesus, see, I'm not comfortable laughing at that."

"It's funny in retrospect. Should I continue?"

"Yeah. I'll fill your plate while you talk. There's good stuff here. We have bread and friggin cheese."

"Mmm. Bread and cheese?! Babe, this is like being on a honeymoon in a really nice hotel with room service."

"Only the best for my wife," he said, smiling brightly at her.

She laughed at him and said, "Thank you, husband. Where was I? Oh, yeah. There was a team who thought of everything. Kali's suicide prevention team or some shit. Different name, of course."

"Of course."

"Everyone gradually became enlisted in the effort to prevent my intensified efforts to kill myself. I killed myself so many times, even with all the preventive measures put in place. I was really good at it."

"I can imagine," said Lev through a mouthful of bread and cheese. "Then one day I realized...that was actually all at once.... I realized all at once, that I wasn't going to be able to kill myself. Those fuckers were better at rewinding me than I was at killing myself. So, I decided to kill everyone else. And man, did I kill a lot of people. Every-fucking-body who came near me started getting killed. I figured if I couldn't kill myself, I had to get rid of everyone else so I could be free from them. Then I could have peace. Plus, if I was going to be forced to live forever with a psychopath, I had the time to kill everyone. But I knew I had to be cool about my new plan. So, I pretended I was better.

"When it became clear I wasn't trying to kill myself anymore, they gradually put away a lot of the Rewinds, and I had less security. It was funny. They didn't realize they'd need to keep the Rewinds around to rewind people around me. They were so unprepared.

"At first, I lied and covered up my murdering by saying shit like, they were running with scissors, or they tripped, or I didn't see it happen, or I tried to perform the Heimlich."

"Now that's funny," Lev said, smiling.

Kali laughed, too.

He handed her a piece of bread with cheese on it and said, "Try this. Taste reminds me of a pre-apocalypse wine tasting I went to."

"You went to wine tastings? Those are for old people."

"Rude. I like wine. And California wineries never checked my teenage ass for an ID."

"We still have the extra bottle of carrot wine," she said as she got up and brought it to him.

He took it from her and she said, "I need more bread and cheese, thank you, please," while holding out her hand to take the bread with cheese he had just made for himself.

"Ok, here, but only because I'm a generous husband," he said, smiling and passing her the bread and cheese.

"Story," he said as he made himself another piece of bread and cheese.

"Yeah. So, with all the accidental deaths around me, they caught on. I even killed Bas a couple of times, but he's got a really dedicated security detail. I couldn't keep him dead for more than 15 seconds. I fucking tried."

Lev was stunned and stopped what he was doing to comment. "Holy shit! You killed that son of a bitch?! Several times?! The fucking guy who ended the world?!"

Kali nodded with raised eyebrows and kept eating her breakfast. "Several times," she said as she chewed her food. "I'd have rather tortured him, because I only want to kill people who deserve death, but yeah, I killed that fucker. You know how crazy I must have been to have killed him rather than torture him?" Kali looked away and shook her head and laughed lightly at the thought. "I killed a lot of people who deserved torture. I kinda lost track of my personal rules for killing people," she admitted.

"I'm so impressed, baby. I can't even make sense of it," Lev said, shaking his head and looking at her in amazement.

"And because I was killing so many other people, that stupid clown didn't even take it personally each time I killed him. But, babe, it was so fucking personal."

"I'm sure it was." Lev opened the bottle of carrot wine and took a big sip. "I'm day drinking before my important work meeting to toast my wife having killed that son of a bitch several times. Want some?" he asked her.

"Yeah," she laughed and took the bottle and took a big sip before passing it back to him. "I really like this wine. I think it's my favorite. So, one day I was at home when Rollo stopped by to talk with Bas, and I walked up behind Rollo, and cut his throat, and jumped in front of Bas to stop him from rewinding him, but he got past me and rewound Rollo and saved him. Isn't that funny? Bas saved Rollo! It's still so funny to me."

She looked at Lev who looked shocked and laughed out loud saying, "You're fucking kidding? Bas saved Rollo Vespry's life? Holy shit, that's dark comedy, alright!" Lev took another sip of the wine and passed it to Kali who also took a sip.

"Rollo thinks it's funny, too. Now. At the time, he was really worried about me. He wasn't ever mad, though. Now, we laugh about it."

"Is that the end of the story?" Lev asked, sounding amazed.

"It can be unless you want to hear about how I got better."

"What? Of course, tell me how you got better."

"So, Rollo's zombie-self told Bas I was too crazy and suggested I be put in Time, inside actual Time, not torture, and see if I could be calmed down. Or, he suggested Bas just finally kill me. I was all for that and begged for that option. Of course, the asshole wouldn't just kill me, so they tried Rollo's suggestion, and I got put directly into Time. There's no torture in Time. That was different. That's when Time and I really got to know each other. Time told me about your mom, and Time and I really learned how to communicate with each other. I felt, and still do feel, really connected to Time."

"Oh. Ok. Hey, I wanted to say, I'm really glad you got to hear about my mom from one of your friends. That's a really weird, but a nice thing to know."

"Time had only really nice things to say about Time's friendship with your mom."

"We'll talk more about that later. Let's hear the rest of this story."

"Rollo told me they took me out of the oven to check if I was done, that's a cooking metaphor, I wasn't actually in an oven that time, or to see if I'd gotten even a little better, and I had.

"The oven thing isn't funny to me at all. That's upsetting."

"To me, too. Let's forget I said it. I had gotten better. I had actually gotten a lot better, but I wanted to go back inside, so I pretended to be more crazy than I actually felt. I insisted I needed more time and they sent me back. It was so nice to be there with Time."

Lev asked, "How long were you inside Time?"

"Time is weird inside of Time, but Rollo said it was 108 years according to Bas's calculations. Time told me it was longer."

"Is time always different in torture, too?

"Yeah. It's all different. Nothing's set. They control the length of your sentence."

"But you age there?"

"Yeah, not your body, unless Bas wants to age your physical body too, but your mind, your consciousness ages. Bas can't stop that from aging. You live the entire experience."

Lev moved his chair next to hers and put one arm around her shoulders and his other arm on the table where he rested his chin in his hand. "How old are you?"

"Pfft. I have no concept of my age anymore, but probably close to 1000 years old. Maybe 1100. I don't know. More than 800. I know of some long stretches off the top of my head that put me over 500, so more than that. Probably less than 1500, but maybe not. I asked Time, but Time wouldn't tell me. Not couldn't, but wouldn't. I trust Time, so I let it go."

"Well, I guess you're 43 years old here," he said with a smile as he rubbed her back.

"Do you see me differently now?" she asked him.

"No, beautiful. I still see you."

"Is it ok that I told you?" she asked.

"Absolutely. It helps me know you better, so thank you for telling me." Lev was pouring them their chicory and moved the honey and the goat's milk towards her. "I think you're worried you'll tell me something that changes my feelings for you, but it's not gonna happen. You can't scare me off. I don't care if you're 1000 years old or 10,000 years old. I've done things to survive here. You've done things to survive, or die in your case, over there. I already accept everything you've done without hearing all of the things you've done. I'll listen to you tell me anything you want me to know. But, you have to know this, you don't have to tell me anything unless you want to tell me. The stuff about killing Bas several times, that was badass, baby. You can tell me all about that anytime. Details are welcome."

Kali happily told Lev the ways she'd killed Bas, and Lev laughed at the stories of that asshole being killed by her.

"One thing I learned from killing Bas was that the people who follow him are more like cult members than citizens of his kingdom."

"How so?"

"Because I killed him. They could have been free. But they fought me and scrambled over me and each other to rewind him before he could stay dead," Kali said nodding her head at him."

Lev nodded, too.

"None of them are innocent," Kali said.

"I see what you're saying," Lev agreed.

They took their chicory coffees to their bed and sat up against the wall drinking them while Lev told her about how he met Dave, Hans, and Cheri, and how he, Dave, Aisha, Bob, Hans, and Cheri ended up at Campus.

"Did you ever find Bob's family?" she asked him.

"Yeah. His youngest, the one in the wheelchair, he was alive. Not conscious, but alive. He was going to die. Bob couldn't do it, so I did."

"Has Bob gotten better at doing what needs to be done?"

"Oh, God yeah. Bob's a scary motherfucker. And that's coming from me. Aisha balances him out. Otis, too."

"Who's Otis?"

"Their son. Bob's only scary if his family is threatened. He lost one family.

He's not losing another without a fight. He and Dave are the same age, or thereabouts. They're pretty tight. Definitely brothers. You look at Dave and Aisha and see two different people, but no. They're the same person. She just smiles more," Lev laughed.

"Did Bob have a problem with you for killing his son?"

"No. He had to beg me to do it. We were standing around the car crash where he was trapped inside their van, and the three of us were afraid he'd regain consciousness. He'd been out there overnight with his dead mother and two dead brothers. It was horrible. Bob tried, but he looked like he was going to lose his mind having to kill his only surviving son even if he was going to die soon anyway. Aisha offered to do it, but she'd known them most of her life and they were family to her, so she broke down and was shaking trying to get it together to do it. Bob grabbed me and pleaded with me to stop Aisha from doing it. He didn't want her to live with the memory or the guilt. She was near the kid saying she could do it. She was really brave. I walked over and fucking did it. Snapped his neck. Bob was never mad at me for doing it. He cried, but he thanked me. It was like when you kill people to end their pain, you know?" he asked her.

"I know. He couldn't have done it. It would have driven him insane. It's good that you saved all three of them by doing it," she said.

Kali climbed over Lev's legs to get herself more chicory. Lev handed her his cup and she made them each a fresh cup using the honey and the goat's milk. Her hair was dry and full now. The pink cosmos still peeked out from her hair and Lev admired her beauty while she stood by the table.

She made two pieces of bread with cheese and handed one to Lev saying, "See? I can cook."

He laughed and shook his head at her while eating.

"You've got a lot of skills, but you should learn a few cooking basics and how to ride a horse."

Kali laughed and said, "Well, I'll improve my cooking skills, but no one's getting me on a horse."

She handed him both of their cups and held on to her bread and cheese as she climbed back up to her spot next to him on the bed.

She leaned against him after he passed her her cup. Lev put his arm around her and said, "But horse riding is fun. We can ride out to the white house quickly. Spend a night there just me and you. No neighbors around. Have really loud sex."

Kali smiled and nodded. "I'm definitely into that, but I'll walk. You ride ahead of me and start dinner."

He laughed at her and asked, "Did you fall off a horse once, or something?"

"No. They're just big and fucking scary. I think they're dinosaurs. They've got attitude. Like they know they can fuck us up. They just tolerate us."

"Dinosaurs?" laughed Lev. "Have you actually met a horse?"

"From a distance. At parades in San Diego. I saw pictures of their skeletons in a book at the library once when I was kid. Their skeletons look like T-Rexes."

Lev laughed at her harder. "No they don't! This is an irrational fear!"

"No, being afraid of spiders is irrational," she insisted, laughing with him. "It's done. It's too late to overcome my childhood children's library traumas. I was left unsupervised with picture books and the damage is done," she laughed adding, "But I'm serious. I'm afraid of them."

"He pulled her tighter to him and said, "We'll start small. I'll introduce you to our goats."

"Oh, I like goats!" she said happily, snuggling up to him.

"You don't think they're baby T-Rexes?" laughed Lev.

"No. They're cute," she laughed. "Also, I feel confident I can take on a goat and win. My dad took me to petting zoos. I fed the goats there."

He laughed at her and said, "James is gonna make fun of you for this."

They were quiet for a few minutes and Kali said, "Babe?"

"Hmm?"

"I'm not comfortable around chickens either."

Lev threw his head back and laughed harder at her saying, "But you wanna go see the bees?"

He was still laughing at her as she protested that bees are pollinators and she understands their mission. "Chickens are so easily provoked! Like little velociraptors," she said, laughing at herself along with him. "I'm not kidding, Lev!" she said laughing as Lev continued to laugh at her.

"I know you're not! That's why it's so funny," he said, smiling and shaking his head at her.

Orders of Business

Lev told Kali that he would meet her for lunch at one of the picnic tables to let her know what was going on and if she was needed in the labs.

"Where are the labs?" she asked as she looked for the slightly burned book about the rabbits in Lev's backpack.

"The entire top floor of this building is various labs. Vespry splashed a ton of money on them and provided Ivy with amazing equipment. It's all like 20 years old now, but he did a good job setting Ivy's RT up for success. Where'd he get all the money to do this? 20 million just for this place?" Lev asked, curious.

"He and Time tried and failed hundreds of times to win the lottery. They eventually hit a jackpot after winning lots of smaller ones. Time says lotteries are rigged. I think Time used a Time-species swear word at some point over the whole lottery thing."

Lev laughed at the information and asked, "But who claimed the money?"

"Time identified lots of good people for that. That was the easiest part, actually. People really are generally good. I was kind of crazy and in Time for some of the plan. Time and I talked about it, but Time told me they had it under control."

"Oh, I see," Lev said, moving her large vase of cosmos to the center of the table she'd cleared. He put his arms around her. "I like your friends, too. Just so you know. I like how they take care of you. I was worried at first. Them sending you here, thinking maybe Vespry had kidnapped you.... You know? But I get it now. It feels good to me that you like the people I care about. I want you to know, I like your friends, too."

"I think they'd like you, too. Actually, Time must already know you."

"I'm going to meet them. I want to. Yeah?"

"Hopefully. Maybe Time will talk to you," she said as they wrapped their arms around each other's waist.

Lev kissed her and asked, "What are you gonna do while I'm in the meeting?"

"Learn how to navigate this weirdly designed building, give Bautista his new book, gloat because I won the bet, get weapons to kill you with, and see if I can find Olivia."

"Where can I find you later?"

"Picnic tables at noon," she reminded him.

"Oh, yeah. That was my plan. I'll bring us lunch. I rinsed out our mugs. Bring them to lunch with you for our drinks," he said as he kissed her again.

Kali took the book about the rabbits Lev had inadvertently discovered during their walk from Front Royal to Ivy and headed off to find Bautista's room with confusing instructions from Lev to guide her.

"I'm not being confusing. The way there is confusing," he insisted when she had asked him to explain the directions a second time and accused him of being confusing.

When Lev arrived for the meeting with the RT, he looked around the room for Bolin.

"Hey, Bol. I need to talk to you," he said, waving him out to the hallway. Bolin jogged out to the hallway and followed Lev a few paces from the open door of the meeting.

"Man, thank you for this morning. The flowers, the breakfast. That was... Do you know?"

"That maybe you two got married? I think I have a sister-in-law. Do I?" he asked, smiling.

"Yeah. We did. You do. I'm a husband. I have a wife. Best fucking night of my life, man. Breakfast this morning, the flowers... Un-fucking-real, man. Couldn't have asked for more."

"I remember the day James and I got married. When you know, you know. I got more flowers. James is going to make a garden of cosmos for her."

Lev laughed and shook his head. "She could hardly handle what you two did this morning."

"Then don't tell her. She'll see them early next summer after she gets used to being part of a family," Bolin said seriously.

Lev nodded. "Ok. You know I appreciate everything you two did for us this morning, right?"

"Yes. I know. Do you know James is completely captivated by Ace? The kid is funny as hell. He's a mini James. You know my daughter has a brother, now? You know I have a son? You know I'm playing guitar again after several years of not being able to? We got you a nice breakfast and some flowers. We didn't do too much. Congratulations on your marriage. We're really fucking happy for you two," Bolin nodded with a laugh.

"Ok," Lev laughed.

"Let's get day three of this wild ride started," Bolin said, as he and Lev walked back into the meeting room.

As Lev addressed the RT he said, "Some issues regarding living and working with Kali. She will not be required to work in the gardens, or with the animals, or in the kitchen. She's lived in Bas's Kingdom since she was 19. I told you all yesterday she only arrived outside of Bas's Kingdom about two weeks ago. She has no skills needed to survive here. She hadn't eaten in days when she arrived here. I hope you all heard enough yesterday to agree we'd be wasting her time and the skills she does have, which we need, if we demanded she learn post-apocalyptic survival skills. She can't cook, she has no farm experience. She is going to work with Bolin to train spies who can be successful in Bas's Kingdom. She's going to be available to us to explain the tech, discuss the 29 things Bas is working on developing which Vespry wrote out for us, and then explain other things we can't imagine today.

"She knows a lot more about our enemy than can be explained in a few meetings. For instance, this morning I was informed that she personally succeeded in killing Bas several times. Unfortunately, he was rewound by his devoted cult members. So, he is killable. That's not an abstract. That information helps clarify our plan. We need to figure out his lock code in order to get inside his Kingdom, separate him from his cult, kill him, keep him dead for just over 15 seconds, let Death Time do their job. I learned that information in a casual conversation with her this morning. If she'd been out in the gardens being taught how to plant seeds, what sense would that make? Are you all getting this? Or do I need to explain further?"

The entire RT agreed wholeheartedly with Lev that Kali should be treated as an essential resource to the mission with different community-related expectations based on her current abilities.

"Ok, good. Three people a week cover her farm duties, me included. Who even knows if we'll make an entire rotation through our names before Bas ends us all," he said darkly. "She'll be treated differently and gossip is toxic. If you hear shit about her receiving special privileges, feel free to shut that bullshit down using hard facts. We need to get into teams and divide up this tech for research.

"Lev, I think we might need equipment from Campus to work with what she brought us. Do we need to consider moving there?"

"Let's go upstairs to the labs today and read the recipe book, decide on teams for each piece of tech she brought us, including a team for the communication tech which is in the recipe book but lacks the full recipe. We need to make contact with Pele. We'll discuss resources. There's a lot of equipment here at Ivy. I know 59 of you are here right now who have lives over at Campus. But all of our present lives are really close to being controlled by Bas. He could figure out how to control two present worlds by lunchtime today. Ivy has a lot of good equipment, too. It's a much smaller community with a lot less going on compared to Campus. We need to work together. We are one team. Communication between teams is going to be really important.

"Plus, it's possible Vespry could show up here with more resources for us. He doesn't even know about Campus. Kali had no idea Campus existed. Bas isn't far from figuring out the worst of his plans. I don't want to waste today, let alone a week figuring out how to move us to Campus. Aisha can have anything we need brought here. Isn't that true?" he asked her.

"We'll work round the clock, Lev. You can have everything you need from Campus brought here by this evening. I'll leave with a list the minute you make one. Everyone at Campus will pack up what you need and deliver it here before we do one more fucking thing. I heard Kali. Tell me what I can do."

Lev nodded at her. Members of the RT spoke in quiet agreement. The RT member who had suggested relocating to Campus said, "I agree."

Lev spoke quickly. "We need to work today. We're wasting this minute talking about stuff not related to what we need to learn. Let's just get our asses upstairs and start working on the recipe book information. We're about to learn whole new branches of physics and math. Maybe more. I don't know what's in this book. You realize you need something? Make a list. Aisha's got us. The quantum computer's already on the list, of course."

Dave got up and said, "Yesterday, I found out I'm gonna be able to see my late wife again after I die. I also found out Bas is going to try and stop me from being with her and will probably enslave her, torture her….. I'm going upstairs to work. If you have people you care about, you'll join me," he said as he left the room and headed to the lab.

"Speaking of wives, Kali and I are husband and wife," Lev told the RT.

"I heard that! Congratulations!" shouted Dave from the hallway.

Lev laughed and stood up. "Aisha come with us upstairs. We'll make that list for you as we decide what we need," Lev told her. "Everyone go upstairs now with Dave. Get into tech teams based on ability more than interest. I'll be up in a minute. I need to speak with Bolin privately."

Lev closed the door to the meeting room and turned to Bolin.

416

"I have math skills that might be useful," Bolin said to him helpfully.

Lev shook his head and spoke calmly to Bolin not wanting to rush the conversation he needed to have with him. "No, man. Listen, I might have gotten you into something you're not going to want to be a part of. I want you to know, you can decline the Intel Team leadership position if you start talking to Kali and realize you don't want to be a part of it."

"Explain."

"Remember how she spoke when she first got here? Dropping comments that sounded too strange to be true? But then they turned out to be true."

"Yes. She's confusing, but then she makes sense when you get more information."

"Listen, man it's bad over there. The torture...It's barbaric. It's part of their culture. Bas is a psychopathic, tyrannical sadist. His cult members are, too. They participate in inflicting torture and enable his ability to maintain power. When Kali clarifies something, it's usually just *so much worse* than I originally imagined. Spies would need to be trained to endure their specialized brand of torture as well as commit it. Their technology enhances the torture, man. I know we need to do this. Ugh... I told Kali yesterday I'm leaving it up to you and her. I'm out of it. She's confident about her role in training the team. She's not bothered by what needs to be done. She's more bothered by the thought of spies who will break and tell Bas about Vespry and Ivy. Are you prepared to be as brutal as is going to be necessary?"

Lev looked at Bolin deciding if he wanted to tell him something else, and Bolin waited patiently. "I didn't tell you what she did to the pedophiles I watched her kill."

"James told me."

Lev looked at him and shook his head.

"Like it was no big deal. She honestly couldn't understand why I wanted her to stop and just kill them. If you do this, I'm going to suggest we keep the team small and local. Just a handful of people. They need to be able to count on each other if they get into the Kingdom. Also, we might need them quickly. A large team…. that's too much work. We don't have time to get a large first rotation trained. We need this team right away. We need spies who can survive this asshole's Kingdom, maybe get us information we need for the tech we currently have, maybe even kill him and keep him dead for those necessary 15 seconds.

"It's like she said to both of us yesterday, no one should be forced to be a spy. I'm not going to force you to lead this team. But if you do, I don't need to know what's going on. You're probably going to learn stuff about her that I don't know. Kali can tell me anything she wants to tell me. Don't you tell me things you learn about her, though. I don't want to know unless Kali decides to tell me herself."

Bolin listened to Lev and remembered that Lev hadn't spent years as a soldier prior to the extinction event as he, himself, had. He understood Lev had no problem killing people, but he was an efficient and quick killer. He didn't take pleasure in the killing. Satisfaction at ending a problem by killing someone wasn't the same as deriving pleasure from the act of killing or from inflicting torture. From what James had told him about Kali killing the pedophiles, she had definitely taken some pleasure in hurting them before killing them. Kali had spent decades being a prisoner of war. Lev accepted that, but he struggled to make sense of the outcome of her experiences.

Lev had seen the sweeping genocide of a madman who used hands-free formulas for the murders he'd committed, but Kali had experienced the cruelty of the madman's hands. Bolin had seen war. He'd seen unnecessary, brutal murders committed by the murderers in real time. He'd seen more than he was willing to talk about even decades after the fact. He hadn't become desensitized to cruelty, but he could identify it without letting it destroy him. He didn't seek opportunities to be cruel, but he knew when it served the right purposes. Like Kali, he could commit what others would deem atrocities without doubting himself or his humanity. Training spies to do what was necessary to defeat Bas, that was crucial to the mission.

"I can do this," Bolin said confidently.

Lev nodded. "Brainstorm an Intel Team. Start by talking with Kali. She was going to find Marty this morning. I'm not going to be involved in the Intel Team. You understand? I wouldn't be an asset. I'm staying out of it and leaving it up to you two. I trust both of you. If you talk to her and decide you're not up for the role, let me know. We'll figure something else out."

Bolin nodded that he understood.

Lev left the meeting room to join the rest of the RT in the labs.

Bolin left to find Kali.

Kali, Ju, and Marty Bautista

"Kali? What's up?" asked Bautista, surprised to see her at his door.

"Oh, I think you know what's up," she said, waving the book about the rabbits under her chin. "I win!" she said, smiling.

Bautista laughed and said, "No, you did not find the book! This is Lev's. Why are you trying to get me into trouble?"

"Do you have a minute to hear the story of how this slightly burned copy of this book got to you this morning?" she asked.

"Sure, come inside. Is anyone else with you?" he asked, looking outside of his doorway and down both sides of the hall.

"No, just me."

"Ok, Ju's here, too," he said as he began to close the door to the room and then decided against it. He opened the door all the way and turned back to look over at Kali as Ju greeted her enthusiastically.

"Hey, Kali!" Ju said, looking up from the couch as she entered the room.

"Hi! Do you live here, too?" she asked Ju, happy to see her again.

"I stay here occasionally. We go back and forth."

"We made a bet, and I won," Kali told her with a happy smile as she handed Bautista the book.

"Have a seat and tell us how I actually won this bet," Bautista laughed as he grabbed a chair from his small dining table and walked it closer to the couch.

Kali told them the story about how she and Lev walked for days and stayed in various houses and how she looked for the book in each one without any success. She told them how preparing for the storm after a long day of walking left her too tired to look for the book at the farm house, but on the return trip, they stayed there a second time and Lev had actually found it without realizing she had been looking for it. Finally, she told them about Lev almost burning the book and how she rescued it from the flames with little time to spare before it would have been lost.

Bautista enjoyed listening to her account of the events that led to his now owning a copy of the book and thanked her graciously asking, "You think it's ok if I mention it to Lev?"

"Yeah, sure. He thought it was funny when he found out I'd made the bet with you. Have you read this book?" she asked Ju.

"Yeah, when I was a kid. I'll probably reread it after Marty."

"Do you prefer Marty or Bautista?" Kali inquired.

"They're the same to me. Whatever you prefer in the moment. Switch them up. I'll respond to either."

Bautista and Ju were both members of a security detail, but Bautista was on Lev's former security team. Team 4 and Team 1 had heard from Bolin and Dave about the attempted coup, and he had happily participated in the execution of Ivy's RT after hearing the information about Heather, Bas, and Kali. Her appearance in his doorway this morning with the book left him surprised and confused at the same time. He had believed the information he'd received from Dave and Bolin and didn't doubt it now, but what was she doing here alone, handing him a book and telling them her own adventure story? After the executions, Dave and Aisha had assembled all of the teams and made sure that every security team member had a clear understanding of the danger Bas and his technologically superior army posed to two, so-called, presents, to Ivy, to the RT, and to Kali personally. They stressed that Kali might not always follow the rules, but to be patient with her during interactions. She was on their side.

Now, here she was in his room, happily telling him about finding the book and winning the bet she'd made with him a little over a week ago while she was on the run with time-traveling technology she'd stolen from a madman. It was a lot for him to process.

"Does Lev know you're here?" he asked her, suddenly concerned that she was not in a room with a guard.

"Hmm?" she asked him, tipping her head to one side.

"Should you be here? Shouldn't you be in a room with a guard?" he asked her with a hint of concern in his voice.

"No. I'm not a prisoner or a guest. I'm just here now."

"Do you want me to walk you back to your room?" he asked her, furrowing his brow.

Kali laughed. "Didn't Dave and Bolin tell security team members who I am and all the rest last night?" she asked, shaking her head and laughing mildly at him.

"Yeah, well, that's what's got me concerned. Does Lev know where you are? That you're here?" he asked her, standing up now.

"Wow. Ok." Kali put up her hand indicating he needed to slow down. "Yeah, Lev knows I'm here, but I could have come here without telling him. I'm not a prisoner. I can go anywhere I want. I'm gonna walk around the building today and try to figure it out, actually."

Ju spoke up enthusiastically offering, "I can walk around with you. I told you it took me months to figure this place out, but really, now that I know my way around, there's a subtle pattern to the hallways and all the false doors."

"Yeah, let's do that," Kali agreed, grateful for the offer.

Bautista scowled and spoke to Ju who was also a security team member, but on Team 3. "I was at the same security briefing as you last night. Dave and Aisha covered a lot of disturbing ground. Plus, I got the earlier information from Dave and Bolin before and after the executions." He turned to Kali. "I'm worried you're not protected the way you might need to be. I'm not trying to be a dick, but I've gotta ask, did you have guards that you slipped to get here? I'll get you back to your room and smooth things over with them if they're pissed off at you. Tell 'em I needed this book and you were just doing what I asked," he said with a laugh.

Kali laughed with him and shook her head, assuring him that, no, she wasn't a fugitive within the halls of Ivy. "I don't have guards anymore. Lev told me how to get to your room so I could give you the book. He's in meetings this morning and I'm exploring."

Bautista looked like he accepted her explanation and asked her, "Do you remember where your room is? Ju can help you find it, if you don't."

"We've got this, Marty," Ju said patiently. She turned to Kali and said, "We already had breakfast, but if you haven't, I can take you to the cafeteria and show you the meal schedules and where things are located. Have some breakfast before we wander the halls?"

"Oh, I'm stuffed. Bolin and James brought us a really nice breakfast this morning and left it outside our room."

Bautista raised his eyebrows and looked at Ju who's eyes swung immediately in his direction while she still faced Kali.

Kali laughed at them and said, "Yeah, Lev and I got married last night. We're in a new room on the first floor."

"Well, congratulations!" Bautista said with genuine enthusiasm. "Williams made it out like Lev was moving down there by himself."

"Mm-hm. We met some of Team 4 last night while we were moving in. They thought it was just Lev moving in, too."

Bautista continued to chuckle lightly and shook his head saying, "You just showed up here bright and early, full of surprises, didn't you?"

"I'm ready to wander if you are," said Ju.

The two of them left, and Bautista sat and considered what he had learned about the world in the past 24 hours.

Bolin and Bautista

Bautista sat and contemplated the unsettling news he had learned the day before until he heard a knock on his door. He was a friendly man, but he knew he wasn't popular enough to have two visitors in a row so early in the morning, and he wondered who could be knocking on his door now. He opened the door and was surprised to see Bolin.

"Hello. Lev said Kali might be here," Bolin said with his usual efficiency.

"Oh, great. Does that mean she *did* slip her guards?" he asked, looking concerned.

Bolin was confused for a moment and then laughed mildly at him. "I see. She was here and left and you think she was supposed to have guards. No. Kali doesn't have guards anymore. She's allowed to do whatever she wants around here and she probably will, so feel free to help her out of any situations she gets herself into."

"That's a relief. Yeah, she was here a few minutes ago, brought me a book. Told me Lev knew she was stopping by. She and Ju went to learn the mysteries of the building together."

"Ok, so the two of them didn't have a destination in mind? I'm going to have to find them in this maze? That's great. Do you know which way they were headed?" Bolin asked with a loud sigh.

"Nah, they walked out and closed the door. I didn't see. But, hey, I want to ask you something. Do you have a few minutes?"

"No. I really need to find Kali."

"Ok. I'll just tell you then. I'm available for whatever this world needs from me. I want to get that guy. I was a cop before this. I put that on my resume when I applied for this position years ago," he laughed.

Bolin didn't laugh. He stared at Bautista.

"I know you gotta go find Kali. Sorry to hold you up."

"I've got a few minutes," Bolin said, looking at him with absolutely no amusement in his expression.

"Come on in," Bautista said as he stepped out of Bolin's way.

Kali, Ju, and Olivia

Kali and Ju had roamed the hallways of Ivy for about an hour before Ju informed Kali that she would have to go do her last day of farm work for the week before the expected rains began.

"Everybody does farm work? Lev didn't tell me that. Maybe I should go with you to whichever garden you're gonna be working in. I'm not going near the animals though."

Ju scoffed at the suggestion. "Don't even think about it. No one else here is helping us get this guy, Bas. You can skip picking bugs off the vegetables and learning how to milk a goat," Ju assured her. "Seriously, I'll do your farm work. I've got an extra three hours a week to spare. Don't even think about it."

"I'll ask Lev later today what I need to do. I've seen one of the gardens briefly, but I've spent most of my time here in Lev's room and in meetings in the basement."

"I'm sure you've helped out the community more by being in meetings with the RT than you would have if you'd been in the gardens. I'll give you the cafeteria tour, and then I have to go."

"In the Kingdom, I ate whatever Bas allowed me to eat, whenever he allowed me to eat. He ordered a lot of his own meals from the past, and my Friend cooked for him once a week, too."

Ju shook her head and scowled into the distance as they walked towards the cafeteria.

"You're allowed to eat anything you want here. Well anything James and the kitchen crew put out for us. The kitchen opens at 6am and closes at 8pm. If you work security overnight, your Team Leader gets you into the cafeteria and food is already made for you in back. No one goes hungry. Unless you're hungry at two in the morning and you're not working an overnight team. Then you wait until 6am. Bolin can probably get in any time he wants to because of James. I seriously doubt James or Lev will let you go hungry. I'll show you around so you're comfortable getting food when you want to eat."

"Will people be annoyed that I'm not farming, though? Maybe I should just have Lev get me my food. He's been doing it so far, anyway."

"That's bullshit. Come on. You didn't escape a madman and risk your life to bring us tech just so we could be mean to you when you want some vegetables and eggs. Jesus, Kali," she said, smiling and shaking her head.

Ju pulled open the door to the cafeteria. "Here are the bowls. Big ones are for two or three people to share. The small ones are for individuals. Are you hungry now?"

"No, I'm still full from the breakfast James and Bolin brought us this morning. I'll just take the tour."

Ju nodded and headed over to the self-serve area. "All meals start over here. This is basically snack time. Foods that aren't cooked, water, and chicory. Eggs are always hard boiled and only served in the morning. Jerky is always available. If you don't see any in this bin, and you need some protein, you can ask the kitchen crew for some or grab some peanuts once those are harvested again in a couple months."

"We had peanuts when we walked to get the tech."

Ju nodded. "What they have left is for situations like that. When someone's gonna be gone for a couple of days. James keeps lots of jerky in back, though. It's mostly deer, but right now, we have a lot of turkey, too. We go through jerky fast. They rarely run out, but sometimes they don't put enough out. Food waste is frowned upon, so take what you can finish or finish even if you're full. You can always go back for seconds if you don't take enough the first time.

"Before I got to Ivy, I heard they caged people for a week and didn't feed them the entire time for wasting food. Water only the whole week you were in a cage."

Kali raised her eyebrows. "That sounds like a rule my husband would make."

"It was him. He made all the rules about farm and food. Actually, I guess he's made all the rules for the community ever since he moved in. Do you have a mug?"

"I used one this morning in our room. Lev told me to bring it to lunch today when we meet at the picnic tables."

"Ok. So, everyone gets one mug. You keep your mug with you. Wash it in your room, not down here."

"Got it."

They sat down at a table against a windowless wall, and Ju pointed to a sink station across the large open space. "When you're finished eating, your bowl should be mostly clean. Rinse it quickly in that sink over there and put it right-side up in the other bowls in the second sink. That one has vinegar in it so the dishes will be sanitized. They make vinegar here to clean a lot of things, but also for cooking with. We basically have no silverware."

"The rules seem simple enough. Thanks for showing me around the building, too."

"Thanks for bringing Marty the book and the RT technology to defeat Bas. It feels weird to be able to name the person who did this to all of us. I lost my whole family. I only found Ivy four years ago. It's been so hard to be alive. Now I hear this guy wants to make it even harder after I finally die? I've been mad for a long time, but I finally know who to be mad at. I'm thankful to be a part of something that may help to bring him down. Whatever you need. Just ask me. Really."

As Kali nodded at Ju, she saw Olivia approaching them from across the room. She waved and called out, "Hey, Olivia! Come meet Ju."

Olivia stood by the table and asked them, "I just got back from Campus. I'm supposed to start my farm duties today, but Tuva told me to come inside and have something to eat before I go over to the gardens. Are there rules? Where are the plates? What am I supposed to do?"

Ju smiled and shook her head. "We'll be right back," she told Kali as she got up to give Olivia the cafeteria tour. Kali sat and looked around the cafeteria. She was definitely going to ask Lev about farm duties when she saw him later.

Olivia and Ju returned quickly, and Ju told Kali, "I'm going to take Olivia to farm with me and show her around there after she's finished eating." She turned to

Olivia and said, "If it starts to rain, we'll move over to the animals. That counts as farm, too."

"Thanks for the help. Tuva's nice, but she doesn't explain things well. She thinks I know what I'm doing, but I don't. Do either of you know if Trent's still here? I haven't seen him in a couple of days."

"Dave said we have a new security team member recruit. It's probably your friend. He's going to train with Team 3, my team, for a couple of weeks. We might see him at farm. I don't know what his schedule is, but he's probably going to do farm every day for a month like most new community members do. New community members spend more time on the farm to get up to speed and learn how to contribute."

"Lev said no riff-raff. Useless assholes who take but don't contribute," she explained, nodding with a serious expression.

Ju and Kali smiled at each other with shared humor when Olivia said that about Lev.

Olivia turned to Kali and said, "Campus is like the cities from the past that I heard about. You know, before the extinction. There's so much going on there. So many people. Everyone was nice to me. I had my own room, and a woman named Anush was my escort." She stared at Kali for a moment as she contemplated what she had seen at Campus. "I didn't know any of this existed. I only heard stories about when the world had large groups of people in it. It was hard to imagine even with all the empty buildings around to remind you of what it must have been like."

Kali and Ju nodded at Olivia and Ju told them, "I was 18 and supposed to go off to college in the fall when the event happened. It took me 13 years of trying to find a decent group of people to survive with before I found Ivy. I walked over the same bridge Kali came over. Marty and Williams greeted me with the usual hospitality Ivy and Campus are known for," she laughed.

"Marty lowered his gun first. Told Williams I looked like a traveler and not a scout for a raiding group. I heard him tell Williams they should find out if I had any skills. I had no idea what they meant. I felt so threatened. After a week in a cage, Bolin finally got to me and had me train with three Team 1 members for two weeks while I worked farm for, Jesus, eight hours a day, I think. I gave it my all. I hadn't seen so many people alive together in one place in over a decade. I wanted to be a part of Ivy, but Bolin sent me to Campus immediately following my two weeks of training, and I thought I'd failed." She nodded at Olivia as she recalled the events.

"Campus, huh? Hundreds of people working together. Everything's run so well. I thought it was intimidating after having been with so few people for so long. I wanted to go back to Ivy, to a smaller community, but I didn't argue. I knew I was better off at either community than I'd ever been since the event. Did you meet with Nova?"

"Yeah," said Olivia.

"So did I. I spent three months there training with their military, and then Nova asked me if I wanted to live at Campus and work in their military or if I wanted to go back to Ivy and work on a security team. I chose Ivy. I grew up in New York City, but I guess I'm more comfortable in the country now. They might offer you a choice about where to live. Do what feels best to you. You can always move later. The communities work together," she explained, nodding.

"I will. Maybe they sent me back because I'm not cut out for Campus's military."

"No, don't think like that. My security team lost three people a couple of weeks ago fighting raiders. That's why they placed Trent with us. Plus, you're so young. Maybe they like you better for a smaller community as training before offering you a role in the military. That's if you want a role like that. No one's gonna make you join the military."

Olivia nodded. "I'm supposed to meet with Bolin tonight. Maybe he'll send me back to Campus." She looked at Kali with a blank expression, and Kali stared back at her saying nothing. "Or maybe he won't," Olivia said, sounding hopeful.

Kali and Lev's Lunch Date

Lev was immediately confronted by Kali's questions about farm duties and quickly tried to put her mind at ease about the expectations he and the community had of her. He explained how the RT would cover her three hours a week which only amounted to one additional hour a week for each of the three people assigned to cover her duties.

When she suggested she might be able to develop farm skills while helping to train the Intel Team with Bolin, Lev explained hornworms to her and asked, "Babe, have you ever picked hornworms off of a tomato plant?"

Kali stared at Lev in disbelief. "You're making those up. Five inch long unicorn worms?"

"No, actually the horn comes out of their tail. We collect them and feed some to the chickens and take some to host plants we sacrifice to them in order to get hawkmoths later. Hawkmoths are excellent pollinators. You like pollinators, right?" he said, smiling at her.

Kali stared at Lev for a few seconds and then said, "No. You're kidding, right? Parasitic wasp...whatevers?"

Lev laughed loudly and assured her hornworms were real and their removal was part of essential farm duties. He continued to laugh at her as he watched her facial expression and body language silently come to terms with the fact that she wasn't prepared to work in a garden or with their animals.

"Maybe I'm not ready for farm duties..." she laughed along with him while still seeming annoyed at herself for lacking a skill.

"You're so good at so many other things, though," he assured her with a smile. "You got us tech. You've already told us so much new information that, this morning, we all decided we need a day off from you just to process what we've found out so far. Plus, you're honestly the best shot I've ever seen, not to mention

425

what I saw you do with a knife. You can fight like a honey badger...." he trailed off, looking at her and they both continued to laugh lightly.

"I wanna see a hornworm," she said.

"Because you don't believe me," he laughed as they ate their lunch.

They continued to talk after finishing their meal and Kali asked, "They really don't want me to talk to them today? There's more I thought of, though."

"We're doing a lot today with what you told us yesterday. Dave's got the prison darts locked in a glass cabinet today, so don't worry about them. The PD team is going to get a separate lecture once he and I go over the formulas for them. We can't have anyone accidentally arriving in Hell. We're in our teams. We got a team I have faith in working on the missing formulas for the comms to get to Pele. We're wrapping our minds around the new science, math, physics, and formulas this morning. Every now and then, someone will say, *'Oh, that's not possible!'* but then everyone else shuts them down and we do what you said, we accept it and move on. It's helping to keep us from getting stuck in some philosophical or whatever debate when we're confronting these new concepts, new formulas. What you said yesterday, really set the tone for us to make this much progress in just these few hours together. We'd known for years the math was missing something. We were close in so many different areas. The recipe book you and Vespry brought us.... So many missing puzzle pieces are right there for us now," he mused.

Lev looked at her and shook his head laughing again. "You don't worry about your contributions here, you understand? You see anyone else eating lunch at a picnic table?" he asked her.

"No. it's about to rain. Do you want to go back inside?" she asked him.

"No. I asked you to meet me for lunch at the picnic tables because everyone else is inside getting Community News about you from Dave and Aisha. No one's gonna give you side eye for not working on the farm. No one else here can do what you're doing."

Lev was looking at her as he spoke and stopped and stared at her with a more serious expression. "I know you know how reality altering a lot of that information you brought us is. I also know you and Vespry have this dialogue between yourselves where you both believe neither of you is smart enough to figure out formulas to take down Bas. I've read Vespry's words from the speech he gave the Ivy RT. Have you read them?" he suddenly asked her.

"No."

"I'll show you his speech. They wrote it down after he left. He sells himself short, too. Even as it's apparent he gathered together a group to help save the world, built this fucking facility, and traveled to talk to them, he's like, *'Oh, I suck at math!'*" Lev laughed and scoffed at the thought.

"Like math skills are the most important thing to have. I have math skills. Doesn't mean Time would have chosen me to help lead an opposition at age 16. The two of you don't give yourselves enough credit. It's all, *'Oh, we need the scientists to save us from this guy!'* But the scientists needed to know what you two know in order to know how to fight back against Bas.

"You and Vespry found the information we need. You think just because you don't know what the formulas or whatever mean, that you're not as valuable as the RT? It's fucking funny, Kali. We need you two. We still need to know what else you know. We're upstairs trying to figure out what you told us yesterday. I don't think we were going to figure any of this out before Bas gained control of the afterlife present. Shit, we didn't even know of the afterlife present until you enlightened us. We didn't know Time existed as a sentient being who's listening in on this conversation right now!" he laughed, looking up at the sky.

"You and Vespry chose what to bring us. You chose the right stuff. No one on the RT believes they're smarter than you. You're really fucking smart. You know shit we need to know. You're also really brave. You got the information to us. Now you're gonna train some stealthy, murderous ninjas with one of the best humans I know. I don't know how to train people to survive in Bas's Kingdom. Do you think less of me?"

Kali rolled her eyes at him and smiled while shaking her head.

"You show me what you know, and I'll show you what I know. We'll work together when we can and separately sometimes, too. We'll grow a garden together after we kill Bas. I'll teach you what James taught all of us here. We'll grow some weed, too. Get fucking high and watch the sunset at the white house," he laughed.

"Ok, I've never gotten high," Kali said, laughing.

Lev laughed with amusement while putting his arm around her. "I'll make us some pot brownies."

"I really like when you cook for me," she said, laughing with him.

Lev and Kali

He was leaning back on the couch watching Kali as she worked towards her orgasm in his lap. The lightning outside briefly lit up their room and was followed by a loud, sharp cracking sound that eventually rumbled across the air filling the room with its sound. Her eyes were closed and she was close by the sound of it. He felt her hands grip his shoulders tightly and he encouraged her. He squeezed his hands on her ass and stopped himself from pulling her down onto himself harder for himself. She wasn't asking him for anything. She was in control.

She felt her orgasm build and heard Lev as he told her in a deep, husky voice, "Come on baby. Come get what you're here for." She felt one of his arms wrap around her lower back while the other continued to grip her ass and knew he was watching her as he liked to do. She called out his name and he groaned, "Yeah, you got this. Fuck, your pussy feels so good." She was moving fast on him now and her arms wrapped around his shoulders as she steadied herself while she came and called out his name and other disjointed words and sounds all strung together as she felt her orgasm hit her brain making thinking difficult. She began to slow down her movements as her orgasm ended.

He was talking now.

"Get on your back, baby. I want a turn. Come on." She felt him lifting her off him and onto her back on the couch with only a little assistance from her as her body continued to enjoy the aftershocks of her orgasm that lingered. Lightning lit up the room again and she waited for the next wave of thunder that would follow. The sound relaxed her body and mind and she enjoyed the sensations caused by touching her husband's skin and him touching hers.

The sound of his voice in the electrically charged air resonated throughout her body and she listened intently to him. "Mmmm, you ready for me? I'm so ready for you," he said without actually waiting to hear from her if she was ready.

She smiled and moaned words of encouragement to him softly as she felt the weight of his body press down on her own and then lift up slightly as he adjusted himself on top of her. She opened her eyes to look up at him as his face moved towards her right ear. She adored the way he looked when he was coming in for her. She felt him kiss her neck as he slid his cock inside of her and begin to fuck her hard and fast.

"I'm gonna cum so fucking hard," he said in a deep voice as he held her tightly with one arm over her left shoulder while using his other to raise her right leg higher. Kali moaned and told him how good he felt and asked him to fuck her harder which he did, telling her, "Say it again, baby," in a deep groan as he pushed himself into her. She said it again meaning it just as much the second time, and she gasped and encouraged him as she felt the pressure of his body around and inside of her as he fucked her harder. He groaned louder as he fucked her, telling her how good she felt on his cock. His pace was fast just as hers had been, and he came quickly after having waited for her to cum first.

Lev rolled onto the left side of Kali on the narrow couch and pressed his face against her neck with his eyes closed. She turned her face towards his and kissed his forehead and he reached for her face with his left hand and held her so he could kiss her mouth. The storm cell was very close to Ivy now and the lightning was persistent. The shock waves of thunder were palpable all around them.

Between kisses, they told each other how the other made them feel.

Lev pulled Kali tightly to him and she smiled telling him, "Babe, I can't get any closer."

"Yes, you can. Come here," he said as he pulled her leg over his side.

They laughed and kissed and stayed pressed together naked, talking on the couch until the very last of the thunder could be heard and Lev said, "I don't know what day we got married, but I think every lightning storm should be an anniversary."

Kali was quiet, so Lev opened his eyes to look at her.

"Kali?" he asked her.

"That was so nice that I don't know what to say," she said quietly.

"Happy anniversary," he said and kissed her.

"Happy anniversary," she said, smiling.

They got up and got dressed.

Experimental Passport Pilot Needed

Two weeks had passed since the RT had headed up to the labs to get to work on the tech Kali had brought them. Lev's priority was creating working passports so that they could eventually find a way into Bas's locked Kingdom once they figured out the lock code. He didn't admit his personal motivations out loud to the RT, but while he and Kali were lying in bed one morning before he headed up to work in the lab, and she headed over to work with the growing Intel Team, he told her, "If you ever get taken, I need to be able to get you back. This tech, the passport with his lock code....That's all I care about."

"Babe, you get the lock code... We need to be able to alert Pele and her army that you broke his code. If I get taken, we need the communication tech to be working. You tell Pele the code, and he may never get a chance to take me back there. Or you and a million of her soldiers can get in and get me out of torture if he takes me."

Lev nodded. "I know. I know. But I'll go in there myself and try to get you back if we still haven't gotten the comms working. I'll find Vespry and tell him the lock code and he can tell Pele how to get her soldiers inside. You two only recently started working with Pele. Maybe the relationship has changed. We don't know. We have to count on ourselves and hope Pele's still on the opposition's side. The Kingdom lock code first. We'll throw it onto every passport we make and get ourselves inside to get you if you get taken and tell Vespry to contact Pele for help."

"What if Rollo's dead?"

"Then we'll get inside and fuck up their lock from inside. Hopefully, Pele's monitoring it all the time looking for an opportunity."

Kali looked at her husband while he spoke and heard the determination in his voice while he looked at her and told her what he was thinking.

She kissed him and said, "I'll wait for you if I get taken back."

Lev noticed that Kali didn't say how long she'd wait for him to get her and nodded. He knew she meant she would wait for him as long as it took him to find her.

Creating passports was surprisingly easy which set a positive tone for the entire RT. Experiencing success at the start assured them all that the information they were accessing through the recipe book, though completely new to them, was well-described and manageable. The tech team used the working passport Kali had brought them as a guide to modify old cell phone technology of which they had plenty in storage. In fact, the passport Kali brought them was made using a modified cell phone.

"They don't manufacture new stuff in the Kingdom. All this tech is repurposed from the past except the Forte Key," Kali had explained to them.

The formulas Rollo had written for them in the recipe book relied upon new forms of energy which took most of the RT by surprise. Containing the energy needed to operate each piece of tech within each piece of tech required the same formula for the energy source with a slight adjustment for the size of the container which would hold the energy. Examining Kali's optical with its energy field contained in the space that once contained a magnifying glass helped the Tech Team understand what to look for in their storage rooms. Shoshi and Carter rode out to Campus to find very small containers for the energy source they needed to put into the passports to power them. Silver chain linked necklaces offered surprising options for containers inside small-scale technology.

"You can fit this in your pocket, but remember what Kali said about losing them. The information remains on your optical. You can't get back what you put on an optical if you go and lose the damn thing. The energy in the optical remains constant. If Bas figures out how to unlock opticals, he might even be able to figure out a way to summon them from their unique energy signals, too. Don't lose these fucking things," Dave told the Intel Team while holding up a one inch optical the RT had created for them.

Kali inspected the new small scale opticals created by the RT and told Lev and Dave, "Yeah, my optical was the smallest optical I'd ever seen. What you have here is so much more stealthy. Maybe you could figure out how to hide an optical on the back of a bracelet or a ring."

Lev and Dave looked at each other and within two days, Bolin was attaching the clasp of a newly designed optical bracelet to Kali's wrist while telling her to go hide various items from the cafeteria and bring them back to the growing Intel Team to see if it worked.

Much to James' dismay, Kali successfully hid multiple items, including dishes, during her walk through the cafeteria with the new optical bracelet. The RT brainstormed additional appropriate options for more stealthy opticals for Bolin's spies.

Members of the RT realized they had frequently come close to some of the new maths and physics on their own, but they had been missing crucial bits of information to find the successes they sought. Creating working passports utilized the same formulas they had developed to move inanimate and animate objects across space, now they had the formula for moving inanimate and animate objects across time. While that was exciting, it was the addition of the formula to move consciousness as a separate and new physical state of matter along with the body which continued to cause RT members the most unrestrained surprise. While they knew that moving plants didn't require the formula for moving consciousness, they decided to test the first passport they created on one of the farm's goats.

"Are we sure a goat has consciousness?" James asked as he led the goat across the compound with Dave.

"No, but we get this guy hooked up to the machines, read what he's got going on upstairs, send him through, and we'll find out soon enough."

Much to every RT member's disappointment, the goat was dead when he returned after one minute in the past. The passport had been fitted with a timer the RT set before they sent him to the past because the goat couldn't get back otherwise. They knew the timer and the pre-set destination worked because they'd tested both of these new functions on a plant first, and then on a snail earlier in the day. The two functions were unique to the RT and not information they found in the recipe book. The RTs were creating new technology tools just as Rollo Vespry had hoped they would.

James took the death of the goat better than everyone else, but refused to serve the goat meat to the community. "Time traveling goats go into the burn pit," he said with authority.

No one argued with his decision even though the general consensus among the RT was that the goat meat would have been perfectly fine to consume.

"We have to send a person," Lev said. "We'll need a volunteer." Several RT members quickly volunteered, even stating that they had confidence in the formulas to be successful with human consciousness, but Lev said no one from the RT could be spared. They'd need a volunteer from the community who could be trusted to return if successful. They didn't want to use the timer for a person, but they decided to engage it in the event that the volunteer died and could not return on his or her own.

Dave, Bolin, and Lev brainstormed possible candidates for the mission and then sent word for the people they felt could be trusted to go to the past and return, despite the temptation to remain, to attend an informational meeting in MR1.

The 14 possible candidates were quickly assembled and sat at the large conference table where they were informed of the potentially life-threatening mission. They were told that no one would be forced to make the potential sacrifice of their own life for the goals of the RT and the technology to fight Bas, but all quickly agreed to volunteer for the task despite having the danger explained in explicit detail.

Gorman was selected after he revealed that he had been an air traffic controller prior to the extinction event. "I can problem solve. I'm good with tech. You tell me what might go wrong to prevent me from getting back, other than I fucking die, and, if I'm still breathing, I'll be able to work with whatever situation I find myself in," he insisted.

"The part about dying is a very real possibility," Lev said soberly.

"I know, but I've got a wife and two babies over in the other present. I'm fine with dying if I'm trying to protect them from that psychopath."

Bolin nodded, asking him, "But you want to live and help make this present safe, as well?"

"Yeah, man. Let me fucking help."

"You survive this, I want to talk to you about our Intel Team. Maybe it's something you'd be interested in joining," said Bolin.

"I'm already interested. Show me how to work the passport."

After some discussion with the other volunteers, which included thanking them for offering to participate in the dangerous experiment, Lev and Dave realized none of them wanted to be excluded from helping to create a working passport. Each claimed a personal history of loved ones lost to the extinction event at the order given by Bas. Lev decided that the other 13 potential volunteers they'd offered the mission to should attend Gorman's attempt at using the passport.

"I want you to see what's going to happen. I want you to make an informed decision about volunteering in the event Gorman doesn't return on his own and the timer pulls him back dead. You can back out if you decide you don't want to go through with it."

All agreed and headed upstairs to the lab where Gorman was immediately given instructions before being handed the passport created by the RT.

Lev told him, "The timer will return you after 120 seconds, but you can choose to return sooner. Once you're there, you only need to be there for a second before you return to let us know it worked and you're still alive."

Gorman had strapped the passport to his wrist by the time Lev had finished giving him instructions. "I'm ready. Let's do this," he said as he adjusted the passport on his wrist without a hint of fear.

The entire RT, along with Bolin and Kali, was assembled as their first human volunteer stood in the middle of the passport lab. Gorman nodded his head at Lev as everyone stepped away from him so they could give him space and watch him leave.

Lev nodded his head back at Gorman and said, "Thanks, man. We appreciate what you're doing for us."

Gorman moved his hand over the passport and manually input the travel destination as the RT had instructed him to do. He was gone in an instant. The entire RT stood still and did not make a sound as they waited, feeling the seconds pass.

"Give him a second to take it all in. He's gone to the past, he might need a minu--" Lev was saying quietly to the RT as Gorman suddenly reappeared with a devilish smile on his face.

"That was fucking awesome, man!" he shouted enthusiastically while nodding.

The entire room erupted in unrestrained cheering as everyone ran towards Gorman to high-five him and embrace him while offering their thanks and congratulations.

Bolin stood towards the back of the room with Kali and looked at Gorman. He had other plans for the man and would wait for his turn. For now, Gorman deserved to be celebrated for his bravery in taking this chance with the passport. He looked at Kali and nodded. Kali nodded back in agreement.

Kali and Lev Travel Together

"I appreciate you going with me. I know you're busy on the Intel Team," he said, smiling at her as she got ready to head up to the labs with him.

"You just think this is going to be an hour off from work and we're gonna get to hang out and hold hands and kiss and --"

Lev was smiling and nodding at what she was saying to him as he drank his chicory at their small table. "Mmm-hmm. I won't deny it. I wanna spend an hour with my wife away from all this bullshit while still managing to be productive so no one questions my motives," he agreed happily.

Kali pushed their shared meal bowl towards him indicating he should eat the extra eggs and vegetables.

"Thanks. I'm hungry," he said as he pulled the bowl closer and kept eating. "You got us enough for three people," he said, looking like he was considering how much breakfast she'd brought them this morning.

"Did I get too much?" she asked him in a tone that suggested she hadn't.

"No. Bring this much tomorrow if I don't go get us breakfast before you," he said adamantly through a mouth full of food while shaking his head. "Must be the exercise."

"Must be," Kali agreed.

Lev had mandated that the RT keep up their physical fitness by adding a daily workout to their already endless lab schedules. "Just do something for a minimum of 30 minutes a day. Longer if you can. We've been at this for two weeks and we need to remember to take care of ourselves. Also, LRs 6 and 7 are gonna have cots brought in by Campus people later today. Take naps there if you need one and you have a chance to get some rest. Stay sharp. LR 9 got exercise equipment two days ago. Dave, a handful of others, and I have worked out so far. No one else. I'm mandating workouts. No excuses. We'll be better at what we're doing if we stay healthy."

"Does farm work count as exercise on days we have farm duty?" asked a member of the RT.

Lev scoffed, "No. That's your vitamin D. Get in LR 9 and lift some weights. Any other questions?" Lev waited.

The sun wasn't up yet, but the kitchen was now serving members of the RT breakfast at 5am in order to let the large team of hungry researchers eat before community members arrived for breakfast. The six lab rooms where the teams were working on the assigned tech stretched the length of one hallway. Five pieces of tech plus the communication tech which was missing some essential parts of its formula were being worked on by the RT. The labs had clear walls between them so that all teams were visible to other teams while working on their tech. Everyone had access to each other so that questions and concerns could be addressed quickly. They had three additional labs across from them for creating and experimenting with the information in the recipe book. The Tech Team also had two labs across the hall as well, and all five tech members were busy working on various projects as requested by the RT as well as being busy sourcing physical materials with which they could build the new tech.

On their first day in the labs, Maren had requested nine magnifying glasses to create opticals for the proposed Intel Team, and Aisha immediately sent them over.

"Lev, I think the Intel Team will need opticals if they can get into the Kingdom. Let's get them made immediately so they can learn how to use them," she told him on day one.

"Yeah, Kali's an expert with the opticals. Let's have them ready for Bolin's team. Dave just mentioned making smaller opticals, too. Bolin's still finding people who can deal with what being a spy entails. People who can survive what goes on inside that hell."

Maren looked at Lev and nodded. "Let's get these large and small opticals ready," she said walking off to the LR 11 to join the other techs.

All of the rooms had doors that led to the hallway and Lev told them to leave all doors wide open.

"We're not Ivy's RT. We work together. Everyone can come and go into a lab for help or to learn from another team. These five pieces of tech do different things, but they also share a lot of similarities. The comms recipe needs solutions. We can learn from all of it. If you discover something interesting, come tell the rest of us. You might be sharing knowledge others need. That's how we got the idea for the timer to test the passport. The goal is to be successful. No one's a hero here. We're one team. No egos," he told them.

After Gorman had successfully used the first passport, he made himself available to test the five additional passports the RT and Tech Team created over the course of the next two days. Every passport was carefully created and no one rushed the process for fear of losing Gorman to a mishap brought about by their own negligence. Each time he left for the past, the entire RT including the Techs gathered in the passport LR and held their collective breaths when he left, and finally exhaled and cheered a few seconds later when he returned.

Today, Kali was going to travel by passport with Lev to familiarize him with various traveling features of the tech.

"I've only ever personally used a passport once, and that was when I escaped the Kingdom," she told the RT. "However, I've traveled a lot as a passenger. We'll travel a few times together and separately so he can tell you the capabilities I'm aware of. Maybe you can learn to do more once you know what it's capable of.

Maybe knowing how it works will help you consider new approaches to figuring out the lock code."

Everyone agreed that the leader of the passport team needed to experience the tech first hand. Lev showed Dave where he kept his notes in case it all went to hell and he never returned.

"Man, the tech's solid. If Gorman can leave and come back, the guy who knows the formulas certainly can."

"Precautions. I'm taking them all," he told Dave flatly.

"You're in charge of Ivy if I don't come back. I already informed Aisha and Bolin. She and Bob will continue to run Campus. You can always count on Bolin here at Ivy. Get his Intel Team into that fucking Kingdom. I'll be in the other present figuring out how to stop Bas from there."

Dave nodded but waved him off with a disbelieving sigh. "What you're worrying about...Not gonna happen. See you in a bit," he said as he went to give Kali a new passport that had been tested by Gorman.

Kali and Lev stood in the passport LR as Gorman had numerous times over the past few days.

"We're gonna be gone for 45 minutes to an hour while I practice using the tech. We'll travel together, separately, and reconnect at designated times in various places. I'm ready," he said, turning to look at Kali and showing her the ready signal he'd mentally delivered to his passport.

"Looks right to me," she said and touched his arm. Lev nodded and they disappeared traveling together using just his passport.

They arrived on an empty beach on a cold cloudy day and Kali asked him, "Ooh, it's cold. What were your instructions?"

"Beach in Virginia Beach 1990. I realize now I should have specified a month. I have to work on my intention with this tech, I guess. Not end up on a cold beach in the middle of the fucking winter," he laughed.

"Yeah, you work on that," Kali shuddered. "Let's check with someone that we're where you wanted us to be."

Lev looked around and laughed. "No one's crazy enough to be out here in this weather."

"We're not dressed for this at all," Kali agreed adding, "Well, we have to confirm, so let's go up to the street area and find someone to ask. Fucking cold, man."

Lev put his around her shoulder while she huddled closer to his body for warmth.

"We can travel to the house I grew up in in California next. I know that specific location and it's warmer there year-round. I can introduce you to my parents."

Kali smiled up at him. "How about only in an emergency? If a passport breaks today, pop in over at your house and ask your mom to fix it."

"Imagine? Hey mom! My wife and I are traveling on these passports a psychopath created using your research. Time says 'hi', by the way."

They both laughed and Kali said, "Seriously, though. Where's a place we can meet if we get separated. I'm not an expert on how to use a passport. I'm only an expert passenger. Let's meet someplace warmer, though. This is bullshit. My nose is running now," she said, sniffing as they continued to walk towards the boardwalk.

"Ok, Miami Beach, June 1st, 1990?"

"Isn't that a big place? I'm not familiar with it. Let's go small and pick a place where it'll be easy to find each other on top of being warm."

"Ok, how about the carousel at Balboa Park on June 1st 1990?"

"Yeah, I like that. I can find you there. Oh, time. Make it for noon," she said.

"Noon, it is."

They approached a man walking his dog on the mostly deserted street of the early morning hour. He told them the year and the date then looked at them asking, "Anything else? You two need a couple bucks for some coffee?"

Lev smiled and thanked him but assured him they had all they needed. As they walked away from the man and his dog, Lev shook his head and looked down at Kali. "What a nice fucking guy. Bas had to go kill nice fucking people like him. Fucking asshole," he concluded by shaking his head in disgust.

"On a happier note, your passport got you exactly where you asked it to take you. You did really good transferring your intention. Entering manually, the way Gorman did, is time consuming but safer for initial testing. The passport team did really well adding the formula to separate consciousnesses of multiple travelers. If we both survived on your passport, that means you could travel with as many people as could touch you. There's no limit other than how much flesh the primary traveler has available."

"So, if you touch me to travel, someone touching you won't also travel?"

"Nope. They have to be touching the primary traveler who initiated the destination."

Kali stopped walking and put her hand on Lev's chest. "Actually, let me be more specific. Put your hand over mine."

Lev did what she asked him to do.

"See your hand covers mine but it's big and also touching your chest?"

Lev nodded.

"That's how you get someone who doesn't want to travel with you to go with you anyway."

"I don't like what you're saying," Lev said grimly.

"Yeah. I traveled that way sometimes, but mostly I was just grabbed. I suppose if you had a group of spies from your Intel Team with you and you wanted to travel with them but one was too injured to place their hand on the primary traveler, that would be helpful. The primary traveler only has two hands to grab people to take with them. Maybe only one person has a passport? The others broke in battle, or something…. You grab the hand of your injured team member and place it on the person with the working passport. Just make sure something, any part of you, is also touching the primary traveler."

Lev nodded.

"I'm just talking this through. I just realized it's something I should tell Bolin and the Intel Team," she said.

"I'll remind you."

Kali continued. "Also, someone chasing you can be transported with you. I've gotta tell them that, too."

"You can't control who comes along as a traveler? If their foot is touching yours, they're going with you?" he asked.

"Yeah."

They walked around a corner to the back of a row of shops and Kali asked, "You ready to travel separately to the carousel?"

"June 1st 1990 at noon. Traveling consciousnesses in alignment."

"See you in a few seconds," she said with a smile and disappeared.

Lev arrived at the carousel a second after she did and said vehemently, "Man, I didn't like it when you disappeared. Not at all. You were just gone. I fucking panicked for a second!" He was shaking his head and put his arm around her shoulders.

Kali looked up at him and said, "Well, even though you were worried, the passport read your intention accurately. That's good. We can tell the team that the tech works around the anxiety of the traveler."

Lev frowned, but Kali kept talking. "This is where we meet if we get separated or lost. This destination works. Ok? You ready to be my passenger? I'll touch you. Don't hold me. Ready?"

"No, wait. You're right, I was freaked out when I got here. I want to leave here and then come back on my own without being so fucking nervous."

"Ok, where will you go?"

"Back to Virginia Beach, same incomplete date," he told her.

"Remember, don't come back here at noon. I'm already here. Come back to my present consciousness. Intention."

"Right," he said.

Kali nodded. Lev disappeared and she waited for a few seconds before he reappeared.

"It's pretty easy once you trust the tech to do what you want it to do," he said, satisfied. "So, where are we going now?" he asked as she took his hand.

"How about New Orleans June 1st 1990 at noon?"

"Let's do it."

Lev looked around. They were definitely in New Orleans.

"Nice. Traveling feels the same no matter how you go. By yourself, as a passenger or bringing a passenger along. Where to now?"

"You choose. Bring me."

"The Alamo, same time."

"Ok."

"Ready?"

"Yeah."

"I can't believe it's this easy," Lev said as he looked up at the Alamo. "I felt like my intention was vague because I've never been here, but the tech had no problem getting us here anyway. I wanted to see if it would get me to a place I didn't really know. Couldn't picture. Fucking nuts. Want to meet at the carousel and then head back to Ivy?" he asked her.

"Sure. Same time?" Kali asked.

"Yeah. June 1st, 1990. Noon to align with your consciousness. I'll see you in a few seconds," he said.

"You like that June 1st date, huh?"

"June 1st is my mom's birthday. 1990 is just easy to remember."

Kali said, "Ok. You go first. See you in a few seconds."

They arrived at the carousel at Balboa park and Lev said, "Well, passport travel is a lot easier than I imagined it would be. We've been gone from the lab for about 20 minutes. I thought this would take longer, but I think we're done."

"Me, too."

"I didn't know what to expect, but it wasn't this feeling," he said, looking down at her. Kali saw discontent in his expression and waited for him to tell her what he was thinking.

"Traveling to the past sounds fucking awesome, but it's actually kind of... I hate to say it, but it feels gross. Dirty. These people are all dead, but I can go get a meal, sit by the koi pond, get a fucking sunburn. It makes no sense. I don't fucking like it," he said, looking away from her and looking at the carousel as it turned with the familiar music playing.

Lev looked back at Kali. "You've mentioned spending a lot of time in the past. I've never heard you talk about it as a positive experience. I get that now."

Kali nodded at him with a knowing expression. "But there's the allure of visiting the past. It's one of the reasons why the formulas, the tech they create, and even my friend Time are so dangerous. To visit the past, to know you can't fuck up the future... It seems so harmless at first. There's no butterfly effect. What's the harm, right? No consequences. But just like a Rewind in the hands of a shitty person, there's a dark side. We can stand here near the carousel we visited as kids and think this passport tech is amazing, but some other person's gonna think, hey, I can go kill my third grade teacher who made me stay in for recess for pushing another kid in line. Even if the death doesn't persist, you can choose to kill a person in the past. It'll feel real, and there will be no consequences. I think a lot of nice, normal people could find themselves corrupted by this information and what it allows a person to do.

"I always hated going to the past because, like you said, these people are all dead. Even if Bas hadn't killed everyone, these people don't exist in this moment anymore. All of these consciousnesses have evolved from this moment whether in this present or in the afterlife present. Why stare at them here in the past? I can't go talk to that kid over there and say something meaningful that helps the kid evolve into a better person. You can't have any impact, positive or negative, on another consciousness by being here. It feels like such a waste of time spending time here. The Universe self-corrects whatever you try to do here. Time never told me if the Universe is sentient, but, I do wonder.

"Your mom told Time people weren't ready to have the information she'd discovered. They were both scientists, curious, smart, and respectful. She was right. People aren't ready for this. We still need to evolve a lot more. We need Time unbound, helping us to become better versions of ourselves before we head on over to the other present and can keep evolving over there, too. Bas sent billions of people into the other present who were still working on themselves. He interrupted Time's efforts to help us evolve our consciousnesses as a species. He's done so much harm that goes beyond killing so many bodies."

Lev wrapped his arms around Kali's waist and said, "Let's go back to Ivy. We can go back to our room and make out in the present for 20 minutes before we head up to the lab. They're not expecting us back so soon anyway."

Kali hugged Lev and smiled up at him and nodded enthusiastically at his suggestion. "I like your plan. Let's travel separately. Remember, instead of a specific time, your intention is for the present time. I've never done that either, but Gorman said it was as easy as going to the past. You go first."

Lev kissed her before letting go of her and stepping away.

"See you in a few seconds," he said.

Lev, Marina, and Arjun

He stood before her and looked at her younger face.

"Do you know who I am?" he asked her.

She looked at his face through the untamed facial hair, and the differences age had made to his features, and said, "Of course I know who you are," and he felt her take his hand in hers. "Come inside. Your father is home today," she said as she turned and led him inside his childhood home.

"It's your birthday, so I knew you'd both be home," he said and reached over and hugged her tightly saying, "Happy Birthday, Mom."

She hugged him back and said, "I thought I'd fixed things. I didn't want this to happen. I'm so sorry. If you're here, I already know it's bad."

"It's really bad," he said, and she could hear the exhaustion in her son's voice.

"Come on. Your dad's out back."

Lev allowed his mother to lead him through his childhood home out to the backyard brick patio his father had laid with his own hands.

As they approached him, Lev could see his father on a small step-ladder picking figs from their prolific fig tree. He turned as Marina said, "Arjun. We have a guest."

"Oh? Who, then?" he asked, turning towards them with a smile. His eyes landed on Lev and he stopped his descent from the ladder and stood frozen looking at his adult son.

"Hi, Dad," Lev said quietly. It was too much to take in all at once and he stopped walking towards his father and stood still staring at each of his parents. His feelings overwhelmed him, and he suddenly breathed in sharply and shook his head saying nothing.

His mother stepped closer to him, still holding his hand, and he heard her say, "We'll do whatever we can to help," and he watched his father put down the bowl containing the figs and walk up to him with his arms wide open and felt him embrace him firmly.

"My son! Look at the man you became," he said proudly.

He felt his mother's arms wrap around him and pulled his arms from both of his parents and wrapped his own long arms tightly around them and cried.

Lev released his parents from his hug and quickly wiped his face roughly with his hands.

"I don't have a lot of time. I've lost someone. I need help finding her," he said.

"Let's go inside and you tell us what you mean," his father said, walking quickly towards the house.

"Has anyone come here looking for me?" he asked them as they walked inside.

"I haven't met anyone looking for you," said his mother.

"Me neither," said his father.

They sat in the living room with Marina next to Lev and Arjun in a chair he had pulled right up next to them so they were all facing one another.

Arjun grabbed Lev's hand and asked, "Do you have time to tell us what happened?"

Lev nodded and explained to them quickly about the near extinction of the human race and the man named Bas who had captured Time.

Marina looked shocked when Lev mentioned Bas and said, "Not Sebastian Bakker?"

Lev looked at her and nodded.

"My God," she whispered.

"We can't undo what's happened, but the woman I'm looking for is... she's important to the fight against Bas, but she's even more important to me. I need to find her. We were traveling together on different devices and something happened.

We got separated. I don't know where she is. I've looked everywhere I can think of. I thought maybe she would come here and wait for me or leave me a message. We had been joking about coming here before we traveled. Said if our passports broke we could ask you to help fix them," he said, looking at his mother.

"This wasn't supposed to happen, though. The passports work. I'm at a loss. I came here as a last resort. I didn't want to upset either of you. To know what happens... To live with waiting for that. I don't even know if you'll forget right after I leave. I'm so sorry. I make mistakes. Maybe coming here was a mistake. But she's not at the carousel. I waited there for hours. I can't get back to the present. Nothing's working." He shook his head and looked miserable.

"What's her name? What does she look like? Or how can we recognize her if she comes to us?" Arjun asked him.

Lev closed his eyes for a second before sighing and looking at his parents. "Her name is Kali. She's medium height, lots of blonde, unmanaged hair. She's a little offbeat, but friendly, unless she's afraid."

"Who is she to you?" his mother asked him.

"She's like you two. She's my family. I'm her husband. She's my wife," he said softly.

"Then she's our family, as well," said Marina while Arjun nodded.

"I kept to myself until she showed up nearly 20 years after Bas destroyed the world. She works for a group in Bas's Kingdom who are trying to kill him and free Time. She's a member of a traitor organization. So am I. She showed up one day at our research facility offering us technology to help us fight with them... Wait a minute..." Lev suddenly stopped speaking and froze.

"What is it?" his mother asked him.

He looked at his father and said, "I must have told you what to tell me. This is why she's lost. This might be Time. I don't know for sure. She said Time can't control outcomes." Lev, looked confused and said, "But Time is always looking for ways to help us defeat Bas. This isn't an accident and it's not luck. This is design," he said, nodding and standing up suddenly.

Both of his parents stood up and his father asked, "I'm confused. What do you mean?"

Lev felt his mother touch his arm and heard her say, "What did you realize?"

Lev put one of his hands on his forehead and asked his father, "You're taking me to get mom flowers for her birthday after I get home from school?"

"Yes."

"Dad, today, you tell me something at the Farmer's Market that I need to know when I'm 43 years old. I was going to kill Kali. Or I was going to let my friend kill her. I didn't care either way. But something you tell me today stopped me from letting her be killed. I stood in front of my friend's gun a second before he would have shot her."

"Tell me what I told you, son," Arjun said in a serious tone.

Lev looked intently at his father and told him, "We were getting flowers for mom and you told me to pick out the flowers I liked best. You said I could choose any flowers I wanted. I told you I wanted to get her all of the flowers. You asked me if mom deserves all the flowers in the Universe, and I said she does. Then you said, 'There's a flower called cosmos. Cosmos is another word for the Universe.'" I liked that. We found cosmos in one of the buckets of water, and the woman who worked the booth wrapped their wet stems. She was handing them to me after you had paid for them. I wasn't paying attention to her holding them out to me, so you said...." Lev froze as he recalled Kali approaching Ivy that morning.

"What did I say, son?" asked Arjun, touching Lev's arm.

Lev looked at his father. "You said, 'Lev, pay attention to the woman with the cosmos in her hand. She's giving you the Universe.' When I saw Kali approach us that morning, she was carrying cosmos. My partner ordered her to drop what she was holding, but she only had the cosmos in her hand, no weapons, and she refused to put them down even when my partner was about to shoot her. She laughed and told us cosmos are her favorite flowers and she wasn't putting them down. I remembered what you said, 'Pay attention to the woman with the cosmos in her hand. She's giving you the Universe.' That's why I stopped him from shooting her. Without her, we wouldn't have a chance against Bas. Because of her, we've got technology, and we're working to get Pele and her army inside his Kingdom. It's a fair fight now unlike before. Kali changed everything in our favor."

Arjun nodded his head and rubbed Lev's arm, saying, "I will tell you exactly what you need to hear today at the Farmer's Market. Don't think that coming here to us was a mistake. If you hadn't, I wouldn't have gotten to meet the man my son becomes. Plus, you've given me an opportunity to assist you in meeting your wife and defeating Bas."

He stepped up to Lev and hugged him tightly and Lev whispered, "I miss you, dad."

Marina said, "Tell us if there are any other ways we can help you."

"I don't think I'm allowed to say more. From what I've learned, the Universe only tolerates small interactions. This one feels big, but I know what you said to me today. Time is sentient, maybe the Universe is, as well. I don't know. Bas is a serious threat to all of us, maybe even to the Universe. How does this even work if you're a shadow consciousness?" he asked his mother.

Marina's eyes opened wide. "Oh, but consciousness is vast. It's not simply contained in here," she said, pointing to her head.

Arjun laughed lightly. "Your mother is trying to tell you that the Universe is more likely to conspire with your good intentions than against them."

Marina nodded at both of them. "Mmm-hmm. But conspiring doesn't offer a guaranteed outcome. Don't give up. And I think you're right. I think Time arranged this meeting today," Marina said to Lev.

"Yes. See if you can find Kali now," his father agreed.

Lev turned and hugged his mother saying, "We'll see each other again."

"I know," she said and kissed his cheek.

"Happy birthday, mom," he said quietly as he hugged her.

He stepped away from them and left for Ivy in the present time and hoped he would be able to find Kali there.

Lev Returns

"Where the hell have you been?! She's been looking everywhere for you! I finally had to wrestle her passport from her after a dozen travels. I think she's planning to come back and get the one with the Kingdom lock code from me by force. She's got it in her head that Bas captured you. She's irrational! We wrestled, man! She's mean when she's upset!" Dave told Lev loudly without an ounce of humor.

"Alright. Stay here in case she comes back for you. Tell her I'm looking for her," Lev said, running towards the door of the lab.

"That's great! I hope she doesn't shoot first!" Dave yelled furiously after him as he ran from the lab. Dave looked over at the other RT members in the lab who had been watching him and Lev. "You back me up when she gets here. Help me tell her Lev's back because I don't know how great her listening skills are right now," he said to them with real concern for his safety.

Lev ran down the halls of Ivy shouting at everyone he passed to tell Kali he was back and that he was looking for her and not to hurt Dave. He stood on a table in the cafeteria and asked the dinner crowd if anyone had seen her. Marco shouted from behind the counter that he'd seen her with Bolin a few minutes earlier near the greenhouses out back. Lev told everyone in the cafeteria to tell her he was back and looking for her if they saw her. He added, "She's really upset right now, so don't get too close." Then he ran out of the cafeteria to the greenhouses hoping to find her before she lashed out at a community member.

As Lev ran to the greenhouses, he saw Bolin walking quickly in the direction of his house.

"Bol!" Lev shouted.

Bolin turned around quickly and immediately began to jog towards Lev.

"Where's Kali?" Lev shouted at him before they had closed any meaningful distance between them.

"She went to your room! Go to your room!" shouted Bolin.

Lev immediately turned to his right and ran as fast as he could across the grounds to the ground floor door that led to their stairway.

He was out of breath when he ran inside the building and bounded up the stairs into their room with his eyes wide open in the dimly lit space as he looked to see if she was in the room. He ran back to the hallway and saw her as she exited one of Team 4's storage rooms.

"Lev?!" she shouted in confusion at him.

He jumped down the stairs and closed the short distance between them quickly saying, "Oh, jeez, baby! Come here."

He picked her up in a sweaty hug, and she hugged him back tightly, telling him, "I thought you got captured. I wanted to go to the Kingdom and get you, but Dave wouldn't let me. I'm so fucking mad at him right now."

Kali had her arms wrapped tightly around him and her face buried in his neck while she told him she was going to use her optical to get the passport with the Kingdom lock codes back from Dave. Lev lifted her feet off the floor and walked up the stairs and into their room with her dangling from him while she told him she wanted to fight Dave for her passport, but she knew he was family, so she couldn't, and that's why she planned to steal it back.

Lev laughed at that and said, "He's convinced you're gonna go back up to the lab and fight him to get your passport."

"Am I allowed to fight him next time?" she asked him, looking at his face with fierce determination for a future fight with Dave.

"Baby, no. Don't fight Dave," Lev laughed as he kissed her.

Inside their room, he put her feet down on the floor as Bolin shouted from the bottom of the stairs asking if he could come up.

"Yeah, come on in. I found her."

Bolin entered looking calm and slightly amused as he told Lev, "Explain to Kali that I don't outrank Dave."

"Bol doesn't outrank Dave. They're equals," a smiling Lev assured Kali who maintained a skeptical expression upon hearing the news.

Bolin asked her, "So, you're not going to get the passport with the Kingdom lock codes 'one way or another,' now, right?"

Lev laughed nervously at that and asked him, "Were you going to enlist James for help?"

"Yes. I was on my way to tell him he'd have to talk to her because no one else had a chance in hell of preventing her from doing whatever she was planning to do. We can't lock you up. Right?" he asked her with a smile, pointing at his nose that still bore the results of connecting with her head in the cage a few weeks earlier.

"Wouldn't you go find James?" she asked him rather than answering his question.

"Yes. But I know Dave wanted to give Lev a little time to figure out how to get back. Bas's Kingdom is locked. Lev's passport doesn't have the lock code. Lev's a smart guy. We wanted to give him a little more time. And look! He figured it out," Bolin said, smiling.

"That was 10 hours ago, but all right, fine. Thanks for trying to reason with me. I didn't know what to do," she muttered, looking away from both of them.

"Did the tech malfunction?" asked Bolin.

Lev looked at Kali and shook his head. "No. I believe the tech did what it did with the help of another consciousness that was directing it, overriding my consciousness, my commands. I need to talk to you about what happened," Lev said, looking down at Kali as she stood next to him. He turned to Bolin. "I want to tell Kali first. Call the RT to MR4 and we'll be down soon. You and the Intel Team need to be there, as well."

Bolin nodded and said, "You'll meet the newest and final member. Signed on today."

"Who?"

"Maren."

Lev looked surprised but nodded his approval. "Ok. Intel Team's complete, then?"

"Yes. Maren, Gorman, Bautista, Santi, and Olivia."

Lev shook his head. "Santi still surprises me the most."

"She wants it, and she's an asset with her skills," Bolin said reassuringly as he turned to leave the room.

Lev nodded and turned to Kali, saying, "Let's go for a little walk and sit over at the picnic tables near the cafeteria. I need to calm down a bit before I tell you what happened." He put his arm around her shoulders and began to walk with her out of their room.

Once they were seated at one of the picnic tables, Lev told her about his multiple attempts to leave the year the passport had him stuck in.

"It wouldn't take me where I wanted to go. It refused to take me to the lab in the present, too." He explained to her that he thought maybe her passport was also malfunctioning since he and the team had created both of them with the same information. He told her he thought of their conversation about his parents and, after numerous failed attempts to find her or get back to Ivy, he decided to look for her at his parent's house.

"I didn't even bother with a year. The years weren't working, but I chose my mother's birth date as I had been doing. I left the year up to the passport."

Lev took Kali's hand as he told her about his conversation with his parents and what he had suddenly realized.

"On the field that morning when you first arrived, I saw the cosmos in your hand and heard my dad's voice as clear as if he were standing next to me. Even after all the years between then and that moment. It's obvious Time was involved in this one. Definitely not luck or an accident. Time's been trying to keep you safe and get the tech to Ivy since the two of us were kids in a twisty Time way. Maybe in another strand, Time felt I, or Bolin, would shoot you. I mean, he was definitely going to shoot you that morning." He shrugged and raised his eyebrows.

"Yeah, I remember," she said, smiling.

They were both facing each other as they sat on the bench at the picnic table while they talked.

"I guess Time couldn't find a way to make Rollo safe enough to bring Ivy the tech, but figured out a way to increase my chances."

Lev smiled and said, "Time might be a little bit of a matchmaker, too."

"I already told you, Time can't make you like me. You don't have to," she said, smiling at him.

"Oh, but I do," he said, closing the space between them and kissing her. "I wanted to tell you what happened first before telling the RT because I feel like it's kind of private. Between us, you know? Do you feel that way, too?" he asked her.

"Definitely. It's part of the story about how we met. Your parents are involved now, too. They know about me," she said, nodding as she rubbed his arm.

"Yeah. I told them about us and they called you family."

Kali saw Lev was overcome with emotions and stood up and hugged him while he remained sitting.

He pulled her onto his lap and buried his face in her neck and said, "They knew about you all this time. They knew you were my wife before I knew. And I know they like you now in their present."

"I can't wait to meet them, Lev," she said quietly while rubbing his back.

After a few minutes, Lev sat up straighter and wiped his face.

"Let's go tell the RT Time is actively on our side in this fight and get back to work trying to protect the afterlife present from that fucking asshole. This is really good motivation for everyone."

Kali smiled and nodded and they got up and headed inside to MR4.

"Please don't try to return to his Kingdom without a solid plan for getting back out," he said as they walked towards the doors of the cafeteria.

"Fine. I'll have a plan for getting back out next time," she said, shrugging.

"Thank you for not beating up Dave," he added as he held the door to the cafeteria open for her.

"You're welcome," she said pleasantly as she entered and looked over and saw Marco mouth silently, 'Thank, god.'

Lev, Kali and the Ginger Wine Crime

Lev entered the room and saw Kali sitting on the couch reading from one of their books. He walked over to their dining table and put down the bottle of ginger wine James had given him as he told Kali, "Hey, James sent me back with a bottle of his ginger wine. I've had it before. I'm gonna be honest. Your goal has to be to get lit, because the taste isn't the reason you're gonna want to finish a glass."

He was looking at her as he finished speaking and she smiled and asked, "Nice. You want to have some now?"

"Yeah, I'm off for the night. We're taking a mental health break for the next nine hours," he said as he loosened the top of the bottle and walked it over to her. "Got Trent heading over to Campus for more resources to make extra prison bullets for the Intel Team. They're so close. I'm really glad we've got Trent. He's available whenever I ask him for something. Doesn't mind traveling to campus at night, either. I didn't think he'd ever be this impressive, but he's a great team player. He's always willing to help."

He took a sip of the wine straight from the bottle and shuddered as he sat down next to her on the couch and flung his arm around her shoulders.

"That's strong. Too much ginger. Needs more raisins or honey... or something. Here. Try it. Let me know if you think it's better than the gin you didn't appreciate," he said as he passed her the bottle.

She took the bottle from him and took a small, cautious sip after listening to his description of the wine and let the flavors touch all areas of her tongue. She swallowed and took a larger sip and handed the bottle back to him nodding her approval.

"It's better than the gin. The gin tasted like I was chewing on an evergreen branch. I prefer the taste of ginger."

He took the bottle from her, took another sip, and shuddered again. "I'd say more for you, but I'm not sure if it's gonna grow on me the more I have," he said, raising his eyebrows and smiling at her.

She stroked the side of his beard affectionately while looking at him and listening to him talk, and he kissed her several times before asking her, "Do you have to work with Bolin and the Intel Team tonight? Or are we both off at the same time?"

"I'm heading back up in a bit. This is my dinner break. Everyone's mastered optical basics now, so I'm training them to use them in other ways. They're gonna learn to transport an item from one location to another on their body. It's a way to remove something, and return it without actually hiding it in the past. It's super quick once you master it."

"I don't know that trick."

"It's just another way to work concealment. Your optical and the object you want stay hidden on you. You don't have to access the energy field to conceal the object. You don't have to recall what you're hiding from the past. You just reveal it through intention. Only trouble is you have to stay focused on keeping the object concealed around you until you can get it to the past. Say I want this bottle of wine all to myself. I have my optical on me and you're not looking as I identify the bottle of wine to my optical using intention. The optical conceals the wine near me rather than hiding it in the past. It's right by me the entire time. It's quicker and easier. Less physical interaction with my optical is needed. Think of it like a hidden space around my body.

"Then I walk into the bathroom with the wine concealed around my personal space by the optical. When I get into the bathroom, I quickly remove the concealment and drink all the ginger wine and then hide the empty bottle in the past. You'll never know what happened to the ginger wine."

"You might be very sneaky, you know that?" he said, laughing at her as she climbed into his lap, straddling him, and took the bottle from his hand, taking another sip before kissing him. He wrapped his arms around her waist and pulled her closer to him, smiling as she spoke.

"I confess my ginger wine crime because I'm unable to live with the deception or stand up straight. I'm drunk. We can't have sex. You forgive me. The end," she said as he laughed and pulled her closer so he could kiss her neck which made her laugh, too.

They continued to kiss for a few minutes, and Lev asked her, "When's your dinner break over?"

"Mmm. Soonish, but I've just decided to be late," she said as he reached under the back of her shirt.

"Yeah, be late," he said while kissing her collarbone.

She turned and put the bottle of wine on the coffee table and turned back to him where they kissed each other with more urgency. Lev stood up with her, and she wrapped her legs around his waist while he walked over to the window as she continued to kiss his neck and the side of his face. He released the dark sheet that was pulled back from their open window in order to give them privacy and kissed her as he walked them to their bed.

Days that Don't End

They had barely seen each other awake in several days as the RT and the Intel Team continued to work round the clock to prepare to take on Bas. Bolin had handed over most security team duties to Anna at this point and served only as a check-in for her. Dave somehow managed to work in the lab seemingly 24 hours a day while remaining an effective Head of Security, and Lev asked him if he wanted to share the responsibility with him rather than maintain the role by himself.

"If I need to do that, I'll ask you immediately. I'm ok for now," he assured Lev.

The Intel Team members were driven, and their enthusiasm for the intended mission to get them into the Kingdom drove their training. Bolin had them training day and night, and they eagerly consumed the hours in the day while trying to learn how best to survive in the Kingdom and ultimately kill Bas. Their energy and commitment impressed Kali as they took instruction and information from her eagerly and developed the skills they would need to use on the field shortly. Santi and Maren struggled with maps, but Kali was working with them to overcome the issue.

Lev's RT surpassed all of their expectations. The recipe book Rollo and Kali had made for them over the course of years contained detailed information that made creating tech and inputting formulas surprisingly easy. They already had their first fully functioning Rewind and used it on one of their goats to test its functionality. When it worked, the mood of the RT went from elation to concern as they all realized how dangerous a Rewind might be in the hands of a shitty person.

"This is a potential torture device. We make enough of these for the mission. No more than that," Lev instructed them. The four remaining Techs agreed. Lev continued, "Anyone who manufactures a Rewind without permission will be sent to meet Death Time to find out if their intention in creating an unsanctioned Rewind was unconscionable. You'll be dead here and you may be dead forever."

Dave stood silently by with his arms folded while nodding and added, "We're born, we live here for a while, we die, we move on to the next present. You all have family and friends over there. Don't succumb to the worst parts of your ego. We're here to protect the other present from Bas," he reminded them more diplomatically than Lev had.

The work on the two teams never seemed to end. Naps and meals were taken when critically necessary.

Kali and Lev found themselves arriving at their room at the same time late one afternoon. Most of their encounters the past few days had involved one person arriving at their room while the other was already asleep. Then the one who was awake, laid down beside the sleeping other and fell asleep. They were rarely awake and together for more than a few minutes.

Today was different. They were both freshly showered and lying fully clothed in bed, facing each other with their eyes closed.

"I really like having sex with you," she told him sleepily.

"I really like having sex with you, too," he said, smiling at the new memory as he rubbed her back. "I'm gonna go upstairs and work with Dave and the passport team. I think that means everybody at this point. You gonna go get some dinner?"

"No. Bolin wants to get the spies together so I can go over the maps with them again. They have to know the Kingdom like they grew up there. Olivia, Gorman, and Marty are already working on interiors of buildings, but Santi and Maren keep getting lost downtown in Bas's capital. After that, we're gonna talk about how to survive in torture devices without losing your mind. How to endure being physically tortured while waiting to be rewound. I think Santi is the most prepared for this subject with her medical skills. She knows the body. She's seen a lot. She can compartmentalize the torture and focus on surviving. Why Santi? Why is she so adamant about going?"

"I haven't asked her, but I think it's because she has a husband and a kid in the other present."

"I didn't know that."

"When she came to Campus, she went to work with our doctor. They clicked instantly. Got married. Had a kid all within a year. He was a lot older than her. He had a heart attack and died in front of everyone while eating lunch in the cafeteria over at Campus one day. She was surprisingly ok after he died. She took it in stride, you know? Maybe because she had their daughter. But then... The stuff with her kid was bad. She was just two years old when she started losing control of her muscles. It was a rapid decline. She's really close to Meabh. I think she wants Meabh safe in this present and her own daughter safe in the other present. Do you worry that she won't be an asset to the spy team?"

"No. I just thought she was too nice to send over there. Now I realize she's angry enough. She hides it well. She'll be fine. She needs to get the maps down, though. I won't tell her what you told me."

"I know. Don't you know I know that?" he asked her with a small laugh.

"I didn't want you to worry."

"I don't worry about anything with you. I need a kiss before I leave. I'll be back late. We might sleep up there again."

"Ok."

Lev finally opened his eyes and looked at Kali. Her eyes were still closed. "Baby, don't fall asleep," he said quietly, moving her hair away from her face.

Kali opened her eyes and smiled lightly at him. "I won't. I'm a good soldier," she said as she pushed herself up from their bed.

Kali and Tracy

Three months had passed since Kali had arrived at Ivy. The summer had ended, and the night air was cooler, even if the days were sometimes still warm.

"Bolin's got James teaching Gorman how to slaughter things so he can hopefully move into a kitchen role in the research compound, Santi's doing doctor stuff for Ivy today, including helping Marty, and then she's coming back in tonight, Olivia's ready to go and is annoyed with all of us for making her wait, Maren's studying tech facilities outside the capital, memorizing names of techs, and getting her fourth tattoo today."

"How many does she have to get?"

"Four to be eligible for Bas's team. She's going in with four. She's going to have to be really arrogant and disdainful of people who question her when they notice her and ask her who the hell she is. But no one gets in or out of the Kingdom. It'd be a hell of an accusation to suggest she was a spy with a face full of tattoos. When I pretended to question her last night, man, she's a whole lot of bitch. She ripped my head off for questioning her. It was funny," Kali said, smiling at Lev.

"What's Marty up to today?"

"He's getting some more scars."

"Ok."

"On his face, arms, shoulder--"

450

"Ok."

"Security is really the best fit for him. It could get him close to Bas. Security is the worst job. A lot of turnover, but he could kill Bas. He'd be so close and have a weapon. Plus, he could prevent someone on security from rewinding Bas."

"I know. He's a good guy. I hate that he has to be scarred."

"Maren's tattoos are scars, too."

"Marty's being branded, though."

"Yeah. That's not easy. He'll be ok, Lev," Kali said kindly, knowing her husband struggled with the reality of torture. "Let's change the subject. I want to go with Tracy to South Ivy to get out and take a mental break for a few hours. Go for a walk in the sunshine. I'm going to be working all night with the team."

Lev shook his head at her. "I'm not your boss. You don't have to explain to me that you need an afternoon off. But as your husband, I wish I could go for a walk with you today. I'm jealous of Tracy. You got a canteen?" he asked her.

"No."

"Let's get you one, then." Lev walked out of their room with Kali following and went into Team 4's storage room.

"Here," he said, handing her a canteen. "Take your gun and your knife, too. It's a well-worn path between here and there, but you never know. Wildlife is a bigger problem than people these days. Does Tracy know you want to go?"

"Yeah, Dave told her. He asked me if I'm sure I want to go with her because she's a bit of a bitch on a good day, and when she found out I won't ride a horse and she has to walk, she was bitchier than usual." Kali shrugged. "I don't care. I'll ignore her and just walk. The fall air is nice today and the trees are starting to change colors. The landscape is pretty. I'll check on James' new bees so I can let him know how they're doing after that storm, and then I'll check on the crops with Tracy."

"Ok. Hopefully the wind and the rain didn't fuck up James' new bee colony or the extra winter crop. Walk the entire perimeter of the fencing because Bol will want details in the event he needs to get down there to fix anything. It should be a relaxing morning for you. I'll be upstairs. You want to meet for an early dinner before you meet with the Intel Team?

"Yeah. Where do you want to meet? The cafeteria?" she asked him.

"Can we meet here instead? Be alone? Hmmm?" Lev asked hopefully.

Kali smiled. "Yeah, I'll get us dinner. A clue for the timing?"

"No idea."

"Ok, so cold deer meat is on the menu tonight," she said, smiling.

"And my hot wife," he said nodding and raising his eyebrows at her.

"Oh, yeah, definitely," she agreed with him.

"Alright I gotta go. Don't go getting stung, please," he said as he kissed her and left for the lab.

Kali and the Cannonballs

She watched as Lev and a team of four other riders came up on her and the two horses she was leading through the field. Lev slowed his horse down as he came near her and hopped off quickly, walking up to her.

"Tracy said three guys attacked you two and you refused to return with her. What the fuck is this?" he asked her, pointing to the severed head hanging down her side from the belt loop on her pants.

"I got it for Tracy," she said.

Lev decided to ignore the head because he realized the pack horses likely posed a more immediate problem.

"And this?" he asked her, looking at the two horses she was leading.

Kali ignored both of his questions and said, "I didn't refuse to leave. They had two carts full of stuff, and I wanted to see what they had, but she was too upset and left. She took off on the only horse that had a saddle. There were these two horses who, I guess, were pulling the carts. I didn't know how to hook them back up to their carts and ride a cart and horse deal, so I just wrapped stuff up in some of their tents and tied it all up on them before I left and started walking back to Ivy. It was so fucking scary, but they're actually kind of nice horses."

"You're talking about the horses being scary?" Lev asked with a look of astonishment mixed with confusion.

"Uh, yeah," she said, pointing to them with wide eyes.

The four riders with Lev included Dion, Bautista, Anna, and Lemming. They had all dismounted and were standing by their horses listening to what was being said. Dion had taken control of Lev's horse without being asked.

"She just fucking left you there?" Lev asked incredulously with more than a hint of anger.

"She got attacked and was pretty upset about it. I cut off the head of the guy who attacked her, though."

Bautista quietly passed his horse's reins to Lemming and went to walk around the horses Kali was leading in order to inspect what they were carrying.

"Uh, Lev. There's a bunch of weapons here. Serious weapons," he said, coming back around to look at him.

"There's a lot more in the carts back at their camp. I threw what I could onto these two, but I didn't know how much weight a horse could carry," she said, looking from Lev to Bautista.

"How much more stuff is back there?" Lev asked her.

"A lot, but I did my best. The carts are full. The harnesses are still there. Hook your dinosaurs up to the carts," she said defensively.

"I'm not complaining. You did fucking great," he said, walking away from her and towards Bautista who was ushering him over to show him something.

Lev and Bautista came back around to the front of the horses and Lev said, "We're going to need to ride back there and get what Kali couldn't bring on her own. Others might show up. Might be a fight. Dion, can you ride Kali and these two horses back to Ivy and ask Bolin to send an entire team out here? I also want Ivy on alert. No, actually, they need to be ready to fight. By the look of these weapons, I think these raiders are looking for a serious fight."

"I already told you, I don't ride horses," Kali interjected.

Lev looked at her in complete frustration.

"Kali, listen to me. This is serious. Get back to Ivy now."

Kali scowled at him. "I see the weapons. I know it's serious. I walked with two horses to bring you the weapons," she said in a defensive and angry tone.

Lev was considering all the worst case scenarios as he walked towards her, and his frustration was obvious.

"Baby, I need you to get back to Ivy now, but you won't fucking ride with Dion. You gotta get over this fucking horse thing!" he said loudly to her as he removed his t-shirt and knelt on the ground in front of her, spreading it out. "Put the fucking head here!" he said, slapping his palm in the center of his shirt.

She untied the dead man's hair from her belt loop and bent her knees and placed the head of the man in the center of Lev's shirt. He quickly grabbed the corners of his shirt diagonally and tied the head up into a bundle so that she could carry it by holding onto the knot he'd created rather than allowing the greasy, bloody head to swing from her side. He stood back up, and neither even noticed that Lev's team was still surrounding them listening to their fight.

"How many bullets do you have left?" he demanded.

"Five of them," she said curtly with her face looking up at his in defiance.

He had his hands on his hips, and his face was full of fury. His stance would have been threatening to any other person standing before him, but not to Kali.

"That's just great! What am I walking into? You tortured three guys?! We talked about this!" he shouted at her.

"You're not even considering how much I might have tried. I was thinking about what you said the whole time. I even shot the first guy and killed him. But I...." She breathed deeply before saying, "He was dead when I did this, ok? I shoved a tree branch through his chest. But he was already dead. So that's not torture. With the other two, I was really quick. It wasn't easy, you know. That second guy, he was watching the other guy go to rape Tracy, and I was standing behind him. I was.... Ok, I had the gun on him and I was going to just shoot him like you want me to. I really was, but then he told the guy on top of Tracy, 'I don't care if you kill her. I'll fuck a corpse'...."

Kali paused for a second after she said that, and Lev sighed and shook his head looking down at the ground and his body language loosened up a little. He went to speak to her, but she suddenly continued. "And I remembered things, so I grabbed my knife instead and I, well I still killed him pretty quickly because I had to get the

453

other guy off of Tracy," she said, shaking her head and shrugging a little. "It was very little torture because I was really trying to do what you asked me to do, and also I had to help Tracy."

"Ok. This is the head of the guy who was on Tracy, then?" he asked, no longer shouting at her.

"Yeah. I wanted to give it to her so she knew he couldn't come back for her. Maybe she'll have less nightmares," she said.

Lev took a deep breath and sighed hard and said, "That was nice of you." He put his left hand on her right shoulder and leaned down and kissed her forehead. "I want you to run all the way back to Ivy. It's only about three miles from here. Whoever these people are, they have a lot of weapons that you just took along with three dead to further piss them off."

Kali waved Lev's t-shirt with the severed head inside in front of him and said, "This guy told me who they are before I killed him. He even said your name."

Lev shook his head and shouted in frustration, "What the fuck, baby?! You saving the best for last?! What did he say?!"

Every person who had ridden up with Lev was standing around him and Kali listening to every word they said to one another as they continued to argue and then briefly make up and argue again in front of them.

"Their gang has some kind of pirate theme going on. He asked if I was one of Lev's, and I didn't respond, but he was sure I was, and he laughed rudely and told me it was too late anyway because the Cannonballs were coming to take you out. He said he was going to do things to me. I won't tell you what he said. It was really fucking gross. Then I hurt him, quickly, hardly even the torture he deserved, and killed him before cutting off his head. He didn't do anything to me. I killed him," she said proudly.

Lev suddenly remembered he had others with him and turned to Dion and said, "Get back to Ivy and tell Dave and Bolin that John's raiders are out here. Send us help. Based on these weapons, send for help from Campus, too."

He turned to the rest of his team assembled around him and said, "You hear that? She's talking about John's raiders. We need to get to that camp they were setting up and get the rest of their weapons if we can. They must have planned to stage there for an attack tonight or tomorrow. The rest of their people will be on the way. We have to fucking hurry. They could be there already."

Bautista said, "These are military weapons, Lev."

"I know. We need to haul ass to try and hopefully get there before others arrive. Then we can get what Kali couldn't bring on her own. Let's go. Kali, Dion, give Anna your guns."

As they handed their guns over to Anna, Lev turned to Kali. "If I need you to get on that horse and ride back with Dion, will you?" he asked her.

"I'll do anything you *need* me to do. I just won't do everything you want me to do," she said with a tone that suggested he should already know that by now.

He mouthed, "Thank you" to her and turned to Dion and said, "Ride back with her as quickly as you can. We're in trouble."

Dion didn't respond other than to walk quickly to his horse and hop on, holding out his hand as Lev took the wrapped head from Kali and helped her up behind him. Lev handed the head back to Kali without being asked, and she wrapped her arm around Dion's waist with the head in her hand now resting between the front of his legs. Dion looked down at her hand holding the head between his legs and said nothing. Lemming handed Dion the rope attached to one of the horses Kali had brought them.

Bautista walked the second horse over and handed Kali the rope to that one. "Let the rope go if you have to," he told her, and Lev didn't argue.

Dion was an excellent rider and managed to lead the two other horses while keeping all three moving forward at an impressive rate given their situation. The two horses being ponied were weighed down with the weaponry tied to their backs and seemed eager to reach their destination and have the supplies removed.

Kali leaned against Dion and held tightly to him with her one arm. He was completely lost in his determination to get back to Ivy quickly, even forgetting Kali was hanging on to him at some points. He even forgot about the decapitated head between his legs. The horse he was riding was considered his own. They knew each other well and he was appreciative of her acceptance of the situation she found herself in. He was a small man, and his horse wasn't used to riding with much weight on her back, let alone a second rider. But Kali was lean, and he had faith in her to get them back to Ivy.

He broke his concentration on riding and leading the horse he was holding onto to tell Kali that she had done a good job getting them the weapons, the horses, and the information. She remained silent, and he asked her if she was doing ok back there or if her horse was tugging too hard on her arm. He felt that her horse was keeping pace, but maybe her arm was getting tired.

Kali said, "The horse is being really good and keeping up with us."

"How are you?" he asked her more specifically.

"I'm afraid of horses," she said, hugging him tighter with her body and one arm.

Dion thought about what Kali had said to Lev about killing and lightly torturing the three men she had encountered in the woods. He thought about her out there alone holding onto the head of the man who tried to rape Tracy and then realizing the horses were packed with weapons. He considered how she had to approach them, and untie them, and then somehow manage to get them to walk with her towards Ivy so she could bring Lev the weapons and warn him that 'cannonballs' were coming for him. She did this despite being in extreme danger and having a perplexing, but demonstrable, fear of horses. No matter how crazy Kali was, and she was definitely out there, she was someone he was happy to have on their side. She was an undeniable asset to Ivy. He understood why Lev tolerated her outbursts and eccentricities.

"How about I try and help you overcome your fear of horses after tonight? We can meet at the stables and take it slow. No cleaning shit from the stables, but we get you comfortable enough to ride independently? It gives you freedom, Kali. I think you'll like that," he said.

"That sounds good, but I might not be able to and you're going to waste your time," she said with a note of concern in her voice.

"Are you kidding? You walked through forests and fields with two horses loaded with grenades and missiles. You can do this," he laughed.

"Ok, I want to try. But I can't talk anymore right now. I'm concentrating on holding onto you and my horse," she said.

"We're almost back," he said reassuringly.

Dion knew the trails leading into Ivy well and could see that they were within a mile of the grounds. He wanted to ride ahead to get help sent out to Lev as quickly as possible along with addressing the rest of his requests. His horse had already carried them for about two miles and he felt she was getting stressed. He told Kali he was going to drop her off with the two horses she'd brought them so that he could make better time and have help sent to Lev and the others. She agreed and he assisted her down while telling her he'd alert the crows that she was coming in from the southern trail. He assured her he would request someone meet her along the trail before she even arrived at Ivy who would help her with the two horses. She told him to stop wasting time and go already. Dion took off on his horse with impressive speed through the forest, leaving Kali to walk with the two remaining horses while carrying the severed head.

The horses were still being agreeable and not giving her any trouble, but her mind was troubled. Lev knew who the man was who was going to attack Ivy. It sounded like a personal grudge between old enemies. She thought he wouldn't have old enemies as he tended to kill them rather than let them devise strategies for revenge. This guy John must have gotten away from him.

Before she could investigate her thoughts much further, what looked like two Ivy guards came riding through the woods towards her. One of the horses she was holding onto became skittish and tugged hard on her arm making her wince. She heard the guards talking to each other, but couldn't make out what they were saying. Two more guards suddenly arrived on foot running towards her. One of the riders suddenly took off in the direction of Lev and the others. The two guards on the ground spoke quickly to her telling her to give them the ropes and hop on the back of the horse being ridden by James. She looked up and noticed James was the second rider and not a guard. She smiled at him and stepped out of the way of the two guards as they tried to determine if riding either of the pack horses back to Ivy was possible.

456

"Hurry up Kali. They have to run the pack horses back behind us," James said, trying to rush her.

"I'll run with them," she said to James as she approached him.

"The hell you will! Give me your fucking hand!" he demanded.

"Jesus, James. I was kidding. Sort of. Not really," she said as he pulled her up in back of him with ease and turned his horse around not even bothering to ask what it was she was holding onto that was now between his legs.

"Hold on tightly," he said and waited to feel a secure hug from her.

He took off through the woods, and Kali wasn't sure she breathed until they reached Ivy and he stopped riding and helped her get down. Her legs were shaking after riding with James, but Lev had said he needed her to ride back to Ivy, so she had done it.

When James immediately took her arm and tried to run with her to the towers, her shaking legs gave way and he had to catch her as she nearly fell to the ground.

"You injured?" he asked, looking her over with concern etched on his face.

"No. I'm shaking," she said, not looking at him.

"What do you mean? Shaking?" he asked her, remaining concerned.

"You know. I'm shaking because I'm afraid of horses, and now I've ridden on them twice, and you're a fucking lunatic. What the fuck, James? Jesus. I'm shaking. That sucked even if you're a good rider. Fuck you. Asshole," she said.

James was incredulous. "I'm gonna laugh my ass off at you about this later, really make fun of you, but right now, you're gonna go to the towers where you'll be safe."

"Fuck you! I'm not going to the towers! I'm going to fight. Give me a gun," she said, scowling at him.

He threw his head back and laughed at her saying, "You can't even walk right now! You'd miss if you shot at the side of a building." He shook his head. " You're going to the tower," he said to her decidedly.

She swatted him away from her and walked quickly away heading towards her and Lev's room. There were guns in there.

James ran up to her and said, "Be reasonable. I heard they have military weapons."

"I, me, Kali, I took a lot of their military weapons from them. Did you not see the two horses loaded with weapons?" She corrected him.

James remained silent as he walked beside her.

"Yeah, that was all me. In fact, give me a missile launcher. I found the weapons. I was bringing them here. I should get to use them. I'm not shaking nearly as much already," she said with a hotly defiant attitude.

"Ok, ok. I was worried about you. I'm not telling you to hide. I hated being essential and being sent to the towers, too. Let's kill some Cannibals together. Me and you, eh?" he said, throwing up a hand for a high five.

She obliged and asked, "Should we report to someone? Dave? Bolin? I can get us guns from mine and Lev's room."

James scoffed and said, "Let's go to Williams and have him give us orders. Dave will give us the safest area he can think of. Bolin will send us to the towers with an armed escort." He laughed knowingly, looking down at her.

"Ok Williams, it is. We'll tell him we want the front line," she said enthusiastically, smiling up at him.

"You know I do!" James laughed as they ran up the stairs to the shortened hallway and headed towards the room she shared with Lev.

"I have to put this in the room," she said, holding up the t-shirt that appeared to be holding a bowling ball.

"What is it?" asked James as they walked in to get themselves guns and leave behind the package she was carrying.

"Some guy tried to rape Tracy, so I cut off his head after I lightly tortured him and then killed him. I want to give it to her," she said, placing the head on the floor and opening a box she had removed from under the bed. She pulled out a gun for each of them.

James stared at the t-shirt that he now knew contained a severed head and remembered she had rested it between his legs while they rode back to Ivy. "That's gruesome. We need bullets, too," he said to her as she stood up.

"Over here," she said, walking to the bookshelves where she grabbed a box and put it on the table, opening it to share bullets with James.

"So horses are your kryptonite?" he asked her, sounding surprised while filling his pockets with bullets.

She shuddered. "You have no idea. I only rode because Lev said he *needed* me to. *Needed me to*," she repeated for emphasis. "He better never fucking *need* me to ride a fucking horse again."

James laughed as they left the room and ran to find Williams and his team.

"They're Cannonballs, by the way. Not cannibals. Like pirates," she said to him as they ran.

"No, love. They're Cannibals," James said, no longer laughing.

Williams ordered James and Kali to guard the entrance to Ivy, but they both vehemently protested his orders until he sent them behind the front line defense.

"You two are fucking ridiculous, and you better fucking survive so you can explain it to your fucking husbands that you refused to obey orders!" Williams shouted as he walked away, furious with both of them.

James turned to Kali and said, "If I die, tell Bolin not to blame Williams. There was nothing he could do," he laughed.

"Same for Lev," said Kali, laughing. They crouched together out in the field behind the front line, far from the entrance of Ivy.

"I heard cannonballs. Why are you sure it's cannibals? Do they eat people?" Kali asked James.

"Sort of, they--"

"Wait!" Kali interrupted him. "There's protein walking around everywhere in this dystopia! Why the hell would you need to be a cannibal? That's fucking stupid!" she said loudly, adding, "I'd understand murdering for carbs, but fucking protein? That's stupid!" She started laughing, and James joined her while trying to explain.

"No, you see, John is this... Ah, he's a cult leader more than a leader. He's got these followers who believe he's been sent by God to pave the way for the second coming of Christ. Initiation is chopping off your pinky finger and adding it to a pot of soup or stew or something and everyone eats from it the day you're initiated into the family."

Kali threw her head back and laughed harder. "Oh, my fucking, *God*!" she shouted as she laughed. "Like the body of Christ?!"

James laughed and yelled, "Yeah!"

"People are so stupid!" Kali shouted while laughing. She breathed deeply to help herself stop laughing and said, "So, this guy John, just keeps finding new true believers in this post-apocalyptic hellscape who believe his bullshit? Lev knew him. Why hasn't he killed him already?"

James raised his eyebrows and said, "Oh, Lev's killed him a bunch of times. It's the followers. They supposedly reincarnate the original John. Lev's become their mythical Lucifer. A John dies, killed by Lev most likely, and a new John reemerges."

Kali laughed uncontrollably at this information. "Oh, my God, James! I can't take it!" She breathed in deeply to calm herself down. "The new John-Squad has military grade weapons, James!" she suddenly shouted and laughed again.

James was laughing so hard that he couldn't speak and held up his hand to try and regain his composure.

"We might die today, and I want you to know, I serve Lucifer, I mean Lev, one hundred percent," he laughed with tears in his eyes.

Kali held up her right hand in the sign of Devil horns and they both continued to laugh as James raised his own hand in the sign of Devil horns.

Lev and the Team at John's Camp

Lev, Anna, Bautista, and Lemming rode quickly to the old campground where Kali and Tracy had been attacked. Lev noticed the lifeless body of the dead man with a tree branch in his chest sitting lazily at the base of a tree as they drew nearer to the covered picnic area. In days past, the covered picnic area would have provided campers and others with shelter during rainy weather at mealtimes. Perhaps the shelter would have been utilized during an electrical storm. Now it was simply an abandoned and dilapidated wooden structure succumbing to the ravages of weather combined with time. The old charcoal grills were still standing, and some tables and benches remained. All were reminders of the good intentions of a society that had wanted to foster humanity's connection to, and enjoyment of, nature.

They could see the remaining supplies and weapons on the two carts that Kali had been unable to load onto the horses she had been leading. Bautista and Lemming quickly went to assess the feasibility of bringing the remaining weapons back with them while Lev and Anna went to look for the other two men Kali had killed. Inside the shelter of the covered picnic area, they found the bodies of the two men just as Kali had described.

"I've seen enough. It's obvious what happened here," said Anna, turning to Lev.

"Me, too. Let's help Marty and Eric. We'll get what we can," he said as they ran to help Bautista and Lemming.

Bautista already had his horse positioned to be harnessed to one of the carts while Lemming's horse balked at the same request he made of her. Anna walked her horse over and they had no trouble harnessing him to the cart.

"Throw off camping shit and anything that isn't a weapon," said Lev to Lemming as the two of them climbed into the carts to inspect what was worth hauling back to Ivy. Anna kept watch on the line of trees behind them and they finished quickly.

Anna and Bautista got their horses to move forward, and Lemming and Lev stayed behind them keeping an eye out for any of John's people who might be arriving. They made haste through the tightly wooded area and reached the field as the lone rider from Ivy approached them.

"What do you know?" asked Lev as the rider named Tuva approached.

"Dion and Kali are with Ivy. We sent word to Campus. Dave and Bolin are setting up a perimeter and Dave's going to utilize any of the weapons Kali brought back that may help," she informed him with professional efficiency.

"Anyone else joining us?" Lev asked her.

"Oh, yeah. Dave's got 20 fully armed coming up behind me. Should see them in a minute," she said confidently.

"Good. You ever fight a John before?" he asked her.

"Yeah. The last one," she said grimly.

"Then you know. This shit's gotta end," he said, and his rage was evident.

"Can we get these horses to move any faster?" he asked Anna and Bautista?

"We're making really good time, Lev. They're moving quickly," Bautista assured him.

Kali, James, and Dave

"Oh, shit," said James, looking wide-eyed at something behind Kali.

"What?" she asked, turning to see what he was looking at.

A furious Dave was approaching them at a speed that resembled running.

"Fuck!" muttered Kali getting up to confront Dave head on. "Hey, Lev didn't want to brag about me, but I'm an excellent shot. I belong here!" she said, trying to preempt his order to get to the towers.

"Yeah?! Is that a fact? Just like the fact that you and Irish here disobeyed orders from Williams to guard the entrance of Ivy?!" he seethed.

"You won't underutilize me," she said defiantly, bracing her body to be dragged from her position near the front line.

Dave raised his finger and pointed at her with a face contorted with rage saying, "You are not thinking strategically! You're a marksperson! Grab two sniper rifles and a DMR from Rodriguez and get your ass to Crow's Nest 2! You shoot anything that isn't Ivy or Campus! You understand me?!"

"Uh, yeah," she said as she shrugged and laughed.

"What about me?" asked James loudly and confidently as he stood up.

"Kali, go!" roared Dave, who then turned his attention to James.

Kali could hear Dave shouting at James, "You're a fucking hunter! You know the woods better than anyone here! Get your weapons and hunt, you stupid son of a bitch!"

James was a faster runner than Kali and caught up with her as she ran to get her weapons from Rodriguez.

"See you at the after party!" he yelled at her, throwing up devil horns as he ran to get weapons for hunting Cannibals in the woods.

Kali in the Crow's Nest

Kali scaled the ladder of the crow's nest tower and hopped onto the platform with two of Ivy's other snipers.

"Hi!" she said energetically while the two of them looked at her with unrestrained curiosity.

"You're Kali, right?"

"Yeah, that's me," she said as she set herself up on a ledge that overlooked the field Lev was going to arrive along shortly.

"Can you shoot?" asked the other sniper.

"I don't want to brag, and I'm not positive, but I'm sure I can shoot better than everyone else at Ivy. Present company included."

The sniper who identified himself as Wang laughed at her and said, "Well, I keep hearing really good things about you, so I'll take your word for it."

The other sniper named Carlos said, "We were told Lev and his team would arrive first. Don't shoot the first thing you see. It could be them."

Kali laughed and looked at him. "You know Lev's my husband, right?" Carlos nodded and Kali said, "If I wanted to kill him, I could any night because he sleeps next to me."

She laughed again as she turned to scan the horizon for anyone or anything that might threaten Lev.

James and Bolin

Bolin wasn't mad at James as James had thought he would be after discovering he had disobeyed the order given by Williams.

"Meabh and Ace are safe, you got Kali back here, I know you want to fight. I just want a kiss before you head off to get shot at," he said as he reached for James' arm to pull him over for a quick kiss before he left.

"Sure, love," James said as he kissed him. "Don't worry. I'm just going hunting. I go hunting all the time," he said kindly as he rested his hand on Bolin's shoulder and rubbed it.

"But these animals are also hunting you," said Bolin seriously.

"Yeah, in my forest. Consider that," said James firmly with years of earned confidence.

"Yes. You're right. I'll have to keep working when this is over. I won't be able to look for you. I always assess damage and outcomes of my team under the tree at the left of the front entrance. Find me there. We don't have to talk. Just get my attention so I know you're alright," he told James.

"I will. One more kiss," James said as he stepped forward and hugged Bolin tightly and kissed him. He smiled at him as he turned to leave. "See you under the tree, love!" he yelled as he ran to get his preferred hunting weapons.

Bolin waved at him, but he didn't like the fact that James was now fighting raiders. His broken arm had only just finished healing from the last fight a few months ago. He considered Lev's intentions for him and James over the years. Lev had wanted them to have a nice family life despite the apocalypse. Bolin preferred peace for his family. He wanted his quiet, mostly stable life back again. He wanted James, Meabh, and Ace safe in the tower, if not at the home he had built for their family. But James wanted to fight for their family, too. That was his right. He decided he would try to kill every single last member of John's most recent cult today. No survivors who could rebuild again could be left alive. This bullshit needed to end once and for all.

Kali in the Crow's Nest

Kali watched as Lev and the others approached. More had joined him. The escort of at least 20 additional riders from Ivy made her feel better. They had gotten the rest of the weapons. Her eyes were clear and her vision was sharp. She didn't need the binoculars offered to her by Wang. "I can see Lev," she said. Carlos looked over at Wang and raised his eyebrows.

"Are we just waiting for John's cult to come at us now?" she asked them.

"Dave said nothing's certain. This is a fight with one rule. Kill everyone, everything that isn't Campus or Ivy. Horses, kids, dogs. Kill it all. We have enough going on, don't we?" Carlos asked her knowingly.

"Yeah," Kali said, "we do. Let's make a pact in Crow's Nest 2. I hear this shit's been going on with the John's being reincarnated and coming for Lev again and again for some time. When this is over, let's go make sure it's over," she said, still not looking at them.

"What do you mean?" asked Carlos.

"Let's find James and go hunting for survivors," she said coldly.

"I'll go with you," said Wang.

"Me, too," said Carlos.

They looked at her as she stared at Lev and his team approaching.

"If the Cannibals ride up with weapons, either of you think you can hit them?" she asked without emotion.

"Hit them or their weapons on the field?" asked Wang.

"Their weapons," said Kali.

"I'll do my best," he said.

"Me, too," said Carlos.

"I'll show you what I mean," said Kali, holding perfectly still.

She suddenly fired her gun and waited for a second before an explosion that lit up the second row of trees behind Lev and his team erupted.

"They're here," she said without a break in her concentration and turned her rifle a very tiny bit to the right before firing again.

Kali tried to watch Lev and the others as they continued to ride their horses and make their way into the safety of Ivy's protected perimeter. She, Carlos, and Wang fired into the woods beyond the field taking out approaching Cannibals, and Carlos demonstrated a need to become increasingly verbal as he fired upon them whether or not he hit his intended target. Kali laughed at him and high-fived him when he took down a horse pulling a cart of what they assumed would be more military grade weapons.

Kali shot at the cart hoping not to hit a missile that would find Ivy. She wasn't certain how such things worked but felt the risk was worth taking. She hoped all detonations would occur at the source and take out Cannibals only. Her shot made contact with something on the cart that caused a fireball to explode outward low on the ground causing people near the cart who were removing weapons from it to be engulfed in flames.

Wang shot methodically at a group of Cannibals advancing from the left and quietly asked Kali for assistance as some got too close to Ivy. She turned to assist him and took down one person before losing sight of them from her position.

"Trees are in my way," she said, sounding annoyed. However, she watched as two riders further to the left went down from a shooter within Ivy's wooded area. She told herself it was James.

Lev and the expanded team dismounted and grabbed weapons from the carts and ran towards Ivy leaving their horses behind. The weapons had to be kept from their enemies. The horses were valuable to them but also to the raiders. They worried less about their horses than they worried about missiles finding their way into the hands of John's cult members.

Kali lost sight of Lev as he entered the woods, and she breathed very shallowly until she finally watched him reemerge. In the meantime, she took out raiders and their horses, furious at the raiders for being such persistent assholes when all Lev wanted to do was help Rollo get rid of Bas. She hated stupid people.

After the Battle

Lev ran to their room to see if Kali was there. He couldn't find her on the field, and no one he'd asked had seen her alive or dead. She wasn't at medical according to Doc, who had surprisingly few patients after the battle. He ran up the two shortened staircases to their room and then came back out quickly into the hallway. She wasn't in their room, either. He couldn't find her. He had looked everywhere he could think of.

The exit door to the right started to open, and Lev held his breath as he walked down the stairs to see who was coming in through the door. He watched as Kali stepped through the door in what felt like slow motion. He didn't say anything as he ran over to her and hugged her, letting relief wash over him. He was filthy, sweating, and covered in blood and nature.

He was still shirtless as Kali hugged him back, and he asked her calmly, "Where the hell have you been? Are you hurt?"

"No. You?" she asked him.

"Not seriously," he said as he continued to hug her. "You did good today, baby," he said, pulling away from her to look at her face. "Riding dinosaurs like it was no big deal," he smiled.

Kali agreed, saying adamantly, "That was the worst part," as he put his arm around her shoulders and they turned to walk together up the stairs to their room.

"You'll need to talk to Dave about what happened out there. Tell him what went down between you and Tracy," he said.

"Yeah. It's bad enough that she was useless, but I feel like she lied about me, too."

"In what way?" Lev asked.

"I didn't refuse to leave with her. I told her we had to look through their stuff before we could decide what to do. She told me to fuck off. Those were her words. *'Fuck off. I'm not rummaging through their shit.'* And I told her no, we have to see what's here. And she said we should go back and send a team to look through their shit, and then she fucking left as I was walking toward the carts!" Kali looked at Lev with an outraged expression and nodded adding, "Just like that! Fucking bitch. Honestly, I considered shooting her as she rode away. But I'd already killed three guys and thought it might become an issue if I shot her in the back of the head, too. But I still got her the rapey guy's head before I left. You know, to be helpful and to show her how to complete a job." Kali shrugged. "It only took a second to get it. I've had a lot of practice," she trailed off as Lev listened.

"You want to take a shower first? I need to go find Dave," Lev said, distracted by his thoughts.

"Yeah. I'll do that eventually, but first, I made a pact with Wang and Carlos in the nest. We're gonna go look for survivors of John's Cannibal cult. No more reincarnations of John. We have more important things to do here," she said as she put more bullets in her pocket from the box she and James had left on the table earlier.

Wang was running fast up to their window calling her name. She walked over to the window and Lev followed her, still trying to make sense of what she was telling him.

"Yeah, I can go. Lev's good. He's not hurt. Ok. I'll be right out. You need guns or bullets?" she asked him.

Lev heard him say they had all resupplied themselves already and that James was going to meet them at the back end of the corral with the others.

"Go ahead, I'll be right there," she said and turned to speak to Lev.

Before she could speak, he took her shoulders calmly in his filthy hands and asked equally calmly, "Does Dave know the four of you, and whoever else, are going to go find survivors and kill them?"

She nodded enthusiastically. "Yeah, I cleared it with him. Very official. He was already so mad at me and James for disobeying orders we got from Williams earlier," she laughed. "Whoo. Man, was he pissed off! I'm trying to be respectful now. Anyway, he said he'd send others to the corral. He's coming, too. He agreed with me, said my plan was good. This bullshit needs to end!"

She smiled and held up her right hand in devil horns and Lev shook his head and said in an exhausted tone, "I don't get it."

Kali smiled and said, "Devil horns. The John cult thinks you're Lucifer! James made me laugh so hard today. They're Cannibals not Cannonballs!" She shook her head, amused at her own mistake in her initial understanding of the name.

"Baby, you know I think you're very capable, but I have to go with you," he said as he put on a shirt and grabbed another gun and a knife and followed her out of their room.

"You don't have to," she said, smiling as they went down the stairs.

"Oh, yes. I do," he said with a laugh.

"It's more fun working with you, anyway," she said, blowing him a kiss as they left through the exit door and headed towards the corral where the others were waiting for them.

The End of the Cannibals

Dave led Kali, James, Lev, Bolin, Wang, Carlos, and all of the others in a comprehensive sweep of the land surrounding Ivy. Dave called them hunters in a nod towards James' skills during the battle and it was agreed that any surviving Cannibals found would be returned to Ivy by three hunters. They wanted an accurate accounting of the total number of survivors their efforts would ultimately produce.

Two hundred military members from Campus had arrived during the battle and they joined Ivy as they scoured the landscape looking for Cannibals all the way to the campground where Kali and Tracy had encountered them to begin with, five miles from Ivy. The three bodies of the Cannibals Kali had killed were returned to Ivy to be burned in the pit.

They hunted through the landscape for several more miles out from that point and determined it was time to return to Ivy to assess their efforts. The far-reaching after-battle sweep netted them nine additional surviving Cannibals. They also discovered numerous wounded Cannibals in the nearby fields and forests surrounding Ivy. In all, they killed a shocking 61 members of the Cannibal Cult.

All Cannibal survivors who were captured alive, wounded or not, were decapitated under Lev's orders. The executions by decapitation were conducted by volunteers of which there were too many to accommodate given the lack of surviving Cannibals. The head Kali had taken from the Cannibal at the campground was tossed into the burn pit along with all the rest of the deceased Cannibals.

Ivy lost one horse during the battle, but gained six from the Cannibals that were not wounded. It was agreed that Campus would take four of the horses because they had a greater need for them in their community. Most of the military grade weapons they had taken from the Cannibals were sent to Campus where Aisha had a better storage system and space to hold military grade weapons than did Ivy.

None of the military weapons the Cannibals had intended to use against Ivy were deployed against them that day. There were no deaths suffered by Ivy or Campus community members. Injuries were mostly mild, with only five members of Ivy having suffered non-life threatening gunshot wounds. One member of Campus was injured falling off her horse when the horse threw her after being startled by gunfire. Most of the other injuries were related to hand-to-hand combat with black eyes, lost teeth, and broken noses being the most prevalent.

Lev, Dave, Bolin, and Aisha held a quick meeting to discuss the Community News they wanted to disseminate to the two communities. They informed their various team leaders of the points that needed to be made and sent them off to inform the people they were in charge of. Lev held two Community News meetings in the cafeteria and informed non security related community members about what had happened.

Dion, Wang, Carlos, Anna, Bautista, and Lemming, also spoke up throughout the community describing to others Kali's willingness to risk herself to save the community. Everyone knew she single-handedly killed three Cannibals and brought back as many weapons as she could to Ivy by leading horses she had packed herself. They also learned that she fired the first shot which had led to a cache of weapons being detonated out in the woods before any could be used against Ivy.

Where before, her positive reputation within the community was based on assurances by leadership about the threat posed by Bas, and her cooperation in assisting the RT in developing technology to help them fight him, having five community members be able to describe personally interacting with Kali throughout the events of the day led to greater understanding of her commitment to all of them. Her own life had been in danger multiple times, yet she continued to put the best interests of Ivy's community before her own. Ivy and Campus community members already knew how dangerous and persistent John's Cannibals were, now they were learning how dangerous and committed Kali was and that she was on their side.

A bonfire party to celebrate the final eradication of John and his Cannibals was called for by Bolin, personally. After the last of the Cannibal bodies was tossed into the burn pit, Bolin had turned to James and said, "I want to celebrate this victory." James had no qualms about throwing open the space around their home to welcome everyone who wanted to attend. The announcement of the planned celebration was circulated enthusiastically and all who wished to attend were told to meet on the property surrounding James and Bolin's house late in the afternoon the following day.

Aisha encouraged the Campus soldiers who had fought against the Cannibals to either stay overnight at Ivy or come back the following day and bring a friend or family member to celebrate the victory, too. She, Bob, and Otis also intended to attend the party hosted by James and Bolin.

Night Shift

The fires in the burn pit were still busy consuming the Cannibals, but the breeze was blowing the smoke westward away from Ivy.

"You said, 'Not seriously.' Those were your words," Kali said, scowling at him in their shared shower. "Did Santi see this? You need stitches. I think I'm mad at you," she said, looking at him with a hard expression.

Lev smiled kindly at her despite her anger and said, "Hey, now. I'm fine. The knife went in, and I pulled it out, and I can still use my arm. Nothing important was hit."

"You need antibiotics, or stitches, or something. And you should tell me when you get stabbed. Stabbing is serious," Kali insisted, shaking her head at him.

"I'll stop by medical on my way up to the lab. Ok? Don't be mad at me. I think you think it's more serious than it is."

"Oh, you want to keep fighting with me? That's all I'm hearing right now," Kali said, getting worked up at his response.

"No, no. Come here," he said, laughing lightly and hugging her under the warm running water.

"Does hugging me hurt?" she asked with concern.

"Not at all. I'll go see Doc. She'll be mad at me, too. I've learned my lesson. Ok? Let Doc be mad at me, not you," he said, kissing her.

"Fine. I'm not mad," she said, relaxing into their hug and leaning against his body under the running water. "Don't think I'm mad. Just tell me when you get stabbed. Let me worry. Let me take care of you sometimes."

"Ok. I will. You and the Intel Team going to work late tonight to make up for the lost time today?"

"Probably."

"I'll be late or never tonight. No one on the RT was injured, so we can be up all night to make up for lost time today."

"I think I just got mad at you again," she said quietly as she shook her head at him as he turned off the shower water.

"Sorry. I mean, only one member of the RT was mildly injured today, so we're gonna work all night." He laughed at her scowling face and took the towel she was offering him. "Baby, I'm fine," he insisted as they dried off. "But you're probably going to have to be on top," he said as he threw his towel over the top of the bathroom door and took her hand to lead her to their bed.

Kali laughed. "See? It's important that you let me take care of you when you're injured." She laughed louder as he picked her up. "Lev! Your arm! Put me down!"

"Oh, I'm putting you down right here," he laughed as he sat on the edge of their bed with her in his lap.

Lucifer Wins

"I don't think I ever heard any of them call me Lucifer," said Lev, determined to win the argument with James.

"Not to your face," said James with a sideways glance that made Lev laugh. "Fuck you, man."

James laughed too and said, "All I'm saying is I don't think anyone survived. We got them all. And that means the Devil won!" They were sitting near one of the bonfires out in back of James and Bolin's house celebrating the eradication of the Cannibals once and for all while they discussed Lev's mythical role in the Cannibal legacy.

"This is gonna be a campfire story for generations of children. You need to accept your role in the legend. You want horns on your statues or no?" asked James, laughing at Lev as he scowled with humor.

The crowd at the bonfire was already large early on and included nearly everyone from Ivy as well as the 200 from the Campus military who had ridden out to help Ivy defeat John's cult. Campus military members brought along their own guests to celebrate, but also brought the family and friends of the Campus RT who were currently living at Ivy.

Tracy was not in attendance. Dave had quickly executed her himself after listening to how she had behaved when she and Kali were in trouble. Rape wasn't an excuse for abandoning your community member. Losing a limb wasn't an excuse. You fought to the death for your community or you were worthless to the survival of your community.

The fact that Tracy had ridden off on a horse leaving Kali behind, appalled all who heard what had happened. Everyone, even Tracy, knew Kali was essential to the fight against Bas. Everyone also realized 60 or so Cannibals might have been waiting at their camp when a small Ivy security team rode up unaware of the danger. They would have been devastatingly outnumbered and likely killed for their efforts to assess the contents of the two carts as Tracy had told Kali was the way for them to proceed. Lev, the Leader of Ivy and the RT, along with his security team, might have encountered the entire Cannibal cult and been killed had they ridden up unaware of the potential risk.

They still might have been killed based on Lev's decision to ride to the camp, but at least he had been able to make an informed decision based on what Kali had told him. Additionally, Ivy's compound might have been confronted by an army of Cannibals armed with missiles and other weapons of war. Ivy could have been defeated and their fight against Bas would be over before it began.

To lose to 60 Cannibals as opposed to having an opportunity to fight a war against Bas was mind-boggling to Dave. He held onto his rage, displaying it even in public spaces, for days following the event. Everyone avoided him outside of the labs. Lev would tell Kali later, "I think he took it so personally because he's counting on defeating Bas so that he can be reunited with his late wife and live without the threat of him ruining that present. Tracy almost deprived him of that opportunity by her actions."

Kali had been at Ivy for a little more than three months now and still hadn't had an opportunity to meet Aisha's husband, Bob. Along with firewood, and lots of food, Aisha had seven metal barrels brought to Ivy to make additional bonfires for the celebration. In addition to the large stone bonfire pit permanently installed by Bolin when he had built their home years earlier, the seven smaller bonfires in the metal barrels were lit throughout the Ivy property around the main bonfire. Tables and benches from inside the cafeteria were brought outside and people were encouraged to bring their own chairs, as well as blankets. Groups of people congregated with friends from both the Campus and the Ivy community and enjoyed the food and drink that was made available to everyone.

Bob was introduced to Kali by Aisha, and he hugged her telling her he was happy to finally meet her. Kali looked at him and remembered the story Lev had told her about how he had nearly been driven insane at the thought of having to kill his own son. She hugged him tightly and told him she was happy to meet another member of Lev's family. He smiled kindly at her and asked, "Can I introduce you to a better man than both Lev and myself?" Kali nodded and Bob introduced her to his and Aisha's son, Otis.

After their introduction, Otis ran off with Meabh and Ace with instructions from Bolin who yelled to the departing kids not to do anything stupid because all of the adults would be getting drunk. Aisha laughed at Bolin and then yelled to the three children that she wasn't going to drink, and she'd be checking in on them from time to time, so they'd better behave. Bolin looked up at Aisha and laughed.

"Meabh, who else is going to be sober?!" he yelled to his daughter.

"You, daddy!" she yelled back, still running with Otis and Ace.

Aisha shook her head at Bolin laughing. "I thought you were serious!" she said.

Bolin shook his head as he laughed at her. Lev watched Kali interacting with Bolin, Aisha, Bob, and Otis and felt good about the fact that he had a family who would welcome her into their circle and look after her if anything happened to him.

Numerous horseshoe pitching areas and cornhole toss games were set up throughout the field and community members congregated around the games socializing and catching up with each other. The families and friends of the Campus RT knew that their reunion was for only one night, and their joy at being reunited after so many months combined with the celebratory atmosphere and gathering.

Three large hogs from Ivy's farm were slaughtered earlier in the day and were being spun over quickly assembled rock pits created by community members. The kitchen staff cooked some vegetables but left many raw and brought them out to the tables where people could take what they wanted. The food Aisha brought from Campus was quickly added to what Ivy had prepared, and people took turns tending to the various stages of food preparation, not leaving the work to any one group so that all could enjoy the celebration. Lev chopped vegetables with Marco and others, while Kali joined a group bringing out bowls in which to serve the food. Alcohol was consumed directly from the bottle with only sober guests and kids being allowed to use mugs.

As more guests arrived, James opened his wine cellar and brought out even more wine, sugar shine, beer, and other spirits he had distilled. Kali went down to his main cellar with him and her jaw dropped at the amount of alcohol James had in his cellar.

"James! You're a hoarder!" she shouted and laughed.

"You don't understand the process! This isn't hoarding as you're calling it!" he insisted. "This is called a collection. It's a legitimate hobby," he explained. Then he told her he had two more cellars which reduced them both to tears of laughter. "This hobby is keeping me out of trouble!" he explained through tears of laughter.

"Yeah, but getting everyone else into trouble!" laughed Kali.

"Not my fucking problem!" James insisted through his laughter.

Bolin arrived with several others ready to carry alcohol up to the party and looked at the two of them laughing and asked, "Do I want to know?"

James stood up and said, "No. Probably not. Unflattering accusations are being made about me which might upset you."

Kali shook her head vehemently and said, "Bullshit. James is knowingly corrupting the community."

Bolin stared at them as they turned towards each other and laughed again and asked, "Are you two already drunk?"

James stood up and wiped away tears as he walked over to Bolin, still laughing, but assuring him neither he nor Kali had had anything to drink yet.

Bolin nodded and asked, "Have you decided what's ready to be brought up, then?"

James put an arm around Bolin's shoulders and said with a sweeping hand gesture, "Everything! There's just under 1100 bottles here, and about 400 to 450 guests expected, right? Whatever. Bring it all up! Let them drink all they want, then take a bottle home. Let's make this a true celebration. Toast the death of all Johns, and Lev's victory over that fucker. But make sure you tell everyone to bring back the bottles," he added in a deadly serious tone.

"They know, they know. But I'll tell everyone again, anyway," Bolin assured him.

"You know what? We're going to war. Bring up 300 more bottles from the small cellar. Campus can bring a bottle back for friends who couldn't make it.

"Wow, you're gonna give it all away?" asked Kali, impressed by his generosity.

James smiled at her and reminded her, "I have two more cellars. Not as large as this one, but we're not about to face an alcohol shortage even with all that I'm giving away tonight."

James turned to Bolin who was looking at a row of vodka. "Can we put aside this bottle of vodka for me?" he asked, hopeful that being married to the owner of the wine cellar gave him special privileges.

James scowled at him and walked over to grab as many bottles of the vodka as he could hold, saying, "Love, I think I can carry five. You grab more. These are yours. Let's bring them upstairs so they aren't accidentally given away. You want anything else from here?" he asked Bolin as he walked by him to hand Kali some of the bottles he was putting aside for him.

"I like your pumpkin wine, too," he said.

"You and me, both," said James, smiling as he looked for the pumpkin wine. "Let's put some in the house. I'll be making more soon, but it won't be ready for a while. We'll go to the second cellar and bring up some of the berry wines, too. I like those," he said aloud while appearing to be considering his options.

James turned to some people who had come down to assist Bolin and dictated to them what should be taken out to the bonfires for consumption during the celebration immediately and made an effort to oversupply the party. All of the sugar shine was going up in the first wave. He then suggested Bolin and the others bring up all of the rest of the bottles and place them on their front porch to be taken by departing guests later in the evening or in the morning as they headed back to Campus.

He turned to Kali who was still holding three bottles of vodka and said, "I fucking love boozy parties. Oh, let me take those from you." He took the three bottles of vodka from her, relieving her of them.

"Can I request a bottle of vodka for Lev?" she asked politely.

James stared at her. "I can't believe I didn't think of that!" he said loudly, annoyed with himself. "Bolin got at least five, so his brother gets at least five. They'll share what Bolin has left if Lev runs out," he said, removing five more vodka bottles to the floor near his feet. Kali smiled and thanked him profusely.

James looked at her and asked, "But what does my fellow soldier want for herself?"

"I heard you mention berry wines. Do you have anything made with blueberries?" she asked

"Mmm. No blueberries, but in another cellar, I have raspberry wine. You want that?" he asked her.

"That sounds great! I'm excited to try that," she said enthusiastically.

"Do you know, I'm eternally grateful to you for getting me out there on the field yesterday? I felt alive. I still feel alive. Thank you for refusing to go to the towers with the kids and getting me out there fighting for the future for my kids," he said to her.

"Yeah, James. I'm not as good with words as you are, but you helped me, too, and you helped Lev," she said to him.

"I'll bring over the raspberry wine tomorrow along with a bottle of your favorite carrot wine just in case you don't like the raspberry. Let's get drunk tonight. Celebrate!" he said, smiling at her.

"Let's do this!" Kali said enthusiastically.

"Here, take this bottle of vodka up to Lev," he said, walking to the shelves and grabbing a bottle for him. Tell him it's his. He doesn't have to share. Except with you, of course."

"Thanks," said Kali.

"Get going, now. I think Bolin's going to play for us, too. Enjoy this night without worries."

"I will," she said, raising the bottle of vodka at him as she left.

She met Bolin on the stairs going up as he was heading back down to grab more bottles and he said, "Kali, I remember you said you play guitar, too. That's why you knew what I would need. Do you really play?"

"I do."

"Do you want to play with me tonight?" he asked her.

"Hell, yeah!" she said enthusiastically.

"I'll bring out two guitars, then," said Bolin.

"Can't wait!"

The sun was just beginning to set, and Kali walked around the bonfire heading towards Lev carrying the bottle of vodka for him. He waved at her and she stepped around and over other people to get to him.

"Hi babe! Look what I got for you from James!" she said proudly.

"Oh! You brought me dinner!" he said, pulling her close to his side as she sat down beside him.

He leaned over and kissed her. "You and James left Dave so unhinged that he dragged me and Bolin to an impromptu private meeting on the other side of the house a few minutes ago," he said as he leaned back on the large tree stump behind their blanket.

Kali looked surprised and said, "I thought he forgave us. Am I still on his shit list?"

"Yeah, well, no, it's me and Bolin he was pissed off at. Told us to stop holding you two back," laughed Lev.

"Dave's so cool," said Kali as she leaned her body against Lev's.

"Where is he?" she asked, looking around.

"Over there." Lev nodded in the direction of a barrel bonfire to their left with Aisha and Bob seated next to Dave.

"Should we join them?"

"They're circulating with the teams. They're doing the right thing. They'll be back. This area right here is for them," he said, pointing to the blanket in the grass beside him.

"Ok."

"I'm doing the thing where I spend time with my wife and people realize I'm a human being."

Kali looked up at him and squinted her eyes. "Who can't see who you are?" she asked, annoyed at the thought of anyone seeing less of him.

"All I need is for you to see me," he said to her quietly as people circulated around them.

"I see you trying to help everyone. They'd better see it, too," she said, looking around at the people mingling about on the property.

Lev opened the bottle of vodka and took a sip, passing it to Kali who took a sip. A lot of people stopped by to talk to them about the progress being made in the labs, looking for reassurance from Lev, himself, that they were finding ways to fight back against Bas. Many asked direct questions they had been harboring relating to the threat Bas posed to them in this life and in the other present.

Kali took the community questions seriously and tried to give good answers. Despite trying to impart helpful information, she still sounded intimidating and a little scary when she told a concerned couple from Campus, "Bas controls everything, and he's immortal, and he's going to torture us, and kill us all, over and over again for eternity."

Lev turned to her and said, "Babe, let's try, Bas currently controls everything, but we're working on how to take away his power. We're gonna win."

Kali nodded and said, "That's a really good goal!"

The couple left looking more concerned than they had when they'd stopped by to speak with them, and Lev laughed at Kali when they heard one tell the other, "I'm completely freaked out. I'm gonna get shit-faced tonight and try to forget what she just told us."

"It's important to be honest with people," she told Lev while he continued to laugh. The next unsuspecting victims of Kali's honesty arrived to chat with her and Lev, and Lev jokingly warned them, "You're probably gonna want to have a drink or two in you before talking to my wife."

Later, Lev watched as Bolin walked over to them and asked Kali which guitar she'd like.

"I'm not picky," she said, reaching out for either guitar he was offering her.

"What do you want to play?" he asked her.

"I was thinking of a song by Traffic called 'Walking in the Wind.' Do you know it?" she asked Bolin.

"I know that song," said Lev before Bolin could respond.

"Do you like Traffic? My dad loved Traffic," Kali told Lev.

"Yeah, I liked them," he said.

Bolin nodded, "Me, too. Great band. Lots of bass in that song, though. Can you play it acoustically?" he asked her.

"Yeah. But it needs some percussive sounds for sure."

"Well, let's wing it and fuck it up together. These people won't know!" Bolin nodded enthusiastically, making a drinking motion with his hand. "You singing? Or is this going to be music only?" asked Bolin.

"Yeah, I remember the lyrics. Do you?" she asked.

"No. That's why I asked. Sketchy after all this time, but I'll join in the chorus. I don't forget music, though."

"Ok. Jump in whenever you remember the words."

"I will. You like the older songs? Do you know From the Beginning, by Emerson, Lake & Palmer? It's a good acoustic song for the most part."

"How does it go?"

Bolin quickly played a part of the song and Kali's face lit up with recognition.

"Oh, yeah! I know that one. I don't remember the lyrics but I've played it before. I might stumble a bit, but I think I can manage."

"Ok, your song first, then mine?" he asked her.

"Yeah, let's do this," she said eagerly.

The sun had set at least an hour earlier, and Bolin went to sit next to James across from her on the other side of the bonfire. The people assembled at the bonfire were definitely no longer sober as Bolin had noted, but Lev had purposely held off on consuming much of his vodka in order to be more aware of the music Kali and Bolin would be playing together. He remembered that he had told her about his musical tastes the evening they spent in the two story house. 60's hippie music. He had told her how his tastes in music had changed over the years. That was more than three months ago. He still knew nothing about her musical tastes. Hell, he didn't realize she was talented enough to play guitar with Bolin. Apparently she felt she could sing well enough to sing along with him, too. Now she was going to play a song by Traffic. He realized he had never found out what music she liked. Tonight he found out that her dad had liked Traffic, but what did she like? He had no clue. He felt bad about that even if he knew Kali wasn't bothered by it. He looked over at her and decided he'd find out later.

Kali began to play, and Bolin waited for his moment to join her. Lev felt that Kali played the acoustic guitar excellently, and he was embarrassed by his lack of knowledge about his own wife. She sang the lyrics to the old Traffic song while playing the borrowed acoustic guitar, and Bolin added depth to the music by focusing on the percussive aspect and playing along with her, humming parts, singing when he recalled lyrics, and joining in for the chorus. Bolin sounded good even when he hummed. It sounded to Lev as if they had practiced together and not just decided to play together on a whim.

Kali and Bolin played a few more songs together after the first two they had decided on, responding to requests when they both knew the music and at least one of them knew the lyrics. Kali made mistakes and laughed, and Bolin sat across from them over the bonfire and laughed at her when she needed to catch up, but he also filled in the spaces expertly like the musician he was.

Olivia decided to let them know she could sing, too, and joined them in singing some songs she was familiar with. Many were songs she had learned as a child growing up alongside an older man named Mike who used to play guitar and sing for their small community during the long, cold winters in New Hampshire.

Olivia had a surprisingly good voice, but she couldn't play an instrument. She expressed a serious interest in wanting to learn to play guitar to Kali who seemed excited to share what she knew. "I'm not a good teacher, but maybe you're a good student!" Kali told Olivia with enthusiasm. Lev laughed at the interaction and decided he would go find Kali her own guitar and kick in as many doors as necessary to find her strings. He decided he would try to find Olivia a guitar, too. Kali really liked her. She might be family.

"The guitar playing, it's really sexy," Lev said to her as she handed the guitar off to a man named Lance who also played.

"Ooh, then you're gonna like that Bolin said I can take that guitar home with me."

"I do like that," he said as he got up off of the ground. "I need a chair to sit on. My back's fucking killing me. I'm gonna grab you one, too. You need anything else?" he asked as he headed towards Bolin's house for their chairs.

"Yes. Food and water," she said.

Lev came back carrying two chairs with a mug of water resting on top of the stacked chairs alongside a bowl containing assorted foods for them to share.

She took her water, and he handed her their bowl of food and said, "I got you the rosemary, garlic potatoes you like."

"You're my favorite person," she said, smiling happily at him.

He put his chair against hers and grabbed the bottle of vodka from the ground near the tree stump and asked, "You planning on singing or playing anymore tonight?"

She had a mouth full of food and shook her head no.

"Ok, I'm drinking a lot more then," he said smiling at her and taking a big swig of vodka.

"I cannot carry you home," she warned him through a mouth full of potatoes.

"The porch," he said, pointing towards James and Bolin's house and the porch that was overflowing with alcohol bottles for the guests to take home with them.

"Ok. That's a plan I can live with," she said agreeably and kept eating.

Lev put his arm around her and listened to Lance and Marco play guitar together while she ate and he drank.

"Want some?" he asked her.

"No. I'm saving myself for you," she said as she leaned against him and offered him a potato which she then placed into his open mouth.

"The hell with the porch, I like your plan better," he said as he chewed the potato and smiled at her.

After the Boozy Bonfire Celebration

It was very late when Lev and Kali walked across the field with the others heading back to the dorms at Ivy after the bonfire celebration had ended. Everyone from Campus was encouraged to sleep at Ivy. Empty dorms, shared dorms, hallways, the cafeteria floor, outside on the ground, the old education center, or wherever else they could find to sleep for the night. Kali and Lev were the only people who entered the exit door near their room as the hallway ended and theirs was essentially the only living quarters near that particular door.

Lev was happily carrying the five bottles of Vodka gifted to him by James, and Kali had a bottle of pumpkin wine, because Bolin wanted her to bring it home. He also insisted she take the acoustic guitar she had been playing and several packs of strings he said she would eventually need.

"He wasn't already drunk when he decided to give away all this alcohol?" asked Lev to confirm with Kali James' state of mind.

"Not at all. He's a hoarder, though. That one cellar was packed. He had to get rid of stuff."

"He usually fills the cafeteria with bottles on the first snowy day of the year and sends a cart full to Campus. Who knows where we'll all be a few months from now, huh?" he asked, looking at her.

"Yeah. This was a great way to celebrate getting rid of the Cannibals," she said approvingly.

Kali opened their closed dorm door, and they placed the six bottles of alcohol on their small dining table with Lev nearly dropping some as they wobbled about like bowling pins after having suffered a near miss. He sat down noisily on the couch making grabbing hand gestures towards Kali as she walked over and sat down beside him.

"So, you're a musician?" he asked her as she leaned closer to kiss him.

"I can play an acoustic guitar moderately well," she said proudly.

"Well, I'm going to be your groupie," he said as he maneuvered her under him on the couch and began to kiss her neck.

"I always wanted a groupie," she said as she made room for him between her legs.

"Why didn't you tell me you could play?"

"I think I did. Outside the music store," she reminded him.

"Mmm, that's right, you did," he said as he ran one of his hands down her side and began to move his erection between her legs.

"Yeah, I told you I play, and you didn't say anything, so I thought we were just talking about Bolin. Focused on finding him some stuff," she said as she ran her hands down his back and then under his shirt to touch his skin.

"I like your hands. I meant to ask you about it. I forgot. It was a surprise tonight, though. You play so well," Lev said as he kissed her. "And you have a nice voice," he said as he kissed her again. "You and Bolin sounded so good together," he said as he moaned lazily and pushed himself against her harder.

"Do you want to get ready for bed?" Kali asked him, touching the side of his face and beard.

"No. I want to talk to you," he said to her as he continued to kiss her.

She wrapped her arms and legs around him and kissed him back saying, "Mmmm, babe, It feels to me like you want to go to bed and fuck."

"Ok, yeah, I do want to do that, but I didn't ask you about the music you like when we talked about the music I like. I didn't know you could play guitar. I didn't know you could sing. Am I rude to you?" he asked her.

Kali laughed at him and said, "No. You're definitely not rude to me."

"You said you play guitar, but I didn't ask you if you need a guitar. I might be a jerk," he said, running his hand up under the front of her shirt to her breast.

"I think you're drunk," she laughed as he purposely tickled her neck by pretending to bite her.

"Just as long as you're not. You're not, are you?" he asked with some concern.

"Not even a little," she said, running her hands over his ass and pulling him onto her.

"Good, because I want you," he said in a deeper voice as he slowly got up off of her and held out his hand to take her to their bed.

"I've never fucked a groupie before," she said, laughing as he pulled her towards their bed.

"I've never fucked a member of the band before," he said, raising his eyebrows and smiling at her as he got undressed and watched her doing the same.

After they had fucked and were lying together in bed dressed with their shoes on, Lev asked her, "What's your favorite song, baby?"

"I've never had a favorite song," she said.

"Really?"

"Yeah. Music is fun and really personal. It's not a competition. Sometimes I like a song just because someone else does."

"I see," he said, looking at her lying next to him with her eyes closed.

Lev Tells Kali the Plan

"I grabbed a bottle of the carrot wine you like. Let's go to the roof and look at the stars and have some," he said as he pulled a sweater on over his t-shirt.

"Your mood is weird. What's up? Why did Bolin cancel work tonight?"

Lev pulled out one of his sweaters for her because she still didn't have much of a wardrobe of her own. "Here, put this on. I'm planning to keep you warm, but it's pretty cold out tonight."

Kali looked at him and didn't reach out for the sweater he was holding out to her. "Why are you being--"

"I know. You're right. I am being weird. Let's get to the roof, open this bottle, and we'll talk."

Kali took the sweater, put it on quickly, grabbed his hand, and walked into the hallway. "Tell me on the way," she said.

"I'll tell you when we get up there."

Kali shook her head and walked quickly towards the stairway that led to the roof while Lev walked beside her holding the wine in one hand and her hand in his other.

Lev scanned the rooftop for a comfortable place for them to sit and walked with her over to a wall that would position them to sit and look up at the sky where the new moon hid among the stars. He sat down and Kali sat beside him looking up at the side of his face pensively.

"The moon's over there," Lev said, pointing at the night sky. "Come back tomorrow, and you'll see a small sliver of it," he said and opened the bottle of wine. "Here, you first," he said as he handed her the bottle and put his other arm around her shoulders.

Kali turned her body to look at him, took the bottle of wine he was offering her, and took a sip. She handed the bottle back to Lev who also took a sip. Lev swallowed and then breathed in deeply while looking down.

The silence between them was prolonged as Lev struggled to find the words to tell her what she needed to know. Kali watched as he struggled and finally shook her head saying, "It's ok," as she lifted herself up and repositioned herself to sit on his lap. Lev put the bottle of wine down and wrapped his arms around her tightly, still saying nothing.

She leaned the side of her head against the side of his and hugged him saying, "Lev, you can tell me anything. Try, and if you fuck up, just restart. Keep doing it until you say what you need to say. I'll listen."

Lev kissed her and took a deep breath. "We're missing some information about the lock code. We can't see it in the passport, we can't find any clues in the other tech or the recipe book. We've all worked on it. None of us can figure it out, but the worst part is, we don't even know what questions to ask anymore. We've run out of questions. Do you understand?" Lev looked at her as she stared at him in silence. "Kali, without questions, we're at a dead end. We can't even conceive of the questions anymore. We've done all we can...here."

Kali sat up suddenly and stared at Lev with a hard expression he could see even in the moonless night.

"Yeah, baby. You remember I told you--"

"Who's going?" she asked with a touch of panic in her voice as she pushed herself away from him to sit up straighter.

Lev nodded and continued. "Come back here," he said as he put his arms back around her. "I told you I was going to make getting him my mission. I'm going to kill this guy."

Lev had Kali pulled against his chest, but she wasn't hugging him back. She tried to use her arms and hands to push herself away from him again, but he held her tightly while she pushed at him and looked into her face explaining, "I'm going use the passport and go to the Kingdom, and I'm going to find Vespry."

"I don't even know if Rollo's alive anymore!" she said angrily through clenched teeth as she continued to try and push herself away from him.

"Baby, you said you'd help me when I told you I was going to make killing him my mission. Do you remember?" Lev asked her patiently as she struggled against him.

Kali closed her eyes and shook her head no, but said, "Yes." She stopped moving and kept her eyes closed, and he watched as she tried to control her breathing.

"I'm going to find Vespry, and I'm going to see if I can find what we need to break Bas's lock code. Pele hasn't gotten into his Kingdom, but I can get inside with the passport you brought us. This guy isn't smarter than me. I can--"

"Lev, I won't know if you're in torture! How will I ever find you again?! If he wins, he'll keep me here and I won't get to die and find you and be with you again!"

"Baby, if he wins, he won't let us be together in the other present anyway. You'll be his prisoner there, too. Maybe he can drag you back here to this present through the past. We think that's how he plans to get people back into their bodies. We don't know. We can't hold back. We have to kill him. We have a plan. Listen to me. I'm not going alone. Santi, Olivia, Maren, Bautista, and Gorman are coming with me. The whole Intel Team you trained."

"But you need smart people from the RT to go with you," she said, angry and perplexed.

"No, I need sneaky fuckers like Olivia and Gorman to go with me. I need Marty who wouldn't think twice about dying if he could kill Bas. I need Maren and Santi who can both get themselves into specialized departments close to Bas and his teams. If, like you say may be true, Vespry's not available, I'll need others who can help me find information. I'll have the passport. Hopefully, I'll be able to get back with some useful information. The others know they may never get back. We talked about it with Bolin. Everyone understands what they might have to endure. I trust these people. You trained them well.

"We know we'd likely be put to work in different areas of the Kingdom and all of us getting together again to transport back here to Ivy by holding on to one another is unlikely. They all know this could be a one shot deal for them, but I'm still going to have the passport because if I find answers, on my own or with their help, or

Vespry's, I'm coming back to the RT, and I'm going to try and break the lock code. That's the only sure way to get the others back. They know they could die there or end up in torture."

"You could, too. You could arrive and be noticed as a stranger. Sure there are two million people there and, yeah, they import new people from Jorge's throughout the year, but you're a big guy. You stand out. You might only last a few minutes there."

Lev smiled lightly and tipped his head at her saying, "Hey now. You're not being positive, and I need a little bit of positivity from you. It's a good plan. If Vespry's there, maybe I can find a way to get a message to Pele, work with her and her team, show them where we're stuck. Maybe I can get you and everyone else into Pele's Kingdom. She could come get all of you. Keep you safe from Bas in her Kingdom. I'd know. Vespry could tell me.

"But being safe anywhere here a little while longer isn't the goal. We need the other present safe from him. We need to go into Bas's Kingdom. I'm the guy to do it. Vespry being there would be fucking great."

Kali was no longer struggling against him and leaned her body against his chest wrapping her arms around him again. "I can tell you where to enter and how to find Rollo's house. Only you should go there, though. I'll tell each of them where they should go. When are you leaving?" she asked him quietly.

"Tomorrow."

Kali tried to get up out of Lev's lap yelling, "Oh, fuck, Lev! No! Fuck that! I'm not ready for that!"

But he grabbed her quickly and held her in his arms again, letting her yell at him while he told her calmly that he would hopefully see her again in this present or in the other present.

Kali stopped fighting him and sat in his arms breathing hard. Lev could feel her heart racing and the tension in her body.

"Kali, I know you know this is the right thing for us to do even if it fucking sucks. I know you know this. Cheri, Hans, and Dave are all in their 60's. They can't go. It's possible a guy my age could have been overlooked for years. They'd have no plausible explanation for themselves. I'll admit there are some others from the RT I'd trust to go because I know they'd endure torture and they specialize in what we're looking for, but I've worked with the passport the most. Others are also great, but they don't fully understand what we're missing. What the answer would look like. I'm the one who has to go. Me going makes the most sense. I'll know the missing part of the formula when I see it. We all know what Bas is trying to do. Waiting a day or two because... Well, because I don't want to leave you and you don't want me to leave..." Lev looked at her face. Her eyes were closed while he spoke to her.

"Baby, can you look at me?" he asked her gently.

Kali opened her eyes and looked at him. "I like the sound of your voice, and I can feel your heart beating," she said to him quietly.

Lev kissed her. "You trust me to do everything I can to stop this asshole and

481

get myself back to you if possible?" he asked her.

"Yes," she said quietly, looking at him intently.

"Remember the last time you thought I was captured? And you were going to beat up Dave and take the passport and go to the Kingdom to find me?" he laughed mildly.

"It's not funny, but yes," she said with a small smile.

"What did I ask you?"

"I don't remember," she said, looking away from him.

"Yeah, you do, smartass," he said, smiling at the side of her face.

Kali took a deep breath and sighed and looked at him saying firmly, "Something about please don't go getting myself into the Kingdom without having a plan to get myself out."

"I knew you remembered," he said with raised eyebrows and nodding at her. "Kali, I'd never recover if I was powerless over there and you showed up and I had to watch you suffer at his hands. The whole time I'm there, I'll already know you want me back just as much as I want to be back with you. The whole time I'm there, I'll be there being your husband. You'll be here being my wife. Can you let me work?" he asked her.

"Yes," she said quietly.

"I know it's not easy for you. It's not easy for me. I'm gonna trust you to let me try."

"I'll be so afraid for you every day," she said.

"I know, baby, but really, that's no different than any day he's still alive. I'm going to figure out his lock code and get Pele's army in. We need to kill him. I need to kill him. We need Death Time to end his consciousness, or rip it apart, or whatever it is they do, so he can't come back ever again," Lev said to her, nodding.

Kali nodded in agreement and rested her head on his shoulder, and Lev looked up at the stars.

"Does the night sky look the same in a locked Kingdom, baby?" he asked her.

"Yes."

"Then you come up here and look at the sky each night, unless it's raining or there's a lightning storm, and you look up at the Universe from this spot. I'll find the same direction over there, and I'll look up at the same night sky with you each night."

Lev felt all the tension in Kali's body leave as she stopped resisting the plan and accepted what was going to happen in the early hours of the morning. She tipped her head up to the night sky.

"I promise I'll do that," she said quietly while looking up at the stars with him.

Lev and the Intel Team Say Goodbye

The RT and the Intel Team were gathered in the Lab along with others who needed to say their goodbyes to the departing members. Aisha had ridden out from Campus with Bob around the same time Lev had told Kali the plan, and they were both there as well. She and Bob had said her goodbyes to Lev already and it hadn't been easy. She was devastated. She had only cried for a brief moment, but everything about her demeanor spoke to her emotional state. Without Bob by her side she wouldn't have been able to pull herself together.

Lev had his arms around Kali's waist and whispered in her ear, "I took the knife out from under your pillow and put your vibrator there instead." Kali laughed a little into his neck as he told her this. "You won't need the knife to kill me anymore. What I want you to do is fuck yourself whenever you think of me. Ok? So, go downstairs and fuck yourself after I leave here," he said, laughing along with Kali who was now laughing harder.

"You fuck yourself, too," she whispered to him, laughing.

"Oh, I'm gonna. Count on it. And when I get back, I'm gonna fuck you the hell up," he laughed as he held her face in his hands and kissed her.

They continued to laugh as Kali stood on her toes and put her arms around his neck running her hands through the back of his hair looking at him with amused affection.

"I'm going to try to get back to you, but if I die, I'm gonna find out how we can fuck in the other present before you get there, ok? I'll be ready for you," he assured her with a devilish smile.

Kali looked at him with merriment in her eyes and laughed at him asking, "You're gonna find out how to make me cum without a body?"

"Yeah, I am. Orgasms happen in the brain, baby," he said with authority, laughing.

"Babe, you're so fucking smart and thoughtful."

"I know," he said as they laughed and kissed.

The other people in the room looked at them laughing, but couldn't hear what they were saying to each other.

"It's gonna be ok. Time is on our side. Lev wouldn't leave Kali if he wasn't sure this was the best way forward," Bob whispered to Aisha.

"Or the only way left," Aisha said darkly.

Bob pulled her closer to him. "I agree, Aish. This is it. They're out of options. They're going to make sure we, the kids, every person in this present and the other, have a future in the afterlife present. If they didn't go, they wouldn't have this chance."

"I'm so afraid for him," she said with a gasp.

"Keep it together. He's chosen to laugh as he leaves," Bob told her kindly, but firmly.

"Ok. Ok. You're right. Kali's doing good. Let's make sure she eats tonight."

"Yeah. If she says she wants to be alone, we'll invade her fucking space and make her fight us."

Aisha laughed at Bob's suggestion. "We're gonna get our asses kicked, then."

Bob laughed and said, "We'll bring James and Bolin and the kids for protection."

Eventually, others started finding reasons to laugh as they said their goodbyes, too, and the somber mood of the room was lightened as Kali and Lev continued to laugh through their painful goodbye, oblivious to everyone else and the humor they had set upon the room.

The Intel Team and Lev stepped away from everyone else and Kali watched as Olivia and the others put their hands on Lev. He looked at her and smiled a small smile at her and nodded his head once before they disappeared. Kali gasped and Bolin grabbed her as she involuntarily huffed a deep breath from her chest that caused her to double over.

"Help me," she whispered to him, and he and James did.

Lev and the Intel Team Arrive in the Kingdom

They had been told what to expect, what the city would look like, what the culture of the people who lived in the Kingdom would feel like, but the reality was still confronting. It was just after 4am, and the early November air was quite cold. They arrived in Bas's capital in Wayne National Forest as opposed to the city of Columbus. They had determined that the walk from Columbus would have aroused suspicion. It was better to take a chance at arriving in the heavily populated capital and assert a legal right to be in the city. They each had paperwork declaring their status as capital workers, but they each needed to find a position immediately.

Santi and Maren left the group with haste after quickly saying their goodbyes, with Maren heading for Bas's technology lab and Santi heading towards the capital hospital.

Maren planned to approach the technology department and demand to know why she hadn't been assigned to a station yet despite her years of provable support for Bas and his mission. The four large tattoos on her face demanded she be recognized as a valuable technology expert. Kali had told her that fear drove many in the capital to overlook inconsistencies. Angering Bas was less desirable than overlooking an inconsistency as long as it was delivered with conviction.

Kali had laughed at Maren saying, "You're a natural for this role. You just go in there and tell them, 'What the fuck, man?! I've been waiting to join Bas's team for weeks. I'm not waiting anymore! You hear me?! Make it happen today!' Kali nodded at her. "Drop Bas's name. It freaks people out."

Maren nodded. She wanted to kill Bas and get back to Vivek. She wanted to be a mother someday, if possible. If not, she wanted the afterlife present safe so she could see Vivek there and meet his parents and his sister who he had told her so much about.

Santi was fearless while also being unusually demure. She was confident in what she knew, and she had a barely perceptible ego despite having a lot of confidence. She wanted her daughter safe in the afterlife present. She wanted her late husband safe in the afterlife present so he could take care of their daughter if that was how things worked there. She wanted Meabh safe in the current present. Santi hated Bas more viscerally than the others on the Intel Team could comprehend.

Kali had needed to take her aside early on and talk to her about her hate.

"I know. Focus on what you want, not on what you hate. You'll lose if you focus on Bas," she had told Santi. Santi had nodded silently in agreement. Kali had faith in Santi to focus. Some of the others worried that Santi was going to get herself killed or put into torture early on, but none worried that Santi would give them up no matter how much she was tortured.

Santi and Maren parted ways at the New Beginnings statue, which was a monument to the extinction event, and Maren told Santi, "If we're still alive one year from now, meet me here at the same time. We can make a new plan together."

Santi nodded and walked away from Maren, heading towards the hospital.

Olivia left without acknowledging any of the Intel Team and headed towards the sanitation department. Her hair was cut close against her head as Kali had instructed.

"You're so young and pretty. Get rid of your hair. They might claim you as a member of the Kept class. Keep your head down. Don't let them see your pretty eyes. Rollo was a janitor. It's a good place to gather intel."

What if I'm Kept? How can I be useful?"

"Oh, God, Olivia. You'll see so much that's useful as a Kept, but you'll suffer. Be a janitor. I don't want you to be Kept."

"Being Kept is better to the mission?"

"I don't want you to be Kept."

"Is being Kept more useful to the mission?"

"Yes. Be a janitor. Please be a janitor. Rollo was a janitor. It's a good position."

"I know you're worried, but I'm over this life. I'm looking forward to the next. Don't worry about me. I know what I'm doing. Time spoke to me."

"What did Time tell you?"

"That I might be able to help Lev."

Kali hugged Olivia, and Olivia hugged her back. "Time didn't tell you to be Kept?" she asked her.

"No, but I told you I want to be useful. Give me permission."

Kali let go of Olivia. "Of course. You have my permission. But please don't try to be Kept. It's worse than you can imagine. Sanitation is still useful."

Bautista looked at Lev and said, "Man, it's been a wild ride with you. This shit's fucked right the hell up. Fucking insanity. But I'm gonna help kill this son of a bitch. Find Vespry if he's still alive. Maybe he can get me onto Bas's security team if I don't manage to do it on my own. Let's kill this bitch."

"Yeah," Lev said with a nod.

Bautista left and headed towards the nearby prison. He planned to appeal for a position on Bas's security team or, failing that, a position on the Orderly Citizens Patrol based on his paperwork. Kali had told him, "Tell them you walked from Columbus on orders. When they ask whose orders, tell them, "Our King's orders, of course! He needs to replace some security who failed him!" Say it convincingly, like you can't believe they'd dare delay Bas the protection he deserves. Say that if you want to, too. Read your audience. People are terrified of pissing him off. You can even look at whoever's holding you up and ask, "What's your name?" That might make them move you along, too."

"They really won't question me?"

"They might, but the affairs of the citizens are so far below Bas's concerns. He only cares about himself and his goals that will make him more powerful. They use technology in research, not in maintaining city records or communication with Columbus. When things start getting out of hand with citizens, Bas orders in some troops to torture and rewind them on public stages. That usually quiets unrest. Citizens' problems are never addressed. He barely cares about how his cities are run as long as he doesn't have to hear about a problem. You show up looking to serve Bas, you got paperwork, scars, confidence in your assumed orders, yeah, they'll give up their authority to you rather than ask Bas if he placed an order for you. They'll pass you along up the chain of command. People above them. They'll do what you did and imply threats if they don't move you through."

"Ok."

Gorman grabbed Bautista's arm as he walked away from Lev. "Meet here in a year if you're still alive. We'll regroup."

"You know it," Bautista said as he nodded and walked away down the street.

Gorman turned to Lev. "You headed to Vespry's house? See if he's still alive?" Gorman asked him.

"Yeah. If he's dead, I'll go join Olivia in sanitation. Get in on the night shift or something like Vespry did."

"Don't let 'em know how smart you are."

Lev nodded.

"The Intel Team agreed to me being the last to leave and to me telling you this. Listen. We want you to know we trust you and Kali. We don't fucking care if we die or get thrown into torture for eternity. We trust you and Kali are doing what you think will save our present and our afterlife present. We're all in. Don't you fucking cry over us. You understand? No guilt. Fuck that. We're in all the way."

"Ok," Lev said.

He inhaled deeply and exhaled sharply as Gorman said, "If this fucker wins, and we end up in the afterlife present rather than torture, we'll find each other there in the afterlife, and we'll kick start this war all over again from there. You hear me?"

"Yeah," Lev laughed mildly, nodding in agreement with Gorman.

"Go find Vespry. Get the lock code formula. Bring it back to the RT. Let's get this SOB," Gorman said as he walked away from Lev with his paperwork that said he was a butcher with 10 years of kitchen service in Columbus.

"Like it or not, Bas has to keep people in the Kingdom moderately fed," Kali had told him.

"Maybe you can get into the research lab's cafeteria. We had one spy in that kitchen for years before she died of natural causes. You just gotta listen. People like to brag across departments about how their department is serving Bas better than some other department. Everyone's trying to be Bas's favorite. They don't whisper. They talk about tech and security issues and other important shit."

"Got it."

Lev in the Kingdom

Lev walked towards the direction of Rollo Vespry's house. Kali had given him directions that suddenly came alive as he walked. She knew the landscape intimately. She had walked these streets. He felt emotionally overwhelmed picturing her trapped here, not knowing him, him not knowing her. No hope. He needed to find Vespry. He needed his commander to be alive.

Lev stood outside of the house at 11 King Street and inhaled sharply. He knocked loudly and waited. Time passed and he knocked loudly again. It was still very early in the morning. The sun hadn't even begun to rise yet. Kali was right about the streets being deserted. Bas really didn't live in fear. He terrorized everyone else, and he ran his Kingdom through relentless intimidation. No one would be on the streets at this hour. Rollo would only expect an official of similar rank to his own, or a security guard to knock on his door at this early hour.

He watched and listened as the door began to open and a voice spoke to him saying, "Apologies. What can I do for you and my King?"

"Vespry?" Lev asked him. The man looked at Lev and said nothing. "Are you Rollo Vespry?" Lev asked again.

"Wanna tell me who you are?" the man in the doorway asked with a threatening tone.

"Hey, man. Name's Lev. Can we talk?"

The bald, bearded man in the doorway was eye level with Lev and he stared at him in a harsh and uncompromising way suddenly as his body language went from respectful to dangerous. The two men stood in silence staring at each other.

"You got the wrong house. Get lost," the man in the doorway said angrily to Lev as he went to close the door.

Lev stopped the man from closing the door and said, "This is the right house."

"Last chance to leave before I have you dragged off to torture," the man in the doorway said coldly.

"Is it you?" Lev asked him without emotion.

"No. Get the fuck outta here," he said as he slammed the door shut.

Lev banged on the door and waited. He banged again and stepped back as the door began to open. He stood and stared at the man in the doorway.

Lev sighed angrily saying, "You gonna let me in? I'm guessing out here... Not good for either of us."

The man moved from the doorway to allow Lev to enter. Lev walked inside and heard the door shut before he turned to see the gun pointed at him.

"I warned you, man. I'll make it quick. Can't deal with your body on my doorstep, but that's why I have hardwood floors," the man said as he raised the gun to Lev's head.

"Fuck. Come on, man. She's gonna be pissed if you send me to the other present this soon."

The man looked startled and asked, "What? What the fuck did you just say?" He seemed surprised but he held the gun steady, pointing it at Lev's face. His willingness to end Lev wasn't in question.

"She told me what you look like. You're Vespry. Confirm it."

"I'm only gonna confirm that you're about to die," the man with the gun said calmly, regaining his composure.

"Ok listen, we're here--"

"There are others? This is too much. You gotta die. It's not personal. It's better than torture," he said as he aimed his gun at Lev.

"I'm her husband. You kill me, she's gonna be so fucking pissed off, man. I would not wanna be you," Lev suddenly laughed and nodded at the man. "She got the tech to Ivy. I wish I could tell her you're alive. She's so worried about you, man. Can you get a message to Pele and tell my wife you're alive?"

The man shook his head in frustration and confusion and looked upward breathing out a string of expletives and various questions all at once.

Lev held up a hand to calm the man down and said, "She wouldn't use her real name. I call her Kali. Don't tell me her name. She's Kali. That's a trust I have with her."

The man looked at Lev. "Like California?" he asked him.

Lev laughed and nodded. "Yeah, exactly. She was afraid the name would give her away. Spell it with a K not a C. It's important to her."

"Yeah, ok. Kali," said the man as he lowered the gun but still kept it pointed at Lev.

Lev said, "Confirm who you are. Tell me who you are already. I'm pretty sure I know, but you gotta tell me."

The man looked at Lev. "Who the hell are you?" he asked Lev.

"Name's Lev. Kali got the tech to us at Ivy a few months ago. We're having trouble with the lock code. Some of us came over to see if we could figure it out by seeing what's going on in the labs here. I need to get inside. I need to figure out what I'm missing. There's something I don't know."

The man stared at Lev. "You said you're her husband."

"Yeah. I am. She's my wife. I left her standing in a lab at Ivy about 45 minutes ago, and I'm fucking wrecked, man. Now I told you who I am. Tell me you're Rollo Vespry, and fucking prove it while you're at it. I'm not afraid of your gun," Lev said, suddenly out of patience.

The man nodded and motioned for Lev to follow him. His gun was at his side and no longer appeared to be a threat to Lev. He opened a wooden box on the bottom shelf of a side table and pulled out a strip of photos.

"We were in Florida. Bas wanted to abduct some people to be citizens before the extinction. There was a hurricane coming in a couple of days. He used the hurricane as cover to abduct a bunch of people, mostly college kids about to graduate with science degrees. He let me take her out one night. I knew the area, being that I'm from there. Kali, as you call her, we went out dancing and there was a carnival. We got our pictures taken in one of those photo booths. He pointed to the row of pictures of himself as a younger man with hair and a younger, smiling Kali leaning her face against his. "That's my girl," he said, nodding. "I bet her I could make her smile. She was so unhappy. I won the bet, but every time I look at these pictures, I know the truth. She was broken inside. She wanted me to win the bet so I'd feel better." He looked at Lev. "Yeah, I'm Rollo Vespry. You're her husband?"

"Yeah, I am."

"Are you nice to her?"

"I am."

"Tell me what's going on," he said as he walked to his kitchen.

"I'll make us breakfast. You like coffee?"

"I'm not hungry."

"Well, you're gonna have some coffee and some breakfast with me anyway. I have a feeling it's gonna be a long fucking day with you here now. We need to eat."

Lev laughed lightly. "I heard you can cook."

"I can. Kali cannot," Rollo laughed. "Oh, wait, was that a secret? Did I just reveal something about her I shouldn't have?" he asked, suddenly concerned.

Lev laughed lightly. 'That's definitely not a secret," he assured Rollo with a small smile.

Rollo sat at his dining room table with Lev after listening to the events which led up to the present moment.

"I knew she could do it. Time was really hopeful."

"Oh, Time was involved in the success of her getting to Ivy without being killed. Time, I'm sorry I forgot to mention what you did to help us!" Lev said up to the ceiling.

Rollo looked curious. "What'd Time do now?" he asked, getting up to clear their breakfast dishes. Lev told him about Time scrambling his passport and the confrontation between Bolin and himself with Kali in the field when she had arrived at Ivy with the tech.

"Man, Time was cutting it close with that, huh?" Rollo asked, amazed.

"Yeah. It could have gone either way, to be honest."

"Time, you're nuts!" Rollo said loudly at the ceiling and then laughed. "Time's cool. Not human, but more human than Bas," he assured Lev.

"Everyone on the team has a role they hope to fill here in the Kingdom except me. Kali told me to look for you and see what you thought was best. I was planning to seek janitorial services if you were dead."

"But you're a scientist? You know your shit?"

"Yeah. Really well. I want to work on the lock code 24/7 if possible."

"Ok. Let me think. We gotta get you into the research labs, but not on a team. That's a sure way to get you fucked. Kali doesn't know this, but Bas chips new research team members. He makes them earn their freedom on their passports. For a couple of years, he knows their every move inside and outside of the Kingdom. That's one of the reasons they're so loyal, too. He trains them to be loyal. Maybe we can get you into the workspace in a janitorial role, like you say. My office is up there. I'm there all the time. I see a lot, but I don't know what most of it means. You gotta be my friend, visit me in my office space on breaks and shit if I can get you inside. We can organize what you find out.

"You need to have a home, too. You just showed up this morning with the other five? I don't know how to help them. They're gonna have to make the best of it for a while."

"Yeah, I don't have a home, but I have papers to get me into sanitation."

"Ok. Come with me to work this morning. We'll be super casual. Get your face in the minds of the people I work with. Kali tell you about these assholes? Not just regular office assholes. Seriously deranged cultists who would go to torture for eternity for this fucking psycho. You gotta know, no one's your friend here. Just me. About 12 others."

"Kali said 17 others."

"Yeah, some died after she left. It was a fucking catastrophe when he started doubting Pele was involved. Realized the opposition had aligned with her somehow. He killed more of his own people than of ours, though. He's a fucking clueless clown."

Lev nodded. "I've heard. But he keeps winning despite that fact."

"Yeah, it's fucking infuriating," Rollo said.

"You gotta change if you want to accompany me into my office today. We're about the same size, so come to my room and pick what you want," Rollo told him.

Lev looked at Rollo and said, "I have to tell you some things before you agree to work with me."

"Great. What?" asked Rollo apprehensively.

"I killed your original 11 scientists."

Rollo stared at Lev for a moment and then started walking to his bedroom. "Ok. Explain."

Lev followed Rollo down the hallway to his bedroom and told him how he came to Ivy, learned about him, and how he eventually ordered the executions of the remaining scientists. When they were finished dressing, Rollo looked at him and said, "You did the right thing. None of us are gods, not even Bas despite the bullshit version of immortality he claims. Time doesn't know the future, and I make mistakes. I'm sure you do, too. Right?"

"Yeah."

"You didn't make a mistake killing the remaining scientists. You did what had to be done. You protected the opposition. I'm not your commander. We're equals, but I know more about this place than you do right now. You're gonna have to listen to me while you get caught up to speed," he explained to Lev. Lev nodded. "Let's get you to my office and see if we can weave you into background and make you invisible so that you can get the information you need to kill this fucking asshole clown."

The sun had risen and there was more activity on the streets now as citizens of Bas's Kingdom made their way to their assigned jobs. Lev and Rollo walked downtown to the city center where the research laboratories were located in several sprawling high rise office buildings. Lev noticed the prison across from the largest building. He looked at the torture arena Bolin had told him to expect. It was as he'd described. He knew not to ask Vespry about it. He didn't want more information than was necessary to kill Bas.

'Protect yourself,' Bolin had told him. 'Some of what you can learn there won't help you accomplish the goals of the mission. Stay focused on the mission.' He had asked Bolin not to tell him things he learned about Kali while working with her to train the Intel Team. But he really didn't need Kali or Bolin to protect him from her truth. He knew. Looking at the torture arena, he focused on Bolin's advice instead of the images that threatened to flood his mind. He turned to Vespry as the man began to talk to him about what mattered to the mission. This was where his focus needed to be.

"This is the building I work in. That's all research on top. My office is up there, too. I'm a high ranking official in Bas's cabinet. You gotta be respectful and speak nicely when you're at work or at a formal party or something like that. Always refer to him as the King or my King. Bas stops by my house, we talk like normal people. Got it?"

"I understand."

"Listen Lev, it's all bullshit here. I've been around long enough that I can get away with some shit. Bas tolerates me, but it's more than that. I help that fucker anyway I can because I'm always trying to help myself. He gets a cake and I take the crumbs that fall to the floor, and I'm grateful for them. This so-called Kingdom is limited. Opportunities are limited. You gotta take what little you can get and move forward with what you can find. Don't rush things. Everyone here is a fanatical cult member. No one's on my side. No one's on your side. You're not going to make new alliances. Don't even fucking try. You got that?"

"I do."

"Yeah? because I get the feeling you're used to working with people who are on your fucking side. This is different. You're gonna feel like shit 24 hours into this. I guarantee it," Rollo said with conviction. "When you start losing hope, let me know. I'll talk you back up from the ground," he said, and Lev could hear the sound of experience behind the words.

Rollo and Lev made their way through the expansive ground floor lobby and reception area heading towards Rollo's office, and Lev admired Rollo's enthusiastic performance as a happy citizen of Bas's Kingdom with all he encountered. He took note of Rollo's untroubled interpersonal exchanges with fellow officials and office staff. Kali had told him Rollo was a theater kid from Miami. He saw that now. He was a showman. His entire body was engaged in the performance. Lev considered that he had lied to the Ivy community about who he was and had kept secrets from Bolin for years. He told himself he was also at least a bit of a showman and could meet this challenge.

He smiled happily at people Rollo introduced him to, showing believable enthusiasm for their introductions as well as for the facility and his charming host. He caught Rollo looking over at him once or twice and turned to him to say, "I'm so happy you took me to meet your work friends! I can't believe you get to spend your days here serving our King!" He and Rollo took turns improvising to their audience as they eventually made their way to the stairwell that would take them to the 23rd floor and Rollo's sprawling office suite.

"You're doing alright, man," Rollo said, sounding genuinely impressed. "I figured you'd play a shy, reserved friend role once you saw how I'm playing it."

"Shy looks guilty in my mind. I'm gonna go big or go home," Lev said, appreciative of the compliment from Rollo.

"You mean or go to torture," Rollo laughed. "Seriously, you're her husband?"

"Yeah. You're still wondering about that? I keep telling you I am. Yeah, I'm her husband. She said that makes you my brother-in-law."

Rollo smiled at that. "Man, that's fucking great news. I like hearing this. Maybe I'll even ask you to confirm it again later. Yeah, I'm your brother-in-law, man. Makes me realize I need to keep you out of torture, though. You're family. Don't fuck up," he said in a more serious tone, glancing at Lev sideways as they walked up to the 23rd floor.

"No elevators?"

"Only the King and his security are allowed to ride in the elevators. This is my very own private stairway, though. I'm gonna die of a heart attack walking up these stairs one day and it'll be a week before they decide to come look for my body. That's how I'm going to get into the afterlife present," he laughed.

"Why do you have your own stairs to the top?"

"So I can't hear secrets about ongoing research. Some motherfucker voiced concern about it a few years ago. Fucking ruined some great opportunities for intel I'd been enjoying," he said, looking pissed off at the memory. "There's a third stairway you'll use if I can get you inside the labs as a janitor. You take that with the others who work as servants in the building. Use that one to get to the labs. Never take my stairway without me. Never use the stairway designated for the researchers. You won't get a warning. Torture is the main deterrent to any offenses committed here. Throw you in for a six month sentence and remove you after five minutes. You come out old and your soul hurts in ways you can't imagine," he said disgustedly.

Lev nodded and flinched internally at the thought of what Kali had endured.

Rollo ushered Lev inside his office after they left the stairway.

"Man, this is your office? It's huge," Lev said as he wandered through Rollo's office space.

"Six rooms. I know. It's obscene. My receptionist isn't even on this floor. I'm the only one here. The other spaces, the other offices on this floor, are all empty. Listen, you did good down there. Keep that happy shit up, Dev."

"Yeah, I'll keep following your lead with anyone else I meet. The labs. Kali told me about the 22 on the 24th floor," he looked at Rollo and nodded.

"We haven't recovered from that, actually. Took out a good number of their research team, though," Rollo said happily.

He looked at Lev pensively and asked, "Where do I need to try to get you in? I'm thinking the quantum cryptography lab? Help me out."

"Tell me the different departments and I'll see what sounds the most promising."

"Ok, don't let on that you're smart with anyone you meet if I get you into janitorial services up there. Friendly's good. Someone realizes you're smart, though, you'll be taken to indoc, chipped, and made a slave to Bas's research team for the next couple of years. Keep that shit on the downlow. You're not smart. Got it? You're fucking nice, but not smart. Your wife will kill me if you get killed or sent to torture, right? I know her. She won't be happy."

"She'll be really upset," Lev agreed, raising his eyebrows and smiling at Rollo.

"Ok. Let's keep you safe. You're stupid while you're here. I can't stress that enough. He can't kidnap scientists from the past, and he's killed a lot of the one's he brought here originally. He's always on the lookout for someone with brains who can learn from the team he still has."

"How big is his research team?" Lev asked, believing he might hear some good news.

"All together, across all disciplines, a little more than 1500 people."

"Fuck," muttered Lev, looking shocked.

"Yeah, used to be twice that, though. He's more inclined to throw smart people into timed torture these days. You know, make you serve a year during your lunch break. It's not easier, man. Believe me. I know," Rollo said somberly.

Lev nodded.

There was a knock on the door and Rollo went to answer it. He spoke with a man briefly and returned to Lev.

"I have to go to the weapons lab upstairs now. See? I have access to the labs without being a chipped hostage. Be a benign dumbass, man. I'll be back. Don't be seen. Wait here for me. Take a nap in back. There's a couch. You can walk around this floor, but don't open any doors except the one that leads into my office. If you see anyone, which you shouldn't, they're all upstairs working in their labs, avoid them. Walk away. Come back to my office. Say you're visiting me. Use my name. Play dumb and ask how to get back to my offices. You know what? Stay here. I'll be back in about an hour. We'll get you some crumbs today. You'll see."

"Yeah, ok," Lev said as Rollo left.

Lev watched Rollo leave the office and watched through the glass walls as Rollo followed the man who had come to speak to him. He sat down in a chair at the front of Rollo's desk and took a deep breath, exhaling with intention. Bolin had taken him aside shortly after the decision was made to send him and the Intel Team to the Kingdom and told him, 'You're too easily provoked. I don't mind it, but I've been listening to Kali for four months as we trained the Intel Team. Your quick response to shit that pisses you off is gonna get you killed in that Kingdom. What good will you be to any of us, to Kali, if you show up in the Kingdom and allow yourself to be provoked? You'll be sent to torture. You want to kill Bas? Then learn to breath before you make a decision to speak. Say less. You told me not to talk to you about Kali and her experiences, but you need to know something... We're all in trouble, Lev. This guy is a living demon. I'm not telling you anything specific about Kali. What I'm telling you is that Bas isn't human. He's a demon. The Intel Team knows it, too. You don't have the details we have from Kali. Believe me, though. Learn how to breathe.'

Lev trusted Bolin as much as he trusted Kali. He realized she'd been trying to tell him what Bolin had told him, but in her own confusing way. He realized she was making sense now that Bolin had spoken to him. Nine hours earlier, Bolin told him what he thought was a potentially fatal weakness in his approach to surviving in the Kingdom. He was still processing the words of a man he trusted to look after his wife in his absence, trying to put those words into action.

Lev stood up and looked at the empty hallway. He might as well familiarize himself with the layout of the 23rd floor while Rollo was gone. He wouldn't need to speak to anyone while he did that. He wouldn't need to open any doors. He looked at Rollo's desk and found a pen and a piece of paper. He wrote a note. "Went to walk the hallways. Back soon."

He left the note on Rollo's desk and walked out of Rollo's office suite.

Lev Meets Bas

"Hey, so when you were gone--"

"Hold on," Rollo said, distracted by the sound of an alarm.

"Yeah about that--"

"This wasn't you, was it?" Rollo asked, squinting his eyes at Lev in actual fear.

"Yeah, so I went to explore a bit--"

"Fucking hell, man!"

"There was a guard of some sort. I knocked him out when he demanded paperwork from me. I think I killed him."

"Oh, fuck! You did not! Asshole! Bas is here. It was probably one of his guards. Oh, shit!" Rollo suddenly exclaimed with a big smile as he shook his head then tipped it flirtatiously. "You sure you're a good actor?"

"Yeah, I can act," Lev said suddenly smiling, too.

"Put your arms around me and kiss me and act like you fucking mean it. You're stupid too, rememb--"

Lev grabbed Rollo and kissed him and then pulled away and smiled and laughed convincingly. He looked at Rollo who looked adoringly at him and also laughed while touching Lev's cheek. Lev realized there was a group of people standing outside of Rollo's office about to enter.

Rollo nodded with an adoring smile while looking at Lev and said, "That's Bas and members of his security team on the other side of the glass wall. Sell this or they'll take you to torture. They might anyway just for fun. Remember, your name is Dev not Lev." Rollo maintained the adoring smile as he tipped his head looking at Lev.

"You got it," Lev said, smiling and kissing Rollo again.

Rollo suddenly turned as Bas and his detail entered the room.

"My King? What a wonderful, but unexpected surprise. How can I be of service?"

Bas looked curiously at Rollo and Lev. "You don't hear the alarms?" he asked him with a tone of irritation he wasn't trying to hide.

"Yes, of course, but we've had multiple alarms this week while testing the new system. I was told to expect at least one today. Is this an actual emergency? How can I help my King?" Rollo said perplexed while sounding prepared to do whatever Bas asked of him.

"Who's this?" Bas asked him, pointing to Lev.

One of Bas's security team members stepped up and said loudly, "That's the traitor who assaulted me in the hallway."

Rollo turned to look at Lev in shock at the accusation. "Dev? What's going on? Did you assault our King's guard?"

Lev hesitated and looked up at the ceiling then turned quickly to look at Rollo saying, "You said you wanted to keep our relationship private." Lev flicked his head in the direction of the guard he had assaulted while still looking at Rollo. "He was following me when I went to look for you. He wouldn't leave me alone. I couldn't get back here with him following me, so I hit him and hoped he'd get amnesia. I guess I didn't hit him hard enough." Lev shrugged while putting his hand on Rollo's shoulder. "I'm sorry," he concluded.

The guard was furious and the swollen eye he was sporting after encountering Lev in the hallway suggested that Lev had actually hit him pretty hard. "I want that man in a time cell. He assaulted a King's guard!" he shouted angrily.

Bas turned to the guard and asked, "Are you telling me what to do? Are you shouting at your King?"

Lev noticed several guards who were near the one he had assaulted moved slightly away from him to avoid Bas's glare.

Lev took the opportunity to talk to Rollo. "Rol, I'm sorry. But you told me you wanted us to remain private. This is the first time you took me to your office to meet everyone. I screwed up." He touched Rollo's arm and looked at Bas. "My King, it's all my fault. I did it. I hit the guy. I thought he was office security. He wouldn't let me come back to Rollo's office. I would never have hit him if I knew he was here to protect my King," he said plainly.

Lev watched as Bas's expression went from one of anger to one of slightly amused sneering as he listened to him.

Bas looked at Rollo and closed his eyes for a second and shook his head mouthing silently, "Really?"

Rollo shook his head and looked at Lev. "No. Dev. This is my fault. You're right. I wasn't clear." Rollo turned back to Bas and said, "If it's ok with you, my King, I'd like to serve Dev's sentence. I wasn't clear with him. He needs more direction than I gave him. He was doing what I asked him to do in some way that made sense to him. I know he's loyal to you and wouldn't assault one of your guards knowingly."

Bas stared at Rollo and Lev.

"Dev, are you loyal?" he asked Lev with a tone of devastating condescension.

"Yes, my King!" Lev answered unnecessarily loudly and firmly.

Bas scoffed at him with amusement and turned to Rollo. "Well, Rollo, if you want to serve Dev's senten--"

"That man assaulted me and should serve the sentence!" the guard suddenly interjected as Bas was about to sentence Rollo to time in torture.

Bas stopped speaking and stood frozen as a look of rage crossed his face.

He snarled, "Take this guard to serve two sentences. He'll serve Dev's sentence as well as a sentence for insubordination to his King."

Bas looked at Lev and said with a condescending tone, "Dev, you appear to have the affections of my most trusted advisor. Let him advise you about how to behave when he lets you outside to play with others. Hmm?"

Lev looked at Bas. "Yes. I will, my King," he said, nodding and looking sincerely sorry for having offended Bas.

Bas seemed satisfied with the conclusion of their interaction and turned to Rollo as the injured guard was escorted out of the room to go to torture.

"Is he Kept, or is he personal?"

"Oh, personal."

"Get him presentable. He does anything like this again, assaults my guards... That's an offense I cannot overlook twice. I'll send him to Jorge's for permanent torture."

"Understood," Rollo said, nodding.

Bas sneered at Rollo and added casually, "Or you could serve that sentence for him. You want to go to permanent torture for this man?"

"Well, I was hoping to ask you if you'd bless our wedding eventually. I just didn't expect..... this to happen," he said, looking overwhelmed.

Bas looked surprised at Rollo's comment. "Oh, so it's serious?"

"Yes."

Bas looked at Lev, and Lev nodded with a somber expression trying to convey respect for the mad King before him.

"Try not to get Rollo sent to torture, Dev. It'd be annoying to have to find a replacement for him."

He turned to Rollo. "Make it official. Stop by the mansion after work tonight. No, that's too early. Come over at 10pm. I'll bless your marriage. No sense keeping Dev private now," he said imperiously as he turned to leave the room with his remaining guards.

Lev stood staring at Rollo after Bas and his guards had left the office. Finally he said, "I'm sorry."

"Don't talk to me," Rollo said calmly, but Lev could see he was furious with him.

Silence filled the air as Lev waited for Rollo to speak. "Man, who are you!? You come banging at my door before I'm even awake. You tell me you brought five others into the Kingdom, you tell me my girl is safe, but then you almost get me sent to torture! You're fucking nuts, man! I can't work with nuts. You don't listen. You're gonna get us both put into torture. We'll both be useless to her if I'm sent to permanent torture. You're dangerous to yourself and to me! Are you dangerous to her, too?!"

Lev blinked hard at that last question and went to speak to Rollo to assure him he had no intention of being dangerous to Kali, but Rollo was indignant, angry, confused, and still scared after the confrontation with Bas. He continued his rant at Lev.

"I haven't even gotten you upstairs as a janitor yet! I just went up there for an hour and dropped hints about the place looking dirty and suggested they let me find them a new janitor. Fucking hell, man!"

Lev listened as Rollo scolded him and nodded in agreement with the comments being made, but he was also suddenly overwhelmed at the situation he found himself in.

He closed his eyes for a second as he tried to compose himself before speaking, reminding himself of Bolin's admonishment, and opened them to look at Rollo before he said, "Honestly, I just stood in front of the man who's tortured my wife for decades. The man I need to kill was just three feet away from me. I'm kinda feeling really fucked up right now and I don't give a shit how you feel. I'm fucked up right now because he left this room still breathing."

Rollo looked at Lev and sighed deeply. "Yeah, ok. I get that. Come on. Let's go to the back and sit down. You did really good improvising there. Saved yourself, and then me, from torture. Gotta thank you for that. You caused the situation, but you cleaned it up really well. Now we're getting fucking married, so thanks for that," he laughed.

Lev looked sheepishly at Rollo before laughing lightly along with him.

Lev sat on the office couch next to Rollo.

"You able to listen to me now?" Rollo asked him.

"Yeah."

"There were eight guards surrounding that clown. Guaranteed eight of them had Rewinds. I'm guessing you know about those, right?"

"I do," Lev sighed.

"You couldn't have killed that asshole. They'd have sent you to the other present if you were lucky, but more likely, torture. Bas would have extended your lifespan, trapped your body in this moment, and then left your mind to a formula that would torture you forever. That's what he does. That's how he can torture a person forever. You showed up here hot to win a war I've been fighting for decades. You gotta trust me. I'm trying to get you into the labs you need to be inside in order to find the information you need to break his lock codes. That's what I heard you say you needed. Am I right?"

"That's what I need."

"Then let me help you. Don't fucking punch people in my work space you fucking dumbass," he said angrily, but then laughed letting Lev know it was alright.

Lev looked over at Rollo. "You're not what I expected," he told him.

"Who the fuck ever is?" Rollo asked with a bored shrug.

Lev nodded and let out a small laugh while looking at the man he'd been serving for years. He told him, "I can't fucking believe we're getting married tonight. She's been so worried about you. She didn't even know if you were alive. I wish I could tell her."

"You know she'd think this was funny as hell."

They both laughed lightly at the thought.

"Let's survive just so we can tell her how I fucked up today and that we ended up getting married to fix my fuck-ups," Lev said with a small laugh.

Rollo laughed and agreed.

Lev sat on Rollo's office couch and contemplated the physical appearance of Bas while Rollo made some calls to different departments looking for a janitorial position in the labs he could work Lev into. He could hear Rollo speak adamantly as he said, "I was just up there. The place could be cleaner. This guy I have in mind is dedicated to janitorial services and sanitation. I should know. You know my work history." Lev laughed to himself as Rollo continued to try to sell him to the person on the other end of the line.

He thought about seeing Bas for the first time after having lived through the actions of the once anonymous psychopath. Bas looked like a young man. His features were soft, not hard. Kali had told them that he'd stopped his aging at the age of 28. Lev guessed that Bas was about five feet ten inches tall because he was only a little bit taller than Bolin. He was trim with excellent posture and appeared to be fit. He had blue eyes and could maintain a benign expression that didn't reveal his psychopathy. His hair was brown and cut short, and his face was clean shaven. Lev hadn't seen a grown man with a clean shaven face in nearly two decades. Trimmed, sure, but Bas was clean shaven and it shocked Lev to see an adult man with no hair on his face. Trent was the youngest man at Ivy and even Trent had a full beard. Ace was the only male at Ivy without facial hair. Kali had told him a lot about Bas, but she hadn't mentioned he was clean shaven. Bas looked like numerous grad students he'd studied with when he was younger. He even reminded him of himself before the extinction. He'd always shaved until that day. He looked over at Rollo who also had facial hair. He had hung up the phone and was walking towards Lev.

"That guy shaves?" he asked him.

"Yeah. Some day, the past is gonna run out of razors." Rollo scoffed. "No other men in the Kingdom are allowed to shave. He considers it a status symbol to be clean shaven. And the color red? He's the only one who's allowed to incorporate the color red into his outfits. He made it illegal for anyone else to wear the color red which is too bad, because I like red. I had to toss my red clothes when he passed the law. I wear all black now because I'm in mourning," he said, laughing mildly.

"No one on the Intel Team was wearing red today," Lev said out loud, assuring himself. He wasn't speaking to Rollo, but Rollo looked at him while he mused in concern about his team members possibly wearing anything red.

"Kali would have told them not to wear anything red. She knows what she's doing."

"Yeah, she does, but she didn't tell me he shaves."

"You're really hung up on that huh? Did she tell you any physical characteristics about him?"

Lev thought about it for a second.

"Actually no. Just that he stopped aging at 28."

"Yeah, that's because she doesn't even know what he looks like anymore," Rollo said with a nod while looking at Lev with a serious expression. "She trained herself to look right past him. Sometimes he makes her look at him, but she hasn't looked at him unless forced to in years."

Lev thought about the day Kali had arrived at Ivy and how she had looked so intently at him and Bolin. He thought about the way she continued to look at him ever since. The way she looked at him was one of the things she did that he really enjoyed. The way she saw him when she looked at his face. He wanted to be seen by her. Maybe Rollo had been the only person she'd seen in years if she could look past people without seeing them.

He sighed. "Alright. Ok. I get it. Let's agree not to reveal stuff about my wife to me. I told her she doesn't have to tell me anything she doesn't want to tell me. I can't get information about her from you. Understand? It'd be a breach of trust. I told you that already. I mean it."

"Yeah, that's fine. I appreciate that. Glad you're not gonna ask me shit about her. I wanna protect her privacy as well. Even from you. But something you should know…. When she left, Bas made it a crime to mention her. She doesn't exist. Don't ask, don't make small talk tonight with him about his wife. He might even try to bait you into asking him something about her just so he can torture you. If you were an actual citizen of the Kingdom, you'd know this. You'd know the law. I'm sure he's fuming that I'm apparently in a relationship while his wife left him. Don't give him a reason to torture either of us. You'll just hold up the work you're here to do. Think about that all the time, man. You could have fucked up today already. Just smile and be quiet when you're not sure what to say. I can't save you from torture if you break this law. Being quiet and looking like you worship your King is your best tactic.

"The punishment for being caught mentioning his wife is public executions for a year. You'll be tortured, killed, and rewound to start it all over again every 15 minutes round the clock for a year. That's tens of thousands of death cycles, each preceded by unbelievable torture. You won't eat for a year, sleep, piss, or shit. All you'll do is scream and die over and over again. Don't think he's too lazy to see it through. We just had a year-long public execution end a couple of weeks ago. She doesn't exist until he gets her back and he lifts the public execution order against citizens who mention her."

"So, he's looking for her?"

Rollo looked at Lev with a shocked expression on his face. He waved one hand in the air for emphasis and said angrily, "Oh my god! Yeah! This guy wants her back! He's got half of his army out looking for her in the past every single day. They're scouring the past looking for her. I'm not bullshitting you for effect. He's convinced she's hiding from him in the past. We're fucking lucky he's not looking for her outside of here in the present where people are scarce and she'd be a fuck of lot easier to find. We gotta kill him before he finds her. He's distracted with her gone. He's been off his game as far as planning to take over the afterlife present, but he's in a constant murderous rage worse than I've ever seen him. Getting her back is 90 percent of what he's thinking about 24 hours a day.

"He lost control of her, and he's scarier than ever. He's not focused on the opposition, Pele, new formulas... He's focused on finding her, and he's passing the time by torturing citizens for fun. This is a good time for you to be here because the people in the labs upstairs are trying extra hard to please him, distract him from the loss of his wife with useful research on how to capture consciousness.

"They're actually allowed to mention her. Finding her are their orders. I sat in a meeting with them three days ago and they told him they can find her if they can figure out what they're missing about consciousness. That got his attention. It was a scary moment. It was like he woke up a little. He's obsessed with getting her back, man."

"Why her?"

"I don't fucking know." Rollo sighed.

Lev looked at Rollo and said, "I fucked up this morning, but, so you know, I'm obsessed with killing Bas and protecting my wife from him. I'm going to break his lock code and send him to meet Death Time."

"Don't mention them. They're the only card we're still holding at this point. If she told you about them, she must trust you completely. They're all we have left. If he finds out, he's gonna change his play for the afterlife present. He'll figure out a new way to take control and avoid them."

"I showed you how I can fuck up this morning, but I'm not always a dumbass. I'm here to put an end to this guy. That's what I intend to do."

Maren in the Kingdom

Maren had to wait outside of the small building where the office for technology assembly and repair was located until it opened. It was still dark outside when she located the building, and she knew she'd be waiting for hours until someone would arrive. The office opened later in the morning because techs were required to travel to the research buildings to assess tech in-house before deciding if the tech needed to be taken in for repairs. The techs had their service calls assigned the night before their day shift, so she had to wait for whoever finished their service calls first to arrive at the office.

As the sun rose higher in the sky, the air remained cold, but the sun warmed her. She was prepared to walk in and demand her assignment be honored immediately. She wasn't certain who worked in the office, so she sat outside it scowling at all passerbys just to be certain she conveyed a bad mood before interacting with one of her future coworkers. Was there an office staff that didn't have face tattoos? She wasn't certain. She decided to treat everyone who neared her as a potential member of the tech department. People arrived on foot to enter various buildings around the technology department building and, for the most part, ignored the hostile looking woman with the large, dark, tech expert tattoos on her face. They assumed they knew who she was. Techs tended to work closely with either their King or with the King's Research Team. No one wanted to further antagonize an already pissed-off looking Kingdom Tech.

When a man carrying a box and sporting four large tech tattoos on his face approached her and asked, "Did you get locked out?"

She glared up at him. "I haven't been let in yet," she said furiously.

The man looked taken aback and asked, "Do you have your assignments?"

"No. I've got nothing because someone somewhere screwed up and I'm sitting here in the cold all morning waiting to meet my new boss. Is this place always so screwed up? I was told when to arrive. I got here on time. I'm ready to do my job. I'm not going to torture for other people who are too incompetent to do their jobs. Our King wants his techs to keep his research going uninterrupted, but when I show up to do my job, I end up sitting on my hands all morning?! It wasn't like this in Columbus. The King's Techs were treated better and encouraged to serve the goals of our King. I might need to speak to my former boss in Columbus," she said in a furious tone while glaring at the man.

The man was flustered and apologized repeatedly to Maren while fumbling with his keys to the building. "Let's get you inside and get you working right away. No need to report this obviously regrettable oversight to Columbus and certainly not to our King. Listen, I have a box of tech inside that needs repairs along with this box I'm holding. We're so behind. Our King recently saw to it that several of our techs were put into six months of real-time torture for not working hard enough to serve him. I was told not to count on any replacements for them, but to get the remaining techs to work harder instead. The team's failure is my failure now. I'm next. We've been working round the clock trying to serve our King better. Everyone's going to be very happy you're here, but I'm especially happy you're here. Don't hold a grudge. It'll impact the work negatively. Come inside," he said, holding the door open for her.

Maren sighed loudly and glared at the man, but got up and said, "Fine. Show me the tech. Let me get to work for my King."

Olivia in the Kingdom

Olivia arrived at the sanitation department on the outskirts of the Kingdom after an hour of walking. Sanitation was located away from the prestigious city center and the research buildings Bas was so proud of. The walk was paved by a crudely laid roadway, but through a miles-long stretch of forest. She saw no one along the way.

Olivia looked at the sprawling one story complex in the early morning sunrise. The Kingdom landfill was located several miles beyond the sanitation complex, accessible only by carts pulled by horses. She considered the possibility that she would be assigned as a cart driver because she knew how to manage horses so well. She considered that she'd be assigned to street cleanup outside the research facilities, and not be assigned janitorial services indoors where she could look for research the RT needed to defeat Bas. She was young, strong, and could endure outdoor work better than older sanitation workers. She stared blankly at the sanitation building and thought of several other possible assignments she might receive if she entered the building and requested work with her forged sanitation papers from Columbus.

Time had told her she might be able to help Lev. Did Time mean she might be able to help Lev if she worked for sanitation? Time didn't clarify for her what Time meant. But she knew one thing for sure after all she had learned about Time. Time didn't tell people what to do. Time revealed options as Time saw them. She knew she had free will in making the decision for herself.

If she turned around now and left, would she encounter Lev heading towards sanitation? Would he ask her where she was going if not to sanitation? Would he be mad at her for not following orders? Olivia contemplated whether or not she actually had orders to go find work with sanitation. Kali had told her she had permission to be Kept. Lev hadn't given her orders to find work at sanitation. Olivia stared at the sanitation building for a few more minutes before turning around to walk back to the city. If she met Lev along the way, if he told her Rollo Vespry was dead and he was going to join sanitation, she'd tell him the truth. She was going to be Kept and she was going to be useful to him and the others. She trusted him to understand her decision and to allow her to do what she believed was best.

She walked with determination and purpose now. She wasn't afraid even with all that she knew of the risks and what she would certainly be subjected to as Kept. She headed into the city, to the New Beginnings statue. She'd wait there until she was spoken to. Someone would want her. She tore the sanitation paperwork slowly as she walked and tossed small pieces into the wooded areas along the way. She removed her warm sweater and walked into the woods and buried it under some thick leaves. She was barely dressed for the cold now. She would arrive in the city unclaimed and with no purpose. She would allow her purpose to be dictated by any research psychopath who chose her. She would make herself vulnerable in order to be dangerous.

Bautista in the Kingdom

Bautista walked through the cold morning air to the prison which was prominently located near the research facilities. Kali had told him Bas liked to hold public executions in front of the prison. As he approached it now in the dim light of the early morning, he saw the elaborate outdoor execution center for himself. She had described it well. The stage for torture and Rewinds, the public seating for citizens who would either want to attend or who were ordered to attend. The architecture was stark, more utilitarian than the Roman Colosseum, but it's purpose was clear. Public viewing of relentless torture facilitated by Rewinds every 15 minutes.

He pictured Kali on the stage only because she had told them the stories herself. Bolin was right, Lev should never be told what she'd endured. Only Kali had the right to tell him what she went through living in this hell. She was adamantly opposed to his knowing. He looked up at the tallest building alongside the prison and determined which office was Bas's, according to Kali's information. That fucker watched the torture he ordered from that window.

Standing in the cold morning air with the visuals before him, the information Kali had given the Intel Team in his mind, and knowing that Ju was waiting for him back at Ivy, propelled his determination to be assigned to a position on Bas's security team. He wasn't faking his rage as he headed up to the doors of the prison which were open 24 hours a day, every day. He pulled the door open and walked inside looking for someone with authority who could explain to him why he woke up this morning, once again, without an assignment to serve his King despite his orders from Columbus.

"I want to know who's denying our King my protection services!" he demanded coldly of the surprised Orderly Citizen Patrol agent.

"I'm just OCP, not even qualified to speak on behalf of our King's security team. Give me a minute to find someone from our King's security detail. We'll straighten this out immediately," assured the woman.

A man sitting next to her stood up and tried to appease Bautista. "Sir, let me get you some coffee while you wait," he offered.

"I don't want your fucking coffee. Get me my goddamn uniform," he growled.

"Of course. What's your assignment?"

Bautista pushed his forged orders towards the man and said, "For the last fucking time, I'm assigned to the King's Guard. Anyone who continues to deny me my orders to protect our King, will meet me on the stage tomorrow because this is getting straightened out today!"

The man balked and tripped as he turned to leave the front desk and go retrieve a King's Guard uniform for Bautista.

"Sir, I'm here to serve our King and facilitate his protection by his chosen guards. I'll return in just a moment with your uniform," he said as he left quickly through a side door while the woman continued to talk on the phone and Bautista glared at her in a rage.

He listened as she spoke to the person on the other end of the phone.

"Yes, that's him. He's furious. I see his orders here in front of me. Everything's in order.... Uh-huh, yes.... Ok."

She hung up and could barely make eye contact with him as she said, "Josephine asked me to personally escort you to our King's residence at 8am because he'll have left for his research facilities by then. You'll be given a tour of his home and the grounds, and the assignment will be described to you in detail by the guards there. Afterwards, I'll escort you to the three main labs. You'll be given tours by each security team in the separate labs. Then, you'll decide where you'd like to be stationed. All areas are in critical need of new guards. I'm to offer you every apology for denying you your ability to serve our King as you were ordered to do by Columbus. The recent loss of seven members of the security team has taken a toll on our overall ability to--"

"Shut up already!" Bautista said in disgust. "It makes me sick to hear you defending why you're failing our King! You lost seven security team members because they were unworthy to serve him! Where the hell is my uniform!?" he asked, as he grabbed his forged orders and shoved them into his pocket.

"It'll be here in a minute, sir. I'll make your badge while you wait. Stand over there for your photo," she said, directing him to the appropriate location with her finger.

Bautista walked to the wall where his photo was going to be taken.

He was officially a member of Bas's security team.

Gorman in the Kingdom

Gorman sat on the bench and watched as Lev and the man walked towards the research labs. He repositioned himself to the right as Lev approached and hoped not to be seen by him. Kali had told them all what Rollo Vespry looked like. The man was definitely Rollo Vespry. Lev had found him alive and was heading inside the research buildings with him. Vespry was alive. This was a success.

He decided he would wait a while before pursuing his role in the cafeteria. Vespry was taking Lev inside the same building that contained the main cafeteria that fed all of the research scientists in the four large buildings as well as the prison staff. He didn't want to distract Lev by running into him in the lobby. The air was warming with the sunrise as he sat and let the hours pass. He decided he would head inside just before lunch began and offer his services during the busy part of the food service day.

He suddenly sat up as he saw Olivia walk towards him. He watched as she turned and headed with purpose over to the New Beginnings statue. She hadn't seen him. Gorman held his breath as he realized her intention for herself and for the mission.

"God, Olivia. No," he whispered, horrified as he watched her sit casually on the chain surrounding the statue that was revered as holy amongst the citizens of the Kingdom.

He wanted to go up to her and stop her, demand she head back to sanitation, but he didn't know if seeking being Kept had been ordered. He had overheard Kali ask her vehemently not to be Kept. Kali wouldn't have sent her to the statue. Bolin wouldn't have. Bolin was a realistic man, and he could be harder than most realized, but for a purpose. This wasn't a sacrifice Bolin would have ordered. Never. Gorman shook his head in imperceptible motions. This was Olivia's choice. He knew her, too. She was committed to this mission to kill Bas. This was all Olivia.

He breathed deeply and he felt as his body shook as he exhaled. He looked at her. There was no doubt she would be Kept. He was going to get a position on the research team's kitchen. He was going to find out which monster on the research team decided to take Olivia and make her Kept. And after Bas was dead, he was going to kill whichever psychopath took this girl and tortured her for their own sick pleasures. He stood up and went inside the research building and asked for directions to the cafeteria even though he didn't need them.

Santi in the Kingdom

"Hi. This is my first day," Santi said while looking around the reception area of the hospital. She yawned and shook her head, appearing to shake off being tired. "Long walk. Even a doctor can't get fucking transportation from Columbus. Total fucking bullshit."

"You walked all night?" asked the receptionist in awe.

"Yes. I was told I was needed today. Morning, afternoon, or night wasn't specified. Torture works. I don't plan to disappoint our King twice." She laughed boldly, looking at the receptionist knowingly.

The receptionist looked scared by the small woman who laughed at having been tortured. "Oh, yeah! I get that. Let's find out where you need to go. Follow me. Deb, I'm escorting Doctor...?"

"I go by Doc in Columbus, but if you've already got a Doc, I can go by Santi," she said mildly, barely acknowledging either receptionist.

"Doc, it is!" said the friendly receptionist. "Deb, I'll be back after I get Doc set up," she said, as she escorted Santi to the back.

"You E.R. or some kind of specialist? General?" she asked Santi.

"Done my time in E.R. I'm coming on to facilitate Rewind tortures. Make the most of them, you know? Make sure every minute counts and the last second of relief isn't missed. Keep those fuckers in torment. Never want a Rewind to miss."

"Oh, you work for the King's Physicians, then. I apologize for how I treated you out front. I'll improve, Doc. Please accept my apologies."

Santi looked up at the taller woman and said, "You make my transition onto our King's staff easier than it has been so far, I'll even put in a good word for you. I'm still so pissed off they made me walk. Someone in Columbus is going to torture for this," she said coldly.

"I agree, Doc. Let's get you into a nice office. How about one overlooking the arena?" the receptionist offered nervously.

"I'd get to watch torture along with our King?" Santi asked, sounding interested.

"Yeah! I know just the office! I'll have it cleared for you immediately! Would you be willing to wait while I do that? I can put you in the King's Physicians private lounge?"

"What's your name?"

"Louise. I apologize for not having introduced myself earlier. That was disrespectful of me."

"Louise, I accept your offer of an office with a window view of torture. You're the first good thing to happen to me since I left Columbus. Show me to the King's Physician's lounge," Santi said imperiously.

"This way, Doc!"

Kali at Ivy

No one let her be alone for too long. Lev had asked everyone to check in with her and keep her busy. Bolin already had a new Intel Team of five and put Kali to work training the new recruits. Despite her sadness and concern for Lev, she remained professional and trained the new team with the same enthusiasm she'd had for the first team.

"We get this team trained, maybe, by some miracle, Dave and the RT will figure out the lock code. We'll send the new Intel Team to extract the others. Maybe Lev will return and need a new team to go in to help get the others out. Let's stay prepared for any eventuality," Bolin had encouraged her.

"I know what needs to be done to help Lev. I'm a good soldier even when it's not easy," she assured him.

Bolin told James, "She really is."

James was standing at her open window in the cold early morning air. "I want to know why Noronha saw you on the roof last night. He just fucking told me that in the chicken coops. I'm furious he waited that long to tell me," he demanded of her without an ounce of humor.

Kali smiled and rolled her eyes at him. "I'm not suicidal. Lev and I look up at the sky together each night. It was his idea, and I fucking like it. I don't want company up there, either, so don't offer to go up with me."

"Ok, I won't, but how about I bring you some carrot wine? You can take it up and have a drink with Lev."

Kali looked sad for a second but nodded in agreement that his offer would be nice.

"The other thing we need to talk about is this open window. It's getting cold and it's gonna snow eventually. You must be freezing at night. Hmm?"

Kali shrugged.

"Alright, I'm not gonna ask permission from you like Bol told me to. He's gonna be here with his engineering team two days from now to build you a greenhouse enclosure right outside here. You can jump out your window and run through the greenhouse door. Anyone chasing you will be confused. Probably run into the glass. He's gonna put a trip wall at the bottom of the door. Hop over it when you're escaping Bas's army. Maybe he'll dig a moat around it, too?" James looked at her and dared her to argue.

"That sounds really nice, James. I accept. I'll thank Bolin when I see him upstairs in a few minutes."

"No you won't. I just spoke to him about what Noronha told me. He told me to talk to you this morning about this stuff and then to take you to South Ivy to check on my bees. I have to winterize their hive. You're coming with me," he said with authority.

Kali smiled and laughed lightly at his bossy approach to her schedule this morning. "Ok, fine. But you realize I still don't ride horses, right?"

"Oh, yeah, I know. I'm going to get us a cart and horse. We're bringing equipment to winterize the hive, and we're gonna see what's ready to harvest, too. Wear work clothes. You got gloves?"

Kali scoffed at him. "No, I don't have gloves, and I don't know anything about anything you think I'm about to go off and help you with," she said and laughed at him.

"Well we're harvesting pumpkins, so it might be a fun day for you."

Kali looked at him suspiciously and asked, "Do pumpkins have those hornworms Lev told me about?"

James laughed and shook his head with great humor at his friend's concern. "No, and he told me about you and the unicorn worm conversation. You're too funny. We're gonna get pumpkins today and then you can work with me and the kitchen crew to prepare some for baking, some for soup, seed collection, and wine."

Kali's eyes lit up. "Oh, James! Will you teach me how to make wine? That's like cooking, right? I want to learn how to make wine," she said enthusiastically.

"Yeah, I'll teach you how to make pumpkin wine. Next month we'll make vodka. You know, to have with Lev when he gets back. He'll like that you made it," he said kindly.

"I really like that idea, James. When I woke up this morning, I felt like the day was going to suck, but you changed it all up," she said, sounding grateful.

"You need to realize we're your family. We don't know what you need, so we're trying to figure it out," he said kindly.

"You're totally nailing it," she laughed while walking away to get one of Lev's sweaters. It was definitely chilly outside. She chose the brown one he'd worn up to the roof when he told her he was leaving and held it under her nose for a minute to breathe in the scent of her husband. It made her miss him even more, but it also quieted her nerves and made her relax. He would be happy for her to go spend a day with James working with the bees and the pumpkins.

James taught Kali how to protect the bee colony during the colder months, and then they used a wheelbarrow to collect numerous pumpkins that were ready to be harvested. They were sweaty and exhausted by the time they rode their full cart back into the Ivy grounds.

James pointed to Kali and Lev's open window off in the distance.

"I see Bol's got engineers out by your window already. You're going to have a warm room sooner rather than later," he assured her.

"I'm so sad," she said to him suddenly.

"I know. Come here. I can't let go of the horses. Get over here and give me a fucking hug," he said, smiling.

Kali laughed and leaned over and hugged him tightly.

James walked the horses slowly up to the compound so he could talk to her.

"You're focusing on what could go wrong. You need to believe your Friend is there and is helping him."

"Do you know my Friend's name?" she asked him.

"Ya. You gonna kill me?" he asked her with a laugh.

"No," she laughed with him. "I know you'd go to torture to protect his identity."

"I would. You know I'd go to torture to protect your identity, too, right?"

"Yeah, same. I'd accuse you of being a sickening loyalist to Bas who's raising perfect little cult members to worship the King. I'd keep you all safe and go to torture swearing you're all the worst of the worst," she said happily.

James laughed at her. "You're always going to say crazy things, aren't you?" he asked with a laugh while leaning against her and kissing the top of her head.

"Probably," she said agreeably.

Bolin insisted Kali take three days off from work on the Intel Team. He told her he could train the new team members to navigate the Kingdom himself using maps she'd created for the first team so that she could catch up on sleep and spend time with James preparing pumpkins for various uses.

"Pumpkins are so versatile. Let James show you all the different ways we use them. He said you want to learn how to make pumpkin wine. That's my favorite wine. Make me some," Bolin had encouraged her.

"Ok."

"I'm not waiting to make you the greenhouse for your open window. It's getting too cold. It should be done in a couple of days. You and James practice escaping out the window and through the greenhouse. Let me know if you don't feel safe enough," he told her.

"I will. Mark just told me about the spikes. I think that's really cool."

Bolin nodded. "I made escape routes in war zones when I was in the navy. Your enemies won't know the traps," he assured her.

"You never told Lev the things I told the Intel Team, did you?"

"Look at me. No," he said firmly.

"Ok. I didn't want him in the Kingdom thinking about me being--"

"He doesn't know what you survived."

"Ok. I'm going to make you some pumpkin wine."

"I'd like that," Bolin said, smiling.

Ju stopped by every night to check in on Kali, and Kali thought it was because she missed Bautista. Three weeks after Lev and the Intel Team had left, Ju confided in Kali that she and Marty had gotten married the night before he left.

"I wouldn't marry him before because he said he didn't want kids. He's a little older than me, you know? Well, 11 years older than me. I don't care, but he thinks it's a lot. He said it would be wrong to bring a kid into this world. He said nothing made sense after the extinction. He was juggling his religious upbringing, his losses, his lack of hope... He had a wife and four kids who all died when Bas ended the world."

"Mm-hm." Kali nodded. She knew these things about Bautista after spending so much time with him on the Intel Team. He knew a lot about her, as well.

"But then you showed up and he found out about Bas. It all suddenly made sense to him. He said, 'Ju, I'm gonna go kill this fucking asshole and you and me, we're gonna have kids. As many kids as you want. Once this world is safe, we're gonna Adam and Eve this fucking landscape.' Ju laughed at the memory and Kali joined her.

"Like rabbits!" Kali exclaimed through her laughter.

"Yeah!" Laughed Ju.

"Are we friends?" Kali asked her suddenly.

"Yeah, Kali. You and I are friends."

"I've never had a friend who's a woman."

"Well, the rule for women friends is that we can talk about our partners, but we don't ever tell anyone what we say. We die with these stories!" Ju said with a laugh.

"I'm a great secret keeper!" Kali said enthusiastically.

Ju nodded and said, "Just so you know, Marty told me he would never talk about you and the Intel Team. I respected that. He never said a word. I'm not even curious."

Kali nodded. Ju didn't have to tell her that. She knew for a fact that James knew everything Bolin knew, but Bautista had taken her aside and told her, 'Hey, Ju and you... I think you two have a dialogue. I'm not here to disrupt that. What you tell the team, I'm not sharing that with Ju. You go ahead and be friends if you want to. I won't let it get weird,' he had told her.

She had worked with him on the Intel Team long enough to know that Marty Bautista was a good man. He didn't lie, he didn't fuck around with your trust.

She nodded at him. 'Thank you. I like Ju. I liked her from the first time she was my guard and she helped me with my bra.'

Bautista had laughed, 'I actually don't know what that means, but she caught up with me that day and told me she liked you, too,' he assured her while still laughing. 'It's an Escher thing,' Kali said, looking at him as if he should understand. 'Oh, I'm definitely more confused now, but I believe you,' Bautista had said shaking his head and laughing.

The new Intel Team consisted of Huong, Mike, Reynolds, Dan, and Walsh. All were from Campus. Kali conducted the same training with the new Intel Team as she had with the first. Their training moved more swiftly due the fact that she and Bolin were now better prepared as trainers.

When Dan broke his wrist breaking his fall on ice one cold morning, sidelining him from training and the ability to use most of the tech, Nova requested to be allowed to join the Intel Team and leave her post at Campus's military. Aisha agreed to her request and Nova moved to Ivy the following day to replace Dan and seamlessly integrated into the Intel Team. She was already highly skilled in military techniques and quickly picked up week's worth of training to catch up with the rest of the team.

Not a minute went by that Kali didn't think about Lev or worry about him being put into torture even as the friends she shared with Lev continued to check in with her and make sure she knew they were all invested in the work he and the Intel Team were doing for both presents.

The RT Makes Progress

In Lev's absence, Dave and the RT continued to work day and night to fill in the missing gaps of the formula for the communication tech. They put aside their focus on discovering the formula for Bas's lock code in an effort to clear their minds from the burnout they were all experiencing as a result of months of effort with no success. "Let's put all our energy into the comms device for now while we wait for

Lev to bring us back something we can use to break that lock code," Dave told the RT.

Kali knew the plans of the RT to switch their focus from the lock code to the comms formula because Dave made a point of stopping by her room the night before he addressed the RT in order to clear his intent with her first.

"I don't want you to think we're not trying to get Lev and the Intel Team back. The comms tech is another way we can get him back. We're out of ideas with the passport. If we can get the comms working, maybe we can contact Pele and see if she can help Lev and the Team."

"I agree," Kali said, appreciative of Dave's efforts as a member of the RT as well as his efforts as a friend to herself to make sure she remained fully informed and approved of the decisions he was making.

"Your optical. You said you have a lot of other things hidden with it. Do you think maybe there's something you hid, something you've possibly forgotten about, that could be helpful to us?"

Kali thought about Dave's question quietly for a minute then slowly shook her head, "I want there to be, but I don't think there's anything hidden with it that would help with the tech you guys have. Maybe--"

Dave held up his hand and sat up straighter, "Anything related to tech, Kali. All this tech was new to us. If you have any tech, any formulas, even if what you have is completely unrelated to the comms tech, for instance, we might find it useful. We might not, but we also might. When was the last time you did an inventory of what you have on your optical?"

"I'll look. But most of what I have is stuff that could implicate Rollo as the leader of the opposition. The rest, you all have in the recipe book. I didn't gather intel and let it sit on my optical. Rollo and I processed what was gathered quickly to make sure we were creating accurate formulas. I never saw the rest of the comms formula."

Kali suddenly looked like she was considering something and squinted and looked away from Dave. Dave sat quietly and waited for her to speak. She shook her head and looked back at Dave.

"No. I don't think it would help, but I have a broken comms device that's at least 20 years old. They use different technology now, so it wouldn't have used the same formulas when it was working. I took it from the trash. When they made the new comms, they threw away all of the old ones."

"Regardless, I'd like to see it if you'll let me," Dave said, nodding his head, hopeful for a miracle.

Kali got her optical and recalled the broken comms device and handed it to Dave.

"I've seen others use their opticals and it sometimes takes a while to get them to respond," he said, impressed with how quickly she could recall hidden objects.

"It takes a while to teach yourself and your optical to respond to your intention. It recognizes you as the operator right away, and it'll hide your objects forever, but you have to learn how to communicate with it before you can get really fast with the commands and requests."

Dave nodded. "That's why you got the new Intel Team members opticals the first day, huh?"

"Yeah. We learned from the first Intel Team to get started as soon as possible with the optical training. Bolin sends the new team on scavenger hunts around Ivy and they have to bring dozens of things to each meeting every day. No one's supposed to notice them stealing shit, either. James told him he had to stop sending them to steal dishes from the cafeteria," Kali said, with a small laugh.

Dave smiled. "Is that right?"

"Yeah."

"Thanks for this ancient comms device. I'll see if the team can do anything with it. I'll let you know."

After Dave left, Kali held her optical and cloaked it. She walked to the bathroom and closed the door, then went and sat at the dining table again. She concentrated her intention on her optical and then got up and opened the bathroom door. She smiled. "Finally," she said as she closed the bathroom door and walked back to the dining table and sat down. She uncloaked her optical and recalled her bath towel. It appeared on the dining table and she let out a small laugh. "I hid it through a wall. I fucking did it." She laughed again before trying to return the bath towel back inside the bathroom. The bath towel disappeared from the table, but she wasn't sure if she'd successfully returned the bath towel to the bathroom hook, or if the optical had hidden the towel in the past. She walked the bathroom and opened the door to see if the towel was there. "Fuck," she said, but she was still smiling, still happy with her success at stealing an item through a wall and hiding it in the past. She recalled her bath towel from the past and hung it back in the bathroom manually. She closed the bathroom door and continued to practice her new skill.

Lev and Rollo

Lev and Rollo had their marriage union blessed by Bas. They had arrived at his mansion at 10pm as he had requested, but he made them wait for three hours before he finally entered the living room and said, "Let's get this over with. Rollo, you sure you want to marry this... Dev?"

"Yes, my King," Rollo said quickly.

"Fine, you're married. Get him a job at the lab so you can babysit him. Kitchen, maybe."

"He's really well-suited for janitorial services."

Bas laughed mockingly and said, "Oh, so that's the attraction? Alright. Tell whoever needs to be told I approved Dev for janitorial services. Find him an open position."

Bas turned to leave but stopped to consider something. Rollo and Lev waited in silence for him to speak.

"Dev, can you read?"

Lev hesitated for a moment, but said, "Yeah, all the important words, my King."

Bas looked at Rollo. "You're vouching for his loyalty to me?"

"Yes," Rollo said with confidence.

Bas considered what he was about to say next.

"He can work in the labs. When you make the arrangements, get rid of Alexis and that fucking guy. What's his name?"

"Dante? The older man with the limp?"

"Yeah, that asshole. Move both of them to cart duty down at the station. Leticia believes someone's been fucking around for the opposition in the labs. Get Dev in there tomorrow. I want someone who's dimwitted around the new research."

Rollo nodded. "I understand."

"Dev, you're going to do the work of both Alexis and Dante. Show yourselves out," said Bas as he left the room.

"Come on, Dev. Let's go home," Rollo said.

The two men walked the three miles back to Rollo's house in silence because Rollo indicated he wasn't comfortable speaking about Bas in the quiet of the night. A light snow was falling and neither man was dressed well enough against the cold.

After Rollo closed the front door of his house, he smiled at Lev and said, "You're in, man!"

Lev nodded, but his expression was one of disgust. "Yeah, and that guy's a fucking nightmare."

"Yeah. It could have gone a lot worse, though. Let's celebrate this victory. You're fucking inside! He thinks you're too stupid to steal research for the opposition. He's gonna tell the lab teams I vouched for you and that you're a fucking idiot," Rollo said happily.

"Uh-huh. This is good. I agree. It's just shocking. This is a lot of fucking bullshit to take in all at once."

"Well, it gets worse. I don't have a spare room, so you're on the couch. I'll get you some blankets and a pillow. Bas shows up here a lot. He'll knock, but you gotta be quick to run the blankets into the back if he shows up some morning."

"Or we say we were fighting," Lev offered.

"Yeah, but let's not burn out that excuse right away. He stops by a lot."

"Why?"

"Because my job is to do whatever he needs to have done. I'm the only one who doesn't fuck up. We gotta get up in three hours. I need some sleep. A lot of good things happened today, Dev."

"Are you really going to call me Dev even when no one's around?"

"Gotta, man. I'll forget and call you Lev and that won't go over well."

"Yeah. Call me Dev," Lev agreed.

Lev and Rollo had been living together in Rollo's house as husbands for a little over a month when Bas decided to stop by their house one morning unexpectedly. Lev was still half asleep on the couch when he realized it was Bas at the front door. He jumped up and ran his blankets and pillow into Rollo's room and threw them onto Rollo's bed. Rollo walked out of the bathroom freshly showered and dressed and looked at Lev's face.

"Bas is here?" he asked him.

"Yeah."

"Alright. Stay here. I'll talk to him. I'll tell him you're still sleeping if he even asks. This is good, man. We look properly married. No worries," Rollo assured him.

Lev breathed deeply. He listened as Rollo opened the front door and warmly welcomed the mad King into his home. Lev continued to listen intently from the doorway and tried to hear what Bas was telling Rollo.

A look of dread suddenly crossed his face and he stood frozen in fear. He ran to the bedsheets he'd thrown onto Rollo's bed and began to toss them around, shaking them out and muttering, "No, no, no, no. Oh, no."

Lev stood up straight and tall. He was in a panic. His heart raced and his breathing was painfully shallow.

"*Fuck*," he whispered, gasping for air. He quickly stripped off his clothes and walked naked down the hallway calling loudly for Rollo.

"Babe, where are you? Did you make me coffee? Rollo?!"

Lev turned and walked into the open kitchen flicking on the bright lights seemingly completely oblivious to the two men standing in the living room looking at him. He walked over to the coffee pot and saw that it was empty. "Babe, I'll try to make us coffee!" he yelled.

He sniffed loudly and scratched his bare chest as he opened the cabinets looking for the coffee. "Where do you keep the coffee?!" he called out loudly, sounding confused.

"Dev?!" Rollo said in exasperation to him from where he and Bas were staring at him.

"Hmmm?" Lev asked as he turned around slowly revealing his full nudity to both men.

"Dev! Our King is here! Go get some clothes on!" Rollo said in shock.

He began to walk towards Lev, but Bas quickly held up his hand and scoffed, "Forget it Rollo. I don't expect your husband to be house-trained yet."

"I'll go get dressed and then I'll make everyone some coffee," Lev said, trying to sound like a positive problem solver.

"No, thank you, Dev," Bas said, looking him over while shaking his head, bemused. "But you know what? Come here. Come on. I was just asking Rollo something. Maybe you can help?"

Lev walked over to Bas despite the look of horror on Rollo's face and asked proudly, "Yes, my King? How can I help you?"

"Well, Dev, I was just asking Rollo to find me a new King's Physician. I put my most recent one into torture for a real year for fucking up a Rewind. Are you following me, Dev?"

"Yes, my King."

"I've got three available at the hospital to choose from. Why don't you accompany Rollo to the hospital this morning and help him choose my next King's Physician from the three that are available?"

"It would be an honor to serve you that way, my King," Lev said proudly.

"Good. It's settled. Rollo, make sure Dev gets dressed, then take him to the hospital and decide who my next King's Physician will be. I have a bunch of public rewinds that have to happen over in Columbus. Citizens are acting up the way they usually do in the winter. You two choose my new KP today and have whoever you choose sent to Columbus immediately. You're driving, Rollo. I want all the backlogged rewinds to happen over the course of the next two weeks."

"Yes, my King," said Rollo.

"My King? We're alone."

"Yes, Bas," Rollo said, sighing.

"You married him," Bas said with a derisive laugh.

Bas looked at Dev and shook his head then waited for Rollo to open his front door for him.

Rollo stared in shock at Lev.

"What the *fuck* were you thinking!?" he asked Lev while gasping for air at the same time.

Lev ran towards the couch and started lifting the cushions. He dropped onto his hands and knees on the floor and looked under the couch and then under the coffee table.

Rollo stared at Lev as he scrambled naked around the living room floor asking, "Have you lost your fucking mind? What are you doing?"

Lev reached his long arm under the bottom shelf of the coffee table and pulled out the strip of photos of Kali and Rollo at the carnival in Miami all those years ago. He closed his eyes and exhaled loudly as he sat on the floor naked against the couch.

"We were almost sent for year-long public rewinds this morning," Rollo said quietly.

"Mm-hm." Lev sniffed and shook his head in agreement with his eyes still closed.

"Gotta agree to put the pictures back into the box before you go to sleep, man."

Rollo walked over to the couch and sat down on it looking down at Lev who was still sitting on the floor with his back leaning against the couch.

"You ok?" Rollo asked him.

"Yeah. You mad?"

Rollo burst out laughing and fell back onto the couch.

"That was the craziest fucking thing I've ever seen, man! You're fucking nuts!"

Rollo kept laughing loudly and fell over onto his side as he recounted for Lev the moment Bas saw him walk into the kitchen with his junk swinging.

"His face! I'll never forget it for the rest of my life!" Rollo howled with tears coming out of his eyes.

Lev's shoulders were shaking as he laughed, too, and he told Rollo how he realized the pictures weren't in the bed sheets.

"I fucking panicked, man! I just ripped off my clothes and started calling for you. I didn't know what the fuck to do!"

The two men laughed until a barely composed Rollo offered to make the coffee Dev had tried to make. They started to laugh again and didn't stop laughing until they arrived at the hospital to find Bas a new King's Physician. That's when Lev saw Santi's name listed as a King's Physician.

"Holy shit! Santi's one of ours! She got in," he said to Rollo happily.

"You're kidding? You got a King's Physician inside the Kingdom?"

"Yeah. I told you about her. We've been friends for 15 years. She's solid."

"Let's get her," Rollo said, suddenly very serious. "Kali and I never had a King's Physician on the team before. Man, it could have helped us out of a few shitty situations."

Rollo looked up at Lev.

"You ok?"

"Yeah, I just didn't know if she was alive."

"Let's put her to work," Rollo said with authority.

Santi, Rollo, and Lev

Rollo and Lev waited in a small conference room to meet with each of the potential King's Physicians to interview them. Rollo arranged the order of the interviews to ensure Santi would be last. He quickly dismissed the first two potential King's Physicians and he and Lev waited for Santi to arrive. "She goes by Doc," the receptionist told them.

Santi walked in and looked at the two men who had requested an interview with her at Bas's request.

"I'm very busy today. Tell me how I can help you so I can get back to work serving my King," she said curtly.

Rollo didn't speak right away, so Lev looked over at him then looked back at Santi and said, "Come in. Close the door."

Santi did as she was told to do and Lev stood up quickly and walked over to her and hugged her tightly.

She didn't hug him back and he pulled away and looked at her asking, "You ok, Doc?"

"Who the hell are you? Why are you hugging me?"

Lev nodded. "This is spy protocol," he said, turning to Rollo. "Doc, this is The Benefactor! Rollo Vespry!"

Santi closed her eyes and put her head back sighed deeply. It took her a moment to move her head forward again and she looked at Lev and said, "I'm so happy to see you!" as they hugged each other tightly.

Rollo stood up suddenly and said, "Call me Rollo."

"I'm so happy to meet you, Rollo!" Santi said, walking over to him to hug him, too. She let him go and sat down as Rollo described to her Bas's request.

"So, I'll get to Rewind people in Columbus for two weeks? Do I have to stay in Columbus? I'm trying to figure out how to get into that crypto bitch's world. Gorman says Olivia is Kept by her."

"Oh, shit. The kid is Kept?" Rollo muttered.

Lev looked sick. Kali would be devastated. "How? She was supposed to be in sanitation. Her paperwork was for sanitation. Kali asked her not to be Kept," he said in frustration.

Santi nodded. "I know. I know. Gorman saw her our first morning here."

Santi told Lev and Rollo about the decision Olivia had made. She told them that Gorman found out a lab researcher in quantum cryptography was keeping her.

"Who has her?" asked Rollo.

"Her name is Robyn. That's a nice fucking name, right? Her name is Robyn and she's a fucking sadist torturing a teenager." Santi looked away from both of them.

Lev noticed Rollo reach out his hand and put it on top of Santi's. "It's not ok. It's definitely not ok. I don't know if we can help her, but I know she's where she needs to be to potentially get some really good information to help break the lock code. Olivia chose well."

Lev suddenly realized he was not ok with what Rollo had just suggested and turned to him and asked, "What? That's not cool, man."

Santi shook her head and looked at Lev. "No, Rollo's right. Gorman knows it, too. We're just really worried about her and we don't want her there, but we know she made the choice knowing what being Kept meant."

"How could she know?" asked Lev.

Rollo and Santi both turned to him. Rollo sighed and Santi said, "Lev, Kali told us. Olivia made the choice. Rollo's right. Let's see if we can make her sacrifice worth what she's enduring."

Rollo still had his hand on Santi's and she placed her other hand on top of his.

"It's really nice to meet you, Rollo. I needed to hear that. I'll remind Gorman, too. He's really upset," she said.

"He needs to stay focused. He's got the researchers who helped design Bas's lock code on his shift if he's working around Robyn," Rollo told her.

"I'll reinforce that with him. He brings me my lunch every day. We get to talk for a few minutes. He and Marty are living together. Marty's working second shift in the crypto lab. He's been trying to get to first shift. He feels like he's become very familiar with the various labs at this point, and he wants to spend more time during the working hours trying to observe the researchers in order to gather intel. Is there anything you two need to tell them?"

"Yeah, if he gets on first shift, maybe I'll see him there. I'm the janitor for most of the labs up there, but I haven't seen him in the mornings. The fucking place is huge. I definitely want to know his schedule," Lev said, sounding hopeful.

"Wow! This is all good news. Wish I'd known I was gonna meet you today, Santi!" Rollo said enthusiastically. "Here's what's gonna happen," he said as he pulled his hand away from hers. "I'm choosing you to go to Columbus. Don't let anyone die. Time those Rewinds without fail. I can't save you if you let someone sentenced to Rewinds die."

"Understood."

"While you go pack, Dev and I, don't call him Lev, his name is Dev here. Tell the others. Also, we're married...."

Santi smiled. "Oh, Kali's going to love that," she said, looking at Lev.

Lev nodded in agreement.

"While you pack, we're gonna brainstorm things Gorman and Marty need to be listening for from the crypto lab researchers. Can Gorman get you information during your lunch encounters?"

"Yes, actually, I have some information from him and Marty already. I was just waiting, hoping to figure out how to find Maren. I think she needs some of this information. Lev you can have it. Maybe you can work with it, or maybe you can get it to Maren."

Rollo continued. "Go pack for your trip to Columbus. I'll arrange your transportation. You got an optical?"

"Yes."

"Hide what Marty and Gorman gave you if you haven't already. I'll pick you up and you give me what they gave you."

"I don't want to take my optical with me to Columbus."

"Ok. I'll take your optical to my house. When you return from Columbus, I'll get it back to you."

"That's better."

"What's your address? I'll pick you up in two hours."

"I have patients all day."

"What you have are orders from our King. Those trump all other obligations. I'll be outside your residence in two hours."

"Are you driving me to Columbus."

"Yeah, that's part of what I do! Your travel home will be arranged on that end, though. You and I can talk about the questions Dev and I are gonna come up with for Gorman."

"Anything else? Can I go and pack now?"

"Yeah, go pack. Wait! Address?"

Rollo and Lev walked back to Rollo's house and Lev noticed that Rollo was unusually quiet.

"Tell me the truth, don't fucking lie. You hot for my sister?" Lev asked, looking over at him.

"Shut up."

"You didn't say no."

They walked in silence for a bit longer.

"Fine. I am," Rollo said, looking at Lev.

"I'm not telling you anything about her. Figure it all out on the car ride," Lev told him with a smile.

"She's beautiful. Mm. When she walked into the room, I was speechless."

"Oh, boy." Lev laughed.

The RT and the Comms

A month earlier, Dave had the RT split into two groups. One group worked to make prison bullets that could withstand the heat of being fired from a gun, while the other group focused solely on completing the formula for the comms device. On the day that the prison bullet team resolved the heat problem Bas's researchers had not been able to solve, Dave called all RT and Intel Team members to an impromptu meeting in the basement.

"I wanted to get everyone out of the labs and out of Intel training for a bit. We're all up there day and night trying to find a way to defeat Bas and his sick intentions for all of us. We all want our people back at Ivy, safe. We had a lot of success when we started with the tech six months ago, but we've hit a lot of roadblocks over the past two months. Seems things we really want to figure out elude us despite how hard we're working. Today, though, the prison bullets? I remember Kali telling us that Bas and his researchers haven't been able to figure out how to create prison bullets that can withstand the heat of being fired from a gun.

Well, we figured it out. This group of people contains the brightest minds left on this planet. Not only the brightest, but the most decent. Sure, Bas has brilliant researchers on his team who have the same degrees all of us here have, but those people, they're fucking monsters. Our decency is what makes this RT better than Bas's research team. We're not smarter than they are. Don't let egos distort who we are. We had a success today.

"I want to destroy the prison darts. Kali's right, they're easily mishandled. Their design is a flaw. It's too easy to be stuck by one accidentally. Ordonez and I are going to destroy the PDs we have. We don't even need to train the Intel Team to use the prison bullets. If you can shoot a gun, you can work with prison bullets. Let's get 'em made for the guns we currently have on hand. Everyone here can shoot.

"Next. Comms device. Who needs a break from working on the comms?" Dave waited. "No one? Alright. I have a new approach I want to try. Three people on a team. Try every fucking thing you can each come up with. Everything. But first, I want us to remember that Time is on the RT, as well. All RT members are now required to sit quietly for 30 minutes in MR4 and listen for Time before we begin up in the labs. Get breakfast then, meet down here at 6am tomorrow. The entire RT needs to shut off their minds and every single one of us needs to focus on listening for help from Time. Lev and the Intel Team left two months ago. We just had a success. Take the rest of the day off and meet down here at 6am. Go on," he said.

Bautista and Gorman

When Bautista was given his choice of assignments on his first day in the Kingdom, he opted to work with Bas's security team in the quantum cryptography lab. Lev and the RT had worked with the Intel Team members to help them understand the kind of information that would benefit their quest to break Bas's lock code.

Bautista was offered a position inside Bas's mansion, and he initially believed that would be the best assignment for him, but he quickly learned that security detail assigned to the mansion had the least access to research. There was also virtually no opportunity to murder Bas while he was inside his mansion. The security role included standing against a wall all night long in Bas's bedroom just watching him sleep along with five other guards. Kali hadn't told them about that function of Bas's in-house security. He wondered to himself at what point did Kali stop noticing the lack of privacy she had lived with for decades. The security detail assigned to the mansion was also required to accompany Bas to his office during the day and on any other business he might attend, but the research labs had specific security detail teams. Bautista knew he'd have more access to potentially useful information by working in and around the labs. Kali had told him it was a rare opportunity to work as security in the research laboratories, but well worth it if he could manage to secure a position.

The labs were guarded day and night. Shifts were 12 hours long and Bautista wasn't certain which shift would provide him with the best opportunities to find information relevant to the RT's needs. Ultimately, he requested second shift, working from midnight until noon, hoping he'd be able to switch shifts later if he found he wasn't able to collect useful information for the RT during the overnight hours.

He kept his optical cloaked and with him during every shift and managed to find time to be alone in various labs as his new security team members ignored him in favor of napping in the hallways outside the lab doors. Bautista learned he would have to pretend to fall asleep in a doorway of a lab he wanted to explore before another security team member claimed the doorway as their sleeping space first. After a few weeks, he successfully claimed the crypto lab doorway as his own by repeatedly getting to it before anyone else had the opportunity. Eventually, the other members of the security team understood that the crypto lab doorway was Bautista's.

Bautista learned that the hours between 12am and 7am were unmonitored enough by the sleeping security team that he could enter the crypto lab and others without fear of being observed. He wondered how quickly he would get caught if he started to hide information and objects on his optical. He decided to do what Kali had done in many instances. He memorized information, went home, wrote it down, and hid it on his optical. He still brought his optical to work each evening in the hopes that he could find something profoundly useful enough to knock on Rollo Vespry's door and give it over to Lev to take back to the RT. By this time, he was already living with Gorman.

His second day working the overnight shift at the labs, he went down to the cafeteria for a meal before heading to his assigned housing. He noticed Gorman working in the back of the meal prep area and realized he should find a way to get his attention. Maybe they could figure out a way to work together. Maybe they could be roommates. He ate his food slowly while he sat in the cafeteria reading a book. He was exhausted after his 12 hour shift, but he watched Gorman and waited for the man to take a break. He wanted to make progress quickly, not wait around looking for a moment that may never happen.

As the lunch crowd dispersed, Bautista watched as Gorman made his way around the counter with his arms full of packaged meals. He got up quickly and headed over to him and offered to hold the door open for him.

"Here, let me get this for you. You need a hand?" Bautista asked Gorman.

"Thanks. Headed to the hospital across the way. You want to help me deliver these meals?" Gorman asked him.

"I sure do," Bautista said with a smile.

As they walked to the hospital, Gorman told Bautista about seeing Lev walking into the labs with Rollo Vespry.

"Ah, that's a relief. That's some good news, right there. Why do you look like there's bad news you're waiting to tell me?" Bautista asked Gorman.

Gorman told Bautista about Olivia's decision to seek being Kept. The two men remained silent as they considered how to help her make the best of the opportunities that would come from such a terrible situation.

"You think someone from the labs got her?"

"Yeah. She was outside waiting to be claimed by someone from the labs yesterday. She wasn't there this morning. Some animal definitely got her."

Bautista listened and felt sick. Olivia was a year younger than his own youngest daughter would have been if Bas hadn't killed everyone. He felt a paternal affection for her and hated that she was so good at being a member of the Intel Team.

"We'll find out who got her, and I'll frame her owner somehow. Get the asshole into torture."

"No. We have to help her be successful. She knows what kind of information the RT needs. Hopefully, she was taken by someone from travel or crypto. Either might be helpful to us. Don't sabotage her efforts. She made the decision because she wants to be useful."

"Yeah, I fucking know. Olivia wants to be fucking useful. Fucking hell. Fuck," Bautista muttered bitterly.

The two men decided to have Gorman move in with Bautista that afternoon. Gorman was ecstatic at the suggestion. "Yeah, I'll take you up on that! They put me in a house where I'm sharing the living room with like 20 other people. No exaggeration. 20 fucking people. We sleep shoulder to shoulder. Told me it was best because the house, if you can call it that, doesn't have heat. It's gonna fucking snow, and I'm gonna have to cuddle up to some unshowered Kingdom cultist who's gonna have a hard on all night for Bas."

"I got assigned a studio. It's small and it's got no furniture, but it's got heat and we can put some distance between us on the floor," Bautista said with a laugh.

"Done. Where's your place?"

After Gorman's shift ended, he went to Bautista's studio apartment and entered quietly so as not to wake him.

"You're awake. Good. I saw Santi at the hospital. She's on staff as a King's Physician. Told her Lev's with Vespry. I'm gonna deliver lunch to the staff every day. That makes three of us with contact, and we know where Lev is even if we don't have a way to reach him right now. This is better than I'd hoped for. How about you?" he asked Bautista.

"Better than I'd hoped for, too. How can we make it work to our benefit?"

"I'm thinking, of the three of us, Santi has the most authority. We find out who's got Olivia, we'll get as close to her as we can to get anything she can find for the RT. I have no idea how to get in touch with Maren."

"I took second shift, but I'm thinking I'd be more helpful to our mission working on first shift. I'll use this time to familiarize myself with the lab, then I'll request the switch."

After Santi had made contact with Lev and Rollo, she had to leave for Columbus immediately. She had to wait until she returned from Columbus to let Gorman know she had direct access to Lev and Rollo Vespry. In time, Santi, Gorman, and Bautista found a way to make the most of their new connection.

Bautista requested a move to first shift so he could work more closely with Lev who was working the day shift as a lab janitor. He approached the request with the same vicious tone he had used in order to get onto Bas's security team.

"Officer Bautista, we don't allow shift changes without serious consideration for the reason the request is being made. What conflict do you have working second shift that would motivate me to approve this request? Are you just too tired to work overnight? I see you have no family. What's your excuse?" demanded a surly looking security official who clearly outranked Bautista. Marty was ready for the confrontation.

"Here ya go," he said, unfolding several sheets of paper. "I made you and my King a time chart of all the hours my incompetent coworkers on second shift have spent napping while on duty. I've included their names in order to facilitate any decisions about appropriate amounts of time to be spent in torture as punishment. See? Gleeson spent 56 hours sleeping last week. So, of the 84 hours he was assigned to guard the King's research labs, simple math, he worked 28 hours. He left the research labs unprotected for 56 goddamned hours."

The higher ranking security official stared at Bautista in shock and asked, "Did you inform anyone else of your findings?"

"Yeah."

"Who?"

"Why? You gonna kill him to keep this information from our King?" Bautista asked in a menacing tone.

The official spluttered and suddenly looked enraged at the accusation being made by Bautista. "How dare you! Your request is denied! You're the one who's going to torture! Guards!"

"Rollo Vespry. I told Rollo Vespry," Bautista said with a cruel smile and a wicked laugh.

The look of horror that crossed the official's face satisfied Bautista immensely. As the guards entered the room, the official turned to tell them to leave, but Rollo was among them.

"So, you've been conspiring against the King's loyal security guard to undermine and threaten the work being done by his research teams?" Rollo asked coldly.

"No! No. I did no such thing!" The official continued to swear his allegiance to Bas as he was led out of his office to torture.

Rollo consulted Bas with the findings of the newest member of his security team and had all second shift security guards put into torture to total the amount of hours Bautista had recorded them sleeping times 10.

Bas granted Bautista a meeting and raised his rank to Trusted King's Guard, affording him special privileges including better accommodations and a new supervisory role created for him by Rollo and approved by Bas.

Bautista would now oversee all lab security. He would have unfettered access to information as he circulated lab teams and determined potential security breaches in advance.

The opposition would never get past Marty Bautista, Rollo assured Bas.

"This is the most secure the labs have ever been," Rollo told him.

Maren and Gorman

Gorman saw Maren from across the cafeteria. A Kingdom Tech inside the cafeteria was not an uncommon sight, but seeing Maren alive for the first time in two months brought a great sense of relief to Gorman. She was staring at him and tipped her head towards the doors.

"I need a water break," Gorman said as he removed his apron. He worked his ass off in the kitchen every day in order to be able to claim a needed break without objection.

"Be back in 10," his supervisor said with a nod.

"I'm finally in the labs. They had me working on tech in the office all this time in order to prove myself. So much bullshit. I'll be here every morning. I have access to multiple labs now."

"Crypto? Travel?" Gorman asked.

"Yeah, both."

"Olivia's Kept by a bitch in crypto, Santi's the lead King's Physician with a mean streak in her for public rewinds, Marty's the fucking head of lab security because he's a ballsy son of a bitch, Lev's a janitor and married to Vespry, and I'm--"

Maren laughed. "Wait. What?"

Gorman laughed, too.

"I know. I'm here in the cafeteria and I'm convinced, as are Marty and Lev, we gotta get Lev's hands on a crypto computer. Santi treated Olivia for a botched Rewind she, herself, engineered so she could be taken to medical. She gave Santi the password to her owner's crypto home computer. Some bitch named Robyn. I don't know if her home computer password is the same as her lab computer password, but who knows?"

"I know Robyn. I was in her lab yesterday. So, I have to get onto Robyn's computer and see if I can find something about the lock codes on there?"

"Yeah."

"Do I need to find Santi, or do you have the intel Olivia got to her?"

"I don't have it. The passwords in crypto are apparently really complicated. I'll ask Marty about meeting up with you. Maybe he'd have a reason to go to the Tech offices given his position as head of lab security. Give me a day or two. Meet here two days from now, same time."

"Ok."

Olivia, Lev, and Rollo

Lev's role as a daytime janitor left him with a lot of opportunities to observe research that was being conducted in the labs. He generally wasn't permitted to enter the labs during active working hours, but he was required to enter labs during down times such as lunch. The research team members paid him no mind at all. He was invisible. They had all been informed that he was Rollo's husband and that Bas considered him an idiot. Bas's description of him was confirmed as various researchers spoke to Lev in such a way that indicated they expected him to struggle to understand what they were telling him or asking of him.

"The men's bathroom has a clogged toilet. Men starts with the letter 'm.' It has two bumps on it, Dev. The women's bathroom starts with a 'w.' Hold up three fingers, Dev. See that? That's the shape of a 'w.' That's how you can tell the men's bathroom from the women's bathroom."

"Thanks. I get it now," Lev said, feigning his appreciation to the helpful, evil researcher who was trying to educate him.

Later he told Rollo, "I have a really hard time reconciling the malevolent goals of that researcher with the helpful demonstration she offered me to help me understand how to read gendered bathroom signs."

Rollo closed his eyes and sighed. "Man, you are *not* gonna force me to listen to hours of this bullshit again, are you?" he asked wearily.

"Yeah, I think it's--"

"No! I'm not listening to you try to make sense of this fucking place and these fucking psychos tonight," Rollo said, getting up to wash his dinner dishes.

Sometime during the third month of being in the Kingdom, Lev and Rollo were busy in the back of Rollo's office using Lev's optical to piece together information Lev had acquired about the comms formula.

"Marty found this. This is something we didn't have. I wish I was looking at this with the RT. I want to talk to someone about this," he said excitedly.

"Take apart my comms again, man. See if that helps now that you have this new information," Rollo offered.

"That won't help. I need to be able to work it, and I can't do that on your kitchen table. Have you heard from Pele yet?"

"No. Don't worry. Getting a message to her from inside the Kingdom is really hard."

"You think she's still on your side?"

"Yeah, I do."

"Why are you so sure?"

"We have an agreement. It took a while, but we came to an agreement. I trust her. You have to trust me."

"Ok, but I really want to let Kali know you're alive and that we're all ok, so far."

Rollo looked at Lev and nodded. "I want her to know, too," he said reassuringly. "Let's get this fucking comms formula and get you back to Ivy. You can contact Pele yourself. It's much easier to work the comms outside of this locked prison."

A voice called out to Rollo from his front office.

"Just a minute!" he shouted pleasantly.

Rollo and Lev walked out to his front office and Lev's breath caught in his chest. He was staring at a battered looking Olivia standing next to a smartly dressed middle-aged woman who Lev knew to be the lead quantum crypto lab researcher. A researcher named Robyn.

"Robyn?" Rollo asked in a tone that wasn't as friendly as usual.

Lev looked over at him and saw him scowl as he looked at Olivia. He knew who Olivia was at this point, but they had not been formally introduced.

"Rollo, I have a favor I need to ask of you." Robyn sounded decidedly put out by the ordeal of having to ask Rollo for a favor.

"What's this?" Rollo asked, pointing to Olivia's battered face.

Robyn sighed in annoyance. "I missed with the Rewind. Now I have to live with this."

"Yeah, you're not supposed to parade around fucked up Kept for the public to see. Bas know you dragged your toy outside looking like this?"

Robyn looked shocked and angry at being confronted by Rollo, but she also demonstrated an awareness that she did not outrank Rollo in Bas's opinion.

"I had to pick her up from the hospital. That obnoxious KP wouldn't release her unless she had an escort. What do you want me to do? I have to finish upstairs, and I need a favor from you."

"This conversation isn't over even if you want it to be. What favor are you requesting?"

Robyn looked at him with a simmering rage and Lev worried that her anger would be taken out on Olivia. "Rollo, let's find out what Robyn wants," he said, trying to act as the middleman.

Rollo stared at Robyn and waited for her to speak without inviting her to make a request of him.

She relented after a minute and said, "I need to leave my Kept here while I run upstairs to finish one thing."

"Fine," Rollo said, glaring at her.

Robyn left quickly and Rollo said, "Olivia, follow Dev into the back room."

"Her work computer password is the equation for the general form of a harmonic oscillation. She changes it all the time. This is the password she's using right now. Use it quickly. You can get into the rest from this point. All the work and access from the quantum computers goes through Bas. He doesn't have to approve access, but supposedly he has techs who look for Pele or the opposition in the system. It's never happened, so I doubt they're very vigilant."

Lev nodded and asked her, "Do you want me to try to get you out of there?"

"No. She's also planning to go away for two days. I just heard her telling one of her boyfriends that she's going to talk to Bas about having Santi sent to torture for being a pain in ass about not rewinding me properly. I think Santi might be in trouble."

"Whoa, wait. What? No. Robyn's the one fucking up. Kept aren't supposed to be paraded around beat to hell. It's supposed to be a private joy for the sadists that call this hell on earth home," Rollo said with impatient aggravation.

Lev asked her, "You want to take the passport and go back to Ivy? You can have it. You've done enough. You got Maren into that bitch's home computer and I'm making great progress on the information about braided time crystals. I think this is it. I'm sure of it. This is how he's locked this fucking place. Marty and I just found more information for the comms, too. You can go home. I'll give you what I got. We've got it all in another recipe book."

Lev was imploring Olivia to accept his offer and when she didn't appear moved by his sincere desire to see her accept, he added, "We're so close. I don't want you to die here and not get to go home. Hey, come on now. Kali will be furious with me if I go home without you."

Olivia remained unmoved. "I don't think you two realize that Santi's in more danger than I am right now. Robyn hasn't done anything to me that I didn't expect. I know what I'm going home to tonight. Kali prepared me, Lev. But Rollo, Santi followed me and Robyn outside the hospital and shoved her so hard that she fell onto her ass in the street in front of a crowd of people. She's embarrassed and furious right now. She didn't just go upstairs to her lab to finish some work. She went upstairs to get Santi sent to torture for assaulting the head of Bas's crypto lab. Give this information and the passport to Santi," Olivia said emphatically.

Rollo seethed as Olivia spoke.

"Calm down. Think first," Lev told him.

Rollo and Santi

When Rollo had met Santi several months earlier, he was instantly smitten with everything about her. From the moment she had walked into the room for the King's Physician interview, Rollo was captivated by her. When she had hugged him after Lev had introduced her to him, he felt his arms wrap around the woman he suddenly realized he wanted to hug for the rest of his life. She was tiny, but she fit against him perfectly in his mind.

When he had put his hand on top of hers to reassure her that what was going on was indeed not good, that wasn't a contrived moment. He had done that many times with others, including Kali, in order to validate their experiences. He considered honesty in the face of terrible truths an act of kindness. To deny someone their pain or truth was a cruelty he refused to engage in with others. But then Santi had placed her other hand on top of his. He was instantly back to being taken in by her.

At the start of the hour and a half car ride to Columbus, he had turned to her and said, "I'm gonna make this weird. Are you single?"

Santi had laughed and said, "I am."

"Do you want to be?" he asked her, looking over at her as he drove the old car.

"We're approximately two minutes into an hour and a half long road trip. You're really not worried about this getting uncomfortable?" she asked him, smiling but without a hint of embarrassment.

"Not even a little. I'm more worried about some bullshit going down in Columbus and never seeing you again," he said honestly.

"We just met," Santi said kindly, looking over at him.

"Mm-hmm. And that already means we're gonna know each other forever. I guess if you're not interested here, I'll check back with you in the other present... If you wouldn't mind. Maybe you already know you're not interested. Let me know."

"Well, how would we date in this shitty Kingdom?"

He laughed. "Carefully, I'm a married man, remember?"

Santi had Rollo tell her how he and Lev had come to be married and he finished the story by telling her how, earlier in the morning, Lev had paraded himself naked through the house in order to divert Bas's attention from possibly seeing an old photo of Kali. Santi listened to Ivy's Benefactor entertain her with stories involving a couple of her closest friends and then told Rollo stories of her own. She told him about Ivy, her friendship with Lev, and how she and James had gotten drunk with Kali the first day she met her.

"My girl's had some fun while at Ivy, then?"

"Yes. We consider her family."

Rollo looked over at Santi. "I can't tell you how much knowing that about her means to me. Thank you for looking out for her. I can see how Lev feels about her, but he's keeping it inside. I don't push him. First day here, he told me not to talk about her, so I haven't."

"Is this our first date?" Santi had asked him.

Rollo smiled, "Yeah, if you want it to be. Let's end this date and go on another."

"Ok, when?" she asked him.

"Now. Now we're on our second date. We'll go on five dates before I have to leave you in Columbus. It'll be like we've been dating for weeks," he said, smiling.

"Ok. Generally, I don't date, but now that I am, I've decided I kiss goodbye on the first date." Santi moved closer to him and kissed his cheek.

"If I pull over, will you make out with me?" he asked her seriously.

"I only make out on the second date," she said with a laugh.

"I'm serious," he said, smiling.

"Me, too. Are we on our second date yet?"

Rollo pulled over and looked at her. "We are now. You really wanna make out, or no?"

Santi moved herself right up against him, wrapped her arms around him, and kissed him as she felt him wrap his arms around her and kiss her back.

In the two months that followed, Rollo was able to justify having Santi visit him and Lev at their residence by telling Bas, "I chose Santi for the position because she was clearly the most ruthless of the three. I heard she finished the two weeks of rewinds in Columbus early by working through the night. We had her over for dinner the other night and she told us how backlogs of rewinds just meant people were having their justifiable punishments delayed. Said no one should feel like they were getting away with breaking our King's laws."

Bas enjoyed hearing how Santi worked the Rewind team in Columbus harder than they were used to and asked Rollo to look into the backlog of rewinds in the capital city.

"Good call choosing this KP. Let's keep her busy if she enjoys the work so much," he told Rollo.

"Will do. I'll invite her over for dinner and let her know I spoke with you and that you want her to keep up the good work."

Bas agreed.

Rollo got to have Santi come over for dinner that he prepared for her, and Lev left them alone to enjoy each other's company. Lev busied himself working on the comms formula, but more so on the information involving time crystals and how Bas was utilizing them to create his impenetrable lock code on the Kingdom.

Rollo was known as a man who liked to cook and entertain. Cooking for Santi, a cruel Rewind master designated as a primary King's Physician, was completely ignored as a potential problem. Santi managed to spend many evenings with Rollo and his simple-minded husband. Rollo walking Santi a mile from his home to her own residence was not considered potentially scandalous to those who witnessed them.

The night before a battered Olivia stood in front of Rollo and Lev and warned them that Robyn posed a serious threat to Santi, Santi and Rollo had agreed they wanted to be married. They had been in Rollo's bedroom for several hours when they came out and interrupted Lev's work on the lock code formula to share the news of their wedding and share a toast with their friend. Lev put aside his research and congratulated Santi first with a warm hug, welcoming her to the family.

"You know Rollo's my brother-in-law as well as my husband, right?" he asked her.

Santi laughed and said, "We're one fucked up family!"

Rollo clapped his hands together and said, "I promised my beautiful wife a toast to our union with our one and only witness. All my liquor is in that cabinet." Rollo pointed towards the kitchen for Lev to see.

"You keep alcohol here?" asked Lev, walking into the kitchen, shocked by the new knowledge.

"Yeah, man, for special occasions."

Lev shook his head as he opened the cabinet and marveled at the assortment of alcoholic beverages Rollo had not told him existed.

"Man, I could have used some of this several fucking times since I got here," he said without humor as he grabbed a bottle of vodka for himself. "He's got everything here. What do you want, Santi? What's your drink order, Rollo?"

Lev and the Time Crystals

They had toasted the happy union between Santi and Rollo, and Rollo walked Santi to her house. When he returned home, he saw that Lev was beside himself walking through the house, taking large sips of vodka.

"I got it, man. I got it. Almost. I know what's going on. I need to get this information to Dave and the RT."

"Really? You got it?" asked Rollo, breathing quickly now. He had never seen Lev so excited.

"I'm so fucking close, man. I need to work on a passport, but I don't have one to work with and I don't have the tech I need to get a unique one going. I need to get this to the RT where they have the quantum computers. I don't know if I should go and risk not coming back if I'm fucking wrong, which I don't believe I am, or if I should send Maren or one of the others back. I can't leave. That would fuck you up. Fuck up my cover. I can't leave you. It'd be too dangerous for you. Maren's gotta go."

"Why Maren?" asked Rollo.

"Because she could go back to Ivy and help them out and then hustle back here. No one would get too upset or ask questions if she were gone for a couple of days. Olivia can't go. Santi would be missed by noon. Bautista is in the labs helping me every fucking day. We don't want to risk blowing his cover. Gorman would be missed, but maybe he could go. I think Maren would be the best choice. I should stay just in case I'm wrong, but I don't think I am. This is it. Kali's gonna be so pissed off, but I'll tell Maren to tell her I'm with you and doing fine. She'll understand."

Rollo, Santi, and Lev

"You're going back to Ivy."

"What? No. No, I'm not going back. Kali expects you to return. You can't send me back. Lev, look at me. What would I tell Kali?"

Lev looked at Santi and explained the options to her as he had explained them to Rollo the night before.

"I thought Maren was the right choice, but Robyn's coming for you. You can't go to torture. Rollo would fucking die if you went to torture."

"I don't want you to go to torture," Rollo said to her quietly.

Santi looked at the two men and shook her head. "I don't understand this tech, time crystals, all this fucking science bullshit. What would I even tell Dave? What the hell, Lev? What will I tell Kali?"

"Tell her I'm safe with Rollo. I was up all night making notes in the new recipe book for Maren when I thought Maren would be going. It's all here. You have to go immediately. Rollo already got word that Bas has decided to put you into torture for a year for assaulting his lead QC lab bitch. They're coming for you now. Tell Kali that. She'll be glad you escaped torture. You know she will be. She'd rather have you escape torture than have me home and know you were sent to torture."

"Oh, shit, Lev."

Lev glared at Santi. "Doc, I'm still your fucking boss. You put this passport on right fucking now, and you get back to Ivy with this intel I'm giving you to give to my RT! You understand me? These are orders. Go!"

Santi looked at Lev and nodded. "Ok. Ok."

Rollo grabbed Santi and hugged her tightly before kissing her quickly. "Don't divorce me and don't marry anyone else," he said with a small laugh while they looked at each other.

Lev grabbed Santi's arm and strapped the passport to it while she and Rollo said their goodbyes. He gave her the new recipe book, her optical, and a nod, saying, "Tell my wife I miss her every day, but that I'm figuring this shit out. I'll be back for her."

Santi nodded. "I will."

Rollo let go of Santi and she stepped back and activated the passport. She disappeared and Lev put his hand on Rollo's shoulder.

"Dave and the RT will work with what I sent them. They have the equipment to make sense of what I'm suggesting. I know I'm right. We have to get this information to Pele. Try to make contact with her again. Get what I figured out to her right now."

"I don't hear you saying I'll see Santi again."

Lev remained silent.

Kali and Aisha

Santi's arrival at Ivy brought the entire community to a standstill. From the kitchen staff, to the RT, Santi's return shattered the flow of the community. Aisha was sent for immediately. Dave, Bolin, the RT, and the Intel Team began to debrief Santi in MR4 within minutes of her arrival while they waited for Aisha to get to Ivy. Kali refused to attend the meeting after she was assured by Santi that Lev and Rollo were safe. She simply walked out of the room without saying a word to anyone.

Bolin told the group, "Let her go. She knows how to ask for help. When she decides to join us, she'll be ready."

He was worried about her, but he knew her by now. She knew Lev and Rollo were safe. That was all the information she wanted to think about for the moment.

Within 30 minutes of the beginning of Santi's debrief, the entire RT was back upstairs in the labs working with the new recipe book Lev had created for them. Santi joined them despite her protestations that she wasn't an informed scientist who could assist the team in any helpful way.

"I don't want to get in your way," she told Dave with a worried expression.

"Stick around. We might have a question you can answer. You're a potential resource," he told her.

Santi sat in the back of the room quietly and watched as the RT worked together to understand the new information Lev had assembled for them.

Aisha's arrival was swift. She dismounted her horse and left its care to someone else outside with a careless shout as she ran to find Kali, Dave, or Bolin. The atmosphere at Ivy was electrified. As she ran inside the facility and asked the first person she encountered where she could find one of them, she was immediately directed upstairs to the labs. Everyone knew Santi was back and that the RT had intel Lev and the Intel Team had collected for them.

She ran upstairs and stood panting in the doorway of the lab as Dave looked up at her and smiled broadly.

"Aish! Santi, you and Aisha find Kali and you tell both of them what's going on. Kali can come up here anytime she's ready, and I'll talk with her, myself. We'll be here overnight. She can wake me up if I'm passed out. Aisha, come back up when you're done. I'll tell you what we're up to."

Aisha looked around the room and noticed Santi walking towards her from a far corner where she had been sitting quietly.

"Is anything secret?" Santi asked Dave.

"From Kali and Aisha?" he asked with a laugh. "No. Definitely not. Aisha, tell Kali I'm feeling positive." He nodded, still smiling.

"Yeah, I will," said Aisha, looking surprised by Dave's enthusiasm.

"I know nothing's secret from Aisha and Kali, but can I include Ju and Vivek?" Santi asked Dave, wanting to speak with the spouses of her Intel Team members.

"Oh, absolutely!" Dave said, nodding reassuringly at Santi. "Ask them to keep what you tell them in our RT, Intel Team family circle for now, though."

"I will," Santi said as she and Aisha left the lab quickly.

"I'm going to find Kali. You find Ju and Vivek and bring them to Kali's room," Aisha told Santi as they ran towards the stairs.

"She was really quiet earlier. It was all good news, but she's still--"

"Kali?"

"Yeah."

"If she's not ok, go ahead and talk to Ju and Vivek without us. I'll stay with her. Maybe she's doing better after the initial shock. We'll find out and go from there."

"Alright."

Aisha and Santi parted ways as they went to find Kali, Ju, and Vivek.

Aisha found Kali in her room sitting on the couch with her feet on the coffee table.

"Santi went to get Ju and Vivek. I still know next to nothing. You want to learn what's going on from Santi along with the rest of us?"

Kali smiled up at Aisha. "Yeah. You know Lev and Rollo are ok?"

"That much I know," said Aisha with a smile.

"I'm so happy, but I'm worried about being happy. Bas always wins even when he shouldn't."

"Lev always wins," Aisha said as she sat down next to Kali.

The two women stared at each other in silence for a bit.

"I have faith in Lev to do his best, but I also have faith in Bas to do his worst," Kali told her.

"So, you're afraid to have hope. Here's what I think we should do. You and me, we combine our hope. We'll believe together that we're going to defeat that fucking asshole even though we're so fucking afraid we won't. You start to doubt, get all fucked up because of what you've seen Bas already do, borrow my hope. I'll do the same with you when I get fucked up and start to doubt we're gonna win. Sound good?"

"Yeah, let's do that. I need that," Kali said and Aisha heard the exhaustion in Kali's voice and watched as her shoulders dropped just a bit as she relaxed at being able to share her fears and doubts.

"Before I headed over here today, I told Bob I'm going to stay at Ivy for a while. I'm going upstairs to my old room. Anytime you need to be reminded to have hope, you knock on my door, ok? Dorm 17. You know where it is."

"Yeah, I do. You do the same," Kali said, offering Aisha a small grateful smile.

A voice in the hallway shouted to Kali from the bottom of the stairs. "Kali! It's Santi. I have Ju and Vivek with me. Can we come in and talk, or do you want to be left alone?!"

Kali, Aisha, Santi, Ju, and Vivek discussed all that Santi knew. She held little back, and Ju and Vivek became emotional as they learned how hard their spouses were working to rid the Universe of the tyrant.

"Every team member has risen to the challenge to defeat Bas," Santi assured them. "I fucked up when I assaulted that bitch, Robyn."

Aisha spoke up first saying, "You said you were defending a child. I don't know how you controlled yourself. Don't you dare think you did something wrong!"

"I could have done better to control myself. Maren would be back instead of me," she admitted, looking at Vivek.

"Stop. You just told me how my wife is helping to defeat Bas. It's not all about me. She wanted this. I support her," he told Santi.

Santi nodded and looked at Kali. She didn't tell anyone that the child she'd been defending was Olivia or that Olivia was Kept. Lev hadn't asked her not to tell Kali about Olivia. Kali would take it hard. She would find out later. There was no need for her to know right now.

After everyone except Santi had left, Kali sat on the couch and looked at Santi. "I'm a spy. The whole time you were talking…. Is there anything you didn't tell them?"

Santi smiled at Kali and nodded in the affirmative. "Yes. I wanted to tell you before, but there were too many people around in the meeting room, and it's family business. Not stuff the RT needed to know."

"Family business?" Kali asked, smiling back at her.

"You told us how trustworthy Rollo is, but you didn't tell us how charming, handsome, and funny he is, so, I wasn't adequately prepared to resist his charms."

Kali closed her eyes for a second and laughed. "Wait. Did you kiss my brother?" she asked Santi with an amused expression.

"Oh, we got married. It's all very complicated what with him also being married to Lev, but we're making it work," she said, laughing.

Kali leaned forward laughing and grabbed Santi's hand absently.

"This is so fucking awesome!"

"It is! But, I'd like to keep it private for now. I don't think it's relevant to the work the RT are doing. Will you keep this between us until we can get our married husbands back?" Santi laughed.

Kali stopped laughing and looked at Santi with a serious expression. "You're my family. I'll do anything you need me to do."

Santi looked at Kali and believed her.

Kali Contacts Pele

Kali woke up to someone calling to her in the dark.

"Kali, it's Dave. You awake? Kali? Wake up! It's Dave. Come on. Wake the hell up!"

"Dave? What the hell?" she asked as she got out of bed and walked to her open door to look at him in the bright light of the hallway.

"Come up the stairs," she said as she flicked on the lights to her room. "What time is it? Is Lev ok?"

"This is about the comms. We got them working. The equation Lev sent us, we figured the rest out. Come upstairs. The comms are working. We gotta contact Pele. You're Rollo's partner. She doesn't know any of us. Come on. Shake off the dreams. This is reality."

"Ok. I'm ready," she said and followed Dave upstairs to the labs.

In the brightly lit lab, Dave handed Kali the comms device the RT had created. "Call Pele," he told her.

"Just like that? What's her number? What do I say to her?" asked Kali, scoffing.

The entire RT including Bolin and the second Intel Team were assembled in the lab.

"It's working, Kali," Bolin assured her.

"Jesus. Hold on. Let me think. What would Rollo say?" she asked herself out loud.

Kali took several deep breaths and exhaled decisively. "How do I turn it on?" she asked Dave.

"Right here," he said as he depressed a button.

"We already made contact, but they didn't know who we were. Do what you do."

"Ok. I've got this," she said with a shrug and pressed the button on the comms device.

"Hi. I need to speak to Pele. Is Pele there?" Kali waited.

"Hello? Is Pele there? If you're there and listening, can you go get me Pele? I need to speak to her. She works with my friend. I need to speak with her right away."

Kali listened to the silence from the comm device and suddenly shook her head in annoyance. "Come on, this sucks waiting to hear back from you. Just fucking argue with me already!" she said angrily.

"Ah, fuck," Dave muttered.

"Hey, my friend Dave thinks I'm fucking up this phone call to Pele. Can someone go get her so I can prove to him he's wrong?"

"Jesus, Kali," Dave muttered.

"He's taking the Lord's name in vain now. I might be fucking up. Someone fucking answer me," she said in a demanding tone.

"Who do you work with?" a female voice asked.

"Um, I hate to use his name. It makes me nervous."

"Who are you?"

"I'm called Kali."

"Like California?"

"Fuck, man. Fine. Yeah."

"Kali, I work with a man in Bas's Kingdom. I need you to tell me this man's name. That's the only way this will work."

"Well, I'm contacting you from a place called Ivy. Does that help?"

"Yes."

"You know of it?"

"Yes."

"Do I still have to tell you my friend's name?"

"Is it Rollo Vespry?"

"Are you Pele?"

"Yes."

"Like, really Pele?"

"Yes."

"Ok. Rollo's my friend. I'm his partner."

"You're his partner? Your name is Kali? Rollo gave me a different name for his partner."

"Well, I decided to change my name. Jesus, I'm not cool with this exposure."

"Kali, are you safe?"

"You know, as safe as a person can be with Bas on the fucking loose," she scoffed.

"Is Ivy safe?"

"Yeah, listen. Our leader sent us really good info on how to break Bas's lock code. Our research team is trying to break the code. They just used info from our leader to figure out how to contact you. Are you fucking evil or are you going to help us break Bas's lock code and blow that son of a bitch up?"

"I'm going to help you blow that son of a bitch up."

"You're seriously Pele?"

"Yes. I want to send some of my researchers to Ivy to help you break Bas's lock code. Would that be acceptable to your people?"

Kali looked at Dave. Dave nodded.

"Pele?"

"Yes?"

"Dave is the leader of this Research Team here at Ivy. He just told me he's ok with your people coming in to help them break the lock code. When is this gonna happen?"

"I'm sending my people now. Don't shoot them."

"Ok."

Kali looked at Dave. "Don't shoot them, Dave," she whispered.

Dave nodded and mouthed, "Ok."

"Pele stop sending people!" Kali said loudly. "There are too many!"

"I sent more to the field," said Pele.

"Wow! Hold up, woman!" Kali said as she walked to the window of the lab to look out on the darkened field.

Bolin suddenly ran out of the lab to go inform the security detail that the people arriving on the field were not Bas's soldiers, but Pele's researchers.

"Can you ask your researchers not to look aggressive while one of my friends lets our security team know who they are?"

"Yes."

Kali watched as the people on the field began to sit down on the grass. "How many people are you sending us?"

"150."

"We've only got like 75 people."

"Kali, can Dave hear me?"

"Yeah."

"I need Dave and any other leadership to listen to what I'm about to say. Tell me when you're ready."

Kali looked around the room with the growing number of Pele's research team members suddenly arriving inside the room and asked loudly, "Um, is Ivy ready to hear what Pele's about to say?"

"Let's do it," Dave said, looking nervously around the room as Pele's people gathered in every available space.

"Go ahead Pele. We're listening," Kali said.

"Rollo said he's working with a researcher named Lev who came from Ivy. Apparently, Lev found information about Bas's lock code that suggested Bas had manipulated time crystals to create impenetrable lock codes that move through time, resetting periodically. The resettings can be anticipated, and calculated, though. That was the biggest problem. Dave? Can you hear me? Bas is using a formula that shatters the time resets of the time crystals but there's still evidence of quantumly predictable patterns. We're sending you some tech to work out the solutions. Rollo contacted us a couple of days ago, but we can't get a signal into Bas's Kingdom to respond to him. Rollo sent us Lev's work. We looked at it. It's good. We've been working with it and have ideas to share. They don't know we received their messages, though. Let my team work with your team. We can do this together, Dave."

Dave looked at Kali and nodded.

"Hey, Pele? Dave just nodded in agreement with you. Let's fucking do this! We have all of Lev's work here. Please don't turn out to be an asshole who ruins everything. I'm so tired," she said.

"Kali, we're going to get rid of Bas. We're going to get inside his locked Kingdom. This is going to end. Rollo, you, and this guy Lev, the people you got inside, you all did good work. I'm going to try to contact Rollo now and let him know what's going on. Dave, can I talk to you?"

Kali passed the comms device to Dave.

"Yeah, Pele. This is Dave."

"You're a scientist?"

"Yeah."

"Kali's what?"

"She's just what we fucking needed, Pele."

"Ok. I'm a scientist. I'll leave my comms open to you, Kali, and who else?"

"Bolin, Aisha, Hans, Cheri, Ordonez, and Carter."

"Got it. My main researcher is in your lab now. Gail, introduce yourself," Pele said.

A short woman with red hair approached Dave. "Hi, I'm Gail. I'm the leader of Pele's research team. Let's get Bas together, huh?"

Dave nodded. "Hell, yeah, Gail!" he said.

The Plan

"No! I go inside! I use the new passport! Bolin, tell Dave he knows shit about Bas and Intel," Kali said in frustration.

"Dave, Kali is correct. She alone knows how to manipulate Bas and work with his likely actions."

"Bol, I can't send Kali to Bas. Lev is important to me. I can't send his wife to that man. I can't fucking do it!"

Bolin glared at Dave. "Are you a member of the Intel Team?"

"No."

"There's a reason for that. Lev understood it. You don't control the Intel Team. You're strictly RT. Kali is a member of the Intel Team. I don't outrank you Dave. I differently rank you. I'm sending Kali into Bas's Kingdom. Kali's going. Don't fucking interfere."

Bolin turned his back on Dave, and Kali followed him.

"Kali, I'm so worried about you. James and I, we--"

"Got it. I'm going in to get my husband. It's a good plan. Pele's onboard, too."

Bolin nodded.

Kali and Bas Reunited

Bas woke up to the sound of his alarm and looked around his room at the guards standing in his bedroom.

"Stay," he said as he headed downstairs to his kitchen for coffee.

It was early, but the morning light was bright enough that lights weren't necessary. He made his coffee without thinking about the all too familiar process and walked with his full cup over to the large panoramic kitchen window that overlooked his sprawling backyard while taking a sip. He liked to drink his coffee while surveying the meticulously manicured landscape which included a large deck, a pool, and gardens that were designed for each season. A thick forest surrounded the back of his property, and he liked to encourage animals of all kinds to make their homes in it so that he could hunt for them and skin them alive in the evenings.

Something outside caught his attention, and his expression hardened as he sighed deeply turning away from the window with his coffee. He unlocked one of the french doors and pushed it open as he walked out onto his deck and headed leisurely towards a long padded built-in bench along the right side of the deck. She looked up at him as he approached and waved, offering him a small, friendly smile.

He sat down next to her and asked, "You're back, then?"

She tipped her head to the left and looked at him with a bigger smile and scoffed, saying, "Well, you really fucked up the world, so I had no place else to go."

He laughed as he turned away from her to stare ahead and sip his coffee. He asked her, "How'd you get out?"

She laughed, too, and shook her head defiantly saying, "Man, you can torture me all you want to, but I'm not going to tell you."

Bas wasn't laughing anymore.

"Did Pele help you?" he asked calmly.

Kali tipped her head quickly to look at him and shook her head no. "No. I'm not friends with Pele. I think you're all fucking nuts."

Bas turned to look at her again. "Are you working with Pele?" he asked her calmly.

Kali turned her body towards him and said, "No. I wanted to see real life, not the past, not what was."

They sat and looked at each other with hard expressions. She knew she had to let him win the silent standoff and said, "I have no interest in Pele's world. I wanted to see the real world," she said as she turned away from him and faced forward.

"This is the real world," he said to her and offered her his cup of coffee.

She took the cup from him and took a sip.

He moved closer to her and put his right arm around her shoulders. "Look at me."

She turned to look at him.

"Why'd you come back today?" he asked her.

"Because I finally figured out how to," she said with a laugh.

"I'm mad that you left," he said to her flatly.

"Yeah, but you're also glad I came back," she said to him, nodding her head.

"Did you fuck anyone else while you were gone?" he asked her.

540

She stopped smiling and frowned saying, "No. There's no one alive out there to fuck, Bas. Do you ever go out there? There's no one out there."

He stared at her trying to decide if he thought she was lying to him.

Kali sighed and looked defeated. "You were right. There's not something better outside of here. There wasn't even more freedom out there. There's no food, no electricity, no medicine, no people...." She turned her face away from him and sighed loudly and closed her eyes. When she opened them again she held out her hand that had the coffee cup in it and slowly swept her hand through the air saying, "This doesn't exist out there. You kept taking me to the past, and I didn't know." She shrugged.

He put his hand on the back of her neck and pulled her face closer to his making her wince in pain. "Ok. But you're going to be punished for leaving the way you did," he said through clenched teeth with a firm nod and blazing rage in his eyes.

"I figured I would be," she said, closing her eyes from the pain of his hand squeezing the back of her neck.

She sounded resigned to his authority over her which pleased him.

He released his hold on her neck slowly and said calmly, "Tell me how you got out. Give me the tech."

She tipped her head back dramatically and closed her eyes saying, "I can't. I like having it. I don't even want to use it anymore, but I like having it. Just fucking torture me. Go ahead. I'm not giving it to you."

They both started laughing, and he sat up and shook his head asking her, "Is it a basic day pass? Did it only get you in and out of here in the present?"

"Yeah, I think so," she said with a laugh and a shrug. "I found it before the trip to Australia. I was going to use it to leave from there, but then I didn't know if it would put me in the present in Australia. I wanted to be in America. I think I could have gone to the past with it, but I didn't want to go to the past, anyway. I really only wanted to see what the world looks like now," she mused, rambling on purpose.

She saw him roll his eyes at her as he asked, "Why were you gone so long?"

"Because I couldn't get back in!" She laughed in exasperation. "I tried! I stood near where I thought all this was and hoped you had guards or something who would see me lurking around. I imagined being inside in different areas, inside your mansion, the New Beginnings statue... Nothing worked for weeks until suddenly I was here a few hours ago."

He laughed mockingly at her and asked, "So, you didn't mean to be gone this long?"

"No," she said as she shook her head and took another sip of his coffee.

"You're dirty. Your hair is a mess. I hate it down," he said, shaking his head at her appearance. "But you look like you finally lost that weight," he said approvingly.

"Yeah, I'm skinny now," she said, nodding. "Starving in a wasteland will get the pounds off," she added with a shrug as she looked away from him. She hadn't lost weight. She'd gained a few necessary pounds after being allowed to eat when she wanted to for the first time in decades. Reflexively, she took another sip of his coffee. He might not let her have anything else for the rest of the day.

"Let's get you cleaned up. Get your hair done. You need to be punished first. Then we'll celebrate your return," he said, getting up. "You'll have guards until I can find whatever you used to get out," he said.

"Ok," she said as she got up and followed him inside his house.

Kali went upstairs and showered because he told her to. Bas was naked and waiting for her when she turned off the water and told her to lie down on his bed. He told her he was arranging for a party to celebrate her return to him later in the day. He said he'd have sex with her after the party, but for now, she had to be punished for leaving him.

He stood naked, pointing to his bed silently, and lit a cigarette. He handed it to her as she laid down on his bed and then lit another one for himself, inhaling deeply and exhaling the smoke as he sat on the edge of his bed next to her prone body.

He insisted she smoke her cigarette while he stroked his own erection and told her about how he had looked for her after she had left him all those months ago. He told her about all the women he considered replacing her with, but how he ultimately rejected the idea of replacing her, expecting that he'd get her back eventually.

He watched as she winced in pain as he burned his cigarette into her lower abdomen. Watching her reaction, he groaned with sexual pleasure as he continued to stroke his erection. He leaned down and inhaled on his cigarette as he pressed it into her skin telling her he was inhaling her body. He told her to remember that her body was inside of him, he had pieces of her in him that she couldn't get back because they were his now. He told her he owned her. He came at the thought telling her no one could make him cum as hard as she could because he hated her so much.

Bas took his time burning her, using four cigarettes to complete his work while he told her he was the only man who could find her body attractive.

"This looks great," he said as he sat up after inhaling the last mark he burned into her. "Wait, just need to touch up this spot," he said and leaned back over her pressing his cigarette into her one last time and leaning forward to inhale, making the heat more intense and inhaling her burned flesh. "It's been too long since I marked you. We need to do this more often," he said approvingly. "Tell me you agree," he said benignly.

"I agree," she said, nodding her head.

He laughed at her. "Still no tears, huh?" He walked into the bathroom while telling her to get dressed and go get her hair fixed for his party. She was sitting up on the edge of his bed as he walked back out for clothes.

"Cover that up. Bandages are downstairs," he said casually.

Kali walked naked out of his room with her exposed burns, past the six security guards who had stood by silently and witnessed her being tortured, and went to attend to her fresh wounds alone. No one would accompany her while she tended to her wounds. They only ever stood by and watched while she was tortured. Well, sometimes they had to help hold her down when she dared to resist.

Bas left for his day job as a mad King, leaving her with numerous security guards tasked with preventing her from doing anything Bas would disapprove of. Three of his overnight security team were walked away, being led by newly arrived security guards who were bringing them to torture for allowing Kali to enter Bas's property undetected.

Kali traveled to the past to the hair salon in Australia where her usual stylist turned her hair into the solid golden blonde shade Bas preferred.

"I'm attending a party tonight. Style it up and make it look glamorous," she told her stylist.

The stylist nodded and added the fringe which Kali knew Bas preferred. Her nails and makeup were done by another woman in the salon, and Kali felt the burden of all that was applied to her body. She hated makeup. She thought she looked like a cartoon as she stared at her reflection in the salon mirror. But she knew what Bas liked. It was what he liked that mattered, not what she liked.

Sitting in the salon chair with the fresh burns hurt. She concentrated on the music being played in the salon. She listened to the music and ignored the cries of pain from her body. The security team traveled back to Bas's mansion with her where several nervous citizens of his Kingdom were waiting for her with dozens of dresses for her to try on.

Everyone ignored the large white bandage across her lower abdomen and all of her scars as they worked to find her a dress that accentuated her curves, but also covered her scared arms and neckline, front and back. They settled on a form-fitting, shimmering purple floor length dress with a ruched center that hid the large bandage below her navel. She chose diamond and silver glittered heels from the closet upstairs in Bas's bedroom. The fashion team had the rest of the clothing taken away and focused on accessorizing her dress. Her hair was woven with delicate silver and diamond strands with silver jewelry for her ears and wrists to match. No necklace. Bas hated necklaces. They were annoying when he wanted to choke her.

Downstairs, caterers and decorators were working furiously to prepare Bas's mansion for the impromptu celebration he had ordered. He wanted to surprise all the members of his government with the return of his wife. The party may have been unplanned, but everyone working on the arrangements knew it had to appear as though they had worked for weeks to arrange it. It had to be perfect.

As busy staff members worked to get various downstairs areas of the mansion ready for the celebrations, Kali was left to wait upstairs in Bas's sitting room with the security detail he had assigned to her. She sat still for hours waiting for him to return. He would either approve of her appearance or disapprove. It was up to him. Nothing they could have done would make a difference to his decision to approve or disapprove of her final look. He knew this morning before he left whether or not he was going to be satisfied or torture everyone involved. Pretending they could change the outcome was a game that made the process and the waiting bearable. No one knew how he would react. Everyone waited.

She heard him coming down the hallway to his room and stood up ready to be judged by him. He stopped a few paces into the room and looked her over from head to toe.

"The weight loss really suits you. You look acceptable," he said approvingly.

Inside, Kali sighed in relief knowing his reaction meant he intended to enjoy the evening he had planned. Maybe he wouldn't torture, kill, and rewind her when he had sex with her tonight. Maybe he'd torture, kill, and rewind her but only once. She could only hope.

"I'll be ready soon. Sit down and wait for me," he commanded her.

The mansion contained a sprawling set of linked rooms designed for lavish parties. A dramatic staircase led to a second floor interior balcony with large french doors that opened to exterior balconies allowing for guests to circle the room from above as well as allowing them to step outside on the balconies to mingle with other guests. The ground floor ballrooms consisted of wide open floor spaces with a large bar and scattered seating areas. A team of caterers would be accessing the party kitchen behind a discreet doorway. They would mingle and serve guests food they knew Bas liked.

Bas had Kali wait upstairs in their room until more guests had arrived. He always made a late entrance, preferring to have the crowd fawn over him rather than greet individuals as they entered his events.

After some time, he stood up and told her, "We'll make our entrance, then stand by the bar. You were away in the past on a vacation, not in torture. I knew where you were the entire time. I even visited you multiple times. Do not eat. I want you to stay this thin. Drink water only. Servers have already been instructed not to provide you with calories or alcohol. You may speak, but don't carry on. If you embarrass me, you'll be sent on vacation tomorrow, straight to torture." He looked at her with less disdain than usual. "I like the color of the dress. I'm going to have fun with you tonight no matter how this evening plays out," he said, nodding to her.

Kali felt her stomach sink because she knew he meant he was going to torture her, kill her, and rewind her many times while he raped her. That was his idea of fun.

Bas offered her his arm, and they walked through the back hallways that led to the second floor balcony overlooking the combined ballrooms. As they stood above the gathering crowd with the music filling the air, the fragrant scents from the numerous floral arrangements, and the chatter of the people, Kali scanned the faces looking for Rollo or Lev. They would be expected to attend this event. She remembered to have hope.

Bas led her down the stairs slowly, appreciating the opportunity to dramatically descend the staircase as people noticed them and began to assess how they would approach him and welcome his wife back from her vacation.

On the floor, people lined up to touch his hand and tell her how beautiful she was, or how happy they were to have her back, or what a gorgeous couple she and Bas made. It was nauseating. No one could see that she was nothing more than his prop. His toy. A dressed up doll for a grown man to rip the head off of later. Kali nodded and smiled sweetly at the compliments offered by his devoted cult members and used her most gracious tone as she turned to look over at Bas and fawn over him, as well.

Rollo and Lev Attend a Party

Lev wanted to use the impromptu party at Bas's mansion as an opportunity to break into his office or the labs and find something they could use to help Pele or themselves, but Rollo was having none of it.

"We have to get there early. We can leave early to do what you want to do, but he's sober now. Everyone's sober. Let them get some drinks in them, loosen up. We'll fuck off outta there early and do what you want, but now's not the right time," he insisted.

Lev grudgingly let Rollo make the call on their plans since he was making valid points. The two men dressed in what Rollo deemed appropriate attire for the occasion.

"What's the occasion, anyway?" asked Lev, annoyed at being forced to wear a suit and tie.

"Did you not hear the city-wide announcement?" Rollo asked, equally annoyed at him.

When Lev shook his head and looked away, Rollo said, "Man, you gotta pay attention to the announcements. That's fucking irresponsible to ignore them."

Lev was defensive and said, "This would be the millionth one since I got here. I didn't know they were all life and death. Most of them just announce who's being tortured and for what crime."

Now he was irritated with Rollo for scolding him as well as for having to wear the suit and tie. "Fuck these shoes," Lev said as he squeezed his foot into a shiny black shoe that was clearly too small for his foot.

Rollo rolled his eyes and said unsympathetically, "Man, I told you months ago to have formal clothes ready for events."

Lev scowled at him and said, "I got the fucking suit, didn't I?" He stood up and shook each of his feet in the shoes that were too small for him.

"Formal footwear is included in that, dumbass," said Rollo, scoffing at Lev.

"How are we the same height and your feet are so much fucking smaller than mine?!" Lev asked, walking past him.

"Jesus Christ. Is your inability to prepare going to turn into a passive dick measuring contest, you asshole?" asked Rollo with an amused laugh.

"What'd the announcement say?" asked Lev, laughing now, too.

"Bas is going to make an announcement and wanted his closest friends and all cabinet members to celebrate some big news with him. He's excited about something, so he probably wants to show off in front of an adoring audience. I don't care if it's that he learned how to ride a fucking bike with training wheels, clap for that asshole like you mean it," Rollo said warningly.

"Got it," said Lev. "Jesus. How do people stand it?" he asked quietly.

"It's a fucking cult, man," said Rollo. "These people eat it up. Can't get enough of it."

Lev sighed and wanted to get to the party so they could eventually leave and see what they could find that would help them help Pele or Ivy. Help himself get back to Kali.

Rollo and Lev arrived at Bas's mansion later rather than early despite their efforts. By all appearances, they looked happy together and excited to be attending the impromptu event being hosted by their King.

Lev was feeling extra hateful towards Bas's biggest fans and went out of his way to engage them in speculative questions about what exciting news Bas might possibly announce at the party, and then deserted them before they finished describing their enthusiastic hopes for what gloriousness Bas would reveal. He relished the look of disappointment on their faces as he walked away seemingly unimpressed by their unfinished suggestions. He hated these people. In his mind, they were all guilty of participating in the torture Kali had been subjected to over the years.

Rollo was beyond the active hate stage that Lev was mired in.

He turned to Lev and, trying to be helpful, said, "You gotta chill or you're gonna burn yourself out with the rage, man."

Lev smiled extra sweetly at his husband and said, "Yes, dear."

Rollo smiled back equally sweetly and tipped his head saying, "I hope your feet are killing you."

They both laughed genuinely at that and mingled throughout the room as a seemingly devoted couple waiting for Bas to show up and tell them all why he'd decided to throw himself a party.

Lev was in the bathroom when Bas descended the stairs with Kali, but Rollo had watched as they made their entrance at the top of the staircase and felt his knees weaken instantly.

With shaking hands, he found a table to place his and Lev's drinks down and walked over to the restrooms trying to think of how he was going to tell Lev about the awful scenario that they were about to have to play out together.

Rollo met him outside the bathroom door and looked at him with wide eyes, smiling and whispering, "You need to dig deep, man. Remain calm. You're a soldier. You hear me? A fucking soldier."

"What? Calm down. What is it?" asked Lev, instantly certain that whatever Rollo was about to tell him was going to be worse than bad.

"Dig deep. She's here. Kali's here. Are you ready?"

Lev stared at Rollo in silence, not breathing, and shook his head slightly, looking horrified. He wasn't prepared for that.

"Not that face!" whispered Rollo sternly with a broad smile. "You want to get her killed over and over again forever?"

"No," said Lev quietly while instantly smiling and even letting a small laugh escape. "What do I have to do?" he asked Rollo.

Rollo looked at Lev and said, "Take a breath. We're gonna walk over there and you'll be introduced to her. You be cool. You don't want to watch her be dragged off to torture. And you….she'll be forced to watch you be tortured if he finds out who you are to her. You understand what that will do to her?"

Lev nodded with a warm smile on his face looking adoringly at Rollo. "What if her being here means we've lost?" he asked Rollo.

"Then why prolong the end of this day? If he wants to play with us, don't let him. Let's get whatever this is over with quickly. Now, breathe, husband. You're gonna go meet Bas's wife."

"I'm ready," Lev said smiling without revealing the fear he felt for Kali to the people around him.

Rollo and Lev walked across the room towards Bas and Kali where they stood side-by-side greeting Bas's guests. Kali didn't see Lev as he approached, but he saw her. She was dressed like a painted doll with her newly blonde hair swept up high on her head. This was why she never wore her hair up even on hot days. By any superficial standard, she was beautiful. Beautiful to look at from any angle. Radiant even. But Lev saw beyond the superficial with her. He saw a prisoner. More than that. He saw his wife was a prisoner. He saw her captor holding her hostage by his side. There was no genuine light radiating from her. She was terrified and trying to avoid torture alongside a psychopath who wouldn't allow her to die. Lev didn't know if her appearance in the Kingdom meant that Ivy was gone, Pele had lost, and that he and Rollo would be discovered next. He knew he needed to stay alive and out of torture until he could help her escape. He didn't care what happened to him after that. She needed to be free from Bas. She had spent enough time in close proximity to the demon.

He and Rollo approached Bas from the left where Kali stood alongside Bas in the long dress that concealed the abuses she'd endured at his hands for decades.

Bas's face lit up with narcissistic joy at seeing Rollo and Lev approach.

"Rollo! Look who's returned home from her vacation!" he said happily, putting his arm around Kali's waist.

Rollo wasn't sure if Bas was going to suddenly declare that he also knew he was the leader of the opposition, but he didn't miss his cue and spoke following the script Bas had begun. "Oh, look at you! I've missed you!" said Rollo enthusiastically, putting out his hand palm up to take hers.

Kali looked over at Bas and waited for him to approve or disapprove of her taking Rollo's hand. Bas looked at her and nodded once, and Kali took Rollo's hand saying, "I'm so happy to be back home, Rollo!"

She let go of Rollo's hand and turned her attention to Lev who was standing silently next to Rollo. He had a bright and happy expression and a believable, easy smile that indicated he was patiently awaiting his introduction to her.

Bas held her waist with his left hand and extended his right arm towards Lev telling her, "Our good friend, Rollo, has finally found his perfect match. Rollo, introduce your husband to my wife," he said, full of his own benevolence for letting another speak.

Rollo smiled and said enthusiastically, "This is my husband!"

Kali waited for a moment, and then laughed lightly. "Hello, husband," she said with a genuine smile, looking right into Lev's eyes, and he felt the warmth of her gaze after so many months.

Lev smiled at her, suppressing his need to grab her and hug her, and quickly looked over at Rollo. "I have a name, dear," he said to him in mock displeasure.

Rollo laughed and said, "I'm sorry! I'm just so excited by our King's news! My own seems to pale in comparison. Please, everyone forgive me. My husband's name is Dev." He nodded and turned to Lev to say, "Sorry about that. I wasn't thinking."

Lev made a face that indicated Rollo shouldn't worry and shrugged it off. "Our King's news is much more exciting. What do I call you?" he asked Kali.

Kali stood silently looking at him with a benign smile and waited as Bas said regally, "This is Mine. You may call her His."

Lev felt an earthquake throughout his body as he considered the branding on her shoulder that said 'MINE' and then processed that he was supposed to refer to her as 'His.'

Nothing in his past prepared him for how to move forward from this moment he found himself in as he stood in front of his helpless wife, himself also helpless.

"His, it's a pleasure to meet you," he said with a smile and a small nod of his head as his heart raced in a panic. He held out his hand as Rollo had done moments earlier, and Kali turned to look at Bas.

"You may," he said.

She took Lev's hand briefly, and then released it.

Kali turned to Bas and asked, "May I speak to you privately for a moment?"

"Yes. Rollo, step away, but stay close," Bas said, waving Rollo and Lev away.

"What is it?" he asked her, not sounding terribly annoyed.

"The edge of the bandage, or some of the tape, caught on the material of the dress," she said, shifting uncomfortably. "I don't want to bleed through. Can Rollo walk me to the bathroom? I need to get a new bandage, and he won't be on my case when I make a stop to get what I need. That guy you have on me jumps every time I blink. It'll take me forever to do what I need to do with him questioning me and running back to you asking for permission. Rollo's easier. I'll be back quickly."

Bas considered what she was asking and shrugged saying, "Yes. Go ahead. Take Dev with you, too. He's useless. Not even decent company."

"Thanks," she said, turning towards Rollo and Lev who had their backs to her and Bas and were keeping his fans from approaching him.

"Rollo. Dev. Come here. Take Mine to the restroom upstairs in my residence quarters. She has to make a stop before, as well. Bring her right back," Bas said to them.

Rollo nodded. "Certainly, my King. May I provide personal escort?" he asked Bas.

"Yes, of course," Bas said regally.

Rollo bent his arm towards Kali saying, "His?" and she linked arms with him and he led her back upstairs with Lev following them from behind.

Bas turned to enthusiastically greet more admirers and tell them how Mine had returned from her extended vacation. Rollo was his most trusted advisor, some might even say he was Bas's friend. Bas didn't even watch as the three of them ascended the staircase together. He trusted Mine with Rollo more than he trusted her with her entire security detail.

Kali, Lev, and Rollo

As soon as Lev closed the door that led to the rest of the upstairs rooms, Rollo said, "Follow me!" and took off running towards the staircase at the other end of the hallway.

"No, Rollo! Stop!" said Kali as she stood between Lev who was beside her now and Rollo who had already darted ahead of them.

"Man, we gotta get the fuck outta here, right now! Does he know? Were you captured? Is Ivy down? Was Pele defeated? We'll use my passport. We'll hide for as long as we can!" Rollo was walking quickly towards her and Lev as he asked her these questions in a state of agitated panic.

Kali was shaking her head putting up her hand to stop him from speaking.

"Let her tell us, man!" Lev said sternly, looking from Rollo to Kali.

Kali was excited but focused and said, "We opened the lock and Pele has our override concealed. Bas thinks I got in on an old limited basic day pass. I didn't. I used a new passport the RT created. They used the intel Santi delivered about time crystals. Pele's RT joined ours at Ivy. They figured out his code last night. She's waiting for me to get Ivy's people and any remaining opposition members out so she can bring in her army. They're gonna kill everyone except Bas. Those are the orders. We have to get our people out of here and out of the way. We can't leave them here. I just need the comms identifiers for the others. Tell me you know them," she said, looking at Rollo.

"Olivia's Kept. But I can get you Maren, Bautista, and Gorman," Rollo said quietly, trying to soften the blow.

"What? No. Not Kept. We need to get her out, too. I can't leave her here! We need to get out now before the military comes in. They might kill her by accident. Plus, this whole thing could still go to shit. They might figure out we're in. Anything could still happen!" Kali said, trying to deny the truth that Rollo was telling her.

Lev touched her shoulder gently. "We'll leave her here for now, but we'll try to get her back later."

Kali couldn't look at either of them as she processed the fact that she would have to leave Olivia behind and suddenly shook her head saying, "Give me your passport, Rollo."

He held out his wrist to her and she wrenched his arm closer while she added the formulas Dave had her memorize which would alert Pele she was ready for her and the extraction team to come get them. Rollo's comms identifier would be communicated through his passport.

"Maren and Marty's comms identifiers," she said curtly. Rollo told her and she added them.

"Gorman's," she said.

Rollo told her Gorman's comms identifier and said, "I gave her the C.I.'s of the 17 before you left for Ivy. The one's in torture will be left behind."

She dropped Rollo's arm. "Follow me!" She ran to Bas's bedroom and flung open the door saying, "That's probably twenty seconds, right? Our override is no longer concealed. The locks are open and they're gonna know it if they're actually paying attention, but fuck 'em. Dave made it so they'll have to figure out his open code he created last night if they want to close the lock again. He thought that was really funny," she said, turning and smiling up at Lev with a happy nod.

Lev smiled and nodded at her. He was speechless as he tried to understand all that she was telling them.

She turned to Rollo. "Pele knows where we are now, though."

"So, Pele's coming to get us now? You have a way out?" asked Lev, looking for reassurance.

Kali turned back to look up at Lev. "Yeah. See? I had a way out like I promised you. Did I scare you?" she asked, smiling happily at him.

"You fucking terrified me," Lev said quietly with a small laugh as he put his arms around her.

Kali put her palm on Lev's chest near his heart and said excitedly, "I'm so happy to see you!"

Lev touched her cheek and shook his head smiling back at her. "I'm so fucking happy to see you, too, but you're crazy, baby," he said with a nervous laugh while she smiled and nodded in agreement.

"I know! Why haven't you kissed me yet?" she asked him happily.

Lev laughed and leaned down and kissed her saying, "Get us home, baby!"

"Yeah, I will. We're going with Pele first. Then back to Ivy after her army gets Bas."

"Kali have you met Pele yet?" asked Rollo, sounding concerned.

"No, why?" She turned to face him, confused by the question.

"There's something I didn't know until she agreed to work with us. You need to know before she gets here."

"Tell me later," Kali said as she grabbed Lev's arm. "Help me stay steady so I can get these stupid shoes off." She held on to Lev's arm as she bent forward and winced in pain as she slid the strap from around her heel. She kicked the first shoe off and did the same with the other one wincing again.

Lev noticed her wince and asked her, "Hey, are you hurt?"

"I'll be ok." Lev didn't look convinced, but she nodded her head reassuringly at him.

Pele's guards had already started to arrive in the room and aimed their weapons at them as a precaution.

Rollo suddenly grabbed Kali's arm with a look of concern on his face and Lev asked him, "What the fuck's wrong, man? You don't like Pele all of a sudden?"

Kali looked at Rollo and pulled her arm away slowly as Pele appeared in the room. Kali was looking at Rollo with curiosity and asked, "What's wrong?"

His expression was one of worry and he turned his head towards Pele and said, "Pele's here."

"Let's go. We don't have a lot of time," Pele said as she walked up to the three of them. "Grab me so we can leave," she said, suddenly gasping for breath as she looked at Kali.

Lev noticed Kali didn't move and asked, "We're going with Pele, right babe?"

Kali still didn't move, and Rollo grabbed Pele's shoulder telling Lev, "Come on! Put your hand and her hand on Pele! Now, Lev!"

Lev glared at Rollo and turned to look down at Kali who was still frozen. He couldn't tell if it was fear or if something else was wrong. He had seen her wince a minute earlier. "Are you ok? Are you hurt? Jesus, Kali, look at me," he said loudly to get her attention.

He placed the palm of one of his hands on her cheek and turned her face gently towards his away from Pele. When she was looking at him, he asked her, "We're going with Pele, right? We're not staying in Bas's bedroom."

Kali suddenly appeared to snap out of whatever had caused her to freeze and exhaled sharply.

Lev took her hand and went to place both of their hands together on Pele. "Is this ok?" he asked her, remembering she had a history of being forced to travel as a passenger on other people's passports.

Kali nodded, still speechless, and Lev touched Pele's arm holding Kali's hand under his much larger hand.

Lua Pele

With Pele's passport, they were instantly transported from Bas's bedroom into Pele's quiet, clean, ground floor office in Lua Pele.

Lev looked at Kali and asked, "What the fuck's wrong?"

Kali still looked stunned and confused as she stared at Pele and backed away from her.

She didn't respond to Lev quickly enough, so he turned to Rollo and asked him, "Rollo, what's wrong? What did you mean there's something she needs to know?"

Kali turned to look at Lev and noticed that his concern was rapidly transforming into anger and frustration at still not knowing what was bothering her. She touched his arm absently and said calmly, "Hey, it's fine."

Lev turned to look at her and asked, "Yeah, you sure? This doesn't feel fine."

Kali rolled her eyes and laughed lightly as she slowly waved her hand in Pele's direction saying, "Yeah, well, it's just that Rollo didn't tell me Pele's my mother." Her small laugh ended with a blank expression and complete silence a split second later as she continued to realize what she had just learned meant. No one spoke. The room was silent.

She closed her eyes and shook her head a little with another small laugh and heard Lev ask her, "Babe, what?" Lev turned to Rollo and Pele and asked, "Rollo, what the fuck? Pele? Is this for real?" He touched Kali's arm gently asking, "Pele's your mother?"

The bemused expression returned to her face as Lev put both of his hands on her upper arms and asked her if she was certain.

Kali nodded and shrugged saying, "Yeah. That's Rachael. But we should confirm. Pele, are you Rachael?!" she asked unreasonably loudly while still standing in front of Lev looking at him in continued bemusement.

Pele hesitated to answer and Lev looked over at her and demanded angrily, "Answer her!"

"Yes. I'm Rachael," she said firmly and stared emotionless at Kali.

Kali suddenly leaned forward and laughed loudly while staring at Lev's chest for a second before suddenly stopping and looking up at him and saying tersely, "I'm in a really fucked up mood right now. I need some air."

She walked quickly away from Lev towards the only door in the office and stopped. "Lev, will you come with me?" she asked as she turned the handle on the office door. "Rollo and Rachael can discuss what else they think would be fun to throw at me today, you know, because I'm not completely insane after having willingly re-entered the locked Kingdom of my personal tormentor where I was physically tortured for breakfast, and then forced to smile happily for several hours this afternoon while waiting to be raped and murdered repeatedly tonight. Thankfully, I was able to find my husband and my friend and escape to another locked city where I should've been able to celebrate this hard-earned success, but it turns out the second locked city I'm stuck in is run by my *dead mother*!" she yelled loudly before turning to Pele and concluding with, "So, I need some air and a fucking adult beverage. Mom, you gonna make sure I get a glass of something strong enough to handle today's events? Bring some for Lev, too. My husband's gonna need several strong drinks to help me deal with my state of mind tonight!"

Rollo went to walk towards Kali and she said firmly, "Rollo, stay away from me. You, too, mom. Send someone else to bring me my very large, very strong drinks."

Lev muttered, "You're fucking kidding me, right now," as he walked past Rollo glaring at him and headed towards Kali to follow her out of Pele's office.

Lev and Kali found their way outside of the office building and walked around the block looking for a place to sit down until Kali quit walking and decided to sit on the edge of the sidewalk with her feet stretched out into a busy street lined with forward facing parking spots.
Lev sat down beside her, and their legs and feet stretched into an empty parking space they had decided to commandeer.

When a driver tried to park in the spot despite their obvious presence, Lev initially waved the driver away fully expecting the driver to comply. When the driver persisted in trying to claim the parking spot from them, Lev stood up and removed the shoes that were killing his feet and threw each one violently at the windshield of the car before getting into an exceptionally loud shouting match with the driver which he felt he ultimately won as the driver pulled back out and drove away.

Kali laughed and leaned against him as he sat back down next to her and stretched his long legs out into the parking space.

He wiggled his socked feet and said, "Those were Rollo's shoes."

They both laughed, and Lev put his arm around her and leaned over for a kiss.

They were still laughing and kissing when a second driver attempted to park in the spot occupied by their feet and legs. They ignored the driver until he beeped his horn several times at them and waved his hand emphatically at them from inside his car.

Lev was looking for a fight and got up again saying, "Oh, you fucker!" He walked past the driver but suddenly turned and pulled the side mirror off of the car with both of his hands before walking into the street and picking up one of Rollo's shoes from the road. He then beat the driver's side window with the heel of the shoe while shouting obscenities at the driver until he backed his car out and drove away.

Lev walked into the busy street traffic, stopping it, and threw Rollo's shoe and hit the back window of the car as the driver drove away. He turned and cursed at the drivers he had held up while standing in the street and dared another to park in the spot he and Kali were occupying when he noticed the driver had turned on the blinker to turn into the spot. Lev yelled animatedly at the driver to go find another spot, which he quickly did.

He sat back down next to Kali, who had been laughing and cheering him on loudly throughout the entire altercation, and they laughed uncontrollably until they were laying on their backs with the top halves of their bodies on the busy sidewalk and their legs sprawled inside the parking spot. People walked past them as they laid down on the sidewalk together, but no one confronted them.

Kali was still wearing the shimmering full length purple evening gown with expensive diamonds and silver accessories adorning her hair and body, but she was without shoes the same as Lev. Lev was still wearing his suit and tie and sat up to take off his suit jacket. He had her lift her head up off of the sidewalk and placed the jacket under her head. He laid back down alongside her and put his arm around her waist and they kissed slowly, lost to everyone except one another, ignoring everyone around them. They hadn't seen each other in four months and they simply didn't care about anyone else at that point.

"I missed you so much," Lev said to her quietly, looking at her intently with his arm around her.

"I fucking missed you, too," she said quietly, running the back of her fingers over his cheek and beard while looking at him. "I want to know if you were tortured," she said to him, and Lev saw her hold her breath as she waited for his answer.

"No, baby. I wasn't tortured," he said reassuringly.

Kali closed her eyes suddenly and took a deep breath and exhaled, whispering to herself as much as to him, "Ok. Ok. That's good." She opened her eyes and looked at him and nodded. "I'm so glad."

Lev nodded and said quietly, "It's ok now. There's not gonna be any more torture."

She smiled at him, clearly relieved, and he smiled in return.

A man in a uniform approached them as they laid there on the sidewalk talking quietly to each other and said, "I'm guessing there's a problem here. I don't need to know what it is, but you two need to move along."

Kali turned herself onto her back and looked up at the man's face. "I'm Pele's daughter, so fuck off," she said and turned back to look at Lev, smiling with mirth in her eyes.

He laughed at her and looked up at the man and said, "Yeah, and I'm Pele's son-in-law. Go inside and tell Pele we're still waiting for our drinks."

They both laughed, and Kali asked Lev, "Really, though. Where the hell are our drinks?"

Lev agreed saying, "Yeah you were really clear about her getting us drinks. She's a decent ally, but she's a shitty bartender."

They both continued to laugh and ignore the man as he walked away and began to speak to someone else.

Eventually, Rollo approached them and leaned against a car parked in the spot next to them. "Pele's got you a hotel room and everything you need's being sent over, including alcohol. Kali, I only found out recently."

"Mmm-hmm. Sure you did," said Kali skeptically while running her hand down Lev's side.

Rollo shook his head and continued despite her disbelief. "I kept trying to get her to work with us. You know we were desperate. She wouldn't agree to work with us unless she knew who 'my team' was. As if I had a team! She didn't trust me. Thought maybe I was a spy for Bas. I told her my partner was Time, but she didn't believe it was just me and Time. She kept asking who my second was. You know I never give up your name."

"Yeah, I heard that about you a while ago. Why is that?" asked Lev, looking over at Rollo while he and Kali continued to lay on the sidewalk and the street.

Rollo walked away without answering Lev and went into the parking spot and waved away a driver who was attempting to park in the mostly empty spot. When the driver said something to Rollo, he shouted, "Because they have some fucking problems, you asshole!"

He walked back and leaned against the car again and answered Lev. "Because she never gave up anyone else's name. Not ever. That's why. She went to torture rather than give up the name of any person working for the opposition. Everyone protects my name, but I found out early on that some people wouldn't hesitate to give up Kali's name. They all knew Bas wouldn't kill you," he said, looking at her. "I killed people who thought that was acceptable. That torturing you was acceptable. Like you've been through it so many times, what's a little, or a lot, more."

"But you gave up my name to Pele," she said, confused.

"She was afraid I was another power hungry asshole like Bas. She didn't want to work with me if all I was gonna do was try to take over after she worked with me to get rid of him. More than once, she suggested I was working by myself, too." Rollo laughed. "She said I was weak and gonna waste her time, and she could beat Bas without me.

We were yelling at each other at one meeting I'd arranged with her, it was a few months before you went to Ivy with the tech, and I told her we were her only way to see inside until they could unlock his space. I gave up Ivy that night. I did that, Lev," he said, shrugging at him.

"It's cool, man. I'm sure you did what you thought was best. My wife's a little pissed off at you right now, but I trust you, man," Lev said with a nod and looked back at Kali who was looking at him with that gaze he had missed while away from her.

"Thanks, because you know what? I had to. I needed to prove to her that I wasn't a one man operation, I wasn't trying to be the next Bas, and I had to show her I was willing to take a risk to trust her.

"She looked into Ivy. Got back to me and told me about her daughter. How Bas had kidnapped her. Said she wanted to get rid of Bas, but she needed information on her daughter. Was she alive? In torture? Either way, she was going to take out Bas, but she wanted her daughter safe if possible. I asked her who her daughter was, and... she knew your name. Your real name. She showed me a picture of you and her and your dad when you were little. I knew I could trust her. I told her you were my partner, that we were the leaders of the opposition."

Kali rolled over onto her back and looked up at Rollo and said, "My real name is Kali from now on."

"Ok," he said, nodding.

"Why didn't Pele come for Kali once she got to Ivy?" asked Lev.

"I didn't tell her Kali was the one who went to Ivy. Time, Kali, and I knew Kali was the right one to go, but, truth is, Pele agreed with our plan even if she didn't know it was Kali who was going. She'd been trying for years to unlock Bas's Kingdom with her people. She wanted to give your team at Ivy time to work with the tech and the notes that were being brought to you. See what you could come up with using fresh eyes and fresh ideas.

"She only realized it was Kali who'd gone to Ivy when Kali contacted her a week ago. We had a very hostile meeting after she learned that. Very hostile. Lev, that was when I told you Ivy got the comms working and Kali had worked out a deal with Pele. Dave said they were close to figuring out the lock code. Everything moved so fast from that moment," he mused. "I asked her to work with you anonymously so you wouldn't be distracted by who she is. I didn't know if she'd tell you, though. Your plan was solid. You had a lot to do to see it through in a really short amount of time," he concluded quietly.

"Fine," said Kali, sounding reluctantly accepting of the events which had led to her current mood.

Lev placed his hand on Kali's stomach and went to ask her if she was ready to get up, but she winced sharply as she had back in Bas's bedroom.

Lev pulled his hand away from her stomach and asked sternly, "Ok, enough. What's that about?"

Kali looked over at him and rolled her eyes and sighed saying, "Bas... hurt me a little this morning. I'll be fine," she said as she began to sit up.

"I'll help you up," said Lev, getting up quickly and offering her both of his hands.

"Thanks," she said, taking them.

"How do we get to this hotel?" Lev asked Rollo.

Rollo pointed at a car down the street from them. "That car. The driver will take us to our rooms. Mine's next door to yours," he said as they started to walk away, leaving Lev's suit jacket on the sidewalk and Rollo's shoes in the street.

"Let's get cleaned up, have some drinks, then we're kicking you out," Lev said to Rollo in a friendly tone as he grabbed Kali's hand.

Rollo nodded saying, "Can you believe it ended like this. We were just standing outside his bathroom freaking out that Kali was there."

"I know man," said Lev, putting his other hand on Rollo's shoulder as they walked towards the car and driver.

Kali was distracted looking around the city. "It looks a lot busier here than what I expected a million people to look like. With a million fighting Bas right now, I thought the streets here would be less crowded. Either that or her Kingdom space is small," said Kali, pondering the possible explanations.

"Yeah, about that.... Pele aligned with one of Time's hidden continents a few years ago. She wasn't just looking to unlock Bas's Kingdom, she wanted help from Time's locked continents if possible because the extinction wouldn't have wiped out their populations. She believes Time helped her access the Pacific northwest continent three years before you headed to Ivy, Kali. She's always tried to seek help from Time. Talks to Time hoping she'll be heard. She described the process as... She was able to chip away at the lock. Like finding a breadcrumb trail.

"She hasn't spoken to Time directly to confirm assistance, but she believes Time took opportunities to help her unlock it. It was Time's lock to break. Only Time could have helped. Pele's convinced no one's smart enough to open a lock created by Time, even if Bas thought he was."

Kali scoffed. "Yeah, but Bas was always lucky."

"The people on the continent, they're not nearly as advanced with math and science, but they had the bodies to lend for an army once they were told what Bas was planning for them."

Lev and Kali both asked Rollo how large Pele's army actually was.

"I told you a million strong because that's what she told me at first. When Lev completed the intel to send back with Santi, he made copies for Pele's team, too. She contacted me and said Lev's information was gonna change the game in our favor. Said we were definitely gonna get in. Called it a bridge. She wanted me to know she'd held back information about the size of her army because she believed it would make us work harder to count on the unlocking formulas for success."

Lev shrugged saying, "I've done that kind of thing, too. Hold back information to encourage another team to perform differently or better."

"Yeah, that's basically how she described what she was doing. She didn't want us to say to ourselves, "Well, Pele has an army of five million, so we don't have to worry so much.""

Kali looked at him. "Well how many people are actually in her army?"

Rollo laughed before saying, "Five million."

Lev threw his head back and let out a yell. "Did five million people go through to Bas's Kingdom when it was unlocked an hour ago?!" he yelled at Rollo.

"Yeah, man! Five fucking million armed soldiers went through and I'm guessing they're tearing the place apart. Pele's waiting for the smoke to clear and then she's going back in to personally unbind Time, apologize, and kill Bas."

Kali stopped walking and turned around saying, "I've gotta stop Pele."

She began to run towards the building where Pele's office was located and Lev and Rollo ran after her.

Inside the office building, the uniformed man who had spoken to her and Lev on the sidewalk earlier, saw them enter and sighed as he walked towards them.

"Not today, man," said Rollo, holding up his hand to stop him from approaching.

Kali ran towards Pele's ground floor office, and no one stopped her. She banged on the door yelling for Pele to open up while Lev and Rollo talked to the office security person.

Kali pulled on the door handle, and Pele suddenly opened the door looking concerned. "Come inside," she said, stepping out of the way. "Do you want Lev and Rollo here, too?"

"Yeah," she said and exhaled, feeling breathless from panic.

"Lev, Rollo?" Pele called to them. "Roger, these three, they're gonna be weird. Just let them be," she said to him, shaking her head and waving her hand in the direction of Rollo and Lev.

Lev and Rollo hurried into Pele's office and she shut the door behind them.

"What is it?" she asked Kali, looking ready for anything.

"I want Bas taken to Ivy for his execution."

Pele sighed and looked away saying, "Really? The rest of us are thinking of a quick and quiet execution with no hint of martyrdom for the son of a bitch."

"That's one way of doing it, but here's my way. First of all, I was his personal, very personal, prisoner for 24 years. In fact, I think it's 25 years now. I want a say in this. I'm not begging. Don't deny me the ability to witness his death. I'll sleep with my shoes on, a knife under my pillow, and all the doors and windows open for the rest of my life if I don't see him killed. Secondly, he didn't destroy your Kingdom. This place looks fucking awesome. Where are we, anyway? He also didn't destroy the hidden continent you aligned with. Rollo just told us about that outside.

"Bas should go to Ivy where the scientists have been working under Rollo and Lev for nearly 18 years now to bring him down. He should die on the land he destroyed. Not in his Kingdom, not in yours, not on some thriving continent Time locked a long time ago. He should die on the land he destroyed. We survived him. I survived him. I want him taken alive to Ivy."

Pele looked at her and nodded. "Ok, yes, you don't have to continue to make your case. We'd planned to have a military execution for him tonight. But, I agree with you. You deserve to take him back to Ivy for his execution. I'm going to go with you, though. I have to do that. I'll need to report to my allies on the continent. I'll bring a lot of guards, too. Is that ok with you?"

"Yeah, that's great," said Kali, nodding enthusiastically.

"You want to go try to get some rest now? We're going to capture him soon, and we can travel to Ivy tomorrow."

"Ok. I want to go back to Ivy as soon as possible. I want this to end, too," she said, breathing rapidly.

Lev nodded in agreement and said, "Thanks, Pele. I think this will help all of us over at Ivy."

Kali saw that Pele was contemplating saying something else, so she asked her, "What else do you want to say?"

"Freddie, my commander, wants me to confirm who they're looking to save. I know you wanted Olivia. Is there anyone else?" she asked them.

"I gave you the names of people in torture who I want back. My people. Not loyal to Bas," said Rollo.

Pele looked at Rollo and shook her head looking very apologetic. "This is going to be difficult to hear, but we can only save people who've been in torture for limited amounts of time. People on your list who were locked away in Bas's torture for extended lengths of time, their minds are destroyed. We're planning a case by case examination of each individual on your list only. I know you mentioned a woman named Lacy who's been inside for at least two decades. We have to look at what that length of time looks like for her in reality. It might have been that Bas let her body age but her mind was in torture for a few years. We can see how strong she is. But if she's been in there for hundreds of years, like so many of his victims have been... she's gone. She can't be saved."

Rollo stepped forward to protest, but Pele continued.

"Bas was a monster. He knew what he was doing. He tortured minds rather than bodies."

Kali huffed disapproval loudly and said, "No, he tortured both. Year-long public rewinds were a personal favorite of his. Plenty of people didn't end up with visible scars even after physical torture."

"You're right. I apologize for saying it like that, especially in front of you. I meant, the people in torture, he knew he could torture their minds forever. He enjoyed the knowledge of their constant suffering. I know what else he did. What he did to you. There aren't words for it.

"Before Kali knocked on my door just now, I was finishing a call with Freddie. Jorge's Kingdom was turned into a living graveyard for the tortured. Not just thousands of people in perpetual torture, but hundreds of thousands. He says the bodies look unaged, but their minds have been tortured for lengths of time that are unimaginable."

"But, no," Rollo protested, "Kali's proof you can survive if your mind is strong. She was in torture for more than 200 years one time, right Kali?" he asked her.

Kali nodded but looked like she agreed with Pele on this subject.

Pele grimaced as Rollo said that fact, and Lev turned his head to the side and closed his eyes for a second, but neither interrupted him.

"Check Lacy. She's strong, too. It was my fault," he said passionately, smacking his chest with his fist. "I got her put inside. She's my brother's wife, or as good as. She's my family," he said adamantly. "Get her out. I'll take care of her even if she's crazy. My wife's a doctor," he said, raising his voice to Pele.

Lev turned to him and spoke quietly, assuring him that what he heard Pele saying was that they would look at each person on his list and assess them. Lacy would be evaluated.

Rollo was unwilling to leave Lacy's assessment up to soldiers, and Lev asked Pele, "Can Rollo be there when they take Lacy out if he wants to be there?"

"Yes. I can arrange that. Rollo, you can be there. Santi, too. It might take a few weeks until they can find her. According to my ground troops, it's worse than you can imagine. Bas was an unchecked madman with extraordinary power for decades. He's left a breathtaking trail of destruction wherever he's gone," she said sadly, taking in a deep, shaking breath. "Rollo, it's not just that she may be crazy. You have to consider her suffering. Will she be capable of enjoying life? Death Time may help her heal her mind. She was a good person. My understanding from you is that Death Time only destroy destructive minds. A broken mind wouldn't be the same thing. She may be healed and have peace if allowed to die. She'd also be able to find her loved ones who are in the present over there. Your brother, for instance. Think about that while we look for her."

Rollo looked miserable, but nodded that he understood what she was telling him.

"Lua Pele and The Continent have decided to outlaw most of the technology Bas used to do all of this. We're going to destroy everything except basic travel passes. Get people from point A to point B in current time. No more going to the past. No more Rewinds. Everything else is too easily corrupted for bad use. Time will be unbound as soon as possible. I can only hope Time will protect Time's self better after this. Not be so trusting of us.

"After Bas is killed, I'm going to drop my wall and my lock. Destroy Professor Patel's research. We'll burn Bas's Kingdom to the ground. Scorched earth. We have to ensure we destroy all the tech floating around inside his Kingdom. Same with Jorge's, once we end the suffering of your people in torture.

"The Continent has asked me to ask Time to let them remain unhidden. We can give the rest of Earth's survivors two places to navigate to if they want. Staying anywhere on earth that's unlocked is always an option. Stay at Ivy. Whatever. Go anywhere you want, but we feel that inviting survivors into our cities will help us all become one supportive community aware of our shared history. We need to learn from this."

Rollo looked for reassurance from Pele, telling her, "But, no one from Bas's Kingdom can be saved. They're all complicit. I told you this already. You can't..."

Pele interrupted him, saying, "You're correct. I thought I was being clear. No one from Bas's Kingdom will be allowed to live. Lacy, the nine or so surviving opposition members, and you three. Maren, Olivia, Gorman, and Bautista are also protected. Maren, Bautista, and Gorman are already back at Ivy. We haven't found Olivia yet."

Lev felt like he was the only emotionally stable adult in the trio and spoke to Rollo and Kali. "Ok, you two? Let's go get some drinks and then some rest. Pele's going to get us back to Ivy tomorrow. That was a really good call, baby," he said as he put an arm around her shoulder. "Come on. Let's go." He said to Pele, "We'll be ready to head back to Ivy early tomorrow, Pele. East coast time, early."

"Ok. I'll be ready," Pele assured them.

"Thanks, Pele," Kali said as she turned away and left with Lev and a still brooding Rollo.

Kali and Lev in the Hotel

The driver took them to the hotel Pele had arranged for them to stay at and Kali asked Lev, "Do you know where we are?"

Lev pointed to a volcano in the distance and said, "I've been here before. I told you when we swapped vacation stories walking to get the tech you brought Ivy. That's Mount Rainier. We're in Seattle," he said confidently.

"I think traveling can still be a problem," Kali said, sounding worried.

"Don't worry. I heard her say it, too. I'm gonna get back to the RT and we're gonna make sure we can put psychopath safety locks on any travel device Pele thinks is safe to put into the hands of people."

"Right?" said Rollo. "First thing I thought was degenerate motherfuckers are gonna travel right into bedrooms and other places they shouldn't be," he said annoyed and shaking his head in disgust.

"You've been around a lot of degenerates stuck in Bas's Kingdom all these years, but people on the outside are a little more civilized," Lev said to him reassuringly.

"People," said Kali with concern.

"We'll make it so you can only travel to a designated street corner. Like traveling bus stops. Very public," said Lev.

"Oh, that's a good idea," said Kali, nodding.

"Yeah," said Rollo. "I like that."

"No one's taking any more people with the tech," he said reassuringly to Kali as he wrapped his arm around her shoulders.

Pele had arranged for them to stay in two separate top floor suites with floor spaces that took up the entire top floor of the luxury hotel. They were essentially expansive one bedroom apartments with panoramic views of Seattle and the various landscapes surrounding the city. They had exclusive access to the rooftop patio and spa and a dedicated 24 hour staff to respond to all of their needs.

Rollo headed to his suite and told Lev and Kali he'd come by when he was done showering. He wanted out of the suit he was wearing and to wash away every reminder of Bas's party and Bas's Kingdom, from his body. Lev told him to give them a little extra time, and Rollo nodded as he closed the door to his room.

Kali and Lev walked down the long hallway to the other side of the top floor to their own suite. Inside, they found walk-in closets with a variety of clothing options, a stocked bar, a stocked kitchen and more.

"I'm not cooking tonight," Lev said, looking at the contents of the full refrigerator. He turned around and noted, "This hotel room must be 5,000 square feet."

"My family's loaded and powerful," Kali bragged jokingly.

"Oooh, I married into money?" asked Lev as he wrapped his arms around her and moved himself against her.

"Ow. Yeah," she said, laughing at him and hugging him back but pulling away from him at the same time.

"Can I see what's wrong or no?" he asked her kindly, helping to keep their hug away from the lower part of her body.

"I'm not crazy about you seeing it," she said, shaking her head and looking uneasy.

Lev sighed. "Are you upset that I asked? I'll shut up about it if you want me to, but I need to know if you're ok," he said with concern, looking down at her face.

"I think it's gonna upset you, and I don't... Then it's like, who's more upset, me or you? That sounds fucking mean. You can be upset. I'm used to doing this on my own," she said, annoyed with herself for her thoughts. She continued anyway. "Or, you're going to want me to talk about it when I might want to shove it deep down inside of me and ignore it. Or you're gonna try to be nice to me and that's going to make me feel worse because maybe I don't even want to feel the emotions. None of them. You know? I might not want to make myself or you feel better. I usually just focus on the physical pain. Then, I don't have to feel emotions. You might expect me to feel emotions. I do. I just do it my own way--"

Lev laughed lightly as he interrupted her. "Ok. You. Stop. How about this? It happened to you. What happens to you, affects me. So, you can't get rid of my part. But, I'll listen to you, and whatever you say about it now, you can say entirely contrary things anytime later if your feelings change."

Kali nodded. "So, if I'm not mad now, I can throw my drink at a wall later?"

"Exactly," said Lev, smiling.

"God, that's the kind of support I really fucking need right now because... It's bullshit what he did!" she said loudly, looking up at him in visceral anger.

Lev noticed her sudden flash of anger and realized he was in uncharted territory with her. He'd seen her in any variety of upset, but he'd never been with her after she'd been physically tortured.

"Ok. I'm as prepared as I can be. But you still don't have to tell me or show me. Do what helps you."

Kali looked pensive and said, "It was terrible. It fucked me up to be back there with him, but it also felt so normal. I've spent more than half of my life with him. I thought I might end up being there forever even though I had a plan to get out."

Lev didn't like the sound of that and struggled to respond. "Kali--"

She closed her eyes and held up her hand stopping him from continuing. "I actually don't want to discuss it even if I want to say some things out loud."

"Ok. I get that. We're doing this together which is different for you. I want to be a part of the healing process, physical and emotional. Let me know what helps you," he said, nodding his head reassuringly at her.

"Ok, I accept this will be different than I'm used to. I'm going to need new bandages."

"See? I can help with that. I'll call down for the bandages. Can you be more specific?"

"Extra-large gauze pads, and tape, and some medicine," she said.

"What kind of medicine? I want to ask for what you need and get it right the first time," he said.

"Something for burns."

Lev winced and swore in a whisper then closed his eyes and nodded as she continued.

"I don't know what Lua Pele has. This city looks really modern, though. Maybe they can travel to the past and go to a pharmacy? Or maybe they have what I need." She looked at him and sighed. "How about I show you what I need this stuff for, and then maybe you decide by discussing it with the hotel staff? Find out what they have available. That's me saying I'll show you if you want to see it. Like an excuse to show you, because I don't know how to ask you to look at what he did to me. I don't know if it's wrong of me to show you. I don't know how you're going to react. I don't know what to do. Maybe you shouldn't see it," she said, looking at him nervously.

Lev nodded quickly. "Alright. I like the plan where I'm better informed. I want to see so I can help you," he said, trying to remain calm despite feeling anxious about how he was going to control his anger once she showed him what Bas had done to her.

"Let's go to the bathroom. I need a shower anyway," she said as she turned and headed towards the bathroom, determined to get it over with quickly.

Lev followed her silently, reminding himself it wouldn't help her if he punched a wall.

The master bathroom suite was very large and included a separate sitting area with a couch, tables, and an elaborate vanity station. Kali looked around the bathroom and headed into the open area that contained the couch.

She turned around to let Lev unzip her dress and said, "Listen, if you don't want to be around it, if you're uncomfortable, just leave. You can tell me that. Let's be honest with each other no matter what. I'd understand. I really would."

"Do you need to see a doctor?" he asked her quietly and calmly as he unhooked the top of the dress and pulled the zipper down slowly.

"No. It'll heal. It's just really fucking fucked up," she said, shaking her head.

He tried to recall a time when she sounded so anxious revealing her body to him, but couldn't. "I'm ready to see this really fucking fucked up thing that was done to you," he said, kissing the scar of the word MINE on her right shoulder.

Kali turned around to him and said, "I think you should sit here on the couch. I'll stand. It's kinda low down low on my stomach."

Lev sat down and watched as Kali roughly removed her arms from the long sleeves of the dress quickly and then slid the rest of the dress off letting it fall to the floor before kicking it away from herself in disgust.

He found himself staring at a large white gauze pad taped across her lower abdomen below her belly button. She didn't waste any time and quickly pulled a corner of the tape and then worked the rest of the tape free from her skin.

Lev inhaled sharply and swallowed hard, saying, "Ok. Fuck. Baby, I... Hold on..." He reached for her hips and leaned forward and kissed her well above the cigarette burn wounds which read 'HIS' in large thick letters below her belly button. Each burn wound was circled in red skin and her flesh was terribly burned within each circle, if not entirely gone altogether in some. The entire wound rested on top of many older scars and stood out in contrast to her older white scars.

He felt her hands on the sides of his head as he pulled back and looked in shock at her wounds again as he sat on the couch. She remained silent as he looked at what Bas had done to her.

He suddenly stood up quickly and sniffed loudly, and cleared his throat saying, "Well, that fucking happened. Would it be alright with you if I was the one who killed him tomorrow? Or do you want to do it?"

Kali tipped her head at him and smiled and said quietly, "I don't want to kill him."

"Yeah. I understand. I get that," he said, nodding seriously and sniffing again to stop himself from being unavailable to her.

He tried to think of what she needed and said, "Baby, this must hurt really bad. There are two rows of burns for each letter." Lev held her face in his hands and closed his eyes as he pressed his forehead against hers. He was speechless, but fought to find words. "You need some pain reliever, too. I'll get you some ibuprofen. You'll take that, right? There are no sedatives in that," he said quietly and nodded and kissed her. "Also, I think you need to see a doctor. There's a lot of burned skin. There's a lot of skin missing. Can I ask for a doctor? I'm not a doctor," he said quietly, feeling slightly panicked and looking at her for approval of his suggestion.

"Maybe. I need to think about it. I need a shower. I need to feel like me. He had me dressed up like this. Bleached my fucking hair again. All this makeup. My hair is piled up on top of my head the way he likes it. I don't feel like me. I need a hug. Are you ok? Do you need a hug?" she asked him suddenly, looking sad and concerned all at once.

"I'm ok. Don't worry about me. Right now you're getting a fucking hug and I'm gonna benefit from that," he said as he hugged her tightly, avoiding her uncovered burns. "I know it won't help fix this, but I'm so glad you're gonna get to see him die," he said as they hugged each other. "Let's get the rest of this crap off of you," he said as he walked in back of her and began to remove diamond and silver chains from her hair.

"Isn't it ridiculous?" she asked him, trying to see his face as he dug through her hair trying to unpin the expensive diamond accessories and updo. "He fucking smokes cigarettes on me, telling me he's inhaling my body into his and then he wraps me up in diamonds and parades himself through a crowd with me hiding the damage he's done to my body. He always makes me cover up what he's done. That's how I got him to let you and Rollo take me to the bathroom."

"How's that?" asked Lev as he continued to suppress his rage and focus on finding hairpins to release her hair.

"I told him the tape on the bandage was pulling on the dress and I was afraid I'd bleed through. So, of course, he let Rollo take me to the bathroom to fix it," she said scoffing. "Called you useless, by the way." She laughed.

"He is an idiot clown just like you said," Lev said, laughing mildly, trying to meet her emotions where they were in her process. He'd deal with his own emotions later, he told himself. "I'm gonna check for more pins in your hair," he said as he ran the fingers from both of his hands from the back of her neck up to the top of her head feeling for them.

Kali stopped talking and sighed as he did that, and he saw her shoulders lower a bit as he gently felt his way through her hair. He leaned down and kissed the back of her neck as he lifted her hair and ran his fingers through her hair a second time.

"That feels so nice, babe," she said as she leaned her head forward.

"Come here and sit down between my legs," he said and pulled her gently to the couch. He sat down and spread his legs so that she could sit between his legs on the couch. He unhooked her bra and she assisted him in the removal of it by moving her arms through the straps. He massaged her shoulders, arms, head, neck, and back and kissed her skin while telling her how happy he was to be with her again after so many months apart. After a while, he wrapped his arms around her shoulders and told her he'd order the medical supplies she needed from room service while she took a shower.

Kali got up and turned to face him and said, "Ok, but leave the bathroom door open."

"You got it," he said with a quick nod.

"Wait. What if he hasn't been captured yet and he can travel here?" she asked him, sounding genuinely concerned about the possibility.

Lev wasn't prepared for an irrational fear from her, but decided against reasoning with her.

"You know what? I can take a shower with you, or just stay right here if you need me to," he offered.

His offer didn't help her and she suddenly looked more agitated saying, "Maybe he escaped. I need a weapon."

Lev decided reasoning with her might be the better option. "Kali, listen to me," he said, standing up and taking her shoulders in his hands, "The guy has five million soldiers hunting him. He's not figuring out how to travel into Pele's locked city and then going to find you in this hotel suite."

She didn't look convinced and he suddenly remembered the time when his passport took him to his parent's house but she irrationally believed he'd been captured and taken to Bas's locked Kingdom. Dave had told him later, 'It wasn't just that she was being irrational, it was more that fear locked her into the irrationality and propelled her thoughts. I couldn't make her less afraid, so she spiraled.'

Listening to her now, Lev started to unbutton his shirt and said, "Fuck it. I'll order what you need when we're finished showering. Go on. Turn on the water. Not as hot as you like it, you lava monster." He smiled at her as he tossed his shirt onto the couch.

Kali had the water ready for them before Lev finished undressing and said, "Look, two shower heads, you snowman!"

She sounded less afraid.

The length of one wall in the large, dual shower contained a comfortable seating area. Kali sat, turned to the side, as Lev stood and took an extra-long time to wash the hairspray and other products out of her hair. She tipped her head back as he used the removable shower head to remove the shampoo and then the conditioner from her hair, making sure not to let the water flow over her exposed burns.

When he went to wash his own hair under his shower head, he watched as she was less careful with herself than he had been. The flow of water hurt her when it ran over her wounds as she tried to carefully wash each of her body parts one by one with the removable shower head.

Lev finished washing quickly and took the shower head from her. "Stop hurting my wife," he said with a joking scowl as he carefully rinsed soap off of her arm. She sighed and shook her head, giving up, and acknowledged he should be in charge of the shower head, not her. He finished helping her rinse her body and turned off the water coming from her shower head.

She handed him his towel before getting her own and said confidently, "We're gonna get drunk, and then we're gonna destroy first base tonight!"

Lev laughed at her and kissed her several times enthusiastically before saying, "I'm actually a really big fan of first base."

They toweled off and walked naked through the suite to the two walk-in closets full of clothes. Kali found soft pajama pants that would sit below her wounds and a bra that fit well enough. She involuntarily shuddered as she told Lev that she didn't want anything to do with the clothes she had been forced to wear, not even the well-fitting purple bra. Lev was still naked when he immediately walked back into the bathroom and gathered all of the clothes and accessories she'd been forced to wear for Bas's party. He dropped all of what she had been forced to wear, and what remained of his suit, in a heap on the floor in the hallway outside the door to their room so she wouldn't have to see any of it ever again. He got dressed quickly and called for the medical supplies she needed, and then she heard him request a person to come remove the items he'd put outside their door.

She found a soft bathrobe and put it on but had to leave it open while she waited for her new bandages to be delivered.

Kali, Lev, Rollo, and a Guest

There was a knock on the door while Lev finished his call to the hotel staff, and Kali got up to answer it believing it would be Rollo.

"Who's there?" shouted Lev, before she reached the door.

"It's me, man. And I have a guest. Open up!" said Rollo.

Kali looked at Lev and realized he was on edge despite appearances. She opened the door as Lev walked up behind her and saw Rollo's excited face as he motioned for them to look down at his side where Santi was standing, smiling happily.

Lev and Kali exclaimed their excitement at the unexpected appearance of Santi and their happiness for Rollo being reunited with his wife. They ushered them into their suite and Santi immediately noticed Kali's attire was loosely covering an injury.

"Let me see," said Santi, pointing at Kali's stomach.

"This is good. Now, you're seeing a doctor," Lev said to Kali.

"Ok, but in the bathroom. It's not a secret, Rollo. Bas burned me this morning-- "

"Son of a bitch!" said Rollo, instantly furious and going towards her.

"No. None of that. Please. I'm dealing with me. Lev's dealing with me, too, actually. You're off the hook for this one. Stay happy. It helps me be happy. Lev, can you make me a fun drink? A big one. We'll be right back," she said.

"What do you mean by a fun drink?" he asked her, confused, but willing.

"Something mixed. Put a cherry in it," she said, as she and Santi headed off to the bathroom.

"Make me the same thing she's having," said Santi.

Lev looked around the bar and told Rollo what Bas did to Kali because she had said it wasn't a secret. He asked him not to bring it up while they celebrated, but to just have a good fucking time for a change.

"How're you dealing, man?" Rollo asked him, sounding concerned about his friend after listening to him speak in calm tones about the horrific injury done to Kali.

Lev suddenly stood still and said darkly through clenched teeth, "I want to be the one to kill him tomorrow."

He was holding a glass and suddenly let go of it quickly looking down at it as he lifted his hand away from it. Rollo walked up to the bar and moved the glass away from Lev realizing he'd almost broken it in his hand. He filled the glass with the nearest alcohol, which was bourbon, and handed it to Lev with a silent nod.

Lev drank what Rollo had poured for him, breathed deeply and finally said, "I can't talk about it right now. I'm trying not to make this about me. I'd have wrecked this place like a coked out rock star by now if I was making it about me. I'm in such a fucking rage, man. I need to drink more." He nodded at Rollo and handed him his empty glass.

Rollo refilled Lev's glass and got himself a glass and poured himself a drink while Lev quickly downed his second glass. "We're gonna change the subject for now, man," Rollo said as he lifted his own glass to Lev.

Lev nodded and Rollo refilled his glass again. He asked Rollo about Santi being in Lua Pele in an effort to change the subject, but also because he was interested in how she had gotten to the hotel. Rollo told him she had been in the suite waiting for him to arrive. Apparently, Pele had sent some escorts to Ivy to ask her if she wanted to stay with him and, according to Santi, she wanted to go, but was afraid it was a trick until Pele went to Ivy personally and assured her Bas was no longer a threat and she could come spend at least a night, if not forever, with him in Lua Pele. He laughed at the thought. "We could actually do that, you know? Move here. I've been in Bas's Kingdom for almost 30 years. It all finally changed in an instant, but for the better. I'm so used to things going to shit in an instant," he said reflectively.

"I'm really glad Doc is here with you, man," Lev said, raising his glass of bourbon.

"Yeah, well, I've been thinking, and I want a divorce," Rollo said, and they both laughed.

"You got it, man! I'm cheating on you anyway!" Lev told him with a shrug while they continued to laugh.

"Mm, I know what I'm gonna make," he said suddenly.

Lev called down to the hotel staff again and asked if ginger beer was available in Lua Pele.

Rollo drank and listened to Lev's conversation with the front desk.

"Really? How are they packaged? Yeah, send me up two four packs. No, wait. Send me three four packs. Do you have that many? Great. You got limes?" he asked the person on the phone. "I need those, too. You got copper mugs?" Lev appeared to wait for the answer to that last question. "Yeah, send me up four of those. Do you have maraschino cherries? ...Yeah, no. I didn't think so.... Sure, I'll take any cherries. Frozen's fine. Thanks."

Lev hung up and Rollo asked him, "What the fuck are you cooking up over there?"

"Moscow mules," said Lev. "The woman said they have loads of breweries and kombucha and ginger beer is everywhere just like the old days. Not a fucking problem. She said Lua Pele extends through all of Oregon and into parts of Idaho. Fucking learned more from the concierge than from Pele. Fucking kombucha. You and Doc should consider moving here. You've already gotten a personal invitation from the Queen of this Kingdom. Is it a Queendom, then?" he asked, nodding approvingly of the idea.

"I'll go wherever Santi wants to go," said Rollo smiling, adding, "Let's call Lua Pele a Queendom. I'm so fucking sick of referring to Bas's Kingdom." He sounded exhausted.

Kali and Santi reemerged and Santi asked where the phone was so she could call down to the hotel staff. Lev showed her and she called and asked them to send some other medical supplies she felt would benefit the healing of Kali's wounds.

After she hung up, she said, "We're taking all of that back with us to Ivy tomorrow so Kali has it while she heals. I'm so glad we get to kill him." She shook her head in disgust while looking off into the distance.

"Where are our drinks, babe?" Kali asked, looking confused as she approached Lev.

"Your bartender is making special drinks that require some ingredients to be delivered. Will you share a glass of bourbon with your husband while you wait?"

Kali walked up to him and took the glass he was offering her and took two big gulps, finishing what was in his glass. "Jesus, finally. Longest wait for a drink ever!" she said loudly while Lev took his empty glass back from her and scowled jokingly at how much she had drunk.

He grabbed the bottle of bourbon and refilled his glass and then another while telling Santi her drink appetizer was ready. Rollo got up and got Santi's drink from the bar and walked back to sit beside her, handing her her drink. He was rewarded with a kiss and put his arm around her shoulders telling her how happy he was that she was with him. Kali watched Rollo interacting with Santi and smiled over at Lev who was looking at her. She had never seen Rollo so happy in all the years she had known him.

Pele's News

There was a knock at the door and Lev went to answer it thinking it would be the food and drink supplies he had requested, but he was surprised to see Pele instead.

Pele made no motion to enter the room and disturb their casual celebration, but remained in the hallway and said, "Hi. I'm not trying to be nosey, but the hotel manager contacted me and said you guys ordered a lot of medical supplies. I don't need details unless you want to give them to me, but I want to make sure you're all ok. We have hospitals. I can get you any treatment you need."

"It's me. But I'm fine. Santi looked at me. I don't want to discuss it. But I'm fine. It's private," Kali said, holding her robe closed so Pele couldn't see her exposed burns.

Kali looked intent on guarding her privacy from her, so she nodded and said, "Ok. I won't ask for more information. Is there anything any of you need that we didn't supply?" she asked as she was leaving.

Rollo said, "Everything's great, Pele. You even brought me my wife! Thank you!"

"I'm really glad you trusted me, Santi," said Pele, looking at her. She turned to Kali and said, "Anything at all."

Kali hesitated then said, "It's very superficial, and I don't want to sound shallow, but do you have brown hair dye?"

Pele nodded. "I'll get that for you. I know what he did. You're not being shallow."

They all told Pele that everything else was wonderful, and Pele looked satisfied as she left.

Lev was closing the door when Pele's phone rang and she said, "Hold on Lev. This is my guy."

Lev walked away from the door but left it open and headed to the bar where he poured two more drinks. He walked over to Kali and handed her one of them and kissed her forehead without saying anything and then took the other to the door and waited for Pele to finish her phone call. All four of them waited in silence as Pele spoke in quiet tones in the hallway. She hung up and looked up at Lev and smiled.

He smiled back at her and handed her the full glass of bourbon nodding his head saying loudly, "Yeah! Come on inside and toast this moment with us!"

With Pele in the room, they all stood up and asked her to tell them what she knew.

570

Pele was smiling and breathless as she said, "They caught him. He was hiding, like the coward he is, in the woods on his property. They'd lit it on fire and he came running out begging for mercy until he started telling them how he could make them all Kings just like him. Offered them power and Kingdoms of their own." Pele scoffed disgustedly. "Bas doesn't know the people from the continent. I gave them tours of the hell on earth he created. They're not reluctant soldiers fighting some politician's war. They know exactly what he is, what he did, and what he was going to do to them next.

"They also found Olivia. They sent her to our hospital, but I'm not sure what her injuries are."

Kali asked, "Is Time free?"

"Not yet. I'm going there right now, though."

"Where's Bas?" Kali asked and gasped for air as she finished the question.

Lev put his arm around her shoulders and Pele said, "I think you'll approve. He's going to be turned over to Dave and Bolin. I went and spoke to them personally after you asked me to bring him to Ivy. They're waiting on news of his capture. I'll let them know he's been captured in a minute. They sounded ready to put him in your prison upon arrival. There were more volunteers from my army willing to escort him and stay at Ivy than Ivy could possibly accommodate." Pele smiled approvingly. "My guy said thousands responded to the request for a hundred soldiers to guard Bas at Ivy before they put out a notice that they had more than enough volunteers.

"That's good," said Lev, nodding along with the others.

"Ivy's currently hosting a hundred of my combined troops under the command of Bolin and Dave. He's not going anywhere except to his execution."

Everyone was happy to hear the good news and they asked Rollo to toast the moment.

He raised his glass and said, "We've captured Bas. That's worth celebrating. Now let's free our friend Time. Time, Pele's coming to release Time, my friend. Kali and I would really like it if Time could let us, or even one of us know, Time's ok the minute Time can!" he concluded with a deep intake of breath that resulted in him becoming choked up. Santi rubbed Rollo's arm and whispered something in his ear before kissing his cheek, and he smiled at her and nodded.

"I'm drinking to that," said Lev and held up his glass where all immediately tapped his glass with their own.

They all took big sips of their bourbon with Lev saying, "To Time!"

Pele shook her head and said, "I'm going to go free Time now. I'm sorry for the role I played in all of this--"

Kali interrupted her saying, "Let's focus on the good things, tonight. My mood is fragile, if I'm being honest, and I want to stay happy."

"I understand. Too much for one day. I'll let you get back to your celebration," Pele said, putting down her drink.

Lev Arranges a Dinner Party

The items Lev had requested were being walked into their suite as Pele left. Santi went through the medical supplies for Kali and was busy separating out what she wanted to treat Kali with now.

"What're you making?" Kali asked Lev as she pointed to the packs of ginger beer on the bar.

"Moscow mules. You ever have one?"

"Hmm. No, but it sounds very much like a recipe you got from your mom," Kali said, smiling.

"This is part of my heritage, baby," he said as he removed a glass bottle of hand-crafted ginger beer from a box.

"The food you ordered smells good. Did you order a traditional Russian meal to go with the drinks?" she asked him as he began to prepare to make the Moscow mules.

"Go see," he said, smiling.

Kali lifted some of the lids of the food that had been wheeled in on the serving cart.

"Lev, is this a California burrito?!" she asked excitedly.

"Yeah, but wait," he said as he cut a lime. "They didn't have avocados, so they won't be perfect, but I --"

Kali grabbed him in a tight hug, careful not to press her burns against him and he hugged her back quickly still holding onto the knife while she told him how great he was.

"This is going to be the best California burrito I've ever had. Definitely my new favorite," she said, standing on her toes and motioning for him to come down to her for kisses she wanted to give him.

Lev obliged. "I'm gonna get you one with avocado next time," he said with confidence.

Kali shrugged, "And I'm sure it will be delicious, but this one's still gonna be my favorite. You know, because of the memory," she told him.

"Mine, too," he agreed.

Santi and Kali headed into the bathroom and quickly covered Kali's wounds using the medical products that had been delivered.

Santi seethed as she applied the antibiotic ointment to Kali's burned skin and said, "Death is too good for that fucker. How the hell are you coping?" she asked Kali.

"Lev's a pretty calming influence, actually. I was afraid he'd punch a wall or something, but he's got calm enough for the both of us to share tonight. I'll have to check if he's ok later, but for now, when I feel like I'm suffocating, I look at him, and I remember to breathe.

Santi nodded grimly.

"Did I ever tell you how Lev and I met?" she asked her.

"No," Kali said, shaking her head.

Santi proceeded to tell Kali how Lev had saved her from a two year long imprisonment after the initial extinction event.

"My scars are inside. Nowhere near as bad as yours, though. I had four older brothers growing up. I guess they all died when Bas killed everyone. Lev found me the day I was rescued. It was like I got all four of them back again."

Kali looked at Santi and said, "I knew you and I spoke the same language."

Santi understood what she meant.

Kali hung the bathrobe and found a soft, loose-fitting black t-shirt to wear.

While Kali and Rollo wheeled the food carts into the large formal dining room and brought plates to the table, Santi approached Lev and said, "She'll be ok. It's a lot to heal, but Lua Pele has a real hospital if she needs more help recovering."

Lev nodded at her, grateful she had shown up and was able to look at Kali's injuries. "Thanks, Doc. I'm really glad you're here."

Lev went to Kali and handed her her Moscow mule and waited for her to taste it.

"Mmmm. This is my new favorite drink replacing any previous favorite drinks," she said to him confidently with a wave of her hand. "But carrot wine's still my favorite wine. That's different," she said, as she took another sip of her mule. "Seriously, this is fucking delicious. James needs to make these. I wonder if he's ever had one?" she mused aloud as she took another sip.

Lev pointed to her copper mug. "And look, a frozen cherry. They didn't have the maraschino kind, but Washington state is famous for cherries. I almost always get my wife what she requests," he said proudly.

Kali laughed at him but agreed wholeheartedly and wrapped her arm around his lower back and gently ran her hand back and forth absently while they sipped their drinks.

They looked out of the large windows in the dining room, down at the city, drinking their mules together and she said, "The sun is going to set in a few minutes, and it looks really clear out. Let's go to the rooftop area later tonight after Santi and Rollo leave and look at our night sky together."

Lev agreed. "Let's do that," he said, looking at her reflection in the large windows rather than looking at the city.

Rollo and Santi approved of the Moscow mules Lev made for them, and the four of them sat down at one end of the large formal dining room table that had room enough for 12 guests. Lev had ordered six burritos for them for dinner. Lev and Kali told Rollo and Santi about the California burrito competition they'd had before they knew each other.

"Did you know then?" asked Santi, smiling at him.

"No. You didn't know her back then. She was extremely confusing. All I knew was that I was confused, too." He laughed and looked over at Kali. "But, that's when I first knew that I wanted her to stay around. I decided I wanted to make room for her at Ivy even if she was crazy. I was making a plan to let her roam around Ivy and do whatever she wanted. Thought maybe she'd want to go surfing with me in Virginia Beach," he said seriously, but with a small laugh, as he recalled the moment.

Kali smiled back at him as she, too, recalled their early conversations as they got to know one another.

"I think he knew. He's just a little stubborn," Santi said, shaking her head at Rollo.

"Lev? Stubborn? What?!" Rollo asked jokingly through a mouthful of burrito.

Their burritos were really good despite the lack of avocado, and Lev and Rollo each ate two. Rollo and Lev finished their small copper mugs of mules quickly and Rollo left and returned wheeling in a cart containing all of the ingredients to make more. He also brought back two large glasses from the kitchen so that he and Lev could make themselves drinks that wouldn't need to be refilled so frequently. Lev taught them all how to make their own while making himself one.

They went back to the living room where they continued to drink and catch up and Santi asked about Pele being Kali's mother. "Her name was Rachael. Why is she going by Pele? She does look a little Hawaiian," said Santi.

"I'll tell you what I was told, but I'm going to have to confirm my family tree with Pele at some point later. I don't know if what I know is bullshit."

"Yeah, tell us whatever you know," said Rollo.

"I want to know what you believe now, so that when you get it confirmed, or get entirely new information, I'll know where you're coming from," said Lev.

"It's got to be frustrating. Tell us what you think the backstory is," agreed Santi.

"My grandparents were Amanda, a tourist from San Diego, who went to visit Oahu, and Malulani, a surf shop owner from Oahu. They met at his surf shop, hit it off, she stayed in Hawaii, they got married, and had Rachael. I knew they moved to San Diego eventually, but that's all I knew. I don't think I ever met them. I still don't even know how she's related to Jorge. Are they really related? Are they twins? I don't fucking know," she said, shaking her head. "Yeah, you three look like you thought I knew more." Kali laughed. "Oh, wait. I know that Rachael died in a car accident when I was seven. I was traumatized. I'll need to speak to her about that," Kali said reflectively with a touch of anger in her voice.

Lev took her copper mug from her hand and made her another drink without being asked, and she looked at him and said appreciatively, "Thanks babe," before drinking it quickly.

"Pele was the Hawaiian goddess of volcanoes and fire. Washington has a lot of volcanoes. Probably why she picked this as her space to lock," Lev said.

"Why do you know that?" asked Kali, confused but smiling at him.

"My dad. He was into goddesses," he said with a small laugh, looking at her affectionately.

"Pele doesn't look old enough to be your mother," said Santi.

"Rachael-Pele looks barely older than me!" said Kali, laughing. She should be in her 70's like Bas."

"He stopped aging for vanity. Maybe Pele stopped aging so she could keep fighting him," suggested Rollo in an effort to find a reasonable explanation for Pele's youthful appearance.

"I think Pele participated in causing all of this destruction and hasn't paid a high enough price for what everyone else had to go through as a result," said Kali, displaying an increasingly angry tone.

"She comes across as haunted to me," said Santi quietly.

"Good," said Kali.

Lev suddenly slapped his leg. "On that note, let's all take our asses to bed. We've got a not-exactly immortal demon to execute tomorrow, and I cannot wait," he said, sounding exhausted beneath the hopeful tone he was using.

"Yeah, it's early, but I'm still operating on east coast time," said Rollo, looking at Santi.

She agreed. "Same. That clock says it's 8pm, but I feel the full 11pm in that number."

Lev and Kali's Night Sky

Kali put the long bathrobe back on for warmth, and Lev grabbed a jacket and a blanket from the closet. The elevator in their room took them up to the rooftop deck where the cold March air greeted them.

Lev turned around once looking at the night sky and said, "There's our sky. Come here." He took her hand and walked to a large outdoor sofa and turned it so it faced the correct direction in the sky. "Help me be careful with you," he said as they sat together on the couch and got comfortable.

Kali pushed her bare feet under Lev's legs and Lev reclined a bit so that she could rest on him with his arms around her to keep her warm. They arranged the blanket snuggly around them and took a minute to warm themselves up under it.

"I looked every night," she said to him while they gazed up at the night sky together.

"Me, too," he said as he stroked her arm under the blanket.

"Even on rainy nights," she said defiantly.

"Me, too, because I figured you would," he admitted with a smile and a small laugh.

Kali kissed him and said, "It might not have been raining where you were. I didn't want you to look alone."

"Thank you. Do you want to go to the white house and look at the stars from there after we get back?"

"Yeah, let's do that."

Inside the hotel bedroom, Lev and Kali laid down on the bed together, fully dressed, in the dark. Lev moved his body up against Kali's as she lay on her back, following Santi's advice about how best to heal. The cold March air on the rooftop of the hotel had chilled them both.

"You warm enough?" he asked while pulling the thick comforter and sheets up over them.

"Yes," she said as he draped his arm over her chest.

He found her feet with one of his own and said, "No shoes tonight. No more shoes in bed ever again."

Kali turned onto her side to look at him.

"Santi said to sleep on your back," he said, scolding her.

"I like my sister-in-law and respect her medical advice, but I'm sleeping on my side facing you and my arm's gonna be around here..." she said as she moved her left arm around his side. "...and my leg will be here," she said as she lifted her leg over his.

"Ok, and can we be close enough to kiss?" he asked as he pulled her closer to him.

"I was already on my way," she said as she leaned forward to kiss him.

They laid in bed talking for a little while before Kali fell asleep. She told Lev how James had taught her how to make vodka from potatoes, and he was genuinely impressed.

"When we get back to Ivy, I'll give you the bottle of vodka I made for you. I made a bunch, but the first bottle I made was put aside for when you got back. By the way, I can make wine, too. I made a lot of pumpkin wine," she said proudly.

Lev shook his head in amazement. "Ok, so I'm fine with you not learning how to cook food. I'll do all the cooking. You just keep up the production of alcohol."

"I will. It's fun, actually, and it's a legitimate hobby," she said, smiling sleepily with her eyes closed. She was obviously very tired.

"Are you worried about sleeping with the doors and windows closed?" he asked her gently.

"I'm trying not to be," she said, opening her tired eyes to look at him.

"Ok. I'll stay awake until you fall asleep," he said, moving closer to her and kissing her. "Go ahead and close your eyes. I've got you," he said quietly as he rubbed her back.

Later, Lev looked at her sleeping peacefully inches from him and let himself feel the rage he had been holding back.

He couldn't wait to kill Bas.

576

Kali woke up to a voice speaking her name quietly.

"Time?" she whispered.

"Yes."

"Is Time free?"

"Yes."

"I'm so happy for Time, but I'm going to miss Time."

"Time will always listen for Time's friends."

"Ok. That makes me happy."

"Time will talk more later."

"Ok."

Kali laid in bed looking at Lev while he slept. Nothing had seemed certain until Time had spoken to her. Now she believed. Time was free. Time didn't say goodbye. She smiled at the thought of her friend finally being free.

She got up quietly to look for the brown hair dye Pele had gotten for her the night before. She looked through the items that had been delivered and found five boxes of brown hair dye. Pele had made sure to include different shades. That was thoughtful, but hardly enough to alleviate the anger she felt towards the woman.

She went into the bathroom and looked at her blonde reflection. It sickened her to see herself the way Bas preferred. She wasn't his toy. He was a grown man playing with her like she was his personal dress-up doll. Ripping her head off when she didn't please him. Ripping her arms and legs from their sockets when she spoke out of turn, or breathed in a way that irritated him. She was excited to have the hair dye and the ability to get rid of the blonde version of herself. He should see the real her when he was executed, not the human toy he'd tortured for decades.

She mixed the dye and applied it to her hair. She had to wait for 30 minutes before she could wash her hair and see the results. She remembered that Bas was in a cage at Ivy. She pictured it in her mind. She imagined he was furious and ranting uncontrollably at Dave and Bolin, demanding his freedom and threatening them. It made her laugh. She actually wanted to see how Dave interacted with Bas.

She took a deep breath as she stared at her reflection in the mirror and then walked into the kitchen to see if there was coffee. There was. Pele and the hotel staff had made sure to consider all of their needs. She didn't know how to use the coffee machine, so she called down to the hotel staff and asked for coffee and two breakfasts to be sent up to their room. "Don't knock. Don't come in. My husband is sleeping. Leave it outside the door. I'll look for it in a bit," she told the man on the other end of the line.

She decided not to endure a second shower, and washed her hair in the large kitchen sink rather than risk water getting on her burns again. After her hair was washed, she went back into the bathroom where she brushed her hair straight down. She couldn't tell what her hair looked like yet, because it was still wet, but it was very dark brown and she already liked it.

She changed her bandage and applied ointment as Santi had instructed her to do. She looked at her wounds. The memories of Bas casually torturing her enraged her. She hadn't felt rage at him for years. The rage usually had no place to go. She had given up at some point. This time was different. She felt like she had woken up from a deep sleep and could suddenly identify the man who had been torturing her for decades. She didn't want to put this latest scarring behind her and move on. All the times she had denied herself the right to be enraged were coming back to her.

She looked at herself in the mirror. "You're not his prisoner anymore," she told herself quietly and considered her new reality.

She looked in the hallway and discovered their coffee and breakfasts had been delivered. The hotel staff had gone all out and included a flower arrangement, a copy of the local newspaper, two carafes of real coffee, and all the rest one could hope for. It still didn't compare to the breakfast James and Bolin had surprised them with the morning after they had gotten married.

She sat in the dining room by herself and drank her coffee while looking out at the dark outline of the mountain Lev had told her was Mount Rainier against the clear, starry night. She pulled a dining room chair through the hotel rooms to a different set of panoramic windows and put her bare feet up on them in front of her as she contemplated what she could see of the landscape in the darkness. She had never been to Washington. She wanted to see more. She moved her chair to look out the windows that offered her a panoramic view of the downtown city. Street lamps illuminated the quiet streets.

She felt some growing rage for Pele building up inside her. Pele didn't deserve to live here.

Her hair was dry and full now. In the bathroom, she looked at her reflection and felt a moment of stunned silence envelop her.

"There you are," she said quietly.

"There you are," Lev agreed as he walked up behind her. "Your hair looks great. I really like it," he said as he kissed the top of her head.

"I haven't had brown hair in 25 years."

"If I could kill him twice today, I would," Lev said in a serious tone while looking at her face in the reflection of the mirror. "You feel more like yourself, now?"

"Yeah, I do."

"I fucking love it," he said as moved her hair away from her neck and kissed her skin.

Kali closed her eyes and tipped her head a bit to encourage more kisses. "Mmmm, you might be underestimating how good this feels," she said quietly as his hands moved along her body while he continued to kiss the back and side of her neck.

He began to massage one of her breasts inside her open robe and kissed her shoulder saying, "I'm not trying to be pushy, I'm just a husband who wants to fuck his wife, and I'm going to stop right now." He stepped away from her and shook his head rapidly while exhaling sharply with his eyes closed for a second. "Ok. Sorry. I'm a fucking animal. Let's go have coffee."

Kali laughed at him and said, "I'm fine with a plan that involves fucking first and coffee second."

Lev shook his head, pointed at her stomach and said, "No, we need to wait until you're better. Coffee first. I need to wake up. Talk about how you're doing."

Kali scoffed at him. "I can't wait. Why do I have to wait? I'm fine. I can think of a dozen positions where this isn't an issue. In fact, I've got a few favorites in mind," she said as she ran her hands up Lev's chest.

"The shower water hurt," he said as he wrapped his arms lightly around her waist.

"That was yesterday," she said dismissively.

"Hey, now. I don't want to hurt you," he said in a serious tone, raising his eyebrows.

Kali smiled lightly at him and took on a more serious tone and nodded. "I know. I don't want you to, either. I wouldn't let that happen. I'd tell you if I was uncomfortable. Maybe we can just lie down together and see what happens," she said, shrugging hopefully.

Lev nodded. "I prefer that plan. Coffee first, then we lie down and see if we can get to second base. I'm fine with hanging out at first base with you, though. Save the acrobatics for next week."

Kali laughed. "Ok, come on. I ordered us breakfast. And just so you know, I'm not waiting a week to have sex with you."

As Lev finished his coffee and the window tour of Seattle that Kali wanted him to see, he said, "Look at all the lights around the city."

"I noticed that, too. The streets of Bas's Kingdom weren't well lit. Everything was dark after the sun set. The research labs and his mansion had most of the power. There were no hotels like this one. No cars on the streets like we saw yesterday."

"Yeah, Bas wasn't trying to lead a civilization. He's a megalomaniac who wants to be the last man standing, knowing everyone else died to serve him or they were killed because they displeased him," said Lev seriously.

Kali nodded but stared silently at the lights on the city streets below.

"I know you're not happy with Pele, and I'm not saying anything about forgiving her or whatever, but this is the Kingdom she's been overseeing. It doesn't seem like a cruel place."

Kali sighed. "I know. But you should know, I already felt a surge of serious hostility towards her this morning."

"Oh. Ok. Good to know, actually. Hey, we can talk. I mean, I think right now all either of us has is questions, but we can talk about the questions you have and try to organize what you need to know from her."

Kali squinted at him. "You're so analytical. I was thinking of punching her in the face."

Lev laughed and took her coffee from her so he could hug her without the danger of it spilling or being thrown at a wall. They laughed and kissed and argued about who had the best approach to getting answers and satisfaction from Pele until they heard a knock on the door.

Family Tree- 4:30am PT

"Hey, we were just talking about you," Lev said with a tone that suggested not everything that had been said about her was positive. Pele looked up at him anxiously and nodded silently. He stepped out of the way, and she entered the room and looked at Kali.

She said, "Time is free. Do you want me to tell you how that went now, or would you prefer Rollo was present for the conversation?"

"I'll wait for Rollo," she said without mentioning she'd already heard from Time.

"Do you want to talk about other things?"

"Not really. I'm pretty mad," Kali said, staring at her coldly.

"I understand, but I think I can offer information that might make you feel less mad. There are plenty of reasons to be mad, mad at me specifically, but knowing more might help."

"Lev, are you willing to stay with me while Pele tries to justify what she did to me, to my dad, and to everyone else?"

"Mmm-hmm. I accept that I'm not going anywhere," he said firmly as he closed the door and walked past Pele to Kali.

Kali turned and walked to the living room and took a seat on the couch with Lev beside her. Pele sat across from them on the loveseat with the coffee table between them and looked willingly vulnerable.

Pele went to speak, but Kali asked, "Who's Jorge?"

"My cousin. My mother's sister had a drug problem. She and her boyfriend had Jorge the same month I was born. They overdosed and died together in their apartment shortly after he was born and the state was going to put him into foster care because no one from either side of the family was willing to take on a newborn baby who might have health issues or developmental issues related to the drug and alcohol use he was exposed to while his mother was pregnant with him.

"My parents decided to move from Oahu to San Diego in order to formally adopt him. They had planned to return to Oahu. They liked living in San Diego close to our grandparents and decided to stay. We were raised as twins, but we always knew our history. Jorge was fine. It turned out he didn't have any long-term problems related to either parents' drug or alcohol history."

Pele looked at Kali and appeared hopeful that her quick response would set a tone for trust.

Kali sat silently for a moment, then asked angrily, "Are you an evil bitch? Why did you align with Bas? Why did you fake your death and let me cry over my dead mother? Why did you let my father kill himself? Why did you let Bas torture me for decades? What the fuck is wrong with you?!"

Lev put his hand on Kali's back and hoped for the best. He didn't know how to calm her down at this point, but he was entirely willing to restrain her if it became necessary.

Pele looked resigned to the accusations behind the questions and didn't appear to take any personally. She nodded her head and answered Kali's questions without a hint of defensiveness, much to Lev's relief.

"Alright. I faked my death so that you and your father wouldn't be in danger. I always had guards on you, though."

"Jesus fucking Christ. My whole fucking life I've had fucking guards watching over me and my life's been bullshit anyway!" Kali yelled. "The guards didn't fucking help, mom!" she yelled at Pele.

Pele nodded. "I know. I thought when Jorge and I left Bas, he'd leave us alone. We left right at the beginning. We didn't know how things would escalate. Jorge was really the brightest of all three of us. Bas isn't that smart. We never expected him to accomplish what he accomplished. We took some of Professor Patel's information with us because Bas was talking about how we could rule the Universe with the information, but the bigger concern was that Bas would share the information with others who were brighter than him, but just as warped, not that he would actually use it effectively by himself. That didn't seem possible. Not if you knew him back then.

"Time was still free. We left to live our lives. We each got married. Jorge had two children with his wife and I had you with your father. We never imagined Bas would have any success. He didn't enjoy math, or physics, or any science when we were in classes together. He was failing his math classes in college when he went for tutoring. Jorge was earning extra money at the student tutoring center. That's how they met. They weren't friends. Bas had no friends. He was a lousy, weird, mean person. It just happened. These things, I've thought about them for decades. Bas is lucky. That's all I can think."

"So you weren't his girlfriend?" Kali asked her.

"Oh, hell no!" Pele exclaimed vehemently, clearly taken aback by the thought. "No. He was demonstrably mentally unstable even back then. Petty, jealous, easily enraged, really fragile ego. Jorge asked not to be his tutor after a few weeks working with him at the tutoring center because he said Bas was difficult to work with.

"You've only known him with power. He wasn't powerful back then, but he was hungry for power. We weren't friends with him. We just ended up in the same circle for a brief moment. The moment when we found Professor Patel's work. That was it. One goddamned moment." She shook her head as the memories overwhelmed her.

"Why'd you fake your death and devastate me and my father. And before you give me some explanation that makes you feel better about what you did, you should know, I really fucking hate you for doing that to us. Fuck you."

"I understand. Just the facts. I'm not trying to change your opinion of me. Jorge and I had left Bas, deciding that meeting Time was enough. Time had said explicitly that Time didn't want to continue talking to us, so we agreed not to bother Time. Jorge and I were content to have this shared experience, this knowledge, and to move on and not use it for anything other than to marvel at the mysteries of the Universe. We both thought the world wasn't ready for this information. I guess that was how Professor Patel viewed the experience as well. It's enough to know. Then walk away and enjoy life.

"It wasn't something we wanted for our futures. It felt dangerous to know something like that. We wanted families, we wanted to raise our kids together in San Diego, go to the zoo, the beach, have family barbeques. Good things.

"But Bas, he was relentless. He wanted the information we took from Professor Patel's notes. He started stalking us, especially Jorge. It escalated over the course of a few years. He actually figured out some of Time's formulas with the information he had kept. He showed up looking young and bragged about halting his aging process.

"The things he'd accomplished in the time Jorge and I had begun to raise our own families was horrifying. Jorge knew part of the formulas for opticals and eventually made what we needed. We hid Professor Patel's work on a hundred of them to keep Bas from ever finding the entirety of her work. Did Time see what he was capable of doing?" she suddenly asked Kali.

Kali sighed and looked down at the floor and then turned to look up at Lev. She looked back over at Pele and closed her eyes and shook her head no silently saying, "Time said Time didn't believe Bas would be successful either. Time believed Bas would give up as most of the strands suggested."

Pele nodded.

Kali suddenly laughed in disgust. "I can't take it if you're not gonna take any responsibility for what happened. You can't be innocent. When you were just Pele I thought, ok, Pele and Jorge were normal people who Bas tricked and beat and they suffered, too. But not now!" Kali suddenly yelled. "This is bullshit! Pele didn't have a kid. Rachael did. Rachael's a bitch! You left me to be tortured! You don't do that to your own kid!" she yelled while Pele looked at her and nodded in agreement.

"I shouldn't have tried to take power away from Bas when I was arrogantly assuming I was smarter than he was. Our plan didn't anticipate Bas's will to win. We were pathetic. We thought we were smart. Our own egos convinced us Bas would be easy to beat, because we knew we were smarter than he was. We didn't consider how determined he was, how cruel. Bas had tried to kill both of us and failed already, but we still believed we could take him on and win.

"Jorge took his family into his own Kingdom to keep them safe. I decided to fake my death and leave you to a normal life with your father while I set up my Kingdom so we could pretend we were going to work with Bas. Really, though, Bas was always ahead of us. Nothing went right for long. We thought we were tricking him, but he was actually tricking us. My plan worked for a while. It worked longer than Jorge's plan for his own family. Right away, Jorge's family suffered inside his Kingdom. Bas was relentless. He was laser focused on punishing Jorge, I think because Jorge was...he was so smart. He was so kind and so smart. Bas was jealous of him." Pele sighed deeply and closed her eyes at the memories as she told Kali and Lev the details leading up to Bas taking control.

"We were so overwhelmed by him. He got his soldiers inside Jorge's locked Kingdom and kidnapped both of Jorge's children who were only nine and five years old. He had them tortured to death and then he had their bodies put back in their beds so that Jorge and his wife would find them the next morning. He was taunting Jorge. He gave him time to change his lock code and then broke it a second time to show Jorge how smart he was.

"Then he took Jorge's wife, Sami. Before Bas kept you, he kept Sami. He kept her the way, I suppose, he's kept you. I heard she died when a Rewind failed. It wasn't intentional, he would have kept torturing her forever if he could have. After he accidentally killed her, he found out about you. I don't know how he found out. He'd mostly ignored me and was more focused on Jorge in those early years.

"He's driven by relentless revenge for the slight Jorge and I dared to inflict on him when we declined to take over the Universe with him by binding Time. The moment we said no to him, he began plotting his revenge. When he couldn't get to us, he went after the people we cared about so that he could hurt us that way.

"Kali, I thought you were in torture all these years. I wanted to get inside, find you, and kill you, myself. I wanted to send you to the other present so you could be safe with your father."

"Oh, fuck," muttered Kali through clenched teeth as she suddenly got up and stormed out of the living room. "Fuck!" she continued to yell loudly and repeatedly in the kitchen, and Lev got up as he heard something being slammed.

"I'm gonna go check on her. I thought maybe she'd need a minute, but I don't think that's going to help. Probably nothing will. We'll be back, though. Don't leave. That'll piss her off more. Ok? Let her throw you out, but don't go running away."

"Yes. I'll stay right here," Pele said, committed to the situation.

"I'm *not* ok!" she said with wide eyes, looking at Lev.

"That's fine. You don't have to be. I'm just gonna risk my life by getting closer to you to see if a hug might help the tiniest bit."

"It *won't!*" she assured him.

"Still, I'm gonna check," he said as he approached her decisively.

Lev hugged Kali and she said angrily, "I just need her to be an unforgivable bitch so I can hate her. You hear this bullshit she's telling me? I want to hate her. I want to blame her. I'm so mad!"

"I know. And this is a bullshit half-hug I'm giving you because I'm worried about your stomach. Let's sit down in the dining room and talk."

Kali sat on Lev's lap so that they could put their arms around each other without fear of bumping into her wounds.

"I'm just so mad, man!" she said, outraged.

"Mmm-hmm. Yeah. That's fair."

"Bas tortured my whole family."

"Ok, that's a different take," he said, sounding positive. Not focusing solely on Pele's role was an improvement in Lev's mind.

Kali looked at him and sighed. She leaned her body against his and rested her head next to his. "Do you think she's lying? Trying to make herself sound better?"

"No, baby, I don't," he said, shaking his head.

"*Fuck.*"

"I know. But, I don't think she expects you to forgive her all in a day. So, this might be enough information for now, huh? Maybe get some more information tomorrow. Let what you just found out settle into your understanding of what happened. Want me to go kick that bitch out right now?" he asked with a smile.

Kali laughed and shook her head no. "No. Let's see if we can find out about Olivia and a few other things first. But, yeah, no more fucking family bullshit. I can't listen to any more of that."

"Agreed. How about I do more of the talking now?"

"Yeah, please take over."

They got up and went back to the living room, and sat down across from Pele again.

"What's the word on Olivia?" Lev asked Pele.

"She's doing alright. She's going to be released from the hospital tomorrow. I'll leave it up to her to discuss her injuries with you."

Kali looked annoyed. "Wait. If she's going to be released tomorrow, when are we planning to execute Bas?"

"I thought today would still be preferable to all," said Pele.

"Oh, you mean preferable to all except Olivia? I just found out Olivia was Kept. That means she was brutalized and still managed to find information that Gorman and Marty got to Maren. That's the information Lev got a hold of and worked halfway through before passing it off to Santi to take back to the RT. That information was needed in order to access the research about time crystals. It all started with Olivia. I'd say Olivia deserves to see Bas executed as much as anyone else who's planning to be a witness. Can't you people wait until tomorrow for Olivia to be released?"

"Maybe she can be released later today?" Pele offered.

"Don't drag her out of the hospital just to execute Bas a few hours sooner. Plan his execution for tomorrow evening. Don't rush her. If she gets released today, she can go back to Ivy and sleep in tomorrow and then go watch that Clown King be executed. Is the Continent pushing for today?" Kali asked, annoyed.

"Actually, the Continent asked if we wanted to conduct the execution tomorrow to give Olivia a chance to be there for it. I said probably not, because I figured you'd want to do it immediately," Pele said, looking apologetic.

"I want him to be executed tomorrow so Olivia can be there," Kali said decisively.

"I'll inform the Continent and Dave immediately," Pele said and pulled out her comms to do so.

Lev nodded at Kali in silent agreement.

"Alright. Dave was glad to hear Olivia was going to be able to see Bas be executed. It's still early, but we can go to Ivy anytime you're ready.

"I want to go now," Kali said, turning to Lev.

"Then let's go now," he said, sounding relieved that their conversation was ending.

"I'll go tell Santi and Rollo. We can all meet in the lobby," Pele said as she got up to leave.

"Hey, I'm really mad, but I'm also listening. I don't want to be friends right now," Kali said sternly.

Pele nodded. "That's good enough for me."

Kali slumped back onto the couch, and Lev went over and gently pushed her over so they could lie down next to each other.

Kali laughed at him asking, "Are you trying to knock me over carefully?"

"Yeah." he said, smiling as he laid down alongside her on the couch.

He kissed her and said, "That was really impressive how you didn't punch her in the face or break any furniture. The neighbors didn't have to call the cops, *and* you're still sober."

Kali laughed at him and said, "It's so fucking annoying that she's even a little sympathetic. That stuff about Jorge and his family really sucked. I felt bad for her losing them all that way."

"Don't overthink things today. You can know all this shit right now, but think about it a few days from now after we're back home and Bas is erased by Death Time. You're not as confused as you were yesterday, and you found out she's got some decent qualities. Give yourself a break."

"Ok."

Back at Ivy- 8:30am ET

Kali, Lev, Rollo, Santi, and Pele arrived near the stables around 8:30am. Santi wanted to take Rollo to their room and then give him a tour of the facility, but Lev told her they had to have a meeting with the RT, the Intel Team, the security team leaders, and Aisha first.

"Go order some water and chicory sent to MR4 and then bang on doors to get everyone downstairs for a meeting in an hour. Get people to help you find everyone. Send someone to get me Dave out here asap," he told her.

"What if they ask who Rollo is?" she asked him, looking over at her husband.

"You tell anyone you want to that this is Rollo Vespry, your husband," Lev said, smiling at her and Rollo.

Santi turned to Rollo and said, "Alright, let's go meet everyone!"

"Vespry, stand on a table and give some Community News to the breakfast crowd. Tell them who you are. Introduce yourself as The Benefactor, then let them know your real name. Tell them Lev and Kali are back, and Bas is in the prison ward awaiting his execution tomorrow afternoon. Have fun with it, man. This is the best audience you're ever gonna have. This whole crowd is on your side," he said encouragingly.

"Ok. I might be late to your little meeting, though. Might have to mingle with my fans, maybe sign some autographs," he laughed.

"Ok, don't have that much fun with it," Lev said with amusement.

"Can Pele join us?" asked Santi, who was aware of the tension between her and Kali.

"Yeah, sure. Pele you want to go with them or hang out with us?" Lev asked her.

"I'll go inside and get familiar with the facility," she said, looking at Kali, knowing that her continued presence wasn't helping Kali to feel at ease even back at her home with Lev.

As soon as the trio walked away, Kali asked Lev who would be watching Bas while everyone was assembled for the meeting. She was clearly agitated, so he asked her who she wanted to be in the prison ward with him rather than making a suggestion of his own.

"James," she said without hesitation.

"You gonna be ok with him here? Let me know. I'll get you anywhere you want to be. I'll do what needs to be done here today and come spend the night with you. Campus, Lua Pele, the fucking Continent, tell me if you can't be here with him down in the basement."

"I'm afraid someone's going to accept his offer of power," she said flatly.

"Let's see what Dave has to say. We'll get James in the room with him while we have the meeting."

"Ok."

They made their way to their usual picnic table and sat down on the bench with their backs against the table so they could lean back and take in the expansive views of the landscape. Kali leaned against Lev and wrapped her arm through his and said, "I just realized I'm not considering that you must be happy to be back home."

Lev smiled down at her and then looked back at the landscape. "I am. I wasn't sure I'd ever get back. Leaving you in the lab that morning was the most difficult thing I've ever had to do. The smallest amount of hope that we'd succeed was the only reason I managed to do it. Nearly fucking killed me, choosing to leave you, knowing I might never see you again."

Kali watched him silently as he looked around the grounds slowly taking in the scenery on the chilly March morning. Community members who were milling about, avoided approaching them as they sat together. It was obviously Lev and Kali they saw sitting at the picnic table, and they knew information would be coming soon.

"You cold?" he asked her as he put his arm around her and pulled her close to him.

"I'm freezing. Pull me closer," she said, smiling up at him.

Lev grabbed her tightly and they kissed until he remembered he had to be careful of her injuries, and he pulled away and said, "Shit. Did I hurt you?"

"No. I told you I'd tell you if I was uncomfortable. Keep kissing me," she said and pulled him back towards her.

They continued to make out until they heard Dave clear his throat and Bolin asked, "Did you two forget where your room is?"

Bolin enthusiastically hugged Lev and expressed relief that he'd made it back alive, then he offered gratitude for the work he and the Intel Team had done to capture Bas.

"You ok?" Bolin asked Kali as Dave warmly embraced Lev and welcomed him back like a father who had missed his son.

"Mm-hm," Kali said expressionless with a quick nod of her head.

Bolin looked at her and knew instantly that Bas must have hurt her. It had been his fear when he'd sent her to the Kingdom. She'd only been there for a few hours. He would have to reconcile whatever injury she had sustained with his own decision to send her into the Kingdom. He shook his head in anger but stopped as Kali shook her head almost imperceptibly at him not to continue with whatever he planned to say to her.

He was furious, but he let it go because she wanted him to.

"About Bas," Lev said, addressing Dave and Bolin, unaware of the mostly silent conversation between Bolin and Kali, "Kali's a little anxious about arrangements for his confinement while we have a meeting this morning. Can we get James to sit with him while we're all unavailable?"

"You bet. Bol, when we're finished here, you want to go get him? Explain what's going on and take him down to relieve Bautista?"

"Yes. I'll do that then head over to the meeting with Marty."

"How long are we going to need James downstairs?" Dave asked Lev.

"Unsure. Won't be all day, but could run a couple of hours."

Dave nodded and turned to Kali. "Bolin, Bautista, and I have been the only ones in the room with him since he arrived last night. Marty's in there now doing the late overnight, early morning shift. You comfortable with that?" he asked her.

"Yeah, but no one else," she said and both he and Lev could tell she was agitated even as they made sure to accommodate what she believed was the best scenario for housing the mad King.

"There are five heavily armed, murderous guards in the hallway outside the door, and one of the three of us inside with him. No one else enters the ward. All he does is negotiate and threaten the entire eight hour shift. I don't think he's slept since he got here last night. We removed the bed, too. Not even a blanket. Just the toilet, the floor, and the four walls of bars. He's got nothing. Don't you worry. He'll be dead tomorrow. Death Time are gonna get that son of a bitch," Dave assured her.

"I'll go find James. He's probably going to antagonize Bas a little while he's down there. I'm on duty after Bautista. Should be interesting to see what happens after James riles him up," Bolin said with a knowing look.

"Let James have his fun, man." Lev laughed, knowing what Bolin meant. James was going to drive Bas nuts partly for the fun of it, but also because he hated him.

Kali looked confused and concerned asking them, "Bas doesn't know I'm here, right?"

Dave shook his head. "Guy knows nothing. The three of us agreed not to tell him a word. He doesn't know he's at a place called Ivy, or in Virginia. He recognized Marty when he relieved me last night, and it drove him insane that Marty refused to tell him what was going on. Kept screaming that Marty was a Trusted King's Guard and was going to be tortured forever for withholding information from him. Marty and I just laughed at him. He's so fucking confused right now. Ours are the only three faces he's seen clearly. Maybe some of the guards outside the door, but he has no clue what's going on."

Kali nodded. "Ok, but, please tell James not to use my name or speak about me."

She looked really worried as she spoke, and Lev went to reassure her, but Bolin spoke up first. "Kali, I'll tell him we're keeping Bas in the dark. I'll tell James. He'll understand. He wouldn't tell Bas anything about you."

Kali nodded and breathed deeply.

"Do I need to be in the meeting?" Kali asked Lev as Dave and Bolin left.

"Don't you want to be?"

"No. I really don't," she said, looking up at him, shaking her head.

"Then, no, you don't have to. I thought you'd want to be, though. Is it because the meeting is going to be in the basement?"

"No."

"Are your burns bothering you?"

Kali smiled up at her husband. "No. I just need a mental break. It just hit me that yesterday was the last time I'd ever be in Bas's Kingdom and it was the last time he'd ever be able to torture me. I might be a little fucked up between that and Pele this morning."

Lev scowled and looked concerned. "Definitely don't come to the meeting then. You gonna go back to our room? Get some rest?"

"Yeah. How long will the meeting take?"

"At least an hour. Give me two hours, but I'll try to hurry."

Kali rubbed her hand on his chest. "You don't have to hurry. I'm picturing James making fun of Bas and I feel pretty good about that, actually," she said with a smile.

Lev looked down at her as she tried to reassure him, but he wasn't convinced. "I'm still going to push the meeting along. I'll walk you to our room now," he said, getting up looking over towards their window. "Hey, is that a greenhouse? What is that?" he asked her, squinting his eyes to see clearly across the field.

"Oh, yeah!" she said happily. "A couple days after you left, worst day ever, Bolin built me a greenhouse outside the window so I could leave the window open all night and not be so cold. It's got traps so anyone who chased me through the window wouldn't be able to catch me."

Lev laughed loudly. "I fucking love it."

She told Lev about the weapons Bolin placed inside the greenhouse for her in various hiding places, too, and he listened and felt his affection for his friend grow even though he hadn't imagined he could care for him anymore than he already did.

"Did it keep the room warmer? Did you feel safer?"

"Mm-hm, and yeah, it really did keep it warmer," she said, nodding up to him as they walked closer.

"Show me the traps and the hidden weapons."

Kali opened the door and showed him the trip-wall, the hole in the ground, and the low hanging spikes.

"The spikes were Bolin's idea. They'd get you. We can take them out now," she said, looking up at her very tall husband.

"Did I say I fucking love this? I fucking love it. You wanna garden with me this spring?" he asked her enthusiastically.

"I do. Let's ask Bolin if we can move our greenhouse a few feet to the right so we can have our window back and have a greenhouse at the same time."

"They took care of you while I was gone?"

"The whole time. Like family," she assured him as he leaned down to kiss her.

"Did Rollo take care of you?"

"Yeah, like family from day one. After he threatened to kill me multiple times that first morning, though." Lev nodded, raising his eyebrows. "He wanted to be the one to tell you how I fucked up the first day I got there and he had to convince Bas to let him go to torture in my place."

Kali suddenly looked concerned.

"But," Lev continued, quickly grabbing both of her hands, "he avoided torture, and we got married that night."

Lev laughed, and Kali looked uncertain about laughing along with him.

"It's ok. It's funny. I learned not to be such a dumbass and we agreed he'd get to tell you what happened. It was all my fault, by the way." Lev continued to laugh as Kali looked skeptical about whether or not the story would be funny.

"Baby, it's funny. I promise. Neither of us went to torture," he said, trying to reassure her.

"I'm asking Rollo," she said, reserving judgement until then.

"I can't believe we forgot to tell you how we ended up getting married," Lev mused as they walked towards their room. "Don't worry, we got divorced last night," he said and laughed as Kali continued to look at him warily.

Inside their room, Lev sighed deeply as he looked around the small space. "I'm so happy to be home with you," he said, shaking his head. They wrapped their arms around each other and Lev put his forehead against hers while they hugged carefully in silence for a few minutes.

"What I said to Bolin about James not talking about me to Bas… I feel like it's not James' business to talk about me to him, but it's different with you. I don't care what you choose to do. Anything you decide to do is fine with me. If you want to go down and shoot him in the leg, or yell at him, or tell him we're married, or just stare at him silently letting him guess who you are…. Lev, I don't care. If you tell me you're not going down there to see him, that's fine with me, too. I wouldn't tell you or Rollo what to do. You both have your own relationships with Bas. It's not my business. You can tell him anything you want to tell him about me, or nothing at all."

Lev nodded slightly with his forehead still pressed against hers. "I get it. Thank you. Are you planning to go down to see him?"

"I don't know yet. I'm still deciding."

"Would you want me to wait and let you decide first?"

"Oh, no. That's not necessary. If you want to go down there now, I'll just go start removing the spikes from our greenhouse," she smiled, pulling away from him to look into his eyes.

Lev smiled back at her. "Ok. So you know, I plan to go speak to him."

"Ok."

"I'm going to head over to the meeting now. I'll be back in a couple of hours. No more than that. If I can't find you here, where should I look for you?"

"I'll be here. I have too many emotions in me right now. I haven't settled on one and I don't want to talk to people. I'm even thinking of closing the door after you leave."

Lev raised his eyebrows and nodded. "You can try doing that. See how it feels. Open it if you start feeling stressed."

Kali seemed thoughtful. "Yeah, I'm going to try to do that."

Lev kissed her forehead and said, "If the door's closed when I get back, I'll knock."

"Oh, that's a good idea," she said approvingly with a hint of concern in her voice.

He laughed. "Yeah. I'm gonna identify myself, too." He considered what he was saying. "Actually, I'm serious. I'm going to identify myself," he said, looking at her without laughing.

"That's… Yeah, that's probably a good idea," she said seriously.

Kali Goes to the Lab- 9:15am

She watched Lev leave, heading for his meeting with the entire RT, all security, and Pele. Aisha and Bob were already at Ivy and would also be attending the meeting. Kali stood by the open door to the room and watched Lev walk down the hallway. She waved at a Team 4 security member she had seen before, but with whom she was unfamiliar, who was exiting the workout room.

"Kali! You're back already?! Was that Lev?" she asked her.

"Yeah, he's back. Williams will be in a meeting with Lev and everyone else for at least an hour."

"Is it over?" the team member asked quietly, daring to hope.

"You have to wait for Williams to inform your team, but, yeah, it is!" Kali said happily. "Don't tell anyone I told you that."

The security team member agreed to keep the news to herself, and Kali went back inside the room.

She walked to the bookshelf and felt for her cloaked optical. She stood quietly with a blank expression on her face, lost to her thoughts. Her expression darkened and she turned suddenly. She had made her decision. She left the room, closing the door behind her.

Kali walked with confidence up to the top floor of Ivy to the unattended labs. The doors were locked, as they should be. Dave was a very good soldier for the opposition. He was careful, even with the people he trusted to help him protect the afterlife present, so that he could be reunited with his beloved wife.

She considered that her respect for Dave knew no limits even when she occasionally wanted to fight him. She understood that they were simply two passionate people who sometimes failed to recognize when the other intended to hold their ground. In the absence of a father in this present, Lev had a father in Dave. In the absence of a father-in-law in this present, Kali had a father-in-law in Dave. That being true, she was still going to have to thwart his best efforts at security. She meant no offense against Dave. He would have to understand. Or he wouldn't. It was up to him now. She was going to do what she was going to do.

She had been practicing for months. She stole a bottle of wine from James' wine cellar. She returned it, though. She took the book about the rabbits from Bautista's room. She returned it. She stood outside the cafeteria and took hard boiled eggs. She ate those. She stood outside the Rewind lab now.

Lev and Dave said it was a crime punishable by death to create a Rewind without authorization. They didn't say it was a crime punishable by death to steal a Rewind. She thought about the distinction. If they had said it was a crime to steal a Rewind, would she still steal a Rewind? Kali stood still and considered the question she had posed to herself. Yes. She would still steal the Rewind. Definitely. She was angry as she considered her answer.

The Rewinds were locked in a cabinet on the far left wall of the Rewind lab. Kali stood outside the glass walls looking at the cabinet where she knew the Rewinds were kept. She conveyed her intention to her optical and hid a Rewind in the past. To be certain, she held out her hand and a Rewind appeared in it instantly. She smiled and hid the Rewind in the past again.

She walked down the deserted hallway to the lab where Prison Darts had been carefully studied and created before being destroyed in favor of Prison Bullets which had been successfully created by the RT. She held still and concentrated, sending her intention to her optical. She held out her hand and felt the weight of the gun loaded with Prison Bullets. She opened the bullet chamber of the gun she was now holding. The bullets each had an IC stamped on them indicating they were Ivy Cage Prison Bullets. She hid the gun with the Prison Bullets in the past. She headed back downstairs to her and Lev's room.

Kali wasn't conflicted. She sat at the small table in the dorm she shared with Lev and considered how much time she had left before he returned. Not much. He was trying to hurry to get back to her. But she still had things to do. She climbed out of her window and exited the greenhouse with her shovel hidden in the space near her body. Her optical knew what she needed. She needed to get the shovel to a new location. She would be quick.

Trent ran up to her as she approached her destination and asked her excitedly, "Kali! You're back already?! Are Lev and the Intel Team ok?"

Kali liked Trent and remembered how helpful he had been since he had arrived at Ivy.

"Yeah, everyone's ok. Olivia's ok, too. Lev's back and in a meeting, but I'm not sure I'm supposed to tell anyone that yet. Can you keep it a secret until your team leader tells you herself?"

"Yeah! Definitely! I'm so excited I don't even know what to do," he said, smiling.

Kali said, "Listen, you helped so much. Lev told me personally how being able to count on you to do things that needed to be done helped the teams a lot. He used your name. I know it's been crazy around here, but if no one has stopped to tell you this, you should know, Lev counted on you."

Trent looked overwhelmed by what Kali was telling him. "I'm just a guy from New Hampshire who had enough skills to get in here," he said seriously.

"No, Trent. You're just a guy from New Hampshire who Time felt could help the opposition. I believe that," she said with sincerity.

Trent looked overwhelmed by Kali's assessment of him and his contributions to the mission.

"Don't tell anyone what I told you. Wait to be informed by your superiors. We won, Trent. You helped us win."

"I'm always happy to help. This is a good life here. Will there be a party?" he asked her.

"Tomorrow. Throw yourself at James and Marco and ask how you can help with the food and drink we're gonna need to feed 700 people!" she laughed.

"The minute I hear from my team leader, I'll head over and offer my services," he said happily.

Trent left, and Kali headed over to the burn pit with the concealed shovel.

After the Meeting- 11am

He knocked. "It's Lev," he said from behind the closed door of their room. Kali opened the door, smiling at him. He shook his head and smiled at her as he walked their bowl of lunch to the dining table to put it down. "You really did it. That was brave, babe. Come here!" he said as he walked over and gave her a hug.

"It wasn't closed the entire time I was in here. I got nervous and opened it a few times then closed it again," she admitted while looking up at him as they hugged. "I left the window open."

"It's still awesome. You closed the fucking door. So you know, you can keep leaving it open. You're in charge of our door. The window, too. I'm not pushing for closed doors and windows. I'm gonna ask for something else, though," he said, raising his eyebrows at her.

"What?"

"We can start small if you need to, but I'm hoping we can sleep without clothes sooner rather than later. Maybe start with bare feet like last night and move on to less clothes?" he asked hopefully.

Kali laughed at him. "I really want that, too. I want to do that tonight."

"No shoes like last night?"

"No clothes, either."

"Well, let's go to bed early then, eh?" he said, leaning down to kiss her.

They ate lunch, and Lev told her about the meeting.

"Dave and I are going to wait until Bas is dead and Pele's army has completely incinerated both Bas's Kingdom and Jorge's before we destroy what the RT created in the labs. The Intel Team members already handed over all the tech they had on them when they got back. Everyone wants to take a breath, get some extra sleep, kill Bas, and then party for two days before we get to work dismantling all that came from discovering Time."

"That's a good plan. You know, I really don't want to see anyone today. I want to stay here in our room. You can leave, do whatever you have to do, but I'm--"

"It's fine. You can do that. Take a day off," Lev assured her.

"No, this morning Pele mentioned talking to Rollo and me about freeing Time. I don't want to talk to Pele about Time. She can tell Rollo, and Rollo can tell me. I can't listen to her anymore right now. Actually, I don't want to ever hear her tell me about Time. But Rollo shouldn't have to wait to hear about Time being unbound. I hate it when she talks about Time. I'm really mad, Lev," she said in a nearly emotionless tone, looking at him with a serious expression.

"Alright. Ok. I've noticed. There's a lot to be mad about. You can be mad," he said, trying to assure her he understood.

"You say that, but I wasn't allowed to be mad for decades. And now I'm getting mad about things that happened to me a long time ago because I wasn't allowed to be mad when they happened. My mind's a mess."

Lev nodded and reached for her hand across the small table. "You don't have to listen to Pele talk to you about freeing Time. I'll go find Rollo and Pele and tell them you want the information about Time secondhand from Rollo only. There's nothing you have to do anymore. You didn't have to go to the meeting this morning, you can skip the execution tomorrow, and the party."

"I'm going to the execution."

"Yeah, I was going to encourage you to go to it," he said, smiling at her.

Kali laughed lightly and asked, "Did you decide who's going to kill him?"

"Yeah. The plan is that I'll kill him unless you decide you want to kill him. You can decide at any time, even the last minute."

"How are you going to kill him?"

Lev knew that question was coming and still wasn't prepared for it. He looked at her and decided to be quick and honest. "This was a problem downstairs when we discussed it. My preference is a bullet to the head. Get rid of him. Don't get fancy with it. One bullet. Celebrate. Some people in the room suggested hanging him. Others advocated for burning him alive in the burn pit. One person, named Rollo, suggested we ask for your input. Hearing you explain how you're doing right now, I'm not sure now's the time to ask for your input. The question's out there, though. If you have a preference, you know, I want to know even if your preference involves torture."

Kali stared at Lev as he struggled to talk to her about how to kill Bas and said, "The truth is, I can't kill him. I can't. Not even knowing Death Time will destroy him. He's existing in defeat right now. This is torture for him. I want him to suffer. He deserves to suffer. He deserves torture. He won't be tortured after he's killed. There is no Hell except for the one he created here on earth. Death Time are going to end him."

"I understand what you're saying. You understand we're killing him tomorrow?" Lev asked with a hint of concern in his voice and a serious look of concern on his face after hearing Kali's thoughts.

Kali closed her eyes and sort of nodded while shrugging saying, "Yeah, I know," in a non-committed way.

She sat with her eyes still closed and heard Lev as he got up from his chair, and then felt him take her hand.

"Come on. Let's sit on the couch."

She opened her eyes and looked up at him. "I'm really fucked up."

"I know."

They sat together on the couch with Lev holding Kali as he told her that Rollo declined the offer to execute Bas.

"He said he might not even go to the execution. He doesn't want to confront him downstairs in the cage, either. Olivia won't be back until later today, and I know we're waiting to execute him until tomorrow so she can witness it, but I've gotta say, you and Rollo are both not ok waiting. I'll go downstairs and put a bullet in him right now if you want me to. No one would stop me. You want me to do that?"

Kali turned her face further into Lev's chest and said, "I can't agree to killing him. I can only let it happen."

"Fucking hell, Kali. I'm worried about you."

They sat in silence while Lev ran his hand down her back and she remained pressed against him with her arm wrapped around him.

Lev decided the best approach would be for him to take charge.

"His execution's going to happen tomorrow at 1pm. I'll kill him. One bullet. If you don't want to be there for it, I'll come get you as soon as it's done. I think you'll feel better once it's over. It's this leading up to it bullshit that's fucking with you."

Kali looked up at Lev and smiled. "Ok. I'll decide later if I want to be there. I won't tell you what I've decided right now because I might change my mind," she said.

"That makes sense."

Lev and Bas in the Cages- 7pm

Lev walked down the stairs to the prison ward and looked at the five heavily armed guards outside the room. "Dave on duty inside?" he asked them.

"Yes. He came on about an hour ago," said one of the guards.

Lev entered the passcode to the prison ward and entered the room, closing the door behind him. The lock clicked as he watched Dave nod his head silently at him. "You want privacy?" he asked Lev.

"That'd be great, man."

Dave got up slowly from the chair behind the desk and took his mug with him. "I'll go get a refill of whatevercoffee and come back down. I'll wait outside the door for you to finish. Take all the time you need."

"Perfect," Lev said as Dave entered the passcode and left the room.

Bas had watched Lev enter the ward and shook his head with contempt as Lev headed towards the cage he was locked in. He watched with his mouth curling in disgust as Lev walked over to the row of cabinets that lined the right side of the room and leaned casually against them. Lev recalled Aisha picking up Kali's shirt from the cabinet he was now leaning against and returning it to her before scolding Bolin for not giving it back to her sooner. He recalled the red mark around her neck from her suicide attempt when she was afraid Bas would find her and capture her easily if she were locked up in the cage.

As he looked into the cage at Bas's face now, he remembered that the bruising around her neck had lasted for days. Bas was the only one to blame for that. He couldn't even fully blame Heather. It all began with Bas. He was the catalyst for so much horror, so much suffering. He looked impassively at Bas, not willing to waste the cost of rage on him anymore.

"You, huh? You kill Rollo, then?" Bas asked him sharply. His tone sounded as if still believed he was a King, Lev's King.

Lev tipped his head, slightly amused at the thought, and let the beginning of a smirk move across his lips. "No," he said with a small shake of his head while continuing to stare at Bas.

"You should have. He'll be coming for me. We'll torture you together," Bas told him with derision, meeting Lev's stare.

"Mmmm... No, he won't do any of that," Lev said, allowing his smirk to grow.

"You think your husband is more loyal to you than to me? His King? You only just met him. I've known him for decades." Bas turned his back on Lev and laughed mockingly at the thought of Rollo turning on him. "You're a fool, Dev. A bigger fool than I'd imagined."

"He's not my husband. I have a wife," Lev said in an irreverent tone, no longer smirking.

Bas turned and looked at him with surprise for the tone with which he used to speak to him as well as for the information. "You remember who you're speaking to," he said menacingly, adding, "So, you played him? You work for Pele?"

"No," Lev said, shaking his head and shrugging dismissively.

"You work for yourself? I know Pele's here. Did you conquer Pele?" he asked in disbelief at the thought.

"I have my own agenda," Lev responded in a threatening tone, deploying a hard stare at Bas's face.

Bas looked confused but also interested and less bored than he was when Lev had first approached the cage. "Did *you* break my lock codes?"

"Yeah, I did," Lev said, raising his eyebrows and nodding. Lev could see the revelation resonate within Bas. He was stunned and couldn't hide the fact that he was thrown by Lev's admission.

He walked closer to Lev and grabbed the bars of his cage. He looked at Lev suspiciously and said with disbelief mixed with contempt, "No. Not *you*. You're *nobody*. That wasn't *your* army that came in. What's Pele's game here?" he demanded, looking for an explanation that made sense. "Answer your King!" Bas demanded loudly when Lev didn't respond.

Lev stared at Bas dispassionately and offered nothing by way of explanation to clear up his confusion. The two men said nothing for several minutes while staring at each other. Lev's calm demeanor unnerved Bas who knew he was lacking necessary information. Finally, relenting, he said, "Dev, listen to me. Clearly, I underestimated you. Probably pissed you off to have your King think you're a fool."

"Mmm, that's not exactly--"

"I'm going to propose something to you right now. Cage or not, I'm still the most powerful man in this room. But you, you're ambitious. You think like me. Neither of us answers to someone else. You figured out my lock. That's impressive, and I'm not easily impressed. You, me... the hell with Rollo. Clearly he couldn't see what you were capable of achieving. The two of us, we'll divide this world between us. I'll help you take out Pele. We can put her into torture today along with her brother. You take over her Kingdom. Two Kingdoms in this world. We'll get the afterlife next. I'm close. You help me see what I'm missing. We'll rewrite the rules of the Universe together."

Lev stared at Bas waiting to see what else he'd offer him in exchange for his eternal consciousness.

"If that's not enough, I'll tell you something else. I believe consciousness keeps traveling forever. There are more presents. The Universe has no end. We get these two presents, nothing's going to stop us. Let's do this together. I've never met someone who might be my equal," he said, trying to sound complimentary but failing as a decidedly patronizing tone slipped through.

Lev shifted his stance against the cabinets adjusting his feet and leaning back with his arms folding across his chest in a thoughtful pose. "We'll get rid of Rollo? I get to keep Pele's Kingdom?" he asked Bas, sounding genuinely interested in clarifying the proposal.

"Of course! If he's even still alive. He's been useful to me as well as to you, but he's nobody. No skills at all to really accomplish anything meaningful. He came onboard as a janitor and he can leave with the trash. He's a fucking human. We're gods. Get that wife of yours, we'll make her one, too."

"You'll make her a goddess?"

"No, you will. She's yours. You do with her what you want. I don't care. Get a new wife. Have as many wives as you want."

"Did you ever do the math?"

"What math?"

"A day inside Time is 108 years for a person. Rollo told her she was inside for 108 years. I'm kinda thinking he got that number from you. But you knew the truth. Didn't you?"

Bas stared at Lev trying to understand what he was asking him.

"Come on, you know what I mean. You put her inside Time for 11 months." Lev watched as some of the color drained from Bas's face and continued. "What are you, like 76 years old? How old is she? It's just addition, really. I'm thinking you unwittingly made her a goddess when you stuck her inside Time because people just don't live that long in this present." Lev stared at Bas as he remained silent. "Goddesses do, though," he finally said, sounding thoughtful.

"What do you think you know about my wife?" Bas laughed with disgust and waved his hand saying, "Mine's definitely not a goddess no matter how fucking old she is. She's probably already dead along with Rollo. She got what she wanted.... for now. I'll get her back from the other present. She doesn't deserve to die."

"No. Rollo's here. He's alive. So is the woman who allows me to be her husband."

"Who?"

"You know who."

"Tell me."

"Mine only ever existed in your imagination, man. You couldn't get rid of her no matter what fucked up thing you did to her mind or her body."

"There's no way. It's not possible. You only met Mine yesterday What is this? You just want her because she's my wife? You think she's a goddess just because she's old? What? You're going after everything of Pele's and think you're actually going to take anything from *me*? You're delusional." Bas scoffed at Lev and turned away from him.

Lev remained silent letting Bas work out all of the new information for himself.

Bas suddenly walked back towards Lev and grabbed the bars of his cage and asked him, "Have you even spoken to Mine? She's too stupid for men like us. She offers nothing of value."

"Men like us, huh? Is that supposed to be flattering? Men like us.... Interesting. You think burning MINE and HIS into her skin made her yours? You ever consider you're the one who's stupid? Men like us.... Yeah, I'm not seeing the similarities you think you see."

Bas stared at Lev silently, but anger and frustration crossed his face as he realized Lev was an adversary he couldn't manipulate or frighten easily.

"Yeah, you're starting to believe me now, aren't you? You tortured my wife, asshole," Lev said darkly.

"She's *my* wife. In this present and any other. I *own* her," Bas said angrily with confidence in his authority.

Lev shook his head while staring at Bas. "No, she isn't, and no, you don't," he said, almost bored with Bas's demand for his agreement.

Bas began to fume at Lev's insolence. "She's *mine*! She wouldn't dare! She knows what I'd do to her," he snarled through clenched teeth. "Maybe you should consider what I'm going to do to *you* just for what you've suggested here!"

Lev pretended to contemplate what Bas was saying. He held up a hand and waved it dismissively at Bas. "She isn't yours, and yeah, she did dare to. As her husband, I don't like what you just implied. You planning to hurt my wife some more? I'm happy to be the one to tell you, it's not gonna happen. The real problem you're facing right now is that you're about to die and meet some *very* judgy Death

Time on the other side. You ever hear about them?"

Bas stared with contempt at Lev and said nothing.

"No? She didn't tell you about them after you took her out of Time? Kept that to herself, I guess. You know, like so many other things she kept to herself. Do you know what her favorite meal is? Her favorite flower? Her favorite wine? Her favorite song? Do you know how to help her feel better when she's upset? Husbands who like their wives know this stuff because they take the time to learn these things. Psychopaths who abduct teenagers and keep them hostage for decades while torturing them... they don't know the answers to those questions. You sure you're her husband and not a psychopath, Bas?" he asked him thoughtfully.

Bas's face revealed the rage that was building inside him, but he remained silent.

"I'm not going to tell you what her favorite wine is, but you should know, we drank it together while she told me how she killed you several times. That's a really good memory. It might be my favorite wine, too, come to think of it.

"Also, I'll tell you something she knows that she didn't tell you. You ready for this? It's big. Human consciousnesses aren't the only consciousnesses living in the other present. Death Time are there, too. Just waiting for unredeemable assholes like you to show up so they can keep the Universe a nice place for everyone else who can manage to get along. Really useful beings that work hard for the Universe. They're kind of like janitors who take out the trash. I think I'm going to have to give you credit for making me consider that analogy. I'll let Rollo know, too. He and I will probably laugh about that for eternity, from one present to the next. Joke's on you, man. Forever," he said with a scornful laugh.

"You're a fool. There's no such thing as a Death Time. I'd know. I don't care if you kill me. I'll get my people and I'll work from the other present. The joke is on you. I'll come get you, Rollo, and Mine, and I'll control all of you either way, Dev," he scoffed.

"Name's not Dev, by the way. My name's Lev Patel. I'm Marina Patel's son." Lev looked at Bas as the new information hit him. He nodded at Bas. "Yeah, I look like my dad." He laughed as he slowly circled the air around his face with a finger.

Bas was rendered silent as he tried to process all that Lev had just told him. Lev decided to keep enlightening Bas to the truth, enjoying watching him come to grips with reality rather than being able to maintain his delusions. "This is crazy, but I heard you killed my mother a couple of times in the past before you figured out killing a shadow consciousness wouldn't stick in either present. Also heard you're going to go after my mom in the afterlife present. I've gotta say, I've got a problem with your plans, man. I don't approve. Now you're telling me you're gonna go after my wife. You should know, I'm not letting you do any of that. I'm sending you to meet Times's less tolerant extended family members tomorrow."

Bas found his voice again and was instantly in a rage as he screamed, *"There's no such thing as Death Time in the other present!* The only thing you can do is keep me alive here forever. Otherwise, I'm getting right back to work. You can't kill me! I'm immortal either way!"

"No. You send someone into Time for an extended period of time, they come back with some juicy gossip. Were you even curious? Or did you just convince yourself that you're a genius and she's too stupid to know something you don't?"

Bas's rage increased as Lev's ridicule of him penetrated his ego. *"Fuck you*, Lev Patel! Fuck you and your mother. I'm going to take Mine, I'm going to punish her, I'm going to make her watch as I punish you, and I'm going to control both presents without you. This cage is nothing. You're the definition of a wasted opportunity just like your mother. I'll get out of here. Someone's going to want a Kingdom. You believed a little fool and her desperate fairy tales. You think you're a knight on a white horse riding in to rescue her. *Death Time doesn't exist! I'd know!"* he screamed red-faced with spit clinging to his mouth.

Lev remained calm and said knowingly, "Man, she doesn't like horses. She prefers to walk. And you ever hear that saying, it's not what you know, but who you know? Yeah, you're older than you look. You know that saying. My wife knows Time. They're friends, actually. Time also calls my mother a friend. Never heard Time describe you as a friend, though. You really should work on your interpersonal, or inter-sentient being skills."

"Mine doesn't know how to talk to Time! She's too *stupid* to know the formula! She sat in Time all those years in *silence*! *It taught her how to shut her fucking mouth!"* he screamed at Lev, pointing his finger at him through the cage bars as he raged.

Lev was still leaning casually against the cabinets and shook his head smiling with affection for a thought he was having as he said, "No, she's still pretty chatty." He turned a harder gaze at Bas and asked him, "You ever consider Time could figure out a formula to talk to her? To Rollo? To the rest of us? You really believe you bound the entire consciousness and every aspect of the free will of a being like Time? Yeah. She said you're not very creative. I don't doubt her assessment, but I think you were also blinded by your ego. It's out of control, man. You should work on that. Anyway, I don't need you to believe what I know is true. You're gonna die tomorrow, man. You'll find out soon enough."

"You know you can't kill me. I'll have free reign over there in the other present to work with my people. You have to keep me alive here. I'll wait all of you out. You'll all fucking die, and I'll finish my work right here in this present. I'll come for you once I figure it out. I'm close, you fucking asshole. Kill me now, I'll get my team in the other present. You can't win. You should have taken me up on my offer. Now, I'm going to come for you and everyone you care about. I'm going to keep Mine. I'll keep her in torture, but I'll pull her out to fuck her in front of you. You'll see who's in charge. It's not you. This? This is almost over. No one beats me. I never lose.

Too bad you chose to believe a little fool instead of taking me up on my offer."

"You're gonna die tomorrow. I'm gonna kill you. And I can't lie, I think I'm gonna take a little pleasure in killing you. I wish I could see your face when you meet Death Time. You know? When you realize you're the trash that's being taken out."

Lev walked away from Bas as he continued to rage against him from inside his cage. He entered the security code to the door and went into the hallway telling one of the guards to monitor Bas through the glass rather than go inside. He looked apologetically at Dave who was sitting on the stairs drinking his fresh cup of chicory. He laughed. "Sorry, I got him all riled up for your shift."

"That's fine. I'm ready to listen to something other than him offering me a Kingdom of my very own, anyway," Dave said with a roll of his eyes.

"He's holding back on you, man. He offered me multiple presents throughout the Universe."

Dave laughed. "That was probably my fault. I told him I'm a simple man. A house with a yard for my dog. A Kingdom is too much work. He was furious. He's never gonna offer me multiple presents, now. Said he'd find me and kill my dog, though."

Lev shook his head and laughed along with Dave.

"I let him know Vespry's alive and here. I'd expect him to demand to see him throughout the rest of the night, but Vespry already told me he's not coming down. He might even skip the execution tomorrow. He's undecided. Might want to give Marty a heads up that Bas knows Rollo's here. I also told him Kali's here and that she's my wife."

Dave looked at Lev in a kind of quiet surprise.

Lev nodded. "After you and Bol left, she told me Rollo and I could say whatever we wanted to say to Bas. No restrictions. She was adamant. Had me go tell Rollo, too."

"Phew. Understood," said Dave, feeling sincere relief.

"I think the information about her is what he's most pissed off about right now. He doesn't know her name, though. I didn't tell him her name. He calls her Mine, just so you know." Lev laughed in disgust.

"This is gonna be an awesome shift," Dave said with an amused smile, standing up from the stairs. He clapped Lev on the shoulder as he walked towards the door to the prison ward and watched through the glass as Bas clung to the bars of his cell and screamed threats at all of them in the hallway.

He turned back to Lev and asked in a serious tone, "It's getting late. Is Kali planning to come down here?"

"I don't know. I don't think she knows, either."

"I'm on until 2am, Bautista's on until 10am, then it's Bol's turn again. We'll give her any support she needs if she decides she wants to come down and face him."

"I'll tell her," Lev said as he left.

Lev and Kali- 8pm

"Do you want me to tell you what happened downstairs?" Lev asked Kali after returning from the prison ward. He placed their dinner bowl on their table.

"Only if you want to tell me now."

"How about I tell you a couple of days from now?"

"That would be way better for me."

"Ok. If you want to know before I bring it up again, just ask."

"I will."

After having dinner in their room, Lev moved their bed from under the window where she had moved it when he was in the Kingdom, back to the left side of the door where it had been when he'd left four months earlier.

"We can see the sunrise from across the room from here," he told her as he dragged the bed back to the place he and Bolin had originally placed it. "Plus, you moved it under the window because you wanted to be able to escape quickly. This is a new start."

She agreed with him that the sunrises were nice to look at together in bed in the mornings.

"Bed's ready. Let's try it out," he said in earnest, raising his eyebrows at her.

Kali laughed at him as he smiled and reached for her. "I wanna be on this side while my skin heals. It's easier to get in and out of bed on the side that's not against the wall," she said as they laid down on their bed together.

"I don't have a preference. I just want to be in a bed with you anywhere in it," he said as they laid down on their sides facing each other.

"How're you feeling?" he asked, looking down to where her burns were concealed behind her shirt and bandages.

"It looks worse than it feels, actually. Santi says I can uncover it in a couple days. That ointment Santi got me is so much better than what I'd been given to use in the Kingdom. It really doesn't hurt that much, and I really want to have a lot of sex with you starting now," she said as she moved closer to him and pulled him closer to her.

"Mmm. Ok. Let's do that. Tell me what's working for you. Don't let me hurt you. I only wanna make you feel good," he said as she kissed him while he tried to talk to her.

They got out of bed, undressed, and then got back onto their bed where they continued to kiss and run their hands over each other's bodies. Lev took her hand and put it under his while he stroked his erection.

"This is all I need tonight," he said, looking at her.

"But, I'm--"

"Uh-uh. I'm worried about your burns. This is what I want," he said, breathing slower. He let go of her hand and pulled her face closer, kissing her harder as she stroked him.

"Let me suck your cock. I fucking love giving you head, Lev. You can stand and I'll sit on the edge of the bed so I can sit up and not bug my burns," she said softly between kisses while she stroked him."

Lev laughed a little and said, "Yeah, ok. You're making a really strong case for that. I'm not going to argue with you, actually."

"No, you're not gonna argue with me." Kali smiled at him as he got out of bed and offered her his hands to help her sit up on the edge of the bed.

Lev ran his hands over her shoulders and through her hair as he watched her give him head. He felt her hands touching his penis, groin, and testicles and groaned as he watched her and felt her at the same time. She knew exactly what he liked, and he had missed her touch, her mouth, and the way she looked as she fucked him. She played with his tip in her warm, wet mouth, using her tongue just right and then reached behind his testicles with her other hand, touching him with his encouragement until he came.

Afterwards, she laid down on their bed and spread her legs for him as he climbed back onto the bed.

"Ah, I fucking love being here," he groaned in a deep voice as he began by kissing her inner thighs.

"You ready to cum, baby? I'm gonna make you cum," he said to her as he slid his fingers inside her vagina and moved his mouth to her clit.

"Mmm, I love when you eat my pussy, babe." She looked down at him and closed her eyes. She moaned as he sucked her clit and buried his face against her and her familiar taste. She ran her hands through his hair as the combination of his mouth on the outside of her and his fingers inside of her brought her close to having an orgasm, but he stopped what he was doing and removed his fingers from her and began to kiss her inner thighs again.

"Oh, we're gonna take a little more time than that to get you there," he said as he softly kissed around her vagina and listened as her breathing slowed down again.

He laughed with amusement at her when he heard her mutter a quiet, "Oh, man" and then he slid his fingers back inside of her to massage her clit as he told her, "You know I'm right," before putting his mouth back on her clit.

He did this several times to her until she said breathlessly, "Lev, stay! Make me cum. I'm so ready to cum!"

So, he stayed until she finished cumming and then kissed his way back up her body to her mouth where he asked her, "Was I right?"

She laughed with her eyes closed and nodded slightly saying quietly, "Yeah, you were right."

Afterwards, they kissed for a while and laughed when Lev declared loudly that sleeping in clothes and shoes was banned forever from their marital bed, adding the caveat, "As long as you're ok with that."

Kali insisted she wanted to wake up naked next to him for the first time, and then told him about Time waking her up in Lua Pele. "I forgot to tell you," she said.

"That's ok. There's a lot going on. I'm glad Time got in touch with you. Do you think you and Time will always talk?" he asked her.

"Yeah. We're friends."

Lev ran his hands over every inch of her naked body in the silence of their room. He told her he enjoyed her in the silence as much as in the noise of a lightning storm and kissed her all over softly and slowly.

Eventually, Kali moved Lev's willing hand back down between her legs, and she began to rub her own clit while Lev used his fingers inside her.

"My wife's ready to cum again, huh?" he asked her quietly as he used his fingers to rub her gently and kissed her mouth. When she started to breathe faster and moaned his name as she looked at him, he nodded and kissed her and encouraged her to cum on his fingers as he rubbed her at the same pace over and over until she came again.

"I missed fucking you. I missed making you cum," Lev said as he smiled at her and she blinked her eyes slowly at him.

She smiled back at him and said quietly, "I missed us, too. I'm so tired, babe."

"I'll bet you are," he said, smiling as he kissed her then got up to turn out their lights. He got back into bed and laid on his back wrapping his left arm over the top of her head while she snuggled against his side under his arm with her arm on his shirtless chest.

"Door and window are closed. We're not wearing anything. If you wake up and you're nervous, wake me," he told her as he lifted her hand and kissed it.

"I will," she said as she drifted off to sleep against her husband who waited for her to fall asleep before falling asleep himself.

Kali's Not Like Everybody Else- 5:15am

Kali woke up and watched Lev sleep. He was breathing deeply and he looked peaceful. She got out of bed quietly, got dressed, and took her optical from the place on the bookshelf where she'd cloaked it the day before. She picked up her shoes from the floor and walked out of the room trying not to wake him. She wouldn't lie to him if he woke up, but he wouldn't like the truth. He would have to make a choice. She didn't want him to have to make that choice because of her. It was better if she made her own decisions without him. He could make his own decisions later. She sat on the short stairway leading to their room and put on her shoes contemplating who might get hurt while she did what had to be done. She would be careful. She headed towards the prison ward in the basement.

She saw no one and no one stopped her while she walked towards the basement. Everyone was asleep, confident that Lev, the RT, and the Intel Team had finally captured Bas. The only security awake were the three guards in the Crow's Nest keeping watch for raiders. They would be relieved at sunrise so they could rest up for the celebrations. Everyone wanted to be well-rested for Bas's execution in the afternoon. Farm duties had been cancelled except for necessary animal maintenance. Breakfast was scheduled to begin at 8am rather than 6am and would be limited to chicory, raw vegetables, and hard boiled eggs. Dinner would begin soon after Bas's execution and would last throughout the night.

The entire community was planning to celebrate Bas's execution. Any Campus community members who wanted to view Bas's execution were told to arrive by noon to get seats on the lawn. The after party would last 48 hours according to the Community News. It was going to be huge. Bigger than the party after the Cannibals were defeated. James was going to release every bottle of alcohol from his wine cellars and Campus would be bringing carts of food and supplies to supplement what Ivy had available. Pele and the Continent were bringing some people from their respective governments, but not many. Everyone would be at Bas's execution to celebrate his death from this present and his complete destruction, thanks to Death Time, in the other present.

Kali uncloaked her optical and held out her hand. She waved a finger over the energy screen of her optical and a gun appeared. She slipped it into her waistband as she strode with purpose towards the stairs leading down to the basement. She hoped Bautista would understand. Either way, she was going through with her plan.

She walked down the stairs leading to the prison ward and stood two steps up from the bottom looking at the five guards in the hall who turned to see who had come down the stairs.

"Hi. It's just me. Lev and Dave said I could talk to Bas anytime I wanted to. I think I want to talk to him now," she said in a friendly tone.

"Oh, hey Kali. Yeah, Bautista's on duty right now. He mentioned that you might decide to show up. You ok? You need a minute?" Carlos asked her.

Kali smiled at him before she shot him with a prison bullet and then quickly shot the other four guards. Through the glass of the prison ward door, she saw Bautista stand up quickly and look to the cage where the guards suddenly appeared clutching their minor flesh wounds. She walked towards the door and entered the code and pulled open the heavy door.

"Hi Marty," she said in a friendly tone as she pointed the gun containing the remaining prison bullet at him.

He smiled, looking at her nervously. "Hey, Kali."

"Tell them to drop their weapons and slide them through the cage away from me and *definitely* away from Bas," she told him.

"You hear her?! Do it now!" Bautista yelled to the guards behind him in the cage while staring at her.

They did what they were told. She heard Carlos tell the others, "I've worked with her. Don't even try to stop her."

Bas was awakened by the commotion and stood up from the floor where he had been sleeping and looked around the ward disoriented trying to understand what was going on. "What is--"

"Shut the fuck up, Clown King!" Kali shouted to him while staring at Bautista.

"You know I'll help you," he whispered to her.

Kali smiled. "I know. But I can't let you. Let's do it my way. Put your cage keys and gun on the desk. I'm gonna shoot you."

"Fuck, really?" he asked as he put the cage keys and his gun on the desk.

"Yeah. Witnesses. I'm the bad guy. Where you wanna be shot?"

"Upper left arm, but listen to me, if you lose control of him, I'm afraid he'll--"

Kali shot him in the upper left arm with the last prison bullet and shouted, "No, Marty! It's all on me. You never had a say in it!" She yelled at him as he appeared in the cage with the others.

Bautista had been blocking Bas's view of her, but with him suddenly sent to the cage with the other guards, she stood by the desk smiling at Bas while he looked at her from inside his own cage.

"Hey, Bas! Recognize me?" She laughed at him while enjoying his confusion. "Yeah, new hair, but it's me, you psychopath! I'm kinda pissed off about the last torture session you put me through. Let's go make it right, huh?" she said as she pulled out her optical from her back pocket and recalled a second gun.

Bas stared at her and shook his head in angry confusion. "Mine!? How dare you speak to me like that! Release me!" he shouted angrily at her with assumed authority over her decisions.

Kali raised her eyebrows and laughed at him as she said proudly, "Clown King, I think you should know, I was always a member of the opposition. It took a while, but I got you, you son of a bitch!" She pointed her gun at him and shot him in the left shin.

She smiled as she watched him fall to the ground with a pathetic yelp of pain. "Really? After all you put me through? One fucking bullet to the leg and you cry like a fucking baby? Jesus, man. You're in trouble!" She grimaced in mock concern for his situation.

"Kali, let me out and I'll help you!" Carlos shouted to her from the cage. The others in the cage agreed, and Bautista stared at her silently imploring her with his eyes to let him help.

Kali looked over at the guards in the other cage and smiled at them. "Thanks, everyone, but this is between me and Bas. I've got this."

Kali took the cage keys from the desk and walked over to Bas's cage smiling. "Hey, Clown King. You ready to meet the real me? I hope you'll understand that I'm a product of my environment."

Bas looked up at her from the floor, bloody and unable to escape her, as she opened the cage laughing at him. She tossed the cage keys through the bars towards the row of shelving on the right side of the room. "Gotta hurry. Can't let you lose too much blood," she said to him in a friendly tone.

Bas's face was contorted into a rage and he hissed darkly at her, "You little fool. I've met Lev Patel. I'm already ahead of him. He's going to lose. Apologize to me now and I'll consider reducing your sentence." He offered her a self-satisfied smirk at what he considered a generous offer for her compliance.

Kali scoffed at him and kicked him in the face hard, knocking him over, then laughed at his shocked expression as he tried to sit up again and recover from the assault. "Hey, Bas, uh, we're gonna need to renegotiate our relationship. See, we were never married. I never consented to it. Now I'm gonna kill you over, and over, and over, and over, and, well, you get the point. Has it been 25 years yet?" she asked him suddenly.

Bas stared at her in confusion and didn't answer her.

Kali waited for him to respond then continued reflectively. "Hmm? You're not sure, either? Yeah, I think it's been 25 years of hands-on torture. Let's get you into some torture for a change. You totally need to see what you've been missing out on."

Kali shot Bas between his legs with her gun and watched as he howled in pain, holding his injury with both hands. She put her gun in her waistband and used her optical to summon a knife she'd hidden 15 years earlier and used it to impale his hands to his groin. "I've been practicing that move on pedophiles," she said with satisfaction as she stomped on the knife handle and drove it deeper into his hands, impaling them against his gunshot wound to the groin.

"You got about 14 minutes to do what I say to restore your pathetic pecker. Or, you know, I can rewind you without one if you want to hold me up. Hmm? Ready? Hold still. I got us a table," she said as she used her optical to recall a rope she'd hidden at least a decade earlier.

"Kali! Give me the keys and I won't open this cage unless you need help!" Bautista told her loudly for all to hear.

She didn't look over at him as she worked to tie up Bas. "Marty, I want to, but I can't! I can't let my friends get in trouble for what I have to do!" she shouted at him.

"Sweetheart, I've got you covered. You're my friend, and my wife's best friend. Let me help you."

Kali turned and smiled at Bautista. "Ju told me she and I are friends, too. We talked about you and Lev every night while you were both gone," she said, smiling at him.

Bautista smiled back at her and nodded. "Let me out."

"No!" She wants to have babies with you!" Kali shouted at him while she finished tying up Bas.

With the rope around his neck and legs, she stood up and looked down at him and laughed at the sight of the self-appointed King.

"Let's go, Clown King," she said happily as she dragged him out of the cage while he screamed at her about the endless torture she would endure for her crimes against him. He was especially furious about her confirming she knew Lev when she had spoken to Bautista.

"Do you actually know Lev Patel? He told me you're his wife! Did you fuck him?" he demanded to know, convinced it was his right to have that information.

Kali looked down at him on the floor and smiled and shrugged happily at him.

Her mocking impertinence enraged him, and he began to loudly describe the torture he was going to personally put Lev through if she had let him fuck her.

"You need to shut the fuck up about my husband," she said to him warningly in a normal speaking voice then brutally kicked him in the face and stomped on his rib cage several times. He stared up at her in shock, but he remained silent, unable to catch his breath through the broken nose and multiple broken ribs he now had.

She entered the code to the prison door and dragged him towards the short staircases as he continued to gasp for air.

Adrenaline coursed through Kali's body as she dragged Bas up the two short staircases to the long hallway. He wasn't a large man, and his injuries left him unable to resist much as she pulled him to their destination. He groaned loudly in agony as she hauled him up the stairs with his broken ribs. She entered the security code to the main security doors of the fourth basement ward and quickly dragged him to a first floor exit next to Santi's medical ward.

The early morning air was cold, and she welcomed it after having exerted herself to get him outside. She felt invigorated and looked down at him and smiled at him in the dark.

"How ya doing?" she asked him pleasantly.

He glared at her with hatred. "I'm going to beat you to death over and over with my bare hands for this, Mine," he said while gasping for air around his broken ribs.

Kali shrugged and waved her hand to shush him. "Hey, Bas, we're gonna go to the burn pit now. That's where I'm going to torture you. You ready?" she asked him as he looked up at her in a rage.

"I own you! Let me go! You're going to be punished for this treason against your King and, I swear, nothing will help you if you fucked Lev Patel. He's not going into torture if it's true. He'll be on the stage and rewound forever and you'll be an audience member every fucking day, you disgusting bitch."

"I've always called you a Clown King behind your back. Did you know that?" she asked him in a very thoughtful tone.

Bas glared at her and took in a painful breath and said quietly through clenched teeth, "I'll get you back in line, you stupid whore."

Kali stared down at him with the rope around his neck and arms and multiple injuries which were preventing him from acting on any of his threats. She pulled roughly on the rope and began to drag him across the field with determination. She didn't stop walking or look down at him as she asked him, "Do you really not realize the situation you're in right now?" with a scoffing laugh.

Bas screamed out in pain as she dragged his injured body without care over the hard winter ground. "Release me, Mine! It'll be better for you if I can recall your compliance with my orders during your mistakes!" he yelled sternly at her.

"No. I'm gonna kill you over and over and over again Bas. You ready? I know I am," she said in a decisive tone as she continued to drag him towards the burn pit.

It was still dark outside, but Kali knew the landscape well. Once she got Bas to the burn pit, she shot him four times using up her bullets in order to subdue him, not kill him, and then hoisted him up first to the top of the picnic table bench and then to the picnic tabletop before using her optical to recall more rope. He passed out at some point from the pain and shock of his injuries which made her work easier. She pulled her knife from his hands and groin and tied him to the table securely before untying the ropes she had used on him in the cage. His body was prone on the tabletop now. She was satisfied.

She was going to wait for him to die, but she was concerned about how long it had been since she'd first shot him in the cage, so she beat him to death with her empty gun then rewound him. She wanted him to be completely healed of his earlier injuries before she began to actually torture him.

Bas looked at her in confusion as he oriented himself to being alive again.

"Hey, Clown King. You feeling better? How are those ribs? Hmmm? All healed? Ready to play?" she asked him with a laugh.

Bas looked at her with hatred. He spoke to her in a quiet and disgusted tone, full of himself now that his body had been healed by the Rewind. "Mine, release me. I've met Lev Patel. He's nobody. He knows nothing. You've known him for two days. I've known him for months. He killed Rollo."

Kali laughed at him. "Man, you know nothing," she said as she shook her head in amusement.

Bas was furious at her for mocking him. "He's Rollo's husband, you fool. I blessed their marriage!" he shouted at her.

Kali looked at him thoughtfully, but said nothing.

She used her optical to recall matches she'd hidden with it on her second trip to the farm house with Lev and started a fire in the pit. "You need to be naked," she said as she used her optical to recall scissors. "Let's cut these clothes off of you. Expose you like you liked to expose me, huh?"

Kali cut off his clothes and pulled them out from under him, putting them into the burn pit to help the fire get going before she added larger pieces of wood.

Bas watched her and sneered at her as she smiled back at him happily. "You always were stupid. Rollo's dead. When we get back to my Kingdom, you'll have nobody." He regarded her with contempt, and laughed at her as she stared at him. "You're pathetic, Mine."

"Is Rollo dead? Is he alive? Is he married to Dev? Am I married to Lev? Am I fucking Lev? What's true, Bas? Do you even fucking know anything?" she asked and laughed at him.

"Lev Patel killed my most trusted advisor, your only friend in my Kingdom," Bas said confidently.

"Trusted advisor, huh? Was he though?" she asked with a grimace and a shrug. She answered her own question before Bas could respond. "Uh-uh. Nope. Rollo's the leader of the opposition, even if he'd argue that he's *not* the leader and that he and I are co-leaders. We'll just never agree on that. I don't want a leadership role. I'm not leadership material. I prefer to work on my own," she said with a shrug.

Bas looked at her in confusion. "Oh, poor stupid, Mine. Did you go crazy again?" he asked her with a derisive laugh.

Kali laughed loudly at that. "No, you stupid Clown King! I did not go crazy again! It's so much worse than that! I went sane! And you're gonna pay for every single fucking minute you tortured me. You understand? I'm here now to make you pay for what you did to me."

"Fuck you, Mine! I've never lost a fight in my life. If you dared to marry Lev Patel, you chose the wrong man. But I'm going home with you today. I own you. I'm going to kill you for this until I can tolerate you again. Probably take fucking years. You ready for that, you fucking bitch? I'm going to beat you to death with your own body parts. Best of all, I'm going to keep your precious Lev Patel alive, and I'm going to torture him in front of you every single fucking day. He's not going into torture where no one can see him. You're going to beg me for mercy I won't give you or him." He laughed with confidence about how the day was going to end for all of them.

Kali laughed with him. "Well that leaves me with very little incentive to do anything you might want me to do, now doesn't it!?" She laughed as Bas looked at her in confusion. "Yeah, we're not in BasLand anymore, dickhead. We're in my husband's community. He doesn't like assholes. You're an asshole, by the way," she said, raising her eyebrows and nodding to assure him he was definitely an asshole.

"You did not marry Lev Patel. You wouldn't dare!" he growled furiously at her in disbelief.

"You're either confused, or in denial. Let me help you out. Rollo didn't marry Lev. I did. Way before you blessed Rollo and Dev's marriage, I was already Lev's wife. You understand now, Clown King?" she asked him with a laugh.

The sun was rising now and Kali looked up to see Rollo running towards her.

Kali, Bas, Rollo, and Pele

"Kali! Stop!" Rollo exclaimed frantically as he approached her.

"No. Go away," Kali responded with virtually no emotion.

"Rollo? Thank god you're alive! I thought that horrible Dev killed you!" Bas exclaimed from the top of the picnic table where he lay naked, roped to it.

Kali rolled her eyes and shook her head at Bas's feeble attempt to manipulate Rollo.

Rollo looked at him in confusion. "Fuck you, asshole," he said in disgust.

"Rollo! I am your King! Subdue Mine, and untie me immediately!" Bas shouted at him.

Rollo ignored Bas and walked to Kali's side. "What's going on, girl? You ok?" he asked quietly as he walked closer to her.

"I'm fine. We'll talk later."

Rollo nodded, but his expression was one of concern. "Who knows you're out here with him?"

"Don't become a problem, Rollo." Kali glared at him angrily, her look warning him to back off.

"You're my girl. I'm not trying to interrupt what you got going on. But this looks serious," Rollo said with a nod towards Bas.

Kali looked over at Bas. "Yeah, but I've got it under control. You can leave now," she said firmly.

Rollo looked at her and shook his head. "Does anyone else know you're out here?"

"Leave," she said coldly through clenched teeth, looking at Rollo with a rage that unnerved him.

"Yeah. Yeah, ok." Rollo nodded and headed quickly up to the facility.

Bas couldn't hide his shock at what he had just witnessed.

"So, you and Rollo are both traitors to your King? My army will be here soon to free me and the two of you will endure years-long rewinds for decades. I'll drink my coffee to them each morning and eat my dinner to your screams every night. You'll see. You were always stupid. Easier to teach a dog to obey."

Kali looked down at Bas. "You cold, Bas? It's fucking chilly out here, but the burn pit is really going now. Let me warm you up."

She reached under the picnic table and pulled out the shovel she had placed there after talking with Trent and scooped up a pile of flaming hot debris placing it on Bas's ankle.

He howled in pain and Kali laughed. "Oh, is that too warm, Bas?"

She walked over to the burn pit and placed the metal shovel into the flames and looked at Bas. "Remember when you branded me? Uh-huh. I do. You talked about it for a week while you waited for the brand to be made. Remember trying to brand my entire body and rewinding me when I had a heart attack and died before you could finish? Remember all the other times you branded me then rewound me to erase the brandings? Well, I'm going to let you experience what branding feels like," she said as she let the metal of the shovel get hotter.

Bas shouted at her in desperation, "Rollo's going to come back and stop you!"

"No, he's not," she said calmly as she walked the flaming hot metal shovel over to Bas and laid it down on his stomach.

He screamed in agony and Kali laughed. "Man, I did not expect that to feel so good," she said reflectively. She picked up the shovel and laid it down on his face to quiet him and he screamed as the heat from the metal shovel burned his nose, mouth and eyes.

Kali picked up the shovel and asked, "Oh, is that too hot? Let me cool you off." She slammed the flat side of the shovel down onto his face with all her might.

She laughed and used her optical to summon a pack of cigarettes she'd hidden when Bas had dragged her to 1979 for a vacation where he drowned her in a hotel bathtub so many times that she'd lost count. "Let's have a cigarette," she said to him as she used her matches from the burn pit to light a cigarette.

Bas looked terrified and screamed in pain from the multiple burn wounds as Kali looked at him impassively.

"Let's Rewind you first. Get you all settled in to this new torture session," she said thoughtfully. I know I need a fresh starting point," she whispered to him with a smile and a nod.

With the cigarette in her mouth, she picked up the shovel and used the edge of it to decapitate him by slamming it against his neck repeatedly.
She rewound him.

"Feeling better, Clown King?" she asked him as she leaned against the picnic table with the shovel by her side. He didn't answer her, but watched in silence as she puffed on the cigarette.

She held up the pack of cigarettes and said, "These things are fucking disgusting. Figures you'd like them so much." She burned his forehead with the cigarette and mocked him when he shouted out in pain. "Man, two days ago you burned your way through to my intestines. I didn't say a fucking word. You're so fucking weak, you know that? I'm so much stronger than you, Clown King," she told him as she burned his forehead again.

This time, Bas gritted his teeth and said nothing while staring at her in a murderous rage.

"Hmmm. That shut your fucking mouth." She smiled and nodded. "You're so easy to manipulate," she said as she laughed at him.

She looked up as she saw movement across the field. "Great. Looks like you're gonna get an audience with the Queen of the other Kingdom," she said, rolling her eyes in annoyance.

Rollo was coming back with Pele.

Kali and Lev

Lev woke up to the sound of someone banging on the door. He looked sleepily at Kali's spot on their bed and saw she wasn't there.

"Hold on. Hold on," he said as he got up and pulled on his pants from the day before and grabbed his t-shirt from the floor. He put his t-shirt on over his head and grabbed his gun. The person on the other side of the door was calling his name and trying to open the door which worried him. If Kali had been in bed with him, he wouldn't care as much. He'd know she was fine. He pulled open the door and saw Pele. Her face was contorted in concern and Lev felt his stomach sink and adrenaline suddenly pump through his body.

"What? Is Kali ok?"

Pele was speaking over him and he said, "Slow down. Where's Kali?"

"She's by the burn pit. She's with Bas."

"Did Bas escape? Is he threatening her?" he asked breathlessly as his heart suddenly pounded in fear and adrenaline flooded his system.

"No. No, she has him!"

They were headed to the exit door and Lev stopped running and shouted at Pele, "I don't care if she has him! I care if she's in danger! Is my wife in fucking danger?!"

Pele shook her head. "There are different types of danger, Lev! Her mind. She's losing it. Rollo tried to talk to her and she told him he's next if he gets in her way. She's out of her mind. That's another way you can lose her. That's a way she can be lost."

Lev slammed open the side door exit and ran barefoot across the field towards the burn pit with Pele behind him. He could see Kali standing in front of the pit behind the picnic table with Rollo standing nearby. Flames were flickering from the pit and smoke was being lifted slowly into the air and blowing away from the scene. It looked to Lev like a body was on the picnic table. As he approached, he could see it was Bas who was roped down tightly to the old wooden table and that he was naked.

"Hey baby," he said as he neared her.

She was standing on the other side of the table closest to the pit with a cigarette in one hand and a Rewind in the other. She smiled at him for a second, but her eyes suddenly focused on Pele in back of him and she looked back at him and said coldly, "Do not stop me."

Lev furrowed his brow and shook his head saying, "No. Never. You want to tell me what you're doing, though?"

Kali puffed on the cigarette but didn't inhale. "Come here. I'll show you."

Lev walked around the table to where she was standing and could already see as he passed by Bas's head that she was burning a word into his forehead with the lit cigarette.

Bas saw him and shouted at him in a panic to stop Kali before she could torture him anymore. When Lev appeared unmoved by his plea, he snarled, "Everything she does to me, I'll do to you, Lev Patel."

Lev ignored Bas and said, "He is shit."

"It's supposed to be shithead. Get it?" she asked with a laugh.

"Oh, yeah. I get it now," he said warily but approvingly.

"I just have to finish the T."

Lev watched as she puffed on the cigarette and added another burn to Bas's forehead as he yelled out in pain.

"I'm not inhaling you, Bas. You're disgusting," she said cheerfully, nodding at him while he yelled out in pain.

Lev noticed burns and cuts all around Bas's naked body. There was a knife lodged into his upper thigh and burning debris covering one of his feet.

"Lev, make her stop!" Rollo pleaded quietly a few feet away from the other side of the table. "It's not good for her to be doing this."

Kali was instantly furious and shouted, "What the *fuck*, Rollo?! This is between me and Bas! Stay the fuck out of our business!"

Lev went to speak to her, and she shook her head no while handing him the cigarette.

"Hold this for me, babe."

Lev took the cigarette, and Kali grabbed a knife that was resting on the side of the table next to Bas's right leg and stabbed him in the shin with it. He screamed out in pain and she asked him, "What? You only get an erection when you do this to me? I'm very confused. I might actually be getting aroused, though. Wait…. No. Just getting angrier."

She pulled the knife out of his shin and placed it next to his leg again. She struggled to pull the knife in his thigh out, and mocked Bas when he screamed in pain as she wrenched it back and forth.

"Give me my cigarette."

Lev handed it back to her and she finished the letter T on Bas's forehead. She held open his eyelid and put the rest of the cigarette out on his eye as he screamed in pain telling her to just kill him. "Been there, done that. Hurts like a bitch, doesn't it?" she asked him.

"Lev, stop her," Pele pleaded.

Kali glared at Pele and said, "Mind your fucking business."

But Pele continued to try and reason with her. "He's going to be executed today. You shouldn't be doing this. It's not good for you!"

"What do you know about what's good for someone who's been tortured for a thousand years? Really, what the fuck do you know? Have you even *been* tortured?"

Pele remained silent.

Kali scoffed. "No. You haven't, so shut the hell up," Kali told her viciously.

Kali picked up the knife again and chopped off several of Bas's fingers on his right hand while he screamed and demanded she stop.

"Scream louder!" she yelled at him as she tossed his fingers into the flames in the pit behind her. "You're never getting those back again!" she laughed.

Lev put a hand on her shoulder and said, "Hey, baby. Tell me what you need."

She looked down at his hand then scowled slightly while looking up at him. "I *need* to do this! And I *need* to know you're on my side! Otherwise I'm alone here with people telling me to stop doing what I need to do! I'm alone, and apparently Bas has the sympathies of the crowd! *Why am I alone*?!" she asked him loudly in exasperation.

Bas was still screaming and Kali started to scream with him, mocking his cries for help.

"Why do you people care about his screams and not the screams coming from *me*?!" she shouted at Rollo and Pele.

Rollo went to speak and Lev said, "Don't speak, man. Baby, you're not alone. I'm here with you."

"You're gonna try to stop me because you don't like torture," she snarled.

"No, I won't."

Kali stabbed Bas in the throat several times.

They all stood in silence as they waited for him to die.

"It's over, Kali," said Rollo.

"Are you *kidding* me?" she asked him with a tone of disgust.

She turned on the Rewind and touched Bas with it. They watched as he gasped for air and all of the wounds she'd inflicted on him healed.

He looked at her in terror as she said happily, "Oh, hey! You're back. Let's do that again," and stabbed him in the throat several times again, killing him.

She rewound him again, and Pele started to walk away.

Lev shouted at her, "Where are you going, Pele?!"

"To get help! I thought you were going to help, but you're clearly not."

"No one's stopping my wife today, Pele! Bring your whole fucking army! No one's stopping her!"

"Really? You're on my side?" Kali asked Lev with a cautious smile.

"Come here. No one's getting past me. You do what you need to do," he said, putting his hand on her shoulder and rubbing down her arm.

James and Bolin were heading towards them from across the field. Both were running as fast as they could and Lev put up a hand as they got closer telling them, "It's ok. Kali's ok. She's just working through some shit with this guy."

"Jesus, Joseph, and Mary! I thought you were in trouble. I heard you screaming, for Christ's sake! Fucking hell. I'm fucking shaking!" James shouted at Kali as he turned to look down at Bas on the table. He was clearly trying to figure out what was going on.

"Ok. Kali's torturing Bas?" asked Bolin as he ran up.

"Looks like it," said James, leaning forward with his hands on his hips, panting.

"Help me! Make this bitch stop. She's nothing. You kill me, and I'll make you a *King!* You can be immortal!" Bas bargained with James.

James looked perplexed and disgusted as he shook his head no. "You're mad," he said to Bas.

Looking at Bas, Kali said, "I need a gun."

"Here, take mine," said Lev, handing his gun to her.

Kali walked closer to Bas and looked at the others saying, "You all should go. Really. This is between us. I don't mind an audience, but I don't need one. And Bas probably likes the attention, anyway."

She motioned for Rollo to move out of the way and waited for him to take a few steps to the left. She shot Bas in the side and listened to him scream. "You were right, Bas! Listening to the person you hate most scream in pain *is* like listening to music. I thought you were making it up," she said in mock wonder.

She grabbed the knife again and stabbed him slowly in each eye, slowly twisting the knife deep into each eye socket, and mocking him as he begged for help. She cut off his ears and told him it would be ok because he could still hear without them. She reminded him why she would know this for a fact. Then she stabbed his eardrums to show him the difference she was all too familiar with. She let him suffer for a while, laughing at his pain, before she cut his throat and waited for him to die.

She rewound him.

"Let me die, and I'll let you live! I'll tell you Time's formulas!" he screamed at everyone except Kali.

Pele was running back across the field towards them with Dave who was running alongside her. Kali was trying to cut off one of Bas's feet by sawing nonchalantly through the bones with her knife as he screamed. She kept screaming back at him mocking his cries for help and parroting him when he begged her to stop. Dave walked over to Lev and Kali's side of the table and she watched the two of them speak, suspicious of their conversation, as she continued to hack at Bas's foot.

"Hey, Dave," Kali said in a friendly, but cautious, tone while Bas screamed in the background.

"Hey, Kali. You got this?"

"Yeah. But Pele's not being cool. Are you gonna be cool?"

"You want me to go get you an axe?"

"That would be great!" she said, smiling at him.

"Hey, Bas, I'm gonna wait until Dave brings me an axe to finish with that foot."

She viciously carved a deep and bloody tic-tac-toe board into his chest and asked him, "Xs or Os, Bas? Which do you want to be?"

He screamed and demanded she stop but she calmly said, "No. You won the last game we played on me, so it's only fair I get a rematch. Xs or Os?"

Dave winced at the conversation Kali was having with Bas, and left to go get the axe for her.

When Bas ignored her and continued to negotiate for help from the people around the table, Kali said, "Guess I'm going first."

Pele yelled at them to stop her and when no one moved to intervene, she started to cry and sat down in the grass, defeated.

Kali carved an X into the center square and told Bas, "X center square. Where do you want your O? And I should warn you, the Os hurt worse than the Xs."

Bas suddenly turned to Lev and mocked him for letting Kali control the situation, screaming, *"Get your bitch under control!"*

Kali ignored his outburst and said, "Bas, I can't understand where you want your O to go. Tell me, or I'll decide for you."

He screamed, *"Fuck you, you stupid bitch!"* at her and she smiled at him and took the knife and drew a large, deep, imperfect circle across his entire chest circling the entire tic-tac-toe board. She turned it into a happy face stabbing to create bloody eyes while he screamed in pain. She laughed at him telling him he looked like the stupid clown he always was.

He began to scream at her that he was going to get free and do worse to her than he had ever done before while she carved circles onto both of his cheeks. He spit at her and she spit back at him laughing and rammed the blade of the knife into his mouth. "No spitting, Clown King," she scolded him as she twisted the knife into the back of his throat while he gagged and choked.

Rollo was walking closer to the table trying to talk to Lev. "Listen, man. I'm trying to help. I've seen this before with her. She went crazy one time. We had to put her into Time to get her back. That's no longer an option. If we lose her, she's gonna stay gone this time."

But Lev didn't know what the best way to help her was, so he simply stood by her and let Rollo talk.

"Lev! Listen to me! I'm worried about her. I'm not trying to deny her the opportunity to torture this piece of shit. I'm afraid of losing her. We finally got the bastard, and we're gonna lose her before she can live in this world without him. Maybe Death Time can fix her. Maybe they do that. I don't know!" Rollo started crying and Dave walked up behind him carrying the axe he'd gone to get for Kali, and put an arm around his shoulders, and walked him around the table away from Lev and Kali. Bolin and James walked over to Rollo and Dave, and Kali could see them all

618

talking.

She watched as Bas died and rewound him. He threatened her instantly but she ignored him, and he began to implore the others for help telling them he could put their consciousnesses inside any person in the past. "I'm so close to figuring out the formula! I can put you inside powerful people! You can live fantasy lives forever. Politicians, rock stars, astronauts! Whatever you want to be. You can ride any person from the past. Try them all!"

While Bas negotiated with the others, she looked at Lev and said, "I told you that story the morning after our wedding. Remember?"

"Dark comedy. Yeah, I remember."

"And then you told me about meeting Dave. He's cool. And about Bob's son." Kali looked at him thoughtfully for a moment. "My story was funnier. I think it was the way I told it, though."

Lev looked at her, and she could see he was conflicted and confused. She noticed that he had tears forming in his eyes and his voice cracked as he told her, "I'm so afraid right now, Kali."

She walked up to him and put her arms around him. He quickly hugged her back and she said, "Rollo's wrong. I need to torture him."

"Ok. Ok. I'm not going to let anyone stop you. But if you need me to stop you, you tell me. Just ask me."

"I will. Right now, I need to burn this bitch," she said, releasing Lev and reaching for the shovel.

"Did you plan this?"

"For a thousand years."

"Ok," Lev whispered while nodding his head and wiping his eyes.

Dave was walking over with the axe and said, "Here you go. We'll keep Rollo back. He's just really worried about you right now. So's Pele. Don't be too mad at them. Lev and I will keep them back."

Bas was pleading with Dave for help, telling him if he stopped her, he'd let him share power with him, but Dave swung and punched him in the mouth breaking his jaw before walking away.

"Dave, you're so cool!" Kali shouted happily at him as he walked a few feet away to the others.

Kali used the shovel to scoop up burning debris from the pit and dumped it right between Bas's legs. He screamed in horror through his broken jaw and Kali walked back to get a second shovelful of the flaming debris. She walked back towards Bas and said, "Watch your feet, babe," as she noticed Lev was barefoot and tossed the burning debris on top of Bas's chest while he tried to scream through his broken jaw. "Bas, I won that round of tic-tac-toe. You're a loser again."

Kali suddenly looked panicked. "I put the Rewind here on the table. Where is it?" she asked angrily.

"I have it," said Lev.

She looked at him with distrust. "I need that."

"Sure, here. I just didn't want it to roll off the table, or get coals on it, or whatever. Take it, baby."

Kali looked at him skeptically while also trying to assess how close to death Bas was. She held out her hand and Lev placed it in her hand quickly. "See? On your side. Why you gotta doubt me?" He laughed lightly at her.

She wrapped her arm around his waist and stood next to him while she waited for Bas to die.

"Bas, I hope you're suffering," she said kindly as he gasped his last breaths through his mangled jaw.

"I think he's dead now," Lev said, encouraging her to use the Rewind.

Kali rewound him and he screamed in fresh new horror at being dragged back from what he expected to be a victorious death where he could begin to plot his revenge on all of them.

"Death is so much better when someone's out here in life torturing you. Huh, Bas? I'll bet you wish you'd killed me now!" Kali mocked him.

The burning coals she had placed on him remained after the rewind and he screamed as the pain from their heat melted his skin once again. Kali used the shovel to roughly scrape the burning material off of his body, tearing his burning flesh entirely off in the process.

"No bare feet on that side of the table!" she shouted to her friends pointing to the hot debris on the ground.

She picked up the axe Dave had brought her and chopped off his foot. She held it up to him as he screamed in pain, and put it on his raw chest. Then she walked around the table stabbing him, letting him bleed out.

She didn't notice Santi coming towards them as she tortured him, but turned when Santi was suddenly standing at her side.

"You need help? I brought my medical kit."

"Can you tell me when he's dead, so I can rewind him?"

"I can." Santi picked up Bas's wrist and felt for a pulse.

"No! I know you! Why are you here?! You're a King's Physician! You work for me!" Bas yelled in horror at what Santi was offering Kali.

"Keep doing what you're doing. I'll let you know when he needs to be rewound."

Kali stabbed him repeatedly and viciously until Santi held up her hand.

"Need to rewind."

Kali rewound him. The two women worked together in this way for several rewinds, with Bas begging Santi to consider that she was a doctor.

Santi laughed and said, "Well, asshole. I'm helping her bring you back to life, aren't I?"

Lev watched as several more people from the community arrived looking to see what was going on. Kali didn't notice any of them. Bolin and Dave turned most of them away, but let Gorman, Ju, Olivia, Aisha, Bob, Maren, and Vivek remain. Ju left to go get Bautista after Kali shouted to her that he was locked in a cage, and Dave told her to tell security not to let anyone else head over to this section of the property. Ju ran across the field to go release Bautista but stopped to turn others away who were heading over. Lev could see the others were telling additional people to turn around. Olivia sat down in the grass next to Pele and put an arm around her and Pele turned to her and cried into her shoulder.

Kali continued to torture Bas, and Santi told her when to rewind him so she could do it again. Kali mocked Bas relentlessly as he alternated between negotiating for help from the others and threatening her. He tried to enrage Lev by quickly telling him about having violent and degrading sex with Kali and reminding everyone there that he was actually her husband, not Lev. He couldn't compel Lev to kill him even after the assaultive imagery, but Kali cut out his tongue and held it up to him and laughed as he screamed through his mutilated mouth.

"This is between you and me. Leave my husband out of it," she said to him with a calm and persuasive tone followed by a loud laugh where she stuck out her own tongue mocking him as he screamed without his own.

She used the axe Dave gave her to cut off his head and then rewound him. She did this repeatedly and laughed at him each time he realized he'd been rewound. He wanted to die, but she wouldn't let him.

She laughed at his outrage after she told him, "Oh, Bas. I *can't* let you die. You know, you really shouldn't have bragged so much about going to the other present to plot how to kill us all from there. So, this is your new reality, you stupid clown."

At one point, she dropped the Rewind as she went to use it and picked it up quickly and rewound him with a second to spare.

Lev asked her, "Do you want me to do the rewinds?"

"Yeah, thank you. That would be great. He was really mean to you. Are you ok?"

Lev closed his eyes and choked a bit on the words as he suppressed the urge to vomit, but managed to say, "I'm ok." He took a deep breath as she handed him the Rewind and composed himself.

Rollo walked up to the table with Bas newly rewound and said firmly, "Kali. I *know* what this is about. You have to stop!"

Lev shook his head no, but Rollo said, "No. I know what this is about. *We have to deal with this!*"

When Lev put up his hand to silence Rollo, he said, "This isn't about Bas torturing Kali's body. This isn't about revenge for what he did to her body. It's about what he did to break her mind. She can't hurt his body enough to make it better!"

Lev looked over at Kali who was staring blankly at Rollo. She looked harmless, but then she tipped her head to one side and he flinched inside knowing it meant she was getting mad at Rollo.

Ju was back with Bautista, and Pele and Olivia were standing alongside them. Santi put her hand on Rollo's arm and stepped back from the table to sit on the grass next to James. He put his arm around her and spoke quietly to her while she nodded her head.

"What's this about, baby?" Lev asked her.

She turned to look up at Lev while Bas loudly demanded Rollo help him, reminding him that in this life and in all others, he was his King.

Rollo scowled at him and said, "*You* did this to her. You did this to *yourself*. No one here's helping you, asshole."

Lev was looking at Kali and noticed her eyes close for a second and her head twitch. He'd seen her do that before. Memories. Really bad fucking memories that she kept hidden deep inside of herself. He put the Rewind in the waistband of the front of his pants and stepped closer to her, putting both of his hands gently on her shoulders.

"What's Rollo talking about?"

"Nothing," she said, looking confused for a second.

"Ok. I'm gonna ask him."

"No. Don't ask him," she said quickly, looking up at him concerned and with a hint of panic in her voice.

"So it's something, then? I can see that, yeah? What I'm gonna do is get real close to you now and maybe you can tell me?"

"You told me I don't have to tell you anything I don't want to tell you," she said defensively.

"Shit, baby. You're gonna use my words against me now?" he asked her with a defeated laugh as he walked his body right up against hers.

Bas was saying something to Rollo and Lev looked down at him and asked, "What the fuck are you saying?"

Bas smiled at Lev and said, "It's not my fault. She did it. She's the murderer."

Rollo grabbed Bas by the throat with both of his hands and squeezed with all of his might snarling, "No. *You* did it. It's *your* fault. You didn't give her a choice. Kali, it's his fault. Don't listen to him."

Kali looked at Lev and closed her eyes saying in a barely audible whisper, "I want to torture him again."

But she didn't make a move to torture him. Instead, she opened her eyes slowly and looked up at Lev and breathed in a deep breath and he felt her shoulders relax just a little bit as she exhaled. She closed her eyes again as she pressed her body closer to him and turned her cheek against his chest as she wrapped her arms loosely around him. He hugged her back and kissed the top of her head.

"I'm gonna need to know, baby. You don't have to worry."

She didn't respond and Lev asked, "Are you gonna stop me from asking Rollo?"

Bas laughed and went to speak but Rollo grabbed his hair and shook his head violently, shouting at him to shut up.

Kali turned to look up at Lev's face with her eyes open now. "Rollo can tell you. I can't. I already tried to tell you once. Don't fuck up the story, Rollo," she said with a small laugh, still looking up at Lev. Despite the small laugh, for the first time since he'd known her, he saw that her eyes looked wet. He saw her blink a few times and the tears didn't overflow onto her cheeks. They stayed with her.

"This asshole wanted to have a kid with her. There was no way in hell she wanted that. I got her birth control pills and, for a few years, we managed to keep her from getting pregnant."

Bas was shocked and disgusted at hearing what Rollo had told Lev and said, "You conspired to deny me an heir? Fuck you two. I'm going to enjoy every minute of punish--"

Rollo snarled at him. "You can't have an heir if you're immortal, dickhead." He wrenched Bas's head up by his hair and slammed it against the table violently, shutting him up before continuing to speak. "But then he took her away unexpectedly on another vanity vacation, and she didn't have her pills. Usually, she'd take enough with her in her shoe or something. Hide them from Bas. Yeah, man. She got pregnant. It was a fucking nightmare. Right, Bas? A fucking nightmare. You stopped torturing her body and you started fucking with her mind in new awful ways including telling her how you were gonna brand your kid with the word, 'OURS' on its back. You ordered a small fucking brand to be made so you could burn your kid with your stamp. 'OURS,' as if she'd ever be a part of that."

"Baby, this asshole told you that while you were pregnant?"

"Yeah." Kali turned her head and put it against Lev's chest again while he stroked her hair.

"I'm not the bad guy. This bitch killed my kid. You killed a baby. Your own baby. Hey Lev, no matter how this ends, I'm coming for you. I'm going to own your consciousness. You'll know what you're doing, but you won't be able to stop. I'm going to make you torture your fucked up wife endlessly. I'll make you kill your bitch mother. You won't be able to stop once I'm in control. You'll see what I can do," he said with confidence in his threat.

Lev ignored him, focusing on Kali instead. He was trying to pay attention to how she felt in his arms. Was she ridged? Breathing? Shaking? What did she need from him? Fuck Bas. He was going to die today no matter what. He had to be here for Kali now.

But Rollo didn't feel the same way. He suddenly started punching Bas and beat him to death with a few blows to the head. Lev looked over and noticed and pulled the Rewind out of his waistband and aimed it at Bas. "Let's keep him alive through this story, eh, Vespry?" he said, looking over at him while putting the Rewind back into the front of his pants.

"Yeah. Yeah. Sorry. I just can't stand it." Lev watched Rollo shake his head and his words caught in his throat as he said, "It was awful. An awful time."

Lev saw how difficult it was for Rollo to talk about what had happened and said to his friend, "I think Bas would rather die than listen to you tell everyone what he did to his own kid. You fucking know this was your fault, don't you, Bas?" Lev asked him quietly as he glared down at the man. He said to Kali, "Baby, I think this is the worst torture this asshole's gonna feel today. Go on, Rollo."

"I was over their house a lot while she was pregnant. I was trying to keep an eye on her, talk him out of beating her and throwing her into torture. He was convinced she could stay in torture because her body would come out fine. I kept reminding him all that shit could hurt the baby. None of us knew what would happen if he put her in torture. I guess he was bored, so he ramped up the mental abuse. She obsessed over how she could protect a baby from him when she couldn't protect herself. He was jealous of the baby even before it was born. But also so full of himself like he was gonna have this kid to rule his Kingdom with. He wanted his kid to be a homicidal psychopath just like himself. Fucking scary.

"Kali I'm gonna tell the rest now. You doing ok?" he asked her.

"Yeah. You're not fucking it up so far. Go ahead," she said with her eyes closed, still pressed against Lev.

"She had her baby. Yeah, that's right, Bas. She had *her* baby. And I went to the hospital to see her, see how she was doing, ask how I could help. I walked into the room and she was sitting up in the hospital bed holding him, looking down at him. Oh, Jesus. Hold on," he said.

Lev watched him shake his head and breathe in deeply trying to prevent himself from getting upset.

"I see her holding him. And it's a perfect picture of a new mom holding her baby and looking at him with so much affection, man. I tapped on the door to get her attention and she looked over at me. I could see her eyes were red and tears were flowing down her face, man. You ever see her cry? I have. A lot. And that was the last time I ever saw her cry. Right, Kali? You ran out of tears after that, didn't you? Yeah.

"I walked over to her and her baby and I could see right away that he was dead. She figured out how to keep Bas from hurting him. She was sitting there alone for, I don't know how long, holding her dead son. She had to kill him to save him from Bas. No one helped her. She had to do it alone. Her own baby. That was the first time she ever killed anyone.

"When Bas found out, he told her she was going to give him another kid. This one he was gonna keep from her. She'd never be allowed to even see it. She lost her mind, man. Started killing herself 24/7 after that. She told me she wanted to be with her son. We all had to have Rewinds. She'd kill herself with a fucking blade of grass. Threw herself into fires and oncoming traffic."

"Baby, we gotta talk about what dark comedy is," Lev said to her.

He felt her laugh and laughed, too.

"He couldn't keep her pregnant. Rewinds only worked on her. Only one consciousness survives a Rewind. She'd lose the pregnancies. Found out you can't put a pregnant woman into torture, either, like he thought he could. Time spent in torture, ended any pregnancies. Then she suddenly stopped killing herself. I told Bas to give her some time. I didn't want him to keep blaming her for killing her son, so I tried to convince him that it was pregnancy hormones, post-partum, some shit he'd have heard about but never looked into. He was buying it and started telling her maybe she could see their next kid if she could keep her shit together. Seemed like it was working, but then people started dying. I mean, I've thought about it. She killed a lot of fucking people before we figured out she was the one doing it. She killed this asshole several times. Killed me once." Rollo laughed at that and said, "I still can't believe you killed me. And then this fucking idiot rewinds me." Rollo laughed and shook his head.

"Ok, baby, you got this part of dark comedy right," Lev said to her.

She opened her eyes and looked up at him. "I told you Rollo wasn't mad at me for killing him."

"Nah, man. Never mad at you. We put her inside Time. It took a long time, but she got better. Kali, I'm so afraid to lose you. Please stop torturing this asshole. Let us kill him."

Kali was still looking up at Lev.

"What's your son's name?" he asked her.

Bas laughed sneeringly and said, "Sebastian Bakker the fourth. And I had the bitch's tubes tied so she couldn't have any more kids. But I still have a son, and I'm going to go get him. So, fuck you, Lev."

Lev ignored Bas and asked Kali again, "What's his name?"

"She never told anyone what she named him. Not even me," said Rollo.

Kali took one of her arms away from around Lev's waist and motioned for him to come closer. "It's a secret," she said, and he leaned down so she could whisper her son's name to him.

"That's a great name," he said as he sniffed and felt the tears fall down his cheeks while he looked at her.

Bas said viciously, "His grave says Sebastian Bakker the fourth, so fuck you all, but especially fuck his mother who murdered him. I'm never letting you die. You'll never see him again. Go on, kill me. I'm going to go get him, and I'm going to tell him what you did to him. No matter what you do, you can't win, bitch."

Lev and Kali were still holding each other and he didn't feel her react to anything Bas was saying to them. She felt calm in his arms.

"Do you still feel alone?"

"No."

"Do you still need to torture him or would it be ok if I killed him? I'm only offering to kill him because I know he doesn't deserve death, and it might bother you to know you helped him die. I can deal with it. You wanna let me do it? Or do you need to torture him some more?"

"You can kill him. Death Time can have him," she said.

"There's no such thing," Bas whispered, suddenly not sounding confident.

"You're in trouble, asshole," Rollo said coldly, looking down at him.

Lev didn't move away from Kali. They stayed locked in their embrace looking at each other while Lev asked for someone to hand him a gun. Rollo wiped away his own tears as he picked up Lev's gun from the bottom of the picnic table and walked it over to him, handing it to him.

Lev looked at Kali as he told everyone to move to the right and waited to make sure no one was in the line of fire.

Kali was still looking up at him, and he smiled.

"Hey, wife."

"Hey, husband."

"I want to take care of some things for you. Is that ok?"

"Yes. Thank you."

"Can I toss the Rewind into the pit?"

"Yes."

He kept one arm around her waist as he pulled the Rewind from the front of his pants. He looked over at the burn pit and tossed it into the fire while she watched his face.

He wrapped his arm around her again and looked down at her and smiled.

"You ready?"

"Yes."

Lev turned, locked eyes with Bas, and shot him in the head.